THEY WOULD ALL BE PART OF HER *HEARTSONG* ...

Manny ... He was her agent, the slum kid who made it big. Now there was nothing beyond his grasp—even Regan Reilly.

Alyson ... Regan's sexy flame-haired cousin, she wanted everything Regan had—and stopped at nothing to get it.

David ... The handsome English film star who offered Regan his name, at the price of his terrible secret.

Jake ... Gifted pianist and stage idol of millions, he was the first man Regan loved—and the last one she thought she could ever have.

Heartsong

Leigh Riker

POPULAR LIBRARY

An Imprint of Warner Books, Inc.

A Warner Communications Company

POPULAR LIBRARY EDITION

Popular Library books are published by
Warner Books, Inc.
666 Fifth Avenue
New York, N.Y. 10103

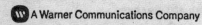 A Warner Communications Company

Printed in the United States of America

First Printing: May, 1985

10 9 8 7 6 5 4 3 2 1

For my family,

and for Mary . . .
who first listened to the music

OPENING BARS

Chapter 1

...What if the dream came true?

In the center of a large stage, highly polished wood reflecting the image of her body, she stood alone, dressed in a gown of gold, flashing light with every movement. The green of emeralds, her eyes were clear and wide. Applause like rolling thunder greeted her, and the people called her name. "Regan!" they shouted. *"Regan Reilly!"* as she whipped the long, tawny hair behind her, head up, chin high—straight and proud and *beautiful*.

Bowing and smiling for the thousands who loved her, she flicked the microphone cord out of her way and began to sing. She gestured with the mike itself, raising it high for the top notes, making love to it during the long, slow ballad that brought tears to the eyes of everyone who listened, misted the green gaze, too. She let the volume soar, not caring for anything but the audience she sang to and the heady exhilaration racing through her veins, pounding in her heart, surely as strong as desire, as strong as love must be. The thrill ran down her spine, like the touch of a hand smoothing silken hair: the touch she had lost, but not forgotten.

As the bittersweet song ended, her heart thumped in heavy rhythm with the burst of tumultuous applause, her limbs went weak; yet she had never felt more vital and alive. More loved.

3

She had captivated them; they would pay anything to see her, to hear the exquisitely trained voice that—

The daydream suddenly disappeared, becoming reality and stillness.

What training? Regan wondered as misery descended like a cloud over the sunny afternoon. There was nobody else in the house, in the room. Alone, she set the "microphone" down gently on the bedroom dresser. Only a hairbrush, after all; a pretense, she thought, like singing in the shower until someone hammered at the door, "you must be drowning in there"; unreal, like all the other afternoons, trying songs out on herself. What did *she* know?

The beautiful young woman in the glass, a *star,* had become just Regan Reilly again, too slender, they said, too ordinary— and worse. In the grip of uncertainty, luminous eyes stared back at her from the dulled mirror; the darker ring of color around the iris had turned black, making them look now like smoky jade.

"Men prefer blue eyes," Alyson had told her after considering Regan at length, and batting long lashes over her own china-blue gaze, which was identical to her father's. "There's no character to your face, either," she'd continued. "Lucky you don't intend to make *your* living on the stage," which had made Regan wince, thinking of her dreams. "But maybe you'll change when you get older," as if Alyson couldn't believe in that possibility for the better.

Regan turned this way and that in front of the mirror now. She didn't find her face disgusting—smooth, light skin, and a regularity of feature. But was Ali right? Was she too thin? And flat? Alyson had matured early, and Regan, two years younger, had been quickly left behind—prodding her chest at night with inquiring, nervous fingers, wondering at the age of ten, eleven, if *anything* was budding, growing.

A silly fear as it turned out, so maybe it wasn't too late now, either, to grow a lush anatomy. Regan glanced at her breasts, arching her back sideways at the mirror to push them out. Nothing to be ashamed of, but still—

Patience, she told herself. But she wasn't patient, and she

didn't want to wait. Alyson had ten pounds more and larger bones than Regan, an inch or so of height. She'd always been better developed in all dimensions—but why don't I have *hips* at least? Regan wondered in frustration. Where was the roundness when she walked, the swing? Men whistled at Alyson, not at her.

Regan couldn't think why people sometimes compared them, as if they were sisters instead of cousins, their blood ties closer. True, they had the same nose, practically straight, and that tilt of the chin when angry. But Regan had always considered herself Alyson's shadow; her hair pale, and Alyson's like fire.

She thought her hair was her best feature, though. The shining, tawny-gold sheen of satin hung, shimmering, to her waist. "Regan Reilly," her aunt had said, goading her to have it cut, "you are full of senseless vanity," which wasn't true. Martha had been dead for three years; but the words still hurt as if she'd spoken them an hour ago.

The wide green eyes looking back at Regan were even darker now. Whistling, she decided, was a vulgarism, anyway; and she didn't want to be whistled at!

Regan's own opinion was that she might well go to her grave a virgin. There were certainly no dates—her uncle discouraged them—and not a borrowed prom gown in her future, much less a decent wardrobe. She was as badly in need of a new dress as the rag doll on her bed.

Some day, Regan promised herself, I'll have a closetful of clothes. And shoes!—a hundred pairs, minimum. Lingerie, clinging and gossamer-light in every color of the rainbow, as sheer as the breathtaking wisp of white nightgown she'd recently bought as an eighteenth birthday present to herself. Jewels and furs and extravagant gowns in silk, chiffon, lace, and satin. She would never wear the same thing twice. She would be famous. Rich. And everyone would love her. Then, maybe she wouldn't miss Mama quite so much.

Regan lowered her head, and blinked. She never cried in this house, and she wouldn't now; but the dream was wasted, the transporting joy when she sang, the thrill, all wasted. Like her mother's love.

When would she ever learn anything except what Paul wanted her to know for his comfort? She thought of her uncle's massive chest and biceps, the ruddy coloring so like Alyson's, even to the cold, opaque blue gaze she could never seem to see through. Thought of the way he had cared for her, once; the way his treatment of her now shifted at a second's notice, so that she never knew what to expect of him, or how to react. It hadn't always been like that, but now the strength she had admired years ago she mistrusted, even feared.

Regan could clean and cook and mend, do the marketing like a slave, juggle the bills and pay them as she could, trying always to please him. But how would she ever learn to *sing?* Her uncle allowed no fantasies about music lessons. A waste of good money, he would tell her; had told her already. Everything to Paul seemed frivolity unless his own welfare was at stake. Or Alyson's.

Regan didn't like feeling so stuffed with envy—but why did Paul draw arbitrary lines between them? Somehow, every year, he scraped money together for *her*—in September, Alyson's junior year at Northwestern, majoring in drama. But in Paul's mind Regan's desire to sing for a living meant exhibiting herself, "asking for trouble," whatever he meant by *that*. So how could she ever make a beginning?

Regan groaned softly in frustration. She went back to the bed, lay down on her side, and cradled her head against her arm. She knew a lot about living in her mind, but she hadn't given enough thought to the real future. After graduation, what then? A dull job in a local store, trying to save money for lessons herself? What was she supposed to do? Fall in love, get married, and forget the rest?

Love. She tried out the word, but it seemed as far out of the range of possibilities as the thunderous applause that still echoed inside her. Regan wondered if she could even recognize the man who might cherish her; if he said he loved her, how would she know whether to believe him? She didn't understand Paul, and he was the only man she really knew.

Closing her eyes, Regan remembered when Mama was with her, and they'd had a home. . . .

Paul took them for drives on Sunday afternoons, she remembered, passing by the great houses strung like perfect pearls on a rope along The King's Highway. Paul had laughed then, his blue eyes warming. At the park, he'd swung Regan high in the air, carried her on his shoulders, fed her peanut butter fudge and lemonade. Her mother had played a game with flowers in the grass. *He loves me, he loves me not. . . .*

Paul had made her mother laugh again.

That night, lying warm and sleepy in her bed, Regan had heard their voices drifting to her from the kitchen. "Next time," Paul had said, "we'll all go, Alyson and Martha, too. She says she doesn't like picnics, but a day like this would change her mind."

"Wasn't the sun glorious?" Then, more softly, "She doesn't like me, Paul. Martha still blames me for Allan's death. He was her *brother,* there's no use trying."

The anguish in her mother's tone; the gruffness from Paul. "It wasn't your fault. It was a hunting accident."

During the long silence, Regan had lain under the blankets, her heart pumping furiously. Her father, dead. Three years old, she didn't remember him. "You think so?" after the pause. "When he'd grown up with guns, Paul . . . that he'd climb over that fence without first breaking the stock?"

The silence had sounded to Regan far louder than their spoken words. Quickly, she'd dismissed the grown-up conversation, thinking instead of the day's picnic. It hadn't been the last outing, she remembered now, only the most joyous. The circus, because of what had happened afterward, couldn't compare.

"Let's you and me get a day by ourselves," Paul had suggested, years after her mother was gone, too. They'd driven to Hartford an hour away, to the civic center where Regan sat high up in the bleachers, entranced by high-wire acts with triple somersaults into space, by the emergence of ten clowns from the tiniest car she'd ever seen—Regan had clapped her hands in excitement—by the smell of elephants and horses. And the sweet, forbidden taste of cotton candy. Aunt Martha didn't allow sugar treats or soda pop. "Isn't this fun, Paul?"

Regan asked, her hand tucked into his large one when she caught him looking not at the center ring, but fixedly at her. "Isn't this just like when Mama was here?"

He had smiled, making Regan almost oblivious to the small muscle twitch at the corner of his eye. "Yeah," he'd said, "just like that."

It was hard to think of him as "Uncle," when he'd always been just "Paul" to her before while her mother was with them. And they'd never done anything half so nice again, because Martha had been furious at their sneaking off for the whole day. "I never get to go," Alyson cried. "Regan does everything!" she screamed.

And with the years, Paul's attitude toward her had inexplicably grown worse, not better. Regan couldn't say why, but it seemed that the more grown-up she became, the more harshly he treated her. Sometimes now, she was certain Paul hated her. She'd always thought that of Martha.

"If Liz were here, that child would be spoiled to the bone!"

But Regan had thought that she wasn't likely to be spoiled when she got so many spankings. And so many hand-me-downs.

Now, her arm fell across the worn rag doll on her pillow as she remembered stopping one afternoon in Alyson's doorway to admire her collection. Porcelain faces, gleaming curls, beautifully painted smiles. The enjoyment hadn't lasted long.

"Keep your grimy hands off my dolls!"

Alyson had flown into the room, seizing Regan by the hair. When she'd stifled a cry of pain, she was shoved away from the shelves. "If you want something to play with, take this!" A flung scrap of cloth, a flash of orange-red yarn, brighter than Alyson's hair. "I'm too old for it, anyway"—an attempt at charity, Regan was to assume. "Almost a lady, Mommy says." Alyson managed a smile, her blue eyes still ice-cold at the intrusion. "Raggedy Ann just needs her dress patched— and if you wash the pinafore, that bicycle grease *might* come out."

Holding the cast-off toy, Regan had already loved it. Even if she wasn't pretty like the others in their velvet gowns and gold shoes, like Alyson. Raggedy Ann was *hers:* a castoff, too.

Why, Regan asked herself, did she always feel guilty for taking up space in Paul Oldham's house?

She buried her face for a second in Raggy's clean, often-mended white front. Then with a sigh, she sat up, reaching for the red scrapbook on the table by her bed.

Opening it—the pages fell automatically to the right spot—Regan took a breath, delighted as she always was by the first sight of the grand old house.

Sun-washed and majestic, the mansion thrust upward against a summer sky of blue: a welcoming fortress of red brick, sandstone, and handsome carved oak, meant to withstand the whims and ravages of time. Even the basement had been cut from solid rock. From either end of the enormous rectangle interrupted by bow windows, a parapet or two, a brief wall of leaded glass (she knew this to be the morning room)—twin wings jutted at angles; to the right of the double-doored entry, a stone tower, four stories high—one more than the rest of the great house—shot straight toward the heavens, wearing its notched pattern of crenelation as if it were an elegant top hat held by some unseen hand against the winds of fate.

Like spikes on a crown, the slate roofs sprouted dozens of chimneys, variously designed in the manner of Tudor architecture, the chief influence—though there were others. The earlier medieval tower, for instance; and the Elizabethan bedroom brought whole from an English manor house. She wouldn't want to use that one—too dark and stuffy. But she wouldn't have to, either; could choose or change, according to her mood, for inside the mansion each room had been furnished in different fashion, and its treasures were renowned.

Regan knew by heart these facts from the yellowing newspaper article, just as she had long ago memorized every detail of the fading photographs. But there was more, far more, than a few words and pictures to dream over. She could see the costly oriental rugs and precious tapestries, yes; but she could also smell the flowers in the gardens, the wafting, rich aromas of cooking for a banquet; feel the satin-smooth linen-fold wall paneling beneath her fingers, the deep color of mahogany almost alive to the touch; taste on her tongue the sweetness of an aperitif; hear fine music from the priceless grand piano that Paderewski had once played and, perhaps best of all, the sound of laughter. Children, she wondered, chasing each other along the broad terrace of sandstone at the rear of the house?

There seemed to be a sense of humor here, not only wealth and grandeur——just as she was well-acquainted with her own, plainer surroundings——and the opposite of smiles. Regan looked about her. Dull but serviceable, the room she had occupied during her childhood and adolescence contained the narrow bed on which she was sitting, a three-drawer dresser badly in need of refinishing, and a bedside table on four spindly legs that threatened any second to dump her white plastic AM radio onto the brown linoleum floor. Regan had hung bright-colored posters to combat the dingy pink-painted walls, and she kept the room itself scrupulously clean, but that was all she could say for it. Nothing to laugh about here in Paul's house. She had never been able to think of it as home, and never would. Unlike the Talbot mansion in the pictures, in her dreams, it was a place to be gotten out of, for good, as soon as possible.

Glancing at her casual attire——brief white shorts and a sunshine-yellow T-shirt emblazoned with the message 'Indescribably Delicious'——Regan decided she fit her present environment only too well, however; and she didn't know how to get out, anyway. But still . . . just suppose she were wearing not the typical teenage garb of a warm Sunday afternoon in May, but a crisp white organdy dress (might as well dream fancy) dripping delicate lace like the frosting on a wedding cake; suppose . . . she did belong.

Shining tawny-gold hair spilling over the pages so that she was periodically forced to sweep it back with one hand, Regan returned her attention to the pictures, that winding, tree-lined drive from the entrance gates and the first glimpse of the house itself. She had never dared to trespass on the property——well, not really *trespass*, as in *against the law*. She did, now and then, scale the high black iron fence; drop down on the other side; slip off her shoes and run barefoot over the cool, uncut green grass. But she wasn't actually violating anyone's privacy, and of course she'd never take anything—not that there was much left inside.

The house stood empty, had been for a long time. Everything in storage somewhere, she supposed. Some windows broken. If someday she was to—ridiculous fantasy now, and dangerous as well—force her way inside, she might be disappointed by the empty rooms, decay perhaps; but Regan didn't believe for an instant that anything about the mansion could be disappointing.

She held the long, loose swath of her hair back with a hand and stared at the words before her, not bothering to read because she heard the words of the article in her mind: "In 1935 Thomas Talbot, a prominent industrialist, purchased this vast property, a tract of land since reduced from the original one thousand acres, and began to construct his dream house. The result is a source of pride to his descendants [said relations having since been reduced, Regan knew, to squabbling over the remaining acres] as well as to the residents of Lancaster. The State of Connecticut boasts no more regal residence, no more harmonious, sometimes whimsical, blend of past and present, of structural beauty and natural location. . . ."

Regan lived in the same town, breathed the same air—or did she? How did it feel to grow up on the right side of Lancaster in such a home? Cherished and well-loved? If only she had never come to *this* house . . . if only she'd never had to.

Regan sighed, feeling the familiar surge of abandonment from her childhood nightmares: She heard her mother singing softly, fell asleep to the haunting melody, then awoke in their small apartment to find her mother missing. When would she forget the terror of that dream? She used to have it all the time, almost every night reliving the misery of coming to Paul Oldham's house, sensing even that first morning that she was unwanted.

She'd learned the hard way—instantly—not to trust Alyson. The surreptitious pinches and bites from her five-year-old cousin were not to provoke retaliation. "Alyson wouldn't do such a thing; that's dreadful to say, Regan. Why would she deliberately push you off the tricycle? You fell by yourself. Go tell Ali you're sorry for tattling."

Regan kept quiet soon enough, grateful at least that she didn't have to share a room in the dingy, mustard frame house. She'd thought life might improve after Martha's death—an impression that brought immediate pangs of guilt—but if anything, it had gotten worse.

"Growing up," Paul had said not long ago, reaching out suddenly to lift her hair off her neck, letting the tawny strands slip through his fingers. Then he'd tilted her chin, staring into her eyes, holding Regan spellbound by his look—as if he loved her, as if the knowledge made him sad. "Don't go sour on me," he'd added.

"Uncle Paul—"

"Where's my dinner?" He turned away from her. "You're not such a great cook to begin with, at least put the food on the table on time."

Regan had felt both happy and uneasy, in the space of several seconds. Well, confusion wasn't in short supply; it had become, for her, a way of life.

Three more days, she told herself. Then she'd be graduated from high school, ready for the world outside the confines of textbooks and this dreary room. Loved or unloved, she had reached majority at last; unscathed, to all outward appearances. Who could see the scars her heart had formed?

With a sigh, Regan decided she was being much too introspective for such a sweet, warm afternoon—and, with a last look at the pages of the old newspaper article, closed the red scrapbook. Somehow, she had to find her own way to make the dreams come true; but she would think about that later. Carefully now, she put the book on the slanting shelf of her bedside table—and at the same time heard the car rattle to a stop in the driveway beneath her window.

Oh God, no! Regan peered out briefly at the green sedan.

ten years old. It was a rust bucket. She hated riding in it. And here was Paul, home from the shop—tired of beating dents out of fenders on other people's cars? How long would that job last? Alyson was away for the weekend. Lucky Alyson, Regan thought. She wanted to retreat into her daydreams again; but far more important, she didn't want to stay in the house with Paul. A small shiver of panic ran down her spine. Where could she go? It wasn't exactly running from him; she'd been thinking about something else to do—but what?

Take a walk? If he was in a bad mood, Paul might ask why she wanted to wander around town, and what was she looking for? If she told him, that is. He was still in the car, listening to a country song on the radio, a song she recognized, and the male singer hadn't hit the second chorus yet. The music was blaring, twangy with guitar and banjo. Regan's mind raced. She could visit the girl down the block who was in her class, ask about the parents' banquet the night before (that Paul wouldn't attend), but no one would be home. This afternoon was the senior recital at the school auditorium, and—

In a rush, Regan dashed to her closet, banged the door back against the wall, pulled out the only sundress she owned, and yanked off her shorts and shirt. She could be ready in a flash. What harm was there in going to a concert, she would ask Paul if he tried to stop her for some reason—or for no reason at all. Even if *he* considered real music useless?

She remembered the excitement at school about the program today. Regan glanced at the alarm clock by her bed. Darn. She'd missed more than half already, but still—

The sundress, a cotton print in cream and brown and rust, slithered down her body, was smoothed into place. She ran a quick brush through her long, fair hair. No, she wasn't quite right about the lineup for the recital. Before the choir sang, there was someone else, a guest *artist*, "a *professional* pianist," one of her classmates had said. Someone whose training had begun right here in Lancaster. Classical training far removed from her own dreams, but wouldn't it be grand to watch him?

With a shaking hand, Regan slashed lip gloss over her

mouth, then hurriedly wiped away the smudges. The back-door screen slammed shut. She raced down the flight of steps to the foyer as Paul was coming through the kitchen, calling her. By the time he thought to look out the front door, Regan would be at the corner of the block, out of sight.

James Harrod Marsh looked out from the wings of the stage at the audience assembled in the auditorium, feeling that familiar clutch of anxiety in the pit of his stomach. His hands, which must be warm and pliant by the time the string quartet finished the Vivaldi, were as cold as January despite the overheated atmosphere. God, why do I play these benefits? Jake asked himself as he had a dozen times in ten minutes. The attack of nerves was no less than a real concert provoked, and the money nonexistent. More to the point, why waste time better used for practice?

Only fourteen weeks left before his tour—a first full-scale tour, and therefore crucial. He was booked with some good orchestras this season and, at last, several fine ones. Not to mention a guest appearance, so coveted, with the best. If the year went well, superbly well...

He didn't finish the thought. A sudden vision of his mother came to mind, blocking superstition. She had looked rather like that middle-aged woman in the front row. From his vantage in the wings, Jake could see graying hair that had once been dark; what looked to be brown eyes; the same slightness of frame. And then, some telltale fidgeting with the handbag in her lap. The woman hated the music. The eyes were soft, but they were vacant, too; though the string quartet wasn't half bad—only a little lacking in passion—nothing of beauty was reaching her. Unlike his mother, he thought.

She had listened to him for hours, and without musical knowledge herself, she had made criticisms that hit the mark nearly every time. An old vow crossed his mind, the stronger for repetition: one day he would repay her hours of concentration, the years of sacrifice for his benefit. Even, if he could repay it, the final sacrifice. Somehow.

The thought made his hands colder than before, and Jake let his gaze wander, picking out a few familiar faces in the crowd. A student of his, a neighbor. But the distraction wouldn't work. If his father hadn't died, he told himself . . . if his mother hadn't become ill . . . if Enid hadn't interfered . . .

In his mother's house, she bustles about, fixing blankets on the bed, smoothing sheets and dispositions. Scolding Catherine to take her medicine. But she's better, Jake thinks—after two years of fighting, she's winning now. Her face, always pretty, looks like a girl's again: the skin unlined, taut against her cheekbones, flushed with color when he makes her laugh.

"Those doctors don't know anything." Catherine struggles to sit up. "The drug makes me fall asleep too fast."

They begin to talk of winter and the coming spring; of the crocuses that Catherine loves; of Jake's music. "I think the piano needs tuning," his mother says. She holds onto the small details of their days as if they were her hold on life itself. Making her well again. "The *Pathétique* sounded off to me this morning."

"It was tuned," Jake answers. "Last month. *I* was off. Not enough practice time"; then he is immediately sorry for saying so. Playing at Steven's roadhouse three or four nights a week to make money, going straight from school, he loses hours at the piano. The music suffers, but she mustn't blame herself.

"You should quit, Jake," Catherine chides. "We'll manage. I'll be on my feet again soon."

But not working; not for a long, long time. Growing back after the radiation therapy, her hair is brittle, graying, as fragile as her body. Her bones.

"No, you let me care about everything. I can handle the lessons, and practice too, and my job."

"That boy," Enid says, smiling at him from the other side of his mother's bed, "was born knowing how to play the piano. Don't you worry about *his* talent slipping."

The frail head lolls upon the pillow; the tired eyes flicker open then shut, then wide again. "I should fix supper"—the little fiction they have perpetuated for nearly a year and a half, since the operation. "In just a minute I'll get something. Jake, what would you like tonight?"

"Steak. And home fries and salad, fresh peas, strawberry shortcake."

Part of the repeated story. Catherine tries to smile.

"And you'll have it," Enid announces. "You should be ashamed, Catherine. This boy will be thin as a rail if he doesn't get some real cooking. I'm taking him home. Lord knows, I've asked often enough. Now I'm telling him. And you . . . you're going to take that medication this minute, and rest."

Frowning, Jake tries to stare her down. How can she talk to his mother this way? Trying to make her feel guilty for something she can't help; not now. Even a lifetime friend hasn't any right. He can feed himself, for Christ's sake. He isn't a baby.

"I can't go. Bring the food here if you want, I don't care, but I'm not leaving her. She needs me."

His stock phrase—except that, usually, he merely thinks the words. A hundred times a day. In school. Practicing. At his lessons. Walking home. Working at the roadhouse. Waking in the night to her groans. If he stays with her, she will never have to go back to that hospital. Never. Between them, they can make her well.

But Enid phones another neighbor to come sit while Catherine sleeps; enforces medicine; steers Jake from the house.

Outside, the air is chill and sharp, and underneath their booted feet, the hard ground seems dead, unyielding. The stars are far away as spring. February. How could any month be worse? He lives constantly with gnawing fear—his own; and pain—his mother's. Will the crocuses ever bloom?

Enid draws a clean, deep breath. "That house smells of sickness. You can't get away from it except by walking out. You should more often, you know. A boy your age . . ."

He doesn't say a word. Sixteen, he thinks . . . hardly a child. Though she treats him like one.

Three blocks from home, Enid opens her own front door. A house slightly better than his mother's, the rooms are larger, the windows bigger and more numerous; the furniture old, though comfortable. Enid forces him down on the tweed sofa. "Sit. Stretch your legs out—My goodness, how you've grown! Almost a man." She brings something from the kitchen. "Try this."

"I don't drink beer."

"You do tonight. And finish it all." Dutifully, he does, and with surprising ease, swinging back and forth in his mind from boy to man to child. Weary, leaning his head against the sofa back, he feels tension drain from him, slowly, as if someone had pulled a plug. He smells supper: vegetables steaming, the broiler being heated, imagines even the aroma of hulled strawberries.

And magically, indeed, she produces the fictional meal. Of course. Her refrigerator and the huge chest-freezer stay fully stocked. Enid's husband, a long-distance trucker, likes to eat well when he rolls in, late and exhausted. A happy surrogate, Jake digs into the food.

Afterward, he feels sated, content, and boneless with fatigue. Every nerve and muscle, every ounce of blood concentrates on the complex process of digestion; still, simpler than the intricate balance of his emotions. He likes Enid now for she seems soft again, warm and easy to be with; but earlier, not so long ago, he had hated her.

She smells like the faintest essence of lily of the valley. Her voice is almost a whisper. "How long since you've gone to a ball game? Taken a girl out? Horsed around with your friends?"

He hasn't any friends left. Only acquaintances now who awkwardly punch his arm at his locker. Sports, clubs, dances are gone, sacrificed to illness and responsibility. Gladly, if only she gets well. And as for girls . . .

"No dates," he says.

"With a face like yours?" sounding shocked, but Enid's smile gives away the teasing. "Last year you went with that redhead, didn't you?"

Yes. Cute, too. "She got tired of me standing her up," Jake says. During those in-and-out weeks of hospital treatment, the endless visits. "She wasn't anything serious."

"What about now?"

"I'm the man of the house," he repeats his mother's charge.

"A figure of speech after your father's funeral, Jake. Catherine never expected so much."

But whom else did she have? Enid, a few neighbors, some friends from church when she could go. Whom else did *he* have?

Enid says, "She knows, Jake. There isn't any cure. And not much time, either. She knows, and if you'd let it come, so do you."

The traitorous tears sting his eyes. He tries not to look at Enid. She touches his cheek, traces the hard line of his clenched jaw.

"No!"

But Enid takes his face between her hands and makes him turn; he directs his gaze past her to the white lace curtains at the dark window. "Poor baby," Enid whispers. "Nothing you can do will save her. Catherine's dying, Jake. It hurts me, too, but she is . . . dying."

"She isn't going to die!"

Isn't. Won't. Can't. *I will not let her.*

Enid's fingers brush his skin. His eyes at last meet hers, a blur of hazel and brown, with that unbearable kindness showing in them. Four, five years younger than his mother. Late thirties, edging into forty.

"I have to go," he says stiffly. "She might need me."

But Enid clutches his hand. "We need each other, don't we?"

And he begins to understand. She's afraid, just as he is; Enid only hides it differently, with gruffness and bustle, not denial. "Jake, I need you for a while," and he rests his head against the sofa, their shoulders warmly touching, hands lightly clasped on the cushion between them. The house feels friendly, safe. Enid is alive, healthy, and so is he. God, no smell of hopelessness here. No fear. Closing his eyes, he feels peaceful . . . until another kind of tension seeps slowly, slowly, through him.

Much later, in a room with old wallpaper and new sensations, he had come to know betrayal, too. . . .

If Enid hadn't interfered, Jake repeated to himself. Now, he listened vaguely to the applause that greeted the end of the string quartet's piece. His music, yes; that was the only way to make up to his mother for the perfidy he tried not to remember; like the night he pushed away now with a faint, physical motion of one hand. Yes, he would gain the reputation on concert stages that he so desperately wanted, needed, for her even more than for himself. With luck, Jake added silently. And a hell of a lot more work.

But today, he had promised the Senior Committee a good performance, and he meant to give one. Where his playing was concerned, he drew no lines. The high school auditorium was no less important, once he sat down at the piano onstage, than the concert hall in Chicago. After all, Jake chided himself, smiling faintly as he began with automatic, almost instinctual, movements to exercise his fingers, he was an alumnus of the school. He owed his alma mater something more than future, and uncertain, fame.

Eight years ago, a senior himself, he'd played at a similar recital. Working his fingers now, Jake mentally raced through a score he had committed to memory while still a child. He despised error, particularly his; and the only way to avoid mistake was to be totally, completely, perfectly prepared. It was his own brand of religion, which he practiced like a zealot.

Excusing herself as she crossed in front of people, Regan slid into the empty seat in the center of the front row to the romantic beginning strains of *The Moonlight Sonata*. Already breathless from hurrying, she glanced up at the stage; felt her lungs fight harder for air—but for a very different reason than escaping Paul.

Oh, how splendid he was!

At the ebony piano, he seemed the essence of what a concert pianist should be. Tall, lean, straight. Better than Liszt, who had been the first to perform with profile toward the audience, being enamored of his own good looks. This man too? she wondered. Her heart skipped and paused, then thudded as she watched.

The overhead lights gleamed in his hair, bringing glints of bronze and gold to deep brown, pooling in rich, thick color like a display of splendor, Rembrandt's opulent portrait; but even the stunning first physical impression soon gave way to something else, like the rhythm of her breathing.

Regan couldn't seem to catch her breath. He might be wearing a conservative dark suit and cautious tie; but there was nothing restrained about his playing. The fact, undeniable, that he was handsome became nothing but a bonus: his versatility, his easy command of the instrument at his fingertips, the keyboard and the music, enchanted her. For a second or two, thinking she could die happy in such a perfect moment, hearing such perfect beauty, Regan closed her eyes.

When she opened them again, he had glanced her way— at least, she thought he had—and she felt sure that the same colors flecked his dark eyes. Or had she only imagined from the distance, briefly, his gaze fixed upon her in some warm communion of spirit?

With a slight frown, he looked away instantly, down at the keys. Of course, she'd imagined. He hadn't even seen her!

Hands clasped tightly in her lap, green eyes riveted on him still, Regan absorbed every elegant note of the Beethoven. Her palms were damp with excitement, and her heart raced. This was what it meant to be trained to a high level of excellence in a chosen field, to be attuned to an instrument as the ebony piano itself had been tuned to perfection. Almost afraid to take a breath for fear of missing a single note, Regan felt she was looking at, and listening to, greatness. Remember this, she told herself needlessly, remember this day forever.

When the piece had ended and the final notes were gone— taken in by the draperies and the walls and the carpet on the aisles—the noise of applause resounded all about her; but Regan sat as still as stone. Her hands could barely move, let alone clap. "Wasn't that *wonderful?*" she heard someone say behind her, and from farther along the row in which she sat, "So moving" in a whisper; but she could only nod in silent agreement of her own with the pattern of her heartbeat permanently disrupted. And stare and stare, mute as a swan, at the stage.

Christ, she's a beauty, Jake thought with another, violent tripping of his heart. She had very nearly made him lose his concentration during the sonata. He meant only to glance again at the woman in the front row who reminded him slightly of his mother, as if he were dedicating the Beethoven to her, and there had appeared beside her this ethereal wonder of innocence. Hardly more than a child, though she looked—idiotic notion, what was wrong with him?—made of spun gold. Too bad she was so young, and didn't seem the type, either, to hang around after the recital— No, it was the aging women who stayed, fawned and encouraged when there was no need, gushing praise he did not require. He always knew how badly or how well he'd done; usually, he could tell before he halfway finished the first piece. Not less than nine on a scale of ten just now, he decided. But look at that hair, that face, the steady, steady gaze. She defied a ranking.

With a quick shake of his head, Jake forced his wandering attention to heel. What next? The program indicated Chopin, lyrical and safe, but Jake felt suddenly reckless. To hell with Chopin! He wanted to see those luminous eyes light up. What color were they? Something magnificent—they could hardly be anything less. Jake looked down at the keyboard, and smiled. At the brief silence between applause and what soon would be a shuffling of impatience, he selected his most solemn expression, squared his shoulders, and began to play.

He might even wake the lady next to her.

Regan recognized the number immediately, but was as shocked by the startling change of pace and mood after the Beethoven and the substitution from the program listing as the rest of the audience. Suddenly, Scott Joplin's stride ragtime rocked the auditorium with rhythm; wrecked the last regularity of her pulse. Scattered applause then, intakes of breath from a few, even a quickly hushed protest or two overrode several bars of the music before everyone settled to enjoy the fun. The woman beside Regan had even fluttered a hand over her heart. Pleased or displeased? she wondered. Then felt that compelling brown-gold gaze upon her.

He *was* looking at her! Yes. For reaction? Why? His eyes seemed to ask her opinion of his daring, even to want her smile. The classical pianist was having a bit of sport, inviting her to share the conspiracy. Or was *she* only enjoying more fantasy?

Regan felt a slow blush creep into her cheeks as their gazes held, briefly. His fingers flew effortlessly over the keys, playfully. She shook her head and bit her lower lip to keep from laughing, and looked quickly down again at her hands, twisting in the skirt of her sundress. But not before she had caught that answering smile from him, that flash of white teeth and personality and mischief that seemed meant for her alone—she was almost sure of it.

Then, in an agony of embarrassment, not sure at all. For the rest of the program, long after the *a cappella* choir had taken over the stage and the piano stood silent, Regan focused her complete attention visually on her fingers, the handbag of the woman next to her, and the shining wing-tip shoes of the man on her left.

Why had she stayed behind? Lingering with the cluster of older women who surrounded the pianist after the recital, Regan was amazed at herself. She hadn't intended to. He was a grown man, a professional, his talent not a question mark, and she had only imagined his interest during the Beethoven, the ragtime, because she *wanted* to think he was smiling at her, to be close to such accomplishment as his. Why didn't she leave now, while she could? Where had the other students gone?

And why was she the only girl in a crowd of women? Gracious and charming, as each of them offered effusive congratulations, James Harrod Marsh used words Regan hardly knew and musical terminology that sounded even more foreign;

and she didn't have the vaguest idea how to flatter him the way the others were doing. Even their smart linen dresses and summer shoes with thin high heels made her own cream-and-brown print sundress with its splashes of rust-colored flowers, and her sandals, appear childish and unsophisticated. Oh, why had she left her hair loose down her back? The gleam of gold satin hung to her waist. Why hadn't she stopped in the restroom beforehand to twist it high on her head? At least she might have looked older that way, a little; but she'd been late and—

His glance flicked toward her, then away. She felt as if she were still under the spell he had cast; as if he had asked her to stay. Don't be stupid! What could she possibly say to him, anyway? She knew practically nothing about music! She was going to make an utter fool of herself, and very soon, too, if she didn't move. Already, people were drifting away one by one, chattering among themselves, ignoring her. He was talking to the only woman remaining (again she dismissed herself from the category), and feeling hopeless and awkward, Regan turned away. It was hard to make her legs move; they might not carry her; she might fall—

Then a voice halted her slow progress. ". . . and the Beethoven, Mr. Marsh, was so very, very sweet." A solid bulk of a woman, skimpy eyelashes batting coquettishly, stood close to him, her immense bosom heaving as he bestowed upon her one of his mesmerizing smiles.

"Why, thank you, you're too kind." Though he didn't sound as if he found her enthusiasm excessive in the least.

Turning back again, Regan could only stare. Straight and tall and lean, he looked deserving of praise, lots of it—and yes, accepting, too, as if the words were his due. He was proud, she decided with the snap judgment of the very young, and he was arrogant. And much too sure of himself—if she was not. Suddenly, Paul's words came to mind again. "You don't need lessons, miss. I got no money for teaching you how to squawk. What makes you think you got talent, or anything more than your mama had?"

". . . very dramatic to use the Joplin after the sonata. Mr. Marsh, I think you are a *master*."

Regan's ears rang with the bulky woman's words. Yes, she thought. And why not? Why shouldn't he be? The lovely afternoon, the spell, began to float away in wisps of despair and reality. No wonder this man's skill made her feel awed and insubstantial. She hadn't a chance to prove herself, none that she could think of, not soon enough; and seeing the result of hard work and real talent that someone had believed in and nurtured only pointed out the vast differences between them. She felt a sharp twinge of unwelcome envy, of helpless anger. This is how the peasants must have felt before the French Revolution, starving to death while Louis XVI and his queen told them to eat cake when there was no bread.

"Well? Think you can top that?"

Startled, Regan raised her eyes to meet a steady, amused regard from brown eyes flecked with bronze light—as if they were the only two people who understood a joke. But she wasn't laughing. A swift glance away confirmed that they were alone in the empty, echoing auditorium. Lost in thoughts of Paul and the clenching unhappiness he brought, lost in thoughts of privilege, she had failed to see the woman leave. Regan looked back at him. It didn't occur to her that he might have deliberately talked to everyone else first. Why did he smile at her like that? She blushed furiously, all the more angry when she couldn't control the change of color in her face. Was he really waiting for her praise, too?

With every ounce of resentment she could muster—which, at the moment, was considerable—Regan searched her brain for the scathing epithet, then poured it over him like a bucket of ice-cold water.

"I—*I* think you are a *cornball!*"

The reaction on his face was instantaneous. "Well, if you know another way to keep them awake, then—"

"Play decently," she said softly, and walked away.

Regan had almost reached the exit when a strong hand closed over her upper arm like a band of fine Damascus steel and swung her around. She had never felt such strength in anyone's fingers, not even Paul's. Her heart raced alarmingly, as if it were trying to leave her body while escape was still possible; but she forced a shaky smile. "I knew you'd do that—make another grandstand play. Like the Joplin."

She hadn't known anything of the sort. Then why this cheeky display, Regan asked herself, when she was trembling inside, searching for Paul's anger in this man's eyes? But he only looked bewildered. "I thought you liked the ragtime." He released her arm. "The song was for you. I'm sorry if I..."

Regan's fragile fury dissolved like sugar in water. He'd been trying to make her smile! "For *me?*" She was blaming him for something he couldn't help. "Oh no," she said, *"I'm* sorry"— giving him a smile, ruefully apologetic. "I only said that— about your playing badly—because you *didn't,* you played beautifully, as you must know ... but after all those women, *I* couldn't think of anything to say, and I—" She couldn't finish.

He said slowly, "You're a bundle of contradictions. Challenging one minute, wistful the next." He began to smile. "Good Lord, you'd stand out in a crowd of a thousand women with that silk waterfall of hair, those green cat's eyes." Stopping, he searched her gaze as if identifying its shade. "No, I shouldn't tell you that, should I? You obviously don't appreciate your own appeal yet, which merely adds to it."

His brown gaze lit the corners of her heart.

"I think we'd better start over." She held out a hand, which he took quickly, as if he'd been waiting to touch her again. "My name is Regan Reilly," she began. "Professionally—"

But he cut her off. "Jake Marsh." His strong fingers warmly joined to hers. He had wonderful hands. She hadn't seen them clearly while he was playing, but it was more than the lean, aristocratic shape of his fingers; she was holding a supple life force, strong and warm and immensely comforting, hands that could never be considered a mere physiological collection of muscles, bones, and tendons. "I'm a junior," he explained, "and there were just too many people in the house with the same name. For a while, anyway. Nobody ever calls me James."

They grinned at each other like awkward dates, blind dates who were both relieved at their luck for the evening.

Jake studied her again with amusement in his eyes. Or something. She couldn't define the expression exactly, but a heated lethargy seeped through her veins, her bones, crept along her spine.

"So," he said after a long moment, "how do you, uh, characterize yourself ... professionally?"

"I'm a singer."

She'd answered so promptly, each word overlaid with pride, that he must think she'd rehearsed them like a song. Well, in a way, she had; today, in her room. Alone, and wondering. And she knew then what she'd been desperately wanting ever since she sat down in the first row and heard such excellence at the recital—from this man. If she took a first step on her own, which didn't cost Paul Oldham a cent, how could he possibly object? Just one little step; maybe nothing more would be warranted. But at least, *she'd* know. At least she wouldn't have to keep on wondering.

"I mean," Regan corrected, "I'd like to be. I want you to— to listen to me, would you? To tell me what you think about my chances; if I have any talent. Just a song or two. Please," she said, not even able to give him one of the smiles she practiced in front of her mirror. "Don't you think one musician should boost another?" Her heart pounded crazily.

"Classical and—what is it you sing—pop stuff? That's like oil and water." Jake frowned.

This wasn't as easy as she'd hoped. "You mixed Joplin with Grieg, didn't you? And Beethoven for good measure? And if that woman thought the effect was—"

He cut her off with an unexpected laugh. "Sweet, can you believe it? I've never in my life heard Beethoven called 'sweet.'"

"Then she gave you a new way of looking at *your* music," Regan said quickly before she lost heart. "You might learn even more listening to mine."

"I might at that," he agreed, giving her an assessing look. "I never said I wouldn't listen, you know. But, first things first. Are you hungry?" He smiled. "I never eat before I perform, so I'm starving now." A teasing smile, she thought. "I'll settle for my place if you will," he said. "It's only five minutes from here, with the requisite piano. And cheap." Then the smile became a grin as he slipped an arm around her shoulder. "I'm an extremely poor judge of talent," Jake added, "when my stomach's empty."

Jake's house—a legacy from his mother, he told Regan with another teasing smile—went perfectly with the battered red VW he drove. White frame and beginning to fall apart from lack of major maintenance—translated, cash investment—it nevertheless charmed Regan. But at the front door, she hesitated, asking, "Is there anyone at home?"

"Only me," Jake replied, fitting his key in the lock.

Regan caught her bottom lip in her teeth, and felt her heart begin to pound. "Well, then, I don't think I should—"

Jake straightened, turning to look at her. "Hey, it's all right. I promise, I'm not an ax murderer." His smile provoked no response. Regan took a step backward on the porch. It wasn't Jake she'd been worried about.

"I know, but my uncle—"

"Is absolutely right to be concerned for you." He opened the door, gesturing her inside. "In this instance, he needn't be. Regan, I'm not going to hurt you." Pausing, he said, "But if you'd rather not sing—"

Regan lifted her chin, then flashed a smile. Paul wouldn't know. And in a way, she had asked Jake to listen to her *because* of Paul. Because, otherwise, she had no chance right now. Brushing past Jake, she quickly stepped inside.

She liked the small and simple rooms, followed Jake on a quick tour—"Don't look at the unmade bed, I was in a hurry this morning"—and thought how like her image of the Talbot mansion was the feeling here, of laughter and people who loved each other. Yes, but the plumbing leaked, Jake told her with an apologetic smile. Nothing had been painted in years, not even the black shutters on the front windows. And in the kitchen, under the sink, during spells of damp weather, toadstools thrived.

"Still, this is a pleasant room." Regan looked around at the red-and-white color scheme, which looked crisp and clean to her, cheerful. "As if someone enjoyed working here—did she? Your mother, I mean?"

"Yes," he said reflectively. "Yes, she did. Maybe I ought to spend more time here myself, but the kitchen and I are at cross-purposes. I hate to cook."

When Regan offered to take over, Jake quickly agreed, setting the table with old, but obviously cherished, blue willow ware and silverplate whose simple pattern was enhanced by a patina of age and use while she fixed their food. Rummaging in the refrigerator; asking where things were; if he liked eggs; what kind of cheese did he have on hand, Regan relaxed, oddly at ease in a stranger's home. *Cozy,* that was the word she had wanted for the kitchen. Not like her uncle's house....

She didn't realize she had spoken aloud, to herself, until Jake asked, "Why do you live with your uncle?"

Regan didn't know how to answer. She didn't know much more about her family than Jake did.

"My father died when I was about a year old," she said slowly. "My mother... left two years later. Paul took me in; his wife was my father's sister." She smiled sadly. "I've always felt that I'm just in the way, though... and Alyson, my cousin—she and I have never really gotten along. I used to try, but..."

Regan trailed off, not able to tell Jake much more, not wanting to. Her throat felt tight, and she blinked several times to clear her vision.

Avoiding her gaze, so as not to embarrass her, Jake set the coffee cups on their saucers and folded two red napkins.

"I guess I was luckier," he said after a moment. "My family was very close while my father was alive, and after his death, my mother and I... well, I knew there were people who'd look out for me, people I could care about, too." *Until the last,* he corrected silently. "You don't feel that way, do you, Regan?"

"No," she whispered, "I don't." But would that always be true?

"I wasn't trying to depress you," Jake said. "The road wasn't easy for us, either." Making coffee, he told her of his father's death when Jake was ten years old.

"Hey, how's it going?" his father's friend had asked, coming by the house one afternoon at five o'clock. Jake liked him; they'd gone to a Yankees game at the stadium one weekend, he and his father and Bill. "Where's your mother, Jake?"

He had noticed immediately the pinched expression on Bill's face, a wavering smile in place of the broad grin. Jake said his mother was shopping. He'd listened to Bill's chatter about the team's chances for the pennant next season while his ears burned and the saliva evaporated from his mouth.

Catherine had known right away, too, that there was trouble. "Bill, where's Jim?" And then, "What's happened?"

Gloom had fallen over the room as if someone had closed a pair of heavy draperies. Jake heard his mother cry out, saw the hand clap over her mouth to stop it, watched the groceries she'd carried fall to the floor, cans and bottles rolling.

"A heart attack," Jake told Regan now. "He was thirty-six years old, no history of problems." And that quickly, it had been over for them. The laughter, and the love. "Four years later my mother got sick," he finished, "and two years after that, she was dead too."

"I'm sorry, Jake," Regan said softly. "Then you were all alone at—"

"Sixteen. Except," he added bitterly, "for a guardian I didn't need, or want. By then, I could have survived by myself; but the court didn't agree." In his mother's will, Enid had been appointed to watch over him. Jake didn't mention her by name; he never spoke her name aloud; tried not to even think it. When he stopped talking, Jake looked up at Regan.

"Your mother must have been proud of you," she murmured.

"She didn't have time to be. But she always said that talent was a gift from God, not to be wasted. My father believed the same," he said with a smile of reminiscence. "Only he tempered it a little . . . which sometimes led to a minor battle at home."

Not the sort of battle he was used to, Regan surmised from

the gentle expression on Jake's face, the softness in his brown eyes. "Mom helped me right to the end," he said. "She didn't have any, as they say, 'marketable skills' when Dad died, and she worked herself too hard, scrimped and saved . . . but it was her small estate that paid for my schooling at the conservatory in Boston, with a scholarship added on." And the reason, Jake added, why the house needed paint and a thousand other things. "She always told me if you want something badly enough, you find a way to get it . . . so I did." He smiled. "It's what she'd have wanted, too. And that's why next fall is so important, my first real tour. Last year I played some good dates, but nothing steady."

"Will you tell me about it?" Regan switched off the gas and carried the skillet to the table, setting it on the cast-iron trivet in the center. "Where will you go, and what's your routine when you're away from home?"

How she envied him his talent, his skill, his achievements. Envy again. But how could she overcome her own obstacles? There was no minuscule estate to keep her, no opportunity for study, no mother who loved her. And then Regan felt ashamed of herself; she smiled in silent apology at Jake's open expression as they sat down to eat. "Please tell me," she said.

"Well, number one, it's not nearly so glamorous as you probably want to believe." He watched her heap his plate with food. "Being on the road sounds romantic, doesn't it, even Gypsy-like? Hell, yes. But there are plenty of lousy hotels, believe me, lots of jet lag and greasy food, not enough sleep, then don't forget the bugs—"

"Oh, stop!"

They were both laughing at the horror picture. Only, she'd love it!

"I'm exaggerating," Jake said after a moment, "but just a bit. Mostly, it's being alone, not having anyone to really talk to—for me, anyway. Strange cities, strange people . . . sometimes literally."

Regan said it before she stopped to think. ". . . Women?"

"Groupies, you mean?" Jake grinned at her. "That's more

a part of the world you've chosen—pop music—not mine."
Jake poured coffee for them both. "Let's talk about you instead," he said. "A young girl, just out of school— Isn't this
the age for diamond rings, or planning to leave for college in
the fall?"

Regan's eyes shone like hard green gems. "I want to sing,
I told you, and that's what I intend to do." Might as well sound
as if she could. "Somehow," she said, "I will. Oh, Jake"—
she softened her tone—"just being here, listening to you play
earlier, hearing all the talk now only makes me want it more!"

"That's what it takes." He gave her that measuring stare
again that saw into her soul. "Guts," he said. "Determination.
Think you've got enough?"

"Yes!"

"And maybe a heart of stone, too." Dropping his gaze, he
pulled his plate closer. "Eat your eggs, they're getting cold."

While they finished the ham-and-cheese omelet she'd fixed,
and a green salad, they talked music and Jake answered her
questions. The cities he would visit sounded exciting: Chicago
and Los Angeles and Denver, places she'd never been, even
Minneapolis and Detroit.

"Competition," Jake said at last with a sigh. He leaned back
in his chair, locking his hands behind his head. "Do you have
any idea how many people in this world can play the piano?"
He grinned. "And I mean *play.*"

"Do you know how many sing?" Then Regan asked, "When
did you begin studying, Jake?", liking the way his name felt
on her tongue. She liked the way his long body lazed in the
chair, too, the graceful motion of his hand as he lifted his
coffee cup, sipping slowly before he answered.

"When I was five. My mother sent me twice a week to the
lady down the street who taught me everything she knew in
less than a year. She told my parents I was a prodigy."

"Were you?"

Jake's eyes brightened with mischief. "No, but I was damn
good for five years old."

Regan laughed, delighted that he could smile at himself.

"You're marvelous now. I love to hear you play."

He inclined his head in thanks. "But I'm running behind the competition, kind lady. How old do you think Cliburn was when he went to Moscow and brought home the Tchaikovsky prize? Twenty-four." He studied her for a moment. "I'm not a *wunderkind* now. I'm twenty-six, Regan. That's why this year is so critical. I can't lose my ground, my momentum. I can't afford to let anything interfere."

A silence settled between them at the hard conviction in his tone, inhibiting the flow of conversation. Regan regretted having asked him to judge her, even that. He had his priorities, and a young girl with no training wasn't one of them. What did she hope to gain from him? Except raw information as crucial to her as Jake's success on tour in the coming season was to him. She wondered if he sensed the harshness in his statement, or her unsure reaction now to being here. In the next moment, unable to believe she said it, even in defense, Regan murmured: "Well, I guess you aren't after my body, then."

Jake shook his head and laughed, reaching out to ruffle the tawny hair that was like silk under his fingers, but she caught the quick flash of undisguised interest in his brown-gold eyes before he stood up, hiding it. "Come on, glutton," he said as Regan scooped the last bite of omelet onto some toast. "I want to hear you sing." Her heart began to trip. "Let's see what kind of a candle you can hold to Beethoven."

Surprisingly, he knew the ballad, slow and haunting, which she asked him to play, rippling off the first phrases flawlessly— what else?—at her mention of the title. He said he'd done some club work for a while to make extra money when his mother was ill, and "This is a steal from the classical, anyway," as he began the introduction, his hands moving easily over the keyboard of the walnut upright. And then she froze.

"I—I've never done much formal singing," Regan said instead of picking up her opening. "Nothing but a school musical once, not even the lead, and I—I try out in the shower now and then, but nobody likes it."

"So this is your big chance. Quit making excuses," and he started over.

There was no hope for it then. She couldn't stand there, staring around the square living room at the philodendrons or the worn, chintz-upholstered furniture or the blue-green carpet on the floor. She had to do what she had come to do, which wasn't to cook or to make pleasant conversation with someone she already liked, and so she opened her mouth at the right time and began. *Do it,* she thought; *you can do it.* He wouldn't bite her head off if she couldn't, would he?

Singing, she scaled mountains and penetrated cloud layers and, losing herself to the amazing union of her voice with Jake's piano, Regan felt as she sometimes did on the verge of sleep—as if she were falling backward over the edge of a cliff, then hurtling through space, faster and faster, with no stops.

"Regan Reilly," Jake said when she finished. He shook his head, saying her name again, hushed, quiet.

"Was I terrible?" Oh God, she hadn't thought so. Despite her nervousness, every note had sounded surprisingly perfect inside, better even than when she sang in her room or the shower, and her voice had come out clear and clean, strong yet simple and precise. "I know I missed the cue at first, almost, but—"

Jake was still shaking his head. "Can't tell a quarter note from a half, can you? A whole from a sixteenth? Bass clef from treble? A sharp from a flat?"

"No," Regan said, feeling miserable. "No." Something in her throat formed a huge lump she couldn't swallow, and she stared at her hands, clenched together.

"That's apparent. Your timing's lousy. Still want to know what I think?"

Her head snapped up. "Yes." Her heart was thundering, and his brown eyes were dark as night, dark and filled with something she couldn't fathom.

"I don't think you have to know anything except how to open your pretty mouth . . . Goddamn, Regan." He grinned at her stunned expression. "You are a natural! Do you know how rare that is? Your simplicity is deceptive because all through it is *emotion*, and that emotion is going to make all the difference, my God, leave everyone else—the rest of the world—behind."

And like a whirlwind, she fell on him, throwing her arms around his neck with a little shriek she couldn't stop, telling him how unfair he had been to mislead her, letting her think she was awful, said finally to herself, "Oh, hush, Regan," and, leaning down, kissed him. His lips were warm and soft and loose with surprise, but his body felt lean and heard as she knew it would. Her breasts nudged against him. A warmth spread through her body. And Regan knew that she would never be able to go back from this day she had wanted to remember for another reason, or from this moment, knew—as Jake began to kiss her back, his mouth moving obligingly over hers—that she didn't ever want to stop falling off that cliff. Then, as quickly as the assault had begun, she pulled away to end it.

"Will you help me, Jake?"

"Help you? How?" He sounded dazed, a little breathless.

"Teach me," she said impatiently. "I want to know about keys, notes, timing, cadenzas, crescendoes—oh, I don't even know the *words* yet—rests and pauses, *everything!*"

She wanted to know what he did; to be as good as he was. If, she thought wildly, he would allow some of his knowledge to modify her ignorance, maybe, just possibly now, she had a chance; and for that one slice of opportunity, Regan decided, she would risk anything. A heart of stone, her life . . .

She seemed to be laughing and crying at the same time, Jake's priorities eclipsed momentarily by hers. Rising from the piano bench, he put his arms around her in a real embrace, smoothing the silken hair down the length of her spine with strong, warm, wonderful hands, making her shiver from a mixture of emotion, calming her though she could feel his heart banging in his chest, too. All her senses seemed to be tingling, full of him, her body to be striking fire. She wondered what it would be like to have those hands make love to her, and blushed at the thought. Yesterday I didn't know your name, she told him silently, but this second I feel as if I've known you all my life; it's so strange, terrifying and magical . . . oh Jake, do you feel it, too?

"Yes," he said finally, firmly. The one word, short and certain, startled her. "I'll help you," he said, sending her heart flying. "I think if you wanted to go to the moon, girl, somehow I'd build the rocket to get you there . . . and I flunked physics."

Chapter 2

I must be out of my mind. Jake breathed in carefully, not to inhale Regan's subtle cologne all at once, and kept his eyes averted from her profile. When he should be working, he was teaching. And he didn't have the patience—or the moral fortitude—to sit at this piano one more night, running scales with a teenaged girl slowly driving him up the living room wall.

A girl who remained totally unaware of her effect on him.

If it weren't potentially lethal, the situation would have seemed funny. "All right," he said with a sigh. "Once more. It's getting late," looking at his watch. "In fifteen minutes I shove you out the front door," *and save what's left of my sanity.*

What was that she was wearing? Something elusive, smelling of wildflowers and woodland paths dense with foliage. . . .

"Jake?"

"Uh, yeah, let's see. How about—"

He glanced through the primer of music theory, but Regan said, "I'm so tired of singing intervals. Could we do a real song again instead?"

"Scales," he insisted. "That's how you learn." When the wide green eyes threatened to melt his insides, he added, "Regan, there's no time for a crash course in music theory as it is—let's try to get the basics at least, okay?" Against his better judgment, he guided her index finger to middle C. "Save the romantic ballads for those million-seller albums you're going to cut one day." The brief touch electrified him.

Regan smiled. "You must have wanted to hit me over the head last night." She ran the scale lightly as she spoke. "Three-four time, four-four time, and I'll never remember how to read flats and sharps, either."

"F-C-G-A-D," Jake recited with a half smile. "Sharps," he said. "B-E-A-D-G. Flats." The notes she'd played lingered in the air, and her gaze seemed to immobilize him. He looked away with effort. "You're wasting money. The meter's running."

Regan laughed, sending Jake's heart rate into orbit, then split the air that had just emptied into a thousand layers of shimmering sound as she trilled the vocal scale up and down its simple range. His breathing seemed to be faster. "Professional quality." He hadn't even touched the keyboard.

Regan smiled at the praise, distracting his attention from the way her firm breasts lifted, then fell, as she sang.

What was he going to do with her? Or rather, with himself? Only four lessons, and he felt as if he needed handcuffs. What if he touched her, and she screamed bloody murder? What if she smiled like that for every guy she met?

As if, Jake thought, Oldham would let her. Which brought his wayward libido instantly to a halt. Glancing at his wrist, he stood up abruptly. "Time's up." Taking her arm, he walked Regan to the door. "I'll see you to the end of your block," he said, knowing her uncle wouldn't want him walking her home. "I'd like to tell you something."

I can't take this anymore. I've got the Brahms to polish before the tour. You shouldn't be here in this house alone with me. I want—

"What is it, Jake?"

Outside, he sucked in a great gulp of warm night air, heavy with the smell of rambler roses. He felt her hand slide into his, the contact jolting him again. "The song you tried for me earlier tonight," he said instead. "Even without theory, you're probably the best ballad singer I've ever heard. I mean that," he added when she turned astonished eyes on him in the darkness. He knew she wasn't used to compliments. "You have tremendous phrasing, a natural sense that you'll never get learning to read the music. With the emotion I heard before, the crystal clarity of your tone— Regan, it's unbeatable."

Squeezing his hand in gratitude, she leaned her head for an instant on his shoulder. "Promise me," he said, his voice husky as he struggled to regulate his pulse. "Promise me you'll never shift too far away from ballads. When you put an act together, you'll need pacing—novelties, a few quick numbers, surprises—but if you ever decide that a good ballad won't knock them on their . . . ears, you'll be doing your audience a grave disservice."

Regan stopped walking. "My audience?"

"Not to mention me," Jake said. "Your mentor," giving her a grin to lighten the moment, which—for him, anyway— threatened to turn desperate. If he didn't shift gears, he would urge her into the deep shadows of that elm tree and—

"Thank you."

Regan's whisper ran through him, a thousand feathery touches on sensitive nerve endings. "What for?"

"Making me feel that I—" She broke off, and he sensed the blush he couldn't actually see. Tipping her head back, Regan laughed in sheer delight. "That I'm really going to be a singer," she finished, chanting the phrase to the end of the block where he had to tell her good night, and leave her. "You pick the songs," he said. "I'll play 'em."

Already anticipating—and dreading—the next lesson, Jake told himself again: *I've gotta be crazy.*

"What's he teaching you?"

Paul's voice seemed to slice through Regan like a knife, but she kept her head down, not meeting his eyes, and continued to clear the dishes from the dinner table—which was in the kitchen because there wasn't any dining room. Oh God, she'd been waiting for this. Focusing her eyes on the gravy-stained tablecloth by her uncle's plate, she said, "Music," and then hastily, "but it won't cost you a dime, Uncle Paul."

"Volunteer work?"

Alyson had been listening to every word of Regan's explanation. Her stomach turned in fear. Stacking the plates with a clatter, she carried them to the porcelain drainboard beside the sink. "There's all kinds of music, Daddy," Alyson said.

Regan's heart tripped over itself, trying to keep a regular beat.

"All kinds," Paul agreed thoughtfully. Ignoring Regan's stumbling second attempt to explain what she'd be learning, he let a slow grin spread over his face. "Beautiful music," he said, but there was no humor in the smile.

Regan ran water in the sink, added a drizzle of liquid detergent, and began hastily to wash the dirty plates. They were mostly cracked and chipped and didn't match. She thought of the old blue willow plates at Jake's house, the soft shine of silver, the feeling of closeness she'd had there, so different from this house, so much more than the lack of color.

In Paul's kitchen, the plaster was cracked along the ceiling, the white paint greasy yellow where she couldn't reach to clean. Decor. The small white enamel table made of metal. The mismatched chairs of wood, one of them needing its back spindles glued. The pattern of black and gray tiles on the floor, a few of them split or with their corners missing. There wasn't a wax made that could shine it. She'd tried them all, just as she'd tried for years to make Paul, and Alyson, love her.

Regan increased the speed at which she worked, washing the dishes in record time. Afraid she'd be late for her lesson with Jake, she dumped them in a plastic rack on the drainboard to dry and shoved the pans into the drawer of the gas stove. She'd wipe the counters later, when she got home. Paul and Alyson wouldn't notice. They were lingering over second cups of coffee at the table when Regan turned to leave. Maybe she could slip past them without saying anything else. But Paul's voice stopped her.

"Regan."

"I swear, Uncle Paul, it's nothing but music," she assured him again. Then swallowed convulsively.

His blue eyes swept over her as if he could spot a lie in the fit of her jeans, the green plaid of her shirt. "I watched you awful close," he said. "All this time, making sure you didn't turn out like *her*." He was on his feet that quickly, his thick hand coming up to brush the soft hair from the nape of Regan's neck, making her shudder in spite of her best intentions not to cringe. The bulky class ring he still wore from high school with its center stone of green caught momentarily in the long, silken strands.

Regan winced. For only a second, she had thought he meant Alyson, who could probably lie or cheat or almost anything else without her father's punishment, but no—Paul had meant Regan's mother, as he usually did.

Was that why she had been so unwelcome in this house, then? Because of something her mother had done? Not only leaving her for Paul to shelter . . . but something else? She remembered the low rumble of argument between Paul and Martha on so many other nights, causing Regan to hide her head in her pillow, trying not to cry.

"Oh, promises are easy, Paul, aren't they? All you do is say the words, then let someone else—*me*—see that they come true!"

"All that's true in this house is your hatred for that girl. I've told you a hundred times—she stays under this roof till she's grown!"

"We don't have enough for extra mouths," Martha's voice whined through the thin walls. "I'm not sewing two sets of clothes when her mother—"

"Accept it, woman! I'm not giving you any choice."

Regan had burrowed into her blankets, heart pounding. She hadn't understood their argument then, only its tone. Did she understand any better now? With a show of calm she didn't feel, Regan pulled away from his hand, smoothing her tangled hair.

"I'm still watching." Paul took Regan's chin in his big, fleshy fingers, held it tightly. "You step out of line, miss, you won't forget. *Hear me?*"

She nodded, thinking that all she had asked was the freedom to spend a few innocent hours with Jake, learning; and that, while his legacy from his mother was a warm house to live in, she had only a tainted memory which she was, somehow, expected to emulate.

Paul let her go, his flat blue gaze trailing her face again, searching for falsehood. "Be back in your room by ten o'clock," he ordered.

"Yes, Uncle Paul. I will."

It took the entire walk to Jake's house to quiet the throbbing of her heart. She had never lied to Paul before; and she promised herself she never would again. But he wouldn't have let her continue the lessons otherwise—and didn't she deserve a chance at life, too? No matter what mistakes her mother had made, what evils she had supposedly passed on to Regan?

But when she saw Jake opening the door minutes later, quickly smiling, she knew she'd been making explanations not only to her uncle, but excuses for herself. There was the music, Regan thought; but there was something more, as well.

The mere sight of him turned her inside out. A smile kept her in rapture for hours. And late at night, arms about her pillow in the dark, Regan invented new fantasies: romantic ones. Jake took her in his arms; he held her close as he had done after she first sang for him; he bent his head to kiss her, his breathing rapid; he asked her to—

But anything more would be sheer speculation, and in the darkness Regan's cheeks flamed. It seemed a near-tragedy that Jake didn't return her adoration.

"One, two, three, four," Jake intoned deliberately. "One, two, three, four..." rapping out time with a pencil on top of the piano, using his left hand as he played accompaniment with the right. "What the hell—Regan, it's a simple signature, read it yourself—" He stopped tapping as the pencil snapped in half, flying across the small living room to land with a ping against the radiator. "Shit," he said softly.

"I'm sorry."

He glared at her. "What are you always sorry for? Why

don't you just do the goddamned job instead of apologizing all over the place?"

Regan began to shake inside at the darkness in his eyes, the way she'd done with Paul when she was little; the way she sometimes did even now.

"Buy yourself a metronome," Jake said, "and use it."

She wondered why he hadn't set the one on the bookshelf across the room; but Jake seemed to prefer the nearest weapon. Tonight, the pencil; yesterday a ballpoint pen; and once, a glass swizzle stick that had shattered, similarly provoking him to curse. It seemed everything did lately. But hadn't there been nights when the laughter and teasing took up more time than work, when they had shared a bottle of Coke without Jake picking a fight?

Because that's what he does, Regan thought. I smile at him, then he destroys me. What was wrong with him? Maybe he'd had a bad day, practicing for his tour. Maybe he just didn't want her around.

Regan looked away from the accusation in his eyes.

"Could we try the ballad I've been practicing?" she ventured. At home, alone in her room, the melody had seemed to lift her spirits, and the rafters, too. She wanted the power again, the exultation . . . and to change Jake's mood.

"'When I Fall in Love,'" he muttered, turning back to the keyboard and squaring his shoulders. "Terrific."

Regan stepped closer so she could see the music. Jake's spine stiffened. She had managed half the chorus before he stopped her.

"Why are you making this so difficult?" Over his shoulder, he threw her a look. "Come around where I can see you," though he'd ordered her to stand behind him twenty minutes before. Resting his hands on the keys, he waited before he spoke. "I shouldn't have said that, about your phrasing the other day. Maybe it was a happy accident at the time." Jake glanced up, not noticing that Regan's lower lip had begun to tremble. "Listen," he said quietly, "'When I Fall in Love,' okay? Old standard, beautiful . . . what could be nicer? Wonderful lyrics, all the work's done for you." He snapped a finger against the sheet music. "So why, for Christ's sake, do you take a breath halfway through the line?" Jake demonstrated, imitating: "When I"—gasping intake of air—"fall in love ... Jesus."

"I'm—" She started to say *sorry*, but didn't. "You were rushing me."

"Fill your lungs at the start of the phrase, then let go a little at a time, evenly. You won't have to rush. You ought to have plenty left until the next *natural* break ... when you breathe again. Got it?"

The tone implied she couldn't possibly understand. Regan drew herself up, switching the weight of her tawny hair back with a motion of her hand. She wouldn't make excuses for him. She'd taken enough for one day. "Why are you condescending to me? What's the matter with you?"

"What the hell's the matter with you?"

"Other than the fact that I don't like you right now?" Regan asked. "Nothing."

Jake's gaze slid away first. "I'm glad to hear it. Let's get through the song this time."

Regan began to wonder where the endless hours of practice, her musical fumbling, Jake's more and more frequent spurts of temper would lead. Was she improving? Or hopeless? Mostly, she couldn't tell.

June was not a month for love, Regan learned, however inexperienced, but a brutal four weeks of bone-crushing effort, correction, approval, then rejection, and of still more toil. Exhilarated by praise, Regan knew she wanted nothing but to go on singing; deflated by criticism, she never wanted to open her mouth again and she could, in fact, feel her throat tighten, her voice close.

"You call that singing?" Jake had stopped playing and was staring straight ahead at the sheet music, not at Regan. She felt as if she were strangling.

"What would you call it?"

"I'd hate to say."

"Can I try again?"

"You *may,*" he nearly whispered, still facing front, "but I don't know if you *can.*" Even correcting her English now! Her heart was thumping. He began to play the wretched song again, but just as before—three times—he stopped dead in the middle of a phrase and sat, as if counting to himself in order not to yell at her. Regan almost wished he would, to break the tension. Then he broke it, but not by shouting. He brought his hands down on the keyboard, crashing unrelated notes together, making her ears ring.

"I am not a voice teacher," he grated. "I am a concert pianist with a helluva lot of preparing to do before September, none of which is being done, so if you can't get it together better than you have been for the last few weeks—"

"That isn't a lifetime," she threw at him, suddenly erupting with her own suppressed anger. "Or a fancy degree from the conservatory overnight, either, but you said I was good once—haven't I learned *something?*"

She hadn't fully appreciated the little putdowns, Regan thought, the increased pressure on her to do perfectly the first try, or the talk that dwindled to painful silences, and the way Jake seemed to avoid looking straight at her.

"Not enough," he said, frowning with the same intensity he showed on the rare occasions when he played his own music for her, and she wondered why she liked that about him, too, even his scowl, and the aristocratic beauty of his hands touching ivory, when he seemed to like nothing at all about her.

"It's my fault," Jake said charitably. "I never should have started with you, I should have known better."

"I didn't mean for you to waste your precious evenings."

"I'm not, but . . . you need a real coach, Regan, and—"

"*I can't pay!*" Through a haze of anguish, she saw her dream rapidly fading.

"I know that. Maybe I can find you someone. I know a few people at the college in—"

"No!" A strange panic welled in her. It wasn't only the

dream of music that was fast disappearing. "No, Jake, please, just give me another chance. I'll work at the sight-reading every spare minute—because I only know what I hear now," she said, "and sometimes I don't understand what you want."

"Of course you don't!" he said furiously. "You don't understand the first thing about—about the music." He ran a hand through his hair. "Seventeen years old, for Christ's sake—you're just a child!"

"Eighteen." *Last month,* Regan added silently. *And I bought my own present. A white froth of a nightie I'll never get to use.*

Jake finally looked at her with what she thought must be a mixture of anger and disgust and contempt. As if he were wishing she would go away without dissolving into girlish tears in front of him. Had they really kissed at this very piano the first afternoon? Had she felt the warmth of his mouth? Since them, he hadn't even touched her. His earlier friendliness, his eagerness to help, had turned to negativism and a newer, more aggressive attitude. An eagerness, oh yes: He wanted to be rid of her. Inept and slow to learn, she was only in his way, and—

"You don't understand anything," Jake said weakly, but she didn't see any further use, either, in trying, not beyond the obvious answers she had just entertained. Going to the door, ripping her light jacket from the chair beside it as she passed, blinded by humiliating tears, Regan ran outside where the heavy evening air promised rain. When Jake called her, she didn't stop.

"Regan!"

Goddamnit. Why hadn't he kept his mouth shut? After a few moments of looking after her, and wondering whether he should follow to apologize—but then what?—Jake went inside and slammed the door. But his anger was more for himself than for her. Regan hadn't been doing much wrong tonight: only standing there beside the piano in his living room, like a lot of other nights, with just the two of them in the small house, and his own barely contained lust for a chaperon.

Why was he having such a hard time keeping his hands off her? My God, he had given lessons on the piano ever since his graduation from the conservatory. But hell, in four years he had never experienced a single desire to take one of his students to bed. Why Regan?

Why not? he asked himself. He was only human. He had wanted her the instant his gaze fell upon her at the senior recital.

But Regan had approached him for very different reasons, giving him an open door to her innocence if he would only hear her sing. The kiss at the piano had been almost childlike, true; yet there had also been an undercurrent of awakening woman. How could he take advantage of her? Regan ought to be wearing a skull and crossbones on her chest, like a poison label. He was going away. He couldn't let anything, especially not a woman, block his path, not now, not this *close*. Particularly a serious woman. And here, Jake realized, was the crux of the problem.

Because Regan Reilly could never be a casual affair. He had known with a terrible certainty, the instant she began her first lesson, that he was going to have a hell of a time keeping his mind on business and his hands to himself. Well, he had to. For Christ's sake. Period.

If not for his career, Jake thought—then because of Paul Oldham. Regan had told her uncle, unwisely, that she was properly chaperoned during their lessons. "What happens if he finds out?" Jake had asked. "Lancaster's small, it's no secret that I live alone."

But Regan had worn that look he was beginning to know very well. Her chin lifted, a blaze of green lit her eyes. "He won't find out. Besides, it's only for a few weeks."

Playing the law of averages. Only, what if she lost?

Jake went into the kitchen and fixed himself a drink. *A cozy room,* she had said. He saw her at the range, deftly making an omelet; at the table, smiling, raptly listening to his tour plans. He could see the need in her eyes when she spoke of her uncle. He wanted to give her the bonds of commitment; the security of home.

Red flag, Jake told himself. Everything he couldn't afford.

He wandered back to the living room and flung himself in a chair. He stared moodily at the ceiling. How could he walk a tightrope for ten, eleven weeks? Or would he have to? Regan had left in a hurry, with defeat and sorrow on her face. Would she bother to show up tomorrow?

Just as well if she didn't, he thought with irritation. If he never saw her again. Hell, he should be practicing. Hadn't he told her so? Nothing but truth. The Brahms had thin spots, moments of confusion and hesitation in the *scherzo*. Taking the glass with him, Jake went to the piano—scene of the evening's earlier debacle—but there he heard, instead of the complex pattern of a concerto, that clear, soaring voice that had made so few mistakes and been reprimanded for beauty.

He saw a slender waist and hips and high, firm breasts, and the perfect translucence of her complexion; the straight nose with only the hint of an upturn to prevent sharpness; that long shimmer of golden hair that asked to be touched; and then, the green eyes, vulnerable to the hurt he'd inflicted, clouded by self-doubt he'd caused.

Jake stopped playing. It was useless to try. As useless, and as hopeless, as trying to hide from himself what was happening—or would, if he allowed it. Why let things go on, not leading anywhere? Yet she seemed to want *him* teaching; and he wanted it too, more than he cared to admit. Much more, damnit.

It was only for a while longer, he told himself. But it had to be less isolated, less tempting. Regan reaffirmed the old conviction that he couldn't handle anything but passion in a minor key—which wasn't what she needed, and never would be.

For long moments, Jake sat staring down at the ivories, sipping his rye and soda. It tasted bitter. And then, like a beautiful, complex chord he'd never heard before, inspiration struck. Their solution—and there was one after all—had a name: Steven Houghton.

What point was there in hoping, Regan asked herself. It was over. She lay facedown across her bed, arms cradling her head, arms hiding the ragged sounds she made. She didn't want anyone to know she as crying; and certainly not why.

At the rap on her door, Regan froze.

"May I come in?"

She'd run all the way home, tripping once and falling on the sidewalk, scraping her knee raw, and it burned now. The knee hurt almost as much as the look on Jake's face had, his rejection. Thank heaven she'd never told him how she felt, and made a worse fool of herself. Regan sat up, wiping a hasty hand over her eyes as Alyson closed the door to her room.

"At least you aren't wearing any mascara to smear." What did she want? Was she looking for contraband? Well, she wouldn't find anything; nothing but Raggedy Ann, who'd been letting Regan soak her cloth body with tears.

"I heard you sniffling. I wondered what had brought on such a deluge." Alyson faced her, but Regan kept her chin up, her profile turned, wondering if her eyes were swollen. "It's Jake, isn't it?"

Regan's chin trembled. She was learning, she *was*. Then why hadn't she told him so? That she wasn't off-key tonight— why let him bully her as Paul did? She thought Alyson's use of his first name sounded too . . . familiar. Did she know him? Was that why she'd smiled in the kitchen, talking about the lessons? Well, what if she did? Regan wished she'd told Jake what to do with his sheet music because—

"Oh, Ali—" She *had* to confide in someone. "I try and try, but he doesn't think I'm good enough!" Then quickly, she was telling about the miserable evening, how hard she'd worked, how little good it had done. When she paused for breath, amazed that she'd actually been talking to her cousin like one civilized human being to another, Alyson said coolly, "And what did his mother have to say about all this?"

"His mother?"

Regan's heart began to drum. She watched Alyson stroll from the foot of her bed to the dresser and peer into the mirror. She picked up a tube of lip gloss, sliding the clear color across her full mouth. Regan sat cross-legged on the bed, Raggedy Ann draped over her lap, her fingers raking through the yarn hair with swift, jerky motions. Alyson knew, *she knew*. And there was no defense Regan could make. What had made her start talking to Alyson, laying a trap for herself this time? What, except her own misery over Jake, her own loneliness?

"I could have made up a better story, if you'd asked me," Alyson said at last, and then scathingly, *"Music lessons,* when it's really Jake you want, isn't it? Just like your mother with all her—"

"What about my mother?" Regan's body tensed. "What about her?"

"This isn't a very big town, you know. I can't imagine how you thought of getting away with it ... or don't you care, either? Well, you've finally outsmarted yourself, just like she did." Alyson whirled from the mirror. "A friend of mine lives across the street from him; he told me about Jake's mother." She looked thoughtful for a moment. "I'm sure Daddy'd want to know before all of Lancaster's talking."

Regan flew off the bed, dumping Raggedy Ann, and swung Alyson around as she turned toward the door. She hadn't known her own strength. "Ali, don't!" Then, like lightning, she saw that her own unhappiness tonight, and Jake's cruelty, were in her favor. Alyson had no levers to pull, no toys to snatch away, no more traps to lay.

"Go ahead," she said softly, releasing Alyson's arm. She went to the bed, pulling back the covers. "Tell him anything you like." She picked up the doll. "I won't be going back to Jake's again. That's why I was crying before; that's what the argument meant. He doesn't want to teach me." And before Alyson could say it, she added, "Music or anything else."

My, don't you sound brave, she thought as the door swung shut; but her fingers shook, and she wished she had blurted out the whole story at once.

"You'd better be telling the truth this time," Alyson had threatened. "Because if you aren't ..."

Sometime deep in the night, the telephone shrilled in the silence. The extension was on a wobbly stand of mahogany veneer at the end of the hall, outside Regan's room. Instantly awake because she had been sleeping so badly, she grabbed the receiver on the second ring, dragging it by the long cord into her room and shutting the door. She didn't want Paul awake.

"You beautiful, wonderful girl," Jake began. "You enormous hunk of talent—"

"Go to hell!" Regan hung up, her voice thick with emotion. There had been no pillow-embracing tonight, no romantic fairy tales. When the bell shrieked again in the silence, she answered hoarsely, "If you don't stop this, my uncle will get up and—"

"Don't slam that receiver down again," Jake warned in a desperate tone as if he had sensed the movement of her hand. "I've got terrific news."

Perched on the end of her bed, which was as far as the phone would reach, Regan pulled the edge of the blanket over her thin blue cotton nightgown. She was shivering, but she wondered if Jake could somehow see through the telephone wires, too, as she managed dryly, "You've sold me to a white slaver."

He tried a small laugh, mainly testing the waters. It didn't sound like him at all. "Not quite," he said, but Regan didn't let him continue.

"I don't care, I don't want to learn any more, or if I do, I'll—I'll get a book and teach myself, so you can just go back to your precious career—"

"I said I was sorry."

Regan took a shaky breath. "No, no you didn't."

"Well, I thought I had." Impatience sounded clearly in his voice. "I am. Sorry. Let my career take care of itself, all right? Now will you listen?"

Jake rushed on before she could agree. He had talked to a friend of his who owned a small roadhouse outside of Lancaster—nothing fancy, he said—but Steven Houghton wanted Regan to audition for him. Jake had only been thinking of a different practice room, but—

"You mean sing for money?"

"*If* you get the job, yes. What do you say? Think you can be ready in two weeks?"

Her pulse was racing. "How about tomorrow?"

"No," he said, "this has to be right. You're going to work your tail off, lady."

"Are you on something? You sound high as a kite."

There was a laugh in his voice, and something more: that quality she had seen in his eyes but could never identify. "I am," he whispered. "Stoned. On you." Still, she wouldn't let him forget their argument that easily, not even with her heart taking such sudden leaps and bounds. For a few seconds, Regan twisted the phone cord in her fingers.

"That's kind of weird, don't you think?" she asked with a smile. "To turn on to children?"

The ancient microphone was switched on, and a piercing shriek of sound whistled through the room. Regan smiled back into the bright blue eyes near her as Steven Houghton adjusted the old equipment, then showed her where to stand. "Not state-of-the-art exactly," he said with a grin meant to calm her shredded nerves. "All right, princess." Steven stepped away, taking a seat at a front table next to Jake at the piano. "Let's hear what you can do."

Regan saw a look pass between them, what she imagined was a kind of male-to-male assent. Steven liked her. She could tell because she liked him, too. Somewhat stocky but solidly built, Steven appeared to be in his mid-thirties, with a few gray hairs threaded among the shock of light brown. He had a pleasant face that focused upon a generous mouth; and a habit, Regan had noticed, of playing with the broad gold wedding band on his finger.

"Steven lost his wife last winter," Jake had told her on the way to the roadhouse. "He's been having a pretty rough time of it."

Which had caused Regan to wonder—instantly ashamed of herself—if Jake could be trying to pass her on to his friend. No, of course not. But their relationship had reverted to practice, during the daytime now instead of evenings, and nothing more. Jake wasn't so sharp with her most of the time, but sometimes Regan felt she must have imagined his telephone call that night and the husky tone of his voice. Except that, now, she was here.

Regan remembered the next hour in a blur of patchy images: the roadhouse itself, a large, wood-frame firetrap with rooms that rambled carelessly into other rooms, like afterthoughts of construction; cracks and gaps in the walls with motes of dust and sun filtering like soft spotlight beams across the tiny scrap of stage; the ascending power of her voice as confidence grew; Steven applauding after she sang.

"Jake, she's absolutely first-rate, you were right!" And her thoughts spun. Jake did think she was good, he *did!* She almost missed hearing Steven offer her a job. Four weeks, he said, to begin, and a salary that didn't amount to much, for which he apologized in advance.

"I'll take it!" Regan said before he could reconsider.

"I use a band on weekends. The kids come here to dance, but we'll try you out between sets then, and during the week if you'd like."

"Oh, yes, I would—I'd like that very much." *Like it?* Her first real job, her first *singing* job? The money made her a professional, like Jake, even if she never went beyond the roadhouse or found the success she had dreamed about and that place in center stage. But what if this beginning was simply the next step in a long, long journey? What if, what if . . .

"Congratulations, Miss Reilly." Jake couldn't stop smiling at her, as proud as a new father.

Paul wasn't so pleased. Or rather, he was pleased, but as usual, for reasons of his own. "So you're gonna get up there in some dive and wiggle your ass—"

"No." Regan was preparing dinner that night, taking more care with the chops and fluffy potatoes than she ordinarily would have, hoping that a special meal would soften her uncle's attitude. She'd already riced and whipped the potatoes, adding lots of butter and light cream the way Paul liked them, and now she turned the meat in the skillet, setting the lid back on it. "I'll be singing," she said, "not on exhibition."

"Is that a fact?" He looked at her thoughtfully, narrowing his blue eyes. "Your mama used to sing, sounded like a bell, I remember. She could have gone a long way with that voice. . . ."

Regan thought she saw something in his smile, an acceptance of her. He so rarely mentioned her mother, almost never with fondness in his tone, nothing but the hints and innuendoes; Alyson's voice sounded inside her, saying, "She was a tramp, your mother." Didn't she have a right to know the truth? She was old enough now. "Uncle Paul," Regan said, feeling emboldened by the flick of a soft glance her way as she checked the pan of lima beans, "what was she like? My mother? I remember the night she left, but—"

"You *don't* remember! You were just a baby."

Regan stirred the beans, mixing spicy tomatoes and peppercorns with them, then turning off the heat. Everything was done. "I was three," she said, "more than that . . . because it was winter; and I must have turned four the next spring. I know what she looked like and I—"

"Because you seen her pictures, that's how you know about your mama. You couldn't remember so far back." Paul left his place, leaning against the kitchen door frame, and took a seat at the table. He didn't offer to help serve. He frowned at his plate. "You can't remember," he repeated.

But Regan persisted. "I have this dream." She'd never told him before, but she wanted him to see that she wasn't starting from scratch about her mother. "I mean I used to have it all the time. My mother was singing to me, Uncle Paul, a lullaby the night she—"

"She never sung to you! Your father didn't give her much to sing about, Regan!"

Why didn't he want her to remember? That was it: Paul didn't want her to; and she knew better than to keep prodding him.

Later, as she sometimes did, she would go up to her room and dig through the red scrapbook for the picture of the slender young woman whose coloring had been similar to Regan's own, the hair a shade darker, the eyes a deeper green without the striking ring of dark pigment surrounding the iris; but their smiles matched. In the photo, her mother wore shorts and a halter, and her legs were straight and tanned. Was she as happy as she appeared? If so, why had she run away? Regan could ponder the photograph for hours, like the pictures of the Talbot mansion; but there were no answers in the smile.

Regan knew it was useless to ask any more questions. She carried the hot frying pan to the table. Paul looked up at her. "You were a funny little kid," he said, helping himself to a thick, perfectly browned chop, "but you've done all right. Got someplace already, haven't you?" But he didn't wait for her agreement. Regan was disarmed by the quiet tone of his voice, the way his eyes had lingered on her face for a moment; holding the same expression they had when he had said how nice her hair was.

Then he asked, "How much is he paying?" bringing her back to reality.

Regan told him what she'd be earning at the roadhouse.

"Peanuts." Paul's thick fingers drew numbers on the green linen. A dollar sign.

"I can't very well ask for more, not yet, when I haven't even done one show for Steven—Mr. Houghton," she corrected quickly. Regan wouldn't look at him. She was thankful that tonight Alyson was painting scenery for a summer stock production in the next town. When she wasn't outnumbered, Regan felt safer challenging her uncle.

Paul dug into the potatoes, poured a deep golden pond of gravy over the mound on his plate. Sitting across from him, Regan could hardly eat.

"I guess it'll have to do, then," he said, the words muffled by a full mouth, and she relaxed slightly. It had been easier than she expected. The first thing she would do was open a bank account of her own and begin saving. For lessons someday if she needed them, for new clothes to wear when she sang, for a place of her own eventually.

"He paying you by the week?" Paul cut into her thoughts. "Yes."

"Then I'll expect the money the morning after you get it—

every seven days," he said agreeably. Then sliced off a chunk of meat and stuffed it in his mouth.

Regan said she didn't understand. Her heart began to pound. "I'll pay room and board if that's what you want."

"You'll pay that, all right. And you can start paying for what you owe, freeloading in this house for years." But hadn't he defended her to Martha?

She said softly, "I do my share."

Paul piled a second helping of mashed potatoes on his plate.

"I didn't ask you to keep me," Regan said. A small, unwanted child again. Her chin lifted, and she stared at her uncle, hoping he wouldn't see her tremble. "I'm not going to give you conscience money if you won't even tell me—"

"I won't tell you." He looked up, his milky blue eyes hard. "I'll ask you—one question, nice as you please. What's the singing mean to you?"

He caught her off balance. "Everything," Regan answered without a second's hesitation, and fell into his trap as easily as she had ever tumbled into Alyson's.

Paul Oldham smiled. It was a cold smile, full of triumph, greed.

"Then you won't miss the money, will you? As long as you can get out there and . . . sing."

Chapter 3

"Get me out of here, I can't do this, I don't know why I ever thought I wanted to sing, *please*, Jake, let me out—I'm going to be sick!"

"No, you are not." He guided her to the small, sagging sofa in the makeshift dressing room Steven had provided. "Sit down. Take a couple of deep breaths." Regan sucked in air, obediently. "And get your finger off the panic button; you'll be fine."

"With all those people out there, drinking, *laughing*, talking? Listen to them! If the band doesn't faze them, how can I stop them long enough to hear some *stupid* song?"

"A beautiful song," he said. Jake sat beside her, holding her clammy hand in his warm one. If only he might stand right next to her when she had to sing, Regan thought, instead of being at the piano ten feet away. "Don't you ever feel nervous before a concert?" she asked in a small voice. "How do you remember all the notes?"

He laughed softly. "Sometimes I don't. So I write my own until I do . . . now that you mention it, I am grateful that I sit while I perform because my knees shake so badly I don't see how I could ever stand up and—"

"Oh, Jake, you're no help!"

But he didn't respond to her wail of despair. "Listen. You're going onstage with so much fluttering in your stomach that you'll think it's a seventeen-year-locust invasion, not butter-flies, and yes, you're going to forget what song I'm about to play; you'll forget the words and the melody; and you'll want to run—"

"*Stop!*"

"—but you won't. You'll stay, and then hear me start..." Jake paused, so that she had to stop staring at his hand and look up. "And you will sing, perfectly—exactly as we re-hearsed." He stood up, pulling her gently after him. "Don't say another word. You've had your fit. Just wait for me to bring you through the introduction, and when you hear your opening, take it."

But Regan couldn't help saying one more thing. "Jake—for heaven's sake, don't hit any wrong notes."

"Me?" he asked in mock horror as he pushed her toward the door. "The classical genius?"

Regan groaned. After what he'd told her about himself, that was no help, either. Nor Steven's kiss, which she didn't even feel as she waited in place, because her face, her whole body, felt numb with fear.

What kind of person, Regan asked herself, wants to stand in front of so many people and sing a ballad they've heard a thousand times before? Paul was right. She was nothing but an exhibitionist. She deserved anything that happened tonight: tomatoes, rotten eggs, catcalls, hissing, booing; everyone get-ting up in a body and stalking out; one of those hooks used in vaudeville to remove the worst acts from the stage.

Her mind raced in wild imaginings. She would stumble. Miss her cue like the first time she sang for Jake. She would slide off-key when she finally started, but not enough to stop and begin again, only enough to sound dreadful. And painfully amateurish. Talentless. If Jake did play something wrong—say, skipped part of the verse—how would she cover? Playing an instrument, one might improvise—but with the human voice?

The rock band began to file past her, the members winking, touching her arm, making jokes she barely heard. Dear God, Regan was praying with a frozen smile on her lips, let this be a quick death. She must be dead white already. And how would *that* look under the spot when she was wearing the same color?

But, no. Touched with cream, the dress had more color than she did. Cut straight across, held by the most slender of gold cord straps, its bodice molded gracefully to her, then bloused softly just above the waist. The long, slim skirt was slit to the knee, and the opening bound by the same gold trim. Regan wore matching light sandals with delicate heels. Her hair had been brushed straight and shining. Her eyes had been the subject of lengthy experimentation with makeup: sooty lashes and eyeliner—which she had never worn before—and a coppery shadow frosted with gold. But did she look sophisticated, as Jake and Steven assured her, or did she look like a little girl playing dress-up? Jake might tease, sometimes unmercifully, as he had backstage just now, but he would never lie and—

Oh no, he was playing the first notes! Not yet, please, she bargained as Steven nudged her. "Go on, princess. . . ." And with no more thought, she was on the stage, alone, a smile fixed on her face, her lips threatening to quiver, the locusts aflutter. She caught Jake's eye as he wound up the introduction—but dear God, to *what?*—and he winked. Her heart skipped a beat at the glimpse of him in navy turtleneck and dark pants, his hair gleaming under the light. And then all at once, as if ordered to, Regan opened her mouth and began to sing.

The audience quieted. Regan's throat relaxed. She did know the words. Jake made no mistakes. The siege of locusts ended, replaced by the gentle butterflies she had expected in their place; and then, halfway through the verse, by the calm of confidence . . . the second chorus, coming so soon, the music soaring, weightless, her voice sounding better than ever in her ears . . . everything working perfectly . . . nothing bad could happen . . . from here on, everything was good—even the sight of Alyson, in front, looking critical, didn't throw her.

When the last tinkling, bittersweet notes of the sad ballad faded away, the crowd let every sound from the piano, from Regan, play itself out. And then, suddenly, what a wonderful thunder began, echoing through the room, growing. Applause!

And she was taking bows, one after another, in a real night spot, as a professional singer, to paying customers clapping for her . . . for *her*. Chills running down her spine, her arms, the back of her neck, Regan thought: Dear God, never let this end.

She sang three more numbers before her set ended and the rock group filed back, but they had to begin the first dance with the applause that belonged to Regan still smattering. Breathless, she made her way off the tiny stage, meeting Jake as he skirted the piano and took her hand to lead her back to the dressing room.

He hadn't even shut the door when she exploded, "I did it! I did it!" and slammed into his waiting arms.

"Lady, you killed them!" His face suffused with joy and pride, he whirled her around the room in gradually tightening circles until they were both giddy from mock waltzing, until Regan was laughing so hard she felt hysterical. Then, hands circling her waist easily, Jake picked her up, holding her high, and spun her in the opposite direction. "Jake, put me down, I'm dizzy, *please,* stop—"

In the center of the room, he did, letting her slide, the creamy dress slipping against the navy sweater he wore, and there was the hard feel of his chest pressed to her overheated body, the brush of his hips, before she reached the ground again, down, down, in slow motion. To an undreamed-of victory as Jake's mouth sought hers, blindly, with hunger. "I'm so proud of you," he breathed against her lips. Then, "Oh, how good you feel . . . baby, baby, *baby,*" and he kissed her again, holding her tight, and again and again, as if he were drowning and she might save him that way, save them both.

Her body warm and weak, Regan was going down herself for the third time when someone said, "Well, I see I have two clear choices. I can turn my back. Or call the Vice Squad." She heard a familiar laugh.

"Steven Houghton," Regan said, freeing herself, but with none of the embarrassment she might have expected to feel, "you should learn to knock on doors!"

"It wasn't closed," Jake pointed out. He sounded dazed, as he had at the piano the first day. He straightened her dress and smoothed her hair, then stepped slightly away. "But you're right," he said to Steven, "she is a whistle away from being jailbait, isn't she?"

"What she is," Steven replied, "is number-one box-office material. I never heard anything so fine in all my life, princess; the band thought so, too, and the *people*—"

"Can I keep my job, then?"

"Is that a serious question? I should sign you to a lifetime contract this minute. I could guarantee myself a fortune."

Jake shook his head, saying with a smile, "Sorry. Her temporary manager drives a very hard bargain."

Fortune and fame, Regan thought, feeling dizzy with happiness. Jake ... and Paul, she remembered, holding all the money. But not even Paul could ruin the evening when she still felt the warmth of Jake's mouth on hers.

"Aren't you going to kiss me good night?"

Sitting in the car in front of her uncle's house, Regan finally had to ask. But Jake only shook his head, running his index finger around the rim of the steering wheel as he said "No," and Regan's joy deflated. What had happened to change his mood? Was it her fault?

"Look," he said at last, "there's no future for us, all right? How would we end up?" he asked softly, not looking at her. "You'd give up your career when it's just starting ... stay in Lancaster with a couple of kids and not enough money ... me knocking my brains out trying to get somewhere and feeling guilty—"

"You're jumping the gun, aren't you?" Regan's voice quavered with hurt. "You won't even kiss me good night! Jake, there are lots of people just like us who—"

"The two-career couple?" he said flatly. "I don't think so."

Maybe, Regan thought miserably, she was only projecting her own love onto him. But the kisses, those lovely kisses, his pride in her, his arms around her—

"Regan, what I understand is the short term," Jake went on harshly. "I mean, women who—who, well, want the same thing I do, just a—a physical act, oh Christ—" She could hear the embarrassment in his voice, cutting through frustration. But it didn't help.

"I see. Well, when I've had . . . more experience, then perhaps I'll apply for that job." She put her hand on the door handle, twisting sharply. Did he think she was hurling herself at him—but then, she had done exactly that, hadn't she? In a strangled tone, she said defensively, "I don't recall asking you to marry me."

Jake reached across to cover her hand. "I'm not trying to insult you. Or to shove you aside, either. But tonight in the dressing room shouldn't have happened." Why not? she asked silently. Oh, why not? And frowned at their hands to keep from crying. "Regan, you've got a great future—and with luck, so do I. That kind of commitment precludes any other, don't you see?" When she tried to withdraw her hand, he held it tightly. "Listen to me, damnit!" Turning to her, his eyes dark with feeling. "You want to hear me say it, do you? All right, I will! I could love you if I let myself; I could really love you—" Only, he was telling her he wouldn't. When September came, as it would all too soon, he would leave. She had thought no one could spoil tonight, not even Paul; but Jake was beginning to. Then why even say it, unless he wanted her as much?

"If things got rough for us," he went on, his voice constricted, "I know I—I'd let you down hard, baby, just like—"

Not finishing, he released her hand, and slumped back in his seat.

"Like what, Jake?"

"Never mind. It doesn't matter. You're going places," he said. "Keep the rest of your life simple."

Regan was baffled. He had been about to say someone's name, but wouldn't. Who had spooked him so badly that he didn't dare to love again? Because, obviously, he had once. Didn't it follow that there could be a second time? Regan wasn't going to give up, not while there was a chance to make him love her.

"I guess I'd better see you to the door before you violate Oldham's curfew. My God," Jake said, "you'd think he would have come to see you."

"Tonight? I didn't expect him to," though Alyson had been there, Regan acknowledged, representing the family . . . more or less. "But you're right, I should go in. If he sees me sitting out here, like this, he——" She stopped herself, but not in time.

"He'd hurt you?" Jake's gaze was sharp.

"I know how to manage Paul."

"That isn't what I asked you. I said, are you physically afraid of him?"

"I can take care of myself . . . better than you might think," she said in a tone that closed that subject as effectively as he had shut her out earlier.

"All right, then"—with a long sigh of exasperation—"let's get you home."

"This isn't my home!"

Why had she said it? Disappointment, buried deep beneath the surface, that Paul hadn't seen her tonight and found out for himself that she wasn't a toned-down burlesque act? Or was it the long years of wanting more than this bleak, mustard-color house with the sagging brown shutters hiding Martha's hostility, Alyson's and Paul's—and the destruction of the only memory she had to cherish?

Regan looked up to find Jake watching her. It was obvious from the combination of emotions in his face that he didn't know what to say to her. She smiled as brightly as she could. "Some weekend before you leave," she said, "I'll take you to a very different sort of house . . . the place I'd like to call home. It's not far from here," not in miles, anyway. "We'll have a picnic," Regan added, wanting only to break the heavy mood between them.

Jake must have agreed. "You pack the food," he said. "I'll bring the drinks and a genuine red-checked tablecloth, how's that?"

"Fine." A start in the right direction, she thought.

Jake got out of the VW quickly, came around and opened her door. He stood her in front of him on the sidewalk, shadowed by night, and put his hands loosely on her shoulders. "Hate me? For spoiling your triumph with the sulks?"

"I couldn't hate you," she said softly.

"No?" He smiled down at her, gently stroked the hair from her temples. "I hope not." At his touch, her senses began to spin again, as if she were still waltzing with him around the tiny dressing room. "You were tremendous tonight," Jake said. "I'm glad I saw that— a rising star." Then he added with a slow searching of her features, "I admit, some sort of concession is needed." And did kiss her, chastely, at the corner of her mouth.

When the taillights of the VW had disappeared from sight, Regan still sat on the front porch steps, watching fireflies wink on and off, singing softly to herself. Then smiling. She had achieved two victories tonight, and suffered one temporary setback. Reliving the show, the applause, the moments in the dressing room, the feel of Jake's mouth, and his embrace, she decided it was quite temporary. *I could really love you. . . .*

"I saw you with Jake, kissing." Alyson was waiting for Regan in the living room when she wandered inside, still bemused by the events of the evening.

"It was only good night and congratulations," Regan explained, wondering why she hadn't seen the draperies lift, or Alyson's auburn hair in the lighted window. But she knew why. Her body and her mind had been able to concentrate on only the feel of Jake's mouth. She wondered if it had looked like more of a kiss from the distance.

"I thought you weren't going to see him anymore," Alyson mused, running a light finger over the arm of the brown tweed chair where she was sitting. "And here you are, triumphant from your professional debut after weeks of practice in Jake's—"

"Alyson, we've been working during the daytime, at Steven's roadhouse, with people around every minute."

Regan dropped her small gold evening bag onto the sofa that

matched the chair. She felt safer on her feet, so she didn't sit down.

Alyson said, "You've beaten me to the stage, haven't you? Tonight, you're a performer while I'm still a student." There was an edge of sadness to her voice, and she picked at the pink nylon skirt of her nightgown, worrying a small hole in the fabric. "I'm so godawful tired of painting sets for that run-down stock company this summer; I feel I'm wasting everything I've learned! Just think of the classes, the workshops I've gone to; the tap and ballet and singing lessons on weekends when I was a kid—"

"They won't be wasted, Ali." Regan perched on the arm of the sofa, more relaxed now. They were talking, and it was Alyson who seemed uncertain, insecure for a change. "When you get your degree, you'll find a wonderful job. Maybe Broadway!"

"That'll take years, I know that much." Regan should have heard the change in the tone of voice, but she didn't. "Unless," Alyson went on, "you could help me."

"I'd like to, Ali, but I don't know how I—"

Alyson leaned forward, uncurling from her relaxed position in the armchair, her body communicating its excitement. "Don't you see, Regan? You've already got the job with Steven Houghton. And the crowd liked you tonight. Haven't people always thought we looked like sisters? I can quit my stock apprentice job so we can have more practice time, and within a few weeks, we could open the act right there at the roadhouse!"

"The act?"

"Oh, Regan, don't play dumb. You and me, together. Why should Houghton care?—Two for the price of one. At least until we give his business a real boost and then—"

"Ali," Regan stopped her, "this doesn't make sense. You're not a singer, and I don't want to be part of a group."

"You're being selfish, as usual." Alyson's blue eyes were icy shards of glass. "You've always taken from me, well, I'd like something back for a change!"

Regan felt crushed under the weight of disappointment. "That's not fair!" She should have known there was another motive than altruism or affection, coming from Alyson. Half of her hard-won job and her first, fragile success for a rag doll and some mended clothing? Alyson couldn't be serious.

When her cousin stood up, she was taller than Regan and heavier, and Regan wished that she'd stayed in her chair. "Think over what I said, Regan. Or if you like, ask Steven Houghton his opinion."

"No, Ali, I won't. I can't. I'm sorry."

With a delicate shrug, Alyson turned away and walked toward the stairs.

Why was it always this way between them? What else could she have said?

Regan's heart pounded as Alyson said over her shoulder, "I don't blame you for liking Jake so well," as if she were changing the subject. "I could like him myself." Without looking back, she climbed the steps.

I could take him away from you, Regan heard in her dreams that night. As if he were hers to lose. . . .

Regan sat with Steven in the empty club after closing. Sharing her last hour before Paul's curfew had become a habit for the three of them, drinking beer—the two men allowing Regan Coke instead because she was underage—and talking. They'd been enjoying a brisk, three-way repartee since the last show had ended, until Jake went to the kitchen for more food.

He'd complained that the ancient upright piano wouldn't stay in tune. "My God, Regan's bringing in enough business. You might at least spring for a new Yamaha, Steven."

"And ruin this delightful ambience?"

"Atmosphere, hell. Considering the notes that come out of this thing, it's a miracle she can sing at all," and he'd kicked the piano for satisfaction, claiming nothing else worked, so he might as well try violence.

Now, Regan grinned at Steven. "You only tolerate me," she teased, "because I take your side against Jake most of the time." She'd claimed the upright wasn't badly out of tune.

"I 'tolerate' you, if that's the word you want, for a lot of reasons," Steven answered. "That's one. Also for talent, beauty, that lovely smile—but you remind me so much of my wife, too," he said. "Ellen," and the smile on his face slowly faded as Steven's hand grazed her cheek.

They were using a table in the club's main room where all the others were stacked with chairs for the night. The tables were small and round, the chairs bentwood, the wooden flooring bare with a weekly scattering of sawdust. The most elegant thing in the place was the bar itself, Steven's pride and joy: a rich, lustrous mahogany expanse that he polished as if it were a fine antique, far older than it really was. Regan, glancing at the spotty display of empty bottles stuffed with candles for the tables, decided that the bar had been the focal point of some grand plan for the roadhouse, abandoned since Ellen's death.

"You loved her very much, didn't you?" she asked softly.

Nodding, Steven sighed. "I wonder if I'll ever stop expecting her to come through that door, fresh from a shopping trip." He turned the gold band on his finger.

"You haven't been without her for very long," Regan pointed out. Only a few months. "It takes time, Steven. No wonder you miss her."

"Well, before I cry in your beer, princess, so to speak—how are things with you two?" He gestured toward the kitchen where Jake had gone for refills of rye and roast beef.

Following his motion, Regan frowned. "Let's just say you can forget knocking on doors before you enter."

Steven covered her twisting hands. "You and Jake have a rare thing," he said gently, "the same as I did with Ellen. Maybe he's circling it yet, but believe me, Regan—he does care for you."

But in the month she'd been singing at the roadhouse, Jake had kept his distance, and she had begun to abandon her earlier faith that she could make him love her. When she shrugged, Steven smiled at her gently, as if she were very young—which she was—and not terribly bright, which Regan hoped wasn't true.

"He's moved around without stopping until now." Steven gave her a searching look. "But I wouldn't worry. He'll tumble soon enough." He patted Regan's hand before releasing it. "If he doesn't, he's a damn fool. If he gets the chance for happiness, and doesn't take it . . ."

Regan guessed he was thinking again of Ellen. She saw raw pain in his face, and put a hand to his cheek as if she might brush it away, like tears. "Oh, Steven," she murmured. As she drew her fingers back, he kissed them lightly.

"Thank you for putting some sunshine in my days again, princess. I can use it. Jake's friendship, too. I don't know what I'd have done when Ellen—after the accident—if it wasn't for him. Jake showed up that morning as soon as he heard the news and ran this place for me as if it were his own. He went from being sometime piano player," Steven remembered, "to raking in receipts, tending bar, paying my bills for me, ordering liquor and supplies, sweeping floors." He paused. "In his spare time, he kept me together, too."

Regan smiled through a mist of emotion. "He loves you, Steven."

"And I think I'd do anything for him."

So would I, Regan thought as Jake appeared with the sandwiches. So would I.

Regan was dreaming, a lovely dream far removed from the old nightmare. Jake took her in his arms, searching her lips with his slowly, firmly, as his hands searched too, moving over her breasts; his mouth against her throat then; and she wanted him to do exactly what he was doing, and more, so much more, oh yes, to find out—

Abruptly, Regan awoke. My God, someone was touching her, creating the dream from which she'd surfaced, aroused and tingling. An index finger ran lightly from her shoulder to her wrist. The hairs stood up on her skin. Fingers running, skating, over her flesh, collarbone to rib cage to the bony prominence of her hip as she lay on her side; fingers racing along her outer thigh. Ohhh . . .

But no, the fingers were thick and short while Jake's were slender, aristocratic, lean and hard and sensitive like him. With a start, she realized it wasn't Jake from the dream, standing by her bed in the darkness. It was Paul!

Regan squinted through her lashes to see him. She kept absolutely still, heart furiously pumping, afraid to make a sound.

The faint light of the clouded moon shone on his features, projected his shadow on the wall. His breathing, always rough and irregular—he smoked too much—seemed harsher. His eyes, in the dimness, looked a darker, normal blue. Regan wished she had pulled the heavier blanket up over the thin sheet. She felt as if she were wearing nothing instead of her blue nightie. Nothing but shame at her own arousal. Dear God, if he touched her now, she'd scream.

Then Regan heard him murmur something. Three indistinct syllables, soft and slurred, as if he'd been drinking; but Paul never drank, because liquor soured his stomach. She saw a tenderness in his expression so alien that she couldn't identify it—like a bird she didn't know, or a flower she hadn't seen before.

Regan was amazed. Eyes bright with moisture that sparkled in the darkness, Paul looked as if he were going to cry. But even when Martha had died, he'd never shed a tear.

He's hungry for someone, she realized. *Just as I am for Jake.* Yearning for whom, though? It wasn't Regan; somehow she felt sure of that. Always, she'd been the thorn in his side; and when, so seldom, he looked at her with gentleness, his eyes had seemed remote. The kindness once-removed.

"Beautiful," Paul mumbled now. His eyes traveled slowly over her body, but he didn't touch her again before he turned away.

Regan lay motionless until she heard the door close, then the shuffling footsteps along the hall. She let out her breath a little at a time, as if she were trying to control the phrasing in a song the way Jake had taught her. Making it last. Using up the air. She was good at it.

How many nights, she wondered. How often had Paul crept into her room without interrupting her dreams? Seen her with her arms wound snugly about the pillow; holding her hunger, too. Did he ever hear her calling in her sleep? Her whole body seemed to shake. *What if he comes again,* Regan thought, *while I'm dreaming of Jake making love to me, revealing mysteries?*

She could put a lock on her door, or a bolt he couldn't force—except then Paul would know she'd been awake tonight. *I've got to get out of here.* But without money, she couldn't; and there was nowhere to go. Regan's heart raced, a futile expenditure of effort, like wheels spinning.

Blankets wouldn't keep Paul out; not locks, either. The next time, Regan wondered, would it matter that she wasn't the right person?

And the next time—would he stop at touching?

Chapter 4

One hot August evening at Steven's, not long after Paul's visit to her room, Regan noticed a dark-eyed stranger staring at her intently from the center table in front. Her heart gave a little leap of alarm. Was it her dress?

Regan had quickly decided that more than one gown would be necessary for six days' work every week, and the cream dress trimmed in gold which she'd worn for her debut seemed much too formal for weeknights. Scraping together enough money from the small allowance Paul permitted from her own salary, Regan had bought a long red prairie-style skirt edged with white eyelets and ruffles. She liked the old-fashioned effect of the long-sleeved, high-necked white blouse as well, its primness softened by the same eyelet trim down the front and on the cuffs. But now, she wondered if she'd made a mistake in putting together the casual, youthful outfit. The expression on the stranger's narrow, olive-skinned face made her uncomfortable.

"Who is that man out front?" Regan asked Steven between sets. "The one in the pinstripe suit." By then, she felt as if she'd put her clothes on upside down. But Steven's answer did little to quiet her heartbeat.

"Manny Bertelli. Owns a few clubs in the Bronx and Manhattan, handles several entertainers; a comedian, I think, and

70

a male singer." He mentioned their names, both of which Regan recognized as second-echelon performers. "Word's getting around, princess. Much as I hate to lose the best act I've ever booked—excluding Jake, of course..."

Was Steven right? Was he really watching her? Regan watched him more closely. That night, and every other night for a week, he occupied the same table, the only motion in his entire body the tracing of small circles on the tabletop with well-manicured fingers. Regan noticed that he never applauded.

But after-hours on the following Thursday, he was waiting for her in the parking lot outside the roadhouse. "Miss Reilly," he acknowledged in the darkness, startling her as she and Jake left the club calling good nights over their shoulders to Steven. "May we talk?" He didn't introduce himself. "My car is here." He gestured toward the black Cadillac Fleetwood limousine, gleaming like obsidian, like his own dark eyes, at the end of the lot. "Perhaps a light snack?" he suggested in a tone that wouldn't be refused.

Heading for the VW without letting her stop, Jake tightened his grip on her elbow; but by this time Regan was too curious not to go. She had become intrigued by the silent attention she'd been paid for a week, even felt vaguely annoyed by the lack of outward enthusiasm; and she could feel the draw of Bertelli's personality. Sheer power and influence radiated from the man. "Don't worry." She withdrew from Jake's grasp. "Mr. Bertelli will see that I get home on time ... won't you?"

Obviously pleased that she knew his name, he said, "You'll be treated like a queen," tucking Regan's hand through his arm. Regan didn't look behind her. She didn't have to. She could feel Jake's brown eyes boring a hole through both their backs; but there had been no more graceful way to leave, and if he was the least bit jealous at this point—not only worried for her about Paul—so much the better!

Now that her routine at Steven's was established, Jake was spending his afternoons at home, working on his own music; twice, he'd been late getting to the roadhouse. It wouldn't hurt him to stew for a change, Regan decided as the big black car drove her with Manny Bertelli to a small country inn nearby.

It didn't take long to learn that Steven had been right about Bertelli's interest. He came very quickly to the point.

"Houghton's isn't a bad place to start," Manny began, adding Chablis to Regan's wineglass after they'd ordered. "Of course, the pay is lousy— Yes, I know exactly what you're earning. You should start thinking about moving on before it feels too much like home."

The wine had begun to relax Regan—no one had asked her age, so she hadn't volunteered—and it cured her nerves quickly enough. At first, settling onto the velvet-upholstered banquette and casting glances at the beamed ceiling, the array of pewter and antique farm tools on the walls, she'd felt out of place, out of her depth. Maybe she shouldn't have been so quick to come with Bertelli—but now, her fingers had stopped shaking and she could lift the glass of wine to her lips without fearing she'd spill it. "What would you suggest?" she heard herself ask in a breezy tone, as if she sat like this every night in fashionable restaurants, discussing her career. *Her career*.

"You need some tough talking-to." Bertelli smiled to disarm her. "That's why we're here." Which was obviously intended to get her complete attention in case he didn't already have it. Which, of course, he did.

Regan studied Manny Bertelli, she hoped with the same objectivity and lack of emotion he'd used on her for a week. Slighter than Jake, shorter, he had a straight, lithe frame that seemed held together by steel wire instead of bone. He reminded Regan of a few boys she'd known in school but was always afraid to talk to, much less date. Like them, Manny Bertelli struck her as a little dangerous. Certainly, he knew more than she did; perhaps wanted more than she could give him. She couldn't help but be impressed by him, by his car, by the chauffeur. But it was a reaction of part fear, part fascination.

"The attention you've been getting at Houghton's is, well, elementary . . . nothing more," Bertelli was saying. "The act is rough. You need the right songs, not somebody else's hodgepodge. That's okay for a start, but it has to change. You'll need your own songs, not just the old faithfuls. Oh, mixing in a few standards never hurts," Manny acknowledged. "When you get into albums, one or two will skyrocket sales. People feel comfortable with what they know, and a new, startling version of someone else's tune wipes out the original as if it never existed." He swept a hand over the tablecloth—which was red to match the velvet of the seats—in dismissal.

"But records are for later," Manny went on. "Forget that for now. We'll talk about recording after you've gotten some exposure—which is why leaving Houghton's is crucial."

Records! Regan barely heard anything after that. Could she make a showing on the charts? Would disc jockeys across America play *her* voice over the airwaves? Thousands of people at once, hearing Regan Reilly? Wow. She wanted to hold the top of her head on, but instead, Regan twirled the stem of her wineglass and grinned at Manny Bertelli, who smiled back, his jet-black eyes sparkling.

"You like the idea, huh? Well, you should."

It didn't occur to Regan until much later that he'd deliberately dropped into the conversation those few words about making records as a teaser, like bait on a line. By then, she didn't care. Regan sat back as the waitress served their food; then set her attention, as did Bertelli, to the delicious Croque Monsieur, all dripping, melted cheese and delicate ham in crusty French bread, quick-grilled.

Bertelli finished first and pushed his plate aside. "I'm going to tell you something, Regan." He watched her working on the fancy sandwich, and smiled at the answering question in her eyes. "All great entertainers make a silence." For a moment, he let the phrase sink in before he continued. "They step up to a mike, sing a note or two, and the whole room, the club or concert hall, goes dead quiet. No rustling. No ice cubes clinking in the glasses. No idle chatter. Even the guy tending bar stops rattling bottles."

Great entertainers! The two words set Regan's mind awhirl, and she forgot the rest of her meal, setting the remains with Bertelli's. Did he mean she could be one of them? It was true that when she sang at Steven's, the house was full of stillness, the very atmosphere that quieted her nerves.

"It happens every night, you know," Bertelli said, leaning forward. "That hush over the club, the spell you weave, making the audience come to you on their hands and knees—and with every song, those people find you more beautiful." His dark eyes slipped over her. "Well, they've got that to begin with because you're not like some singers who have to overcome their looks and force their fans to adore them. You've got the face to launch a career overnight, Regan. I guarantee you can climb so fast, so high, you'll need extra oxygen to breathe." Then he laughed at the expression on her face. She knew she must look stupefied, and her heart was behaving oddly. "Think I'm selling you a piece of the Brooklyn Bridge, do you? Well, I'm sure as hell not. I grew up in a neighborhood like the Bronx Zoo behind bars, and I like it a lot better out here, let me tell you. So will you. Everybody does. In a way," Manny said, shifting his gaze to contemplate the last of his wine, "I'm a phenomenon myself."

Then he looked up, straight at her, and she felt again the pure force of his will. It frightened her a little, it was so strong; excited her. "That's what you are, Regan Reilly—a *phenomenon.*" His voice was nearly a whisper. Jake had called her a natural, which was heady news in itself to a girl who only sang in the shower—but a *phenomenon!*

"And you're going to be what all good girls with such prodigious talent ought to be—a superstar."

Regan could hardly take in what he was saying. Every sentence carried her higher into the clouds, lifted her off the mountaintop she had scaled with Jake the first afternoon, pulled her toward the stratosphere. A superstar?! Regan bit her bottom lip to keep from smiling too much. She didn't want Manny Bertelli to think she was completely giddy, though inside she felt awfully close to getting up on the table and shouting, "Here I am, people—look at me, Regan Reilly! I'm going to be a star!" Wouldn't Paul scold her for a show-off if he heard *that?* And Martha, who told her she was full of vanity for no reason? Maybe, just maybe, they were wrong!

"I'm making this sound easy, but it's not." The dark eyes grew darker. "You're not looking at simple choices, Regan. You decide."

"I know what I want, Mr. Bertelli. Getting there may not be simple, but that doesn't scare me." *Liar,* Regan chided herself. She was all but shaking in her shoes. Jake was one thing, Steven another, but this—

"We work together," Bertelli said. "Your choice again; we do it with first names." His fingers moved on the cloth. She wondered if he was going to reach for her hand.

"All right," she said, "Manny." But he didn't touch her.

"I own the Birdcage, in Manhattan. The headliner I've got now is a comedian—but he could be better. I can use a good warm-up." Manny's voice became rapid, and his eyes held hers. "You know what I mean by that? You come on first, get the folks in a good mood; they laugh at the jokes during the main event—and they buy more drinks."

Regan felt slightly disappointed. But what had she expected? Las Vegas at The Sands? What was she doing at Steven's except keeping the crowd happy for the rock band between sets? A second act. Well, she already was one; but she wouldn't always be. *Guts,* Jake had said. *And determination.* It looked as if the time had come at last to try them out.

Manny was smiling at her. "Cheer up," he said. "I'm going to give you a raise. And hire a new accompanist."

Her eyes fixed not on his face, but on the gold of his cuff links, Regan said she preferred Jake.

"But unless he's a magician, he can't be in two places at once next fall, can he?"

Regan's chin went up. She hadn't wanted to think about September. Or the shaky future that she wanted so badly but that Jake denied, whatever his reasons. She watched Manny fold his arms over his chest, settle back in his chair, and let his dark eyes wander over her. Strangely, he didn't make her feel like a piece of cheesecake, not cheap and tawdry, as Paul could. Her senses didn't whirl, either, as they would have under Jake's regard. Manny's gaze remained steady, but open—as if he were wondering now whether she could go the distance.

And though he couldn't have been more than half a dozen years older than Jake, Bertelli made her think of a father, his look appraising, then approving.

"Marsh is smart enough to take care of his own career," Manny pointed out, as though Regan needed the reminder. She felt the bottom of her stomach drop when he added, "So are you, sweet. Shall we talk hard business?"

"That must have been some talk."

The following night, in Regan's dressing room at the road-house, dozens of white roses awaited her with a rectangular card, off-white, stamped in gold: *Emmanuele Bertelli*. Holding it, Regan turned to find Jake in the doorway, leaning against the frame, frowning at the flowers.

"Yes," she said, "it was." She had wanted to tell him, had been bubbling over with excitement, but Jake had been unusually quiet during the quick run-through before she came backstage to dress. He had played. He corrected. He even praised her when the new arrangement went extremely well. But the closeness had been missing, the easy conversation, and she had decided to wait for the right moment.

"I wondered," he said, "if you'd get around to telling us. Me. When do you jump ship?"

"How did you know—"

"For Christ's sake, what the hell do you think I thought Bertelli wanted? To go joyriding? You've taken him on, haven't you—as your manager?"

"Oh, Jake, he made me such a good offer—two whole weeks to begin at the Birdcage, in *Manhattan*, Jake, just think." She could hardly contain her excitement. "And more money!" She explained about the club in SoHo while Jake listened, or appeared to, without ever smiling, his brown-gold eyes watching her. "I'll be earning twice what I get here, and we even talked about records. Manny says if I get one hit single, a song all my own, he's sure I can have a major recording contract and—you're not pleased," she finished weakly, taking note of his darkening expression.

"Not if Bertelli's involved, no."

"But he's charming," she said, unable to understand Jake's attitude.

"Tarantulas are soft and furry, but you really mustn't pet them." Jake looked uncomfortable, as if he didn't want to disillusion her. "Regan, he's a manipulator—and that's the kindest thing I can say about him, so how can you expect me to—"

"Who told you so?"

"People I know, people in the business. It's like a fraternity, music. . . ."

"Well, I *need* someone to manipulate my career," Regan insisted. "I'm not as good at that as you are." She tried not to sound panicky. "Jake, you're going away soon. What would you have me do?"

"Stay right where you are."

"And stagnate at Steven's while you keep going, getting better and better?" She stared at him, not believing he could be serious. "You didn't expect me to stay before. You said I'd leave the roadhouse and—" Regan broke off, looking at him more sharply. "I think you only want Steven watching out for me—but why, Jake?"

If he was jealous, let him say so, and set her fears to rest. If the issue was male and female. She would understand that, welcome it.

"You need seasoning, confidence," he murmured. "To be certain of where you want to go. Regan, you've got time."

"I *haven't* got time! I need to take my opportunities as they come, the same as you do"—he was looking at her now as if she were a stranger—"because the chances don't come that often, Jake. Maybe they'll never come again! Manny says I'm a *phenomenon*—but will anybody else feel that strongly? By January, he thinks he can get me some bookings out of town . . . oh, not as a headliner yet—but even second acts get to be seen, don't they? That's the point, and if you'll play for me at the Birdcage . . ." She didn't tell him that Manny wanted someone else. Anyone else, had been the impression.

"I won't play for you there," Jake said. "If you leave Steven, that's it, Regan. That's as far as I go. I've got my own headaches." His voice was tight with anger, making her determination falter.

"But—we were going to work out the new set of songs and—"

He had straightened from the door frame. She wondered why he looked almost sad. "Do you have any idea what sort of life you're staring at? What going on the road is like—especially for a woman?"

"Bugs," she said harshly, "the same as it is for you! Bugs and bad food and no sleep and missing—yes, I know, you told me already, and maybe you *weren't* exaggerating, but Jake, I have to learn for myself!" Then she backed off at the expression in his brown-gold eyes. "Oh, please try to understand about Manny," she began again. "Jake, a few months ago, in May . . . I thought I'd be stuck in Paul's house for the rest of my life if a miracle didn't happen."

She tried to make him look at her, but Jake's gaze had shifted to the whitewashed wall behind her shoulder. "Then a miracle did happen," she said. "I met you, and you told me I could be *good* when nobody had ever believed in me before. You gave me the start I had wanted so badly. Jake, you were the one who said I had to want it, *really* want it—"

"Well, I'm glad to have been of service."

She had taken the wrong approach, but how could she pretend now that the words didn't exist? She had already said them, meant them; why was he twisting them?

"I haven't used you," she said. "I think you're clinging to some ancient double standard—expecting me to put on the brakes when the only thing to be done, Jake, is to step down hard on the gas. Which is exactly what you'd do, and will do in—"

"Nobody's going to stop you, are they?"

His voice had been savage.

Regan's throat so closed off she couldn't speak. She turned her back, facing the flowers, rearranging a spray of fern. She wouldn't let him order her life, as Paul had always done. If

ـake didn't want the best for her after all, she wouldn't break down and cry in disappointment, either. Anyway, she'd already accepted Manny's offer, and she couldn't change her mind.

"If you're going to fight with me," she said at last, "why don't you leave instead, so I can get dressed?"

But she felt him close behind her, so close she could feel the heat of his body, and its tension. "Bertelli overdoes it, don't you think?" he asked. "Besides, you're not a rose person." And she thought he wanted to keep the argument going when she wished with all her heart that he would pull her into his arms.

"I love roses," she said, her voice quivering.

"They're too stylized," Jake insisted. "Much too formal. You won't ever get them from me—even making allowances just now for the cost. I'd always give you something simpler, fresher . . . daisies," he said.

She held her breath, not certain what he wanted; angry enough to hurt him if she could, as he'd hurt her. "Some lover you are," Regan murmured.

Jake, his voice sounding strained to the breaking point, said after a silence having nothing to do with great entertainers, "I'm not your lover."

Late that night, Regan followed Jake mutely to the VW. He'd barely looked at her throughout the evening, and she had the feeling he'd increased the tempo in the last song just to see if she could keep up. Well, by heaven, she had, Regan thought as Jake started the car with a furious rush of gas.

Each mile of the dark, winding road only strengthened Regan's anger and a growing sorrow that tasted like bile. If he never talked to her again, that was fine with her! Who did he think he was, anyway, ignoring her most of the time, and teasing her like a child the rest—holding her at arm's length (fancy anything else!) to make his eventual leavetaking simpler. Simple, simple. *You're going places, don't get involved* . . . and then what? He blamed her when she took the opportunity. Regan wanted to scream at him. How dare he drive so fast, eyes straight ahead at the road, as if he couldn't wait to get her home? Why wouldn't he give in again as he had the night she opened at Steven's, whirling her around the dressing room, kissing, kissing as if he'd never let her go, when now—

"Jake!"

The blown tire exploded in the quiet black night, echoed by Regan's quick cry of alarm. Swiftly, he slid the shift through the gears, fourth to third to second, one hand holding tightly to the wheel, his eyes riveted on the stretch of twisting pavement. She felt the car reeling, drifting, jerking, the sharp slap, slap, slap of deflating rubber against the road like a punishment for her thoughts. She didn't dare to speak again; the pounding of her heart shouted for her.

Then they were stopped by the side of the road, inches from the deep pit of a ditch that substituted on The King's Highway for a shoulder. She heard Jake's shaky breath, a convulsive swallow. "Christ," he muttered, and flung open his door to take a look.

The highway was deserted, not another car in sight. Thank God, Regan thought in relief. She followed Jake on trembling legs that threatened to dump her on the pavement. The left front tire was flat to the rim.

"Kids on my street," Jake said tautly. "They litter the block with broken soda bottles. I knew I'd picked up a piece or more on my way to Steven's, but I forgot to check later."

Because they had argued, Regan added for him. Because of her. She wished she could say something, but she couldn't. If there'd been another car coming from the opposite direction when Jake fought the VW past the center line and back again. . . . Regan was shaking from head to toe.

"Are you okay?" He had turned and was peering at her in the dark. Didn't touch her, though. Stayed a safe six inches away. His eyes concerned, but angry still—at the car, at the boys on his block, at himself for negligence, preoccupation . . . at her? Probably the last.

"Yes, I'm all right."

"See if you can find the flashlight in the glove compartment. You can hold it while I put the spare on."

A joint effort then, locked into a midnight intimacy no one could appreciate, a stall. A fresh chance at living, Regan corrected. She was still imagining what might have happened when Jake finally grunted, straightening from his haunches to stand upright again. He stamped his feet to restore circulation in his cramped legs, wiped his hands on a rag, but she kept shaking. In the car again, shoving the flashlight into the glove compartment, she couldn't control the motion of her own hand; heard herself take a quick, deep breath more like a sob; and then she was in his arms, held hard, crying into his shirt, which smelled like grease; and Jake was saying, "Oh, baby, I'm sorry. I'm sorry this happened; I'm sorry you're so scared; I'm . . . just sorry. About tonight."

"Me, too. Oh, Jake——"

His mouth on hers, the thunder of his heart, the trembling of his arms that echoed her own shivering. His mouth, his mouth. Wet kisses with her tears. What had she cried at the instant of the blowout? His name—not to warn him, but to have it on her lips, the last thing she ever said. *Jake, Jake. . . .* She felt weak and pliant, full of remorse and wanting. I love you, she thought, clinging; please, please love me.

But as he had done before, Jake lifted his head. "I'd better get you home," drawing away from her lips when she would have begged him to kiss her again. "It's late now, and by the time we get there——"

Regan didn't hear the last of his excuse. A kiss of apology, she thought with disappointment; a kiss of relief.

But at least, Regan told herself as they sped along the highway, we aren't fighting now. Touching Jake's arm, she said, "Remember that house I mentioned to you once? It's not far from here, along The King's Highway. Do you suppose—could we have that picnic tomorrow, Jake? You could practice until noon, then we could go until sundown. . . ."

He'd refuse, of course. Hours he needed for his work, and she immediately wished she hadn't opened her mouth. But he surprised her.

"Sure, why not? Christ, after tonight we deserve a holiday," with a quick flash of the smile she adored. Jake, looking care-free and accepting, as if his smile were a preview of Saturday. The Talbot house! Regan wanted to hug herself the rest of the way home. And Jake didn't even say he was sorry for the kissing this time.

"Want me to speak to your uncle?" he asked in front of the house, his voice low as if Paul could hear them. "It's after three."

"No. He'll be asleep. Good night, Jake."

When she slipped into the silent foyer, Regan didn't know whether her footsteps woke Paul or whether it had been the simultaneous haunting whistle of a freight train rumbling through the valley not far away, but suddenly he appeared, rumpled and combing his fingers through his hair, in the upstairs hall. "Where you been, miss?" He did not, on second glance, look as if he had been sleeping. He looked enormous and fully prepared for trouble as Regan continued up the stairs.

"You know where," she said. "Working." At the top of the flight, she tried to ease past, the very picture of fatigue, but Paul stopped her. "Jake's car had a blowout on The King's Highway tonight!" she went on in defense. "We might have been killed—"

"And you just might be lying!" In the hall, his features were cast in grotesque shadows by the bare ceiling bulb. "Again," he added softly.

What was he talking about? "I haven't—I haven't done anything!" But Paul's big hands shot out with no warning, taking her by the shoulders, half crushing the fragile bones, making Regan gasp with shock and pain.

"I know where you've been half the night! Not singing, not fixing tires," Paul shouted. "You've been having your own brand of nightcap—just like your mama—only this time, you stayed too long in Jake Marsh's bed!"

"No!" He had no reason to think so. Regan stayed still and stiff under his hands. Then she heard the door close, almost soundlessly, at the end of the hall; and the dull uncertainty, the confusion at this outburst, became sharp-edged and finely honed, like a knife blade. Of course! Alyson had been waiting, waiting until she was late one night, waiting to pay her back for imaginary crimes.

"Oh, God," Regan cried, "no, Uncle Paul, I—"

"I warned you about trouble if you got out of line, didn't I?" His voice came at her like hailstones. "Didn't I?"

Paul let go of her shoulders, turning Regan weak with the release of pressure and tension; but she was grateful too quickly. The interval of relief was shattered by force as Paul struck her, hard, across one cheek. And back again, her head snapping until her neck went limp like the old Raggedy Ann doll, tattered and frayed, its pinafore dirtied and torn. "I've never done anything, I only went to practice my music. We don't even work at his house anymore!"

"Nobody there, *was* there? You think I'm stupid? His mother died ten years ago," Paul said hoarsely. "So unless he's got a petrified mummy propped in a chair, it was just you—and him—and your filth in that house!"

Then he shoved her away, letting Regan slide to the uncarpeted floor. Her head bumped against the boards. "Just like *her*," he said. "You got anymore lies tonight? Clear the air, miss, tell me your lies. . . ."

What was the use of explaining? Paul believed what he wanted to believe. She could almost hear Alyson's words of poison. It didn't matter that she had been telling the complete truth, that she still felt shaken from the loud explosion, the swerving of the small car. No, Alyson had planted mistrust based on one small, harmless fib.

"No," she whispered, "no more lies."

"Get up."

Paul's hands closed over her wrists, hauling Regan to her feet. She could feel the bruised flesh beginning to swell on her face, and in her mouth was the metallic, ferrous taste of blood where her teeth had cut her cheek. Was this the same man who had looked at her so tenderly?

"Don't make me do that again," he warned. "You might not get off so easy next time."

"There won't be a next time." He took it as submission,

but a small seed germinated in Regan's heart and took root as easily, with as much determination, as Alyson had planted doubt in her uncle's mind. Regan would never let Paul Oldham touch her again. Not her body, and not her spirit; nor stare at her in the night, either, wanting someone else.

The next afternoon, in a mixture of love and defiance and unconscious will, she made certain of it.

Chapter 5

The King's Highway West, benign again in the bright sun of midday, curled like a satin ribbon unrolling before them. When they drove past the site of the accident, she shut her eyes tightly. Regan had considered not going with Jake on their picnic after all—but only briefly considered. She knew she needed to go. More than ever.

Both cheeks that morning had pink-and-white welts, but an ice pack and a generous application of makeup repaired the damage well enough. She looked normal, even to herself, and Jake didn't notice anything other than the navy shorts she wore, the soft cotton blouse in primary stripes, and the sweep of tawny hair loose over one shoulder, partially disguising the cheek nearest him—just in case. "Hi," he had murmured when she got into the car, setting the picnic basket on the floor. "You look festive today. How'd you sleep last night?"

"Fine," she muttered, shutting the door on the subject, too. Then, with a glance at Jake's trim white jeans: "I hope you remembered the cloth for us to sit on, or you'll be one big grass stain." Though she thought he looked very handsome in his French-blue polo shirt. She liked watching the muscles in his upper arms work as he drove, and forced herself into a better mood so he wouldn't ask her questions she didn't want to answer. As long as he didn't see the large bruise on her shoulder, she could pretend that nothing had happened. Even to herself.

"Look." Regan pointed now at the road. "Here's the turn for the drive. You can leave the car up against the gates," which were padlocked.

She all but leaped from the VW as soon as it stopped. Taking deep breaths, she looked around in wonder. Even abandoned and decaying, the grounds and the house itself were like a clean white canvas for Regan's bruised imagination to paint with elegance, color. The property, bounded by a New England stone fence in a state of advanced disrepair; its rusting iron gates entwined with a scrolled letter T where they converged, seemed to her like love, long-denied.

"T for 'Talbot,'" Regan explained, taking Jake by the hand. "The house has been empty for years since the last member of the family died a bachelor. But extended family from the four corners of the globe keep the will in litigation, and this place a shell."

The driveway, overgrown with grass and weeds thrusting from the gravel bed, wound through a stand of pines, secluding the mansion. Regan watched Jake's face when the house, in a once-beautiful clearing, came into view at last, saw him gape at the apex of the graceful circular sweep of drive, at the immense house itself. Not even the neglect of years could destroy its first impression of grandeur. But she'd never before been this near the mansion itself.

"Oh!" Regan cried, "I told you this was the perfect spot for a picnic! You don't know how long I've wanted to come here."

"A picnic?" Jake echoed, grinning. "More like a bacchanal."

They sat on the broad front lawn under an oak tree, eating lunch off the red-checked cloth and soaking up the bright sun. Watching Jake enjoy his cold fried chicken and green salad, Regan felt curiously proud of the place—as if it really were hers, from the dozen-plus chimneys to the double front doors with their heavy, now-tarnished brass pulls.

"If they ever sell this place," Regan mused, munching on a piece of celery heaped with cream cheese, "how much do you think it would cost?"

Jake speculated silently, squinting up at the square tower that housed the main stairway, at the sun glinting on its stained glass windows; then he laughed. "As the old saying goes—in reference originally, I believe, to yachts—if you have to ask the price, you couldn't afford to live here." Then, when she made a disappointed face, saying she hadn't expected to—though her heart asked, anyway—he added, "But if you're a very good girl, someday I'll buy it for you," and ruffled her hair.

That day, however—after Paul—Regan didn't want joking. She had never seen the house inside, she said doggedly, and if it would be a present, she thought Jake should make sure it was worth the price. He told her she was being silly and finished his dessert, a thick slice of chocolate layer cake. During which Regan, with unaccustomed petulance, argued him into agreement. At the far end of the long veranda at the rear of the house, she had found a likely looking window.

"We'll have every cop in the county on our asses in five minutes," Jake grumbled—but, receiving only her set look for reply, he quickly drank the last of his lemonade, then pried the frame open. Regan wriggled through.

"Hey," she heard him call softly through the opening, but didn't answer. Couldn't. Even taking into account its present condition, the house was a dream come true. The house would be worth any price, she thought.

"Jake!" Regan was laughing. On the terrace he found her standing in the now-open French doors, looking as if she truly lived there. "Delighted you could join us this Sunday, my lord," she said, taking his hand to draw him inside. "Welcome to my ancestral home."

"You're nuts."

"Shhh." She put a finger to his lips. Her hand trembled with excitement. "If you're coming inside, you must play."

"You're crazy," Jake said again, but he mumbled it this time; and, smiling, he followed her.

From the terrace she led him into a cavernous room, two stories high, the ceiling beamed with dark wood against white plaster now flaked and crumbling. "This is the Great Hall,"

Regan explained. "A kind of living room—family room, I suppose. The furniture is in storage somewhere, but in its heyday, this room was exquisite."

Jake laughed. "You sound like a tour guide."

"I could be." She removed the carefully preserved pages from her totebag to show him ancient clippings faded yellow. "These tapestries, which hung on that far wall, were mostly fifteenth-century Flemish, and there"—she pointed to the huge sandstone-faced fireplace that tapered toward the ceiling— "was the coat of arms the Talbots used as a motif in many of the other house carvings and moldings."

She walked Jake through empty rooms echoing with footsteps and the past: the music room, the dining room, and the library; the breakfast room and a billiard room; even the shambling remains of the indoor swimming pool downstairs. Upstairs, they quickly lost count of the rooms, wandering along halls that bisected other halls, as Regan flung open doors and more doors. "And this room," she said gaily, twisting the knob, "is . . . Oh, Jake, *look* . . ."

Her voice trailed off on a sigh of delight. Immediately, she loved the room, which was modest in size but had great appeal. Simple and tidy, the fireplace here had, instead of a mantel, delft tiles of blue and white around its opening. A wide shaft of sun angled across the floor to strike the opposite wall like an arrow, sent flying with truest aim. By Cupid, Regan promptly decided. She didn't care what it had been once. To her, it was a room for lovers; and her heart began to pulse strongly.

"Over here by the fire, I'd have two small wing chairs in gold velvet—so the light would turn the fabric different shades and textures."

Jake kept looking at her with that even, amused expression that puzzled Regan. She had learned that he wasn't going to laugh at her, but she hadn't learned more than that. "Sheer curtains, my lord," she told him, involved in her daydream, "because there's no need for privacy here. At night, they'd let in the moon. . . ." She touched the windowpanes, filmed with dust, imagining them sparkling prisms for the sun.

On one side wall, she tried a locked door that wouldn't give. "Probably a nanny's room," Jake guessed, "and this would connect to the nursery."

"Oh, you think?" Regan ran to see, and coming back said yes, wasn't it grand; there was even a small kitchenette next door for making hot chocolate and cinnamon toast on winter nights. "Imagine having a nurse to live-in!"

Not waiting for an answer, she opened a closet door, a big walk-in with drawers and shelves and endless compartments. "Umm, must have been a well-dressed governess," Regan mused. She pawed around inside the deep closet and came up with an old muslin cover from some piece of discarded furniture. Jake began to cough as the first haze of dust rose into the still air of the closed room.

"For God's sake, Regan, what are you doing?"

Dragging the muslin, she positioned it at a right angle to the window, flipping the material like a cloud, choking herself as the cover billowed to the floor. "This is the bed, of course. Large and brass, perhaps, yes—with a canopy and side curtains. Very medieval . . . and sexy, don't you agree?"

Jake frowned at the image she'd presented. "I think we'd better go," he said, but Regan only shook her head, putting her arms around his neck before he could prevent it, her heart picking up speed as she reached up to kiss the corner of his mouth. The kiss last night went through her mind, her senses. The kiss, and Paul. "This room . . . this house," she whispered, "were made for pleasure." And moving her lips over his, started kissing him: soft, glancing kisses at the start, then increasingly hungry and pressured.

"Regan."

"I won't hurt you." She tried to smile; but her memory of Paul wouldn't let her. "Pretend," she said fiercely, no longer teasing as Jake's arms came around her lightly, barely holding. "Pretend, my lord, that you care for me, even a little—"

"I care," in a ragged tone, his brown-gold eyes darkening as he searched her features. "You know I do, but—" He drew away.

"Then want me— Don't you want me, Jake?"

"God," she heard him whisper. And it was as if someone had blown a wall apart between them. "My God, yes." Like last night when the tire on the car had shredded after exploding. Something in her words, her tone seemed to blast away his last defenses, and somehow they were lying together on the muslin cover with the muted sun beaming through dusty windows, nothing separating them, Regan thought, now or forever, as Jake's hand slipped under her shirt to touch her breast. Not a dream, no . . . but real and present, happening now, oh . . .

Beneath his palm, the nipple went taut and hard, as eager as the rest of her for his touch. Jake fingered it, kissing her deeply on the mouth at the same time, taking quick command, his breathing harsh and shallow.

Regan breathed carefully, savoring each sensation, as if the slightest untoward movement on her part might make him stop. So much newness, she thought. I want to know it all, everything, to have him, and I will. . . .

She watched intently while his fingers worked the buttons on her blouse, the front closing of her bra, baring her to his dark gaze. "Oh, Regan," he murmured. Then he turned her slightly to slip the shirt from her shoulders, and his voice changed. "Oh baby, no—"

She had forgotten the purple bruise along the bone; but it was too late to hide it. He'd already seen, was sliding down to take her in his arms. "Regan, why didn't you tell me? Baby, why did he—"

"Don't, Jake, please. I don't want to talk about him now—"

And he pressed his mouth to the roundness of her shoulder, then the darkened bruise itself, softly, softly, his lips as light as the butterflies in her stomach when she sang; his touch, healing where she hurt. But Regan felt the tenseness in him of anger, and she whispered, "Touch me," pulling his hand to her breast again.

Long moments of close silence. Jake's kisses changing, deepening, probing; long moments when she realized that if he might have left off before, he wouldn't now. His mouth, following those clever fingers to her breast. His hand, sliding

along her stomach; his hand between her legs, warm, so warm
through her clothing; his hand, parting her thighs, eager and
open; his hand, finding its way gently up the brief leg of her
shorts, fingers finding her softness, wetness. She couldn't have
let him leave; there was fire in her veins. Dear God, she could
never have imagined—

"Jake," she moaned, but nothing else came out.

His voice was husky, strained. "Say no, then. Regan, hurry
up, say it!"

He thought she was afraid; but she wasn't. The minute she
had seen him, heard him play, received his smile, there had
been no one else she wanted, no one who was better now at
what she needed, touching her even as he spoke against it,
couldn't help himself, touching her in all the places she'd never
been touched before—her body, and her heart.

"Yes," she whispered, "be first for me, oh Jake, yes . . .
please."

"Regan," he breathed, "Jesus," his mouth against her throat,
its tender hollow brushing across her collarbone. "Oh God, I
don't think I'm any good with virgins. . . ."

He groaned. He made promises. To be gentle, not to hurt
her, never to hurt her, to stop if she wanted him to. But all
the time Regan was twisting under his guidance, letting him
remove her clothes, then helping with his, turning into and
beneath him, barely able to wait, knowing—thank God, knowing—he couldn't stop, no matter what he said. The initial
pain, sudden and sharp, was just as quickly gone on a long,
slow wave of liquid pleasure. And even when the gentleness
did finally give way to force and drive and heat, she urged
him on into a world of their own making where there was
nothing but Jake's hands at last upon her, his mouth, his whole
body loving hers. Loving *her.* As no one ever had before.

Feeling flushed from love a long while later, Regan drew
a finger lightly along his jaw as Jake, raised on one elbow,
studied her. She had never belonged anywhere but in this room,
in this moment, with wide stripes of afternoon sun across Jake's
body.

"I want you out of that house," he said suddenly, his other hand caressing the roundness of her shoulder, gingerly touching the darkened bruise. "I'll help you find a place closer to Steven's, or maybe near the station so you can get the train to New York when you—"

"Jake, I can't."

Her heart began to pound, but not with excitement now.

"Why not? You told me after the audition at the roadhouse that you were going to save your salary, and by fall—"

"I haven't saved . . . very much." She looked away from the growing suspicion in his eyes. "But I will, Jake, when I start working at the Birdcage. You mustn't worry about me, I'll be all right." She eased her shoulder from his touch, and tried to smile at him. She hadn't expected this.

"Sure you will. I love the way you handle Paul." Jake's voice was deceptively soft. "This isn't the first time he's put a hand on you, is it?"

"Jake, he's only miserable just now because the shop is closing, or about to, and he doesn't know how to pay his debts, except for my money, so—"

Oh God, no. She hadn't meant to ever tell him, but out it came before she could think.

"Your money?" Jake tipped her chin up, forcing her eyes to meet his, cloudy with anger. "You mean he *kept it*, made you give him your pay? Regan, you can't possibly be signing the checks over to him like that, without even—"

"I sign the checks over," she said flatly, pulling away from his hand. "Just like that. Now, could we please stop talking about him? I want to forget last night!"

"Jesus Christ!" Jake exploded. *"Jesus H. Christ!"*

He was sitting up, staring at her, and she could see the muscle working in his jaw. He was furious.

"Jake, he wouldn't let me sing, otherwise! He'd make me stay home, get a job I *didn't* want, and maybe—maybe he'd have taken *that* money, too. So what difference does it make where the checks come from? I don't care about the *money*— I only want to *sing!*"

She was almost shouting. How could she hold onto the last few hours now? Forget about Paul when Jake wouldn't let her?

Her glance met Jake's darkened eyes, which were touched by softness and something else, too.

"You really want it, don't you," he said. "The singing."

"As much as I want you," Regan answered. She reached up to touch his face, the line of his jaw. Why did she think it was fear in his eyes?

Jake was silent for the length of a heartbeat or two, then he said softly, "Maybe more." His fingers brushed the loose strands of hair at her temples, his eyes swept over her nakedness, and changed expression. The room was back again, the sun; and she blocked Paul from her thoughts as easily as Jake blotted out the shafting light when he moved over her. "I guess I'll have to love you hard enough to make sure I keep you," he whispered. "Hard enough to make up for everybody else." And she drew him down again. "Please do," Regan said as the passion began to grow.

Jake's mouth teased hers. "Dual-career couple, huh?"

"Oh, yes."

Regan smiled, knowing precisely what the puzzling, warm, accepting look in Jake's eyes had meant from the beginning.

Driving back to Lancaster, his eyes narrowed into the sunset, Jake said with the resigned air of a man reaching a tough decision, "All right, how long will it take you to collect your gear?"

"Not long." Regan stopped in the middle of a luxurious stretch. "But why?" She pulled her striped shirt down into place again and peered at Jake.

"Because you're moving." He didn't even look her way, looked instead as if he were contemplating violence. "You won't spend another night in his house. You wanted to get out, and you are." Then his right hand lifted from the gearshift and seemed to find her face by instinct, his eyes remaining fixed on the road; his fingers skimmed her cheek, lightly, as if he had kissed her. Was she going crazy? Dreaming again? Even after today, she wasn't sure. Nothing had ever been as important as his work to Jake, certainly not a woman.

"I should have taken you home to stay the day I met you," Jake said, answering her question, making her pulse race. She tingled from his touch, from anticipation. Not having to be afraid of Paul, his moods and his criticisms; having Jake to look at, to love, anytime she wanted? How could she possibly absorb what was happening so fast, after waiting so long? Jake looked at her and smiled. "How would you like a night off? I'll call Steven while you get settled and—"

"But Jake, it's Saturday, the busiest time for the road-house—"

He grinned. "Well, for one night Steven can play Muzak between sets for the band. I need you to myself."

"Jake—"

"The piano player's taking a holiday, so you might as well." He reached for Regan's hand. "Besides, I have ulterior motives. Tonight," Jake said lightly, "I'm going to make love to you in a proper bed."

"You're late!"

With a grim look in Jake's direction, Paul Oldham rose from the kitchen table, throwing his knife down with a clatter against the ironstone plate. When he moved toward Regan, Jake spun her around. "You go upstairs," he ordered softly, giving her a gentle push. "I'll do the explaining."

"I've heard all the explaining from you—years back—that I'm gonna listen to!" she heard Paul say as she rushed up the steps.

Pulling clothes from her closet in a tangle of fabric and hangers, stuffing everything into an old suitcase, Regan tried to block out the rumblings from downstairs. Her heart pounded until she felt breathless. Dear God, keep Paul's temper under control until we leave. She too remembered the night Jake had first come here after walking her home. The last thing she packed was Raggedy Ann, jamming her in on top. Everything else belonged to Paul.

Without a backward glance, Regan walked quickly from

the room, down the hallway, bumping the suitcase down the stairs, hauling it to the living room where the voices were now. Paul and Jake, facing each other, were talking in low, angry tones, but she couldn't make out their words. From the doorway, Regan saw Alyson run her hand along Jake's forearm, saw him pull out of reach. Calming, making peace? Or—

"I'm ready," Regan said clearly. Jake turned, but Paul didn't move.

"Where do you think you're going, miss?"

Jake answered for her. "Don't try to stop her, Oldham, she's of age. You don't give a damn about her, but I do, and I know enough of what went on here last night—"

"That's between her and me!"

"Not anymore." Jake took the suitcase from Regan, his eyes gesturing toward the front door. His eyes saying, Hurry. He nearly shoved her outside. Paul shouted after them, "You take what's mine from this house, you'll pay!" But Jake kept walking, nudging Regan before him. Alyson hung on Paul's arm, crying, "Daddy, *don't,* she's trash, let her go!"

At the car, Jake ordered tersely, "Get in." He tossed the suitcase into the back, slid into the seat and started the engine. Wrenching the gearshift into reverse, he let out his breath as if he'd been holding it ever since they entered the house— which he probably had, Regan decided, because she had, too. But she felt strangely calm now; at least from the new vantage point of safety.

"Thank God I read him right," Jake said minutes later as they were speeding along the streets of Lancaster. "The last thing I need is a fight."

Regan put her hand over his on the shift knob. "My champion," she said with a smile. "But where, my lord, is your white horse?"

Jake prepared spaghetti with leftover sauce and offered the last half of a bottle of Chianti. "I'm sorry," he said politely. "I didn't know I was going to be kidnapping a young maiden, or I'd have shopped."

Regan felt ill at ease. Her peace had been short-lived. The

first business of getting settled in the small house had been dispatched far too quickly. Jake had assigned her several drawers in the bedroom dresser, then the right-hand side of his closet, and within minutes she had folded and hung her scant collection of clothes, feeling all the while like an interloper; an intruder.

"You can take me back," she said now, instantly losing her appetite.

"No, I can't." A wide smile as he filled her glass. "You're non-returnable."

Regan's face paled. "Damaged goods?"

"Regan, that isn't what I meant." He looked shocked. "Not feeling guilty, are you?"

"Well, no, but I don't leave my girlhood behind every day of the week, either. And this house—I mean, would your mother approve?"

"My mother," he said, "would have wondered why I didn't marry the day after my graduation from the conservatory."

For a second, Regan wondered insanely if he would propose, but Jake began to clear their plates from the table. And besides, she knew he had no intention of marrying. He caught her looking at him and smiled. "My house," he said firmly, "is your house. Give me a hand with these dishes, then we'll relax."

Slim chance, Regan thought soon enough. She was still drying pots and pans when there seemed nothing left to say other than, "Where should I put the colander?"

"You're looking guilty again," he said, hanging up the dish towel he had pulled from her hands. Then he smiled. "Come on, you might as well tell me now. What sort of repulsive personal habits are you hiding? I'm bound to find out sooner or later."

"No, you won't," Regan said, managing to smile back. "I've got my one vice well under control. Not even Paul and Alyson know about it."

Jake's smile grew broader.

"Yeah? Then it can't be squeezing the toothpaste in the middle, so—"

Regan looked down at the kitchen tile floor and confessed, "I'm a chocolate addict. Once I start, I can't stop . . . but I've reformed, sworn completely off the stuff." She looked up to find him grinning at her. "It makes my face break out," she said, grinning, too.

"My God, now *I* feel guilty—for bringing home an adolescent who's still prone to acne and obvious hormonal imbalance." But he was laughing. "Hey, you haven't heard anything yet. You've just moved in with a man whose secret passion is onion sandwiches after midnight."

"Ugh!"

"Onion on rye—or sometimes, pumpernickel with hot mustard. Bermuda onions. Great big, thick slices," he said, then noticed Regan's nose wrinkled in distaste. "But I only indulge when I'm entirely alone . . . and likely to be for the next three days." Then he steered her from the kitchen. The few moments of teasing should have relaxed her more, but something kept getting in the way.

The evening stretched like a yawning chasm before them. In the living room, there were sudden spaces in the conversation. To fill the gaps, Regan supposed—Jake must have felt them, too—he brought out a box of snapshots, not neatly arranged like her red scrapbook, but piled together any which way. They sat beside each other on the green-and-blue chintz sofa, and Regan eagerly selected a picture.

"Are these your parents?" She studied the chestnut-haired woman with laughing eyes, the dark-haired man whose smile seemed to radiate from the photograph. "You said they were happy together. They look it."

"Yes. Very."

But the hard muscle of Jake's shoulder tensed against her softer one as Regan reached into the mess. "Who's this?" she asked, pulling out the color image of a woman in a print housedress, walking shoes and bright garden gloves. There was a smudge of dirt on her face, and she was smiling broadly.

Taking the photo from her, Jake tucked it quickly underneath the rest. "A friend of my mother's." Regan had the oddest notion that he wanted to wipe his hands. "My mother's friend

Enid," he continued tautly. "She lived a few blocks away, but hung around our house all the time. Her husband drove a truck and was never home. After my mother died," Jake added, "she became my guardian for a couple of years."

"And you didn't like that," Regan supplied, wondering why. To her, the woman looked pleasant, her hazel eyes warm with laughter, like Jake's mother's.

"Not very much, no."

Regan glanced at him, surprising a look of anguish on his face. "Does it bother you to look at these?"

He took a moment to answer. "No, not really," but he pulled the box onto his lap, making the next selections himself and handing them to her. Regan's eyes softened at the picture of Jake with his father. Both of them wearing baseball caps, blue with large white letter *Y*'s, Jake holding a bat in one hand. "A prodigy *and* a Yankees fan?"

"Rabid . . . I think I was about ten at the time."

Jake's frown eased into a faint smile as he looked at the photograph. There'd been some running argument in the house over that issue, he told Regan. "To my mother, my music was a gift, and sacred . . . but Dad didn't want me ending up one-sided. He loved the game, too, and it wasn't enough driving into New York to watch other people play. He'd done a lot of sandlot ball himself," Jake said, "and he got a real kick out of teaching me."

"What did your mother say?"

"Not a word for three days." Jake laughed at the memory. "That was some silence in our house . . . then one night after dinner, Dad asked me to take a walk with him. I figured he wanted to get out, away from the daggers Mom was shooting whenever he tried talking to her—but he walked me to the old cemetery . . ." Jake shook his head. "God, I didn't want any part of that place. But Dad pointed out that it had the only stretch of ground in the neighborhood not surrounded by trees. Then he pulled a brand-new baseball from his pocket and fired it at me." Jake remembered his admonition: "For God's sake, just be sure you don't jam your finger!" And from that night, they'd shared a secret passion. "We played there for years—I'd been about six at the time—and I'm sure Mom knew all about it. I think she gave in just to keep him happy." He looked fondly at the photograph in Regan's hand. A serious, dark-eyed child and the man he'd worshiped. "And he was the first one to insist I practice the piano when I wanted to play outside. I guess I owe my father whatever success I find . . . just as much as I do my mother." With a last glance at the picture, he laid it in the box. "I think that must have been taken only a month or so before he died."

Regan remembered the afternoon in this house when Jake had passed judgment on her talent, and made very clear his own priorities. How could she stay here, in these small rooms, distracting him, bumping every day into his practice time, his memories, getting in the way of his future?

"Now what's the matter?" Jake was watching her face.

"Nothing," she said lightly. "I didn't say a word."

"No, but your features are a study in dismay—however beautiful."

"I shouldn't be here," she said quietly. "Interfering—"

"Are you *serious?* I want you sharing my meals and my bed and my time." He smiled, but it was not returned. He cupped her face in his hands. "Regan, listen . . . in my adult life I've had one goal. My music. But this summer, there's been you," he said. "I fought myself, yes. But I'm not fighting anymore. Since that afternoon in May, I've had two priorities of equal weight."

She began to smile.

Jake leaned close to kiss her. He closed the box of photographs.

But how would he keep the balance? Regan wondered as Jake drew her, slowly and gently, to her feet. His eyes had darkened. "Your turn first in the bathroom. If you want a shower, let the water run for a few minutes, or you'll turn blue." He stayed in the living room. "Fresh towels in the bedroom closet," he called. "Top shelf."

Suddenly there seemed to be too much courtesy in the air

again. And promise. And the remembrance of an afternoon
that Regan feared could never be repeated. Though they were
obviously going to try. She couldn't relax. Not even in the
steamy environment of the shower, or drying off afterward.
And when she had slipped into a fresh nightgown, white and
lacy—that eighteenth-birthday present from herself—Regan
wanted to hide.

The fabric was nearly transparent! In the bathroom mirror,
wiped clean of humidity, she craned to see herself: twin dots
of rosy color above and a dark blond triangle below. The
afternoon had seemed so spontaneous and trusting. The edge
of Paul's assault had been blunted by first-lovemaking and
wonder, but now . . . could she stay in the bathroom all night?

Jake rapped at the door.

"In a minute," she said, stalling for time to compose herself.
He had been playing the piano while she prepared her shower,
still running over the keys in some light melody when she
finished. Why hadn't he stayed there? So she could slip into
the bedroom and retrieve her other, more modest blue gown
from the drawer? *Why did I buy this wisp of gossamer? Like
something from her daydreams.*

"Regan, come out here."

How had he guessed at her reluctance? She felt more virginal
than she had at the Talbot mansion. Steeling herself, Regan
opened the door slowly, and stood in the light because there
was no escape from it. Jake was blocking the exit. His eyes
took in everything and narrowed in desire, and the soft smile
of understanding seemed to get wiped away like the moisture
on the mirror.

"Good God," he said in a shaken tone. "No wonder I'm so
damn nervous."

"Are you?" It seemed to make everything better. She let
him take her hand and lead her to the bedroom, which was
predominantly rose and soft white. The lights were dimmed.
The pink top sheet had been pulled back on the double bed.
And Regan wondered if anything in her life would ever again
be as pure as the rush of love that swept through her, cleansing
hesitation.

"I wanted tonight to be right," Jake said softly. "But dinner was nothing, and this house isn't much either, and I—"

"It's wonderful," she said. "It is, Jake."

Slowly, he took her in his arms. *"You're* wonderful." Lowering his head, he kissed her, parting her lips. His body felt warm, hard, hot. Regan twined her arms around his neck, and Jake bore her gently to the bed. "Are you all right—after today? I mean, not . . . sore?"

"No." She smiled at him, a womanly smile full of new knowledge, her fingers playing with the hair at the nape of his neck. "I'm fine. Jake, I want you very much . . . and very soon."

Regan watched him undress, feeling quick pleasure at the sight of him, noting the gleam of light across his back, the satin sheen of his bare skin, the ripple of muscle underneath the flesh. He had a spare, exciting body without any excess or lack; and fiercely, she wanted to own the rights to that body, to his heart and soul forever.

"Jake, I feel like a bride," she whispered when he came to her. He smiled gently and began to caress her. Feathery touches grew rapidly bolder, kindling newness into a greater, more fiery passion. All at once, neither of them could wait. Jake moved over her. "Baby, I love you," his eyes full of need and urgency. "I do. . . ."

And taking him in, Regan thought: Even if I never marry, him or anyone, this is my wedding night.

Chapter 6

Regan squirmed away from Jake's touch, and smiled at the pages of the book in her lap. "What are you grinning at?" he asked, opening one eye. Lying down while she sat next to him, he'd been barely listening to her read from the dry volume of music history.

"You and me." Then she laughed aloud. "And Raggedy Ann." Jake laughed, too. It didn't take much to amuse either of them lately.

Here, on the ridge above and behind the Talbot mansion, affording a spectacular view of the estate, Jake and Regan had lazed away the weekend dog days of August. The grass, burned out by summer heat and little rain over the rest of the parklike grounds, remained tall and lush and green on the hill, sheltered by sweeping trees. On this Sunday afternoon, a hot, rustling breeze fanned the grass and rippled over Regan's skirt.

Jake's hand toyed with the hem; a finger running idly back and forth, persistent underneath the blue paisley fabric, along her bare thigh. Shifting once more, she tried not to answer the call of her senses, which seemed to be near the boil most of the time.

Jake gave up for the moment, replacing his arm across his eyes.

"I thought I'd seen everything," he commented, "until you

102

unpacked that doll." Regan could still see the look he'd given her as she took the floppy rag companion from her suitcase, placing it on his bed. "I didn't realize I'd gotten myself into a *ménage à trois*," he'd said, watching Regan arrange limp arms and legs on the pillow.

"She went through the bad times at Paul's," had been the explanation. "I thought Raggie deserved to get out, too."

Now, she looked up to find Jake watching her with the same smile on his lips, the same serious expression in his brown-gold eyes.

"I think I'm getting used to her," he said, "but even if she keeps sharing our room, she'll have to get her own guy."

"Selfish." And then, before she knew she was going to, "Would you have preferred Alyson?" remembering her hand on his arm.

"Alyson?"

"She seemed quite taken with you." The uncomfortable image flashed through Regan's mind of her cousin saying, "I could like Jake myself," which made her probe for his reaction. "Don't you think she's pretty? With that auburn hair and those china-blue eyes? I always thought she was prettier than me."

"And she probably thought you were," Jake dismissed the comparisons. He reached a hand up to her long, tawny-gold hair, flowing free and stirring gently in the mild breeze. "I just told you I don't like redheads that much." His fingers combed through the silken strands, came to rest on her shoulder. "Green-eyed blondes," he murmured appreciatively.

"I wasn't fishing," Regan felt obliged to say.

"Of course you were. All women do. Well, you've got the compliment, enjoy it." He gave her a lazy smile, and ran a hand down her bare arm, sending quick shivers through her body.

Had she been searching for the reassurance? Then why didn't she feel any better? Maybe it wasn't a struggle Jake could help resolve, but only Alyson—who wasn't likely to. Thankful for what she'd found with Jake, Regan stared at the book in her lap, trying to bring her color back to normal, which was difficult when Jake kept looking at her, smiling that way.

She moved slightly away from his hand on her thigh again, because she couldn't even think when he touched her. In a businesslike tone, she asked, "All right, if you're so smart about Handel—" she scanned the page again—"how many pieces are there in the *Water Suite?*"

"Originally? Twenty-five. Now usually played in six movements." Then Jake took the book from her, tossing it in the grass a few feet away. He leaned up on his elbows and studied Regan until she turned an even deeper pink. "You are a work of art yourself, did you know that?"

"Don't, Jake, that's embarrassing—"

"A masterpiece," he affirmed. "Every part of you," as his eyes roamed over her, familiar and knowledgeable. "You like it, too," he said, "being a woman, knowing—"

"A little."

"More than that," he murmured, shifting closer, turning toward her. "Tell me, baby."

Her whole body felt weak with the flood of response. "I like it a lot," she said, even managing to meet his eyes, which were growing darker by the second, no longer simply teasing. She loved being on her own, away from Paul, being with Jake and getting to know him, learning with every look and touch new ways to arouse each other. And it seemed she could recall every moment of their lovemaking since that first afternoon in the Talbot mansion, visible now beneath the crest of the hill. "You know what I like most?" she asked softly. "I love your hands, Jake," drawing one of them toward her, planting a kiss on the palm. "I love watching you work, knowing when you perform on a concert stage that those same hands can make me so happy. . . ." Which was a relatively new discovery, one she couldn't begin to appreciate the day they met. "I love the way you make me feel," she whispered.

But she was still so unused to happiness, to *their* happiness and their mutual pleasure, that she sometimes—like a few minutes ago, thinking of Alyson—wondered fearfully if it could last. Then Regan pushed the unwelcome thought away, like the book that had been discarded for another kind of music, and let Jake roll her gently, slowly, both of them softly laughing as they touched, into the warm, sweet grass.

He fell in love all over again each time he saw her. Whether she was singing at Steven's roadhouse, wearing the white gown slashed with gold, or naked in their bed, showing even more magnificence, or now, in worn blue jeans and a hunter green sweatshirt, Jake couldn't believe his luck. Watching Regan rehearse for her opening at the Birdcage, he shook his head in wonder.

She deserved the setting, he admitted, which was more modern than Steven's run-down bar, and lavishly decorated—soft lighting, thick dark carpet, gleaming tables of teak, and filmy azure draperies. From the beamed ceiling were suspended numerous cages of wicker and brass, housing green plants instead of birds; and the stage itself where Regan would perform was a semicircular glow of wood backed by a floor-to-ceiling latticework in the shape of an enormous cage, but open at the front. The club boasted a first-rate sound system, of course, and the piano was new, in perfect tune. Jake didn't know why—unless it was Bertelli—but he had immediately resented this relative splendor at the same time he acknowledged the career step up for Regan.

Standing just inside the doorway on a weekday afternoon, he listened to the sound of her singing reverberate off the walls, the draperies, the empty tables. She was in perfect voice, not missing a note, and he couldn't understand, either, why Manny Bertelli, resting one hip against the next table, was frowning more and more at every golden phrase.

At first, Jake thought it was because Regan and her new accompanist were like opposite poles on the globe—a mutual frost passing between them as they worked. Bertelli had hired Peter Noel, a small, intense bird of a man (perfectly keyed to the setting, Jake observed) with a spritely touch at the keyboard; but for reasons that were not obvious to anyone, including Regan apparently, she disliked him. Peter was steady, stable, and possessed of keen insights about her style. Already, he'd added up-tempo pieces to the act, giving Regan's repertoire balance. Julliard-trained, he was competent beyond a doubt, and Jake wasn't sorry he had refused to play for Regan here— he was practicing full-time himself at last—but, "Peter makes me uneasy," she kept saying, offering nothing more, making Jake feel at odds, too.

Now, he caught her eye and smiled, and the song went soaring, raised the hairs at the nape of his neck. He glanced at Peter Noel, effortlessly fingering the keys with the long, spidery digits tipped by spatulate pads that were supposed to be standard physical equipment for the very best pianists. He'd never thought it made any difference; but then, he could be defending himself. A bird, Jake decided again; and, with that almost-black hair and the small, bright eyes to match, perhaps an eagle. Maybe Regan had a repressed aversion to birds of prey. Shifting his glance to Bertelli and his hawklike scowl, he hoped so.

"Jeez, I ask those two to run through the first number for me, and what do I get?" Manny demanded rhetorically, his dark eyes barely touching Jake in return. "Moonlight and roses," he said in disgust.

"It's a pretty ballad," Jake pointed out.

"Yeah, well, pretty songs don't sell drinks. And they don't hype the customers to laugh at the comic I got on next, either." He glared at Jake. "I'll tell you what pretty ballads do. They make people pay the bill so they can run home fast and jump on the mattress together and—" The song hit a sequence of spiraling high notes, clear and true. "Ah, Christ, Regan!"

"Bertelli, let her finish."

Manny whirled, shrugging off Jake's hand from the sleeve of his brown silk suit.

"Listen, you . . . let's get this straight. I didn't like you the night I picked her up at Houghton's dive, and I never will. You may be getting in her sweet little pants right now, but that's all you got, understand?" His jet-dark eyes bored into Jake, whose pulse had begun to throb at his temple. "This is my club, Marsh, and that"—pointing to Regan on the stage—

"is *my singer*, and don't you forget it! Now, you can either stay or you can go back where you belong, playing longhair music for your longhair friends, but if you decide to stick around, take a seat"—he slammed a chair from the tabletop where it was stacked with the others onto the floor—"and keep your highbrow mouth shut!"

Forewarned, Jake thought, forearmed. What Bertelli wanted was written all over his features, tight with anger . . . and desire. He tried not to let his feelings show, but they were plain enough, obvious in the low, taut voice and the random violence with the chair; and in the ever-present tenseness belonging to a street kid who'd hustled his way to success. A singer for his club, yes; but he wanted the part he didn't have, too.

Jake's heart felt as if he'd run the three-minute mile without training first. He had a temper, sometimes bad, which his mother always schooled him to control, and sometimes, even now, he let it get the better of him—but he'd be damned if he'd be drawn into a brawl with the likes of Manny Bertelli.

"I'll stay," Jake said, pushing the chair back hard against the table. He'd be damned if he'd sit down, either. "I'll stay, Bertelli—because I don't like the way you look at her."

"Then don't watch."

He saw the back of Manny's custom suit through a red haze of fury, but at the same instant the song stopped short of its ending, and Regan asked, "What is it, Manny?" her dark green eyes skipping between Jake and Bertelli, who was walking toward the polished stage.

"How are you gonna get these people to listen, sweet?" He gestured at the round tables, like so many ellipsis marks in straight lines across the room. "You can't open with a ballad. They'll fall asleep—or worse, they'll leave. Every singer knows the unwritten rule. You open with something flashy, loud— like hitting a mule over the head to get his attention, you see what I mean?"

Regan stared for a moment at the carpet before she spoke. "I like this song, Manny. I feel comfortable, I know it isn't new, but the arrangement is special, innovative and delicate.

Nobody has ever sung it in just this way. Didn't you tell me how well that freshness works on records, with old standards? Older than this one." Regan's chin lifted with what Jake knew to be determination. "I think we should take the chance."

"A big chance," Bertelli grumbled. "You lose the audience with the first number, you lose them for the rest of the set! Then what? Our friend, Dale Lester—the big-shot comic, he thinks—comes on to nothing but—"

"I'm not going to lose them, Manny." Nobody moved. Nobody spoke. Regan's voice rang through the room, through the sound system, and Jake wondered if she had spoken into the silver microphone for effect. "You were the one who said I make them come to me."

"So I did," Bertelli acknowledged. He turned slightly. "Noel? I'm not paying you to sit like a stone on that piano bench. Do we switch to the circus number? It's a novelty, but no one's going to forget that in a hurry. They'll walk out of here night after tomorrow, humming as if they'd seen a parade, and—"

"I think she's right, Manny," though he said the words grudgingly.

Regan took a step forward, putting herself between Bertelli and Noel. What's his problem? Jake wondered. Noel looked scared to death of Bertelli. Maybe Regan was right about him. He might be stable, but he didn't appear to have much backbone.

"If I don't warm up the audience for Dale Lester," Regan said firmly, her eyes deep jade and unwavering on Bertelli's face, "then I won't have done the job you hired me to do, Manny—and you won't have to pay me."

Bertelli stared at her in amazement. *"Not pay you?"*

Jake thought immediately of Paul, keeping her pay from Steven's, and then of the look on her face when applause sounded at the end of a number. What did she sing for? Not for the money, as she'd told him, no; but for the adoration of a few hundred people at the roadhouse, at these small, round tables of teak in a New York club. As she turned toward him now, her face glowed from the battle. How different she is already, Jake thought; not unsure of herself, but standing straight and determined, hands on her slender hips, that satin swath of tawny hair hanging down her back, the soft lights of the empty club turning her green sweatshirt a deeper, more sensuous hue.

"Jake, what do you think?"

And he forced the smile she wanted. There was no way she wouldn't get paid. "I think you're doing fine," he said, "all by yourself."

"Curtain time!"

With the bright announcement, Jake poked his head in at the dressing-room door. But Regan wasn't where he expected her to be. The pleasant room—a far cry from the makeshift changing area at Steven's—was empty; the tan sofa and chair deserted. Her gown still hung over the screen of brown and yellow plaid, the jars and bottles of feminine mystery on the dressing table appeared untouched.

"Regan?" he called. "Noel says the sound check is okay—" Then he heard the unmistakable sound of retching. Flinging open the door to the tiny connecting bathroom, Jake found her in bra and panties hunched over the porcelain bowl as if it were the only stable object in her world. More violent activity. "Oh God, I can't go on tonight!"

Jake held her head and groped with his free hand for a washcloth on the stand. Finding a thin piece of yellow terry-cloth, he dipped it under cold water, applying the compress to the back of her neck.

"Don't, Jake, you'll get my hair wet!"

"If you can still protest with such vanity, you'll be fine," he said. "Mind over matter." And within minutes, Regan was managing a feeble laugh. "Good heavens, if I do this every night—"

"Not every night," Jake said blandly. "Only when you open."

"You make going on the road sound worse and worse. Almost every night will be an opening, won't it? I think I'd rather catch bubonic plague."

"As you well might, in Texas and Louisiana."

She gave him a stagey laugh and managed to stand, reaching for his wrist, examining Jake's watch. "Oh no, nearly eight o'clock, and I'm not even dressed!"

"Lucky for your costume," he pointed out.

"You know something? Someday I am going to come watch you play a major concert—just for the sheer hell of seeing *you* turn green with panic."

"My color is more the white of rising bread dough."

Regan stuck out her tongue at his humorous attempt to calm her—again—and slipped into the new gown she was to wear. "I'd better be good tonight," she said. "After that bit of bravery with Manny, I don't dare be anything less." She looked at Jake. "By the way, what were you two arguing about?"

"The same thing," he hedged slightly. "Don't worry. You'll be great."

She wound her arms around his neck. "Love me?"

"Love you."

In the muted beam of light she stood, wearing a gown that hadn't been popular for three-quarters of a century, though it was new to her, a treasure from a secondhand shop: a lace sweep of a gown, intricate and puffed and ruffled, slender at the waist and graceful at the hip, a long fall of ivory delicacy hugging her round breasts, braceleting her wrists with pearl buttons. Every inch of skin covered, and her hair piled, as if at a second's intention, upon the crown of her head, a silken spill that could be released with one deft move of a man's hand, the pull of a pin or two, the slide of satin falling into his hands, to his lips as he fought to catch his breath. My God, Jake thought, she's the most beautiful woman I've ever seen....

Then, slow and drawn out, clear as a chime in the still night, Regan began to sing; and with the first notes all extraneous shuffling stopped. The talking ceased, and orders for dessert, for drinks were waved away. At the end of the first number— the ballad which had so alarmed Manny Bertelli—there was a collective release of held breath, a moment's pause before the first applause, then a rising tide of clapping until the room seemed full of it, ears deafened by the shouts and whistles. Regan, like a victorious queen, regal—like her name—and in full command, took her bows with a generous smile upon her lips. She had made them come to her, all right; and, Jake thought, she always would.

He didn't hear the spate of tepid jokes from Dale Lester, the headliner. "Manny, you better pay this little lady what she's really worth... Have you people heard about Bertelli? Why, he's so tightfisted..."

Jake heard nothing but the pounding of his own heart.

On the way home, Regan kept glancing at Jake apprehensively, but he kept his eyes glued to the busy stretch of I-95 that led to Lancaster, the race of tractor-trailers flashing by the VW; his mind resolutely on the rocking motion of the afterwave of air, the arrhythmia of his own heart.

"Jake, what's wrong?"

"Nothing. What could be wrong? You were colossal." He tried to flash her a grin, but failed. His glance stuck on the glowing sight of her, triumphant, radiant; wearing his suit jacket against the unexpected August chill. The heater in the car didn't work. "I'm very proud, more than at Steven's. I'm thinking I ought to buy you a fox fur coat, or maybe mink." As if he could.

A quick picture in his mind. Regan rushing into his arms; Regan laughing, "I've done it, I've done it"; his own embrace; the giddy whirling dance around the roadhouse dressing room; the pure joy racing through his veins. For her. Why not now? This time? It wasn't only Bertelli....

"No, you're not happy," Regan said quietly. "How do you really feel?"

"Inadequate," he said without a pause. "And...sad, I guess—and guilty for both feelings." Her green eyes were dark in the dim light of the car, then just as quickly illuminated by passing headlights, a dark jade with an ebony cast. "You don't need me," he admitted. "And it hurts even more than I thought it would."

Her answer was delayed for a few long moments while he thought: But I am proud, I'm so proud I could stop traffic in the middle of this lethal highway and shout at the world going by about its business: *This is Regan Reilly, and she's mine.* He wondered why the thought wouldn't make him happy.

Regan's voice was husky, soft. "I'll need you for the rest of my life, Jake."

And then, he wondered why he didn't believe her.

Regan knew that Manny and Jake didn't like each other, but she was much too busy to dwell on the reasons why—and far too preoccupied with Peter Noel and company to search for them. It had taken her weeks to discover the real cause of her own resentment toward her new accompanist, and when she did, she couldn't even smile about it.

Thin, serious, and dark in coloring, Peter seemed at once strange and known. Another two inches of height, she would think, another twenty pounds, a straighter posture, an occasional smile . . . but the plain truth was, he was still Peter Noel, and an unwelcome replacement for Jake. Manny had decided that more backup was needed for the sound he wanted at the Birdcage, and so, in addition to Peter, Regan sang each night with Sam Henderson, a small, ascetic-looking black guitarist, and a big, shaggy, russet-haired, gray-eyed drummer called Kenny Williams. If at first she thought of Kenny as a huge teddy bear, a hulking presence of a man, large-muscled and tall, with broad shoulders and heavy bones, Sam had to be his opposite number: quiet compared to Kenny's boisterousness, studious where Kenny was always ready for a party.

Sam had a neat, springy black Afro and the most serious brown eyes she'd ever seen (without Jake's bronze light), but when he went out into the sun—where she rarely saw him because they worked half the night—his hair took on a blue-black satiny sheen, and his smile shone too. Before their first week together had ended, Sam Henderson was a friend, and Regan didn't imagine for a minute he'd ever be anything less— though she felt unsure about Kenny. Bitterly divorced, Sam seldom discussed his ex-wife, but had no tolerance for Kenny's casual treatment of women. Although the guitarist and drummer were close, their arguments on the subject were legendary.

Kenny told Regan, "Sam's just gun-shy." Kenny leaned his forearms on the teak tabletop where he and Regan had been sharing a coffee break during rehearsal. "What Sam needs now," he pronounced with a grin, "is another broad to keep him warm, but he won't even pay for it. Why, Sam's so shy, he—"

"Never mind, Kenny," Regan stopped his imitation of Dale Lester. "I get the idea."

Privately, she thought Kenny himself could do with a bit more reticence. But that seemed to belong to his wife, Linda, a petite, dark-haired girl who would have been quite pretty if she'd smiled more. The only time Regan saw Linda's lips curve upward, gently and sweetly, was when she looked dotingly at her infant son, her constant companion.

"Doesn't the baby get tired, staying up until Kenny's finished every night?" Regan asked once, receiving only a silent stare for an answer. Then it occurred to her that Linda never spoke to Regan first, and that she did smile, not only at the baby, but at Kenny—with adoration—and at Sam too, with a look of open friendship, which Regan began to covet soon enough. Despite her best efforts to gain Linda's acceptance, however, Regan failed miserably.

"How old is the baby?" she asked brightly.

"Five months," was the grudging reply.

"Would you let me hold him?" she tried again. "I used to be a good baby-sitter, and maybe you'd like a few minutes with Kenny and Sam." Linda, she had observed, could talk music as well as any professional.

But, "No, he's about to fall asleep if I keep rocking him in my arms." Then, a quick upward glance from cool eyes. "He doesn't like other women holding him. Strangers."

Maybe she thinks I'm playing hotshot career woman, Regan thought, while she sits at a side table every night, watching from the fringes.

"Ah, hell, don't pay any attention to Linda," Kenny said flatly. "She's got some tick in her pants, that's all. She's afraid you're going to pull out of town and take me with you." A pause for effect, a grin that could conquer the world. "You are, aren't you?"

"Manny's lining up some out-of-town dates after the first of the year," Regan admitted. But she wondered if Linda's jealousy—why hadn't she seen it before?—was more sexual than professional. How could she make it clear that she saw Kenny just as she did Sam, only as a friend? None of her attempts so far with Linda had proved successful. And if they began to travel—

"Whenever and wherever," Regan said, "of course you're coming along, Kenny, you and Sam."

She tried not to notice how her heart flipped over when he grinned.

"And Peter the Noel." Kenny's grin broadened as if it might split his ruggedly attractive face. "Goddamn, he ain't no Kris Kringle, is he?"

Regan bit her lip against a smile. "I wouldn't say so."

"We go on tour," Kenny continued, "Noel's going to be one heavy dude. On a bus, middle of the night, everybody loose— except old Pete."

Then his gray eyes turned dark, leaden, seeing things Regan knew nothing about. The expression alarmed her like the worst of Jake's preachings about the evils of the road, dampening her enthusiasm in an even more sobering way. This melancholy side of Kenny showed itself now and then, at unexpected moments; and it was guaranteed to frighten because she couldn't understand that obscuring shadow. Just as well for now, she told herself. She had enough problems. But Kenny's expression lightened as quickly as his gaze had darkened.

"Maybe we can make Noel ride with the equipment, how's that sound?" the grin back in place as if it had never been disturbed by some deep, inner demon.

Regan tried again to hide her own smile and her apprehensions, all of them.

"I have the distinct impression, Kenny Williams, that you spent most of your school days sitting in a corner, standing in the hall with your face to the wall, or—"

"In the principal's office," he confessed sheepishly. "But wait until you get to know me better," with a deep wink of one clear gray eye. "You're gonna love me, sweetheart."

Regan wished she could smile at the rest of her life as easily as she'd laughed at Kenny's teasing. But the unavoidable fact remained: Jake was leaving. If she hadn't fully appreciated the inevitability before, Regan had to now as she packed his clothes, distracting herself from misery while Jake ran through the Brahms at the piano, perfecting—always perfecting.

The more edgy he'd become, the more distant and less involved with her, the more unhappy Regan grew. Sometimes now, she felt like a piece of furniture, little more than a convenience in his life. When she should have been giving Peter and the band her best, instead she held back, taking refuge in domesticity. Volunteering to pack for Jake, she'd wanted to feel his shirts and ties and underwear in her hands, as if she could hold him closer, keep him.

But hadn't she known from the instant they met that Jake would leave in September? And of course, she didn't want to hold him back. Regan inhaled the fresh, laundered smell of a T-shirt. It was just that she didn't want him to go, either. She couldn't imagine being in the little house alone. But what other choice was there? Manny had extended her engagement at the Birdcage, playing to capacity crowds six nights a week and—

"Regan, listen to this!" Jake's voice called her to the living room. He replayed a passage for her, his fingers gliding effortlessly over the keys. When he had finished, Regan murmured, "Perfect," which seemed not to soothe but to enrage.

"How the hell can you say that? It's a disaster!"

He began to play again, and over again, until she had heard the same passage three times. "It was much better the second time," she said, having carried a folded shirt with her to the doorway so she could watch him work, see his reaction. Silence. Jake frowned more deeply, the characteristic intensity he wore when concentrating hardest; he looked at her, then through her, a pose which Regan had also learned meant he was replaying the notes in his mind. "Yes," he said, breaking into a smile, "no question . . . it was stronger, wasn't it? You've got a damn good ear, lady. I think I'll keep you."

Arms around his neck, Regan kissed him. "I certainly hope so." He wasn't gone yet. Take me with you, she wanted to plead . . . but she couldn't go, either. Just as he couldn't stay. And underneath the moment of closeness, she was afraid.

The morning was warm and still and damp, wringing perspiration from them. Jake left the piano to get a cold drink, but Regan decided on a quick shower instead, cool and refreshing. When she had finished and was pulling from her dresser clean shorts and a scoop-necked orange top, she heard Jake working again. The music sounded brilliant to her, better than ever, as a sense of elation winged through Regan, followed by despair. Casting the clothes aside, she grabbed the new dress that Manny had purchased for her and slipped it on. An impulse, this reminder to herself that she too was preparing for something—the road, even a single club date out of town?—eased the growing loss inside.

At the bedroom doorway, she paused, hesitant to interrupt Jake's practice. But when he saw her, he stopped. Explaining, Regan said, "I wanted to show you this since you won't be here next week, I wondered what you'd think of it. . . ." His gaze skimmed the wine-red gown. "The dress," he said, "or the obligation that goes with it?"

"What obligation?"

Regan's heart began to pound as Jake slammed the piano lid closed. "Oh come on, he expects something for his investment."

Her throat tightened. She couldn't tell him the rest now: that Manny had paid for three other dresses as flattering and dramatic as this one. A yellow silk, a long velvet skirt of rich green, a black-and-white print crepe that made her feel worldly and sophisticated. But Jake seemed to know, anyway—as he always did with Manny, by some primitive male instinct.

"What would Manny see in me, Jake?" she reasoned. "What would he want me for?" She was hardly his type, Regan thought. He preferred women of a bolder sort—large-breasted, wide-hipped, exotic girls. Showgirls. More like Alyson, she thought. But Jake only looked at her, unbelieving, and shook his head, not quite able to suppress the smile—though it was one of the few times he would ever smile about Manny Bertelli, and not a happy smile at that. "Jesus," he said under his breath.

"Well, I can't sing in rags, can I? You may be able to wear a clean shirt and the same black dinner jacket every night, but a woman can't get away with the uniformity, Jake. Besides, when I do go to other cities, sooner or later——"

Jake's blood pressure rose with his suspicions.

"And who pays for that?"

"You know darn well that this arrangement is nothing more or less than a hundred other performers might have, Jake! Manny *believes* in me. He's willing to make the investment now because he has the money to do so, and he *knows* I'll earn more than enough in return; and *when* I do, mister, his percentage slides up the scale." Despite the apparent self-assurance in her words—where were the blacker times when she wasn't at all sure she'd ever get another booking, let alone make money?—Regan felt sick at the unexpected argument, and her heart seemed to shake with every beat.

"Manny expects me to look right when I appear." She lowered her voice with effort. "At the Birdcage, or anywhere else. I wouldn't have shown you this dress if I'd thought for one minute you'd be so upset." But Jake had to appreciate the reasons for a fine wardrobe; a good impression; the proper start. She wanted so much for him to like what she wore; wanted to see his eyes full of love, not hard bronze flecks overcoming the softer brown.

Carefully, Jake took a breath. His teeth clenched around the words. "I am not upset." But why couldn't Regan see Bertelli for what he was? "I merely dislike his taking . . . liberties that do not belong to him."

"With me, I presume? Such a charming, if archaic, phrase to say so. That kind of thing belongs at the Talbot—"

"I'll say whatever I want to, damnit! This is my home, remember?"

Regan's heart lurched. Paul's words; the years of growing up in that house, unloved, unwanted, a house she had escaped with Jake's love. And now—

"How could I forget? I'm always in someone else's home! Well, if you want me out, Jake, just say so—"

"Christ, who said anything about your leaving?" Jake's expression was bleak, withdrawn. They had exchanged one bad topic for another, even worse. Regan tried to restore their equilibrium. "When I earn enough money," she said, "I'll pay Manny back, if that makes you feel better." And there the argument might have ended. But Regan kept hearing *my house, my house.* Brushing the skirt of the fluid, low-necked gown, she added, "For the time being, Jake, I happen to need what his money can buy."

Looking her up and down, he made her intensely aware of the new burgundy silk clinging like another skin. Then slowly, deliberately, Jake walked to the door. "Okay, fine," he said. "Let Bertelli peel off the bills and pay for those fancy bolts of cloth. But if I were you, baby, I'd make damn sure your body isn't part of the price—like sales tax!"

He slammed the door behind him so violently that the small house shook.

Jake came home late, long after Regan had returned from New York; but he didn't sleep with her. In the morning, he mutely placed a sheet of staff paper in her hands, folding her resisting fingers around the page. Not wanting to, she saw the sequence of notes as distinctive as Jake's handwriting, the strokes and circles bold and dark and creative, like him.

The song he played for her was more than apology; it was a love song from the heart, lyrical and sweet, filled with metaphor:

"You are all the constellations of the stars, a roaring rocket ride to Mars..." And in the second chorus, "You're all the words I know, old and new...but of all the words I know, the only one I care to know is 'you.'..."

The last notes faded, echoing briefly in the still room. Regan's green eyes locked with Jake's, dark brown. "Is this from the classical, too?" she asked.

"No," he answered, soft as a whisper. "Just for you, from me." With a hesitant smile, he added, "I'm sorry I couldn't say 'moon.' It wouldn't rhyme."

Regan tried to smile back, but her lips quivered. "Mars will do nicely. Thank you." And she turned into his arms, held tight where everything that made her afraid for them seemed far away, remote as the three-digit number of Jake's scheduled flight; as distant now as their argument.

Winding her arms around his neck, Regan said, "Oh Jake, I don't know what I'll do if you ever stop loving me."

He bent his head to kiss her. "Impossible," he said against her mouth. And she even felt that it was true.

VERSE

Chapter 7

"What the hell happened to the grace notes?" Peter Noel's angry voice stopped rehearsal in the middle of a song. "Have you decided to save them for a rainy day? Transpose them elsewhere? Or did you send them off in your boyfriend's luggage? Do you even know what I mean by grace notes?"

Regan despised him. Why was the part in his hair so straight and at an angle so familiar? "I forgot," she said. "Yes, I know what they are."

"And will the people who come to see you tonight 'forget' to pay their tabs? Or in Des Moines, neglect to purchase tickets? In South Bend? Oklahoma City?" His voice rose on each query. Regan, Sam Henderson, Kenny—the only one stifling a smile—stared at the floor.

"No," Regan said, "I suppose not."

"Perhaps, then, we do owe them something in return." He signaled for the opening once again. "Lester's still counting on you to prime the audience, you know. You can give in to your romantic depressions later—on your own time. Which is after two A.M."

Regan glared at Peter's back, all the more furious because he was right. She couldn't work, couldn't concentrate. She kept thinking about Jake's leaving her, saying in a husky tone, "I'm going to miss you."

"But you know where I'll be," she'd said, putting her hands in the thick darkness of his hair. "Here," she said, holding his head, "and here," touching his heart. Then, violating her own resolve, she had begun to cry.

"Hey," Jake whispered, "none of that. I shouldn't have started feeling sorry for myself. Now look what I've done." Raising her face, he had kissed her mouth, slack with tears so that he had to do all the work. "I'll be back," he'd said lightly, but she only clung to him. "Baby, I'll always come back."

Already she was counting the days, unable to appreciate any piece of music other than the beautiful ballad Jake had written for her. Their song. Regan would never think of it without thinking of Jake, of the unbalancing quarrel that had given it life. The house, Bertelli, the compulsive playing to get his music right, all the moments together when both of them had known the summer was going to end—none of that had mattered when Jake got into the VW and drove away with her happiness inside.

It was one thing, she told herself now, to be driven by a taskmaster who loved her and quite another to be bullied by Peter Noel.

But when she sang, the grace notes were there, delicate and in the proper places, making the piece completely different from the plain delivery before. She would never manage to like Peter, Regan decided on her way to the dressing room after rehearsal, but she would have to find a way to work with him for now—no matter how he condescended to her. Though she also knew she would never be able to reconcile his differences with her need for similarity to Jake.

Someone knocked at the door only seconds after she had closed it. "Yes?"

"May I have a moment? It's Peter."

Well, she would tell him a thing or two as well. In private. She wasn't as green as he thought.

"Come in," she said coolly, summoning every ounce of self-respect she could find. "Would you like to sit down?"

Peter folded his wiry frame into a chair. There was a protracted silence. Regan remained standing by her makeup table. Then Peter cleared his throat. "I am a perfectionist," he began. "I expect perfection in those around me—especially if that state can be achieved, as, in your case, it may well be."

"Are you apologizing, or preparing to resume your lecture?" But she felt the slightest pleasure in his awkward compliment. At least he thought she could sing.

He attempted a smile, but Peter's smiles nearly always turned out to be more grimace than grin, as if he were feeling minor pain. "I do believe in you," he said. "That's for the record. You're destined for stardom, Regan. That's no idle pat on the back, or any attempt from me at getting in your good graces. I have the feeling I couldn't, anyway; and, besides, Manny's already told you the same thing—but in two or three years, five at the most, you're going to be on top of the heap." He paused. "And I—I want to be there with you."

Amazing, Regan thought, sitting down before she fell down. How the mighty are fallen. Peter Noel, stepping down from his lofty perch. He sounded almost human.

"I'm not convinced we can work together, Peter." She remembered Kenny's comments about Noel, dampening everyone's enjoyment of a road tour—if there ever was one.

"We will work together," he insisted. "Because—because I don't want to go with anyone else. That isn't saying I couldn't, mind you, but even superior musicians"—with the ghost of a smile—"don't earn much money as a rule. As soon as Bertelli's offer came, and I heard you sing, I knew we could help each other, Regan."

She stared at him silently for so long that at last he said, "I suppose you're due the real explanation, at least a capsule version. Regan, I need a real future, musically and financially. I've got a mother upstate with a bad heart— No, never mind the sympathy. I'm quite used to the problem by now and so is she, as a matter of fact—but she's bedridden much of the time, requires a nurse-attendant round the clock—"

"Which means a great deal of money," Regan supplied. And a lot of devotion, as well. Her estimation of Peter—whether he had calculated or not—went up several notches, and she couldn't help but think of Jake caring for his own mother when he was still a boy.

"Which means I hitch my wagon to a star," Peter said. "Regan Reilly, to be exact—because I want the best. You've been getting lazy out there in the last week or two, but I'm willing to write that off as temporary pining on the part of a young girl who will know better very soon—as long as you agree to keep it off the stage. There's a lot of work to be done, but you have to be willing—and willing to make the sacrifices, too."

As long as Jake wasn't one of them, she thought. And then felt guilty for doing her job—the job she was paid to do—so lethargically over the last weeks as Jake came closer and closer to leaving Lancaster—and her. She owed Manny, Peter and the rest of the trio; Dale Lester; and above all, her audiences much more than indulgent self-pity because she awoke to cold sheets on the other side of the bed. Did she want to be a singer, or didn't she? How could she blame anyone for observing the truth?

"I'm sorry, Peter. You're right. I have been getting off the track."

"Agreed. This is a trade, Regan," he went on firmly. "A very skilled trade, every bit as much as it is an art. You need technique. In a business like this, knowledge is power, for sure—the more you know about what you do, the better your advantage." His eyes bored into her. "There is nobody in this world, mind, who could teach you to be a star—not me, not Jake Marsh, not the finest voice coach who ever lived. But if you take native talent and that sixth sense you already have about your audience, that inborn gift for . . . all right, *acting*, if you will . . . and add a solid feel for what's going on behind the song, within its notes and measures, its entire structure, nothing can hold you back . . . nothing."

She was a natural, Jake had said. But was that enough? Enough for Steven's maybe, even for the Birdcage. Manny had called her a phenomenon, promised that she'd become a superstar. It had seemed like so much talk then, exciting to be sure, but now—

"I think this is only the introduction," Peter continued. She couldn't seem to say anything herself, or to look away, either, from his dark eyes and the swift, birdlike motions of his hands. It was the first time she'd felt good about anything since Jake had left—and oh, such enticing vistas lay, according to Peter, at the very edges of her sight.

"Like the songs you sing," he said with an eagerness she had never heard before. "The first bars, then the verse, the chorus—and who knows what kind of songs you'll be singing five years from now? . . . ten?"

Where *could* she go, with work and talent and technique? How far? To the moon, Regan thought, to Mars. How many worlds could she conquer?

"Streisand hit Broadway," Peter was saying as his thin hands took hers. "So have other singers. Do you think people could stay away from a theater with *you* on a stage, in the perfect vehicle?"

"Peter, now you're having delusions of grandeur." Regan found her voice at last.

"You think so? Listen, I believe that once in a score of years, or half a century, someone comes along in this business who's so enormously special that the world turns inside out. I know you think I'm a very unpleasant man, Regan—but if I seem unbearable, it's because anything less than your finest effort should be a class-A felony."

He meant *her*, turning the world around! Regan sat, clasping her hands in her lap, willing her pulse to slow down. But if she worked as hard as Peter wanted, if she focused toward Jake's excellence—could she truly achieve stardom? Oh, not Peter's suggestion of Broadway—light-years removed from her wildest dreams—but in the recording industry? Concerts in Vegas and New York and Chicago; in LA and San Francisco and Miami? In Europe and the Far East; Japan and Australia; England and France and Spain, Italy . . . ? Perhaps.

Regan's heart only beat faster as she thought. What if all

of the dreams she'd had for herself, and that other people seemed to have for her now, came true? Records and television specials, a video on cable's MTV with flashing light and sparkling sound. She closed her eyes, envisioning applause, the love she'd feel when hearing it, the heart-thumping thrill every time she sang. In her mind danced visions of gold records lining the walls of her home—wherever that might be—and Manny's office, too; a collection of platinum albums fanned out like cards in a deck. A shelf full of Grammys, those shining miniature Victrolas gleaming back at her like smiles.

What if . . . ? Regan's head felt dizzy at the future possibilities. In the meantime, it seemed, she had her work cut out for her. Grinning, she looked straight into Noel's eyes.

"I accept the challenge, Peter. How do I get perfect?"

It wasn't gong to be easy. Regan decided that she'd been enjoying beginner's luck, the kind of success that had permitted her a 140 score the first time she'd bowled and a perfect run of gutter balls the second. She could only hope that she was more talented at singing than as an athlete.

But did Peter think so? His tirades didn't abate, as she might have expected after his rousing pep talk; and the voice coach he'd hired for Regan three days a week wasn't any more inclined to kindness. Since Regan could barely pronounce the woman's name—she was a Madame something-or-other, Eastern European, with a lot of consonants and no vowels—she couldn't place blame. Regan gritted her teeth and practiced musical scales, hating them even more than she had at Jake's during the summer; learned to emote in her phrasing and to draw power from her voice. The long Indian-summer afternoons in Madame's third-floor apartment—no screens at the windows and not a fan in sight—might have helped Regan's delivery, even polished her repertoire. But they did nothing for her disposition.

The only thing she and Peter seemed to agree on, from Regan's viewpoint, was her solid position as a singer of ballads. Jake's suggestion that they focus her act and modify her style to concentrate on standards and love songs impressed Peter, too.

"We'll begin casting about for something all your own, though," he added. "Manny's right about that," which led to Regan's introduction of Jake's song within the first month after his leaving. The ballad became an instant favorite at the Birdcage; and Manny, at Peter's urging, had been exploring the possibility of making a record.

"I think you're almost ready," Peter said to her. "At least, you will be by the time we've got a studio and some tape." By the time I get through with you, Regan added for him. She'd been falling asleep at night with the sound of Madame's grating, guttural voice calling cadence echoing in her ears. One, two, three, four . . . as Jake had done once. Only, Madame sounded more like a rusty metronome.

"Vun . . . two . . . tree . . . furr. . . ."

Still, the crusty, white-haired dowager with the heart of a storm trooper seemed preferable to the hecklers that had appeared in her audience at the Birdcage. Beginner's luck, Regan repeated to herself with an inward groan every time she stepped up to the microphone and encountered verbal assault from the other side of the lights. Why did it seem to her that the insults had begun—the catcalling and baiting—as soon as Jake left town?

"You have to learn to handle 'em, that's all," Dale Lester advised. Which was far easier, Regan thought, if you were a stand-up comedian to begin with. She did her best, wondering why the occasional animosity now, when her first weeks of singing for salary had been so insult-free? Was she just off balance, more aware, because Jake was gone?

"You can't afford to believe the critics," Jake told her by telephone, as if she had reviews instead of plain old hecklers. "If you do, the good ones will destroy objectivity, and the bad ones—there are always some of those—will make work impossible." He added that he was his own best, and most severe, critic; and remembering the morning he had asked her opinion of the Brahms, Regan agreed.

"Words of wisdom," she said gently, "from the man who had a standing ovation in Minneapolis."

"Easy for me to say, huh?" She heard the smile in his tone, the pride.

"I miss you," Regan said, rolling over on the bed to pull the second pillow close. She was speaking to Jake from new quarters. With Regan based in Manhattan and Jake away much of the time, they had decided to rent out the house in Lancaster. "I'd rather save my cash for flying to see you than for paying the mortgage," he'd said.

Her move had been quickly accomplished into a modest suite at the Shelton Hotel on Sixth Avenue in the lower fifties: two bedrooms; a sitting room; a huge bath with old-fashioned porcelain fixtures, including a clawfoot tub big enough for two; a few touches of wicker here and there. Regan liked the rooms, and although the imitation Chippendale scattered around wasn't her style of furniture, she could live with it because the colors—clear green and white for the upholstery, a lighter apple-green carpet, and neutral walls hung with pleasant Impressionist prints framed in gold—appealed to her. She finished telling Jake about the suite, laughing. "This whole place matches my eyes."

His reply came softly. "Then I already love it," followed by a more intimate, "How's the bed?"

Enormous, and lonely. "Is that all you can think about?"

"These days, mostly, I'd have to say so."

Regan smiled into the telephone. "I couldn't agree more," she said.

Anticipating Jake's imminent homecoming, Regan was whiling away her free time between sets at one of the tables that Friday night with Sam, Kenny, and Linda. "Would you like another drink?" she asked, beckoning the waiter. "I'm buying. Kenny . . . Sam?"

It was a small joke, since the drinks were on the house and Manny, but both men quickly accepted, shoving their empty glasses over the tabletop toward her; only Linda stared into her half-finished gin and tonic. "No, thanks. I've had enough."

The ice had melted, and a wedge of lime was floating in the diluted mess. When Sam and Kenny drifted back to the bandstand—minutes after Dale Lester departed the stage—to fuss with drums and acoustic guitars, Regan said gently, "Linda, I've been getting the impression for weeks now that you don't like me very much." She reached over as she spoke to let Linda's baby take her finger, gripping it tightly in a warm, moist embrace. "I'm trying to be your friend."

"I have all the friends I need."

Regan tried not to notice when a few drops of clear drool ran from the baby's lips onto her bare arm. Thank heaven she wasn't wearing the lace period piece tonight—that long-sleeved Gibson—but a simpler gown, the black-and-white crepe halter dress which Manny had bought, in which she felt sophisticated and quite bare. She could feel Linda's hostility like a physical force, knew without a doubt she wanted to pull the baby's hand away from Regan's. When Linda glanced at her, the brown eyes were harsh with unexpressed anger. But Regan, having opened the subject, plowed ahead.

"Look, if you're afraid that this job means Kenny's going to be gone too much . . . well, I don't even have a tour lined up, Linda. I may never get one and—"

"You will. And Kenny's been on the road before. I can't stop him this time, either."

There were so much pent-up frustration, professional and sexual, behind the terse words that Regan held her tongue and waited for more. She felt as if she'd been smiling into those infant gray eyes, just changing from newborn blue into the very image of his father's, for at least a year before Linda said anything more. And then, "Kenny's been playing local jobs, doing mostly studio work, for a year. Before that, he worked with a middle-level rock band, touring ten months of the year— and there's nothing worse than being just good enough, believe me, no money and no working capital to improve the act, but plenty of dates, pressures, ego padding, travel, and . . . well, anyway, it's a rough life, keeping up appearances, you might say. Better than the jazz gigs he tried first, but not much."

"That's what Jake keeps telling me," Regan put in, thinking

it couldn't hurt at this point to mention a relationship of her own.

To Linda's blank stare, she said, "The man I'm—involved with." She didn't know how else to describe him. Linda had never met Jake. The night Regan had opened at Manny's, the baby had been sick, forcing Linda to stay home. And after that, Jake had stayed in Lancaster. "He's a concert pianist, and he says touring is the pits."

Linda managed a smile. "Of course, you don't believe him."

"Not yet," Regan said happily.

"Does he have—" She seemed to be searching for a way to say something painful. "Does he ever—on the road, I mean—have troubles?"

"Troubles?" Regan looked blank. Did she mean women? Jealousy again, she thought. Maybe Kenny couldn't pass up a pretty smile, even if she had always assumed his come-ons were a joke. If they weren't, that would explain a lot.

Linda's grip on the baby shifted, and Regan lost his fingers. He shoved his own fist into his mouth after a second or two of aimless searching. "I meant ... migraines, sour stomach, that sort of thing," Linda said. "Montezuma's revenge, the usual traveler's ailments."

But the tone of voice wasn't any more convincing than the lesser troubles Regan was she she'd substituted for real ones, worse ones. What was wrong between Kenny and his wife? Why had Linda almost confided in her, then stopped? Because of Regan's apparent ignorance? Disappointed, she supposed so.

"Jake says he ought to own shares of stock in a drug house that makes antacid tablets." She caught another weak smile from Linda, who was now jostling the baby gently to quiet his increasing fussing. The club was full, and Regan doubted anyone could even hear. "He claims he'd be a rich man just from his own purchase of the company product."

"You sound close to each other," Linda said. "Is he good at the piano?"

"Wonderful."

"I've never heard Kenny play a bad night, either. Not even—" Then she broke off, staying silent for an instant before she adjusted her blue sweater and put the crying baby discreetly to her breast.

For a few moments, there was only the sound of drink glasses clinking at other tables, the hum of conversation, and the soft, suckling noises that made Regan suddenly yearn for a child of her own. Jake's child. How tempting, she thought, to go back to Lancaster, to paint the shutters and weed the garden, plant bulbs for spring, and keep the mushrooms from under the sink when it rained; to wait for Jake for a day, a weekend, a long holiday, as she was waiting now. To forget Peter's urgings, Manny's plans, her own ambitions. Not to want more than the touch of Jake's hands on her skin, his mouth against her lips and her breast, the lovemaking they both missed. Not to want less than that. Couldn't it be enough? The thought was seductive in itself, especially when she missed him, even more so when she kept looking toward the door, wanting his arrival in the next second.

Regan frowned, biting her lip. Would it be so wrong to give up now, before she'd really tried?

Linda was studying her. "It's lonely, isn't it? Without him? It's not easy when one of you is always gone, especially if you're just starting. The last time, I asked Kenny to stop touring—I said I'd leave him if he didn't." She laughed softly in amazement. "I couldn't believe it when he listened." She eased the sweater down, then propped the baby against her shoulder to bring up air by thumping him gently on the back. "But basically," she said, "he's a vagabond. He can't wait to chase you all over the country, looking for the big chance."

Regan didn't know what to say, but she hoped she understood Linda a little better now. And hadn't their antagonisms lessened? Two women in love with musicians, one who yearned for the road and one who didn't, but who endured it to find his own success. Am I more like Kenny? she asked herself. And again, what troubles? But Linda had turned the baby around, and was, to Regan's complete surprise, handing him across the table. "Here," she said. "You wanted to hold him once before, and he—he seems to like you. His name is Kenneth, Junior, but we call him Jeb. Give him to Kenny for a few minutes while I order another drink."

"My treat," Regan said with a smile. She rose, pressing Jeb against the front of her gown as she walked toward the bandstand, feeling free and light despite the burden in her arms. She rubbed her cheek against the fine, fair hair, relished the soft warmth of his skin.

"So you got saddled with Attila the Hun, did you?" Kenny asked with a grin. "We haven't had a good night's sleep in five months or more."

"You make a tender father, Kenny Williams," Regan joked. "And you don't even know how old your son is—try six months. He gets older every day, you know." The baby cooed and gurgled, looking with interest around the small stage, at the instruments. "You should be more devoted," though she knew how much he actually doted on the baby. It warmed her to see Kenny's big hands on the small body of his child, lifting Jeb high overhead until he giggled. "Besides," Regan continued, "I think he's going to grow up to become a drummer like his daddy."

"God forbid," with a vehemence that didn't seem all pretend, then just as quickly, "but talk about devoted, songbird...." Kenny was grinning at someone behind her.

Regan turned around to find Jake smiling at her, a navy garment bag slung over his shoulder. His hair was tousled from the wind outside, and he looked marvelous. "Jake, oh Jake! It's you!" Her eyes seemed to hold him in a very private, special place, as if the vast, crowded room and the talking people and the curious glances—Linda's among them—and even Sam and Kenny had disappeared. "Oh," she whispered, "hello."

"Hi." He bent forward, planting a warm kiss on Regan's lips, then laid a hand on Jeb's silky head. "And hello to you, little one," with a pointed look at Regan. "Trying him on for size, are you?" Which made her blush because, in a way, she had been. Envying Linda and Kenny what appeared to be—

though she guessed it wasn't, underneath—a simpler life together. "Thinking of getting yourself a big belly for the winter instead of a hit record?"

She grinned back, her heart increasing its beat. How could he have gotten more handsome, being away for only a week? "Not on your life, James Harrod Marsh—and don't you forget it!"

Then she decided to make certain that he appreciated her position—or to reaffirm it for herself, perhaps. She couldn't quit now. Guiding him to the table she'd been sharing with Linda, Regan introduced them. "Nice to meet you," Linda said with a smile more genuine than any Regan had seen before. "Have a seat, Jake."

"Hi, Linda. You have a beautiful son," as Regan handed the baby over to his mother again. Her eyes met Linda's briefly, found them glowing with what she took to be a total absence of jealousy, and a tinge of friendship. At least for the moment. Regan kissed Jake quickly on the cheek. To be fair to Linda, she had probably fought off her share of competition since meeting Kenny, who remained a free spirit, husband and father or not.

"You two get acquainted," Regan said. "I have to go to *work*."

By the end of her first number, they were doing famously, and toward the end of the set, Regan glanced over to see Jake cradling a sleeping baby in the crook of his arm and nursing his own Scotch with the other hand. She turned to Peter in sudden inspiration, amazed when the quick grin split his stern features at her suggestion, and he nodded. As the new intro began, Regan said, "This is an old one, ladies and gentlemen, but the words are as true as time. . . ."

It was a showstopper, substituted for a light ballad that wouldn't have prepared the crowd nearly so well for Dale Lester's last show; and, as ambiguous as the song might seem, even to Jake, she felt sure he was getting her underlying message. A squirm of discomfort at the start, then a slow, unwilling smile crossed his face as she sang:

Baby face, you've got the cutest little baby face,
There's not another one can take your place, baby face,
My poor heart is jumpin', you sure have started
      somethin' . . .

Regan threw everything she had into the song, body and
facial gestures; a tongue-in-cheek rendering that brought the
audience to her, wild. Then the spotlight swung away from
Regan and the trio—all of whom were smiling, even Peter—
swept over Linda's surprised face, and illuminated Jake holding
the baby in his arms as Regan finished with maximum volume
and an overload of campy style.

Baby face, I'm up in heaven when I'm in your
      fond embrace,
I didn't need a shove, 'cause I just fell in love,
With your pretty baby face . . . !

The crowd, revved up for Dale Lester as it had never been
before, was a hand-clapping, toe-tapping celebration when Lester himself, capitalizing on the emotional momentum, joined
her for a last repeat of the chorus. As his heavy body lumbered
in a dance parody to the microphone, and the spot immediately
switched to him, to Regan, she read clearly Jake's lips moving:
Wait until I get you home. Then he threw back his head and
laughed.
    "You like corn," Regan said later, snuggled into bed, "so I
gave you some. Everyone thought you looked adorable with
Jeb. Maybe *you* ought to stay home and have a baby." Then,
with a kiss to soften the rest of the message, "I told you I
meant business," because as much as she loved Jake's music,
it couldn't be the only music in her heart, in her life. Crawl
back to Lancaster, Regan asked herself, and wait for him?
Make the rare, languorous nights of loving the sole focus of
her life? No, not when the girlhood dreams might become
reality yet—no matter how much she loved him.
    Because Jake's success wasn't hers.

Chapter 8

"You got a lot to learn, little lady," Dale Lester admonished as Regan paced her dressing room one night. "It's kind of like being in the army. Hurry up and wait, hurry up and wait some more." He gave her a kindly smile, though. "And then what do you think? *Bam*, some morning you're going to find yourself so frazzled from racing around, keeping up with this business, you'll wish you were back on line at the Unemployment."

She knew his was the voice of experience. At fifty-four, Dale Lester was a veteran, to say the least. Originally a borscht-belt comic playing the Catskills resorts as a fill-in for canceled acts far better than his, he'd certainly served his time, and he was quick now to preserve his hard-won territory. Regan didn't care for his humor—mostly name-calling one-liners—but underneath he was curiously gentle, and she liked him. If he was sometimes given to surreptitious pats and pinches of various parts of her anatomy, he never went farther, so she always forgave him. Lester had lent her money between paydays now and then; made certain to boost her during his act each night. They'd been friends—after a slow, cautious circling of each other for her first weeks at the Birdcage—ever since the night she'd sung to Jake and the baby.

"You have those people in the palm of your hand," he'd exclaimed when the song ended, leaning over to hiss the words in her ear. "What an ending, what an opening for me— Say, why don't we use it every night, me coming on to finish the last chorus with you? It's a natural segue, don't you see, keeps the flow . . . nobody's going to leave their seat in the middle of something like that; we just won't give 'em an ending at all."

"If you don't think I'd be stealing your thunder, Dale." Regan hadn't been so sure it would work. But it amused her to be so quickly matching his clichés.

"Hell," he replied, looking her over with a leer that was far more comical than sincere, "I'd be a damn fool to even try competing with this little package," as his plump hand found her bottom. "If you can't beat 'em, join 'em, huh?"

Regan couldn't help laughing. "Right," she said before shifting away from his touch and adding more firmly, "Here. You seem to have misplaced your hand."

But the short duet did work, and wonderfully. No matter the song she selected for the finale, Dale Lester joined in, doing his best to carry a tune and pulling faces for the audience as he sang, the buffoon to Regan's straight man—or rather, woman—routine. She was learning to handle people, too—not the least of them Dale Lester of the spreading paunch, balding pate, and harmlessly roving hands, who wore the most ill-fitting suits, expensive ones, she'd ever seen. But if he didn't know a decent tailor or couldn't keep his hands where they belonged, he knew the business cold, and when Dale said, leaving her dressing room, "It's gonna happen all at once, Regan," she had to believe him. Believe him, she added, or go crazy. Which didn't make success happen any faster.

One person had noticed her developing career, as usual, with a selfish motive. Regan knew it the second she answered his knock at her dressing-room door to find Paul Oldham standing in the hall.

"Well, well." He shouldered his way into the attractive but simple room. "Looks like you been moving right up the ladder while I was stuck in Lancaster trying to hold body and self together."

"I wouldn't exactly say 'climbing ladders,' Paul." She stepped out of his way. There was no telling what he wanted, and she was apprehensive, her heart behaving badly, her palms growing damp with tension. She hadn't seen him since leaving his house with Jake—whose absence now must have been noted also—and she didn't want to see Paul, period.

Sitting in the tan easy chair by the brass floor lamp, he crossed his legs, pretending to pick lint from his gray trousers, which were, as usual, unpressed and bagging at the knees. Paul made Dale Lester look like a fashion plate. Staring at him, Regan took a deep breath.

"What's on your mind, Paul?" Might as well get to the point, if possible. With Paul, she never knew how long it would take, or what might happen when they got there.

"I come to see my favorite niece, and what do I hear?" He mimicked her edgy tone accurately enough: "'What do I want?'" Then, after a pause that made her squirm, he repeated the phrase, studying her with those glass-blue eyes she had never been able to see through. Regan wrapped her long white terry-cloth robe more tightly around her body, as if it might protect her. "A little respect, if you please," he said. "And maybe... maybe some help—that's what I'd really like, a little bit of help from those with better luck in this world."

"I suppose by luck you mean money."

Good God, she thought. Two months ago, I'd have been terrified to speak to him like this; then she realized she still was; that her throat was dry.

"You're slightly late if you mean to ask for my paychecks from Manny, too," Regan said, nervously brushing a strand of hair from her cheek and tucking it behind her ear. Turning her back, she pulled a jade-green skirt from its hanger, unbuttoned the biscuit-colored satin blouse she would wear tonight. She went behind the dressing screen. Maybe she'd be braver still if she didn't have to watch his face.

"Now what makes you say a thing like that?" he asked. "Alyson and I needed extra at home when you were singing at Houghton's roadhouse; you had money and we didn't, the shop closing and all. Besides, you were eating off that table, too, weren't you?" He waited, but she didn't answer.

Her hands were shaking, fluttering as she slipped off her
robe, quickly slid into the sleek, warm satin blouse and worked
the fabric buttons closed. Putting on armor, she thought. "I'm
not asking for a handout," he said. Regan heard a rustling
sound and glanced up. The velvet skirt slid from the top of
the screen where she'd thrown it while she finished the blouse;
the skirt was in his hands. "Very fancy, nice and soft." And
she could see him in her mind, smoothing the material through
his thick fingers, his brain calculating how much the skirt had
cost. How much she could spare, or be talked out of. Threatened for. Should she tell him it was part of Manny's contri-
bution? No, she'd have to be completely insane to make that—
or any other—admission to him; it had gone over badly enough
with Jake.

"Give me my gown, Paul." She held her breath, waiting;
but nothing happened. Then Paul said, "Look, Regan, I got
me a problem." He paused a moment before continuing, "I
need a job," his voice muffled and indistinct. "I—I thought
maybe you could talk to Manny Bertelli, put in a good word
for me. . . ."

Regan stood, stunned and speechless.

"Nothing I couldn't handle, understand," Paul went on.
"Just a start, you know . . . running errands, maybe driving for
him—I'm not a bad driver, Regan—and who knows? After a
couple of months, a year—"

"Paul, I'm not sure. I can't speak for Manny," Regan said
helplessly. She'd never heard Paul grovel before, but that's
what he seemed to be doing.

"I'm family," he said in a defensive tone. "I'm all the family
you got, me and Alyson. It's not like I'm looking for charity."

Regan gnawed at her bottom lip for a moment, wondering
what to say. It was true, Paul and his daughter were the only
relatives she had in the world—and hadn't she always wanted
them to love her? Why live with the unhappy past, now that
she was grown up and standing on her own? In a way, he was
right—that she'd been luckier. Though Regan attributed whatever success she had more to hard work. Still, if Paul worked
for Manny, he wouldn't be so likely to ask her for money she

didn't have. Or to resent her, either. And couldn't Manny keep Paul under control if necessary?

Squaring her shoulders, Regan said with a small sigh, "All right, Paul. I'll see what I can do."

Suddenly, the skirt came flying over the top of the fabric dressing screen. Regan caught it, then slipped it on before Paul could change his mind. When she was completely dressed, except for shoes, she walked from behind the screen. Paul was standing in the center of the room, his eyes cast down at the floor. He wasn't going to thank her; but then, she didn't expect him to. Though it occurred to Regan that she'd rarely—except, perhaps, for that strange night when he had come to her room—seen Paul looking helpless. It must have taken a lot for him to come to her now. "I don't see Marsh hanging around," he muttered, flicking a glance at her. "Looks like love ain't all it used to be."

"Jake's away on tour, Paul."

His gaze found hers again, and held. "He put a ring on your finger before he left?" Though of course he'd seen that her hand was bare.

"No, he—"

"And he isn't going to," Paul said flatly. Despite the growing discomfort she felt, Regan saw the unhappiness in his eyes. "Shouldn't have messed with him, I told you that. You know I wanted more for you, Regan. . . ."

"We'll be all right, Paul," she assured him, not feeling that confident herself. Regan walked closer to him, wondering if she ought to defend Jake, try to make Paul see that he'd been wrong from the start about him. But where Paul was concerned, she didn't trust her powers of conviction. Didn't want to give him any further opportunity to make his point. "Would you like to hear me sing tonight?" she asked, diverting his attention. "I can get you a table."

"Some other time," he said, lightly touching her cheek. "Alyson's coming home in a few months. If you're in New York the middle of March, we'll both come to see you." He gave her a smile. "And if I get in with Bertelli, I'll see you all the time, won't I?"

Regan's heart sank. "Did I—Did I tell you that I'm going to make a record, Uncle Paul? Maybe . . . maybe you'll hear me on the radio and—"

"I'll turn it up real loud," he promised. "You let me know when." And he turned away, walking quickly to the door. "Don't forget to talk to Manny."

After he had gone, Regan slumped into the tan easy chair. Staring hard at the closed door, she kept blinking back the tears until someone called for her to go onstage. *Oh Jake, why weren't you here?*

Peter Noel's stormy features intruded into Regan's protective daydream. Standing before the microphone, she'd been lost in another realm of existence, seeing Jake's face and his brown-gold gaze, so much warmer than the one that now penetrated her fantasies.

"Come on, Regan. See that guy in the control booth? He needs some levels."

"Peter, can't we call this off for today?" The rising panic washed over her in waves.

"On account of your nervous attack? Hell, no." He spun her around to face the control room and the scrawny man at the mixing desk, his bald head shining in the glow of colored lights, his scraggly beard like a misplaced wig. Almost hysterical, Regan wanted to giggle, but she knew where that would lead: to the tears that were even closer to the surface than nausea. *My God, why had she agreed to make the tape? My God, wasn't it enough to sing at Manny's without getting sick? How could she even entertain the notion of going on the road, opening in a different city every night? And this, this was a whole different world.*

"Listen," Peter was saying, his strong, thin fingers digging into the shoulders of her sweatshirt. "You keep your guts where they belong! There's nothing to be afraid of, Regan. There's plenty of tape. That guy in there is one of the best on a small scale, a very personal operation, attention to every detail, he's going to make us—you—sound like a Grammy Award winner. Now, damnit, what's the holdup?"

"Peter, I'm so scared! I can't help it!" She made a wild gesture toward the genius in the control booth. *"My God,* it's like *Star Wars* in there; the whole place is switches and dials and levers and eerie-looking lights—"

"I don't care if it's the whole galaxy exploding! Your business isn't to pay attention to the technicians or the colors, or to worry yourself literally sick about how many tracks we tape today, or tomorrow, or the day after that. Your only concern is to stand right here"—he wound her stiffened fingers around the mike—"and to *sing!*" Then he gave her a long, searching look that asked for perfection. "Well? Are we going to make music for these people?" with a flick of his dark head toward the booth, toward Kenny and Sam, who were contending as best they could with their own anxiety. Glancing back, she saw Sam hunched over his sheet music, biting on one fingernail as he skimmed the page with a frown; and she saw Kenny, tapping out time with a foot, adjusting his drums, smiling to himself in a way that reminded her of animal rictus more than mirth.

Regan smoothed her damp palms one at a time along the thighs of her jeans. She could feel perspiration trickling from her armpits, wetting the heavy shirt. She should have worn something cooler. She looked around at the bare, dreary room that was the studio where she would record her first commercial effort, and she tried to stop shaking inside. It was Jake's song, she kept thinking; so why couldn't he be here instead of Peter?

Because he didn't want to be, Regan answered herself. Jake's reaction to her first recording attempt hadn't been what she expected. It had seemed fitting to her that he play piano for the tape, but Jake had refused. "Baby, I don't have the time," he'd said.

"But it won't be the same record without you," Regan argued.

"Maybe it'll be better."

She'd argued with him, too, about the song itself. Jake insisted upon signing away all his rights to the ballad.

"But what if it's a hit?" Regan asked, hoping to change his mind.

"Then you'll earn that much more from it. I wrote the song

for you, baby, as a gift—not for profit." Besides, he'd added, he had no intention of writing another.

His last words to her that night had been, "You're really feeling your oats, aren't you?" without the amusement in his voice or the encouragement that she'd wanted to hear. Maybe that was what did it. Regan ran her hands through her hair, shaking out the tresses, then grabbed the microphone again. "All right, Peter," she said, sucking in her breath. "Let's make some music."

The session turned long, exhausting. The floor became littered with cigarette butts—from Sam; and beer cans—courtesy of Kenny; and then with pages of staff paper containing Peter's aborted corrections to the score. He didn't like the ending. He wanted the time changed for the beginning. He felt the bridge to the chorus was too short, choppy. "Aw, Christ, Pete," Kenny said in disgust, punctuating his anger with a loud, complicated drumroll. "The bridge is fine; the opening's terrific; Regan sounds like an angel; now can we, please, for Christ's sake, get outta here and have some supper before my old lady starts heaving skillets at my head for being late?"

"I'll decide when we're finished . . . with the help of the pros in there," pointing a finger at the control room. "Let's take it from the top once more." And then, of course, again.

Regan's voice felt raw, and she was sure the tape wouldn't be any good now; that the huskiness would come through and nothing else. But she said nothing. She was too tired to speak, only exchanging weary glances with Sam. At the microphone, she squared her shoulders. At least, she thought, I *can* sing— even if it sounds bad—and the nausea's gone. It wasn't so much different after all from singing at the club, once—

"Jesus, Noel, slow the damn thing down. It sounds like hell in here, what are you running—a race?" The voice, disembodied, came from the mixing desk in the control room. Peter flushed. "The last run-through sounded pretty good. Why don't you give me another like it?"

The opening, the bridge, the tempo . . . all fine. Peter, having his own fit of nerves now, she supposed; fatigue taking its toll of the trio, too. The shared weariness seemed to give Regan another charge of energy, like hitting the wall in a marathon, finding that last spurt of determination, will, the physical resources to finish and make a showing. She sang her heart out, knowing that a great part of the effort now was for Jake, who wasn't with her, for Jake who had written this song because he loved her. But that ending—she was spinning the thoughts before she got there—the ending had to be different, slightly; not the alteration Peter had proposed, but sleek and soaring, a finish no one could ignore or forget. And when she reached it, out came the notes and the volume and then the embellishment she wanted at the last, that little curlicue of notes completely separate from the music behind, from Kenny and Sam and Peter, for herself and Jake.

"... 'the only one I care to know is "you."' ..."

Holding to the notes, Regan put one hand on top of her head, using the huskiness in her voice for added emotion as she raised her other arm in a fisted salute. Then the volume dropped at last; the words trailed away into a hushed silence.

"Beautiful," came a whisper from the control booth. "Wrap. It. Up. Thanks, folks."

Peter, gaping at her as Kenny and Sam whooped their delight, both hugging her at once. Wow, she thought. *Wow!* "Great, Regan," from Sam, and *"Dynamite,* songbird," from Kenny; but her eyes were holding Peter's.

Regan asked, "Perfect?"

And he grinned, his whole face lighting up like part of the mixing desk in the control room. "Getting there," he conceded.

Chapter 9

Elegant in white tie and tails, Jake walked slowly onto the stage, acknowledging the applause of greeting from the audience, feeling the licks of anxiety in his stomach and the stiff awkwardness of his hands, which wouldn't be warmed. His knees shook as he sat down at the bench before the gleaming mahogany Steinway grand—the most perfectly tuned instrument he'd ever played. Chicago is important, his pounding heart kept repeating in sickening, pulsing waves. Rehearsal had gone well enough, but he wasn't so confident now. Worldwide attention for this symphony orchestra always; and tonight, for him.

Jake cast a quick glance toward the front row, from which Regan had caught his notice in a different auditorium only six months ago. She wasn't there now, of course. The row was filled by alien bodies, not a single face he recognized. My God, why couldn't she be here? Was it so much to ask that she hold his hand, his head if necessary? Apparently yes. Yes, it was.

Why couldn't she share his successes, too? His performance nerves? Granted, on the telephone Regan enthused endlessly about each of his concerts, begging Jake to read her the reviews he didn't care about as soon as they'd come out—but she'd never seen him play. Perhaps that explained his own lack of enthusiasm when she'd made the all-important demo tape. Not that he wasn't proud of her.

He knew about working hard, waiting for a break, praying it would come one day. Yet, hearing about the studio session, the club dates Bertelli had arranged after the first of the year—only weeks from now; and having seen firsthand how well people accepted Regan at the Birdcage, Jake felt a continual, gnawing pain. If only they could spend more time together. . . .

But success also meant one long series of empty rooms without her. And he'd guessed—though Regan wouldn't tell him—that part of the Shelton suite's tab must have been funded by Bertelli, waiting in the wings. To keep from asking her the direct question, Jake had diverted himself by teasing. He also felt slightly ashamed that he hadn't been able to share her good news about the record. "You ought to see this hotel," he'd said. "This *town*, for that matter. I doubt there's a female in five counties under the age of eighty."

"Are you looking?"

"That's all there is to do." And then, aware of the tenseness in her question: "Regan, I miss you so much I'm half crazy."

"I wish you were here." She laughed, realizing what she'd said. "I sound like a boring postcard, don't I?"

"I wish I was there," Jake had answered, not laughing at all. Which had made her ask if he was okay. "Nothing you couldn't cure," he said lightly, dismissing the subject.

Then he'd made the mistake of asking her to join him in Chicago, tonight.

"My God, why *can't* you come? This is the fourth time I've asked since I went on the road. Are you that enamored of Bertelli and his plans for you?"

"That's unfair, Jake. I'm tired," Regan had said. "We finished recording only last night. I was up until three A.M. at the studio, my only 'night off' this week—with rehearsal all day today at the club. It has nothing to do with Manny." Jake had heard her take a breath before she promised, "I'll come next time you play."

But would she? For now, he had to stop pondering the possibility of her saying "No" again. Jake straightened at the piano as the French horn played the opening notes to the Concerto No. 2 in B-flat Major, and willed himself to concentrate. But feeling no better one second than a little boy who didn't get his way, in the next Jake decided he had been perfectly justified in his anger. *I need you too, baby.*

He took it out on the delicate Steinway, playing that night with a fierce, aggressive precision totally unlike his usual style. Pounding shit out of the piano, punishing the instrument instead. When he finished, Jake was bathed in sweat, even his hair soaking wet. As he left the stage after taking his bows, he felt ashamed.

Later, the newspapers would print amazing reviews far removed from Jake's opinion of himself. "Every spine of every person in this sellout audience must have been tingling, every hair standing on end, to hear such impassioned Brahms." But Jake knew he didn't deserve the praise. Just as Brahms didn't deserve the beating. Taking his bows and more bows, hearing the whistles and the cheers, he had thought: Not here, *not here.* Why can't she understand the loneliness of the road, the need to fill that empty seat? Well, the hell with her then. . . .

But Jake was on the morning plane to New York, he and the pulled tendon in his right wrist. Shooting, burning spikes of pain when he moved the wrong way. Served him right, he decided. But if he hoped to play on Tuesday evening in Philadelphia, he'd have to rest the whole arm for the weekend. He cradled it against his stomach, feeling chastened by his vicious performance. Better find a way, he told himself, to manage the duality of his life—the tour and Regan.

A month later, he was still trying.

"You'll like California in December," Jake coaxed. "A complete change of scene—no snow, no cold, no wind. Just sunshine and blue sky—if the smog lifts."

"Then how can it be Christmas?"

"You want me to come home?" he asked by phone from Denver. His voice picked up. "Why not? I'll kidnap your enticing little body; we'll go up to the mansion. . . . We'll gather tree limbs and twigs from the woodlot, build a roaring fire.

I'll throw a sleeping bag and some pillows on the floor in the room you like; we'll drink cheap red *vino* and screw all night. . . ."

"Jake, *stop.*" She missed him terribly, Regan told him with a breathless laugh—hugged her pillow at night as substitute—and even the tone of his voice, made intimate by the vision in his mind, had caused hot blood to course through her veins. "I have to work on Christmas."

"Oh, shit, you do."

"And so do you," she said reasonably. "You *can't* give up one of your concerts."

"No." *But why won't you?*

In Los Angeles, the telephone short-circuited sleep long before he wanted to gain consciousness. Fumbling for the receiver with his eyes still shut, Jake yawned. "Yeah?"

"This is your obscene wake-up call," Regan said. "Merry Christmas."

"Oh . . . *baby.* . . ." He struggled up in bed, blinking against the light. "Merry Christmas." He squinted at his alarm. It was only six o'clock, nine in New York.

Regan rushed on. "Jake, I love the daisies!"

She'd been awakened at dawn by the delivery boy pounding at her door. As a surprise, Jake had ordered the huge basket of white marguerites, unable to imagine a more fitting gift than the fresh flowers he always associated with her. "There must be hundreds of them," she added. "My room looks like a garden."

Jake smiled. "And I love the piano," he said, acknowledging her present to him, which had come the day before.

Regan explained breathlessly that she'd spent the better part of last Saturday hunting the perfect gift. There'd been no question, once she spied the music box from Austria: a shining ebony miniature grand piano that played the opening to the *Moonlight Sonata.* "Cornball," Jake murmured, remembering the senior recital where she'd heard him play it. The only time she'd seen him perform. More awake now, he ran a hand through dark hair tousled by sleep. "Listen," he said after a moment, "get your ass on a plane. You can be here before I play tonight if you hustle. I'm doing the Beethoven—for you. And then afterward, we'll—"

"*Jake*."

"Yeah, yeah, I know . . . Manny's got you trussed up like a turkey tonight, but—"

"Please understand, and don't argue. It's a holiday."

"I *know* it's a holiday."

"Then be nice. Next year we'll plan ahead."

"Dual-career couple," he said with exasperation. Was he being unreasonable? "We need more split-second scheduling than the President." Then, after a silence, "What'll we do this year?"

He heard the smile in Regan's voice. "Talk dirty on the phone, I guess."

But when they had hung up, Jake felt less aroused than lonely. At the windows of his hotel room, he looked out on the flat landscape and the haze of Southern California, where there was no holiday snow. He shivered from cold anyway; but there was no Regan to warm him, either. He felt suddenly as if he were hanging onto his concentration—always so carefully nurtured—like a man clinging to a ledge by bloody fingertips, someone about to step on his hands.

Regan dashed madly along the terminal concourse from the plane, her opened camel's hair coat whipping about her legs as she ran. Into a fast-paced existence had come, with the beginning of the new year, some sporadic travel. Tonight, she was meeting Jake in the airport for dinner. Regan hadn't seen him in more than two weeks, and she felt like a starving woman—but not for mere food. What she needed was Jake, and time, but she was en route to—

"Where am I going?" she asked him with a laugh, embracing him again before they sat down in the terminal restaurant. "In fact, where are we now? Have you noticed that every airport looks the same?"

"No character," Jake agreed. He kept smiling at her, and

she kept grinning back until Regan felt certain everyone in the restaurant was looking at them, wondering if they were demented. Jake consulted a pocket notebook. "I think we're in— Detroit. Yes, I'm sure of it." He glanced toward the windows, his eyes sparkling. "Snow and ice ... January twenty-eighth ... this must be Michigan. It's Tuesday, isn't it? So I've got a hop to Rochester tonight."

"Then I'm on my way to Louisville." Regan took his hand. "I'm so glad to see you," she breathed, her whole heart in her eyes.

Then she became unaccountably tongue-tied. She had such news, but couldn't seem to tell him. Instead, Regan heard herself thanking Jake for the daisy bouquets delivered to her dressing room before every opening night. Since Christmastime, she'd been enjoying the velvety white blooms. Bringing a flower to her lips, she'd remember the game her mother had played long ago. *He loves me, he loves me not.*

Now, Regan's heart rate increased as Jake said, "You're quite welcome. They reminded me of last summer ... before you became such a busy lady."

He trusts me, he trusts me not.

Why so little time together now? So much insecurity about them? And why spend what time they had in obscure small talk? Jake knew that Manny had taken her demo tape to the right people, who'd proclaimed it "astoundingly commercial." Manufactured and packaged, the record itself had reached the stores seemingly overnight. A genuine recording of her own, not a dream and not a trial run. Something to hold in her hands, to hear on the radio, as she'd promised Paul. Why couldn't she tell Jake the rest?

Regan hadn't mentioned her reviews, either. From the Cleveland paper: "Miss Reilly is refreshing. The clarity of her voice and naturally intimate style illuminate an exciting new star on the musical horizon." A critic in Toledo had topped the *Plain Dealer* two days later: "Of all the words *this* reviewer knows, *good luck* are the two Regan Reilly will need least." New to her profession, Regan—unlike Jake—wanted to believe them. Praising his press notices, she'd told him so often enough—before she had any of her own.

"Isn't there something you want to say?" he asked now, bending slightly over the table to look into her eyes.

"Like what?"

Jake grinned. "I know what you're hiding. You've hit the charts."

And Regan's pride took over, ending the brief, unhappy mood. "Number fourteen, Jake! I can hardly believe it."

"Twelve."

"Twelve?" Her voice had risen in surprise, turning the heads of several other diners nearby.

"You and Bertelli don't know everything. I heard on a top-forty radio show before I left the hotel to meet you. The recording sounds great, baby."

Regan sat, smiling at him in a daze. That high? Why had she been afraid to mention the showing to Jake before? His obvious pride was written, too, all over his face, in his brown-gold eyes. Perhaps she'd imagined his lack of enthusiasm about the taping, her new club dates, and Manny's ongoing preparations for a tour in the spring. "I'm sorry I didn't tell you," Regan said. "It just seems that lately we don't talk to each other the way we used to, Jake—" She broke off because his smile had faded, and a frown creased his forehead.

"No," he said, "I suppose not. There are times when I feel so wound up after I play . . . but hours pass before I get you on the phone, and by then the feeling isn't the same."

They sat staring at each other with silent understanding.

"Linda said that relationships like ours were never easy to maintain," Regan said.

But he answered quickly, "We're doing all right," and looked away, attacking his salad. She noticed that he set the onion rings aside, and would have smiled at his neglected passion, but there was a curious pain running through her. When neither of them did justice to the seafood they'd ordered, Jake put his fork down, his voice low and somber.

"I love you, baby."

She felt her bones melt, the ache subside. "I love you, too."

But with a groan, Jake looked at his watch. "Time to go," he said, then gave her a piercing glance. "Unless you want to miss your plane . . . and I'll miss mine."

Why not? Why not a night together now? She wanted him so. But Regan laid her napkin beside her plate, shaking her head. "I can't," she said. "We can't."

Their flights left within twenty minutes of each other. In less than half an hour, Regan's would taxi first down an icy runway. Lifting her gaze from their entwined fingers, Regan encountered more than a few curious glances from nearby diners. "Everyone *is* staring at us," she said, wondering if she was going to cry.

"Because you're so pretty," Jake answered.

"Because you're getting so famous."

Immediately, she regretted saying so. It put a different slant to the conversation, one that had hovered dangerously near them the minute she'd refused to miss her flight. She set the rest of her uneaten lobster aside with Jake's and tried to drink her coffee. "Because we make a stunning couple," she added after a moment, smiling as best she could.

Jake groaned again. "Don't remind me."

Walking her to the gate for boarding, he kept his fingers loosely laced with hers. But although the slight pressure warmed her, Regan couldn't help feeling that it seemed to hold her back. The closer they came to Sam and Kenny, who were waiting with Peter against the wall, the more she felt it. At the gate, Jake stopped her, kissing Regan hard on the mouth. "You're becoming pretty famous yourself," he said, dragging his lips more lightly across hers.

Regan felt the thrill and the pain both at once. "It's not a competition, you know."

But then, she wondered if it was.

Each time Regan landed at Kennedy or La Guardia or Newark, the report of sales on her single of Jake's song had grown again, like the very first flowers of spring bursting from the cold, hard earth. By late February, "All the Words I Know" had sold five hundred thousand copies. Halfway to a gold record! Returning to New York after a month of on-again, off-again travel—mainly through the Midwest—Regan wanted to hug herself. Blustery as the weather was—as only New York at the end of winter could be—she suddenly felt summer in the air. In fact, she walked on it!

In celebration, Manny decided to throw a private party at the Birdcage, closing the club for the night, with plenty of press invited.

"You have a stake in this, too," Regan argued, trying to convince Jake—who was staying over just one night—to attend. "It's your song, Jake, please."

"And Bertelli's celebration. If I can't see you alone," he said, "I'd rather get some sleep before I leave for L.A. tomorrow instead of drinking too much. I've got to shake this head cold somehow." He was blowing his nose for the hundredth time in the hour since he'd arrived at the Shelton suite. "I've had the bug since we met in Detroit, and I'd really like to see the keys when I play, so enjoy yourself."

Regan assured him icily that she would. He hadn't invented the illness: she could see the dark rings around his eyes and the pallor of his skin. But if he wanted to stay home and sleep away their visit as well as his cold, let him. If he wouldn't make the effort this once . . . *she* intended to have the time of her life.

When Regan arrived at the party, the Birdcage was already awash with empty bottles, tipped-over glasses with melted ice running onto the tabletops, onto the carpet. And the heavily laden buffet table itself contained a mess of crumpled napkins and discarded plates; the remnants of roast beef, ham, and turkey; rye and pumpernickel bread rounds; Dijon mustard; spiced mayonnaises; potato and macaroni salads; and a dozen other concoctions she couldn't readily identify, not to mention the well-used pots of caviar, now a glutinous mass of tiny, marble-eyed fish eggs without elegance.

She shouldn't have taken so long to dress. She was late, and people were entertaining themselves hugely with drink and dancing. The day before, Manny had handed her a sheaf of bills, large denominations plainly visible, and said, "Get something to make their eyes roll back in their heads, sweet."

"Oh, but Manny, I—"

"Take it," he said, adding with a grin: "It's your money, isn't it?"

She had bought a dazzling piece of green silk jersey, the exact shade of her eyes when she felt happiest, when they were most clear and sparkling. The dress was knee-length, showing her legs and the matching silk delicacy of her shoes, which were sling-backed and slender-heeled. The halter style of the design left her back completely bare to the waist, and in front scooped down in a flattering U shape to skim the swell of her breasts. Regan felt smashing in the outfit, carrying a slim mushroom-colored satin clutch (trimmed in the same green) to relieve the monochrome effect; but she couldn't stop remembering Jake's reaction—or rather, the lack of one—before she left the Shelton.

His eyes had gone over her as before, viewing Manny's investment, but this time without comment. She had felt the quick surge of self-righteous anger again.

"Thank you very much," she said. "I'm glad you like my new dress. Which I paid for myself." And she had slammed the door to the suite on her way out.

Now Regan tried to push away the last of her frustrated fury. As she left her serviceable camel's hair coat with the Birdcage's cloakroom attendant, Kenny spotted her and quickly crossed the room.

"God, you look sensational!"

"Thank you," Regan said with a smile. "But anybody would look good in this. It comes with a guarantee."

Beaming, Kenny swept her into his arms.

"Come on, let's dance before everyone else finds out you're here."

Which didn't take long, but at least they had a few turns around the floor—cleared for dancing by jamming the tables closer together, away from the bandstand. Kenny danced well, his body accommodating to Regan's automatically. "Where's the old man tonight?" he whispered in her ear, barely managing to be heard above the noise around them.

She flashed him a sour look. "He wouldn't come," she said, though she wasn't going to admit why.

"Because of Bertelli?" Kenny laughed. "I thought you were the one with the green eyes."

"Ha-ha, but you're very perceptive, my friend." She felt his hand on her skin, and wished it were Jake's. So much for her defenses of anger. "Oh, Kenny," she said, "we see so little of each other, but when we do, nothing goes right except—" She stopped herself, but he had caught her meaning. Regan flushed.

"Yeah, me and Linda too, when I was on the road." He whirled her with the music, and her hair swung out behind her like a silken lash. "That's how we started Jeb-boy," he added with a laugh. "Better watch yourself making up, nightingale. I don't think the *maestro* would be too unhappy if you ended up on the sidelines for a while."

Regan remembered the night Jake had come to the club to find her holding the baby. She'd never imagined he would really want a child; after all, she knew how he felt about getting married and having unwanted responsibilities—but if that responsibility kept *her* at home, not away on tour? And away from Manny? She'd thought then he was teasing, but—

"Is it so obvious?" she asked Kenny.

"Well, I ought to know," he said. "Linda gave me my orders, or I'd have stayed on the road forever . . . even as bad as—as bad as it can be." Linda had told Kenny she'd leave him if he didn't come home. And he'd listened, to her amazement. But could *she*? If Jake gave her an ultimatum about her career, and their relationship . . . ?

Regan slightly turned as they danced, and saw Linda glaring at her across the room. Two demerits, she thought, just when I was working on a medal for good behavior. She murmured, "I think you'd better dance with your wife," then she maneuvered Kenny quickly to the edge of the dance floor, stopping in front of the dark-haired girl. "Linda, he's done his duty for the night." She looked appreciatively at Linda's simple but flattering cranberry crepe. "I love your dress. Thanks for lending me a dance partner."

Linda managed a smile. "I wouldn't mind at all if I'd gotten a turn with Jake. Where is he?"

"I'll let Kenny tell you," Regan said over her shoulder as she moved on. How many people would ask about Jake's absence before she began screaming loud enough to quiet the rest of this raucous party? She didn't stop to count, for fear the total would make her lose control. Instead, Regan smiled and laughed and sparkled; she talked with people she knew and met others she hadn't known before; she accepted congratulations and, from Sam Henderson, advice.

"What do you mean, Jake wouldn't come? When you've gotten half a gold—" Then he saw the greater sparkle in her eyes, the downturned mouth that wanted to tremble. "Hey, he'll work it out. You'll be okay," he reassured her. "You love each other, don't you?"

Another voice of experience, Regan thought with an inward sigh. But she wouldn't hurt Sam by saying so. His broken marriage had made him shy of other involvements, but it had also given him a touching, childlike faith in other people's. As if, she thought, he or Kenny could keep anyone else from having troubles or making mistakes. "Yes," she said, "I love him."

When Sam had wandered away, Peter Noel came to her, a morose expression on his face. "You having a good time?"

"Is there a penalty if I am?" She didn't want to see his scowl tonight; she'd had enough of Jake's before she left the hotel.

"No," he said with a slow, thin smile. "But God Almighty, who could have fun in the middle of all this?"

"Manny, apparently."

Regan gestured toward him: dancing, wearing a gray silk suit that looked lustrous under the lights and a smile that proclaimed he'd had too much to drink. "It isn't every day we almost get a gold record, Peter."

"No, but don't count on another if Bertelli has his way.

He's already talking plenty of echo and a full orchestra for the album before—"

"*Album?*"

"Oh, damnit to hell, I shouldn't have taken this one myself." He tossed down the last of his drink. "I won't say another word. Talk to Manny yourself when he—" Then Peter interrupted himself. "Say, I thought Jake would be here."

Regan stalked away with dual purpose before the screaming started. She left Peter with his mouth open, but she didn't care. For once, she wasn't going to make any explanation for Jake's rudeness. Feeling impolite herself, she caught Manny by the arm and drew him aside. "Excuse us," she said sweetly to his companion, a well-padded blonde—probably artificial, Regan thought, on both counts. "Manny, what's this about an album? Peter said—"

"Goddamn, that Noel could ruin a christening!" He slipped an arm around her waist, leading her toward the bar and a tall, slender man in a dark blue suit who was sipping contemplatively at a martini. "I want you to meet a friend of mine— yours, too. Regan, this is Bill Houston, he's the AR man for Worldwide Records."

They shook hands, Regan looking puzzled. Her heart began to hammer.

"I think Bertelli and I have got the agreements straightened out," Houston said with a smile. "Except, of course, for your signature and the go-ahead." He had a rangy body and a thin, long face to match. "It's a three-album deal, Regan . . . may I call you—"

Regan whirled around to Bertelli's grin, which slashed from ear to ear.

"A recording contract? Manny?" She was starting to grin herself, forgetting Jake's melancholy for the first time all evening. "*A contract? For me?*"

"Surprise," Manny said softly. "I wanted to give you something special tonight."

"Oh, *Manny!*" A contract? It was a major step forward, every bit as important as the spiraling sales on the record— and Jake's song had made it possible. Oh, why wasn't he here now? Worldwide Records! Not as big as RCA or Columbia, but very well regarded, with a small but select stable of artists. *Worldwide.* . . . Regan was in near ecstasy. She had a sudden vision of herself standing before the old mirror in her bedroom at Paul's house. Dreaming, when it was still just that.

When they were alone, she said, "Worldwide, Manny! I couldn't believe it when I met Mr. Houston."

"He couldn't believe you, sweet."

She smiled at him, though she wasn't sure his eyes focused on her that well. "Thank you, Mr. Bertelli," Regan began with mock sweetness, but without warning he reached for her. He'd had too much to drink. Heart instantly racing, Regan pulled away. "Don't, Manny, don't—"

"Let me kiss you. I've wanted to for weeks, ever since I saw you at Houghton's, Regan—"

People were staring at them. Regan caught Sam's alert posture; then a sober look from Kenny.

Manny dropped the awkward embrace. "Why?" Straightening on the bar stool, he smoothed his hair into place. "Because of Marsh? Waiting for you at home? Pouting, I hear, like a spoiled prince?"

Who had told him? A dozen people, Regan answered herself.

"He isn't pouting," she excused Jake. "He felt sick."

"Give him my regards for a lightning-fast recovery." Manny's tone said exactly the opposite, and he added: "I wouldn't want him to miss his plane." Then he stroked one finger down her cheek. "You and I, Regan," he observed, "we're going a long way together—just the two of us. *Capisce?*" Leaning close, he kissed her on the forehead. Regan struggled inwardly not to jerk away from the brief touch. "Someday," he said, "I'll make you want me, too. I just picked a lousy moment to try."

It was late, nearly five in the morning. Regan undressed quickly, then slipped into bed. There was no sound from Jake; no deep, regular breathing that would have told her he was asleep. "Hi," she whispered, her body finding the contours of his by instinct. "Quit pretending. You're not sleeping." But almost imperceptibly, he shifted away. Regan snapped on the small porcelain lamp by the bed. "You said you didn't want to go tonight."

Jake squinted against the sudden rush of light and, leaning over her, switched off the lamp again. "I didn't."

"Then why are you so angry?"

"I'm not angry." He sat up, his skin gleaming in the dim you—What's so paranoid about that? And if—if he hasn't hand over his back the way Manny had with her. But when she did, tentatively, he swung out of bed as if she had burned him. "I'm only surprised," he said, "that you made it back here—for part of the night, anyway."

"Meaning?"

"I don't want you after *him* . . . I don't want you stinking of Bertelli!"

Regan felt stunned. "Dear God, Jake, that's paranoid!"

"I'm on the road too damned much, while Bertelli's with you—What's so paranoid about that? And if—if he hasn't already, it's just a matter of time before he drags you into his bed. That isn't paranoia, that's proximity!"

Regan stared in disbelief at the stiff set of his shoulders. Jake sounded like Paul, accusing her of something she hadn't done, and the similarity made her heart twist.

"Is that what you think of me, Jake?"

He gave her a flat look, then crossed the room, his body moving like a tin soldier wound too tightly. He poured a drink from a bottle on the dresser. "No," he said after a moment. "It's what I think of him."

Regan sat up, her heart pounding. "Then why wouldn't you come to the party tonight? Why wouldn't you protect your *property?*"

Jake still had his back to her, hadn't raised the glass to his mouth.

"You think I don't know he pays for this place?" he demanded. "You're not making enough money to rent a two-bedroom suite in a hotel, especially when you're out of town more than you're here!" He reached for something on the dresser. "Well, I'll tell you this much—he isn't paying for my side of the bed!"

Regan saw the soft-leather gleam of his wallet. "Don't you dare!" she cried. "I'm not taking money from you!"

"Why not? You don't mind taking it from him."

But he shoved the billfold back against the mirror without opening it.

"Tonight was very special to me," Regan said in a low, thready voice. She felt cold and clammy. "Why do you keep harping about Manny if you won't—" She broke off, feeling the tightness in her throat that choked the words. "Jake, tonight I got a *contract* with *Worldwide Records* for three *albums* and you—you—" Regan took a heaving breath. "If I ever went to Manny, it would be you who sent me there!"

She had certainly never felt farther away from Jake. Staring at the hunched set of his shoulders as he stood motionless at the dresser, Regan wanted to get up and put on a nightgown, hiding her own nakedness; but she didn't move. It wasn't Manny, she decided, not really. Jealousy was only part of the excuse. She'd been right: they were competing, and it was a contest like her struggle with Alyson, or like trying to win Paul's favor. And just as futile? Hadn't Jake warned her that two careers was one beyond the limit? She stared at him moodily until he spoke, not expecting what he would say. "I'm sorry, baby."

When he turned around, she saw the anguish on his face. "That's so great about Worldwide, I mean it—" as he looked at her miserably. "But sometimes I find myself looking at a whole set of attitudes I never thought I had, that I don't like or even know how to resolve." A shrug of defeat. "All I know for sure is, the Jekyll-and-Hyde existence is really getting to me. I've never felt like this before, Regan. God," he said harshly, "I hate being keyed up all the time. The tension keeps getting worse; it affects us, my own commitments; even the pleasure I might feel because of your albums." He paused for a long moment before going on, "In Toronto—did I tell you—I forgot an entire passage to the Brahms that I've played a million times. I ended up all over the keyboard, faking until I could remember where the hell I was supposed to be. Christ, half the time I don't know where I am, what city or—" He shook his head, not continuing.

Regan's heart pounded painfully in alarm.

"Everybody has bad nights, Jake. We need a little innovative scheduling, that's all. That's what you said."

What were they telling each other? She didn't understand. Jake flicked another glance her way, unhappier still, his dark eyes seeming to take in her nakedness with only abstract interest. "Yes. I did," looking down into his glass as he swirled the ice. But the Christmastime joke, the amusement now and then at being part of a new social phenomenon—the dual-career couple crossing continents to spend a few hours in each other's arms, meeting in airports for meals nobody could eat—didn't make him smile now, if it ever had.

"Jake, everything to me is new and exciting," Regan said. "Don't you ever feel like I do? Tonight, Manny said I'm almost sure to get a platinum album if we pick the material carefully—with your song as the lead, Jake—and as soon as we finish recording, I'll be off on my first tour! I can't help being as high as the sky! Why, I feel like"—she laughed—"like Dorothy in *The Wizard of Oz*, stepping out onto that golden highway full of adventure, glittering—"

"It was yellow brick."

"That's all?" she asked. "No more excitement for you?" Though as successful as his tour had been so far, Jake was spending three-fourths of his time, Regan realized, on airplanes or in baggage claims or on his way to or from terminals. To see her, if not to play somewhere. Regan looked at him closely as Jake sipped his drink. He had lost weight, and his face was pale and tight, not only from fighting a cold; his skin had an unhealthy translucence. And he had not answered her question.

"You haven't slept tonight at all, have you?" she said softly. Jake shrugged. "I will during the flight tomorrow."

"You never sleep on planes," she said. "I do."

He shrugged again and set the drink down, barely tasted, as the words were drawn from her—agonized because she wanted him with her every minute. "From now on, you come to me only when *you* have the time, Jake, and—and want to."

"I always want to." He looked at her oddly, as if she had disappointed him somehow. Then he walked across the room in watery moonlight, his features shadowed in the dimness. He sat down on the bed, facing her, and placed his arms to either side of her. Slowly, Regan drew him down, insistent against the first, resisting tautness of his muscles. She could hear the rush of his breathing, feel the increased pulse-rate of his heart.

"Please," she murmured, "don't be so intense and Byronic on our only night together for three weeks." And Jake smiled slightly. "Oh, baby."

But it was Regan who kissed him first, who urged and whispered moments later, "Love me, yes . . . like that, love me"; who caressed and aroused, guiding his hands, his mouth, until the tension of passion grew fierce, harsh, explosive, and was finally released.

Afterward, Regan lay awake while Jake slept deeply, quietly, exhausted. *We'll be all right,* she thought; and in the next breath, *It isn't true. The natural communication of our bodies isn't the only way we touch.* But for the first time, she sensed distance between them far greater than a phone call—or the three-thousand-mile span of a continent.

Chapter 10

A steady stream of taillights had Regan perching on the edge of the cab's backseat as it seemed to inch northward on Sixth Avenue toward the hotel. Why were they the only ones not moving faster? Regan drummed her fingers impatiently on the toast-colored leather of her handbag. Why had Jake come home a day early?

He hadn't been very understanding that afternoon when she tried to explain about the album. "We've got a session tonight, I'm sorry. We've been taping all week, trying to finish before I go on the road." But Jake, at the Shelton, apparently hadn't liked the explanation any more than he'd liked the cancellation of his last L.A. concert because of a union strike. "If you'd called before you left the Coast, Jake, maybe I could have—"

"Well, Christ, I had some nutty idea you'd like to be surprised." There had been a long, stony silence with audible breathing at both ends of the line while the hours stretched before Regan like a marathon. Rehearsal all afternoon, then the taping. She knew what Jake must be thinking: that he should have kept going, straight to New Orleans without the detour to see her. But Regan didn't know what to say. She only knew that—because of Manny—asking Jake to join her at the studio tonight for a few hours would be pointless.

A short phrase, *oil and water,* ran through her mind in the stillness before Jake had said with a sigh, "All right, baby. I'll see you when I see you."

Regan leaned forward now, as if she might push the taxi to the Shelton that much faster. Pleading hoarseness to end the taping early, she'd left Kenny and Sam to soothe Peter, who hadn't appeared to believe a word of her excuse. She didn't care. She only wanted an end to the arguments she and Jake seemed to be having far too often.

When the cab at last reached the hotel, Regan paid the driver and tore into the lobby, catching an elevator just before the doors slid shut. She wished she'd worn something dressier that morning than the charcoal slacks and camel's hair sweater that matched her coat. In the hallway on her floor, she slipped a ready key into the suite's lock, calling out as the door opened, "Jake, I'm home!" sweeping the flying mane of tawny hair from her face. "I told Peter to—"

She stopped just inside. Why such surprise? That furtive look on his face as Jake crossed the sitting room toward her? He moved slowly, had taken too much time closing the bedroom door behind him. "Christ, Regan, I—" he began; then she was in his arms, launching herself at him, laughing at his expression.

"Didn't you miss me?" She kissed him again, a long kiss that tasted, on Jake's mouth, of whiskey. Breaking the kiss, she asked, "Am I in time to join you?"

She could hear the shower running hard, though Jake was still dressed, two buttons on his shirt undone and the sleeves rolled back. Then, seemingly by itself, the water shut off. "No," Regan said softly, "I guess not." And in the space of seconds that felt like years, a woman appeared in the bedroom doorway, the soft light making a halo of auburn ringlets; and Regan felt the world go dark. Her heart didn't seem to be beating at all, certainly not in any rhythm she recognized. *Oh God, oh God . . .* she was on the back side of the moon. *Dear God, no.*

Blue eyes bright with malice, Alyson was smiling. "Well. We didn't expect you so soon." She was wearing Regan's rust-colored velour robe, barely concealing her breasts, stopping well above her knees.

"Get out." Regan spoke in a deadly whisper, not knowing how she formed the words. Her heart was working again, pumping blood and adrenaline through her body in sickening, pulsing waves. *I could like him. I could take him away from you.* When Jake said her name in a guttural, stricken tone, she whirled on him. "You just answer me one thing," she breathed. "Is this before—or after?"

But it was Alyson she heard. "You and I have always *shared* our belongings, Regan, haven't we?" looking straight at Jake with a sated expression.

"Alyson, Jesus!—"

Jake's explosive protest; then her own hissed command:

"Get out, no, don't take your clothes, just—get—out!"

A hasty retreat into the hall, and then, "When you've finished here, lover, I'm in six-oh-seven . . . remember?" The door closed Regan and Jake into a weighty silence. Every cell in her body seemed to be shaking.

"Regan, come on, put the ice pick away." Jake came toward her, his voice slower than normal, his enunciation cautious. "I know what she said, but if you believe that garbage, she's getting what she must have wanted, coming here—"

Regan clenched her hands into fists. "Not a shower?"

She wasn't making sense, Jake argued. How could he have asked Alyson—or even known where she was in order to call—when he'd gotten into town himself only that morning, exhausted? Which didn't explain to Regan the rest of the day, or the evening.

Her gaze swept the room. "However did you manage the party? And the bedroom Olympics?"

"I didn't! Yes, I was angry, so instead of getting dinner, I took a nap, then had a shower and a few drinks—as you may be able to tell; and then *she* came to the suite and said you'd invited her."

"Me? Why would I? We've never been close, you know that."

"Then why would you think I'd take her to bed, for God's sake?"

"Force of habit," Regan said softly. She saw at once every woman who had ever given Jake a measuring appraisal—at the recital when they met, at the airport in Detroit, on the street, everywhere. She began to pick up the empty glasses scattered about the room. A few drinks, yes—but not alone. And how many other nights, in other hotel rooms? With other women? "Jake keeps moving," Steven had told her with a smile; but whatever made him think Jake would stop for her? Or that he wouldn't want, no matter what he said, a redhead one night instead of a green-eyed blonde? But why Alyson? If he'd chosen anyone else in the world—

"Regan, what the hell's wrong with you? I didn't touch her!"

"Am I supposed to believe you because you've got your pants on?"

"Goddamnit, you crazy woman!" He reached for her, but missed.

Regan took advantage of his momentary imbalance and the obvious effects of liquor to start for the bedroom, tears in her eyes, shouting, "I don't believe you!" On the threshold she froze at the scene there, too: clothes everywhere, damp towels, the bed unmade. *Their* bed . . . our bed.

Jake had followed her into the room. "If I had to buy your story about Bertelli, why won't you believe me?"

Was that it, then? Had his jealous fantasies, particularly his envy of her career, made Jake want to hurt her—with the one woman who really could? Regan looked at him evenly, briefly, before brushing the room with a glance that she wished with all her wounded heart might cleanse. Then she bent to pluck Alyson's clothing from the green carpet as if she were daintily picking flowers in a field . . . white daisies . . . her hair hanging, shining.

Will you help me, Jake? . . . the audition for Steven . . . the Talbot mansion . . . and Jake's face, so loved, his body moving over hers in that sun-filled room on a bare floor . . . *be first,*

Jake, please . . . be first, she had prayed, and last, and always . . . so certain she could trust him, then.

"Please," he said, his voice husky, "if you want me to prove how I feel, Regan, I will . . . but tell me how?"

Silent, she kept on harvesting the clothes, soft blue blossoms of fabric, and memory.

"Oh, God, listen," he said. "You want to get married?" in the reluctant tone that he'd used when taking her from Paul's house to live with him. Interfering with his plans. "I mean, maybe we should have done it a long time ago."

"You don't have to marry me."

"What do you mean, I—" He was trying to control his impatience. "Christ, maybe I want to— Look, we could even sell the house in Lancaster; hell, then you'd never have to see your cousin again. We could buy a new house somewhere else." He attempted a smile, but she looked up and away before it took. "Sure, in Kansas City, why not, baby, like the hub of a wheel, a center, it would cut down on some of the traveling—"

"No, Jake."

My God, why wouldn't he stop? She couldn't look at him, felt scarcely able to fit two thoughts together; they were disengaged from her feelings, none of the cogs in her mind meshing properly, her whole head cottony with shock, reaction, anger, pain that threatened to tear her apart. If he'd asked her to marry him the first night in his house, oh, she'd have believed him then, wouldn't she? But now—

"Damnit, why not? Listen, there's a whole world out there conspiring to keep us apart—but it doesn't have to be that way! We get married; we work at it; and in a few years—who knows?—maybe we'll even start a family. Regan, you're crazy about Linda's boy and—"

"I don't want a baby!" Her voice rose again, and she had to force it down. "Kenny told me that would make you happy," and Jake sounded not at all romantic or committed to them, only desperate. Why? Because he'd been caught with Alyson and was shoring up lies with more lies? *He'll never put a ring on your finger,* Paul had said. His awkward proposal might go far in calming her down for the moment, though. But was marriage, in fact, what she wanted? Had wanted from him all along? If so, Regan didn't want him this way. "All you're doing, Jake, is laying traps for me—like my uncle, like Alyson! You don't mean a word you're saying— Oh God," she said brokenly, "maybe you never did."

"Regan."

Her lungs rasped with each effort to speak, her voice thick and raw. "No, I don't want anything from you, Jake. I don't want . . . I don't want to marry you. I don't want your baby, I could *never* want your—"

"Don't say that." His voice was barely audible. "I love you," he insisted. "I promised that—"

"Oh yes," Regan breathed in sharp little gasps, the words shaking when she said them, "your beautiful promises."

I'll love you enough to make up for everyone else . . . I do love you . . . I'll never stop loving you . . . but no one had ever loved her, so there must be another side to the promises, too; another side to Jake. *You really want the singing, don't you . . . more than you want me . . . you'll need a heart of stone . . .* Yes, Regan thought miserably, perhaps she would. Straightening at last from her carpet garden, turning to the bewilderment that seemed genuine in his brown-gold eyes, holding the garments like a dying bouquet, Regan thrust them at him. She wanted to run for the bathroom, to wash her hands of Alyson. *I don't want you stinking of Bertelli.*

Regan's throat ached with unshed tears. "But how could I forget the rest?" she whispered. "How gifted you are at the breaking of promises . . . and letting people down."

"Ah, Christ."

Jake looked as if she had stabbed him with that imaginary ice pick; the light dying in his eyes, their future. And Regan knew her memories were dying too, with the defeat in his expression, and the bunch of dead flower-clothes in his hands.

Trailing the aftermath of argument like a ruined bridal veil of muddied lace, Regan met Steven the next evening for dinner. She wore a skirt and sweater of rose-colored wool. The three of them had been planning the event for weeks, and Regan had hoped that Jake would simply show up at the restaurant near the Birdcage to surprise her, to apologize. When he didn't, Regan's anxiety peaked once more.

Steven was understanding, but not entirely sympathetic.

"If Jake wanted another woman, he'd have found one before this," he scolded gently. "Regan, he loves you too much to wreck everything. Especially"—he repeated the word—"with your cousin." Hadn't Jake been knocking himself out, Steven argued, sacrificing his own rest between engagements to be with Regan?

"I know," she said miserably, feeling so diminished in the light of a rational day that the night before struck her with horror. How could she have flung those horrid words at Jake? Of course she wanted him: his love, his life, his children. Why hadn't she let him explain?

"He was right, Steven, calling me a crazy woman last night." But she couldn't even grant herself insanity for an excuse. And a woman would have handled the misunderstanding by listening, at the very least, even by accommodating with humor, as Jake had tried to at first. Above all, by being willing to forgive. Like an adult. But Regan had handled circumstantial evidence like the child she really was. She had been foolish, letting Alyson get to her so easily, falling back on her training in Paul's loveless house.

Regan felt a stab of despair as strong as her eagerness to forgive. For hours after Jake had left, she had searched her mind and heavy heart, waiting for Jake's key to turn in the lock. If he had only opened the door, she kept thinking, with all their anger spent—

"He'll probably be at the club," Steven said now. He paid their bill, ushering her from the restaurant where Regan had picked at her food and watched him eat. "With dozens of daisies," he added, kissing her cheek.

Regan looked at him soberly. "You really believe in love, don't you?"

"Like gospel. And so should you, princess."

The Birdcage was only a few blocks from the restaurant, and they walked the distance quickly in the sharp night air.

Regan had begun to feel somewhat better when suddenly Steven stopped her, his hand tightening on her shoulder. Following his gaze she saw them, too: several men running from the alley beside the club, their bodies weaving, scattering across the deserted street. "Now I wonder what—" he began. Then they both heard the awful sounds.

Steven bolted from her side, leaving Regan to follow, reaching him first, well before her leaden steps of growing apprehension. "Steven?" Calling softly, Regan went into the alley. And froze. She saw Steven on his knees, bent over the stilled form that began to writhe in pain, all thrashing arms and legs, a body she knew as well as her own.

"Jake!" Regan's scream brought Steven's head around, and he shouted at her. "Get away from here, do you hear me? Go inside, call an ambulance, Regan, hurry—Don't look, damnit, go on!" But the backstage watchman had already telephoned, and simultaneously she heard a siren begin to sing harmony with her, sliding up a scale as Regan's voice spiraled down from screams to a keening cry. *"Jaaakkke, Jake—"*

Closer the siren sounded, louder, as loud as her pulse of terror, throbbing, pounding; a horrible, echoing quaver that wouldn't stop, like the violent trembling of her limbs so that she couldn't move, either.

When she called out to Steven, he didn't seem to hear. "Easy," he was soothing as his hands pressed Jake down. "Easy now, try not to move—" his voice breaking. "Oh *shit*, who would do a thing like this? Jake, don't move—"

But with a groan, Jake had raised himself, was turning on one shoulder, letting his forehead drop against the cold paving stones of the alley. Regan clapped a hand over her lips and thought with the stunned, giddy detachment of shock: *Backstage nerves, that's all,* and then, *Oh my goodness, he's ruined his jacket* when she saw blood, too, running from his mouth.

Then Regan was roughly pushed aside, jostled from her daze. The unreal, pulsating red shadow of revolving light on top of the ambulance had filled the alley as the siren wound down at last, and stopped. Two paramedics ran past. She lost the scrap of tissue she'd been hunting from her purse a second ago, saw it flutter to the dark pavement. On legs as weak as matchsticks, she fought her way through a growing crowd to Steven.

Immediately, his arm went around her; but the sensation of being touched came from a distance, and seemed as unreal as the grotesque light. When Steven tried to press her head to his shoulder, she cried, "No!" *Was he dead*, oh God— She heard herself scream the words.

"No, princess. Hush, he's going to be all right—"

But she had to see for herself. Tearing free, she pushed back into the mass of onlookers, chatting as if there were a party . . . but he was alive!

Weakly fighting the oxygen mask, he was tossing his head from side to side as the attendant eased him onto his back, Jake's chest heaving at the same time. "Don't you see?" she shouted. "He thinks he's still being attacked!" And the paramedic, struggling with the apparatus and a pair of flailing arms, threw her a grateful look.

"Take it easy, buddy . . . It's only nice, clean air."

"Jake, let them help you!"

With the words, he suddenly quieted, going limp and still. After that, she didn't know exactly what they were doing for him. Regan's gaze stayed riveted on his face, a bad combination of gray and—at intervals—a flush of unhealthy pink from the swirling ambulance light that swept the buildings on either side of the alley. But there was a needle in his arm, she saw; a bottle of clear fluid held high by one attendant; and then, a metal stretcher rolling by. When they lifted him, Regan's blood chilled at the helpless groans that Jake couldn't stifle.

"Ohhh . . . *Jesus.*"

Feeling his cries as if they'd been her own, Regan scrambled after Steven into the waiting van, which screamed off into the night; hovering as close to Jake as the medics would allow, she took the ride with him through crowded city streets, crosstown, uptown, until at last she smelled the river.

But Regan's mind had long since stopped trying to comprehend anything beyond the same frantic thought, echoed and re-echoed like the siren's wail as she clutched Steven's hand, watching the pale face of the man she loved. *Oh God, Jake, dear God, what have they done to you?*

Chapter 11

No! Not again, Christ, no . . . !

He is spread-eagled on the pavement, held down, his mouth gagged by thick cloth. His body cushions the forward thrust of heavy blows.

"This ain't gonna take long," someone grunts: a man who enjoys his work. The skin beneath Jake's chin splits under pressure from knuckles smashing into bone. "Mess him up good, damnit!"

How many are there, pressing him, pinning his arms, weighing him down, down, like stones? Silent, because he has no air left for speaking . . . struggling. He begins to pray—if he passes out, will they leave him alone?—but he can't seem to lose his hold on consciousness, or terror. Time slowing down, almost stopping as he wonders: *What are they doing to me? Why?*

And then, in fresh waves like breakers against a jetty, the real pain crashes through him. Startlingly aware, he feels every fine bone break; cartilage and tendons giving way under some awesome force . . . crushing, like cement or bricks . . . crushing. *His hands . . . !*

In the high hospital bed, Jake thrashed from the pit of sleep into daylight, softly groaning as the drugs wore off. Cracked ribs made him rasp for every breath. The stitches in his face throbbed; his body had become one giant bruise. The bandages, tight as a death grip. How long had he been lying here, wherever, full of tubes, breathing sand with every attempt for air? How many days, nights, awakenings like this, then giddy driftings into careless sleep?

Morning now? Afternoon? In early spring the sun shone weakly, and it was difficult to tell. Or was it even March still? Jake tried to watch the light blue sky outside his window, and the mare's tail clouds high up, drifting and soaring like his mind. It wasn't easy to think.

He knew Steven had been with him, when the room was dim. Nighttime, then. And he thought he'd glimpsed Regan at the window of the unit, looking in—and once in the room beside him, her face a white sheet of haunting. But he couldn't be certain of her, any more than he was certain of his life; and each time he wanted to speak—about his hands, or Alyson—Regan disappeared, or he floated away.

Jake stopped watching the clouds. They were making him dizzy. The drug had worn off completely; there was too much pain coming at him now—like those faceless men in the alley, making his heart race and his mouth go dry. He didn't want to think about the night before *that*. He wanted to shut off this interlude of thought, to sink again, oblivious; but, between the deep sleep of medication and the fierce agonies before another blank relief, was this monstrous time when the pictures kept coming, coming, as clear and sharp as pain. And what had happened in that alley seemed almost pleasant by comparison.

At the Shelton that evening, Jake had waited for Regan, worrying. In Los Angeles he'd spent too much time thinking about her and that look she had of half-veiled innocence mixed with desire; wondering how much longer she might belong to him. When the knock had sounded at the door, he'd imagined it must be Regan coming back early. Only, of course, it wasn't; and opening up, he'd been annoyed.

"What do you want?" he'd asked Alyson Oldham, thinking that he shouldn't have been holding the half-empty glass of liquor. Brilliant, not a single system functioning.

"To see Regan, Jake," she'd answered. "I'm on spring holiday." She'd promised her father the visit with her cousin. "Do you think I'll have a long wait?"

"You don't have to wait."

But without invitation, Alyson had stepped inside, asking Jake for a drink. She wouldn't think of going back to her room without saying hello. Taking the glass he reluctantly offered, she ran red fingernails lightly over his hand. "You should smile more, Jake. You're quite a heartbreaker. How do you put up with Regan—keeping you on hold all the time?"

After the phone conversation earlier, her words hit home; but he didn't answer. He tossed off the last of his Scotch and made a refill. He felt fuzzy around the edges.

Why hadn't he eaten? Alyson kept talking, but he didn't listen closely. She told him about drama school, and that she knew Regan would be important soon, with the right connections to help her. Not helping with the talk, Jake fixed more drinks.

"Do you know I used to watch you in Lancaster?" she asked. "No, of course you don't," she said, not letting him answer. "You were always watching *her*." His throat felt tight as Alyson's eyes moved over him with the frank speculation a man might give an available woman, and provoked a mild response. Well, why not? Jake reasoned. "Do you mind if I freshen up?" Alyson asked.

She was already heading for the bathroom before he had a chance to say he did mind. If he could have said it. The room was beginning to spin, very gently and slowly, revolving on its axis around him.

Jake heard the water come on loud, sounding like a torrential downpour. He went slowly toward the bedroom, into the bath where Alyson's full-breasted figure made an alluring silhouette through the frosted glass door of the shower stall.

A slow, unwilling fire kindled in his loins. He was staring at her, transfixed and bleary, from the bedroom doorway when the lock clicked and the sitting room door swung open. "Jake? I've escaped, my love, home earlier than I'd dared to hope."

He was sober that fast. Stunningly sober. At that instant,

he could have walked a straight line from New York to California. He had her in his arms, his mind casting for excuse, when the shower went off. And Regan's face turned pale with that glazed look of disbelief, the laughter fading from her eyes. And everything went to hell.

Now, Jake twisted in the hospital bed. It was like an oversized crib, the mattress hard, and the pain was starting to engulf him again. He couldn't think... but he had to... had to, damnit... *concentrate*. Talk to... Regan. Make her see the truth. Tell her... *I walked all night under cold stars*. And— Oh, *damn*. Jake ground his teeth as a thrust of unprotected misery shot through him.

But it wasn't only pain.

The morning after his argument with Regan over Alyson Oldham, Jake had pushed his way into Bertelli's office, past the flustered secretary and Paul Oldham. He hadn't been surprised to see Paul there; Regan had told him that her uncle was running errands for Manny, and Jake's impression had been that the two suited each other.

"I don't want to sit down," he had declined Bertelli's halfhearted invitation. "What I'd like is to beat the shit out of you!"

"If you'd feel better, you're welcome to try."

But Jake only shook his head, his eyes hard and metallic, bronze.

"I make my living with my hands. That would be an expensive satisfaction." Then, with a flick of a glance toward Oldham, "Where's Regan?"

He never interfered in lovers' quarrels, Manny said. She was tied up for the day: various appointments. Fittings. Rehearsal. She'd have to decide for herself whether she wanted to see Jake later, after working hours.

"She'll see me. Oh, she'll see me," Jake repeated. "And by tonight, Bertelli, you'll be looking to skim the cream from somebody else's milk!" He stalked to the door, stopped to throw an angry glare at Paul. Theirs was an instinctive animosity— not unlike Manny's for Jake—that wouldn't improve with time.

Jake kept his eyes on Oldham and asked, "Why not give Alyson the star buildup, Manny? I'd wager—to coin a phrase—that you two are thick as thieves already. Or should I say three?"

Oldham, tensing; trying to decide whether his daughter had been insulted.

"Back off, Jake," Bertelli murmured. "You don't look so good—tired, strung out, not getting enough rest. You ought to take better care of yourself. I think you're pushing too hard."

Had Bertelli's words really been a warning?

Jake struggled to organize his thoughts, which moved swiftly now, free-form . . . black and white bars of Beethoven flashing by. Brahms. He could hear the notes, feel the keys under his fingers. Schumann. Then he felt as if he were falling, falling . . . and oh Christ, his hands! Regan, *please* . . . baby, they won't hurt any worse if I know for sure, tell me, if you love me, baby . . . I love you—

"Please!"

He heard his own voice, shouting. Then the nurse bent over him, her voice soft and lush and soothing. "Quiet now. Rest, Jake," and the needle pricked a vein, fluid coursed through his body again, absorbed, absorbing. Once more, he floated toward nothingness, to wake later—but how much later?—to give in, by degrees, to those igniting flashes that fired every part of him, that left him weak and gasping and out of thought. An animal, moaning and begging. Reminding him of someone else. . . .

Oh God, his mother. He had hoped never to see her kind of suffering again; but now he sounded exactly the same. The same as she had, that last night.

Steven walked slowly from the sitting room into the bedroom of the suite. There were no lights on, but it was nearly dawn, the first flush of pink streaking the gray sky, and he could see her clearly enough, as he had been able to pick his way through the dark rooms.

Regan was lying on top of the covers, one arm flung across her stomach, the other out to the side. Her hand was clenched into a fist, in frantic sleep. When had she finally drifted off at last, this time? Three nights; his own vigil at the hospital in the horrid, too-bright waiting room full of old magazines and stale cigarette smoke and the rank smell of fear. Like sentinels, he and Regan had kept alternating guard—her days, him nights—sleeping when they could.

"Steven?"

She had opened her eyes, dark, soulful green, and was looking up at him, not as sleepily as he would have wished. Every night, coming in at this same hour, he had found Regan the same way—or, if she couldn't sleep at all, then propped on the pillows, her slender body rigid with hope, and its antonym, despair. A few minutes of dozing tonight, he guessed; a half hour at most. He was becoming too familiar himself with the interrupted cycles of sleep, just as he could read, like a mirror of his own mind, the naked, often-asked question in her eyes.

"No difference," he answered. "They let me into the ICU for a few minutes, but he was . . . unconscious. Still some internal bleeding—seeping, they say. I'm sorry, Regan, I wish I could have brought better news—some sort of change."

She said in a small voice, "I always wish the same for you."

He sat on the edge of the bed, and she made room for him, rolling onto her side. Steven took her hand. He thought she looked like a doll, small and defenseless and exquisite; but in contrast, the tawny, waist-length tumble of hair, the astonishing green eyes—irises overwhelmed by the ring of pigment around them—formed a sensual display.

"Why don't they catch those men?" she whispered. The newspapers had been full of the story the first day ('Promising concert pianist, brutally beaten by unknown assailants outside a downtown club . . .'); but, as often happens, media interest had quickly waned. No one had stuck around to find out the result; public fascination had fled like—

"Phantoms," he said bitterly. "No, princess, it was a garden-variety mugging, I'm afraid, standard operating procedure. The cops will never find out who they were or why they did it. Probably they just wanted to, for kicks."

"Steven!"

Regan's face had gone ashen. "Sorry." But, damnit, the thought—and the sight, earlier—of Jake, with the broken ribs and contusions, made him hurt too. Sure, everything was neatly sewn together again—or was it that neat? What if the doctors couldn't fix—

Breaking off the thought, Steven stroked Regan's hand in apology for venting his own frustration. "Maybe he didn't have enough money on him to suit them." But he felt more comfortable with his first answer. There was a senselessness about it that he knew only too well—as he knew lack of sleep, like Regan, and a constant anguish without words.

He closed his eyes for a moment and pictured a car, sliding into the rotten wood guardrail on a curve one snowy February night only a year ago, the blue sedan pitching over the edge and rolling end over end to a finish in the ravine below. Flames from the exploding gas tank had turned the white fairyland into a charred black hell for a radius of fifty yards. His life, too. Oh, Ellen. . . . God, would he ever stop missing her?

And now, there was Jake—bandaged, with possible organ damage, his hands *broken*—and this young girl he didn't know how to comfort. Opening his eyes, he looked into Regan's somber green gaze.

"I keep remembering him, fourteen years old, walking into my club one afternoon, asking for a job." Steven's voice was hoarse. "He was underage, but didn't especially look it. He told me how sick his mother was, and how he needed to take care of her. Said that—that playing piano was what he knew best."

"You hired him," Regan said.

"And he never missed a show. When he started, he didn't know much but classical repertoire. He brought a stack of sheet music with him at first—but after a couple of weeks, princess, he could play anything. Anything at all."

"Because most of the standards come from the masters, anyway," Regan said with a tiny smile. "He told me so. Chopin . . . beautiful melodies to put words to."

She pulled her hand away, her glance shifting as she sat up, then got off the bed to stand before him. Her body, clad in a thin peach-colored gown, was like a young wood nymph in a painting, clean lines and gentle curves and the soft swell of good, but modest, breasts. How he had envied Jake this girl the afternoon of her audition at the roadhouse. What would it be like, he had wanted to ask, starting fresh? With someone so alive?

"Shall I order coffee?" Regan asked as she tied the sash of a white robe that looked new enough to still have tags on its sleeve. "Or will you try to sleep?"

"Sleep. I'll relieve you at the hospital around five. Is that enough time for you to get to the Birdcage and dress?"

"Yes, plenty. Thanks, Steven."

As she leaned down to kiss him, as he still sat on her bed, he thought how quickly, if painfully, they had organized a routine devoted to constant emotional maintenance of Jake's fragile hold on life.

With a sigh, Regan sat back in her chair that night at the Birdcage. The club had long ago emptied of customers, and the lights were down. Staring at Manny across the table, she felt momentarily at a loss for words. They'd been arguing for over an hour, not much being gained on either side; and all Regan could think of, anyway, was Jake, who had tried to smile late in the afternoon—had tried to speak!

"Romance is a wonderful thing, sweet." Manny traced a circle now on the teak tabletop with his forefinger. "But it never built a career." The tour was important, he kept on saying until Regan wanted to scream, "So is Jake," but instead, she spoke calmly. "He almost died."

"Well, he's alive today—and better. You said so."

Regan tried to explain how fractional the improvement was. When Jake had opened his mouth slightly, she'd stopped him. "Jake, don't . . . not yet," making a quick gesture, afraid to touch him. "I'm here," she told him, "there's time." And he had slipped back into the void of darkness. It would be impossible, she informed Manny, to leave New York.

"Why?" he demanded. "Jake's doped out of his head. He isn't about to make conversation no matter what you want to think. Look, sweet"—Manny reached for her hand—"you go on the road day after tomorrow, do the concerts, and stop fussing. Give him a few weeks. Recovery takes time."

But Regan wouldn't budge. "I can't go."

"I don't want to mention this," Manny said softly, "but if you keep being so stubborn, I'll have to induce you to ... reconsider." He released her fingers. "Legally."

"Take me to court, then. I don't care."

"You care," he said. "So would he. Marsh would wake up one morning to find you with no career, no future; all because you wanted to hold his hand while he slept." Manny smiled, a slow smile that spread across his hawklike features in stages. "Regan, Regan," he said quietly, then stopped, making time to think.

He couldn't afford to say the wrong thing. Regan had enough spunk to walk out for good if he did, and a messy court battle wasn't the only thing he stood to lose. In a few short days everything had changed; the odds were in his favor; and Manny Bertelli wasn't about to blow his opportunity—not after all the waiting.

If the truth were known, he told himself, Jake's condition was largely his own fault. A hot temper was a death warrant for sure—one reason he still felt leery of Oldham, too. *Highbrow, lowbrow,* Manny thought; *what's the difference?* Both losers.

But Manny didn't intend to lose his temper or the battle. He stared at the girl across from him now. Passion or not, she'd be out of town so fast. . . .

Manny kept his smile fixed firmly on Regan, who looked down at the floor without returning it. *Careful,* he thought, Marsh hasn't lost her yet.

"Regan, sweet, you know this kind of thing isn't necessary between us. You're not about to give up what you've worked so hard to get ... not when there's so much more to come." The voice of reason, cool and sane. Manny watched for her reaction.

Regan sighed again, heavily; looked around the darkened club, her eyes pausing at the bandstand, the microphone, the piano, then swinging over the tables stacked with upended chairs for the night. "I'll have to come back after Baltimore, Manny." He heard the resignation in her voice as he shook his head.

"Atlanta show is two days later, with rehearsal between."

"Then cancel," she said.

"Contracts, sweet, we keep coming back to that."

Regan stood up, her green eyes snapping. She wouldn't give in so quickly after all. "Damn your contracts—do you hear me?" She snatched her coat from the back of the chair. "I'm not leaving him! I'm not going to Baltimore or Atlanta, either—so you'd better postpone this tour or call your lawyers, Manny!"

Stalking toward the exit, she missed Bertelli's smile.

Chapter 12

She hadn't quite managed to slam the heavy door behind her, either. But as she pushed from the club into the cool night air, Regan didn't notice anything except the crazy circling of her thoughts. What would she do if he brought the lawyers down on her? Could Manny ruin her? Why would he want to? Was Jake right about him, after all? Manipulation, she was thinking. And slick attorneys who knew every loophole. But they wouldn't need any. She had agreed to the tour, hadn't she?

Agreed? She would have sold her soul for the chance—and perhaps she had. Baltimore first; then Atlanta, and quick stops in Virginia, a far southern swing after that, ending in New Orleans before the band headed back north to Philadelphia weeks from now. Weeks without Jake, without knowing . . . if she went. But how could she back out now when—

Regan's mind made a crash landing. Immediately, she had recognized the man who stepped away from the building entrance when the door shut. It was Paul, and her heart began to slam harder than before.

Scowling, he moved quickly, pinning Regan against the building wall. The street was deserted, black and slick with rain; as dark as Paul's menacing stare. Regan took a quick, deep breath to calm herself. No stranger to Paul's mercurial moods, she wanted to keep her wits about her. "I've just had a fight with Manny," she said quietly. "I don't want another one with you."

Paul's features were tight, carved by anger as they'd been the night he struck her to the floor in the upstairs hallway of his house. Regan's few happy memories of her uncle fled, like Jake's anonymous assailants. Gone was the image of his face softened by tenderness and even humility when he'd asked about a job with Manny, expressed concern for her with Jake. And as if she could feel again the bruising pain as the wooden floor met her shoulder, she wanted to cry out.

"I know you been under the weather," Paul said harshly, "but you better make things right with Manny. He's a smart guy, miss—better for you in the long run than that piano player."

Regan's heart lurched again. She tried to bolt, struggled under his grip, but Paul's greater strength only pushed her harder against the wall. Regan felt the cold brick pressing against her spine through the fabric of her coat. "You get on that bus to Baltimore like Manny told you! You don't want to be out of a job just when you got a chance to get somewhere," Paul growled, "and neither do I."

Mutely, Regan stared at him. Her heart beat faster. What was he really saying? "But I don't want to leave him—Jake," she managed, pleading, "not when he's so sick and needs—"

Paul's hand wrenched her wrist. "You listen to me, and listen good!" His face, inches from hers, blocked out Regan's vision. "You pull any funny business with Bertelli, I'm warning you"—his eyes flashing fury—"I'm *telling* you, miss—Jake Marsh will wish he'd died in that alley the other night! Because his hands won't be the only part of him not working any—"

"Uncle Paul, oh God, I don't know what you—"

"You don't have to understand!" He released her, and Regan nearly fell to the pavement. Her legs were weak as water; her heart skipped, then pounded. "You don't know what's good for you, but I do!" He gave her a light shove that nearly sent Regan to her knees. "Be on that bus, you hear me? *Be on that bus!*"

The words relentlessly crashed through her as Regan began to run, blocks and blocks of pavement pounding beneath her feet until her lungs wheezed for air as Jake had done . . . oh, Paul . . . running, running. "His hands," she cried, racing through the dark night for the hotel . . . *his hands*.

At dawn, Steven found Regan huddled on the green-and-white Chippendale sofa in the suite's sitting room, fully clothed. Every light blazed. When she glanced up at his entrance, her green eyes—looking twice-normal size—didn't seem to focus. She shook like a slender sapling in high wind. "Regan, what's wrong?"

But she only shook her head. Quickly, Steven fetched a blanket from the bedroom, wrapping her snugly in it before he held her. She's breaking down, he thought; too many nights of waiting, too much pain to watch. Steven gently forced her chin up now so he could look into her eyes. "You scared me so, I've neglected my news," he said. "Listen, Regan . . . they're moving Jake this morning out of ICU into a private room." It was the change they'd been waiting for, praying for. "Regan, he's going to make it! Do you hear me, princess?"

Her face gaunt and hollowed, she looked at him. "He's going to get well." Then, in a broken voice, "Oh God, he's going to get well." She went limp against him. Steven cupped a hand over the back of her skull, warm gold silk under his palm. After a moment she said, "Tell me the rest."

He smiled slightly, impressed by the show of strength when he'd thought her down for the count. "The news isn't all good, princess, that's true. His hands— The orthopedic men have set the bones, but there's restorative work ahead; plastic surgery when he's stronger. He's going to need one hell of a lot of fine care." Steven paused, not wanting to go on. "Regan, he's one of the worst cases they've seen in Special Surgery."

"He has to play again," she whispered, shaking her head in denial. "Steven, it will kill him if he can't!" *He'll wish he'd died. . . .*

Steven twisted the gold band on his finger, feeling frustrated. She was right, of course. "Expensive operations, specialists—

those guys don't come cheap... weeks and weeks in the hospital yet. Whatever insurance Jake carries can't cover all of that." He grew silent, suddenly depressed. "Well," he said at last, "I've got some money put by from... Ellen... life insurance, just a little but—"

"*We'll* pay." Regan straightened, sweeping the tawny hair from her face. Steven saw the light of absolute conviction blazing in her eyes, like fire. "We'll pay whatever we have to."

She had told Steven *we;* but she had meant herself.

Paul's threats kept revolving in her mind as if she were still going through the lobby doors into the hotel the night before. But she could still help Jake. And she would, in a way that seemed fitting—like justice.

"I'll go on the road as I promised," Regan told Manny. "I'll sing, and I'll fulfill my contracts. But I want you to do something for *me*."

"Anything, sweet."

"Jake needs special treatment. I want you to lend me the money. And use your contacts to find the best plastic surgeon there is for him. I won't get on that bus, Manny, until you do."

"You're growing up fast, sweet. Making tough demands." Bertelli's eyes skimmed her body. "You want to put Humpty Dumpty together again—after the battle you must have had?"

"I want Jake exactly the way he was," Regan corrected coolly.

He ran a finger thoughtfully over his upper lip. "You're asking me to fix somebody I have absolutely no use for," Manny observed, and Regan's blood turned to ice water. How dare he look so bland and innocent? "Is that why you sent them after him, then?" she said. "Why you had Paul warn me yesterday? I never thought when I asked you for a job for him that—"

"Warn you?" Regan had startled him, but he wouldn't let it show in his face. The deadpan expression was a stock-in-trade for Manny, acquired like his charm. Already a street fighter from Brooklyn when Jake Marsh was learning his first classical piano pieces, Bertelli had spent his adolescence in and out of reform schools. The polish had come later, and with effort, unlike Jake's innate elegance. But the school of experience had taught Manny some lessons that Jake had never learned. "I didn't hire those thugs, sweet, if that's what you're thinking." Manny stared earnestly into her wide green eyes. "I'll prove it," he said. "I'll make arrangements with the hospital. Place some calls for that doctor you need. You get some rest, and pack. By the time you leave town," he added with a smile, "the musical wizard will be on his way to perfect health."

So long as it suited his purpose, Manny would fix anything. Even Jake Marsh, who had been standing in his way for much too long. It wouldn't matter now. With his hand riding lightly on her waist, he walked Regan to the door.

"I'll pick up the tab," he said. "No loans, no repayments. We'll call this my part in keeping your trust. I'm a little hurt that you don't trust me, sweet."

What does trust have to do with it? Regan asked herself. She had done the right thing—the only thing she could do—for Jake.

"I think you're making a big mistake," Steven told her the next day as Regan—trying not to hear his disapproval—packed the last of her clothes, folding gowns and lingerie neatly into matching cordovan luggage with her initials stamped in gold. But she couldn't begin to appreciate its luxury, its newness, or the fabrics and colors, the sheer quantity of her wardrobe, either. Not now. Just as she couldn't tell Steven about Manny's threat—or had it been only Paul's?

She was still afraid of her uncle and uncertain of Bertelli's innocence; but despite fear and confusion, she had made the bargains that were necessary—and one broken man, she reasoned, was one too many. How could she jeopardize Jake's closest friend, and hers? He was better off not knowing anything except the most basic details. In time, she'd learn the truth for herself, and then—

Regan stared into the suitcase piled high with finery that blurred into a single, meaningless color as she blinked.

"If my staying would help him, Steven," she said, "I would. But Manny is right. Jake won't be able to communicate for a while, and even if he could"—she paused, finishing weakly— "I'm not sure he'd want to." Oh, but hadn't he smiled at her, just a little? Hadn't he known she was there?

"What do you mean, *if?* Why do you think he was at the Birdcage that night—he was looking for you, damnit!" Steven was watching her closely. "Do you honestly think that Jake would want Bertelli paying for him? If Manny sends you away now, legal or not, how do you think Jake's going to feel? Regan, he's a proud man, maybe too proud for his own good, but—"

"How else is he going to get what he needs *right now?*" Regan asked in a hard tone she'd never used before. Manny had found the doctor, hadn't he? And, guilty or not, he certainly wouldn't miss the money. She said doggedly, "You were the one concerned about the costs! Well, I've fixed that." Why was Steven judging her so? He was the only other person who appreciated the importance of Jake's music to him. "I *have* to go," she insisted. "I haven't any other choice. And neither does he."

What choice, indeed? Steven wondered. She'd been brainwashed by Bertelli. Poor kid, he thought. Growing up the way she must have, with no real home, no family who loved her, he couldn't blame her for being so excited by the lure of success, which was a kind of love. Or maybe, a balm of approval. And somehow, he couldn't fault her for taking off to follow that lure now. Yet he did blame her, damnit. As far as she and Jake were concerned, Regan was doing the worst possible thing; but he couldn't convince her of it. What more could he do?

Regan closed and latched the last case and let him pull it off the bed to stack with the rest beside the door. Then she touched his cheek, her eyes misting. That look, he couldn't help thinking, was going to get to a lot of other people too, and soon. He felt suddenly ashamed of himself. These last moments weren't any easier for her.

Steven took her gently in his arms. "Have you got everything, princess?"

And after a long moment she whispered, "Yes," slipping away from him, hiding her face in the curtain of her hair. "Everything that's going." She picked up her handbag and coat, then made a needless search of the room. Steven thought how lovely she looked in the sheer wool paisley skirt and black knee-length boots and white silk shirt, tied with a deep red chiffon scarf around her throat. How lovely, and how sorrowful.

"The bellboy will be up," she said. "Will you see that he gets the bags? I'll check out before I'm late." Regan made a little circle, taking in the rooms, then opened the door.

She and Jake had shared this suite off and on for months, through so much that had been positive for them both, that it must seem like some kind of home to her; yet there was something new about Regan that wouldn't let her say so. Or ask the question, either. Did she feel guilty, leaving, with her career rising and Jake's on the ground? Had he made her feel more guilty than he meant to?

"It's all right, princess," Steven murmured as she stepped into the hall. "I'll watch out for him."

Chapter 13

This isn't going to work, Regan told herself in panic. The house lights had already dimmed on the overflow crowd. Regan stood before the microphone in a long fall of palest green chiffon with an underskirt of white that made the dress more fragile in color and intensified the emerald of her eyes. She had kept her hair loose because audiences seemed to prefer it that way, and she wore simple gold jewelry: a pair of bands around her upper arms, a delicate swing of earrings. Gold sandals. But she had never felt less glamorous in her life; or more nervous. Which was saying quite a lot. *What am I doing here?* she asked herself as she opened her mouth for the first phrase of the song. *Why didn't I stay in New York?*

They didn't want her, that was clear. Hadn't paid to see her, but the act she was opening for—one of the middle-level rock groups Linda had warned against. And she couldn't have felt more out of place. Oh, they knew the ballad well enough, and so did anyone else who listened to the radio or frequented the record stores—but once she'd finished "All the Words I Know," and the last, trailing notes had ended, what was left? The audience fidgeted for the main event.

Before, up north, hadn't she made people come to her? Except for a few bad nights, hadn't she kept her audiences at Steven's, at the Birdcage, in a dozen lesser cities of the Midwest, enthralled by her music?

Tonight, she heard shufflings and coughs, conversation above the noise of the band. Peter mouthed, "Do the circus novelty..." But it fared no better.

Perspiring, Regan came offstage with her gown plastered to her body, the gown ruined. She could only describe the applause as tepid. The only person she'd warmed up was herself.

"Take another bow," Peter said.

"Are you kidding?"

She took a shower instead. And cried under the stream of hot water.

But if they had liked her somewhat in Baltimore, slightly less in Atlanta and Alexandria, in Nashville Regan was a disaster. As she could plainly read for herself.

She threw the newspapers aside, cluttering the cheap hotel room.

"Lackluster reviews on all sides, Peter," she announced.

"I think we ought to try some upbeat numbers," he suggested. "Open with the single, a hit they all know and like— but then something more flashy, fast; hit them right between the eyes." But she could see he was confused, too.

"I know." Regan tried to smile. "Like a mule. The way Manny wanted."

"Well, he might be right in this case. Not the novelty—we used that once without effect—but I'll scout a couple of others."

So she tried them—two bright, breezy numbers which people recognized—and for a while, she felt better. But not enough.

Why had Manny sent her on this southern swing? "Nobody knows what I'm doing here," she fumed on the telephone from yet another beige-and-electric-blue room where the television set (which barely worked) was chained to the wood veneer table. "And I'm no more certain than they are. Manny, morale with the band is rotten. Half the places I sing, my name is added to the bill *after* the show's sold out!" And, of course, there was something more on her mind. "Manny, I want to come North. I want to see Jake."

Silence. She had nightly reports, solicited from the hospital switchboard at worst, at best from Jake's doctors. Gleaned occasionally from Steven, too. Fair, stable, resting comfortably. But the words seemed innocuous, like the greeting cards she'd sent . . . that Jake probably never saw. He had no telephone in his room yet, either. And nothing could have soothed her anxieties about him, anyway—except for seeing Jake herself, talking to him.

"Sweet, listen to me," Manny broke the silence at last. "Your schedule's full, no dead time right now. You just keep singing like a bird until the tour swings north. By then, he'll want visitors. . . . For now, you're working, aren't you? Being seen? Making contacts? And people are buying records, Regan. The album's taking off on the strength of the lead single." Then his voice lowered, sultry and cajoling. "I know what I'm doing, sweet."

"Well . . . " How had she let him defuse her so quickly?

"Maybe they don't clap so loud in Nashville," he said, "unless you're Dolly Parton or Tammy Wynette—but they must like what they see. I'll send you the sales figures."

"But Manny . . . there's another thing, the bus—"

Only Regan was talking to a dead receiver.

Mortally tired, she wished she could go to sleep; but she couldn't. Following the usual noise to its focal point, Regan wandered across the hall in the middle of the night and joined the party in progress. The members of her band here already there in the suite belonging to the headliners of the evening. The Country Band. Capital letters, and descriptive as all get-out. Regan hadn't understood much of their music; but then, she supposed they might say the same for hers. *More oil and water.*

"Say, Miz Reilly, grab yourself a beer and set a spell!"

"Whooee, this little gal is gonna come with me inside." The Country Band's drummer flung open the connecting door to one bedroom. He reached for Regan, who stepped back.

"I think I'll settle for the drink."

"Well. Sure enough, little *lady*." The door slamming shut. "Wouldn't want to disturb the goings-on in there, anyway," as a fit of giggles and a deeper rumble of laughter seeped under the door. Regan noted one missing guitar player, not hers; and then, several stray girls who seemed to have materialized from nowhere—young and hard. Such deadly vacant eyes, she thought.

"Here you go." Someone slapped an ice-cold bottle of Miller's in Regan's hand. "Plenty more where that came from and all night to put it away. Hell, I ain't drivin' tomorrow . . . you either, huh, Regan?" He said her name with a long, exaggerated *e*. Like a drumroll. The whole band did.

"Me either," she said and took a long swallow, shuddering at the sour taste. The room around her was a mess: liquor bottles on the carpet; plastic glasses everywhere; a large, unidentifiable stain on the shiny blue sofa. The food had long ago disappeared, but the bowls and serving plates remained on the long, fake-walnut dresser; and the mixed aroma of spaghetti sauce, take-out chicken, and greasy pizza hung in the heavy air, somehow overcoming the low-hanging clouds of tobacco smoke. In the corner, a portable cassette player, big as a suitcase, blared the group's last album from twin silver speakers.

Kenny was dancing with a scrawny dishwater blonde who wore her white gauze blouse mostly unbuttoned. They were dancing close, Regan noticed, and not in particular time to the music, either. Maybe I ought to cut in, Regan thought—but she didn't suppose Linda would thank her for it if she ever knew.

She didn't realize until he spoke that Sam had joined her. "That guy's looking for one peck of trouble," Sam grumbled. "If she's a day over fifteen, I'm Igor Stravinsky."

"Hello, Igor," Regan said with a grin. "She looks closer to fifty-five from here," though she knew what he meant. About the trouble, too.

Regan steered Sam away from the group, who were discussing the relative chart placings of songs she'd never heard of. "Sam, where did Kenny come from?" Seeing him with the girl had piqued her interest in the drummer.

"To hear him tell? From the bowels of hell, my dear." Sam swigged from his half-empty bottle of beer, which had loosened his usually reticent tongue. "Actually, it was a small town in Vermont somewhere, lots of snow and ski slopes. His Dad was a physician. Beat Kenny up when he got in a bad mood. So much for the upper classes. His mother drank. They lived in a twelve-room house built before the Revolutionary War—and sent Kenny to Harvard to show him they loved him. About eleven thousand dollars' worth of affection his freshman year—after which he flunked out."

Regan kept her eyes on Kenny and the dishwater blonde, pressed closer together in the corner, not dancing at all. His hands were under the gauze blouse.

"He's sublimating," Sam said. "Wishing she was you. Keep away from him, Regan. Not only because of Linda. Or Jake, either."

Why the warning? she wondered. And what was the truth about Sam? She decided, after a few beers had alleviated much of her earlier tension, to ask Kenny—who seemed the logical choice. He and Sam were inseparable.

"I'm getting to know my band, that's all," she explained, ignoring his wary look when she questioned him. "It seems to me that Sam has some, well, ax to grind."

Kenny nodded, running a hand through the unruly mass of russet hair which always looked as if it needed combing. After the wrestling match in the corner, it looked worse. But his gray eyes were serious, not in the least bleary from drink, and the dark blonde had long since switched her allegiance to the Country Band's drummer.

"Sam's our moral conscience on this trip," Kenny said. "He's forgotten how to have a good time himself, and he's damned if anyone else will. Ever since Polly, Sam's been evangelizing about decency to hide his own hurt."

"Who's Polly?"

"His ex-wife. She's done all right for herself; took what she

wanted from Sam—his contacts, his knowledge, his love—
and made herself a nice niche in the business. She's a singer,
Regan, bases herself mostly on the West Coast, where she lives
with husband number two . . . Big house in one of the canyons
around L.A.; he's a songwriter, works the movie studios—I
think he won an Oscar a few years back."

She could hear the distaste in Kenny's voice.

"Been warning you off me, hasn't he?"

"Well . . ."

"Sam wants to keep you from getting burned, nightingale.
Because he loves you." Then, bending his head, Kenny tilted
her chin at the same time, gently, slowly, his breath on her
cheek smelling of brandy. "We all do," he whispered. "Don't
you know, songbird . . . Men are going to be falling in love
with you all your life?" His hand trailed from the curve of her
ear to her throat. "And women"—his mouth came closer—
"are going to hate you for it."

At his touch, Regan's body grew languorous and warm.
Kenny would have kissed her if she hadn't moved, horrified
by her quick response—then seeing Sam, his dark eyes angered. Kenny saw him, too, his hands falling away from her.
"Oh, Henderson, *Christ*—"

"You've got money," was the only comment. "I told the
boys we'd find a bar open and con them out of another bottle
of gin—but you'd better hurry because closing is in ten minutes
around here."

Kenny was on his feet, running a hand through his hair,
tucking in his shirt, giving Regan a quick rueful smile. "All
right, Sam. All right, you win. For now."

She was still trying to check the staccato beat of her pulse
minutes after the two had left, when the Country Band's guitarist said, "Hey, Regan—you ever heard the one about the
guy on the road, he's been traveling for about four weeks,
missing his old lady. . . ."

Regan gritted her teeth and smiled through the bad joke.
She hated the stories, and particularly the expectation that she'd
like them as much as the other female visitors to the band's

suite. But she had to work with this group for the next few weeks. And she didn't want to go back to her own room and wonder why Kenny's arms around her had felt so good.

Away from the cardplaying and the softly insinuating jokes, the sexual conquests remembered from other tours, Regan subsided into a dark and gloomy silence, hunched into her seat in the rear of the bus. She wasn't sorry to leave Nashville after a second, even less enthusiastically received concert. Warming up for The Country Band? She had delivered the audience lukewarm, if that, and she would die on stage every time until they turned this bus north again.

Yet she almost welcomed the deep intimacy of the darkened bus, the already familiar smells and sights and sounds. Humming along the road in a green, eerie stillness, the dash lights softly glowing while a member of the band picked out tunes. Sometimes, Regan sang along when she couldn't fall asleep. The nights of driving were an interlude of peace—and hope: that she could see Jake again, one day sooner. That tomorrow, the next town, the next concert, the next warmup—they would like her again.

"Want something to eat?" Kenny was standing over her in the aisle, shifting his weight to keep his balance as the bus swayed along the road. "I've got potato chips, pastrami sandwich, two hamburgers, Doritos—" The constant supply of junk food.

"Pastrami, thanks." Regan took the sandwich, and Kenny dropped down beside her in the aisle seat. What she wouldn't give for a good meal! The pastrami wasn't bad tonight, but she'd never tasted anything like the hamburgers. Regan bought bags of fresh fruit, apples or bananas, and passed them out on the bus like candy. But everybody else seemed to prefer these lesser offerings. *Bad food,* Jake had said; and he was certainly right.

Regan munched on the sandwich, enjoying the quiet. Kenny was devouring both hamburgers and a bag of Doritos, so there was little talk. Peter, she could see up front, was poring over song scores by the pinpoint overhead light at one of the tables. The bus had been converted into more or less livable space— a few tables for eating and cardplaying and work; reclining seats; a small kitchenette; the tiny bathroom—all done in silver and navy blue. Most everyone else was sleeping, except for Sam—softly chording on the guitar, a song he'd been trying to finish, which he hoped she'd like. Just now, Regan couldn't tell, but she thought it might be too ... well, quiet. In Nashville, they didn't like quiet. At least not her brand. Hushed, she thought; like a hospital.

"Hey, nightingale," Kenny interrupted her thoughts about Jake. "How's your sex life?"

She had to laugh. Regan had been curled against the window, digesting her sandwich, resting her chin on one fist. At the absurd question, she straightened. "Nonexistent, thank you."

She tried to smile at him in the dark. Big, imposing body; that russet shock of unkempt hair.

"How's Jake?"

"Kenny, your connections aren't very subtle."

"Neither are the raindrops in your big green eyes," he said.

Regan sighed. It was the truth; why hide it? "Oh, Kenny— I don't know. The reports are all the same. Tonight, Sam passed on a message from Steven—that's my friend in New York, Jake's friend, too—that he's stronger, not having as much pain as before, but ... nothing else. I feel so frustrated that I can't see him. I wonder what he must be thinking, feeling." Regan took a shaky breath, her voice growing husky at the sympathetic look in Kenny's gray eyes. "Why do we have to spend two months in the Deep South, will you just tell me that? With no chance to see him at all?" Contracts, Regan answered herself; always the contracts. "If we're not jammed on this bus," she went on, "then we're crashing in some sleazy motel. . . ."

When she trailed off, unable to continue, Kenny had reached for her hand, wrapping it in both of his, running a thumb lightly over her palm.

"As you may have noticed," Kenny said, "life on the road gets lonely. A couple of good-lookers like you and me, for instance"—his voice dropped in the stillness to a near whisper—

"what do you say we save a few bucks... share a room next time we land?" His thumb stroking, his mouth near.

Regan looked at Kenny in shock. "I know this is going to sound puritanical"—like her surprise at finding Jake with Alyson?—"but what about Linda? The woman you love?"

Kenny drew back to study her face in the dim, greenish light. "The faithful type," he said. "But you're tempted, nightingale—aren't you? You want to find out what I'm like in the sack, don't you?" he pressed. "And believe me, I want to show you. I can see it on your face, you've been a long time without, and—"

"I see." Regan's tone hardened. "On the road we just forget about the people we love and make do with what's available...? Well, I'm sorry, but my answer's no. Kenny, don't you think Linda's just as lonesome when you're gone?"

She heard the edge in his voice. An excuse he couldn't possibly believe.

"Maybe she's not alone, so why should I be?"

"Is that why you fool around with girls you don't care about?"

"I care about you."

Regan turned away and stared out the window. How easy it would be to turn into Kenny's arms, in the deep intimacy of this nighttime bus, to kiss and hold and touch until every cell of her body felt on fire. But it wouldn't be the same. He wouldn't be Jake.

"Besides," Kenny argued after a silence, "the kid keeps Linda busy."

"Wasn't that thoughtful of you between tours?" Regan could hear Jake asking if she intended to be pregnant this last winter. Saw Jeb's blond head and baby grin, and felt ashamed of herself.

"There wasn't supposed to be another road trip," Kenny said, sounding sullen. "She's already making noises about pulling out because of this one." Then he fell silent for a few moments, presumably pondering his alternatives. Regan didn't know what to say, so she kept studying the road whipping past the dark windows until he said abruptly, "This is a long trip,

Regan, a lot of miles, a helluva lot more long, black nights alone. When you're high from a show and can't get down, can't sleep ... how do you blow the tension, songbird?"

But she wouldn't answer, thinking about the trials of the trip so far—only one of which was the pastrami sandwich churning in her stomach—and about the party she hadn't cared for in The Country Band's suite. Why did Kenny stay on the road if Linda wanted him with her? And then, Regan asked herself, why do I? Though she wasn't sure Jake wanted her now.

"Kenny, don't you miss home?" she asked softly.

"I haven't got a home."

"Don't you think about Jeb and Linda, and New York?"

He looked at her, surprised. "Oh, sure ... sure, we've got our problems, but most of the time we handle them okay." A silence. "You know, for a minute there I thought you meant ... my folks. Vermont; and the big house on Cedar Street. Funny," he said with a frown showing on his face in the dimness, "how you fixate when you're little. Home and family; my kid brother—he's a surgeon now; the car I got for my sixteenth birthday, a Pontiac monster—cracked it up a couple of months later. . . ."

"But you haven't been back in a long while?" Regan asked.

"No. Left when I was eighteen. Met Linda after I left school and started traveling, playing jazz gigs here and there. I guess you're right," he said. "She's where home is now." But there was that dark shadow again. Even though Regan felt sure that Kenny loved Linda and their child. Maybe *her* home would always be with Paul, Regan thought, warring with Alyson, trying to be accepted—and leaving his house with Jake that afternoon was nothing but a physical act. Maybe she'd never stop looking for a place to belong, to be loved. Are we alike, she wondered, as she felt the bus rocking over a rough stretch of road, Kenny Williams and me? Two homeless souls on a miserable trip to nowhere?

Gripping the seat back in front of her until the motion stopped, Regan glanced at Kenny, eyes closed and the frown gone. At first, she didn't see the hand-rolled cigarette dangling from his fingers until he lifted it to his mouth. Lost in her thoughts, she hadn't even heard him light it. Then she caught the sweet, heavy scent, so telltale. "Take a drag," he said, offering the joint. Regan shook her head. "Smoothes out all the wrinkles."

"It's also illegal." He opened one eye to look at her in disbelief. "Kenny, I don't want that stuff on my bus. I don't want it in the hotel, and I don't want to smell it on-stage."

"Hey, take it easy, what's a little grass—"

"It's against the law! How many ways can I say it?"

He was glaring at her now, wanting to hurt, his voice rising to match hers. "Well, let's see, songbird, you don't want to go to bed with me and you don't want to share my stash—so how *do* you get down after a show, Regan? I only know two ways, but—"

A hand slammed down hard on Kenny's shoulder. For such a small man, Peter looked very imposing. "Get back to your seat, Williams, before I decide to forget your paycheck—or better still, throw you out in the middle of this highway! *Then* you can worry where you'll be sleeping."

Kenny ignored him. "Not booze," he said deliberately to Regan, "not pills; no men, either . . . your bag's gotta be—"

"Leave her alone." It was Sam's voice now. Shrugging off Noel's hand, Kenny was on his feet in one lithe movement, curiously graceful for someone so solidly built. He towered over Sam, seemed to make two of Peter Noel.

"Hey, man, get off my case before—"

Sam's dark brown eyes drilled into Kenny. "You're too mellow to take a swing at me."

And to Regan's amazement, Kenny grinned like a little boy, following Henderson to another seat as if he were a tamed wildcat, gentle as a tabby. "I need something to drink," she heard him say, then the sound of a pop-tab snapping loudly on a beer can. Peter took Kenny's vacated seat.

"He didn't mean any harm, Peter," she said. "Kenny likes to talk, that's all."

"I heard the whole thing, and if you want to accuse me of

eavesdropping, go right ahead—but if you don't watch yourself, you're going to get in one hell of a jam . . . guys like
Williams, a night here and there, cheap thrills—"

"Peter, don't make a deal out of nothing," though the encounter had shaken her.

"He's a damn good drummer, Regan—but he scares hell
out of me. Some night he's going to shoot himself full of crap
and—"

"Drugs? Kenny?"

" 'Drugs and booze'—am I quoting him correctly?"

"I thought he wanted to shock me."

The dark shadow she glimpsed in Kenny Williams, as she
had seen it when he spoke of Vermont, his family . . . Had
drugs been the trouble Linda skirted that night at the Birdcage,
asking about Jake's tour? Regan lowered her eyes from Peter's,
looked glumly at the front of her faded green T-shirt, the soft
rise of her breasts through the material, at the worn Levi's she
had thrown on for the trip after tonight's show.

Peter said after a moment, "But he was giving you the truth
about himself, too. You think he really cares for that girl? Or
the kid they made? Hell, it's the other way around—She's nuts
about him, Regan, but Williams wouldn't care if it was three
in the bed. . . ." He kept his voice low. "You want to be the
third, Regan?"

Shaking her head, she crossed her arms protectively over
her chest, hiding from further blows. Hoping Peter would disappear. "Go away," she said, but he only sat there watching
her in the dimness while the soft strumming of Sam's guitar
filled the silence.

"You want to be perfect; then keep your mind—and the
rest of you—focused on the work. So far this tour stinks, as
we both know, but shagging Kenny Williams isn't going to
make it better!" Peter forced her to face him, his touch surprisingly strong, his dark eyes like two black marbles against
a pale face. "These are the best bookings, steady, that you're
likely to get just now. Manny's right. A week in Cleveland or
a month in Chicago won't get you the exposure, not enough
people see you. The single didn't make you a star, either, and

it isn't going to—though it helps. That goes for the album, too. Your sales are good, terribly good—but nobody's killing the next guy in line for the last ticket to hear you sing!"

Regan shivered at the diatribe. *How do I get perfect, Peter? Getting there,* he'd said. Then why did he criticize every time he opened his mouth, as if he hated her? She almost wished she had crawled into the rear seat with Kenny and let him hold her; never said a word about loyalty or provoked the argument about the grass. Never started thinking about Jake. What did Peter want from her? She was trying as hard as she could, and still—

"I'll do my job," Regan murmured. "Don't worry about me."

She hugged herself to keep from shaking, from crying; drew her knees up under her chin for added protection, watching Peter who was watching her. "I'll worry." He stood in the swaying bus to remove his worn tweed jacket. "It's my nature," tucking it around her shoulders like an apology. "Get some sleep. Memphis is waiting with a twenty-one-gun salute. Maybe even a clean motel room," he added, "and a halfway decent steak."

Memphis hated her. Regan—ready to sing the next night, already onstage dressed in sinuous, smoky-gray silk crepe de Chine with a plunge front and a pair of deep side slits that showed her thighs when she moved—felt hostility emanating toward her in waves from the seated audience. She should have worn her hair down, not loosely piled at the crown of her head, stray tendrils casually escaping. Everything simpler. My God, she was warming up for a country group here, not the Metropolitan Opera Company. Why hadn't she worn a long skirt and blouse instead? But she had wanted to feel good for a change, and the gray crepe de Chine made her feel like a million dollars.

Regan sighed inwardly, and pasted the brilliant smile on her lips. She lifted her head and flicked the microphone cord out behind her. The show of confidence was counterfeit, but she was being paid to sing. And sing, by heaven, she would.

She sang to a constant, low level of superfluous noise: paper-rustling, whisperings, the usual coughs and throat-clearings, a few latecomers who loudly excused themselves as they crawled over other people in the row, even some catcalls. In the last chorus of the love song, she heard shouted, "Take it off, honey—Let's see what you got!"

When she had finished, Regan stood stunned by the words, and the halfhearted applause, a smattering instead of a storm. She swallowed the huge lump of disappointment in her throat, stuck there like a giant fish bone. *I knew they hated me. I knew as soon as I walked onto the stage, before the music started. They didn't like her; and they never would.*

Regan came offstage, followed by the band. Peter, Sam, Kenny; the other sidemen, a bassist and the second guitar player. "It's okay, songbird, you were fine, the last song really got 'em, don't worry about it, kid, in New Orleans you'll be a hit." But she didn't stop to see who was talking. Their words ran together in one meaningless stream as Regan swept past the boys from The Country Band, grinning, touching her arm, saying, "Thanks," as if nothing horrid had happened. *Thanks for what?* she asked silently. *Making your job that much easier tonight? After Regan Reilly, anyone would look good. For what?*

"Regan . . . ?"

"Don't talk to me," she said, her face held together—nose and eyes, cheekbones and mouth—by sheer effort of will. "Don't say a word."

Be by myself, Regan chanted inwardly. *On my own, with the door to my single room shut tight and locked behind me.*

Take it off, honey, let's see what you got.

Stripping off the smoke-gray gown, Regan let it slither to the dingy carpet. A bath, she thought, until she could forget tonight, tomorrow—even the party starting next door, already loud with male laughter and music. A very hot bath.

Letting the faucets run full-blast, Regan sank into the steaming water before the tub was half filled. Her skin tingled from the heat; she felt her muscles begin to relax. Closing her eyes, she let her hair slip into the bath water, wetting and weighting the silken mass. *Where am I going?* she asked herself.

Regan opened her eyes to hunt for the soap. *On a wild goose chase,* smiling in spite of tonight's misery. Chasing fame. You might as well be standing in front of a mirror, Regan Reilly, holding a hairbrush for a microphone. At the cloudy glass, she could at least imagine that people liked her. That she was good enough. The old doubt again, but what else could she—

Regan splashed upright in the tub. "Ohhh! Oh, my God!"

She was staring straight at a horror show. In the moist environment of the steamy bathroom, a creature of dampness was emerging from behind the medicine cabinet on the wall by the tub. One giant feeler first, then the other. Regan's heart pounded in her naked breast. A body, shiny and black and endless, wearing a hard-crusted shell. Legs, and more legs. Regan thrashed to her feet, water streaming from her body, soaking the gray bath mat as she hit the floor, trailed water over the cracked tiles into the bedroom, puddles of revulsion. *My God, my God . . .*

Just a water bug, you've seen them in New York. *Just a water bug . . . ?!* She grabbed for a shoe from under the bed. Not a high-heeled slipper or tonight's silver sandal. A substantial, heavy leather walking shoe for jeans, for hiking . . . for killing. She ran back into the bathroom. The thing had tumbled to the floor. With one hand clapped over her mouth to stifle a shriek of fear, Regan slammed the shoe at the black bug. Hitting, hitting, flattening, pulverizing. She murdered it a thousand times over, unable to stop, unable to look when she had done.

What was I killing? she asked herself. Regan left the shoe over the body, then turned on every light in the two rooms and searched the place for more. Thank God, nothing. She drained the water from the tub, gingerly pulling the plug, not wanting to touch anything, and, naked, dragged herself to bed, shaking out all the covers first. Shaking Raggedy Ann, too. Just in case. Contamination. Manny's bookings; the people who thought she was a stripper, not a singer; The Country Band who needed the wrong music; her own hopelessness. . . . Kill it, how could she kill it? Not as easy as a bug.

Desperately, she wanted to call Jake. But she would only get the floor nurse again, nothing more. Regan rolled over in bed, pulling the covers to her shoulders, leaning her cheek against Raggedy Ann's cloth body. She could hear the rumble of men's voices through the wall, the thump of bass and drum in the music, a high, shrill, feminine laugh. *A natural,* Regan thought; a *phenomenon,* a *superstar.* A washout.

She felt the tears begin to come. She'd thought that touring with the band would be different from Jake's isolation on the road; easier, even fun. But all she felt was lonely and afraid. What if she kept failing and never got a better tour, another song to record . . . never became a headliner herself? Where would she go then?

Regan soaked the doll with giant tears, making up for all the years in Paul's house when she wouldn't cry. "Poor Raggy," she crooned; then the tears became sobs—loud, wrenching sobs that tore her heart out. *Where's that heart of stone when I need it most? But no, hers must be like Raggedy Ann's, just a lump of cotton batting, sodden and—*

"Regan?" There was an insistent pounding at the door to her room. "Regan, it's Kenny. Let me in."

She stayed still, one arm wound around the doll, her face pressed to the cloth pinafore, warm and wet. "Go away, Kenny," she whispered hoarsely. She wondered if he was drunk. The party blared from his room, so much louder now that she guessed the door was standing open.

"Come on, nightingale."

"Let her be, Williams."

"The chick doesn't want your company, Kenny—" Regan heard shuffling, milling in the hall. She raised on an elbow, listening to the scuffle. "Christ, what do you think I am? The lady's crying her eyes out and I—"

"Girls like to cry. For them it's better than a fistfight."

"You want a fight? You got it, come on, come on—" At the sound of breaking glass, Regan ripped the white top sheet from the bed, wrapping it around her as she ran.

The door opened onto a crowded scene. Her eyes saw every one of her own band, a couple of sleepy members from The Country Band, and their leader, Clive Dixon. In the center of the group—all of whom looked slightly confused, as if they didn't know whether to be amused or alarmed—Regan spied Kenny and Sam. Kenny had obviously been holding a beer bottle when he knocked at her door. He had smashed it against the wall, breaking the neck off, and the jagged glass shone in the light. There was blood running down his hand, but he didn't seem to notice or care.

"You can't leave it alone, can you?" Sam was taunting. "You got to get some for yourself . . . well, let me tell you, Kenny—two musicians in one family is nothing but hell! How's it going to work, you tell me that—always in a contest, both of you: that's how it would be, man, always wondering who's best!"

Kenny's voice was a blind shout of rage. "We all know who came out first in your house, Sam! Just because your woman got herself a big name and a new guy to match—" He raised his arm.

"Sam! Kenny!" Regan threw herself between them, oblivious of danger from the brandished beer bottle. "My God, stop, both of you!"

Silence. Kenny, staring into her white face as if he didn't know who she was. Sam, chastened and looking at the wall. Peter Noel, standing in the door to his own room, directly across from Regan's, wearing an I-told-you-so look meant for her alone. The others, shuffling away as they were told, mumbling, muttering. The shattered bottle dropping to the floor.

It was Sam who broke the eerie stillness. "What are we doing?" he asked in a tone of wonder.

"I'm sorry, man," Kenny answered. Trickles of blood ran from the ends of his fingers onto the rug. "She was crying, that's all. I swear."

"You were right. I was preaching again, and—besides, I was never good enough for Polly."

"That's not true, Sam. She wasn't good enough for you, she—" Kenny's voice broke. "You're my best friend. . . . Sam?"

"Yeah. Yeah, sure . . . I'm your best friend."

Peter Noel cleared his throat. "Kenny, you take the extra bed in my room tonight. Come on, I think I've got some Band-Aids somewhere for that hand." Then he looked straight at Regan. "Almost every band I've played with has been broken up by its girl singer. It isn't going to happen this time."

Regan crawled back into bed, aching with reaction as if she'd had the flu for a week. *Two musicians,* she heard Sam say. Someone might have gotten killed tonight—not only a harmless water bug. *What are we doing?* Kenny's face, and Sam's. Both of them as confused by their fight as she had been by the last weeks of failure. Hadn't Jake tried to tell her about going on the road? Two musicians, Regan thought. *It's not a competition,* she had told him. Oh Jake, Jake . . . *what are we going to do with all the long, black nights?* With Jake, so broken now; as broken as she felt herself.

Chapter 14

"You and me," Clive Dixon said at last, "got to have ourselves a little talk."

Regan's spirits sank even farther toward her shoes. After two weeks of her warming up for his Country Band, it must have been just as obvious to him that she was all but dying onstage every night. Except for the way he kept drawing the vowel out in the middle of her name like a pig call, Regan liked him. A soft-bellied man given to two-day growths of beard, runover cowboy boots and floppy Stetsons—a style Kenny had immediately taken for his own—Dixon wore a diamond horseshoe ring on his little finger and capped his attire with fringed Western shirts in Day-Glo colors. Regan couldn't decide whether these outfits were a projection of an image or a true manifestation of Clive's taste. But she felt certain he was going to read her the riot act about her work, and she was sorry to have disappointed him, too.

"I know, Clive," she said. "If your fans weren't so eager to see you and the boys, there'd be nobody left in the seats when I finished." She stared at his blank expression unhappily. "I'm perfectly willing to tear up the contracts if you are, call Manny, and—"

"Whoa, hold up there!" Clive's big hand shot into the air. He motioned her to a chair in his dressing room, which was

a strangely artful clutter of shirts, trousers, string ties, mismatched boots, and various musical instruments, both in and
out of cases. Regan sat down too hard on the straight wooden
chair, wanting instantly to rub her bruised bottom.

"Now, look here, Regan——" Clive grabbed a second chair,
turning it around and straddling the seat. "When me and the
boys began our first trip, we was way outa place, *whooee*—
playin' for a whole string of burlesque joints, you know what
I mean"—with a brief pause until she nodded, wondering why
she felt like smiling when she was about to lose her job. "Every
night we'd roll in and set up and pound out music that nobody
wanted to hear because, hell, they weren't there for no country
jug band—at that time—no, they just wanted to see those
pudgy little girls take off they clothes."

Regan gave in to the smile.

"That's better, honey." He patted her hand with one of his,
big and soft. "No need to look so miserable scared, Clive ain't
gonna tear you up and feed you to his dogs for dinner . . . now
you listen, here. What is the matter is simply this, sugar: you
got a beautiful voice and the rest to go with it, honey; you
can't help but be a big-time star, smart little girl like you . . .
but you are singin' above all these people's heads, that's all."

"I don't know how else to sing, Clive."

"Sure you do. What you need is a little variation on a theme.
Love's a fine topic, you see, but my kind of people—which
is who we are playin' to—they want to hear about cheatin'
love, no-good love, three mouths to feed, and they daddy's
run off with some low-down woman, left this little gal alone—
They want to suffer, want to cry a bit."

Regan thought for a moment.

"You a woman, ain't you?" Clive Dixon's small, bright eyes
slipped over her. "Honey, there's not a woman alive hasn't
been done dirt by some man, some time or other—and come
to think, it prob'ly works the other way too." He grinned at
her. "I know it did for me, first time around; don't try to tell
me you ain't never been in love yourself and can't sing about
how it hurts just as easy as you can sing about how it feels

good, sugar—even if somebody let on to me this mornin' that you just got a nineteenth birthday comin' up soon."

"I've been in love, Clive," Regan murmured, feeling the familiar lump in her throat when she started to dwell on thoughts of Jake.

"Then you home free, sugar," he told her. "It's the human condition, as they say." Then he leaned over the chair and kissed her soundly on the cheek. "You know, it's gettin' to the point in my life where I take offense at someone bein' so young. . . . Except you're so pretty, honey, I can't get mad at you." Dixon stood up, ending the meeting. "You let me see what I can do, Regan. I just may get me some bright ideas where you're concerned."

It was Regan's turn to plant a kiss on Clive's whiskered jaw.

"Thank you, Clive. Most of all, for patience."

On the bus from Mobile to Birmingham, Regan celebrated her birthday, complete with gooey chocolate cake and vanilla ice-cream cups. There were gifts, too, mostly novelties, though there were a few serious ones. A warm, ivory fisherman's sweater, hand-knit, for cool nights near the ocean when they got there, and on the Gulf of Mexico. A full-color picture of the band, with Linda and Jeb posed in front.

In the days following what would always be referred to in Regan's troupe as "the beer bottle incident," Regan had been forced to make a basic decision. She didn't want to break up the band or the road trip—as Peter seemed to expect—but she couldn't keep dancing away from Kenny, either. The placing of one telephone call had eased her mind.

"Kenny's morale is as low as the rest of ours," she'd said, "but I can only import one wife. Please come, Linda."

The hesitation had been perfunctory, Regan felt. "He won't quit to be with us. At least if we come along, I can keep an eye on him."

On the first of May, Linda and Jeb had joined the busload of musicians on their thus-far unsuccessful odyssey through the South. Regan was glad to have another woman on tour, a civilizing influence—and, perhaps in time, a friend.

Now, she rooted through the rest of her birthday presents, laughing at the huge box of Kleenex someone had bought "for your next crying jag" and, from Kenny, a rubber chicken with red-orange claws and beak, a tag attached to its scrawny neck: *"What are we going to do?"* Regan read aloud, reducing the party to gales of laughter again, Kenny's loudest of all.

After his fight with Sam, the phrase had become standard with the band. In the middle of rehearsal, on the bus at night— even when someone had lost a wallet between Memphis and Mobile—the cry would go up, "'What are we going to do?" followed by "Chicken Little, the sky is falling!"

She grinned at the ridiculous gift, knowing at the same time she'd always treasure it.

"Nobody ever had a nicer nineteenth birthday," Regan said, retiring with her booty to the rear of the bus. She sat across from Linda and Kenny and thought she could see how relaxed Kenny had become. Hearing him talk softly to Jeb as Linda tried to get him to sleep on the facing seat, Regan felt pangs of near-jealousy again: that they were together, loving, while she still relied on Steven's reports—most recently, that Jake had been allowed a wheelchair. She counted the days until the tour swung close enough to New York so she could see him again.

Regan covered herself with the new sweater because she felt chilled, and remembered her talk with Clive Dixon so she wouldn't become depressed. She hoped he came up with that bright idea. She didn't have one herself.

Groaning inwardly, Regan shifted in her seat, striking up a conversation with Linda, who had relinquished Jeb to his father. It was female talk, and Kenny didn't bother to listen as Regan noted Linda's attractive skirt and blouse, matching soft cotton in a batik print.

"Oh, thank you," Linda said with a shy downward glance at the outfit. "I made it myself. I sew a lot of my own clothes, Regan—not only to save money, but because I like my workmanship much better than that I find in the stores . . . except for the big-name designers I can't afford."

Regan looked at her own crisp navy-and-white sundress, peeking out from under the sweater she'd used for a cover. "Lucky you," she said. "I paid more than I wanted to for this, and it can't have ten dollars' worth of fabric in it."

Linda's smile was understanding. "If I can get Kenny to part with some money, Regan, we'll pick up a used sewing machine in Birmingham. I'd be glad to run up a few things for you, and"—with a quick glance across the aisle—"with a figure like yours, the design and fitting will be easy."

"Money?" Kenny opened one eye and gave his wife a jaundiced stare. "Who's spending my hard-earned money?" with a grin.

"Two women," Linda answered, smiling at Regan. "This man is a master at selective listening, hears only what he wants to. . . . Hand Jeb to me, Ken, and I'll get him back to sleep so you can rest, too."

How easy they were together, Regan thought. Kenny obviously adored his son, and seemed good to Linda, too.

Regan wondered what had prompted him to chase after her in the first weeks of travel; why Sam had so readily assumed the worst. Loneliness? The constant pressures of the road? *Proximity?* Jake's word for Manny and herself. Some truth to it, she supposed.

Regan glanced at Linda, cozy with the baby in her arms and her dark head on Kenny's shoulder. At least she could be proud of finding a solution to one problem.

Regan's thoughts were interrupted by the low, clear sound. "Linda?" She leaned over, gently shaking the other girl's arm. "What is that you're singing?" A pair of startled eyes met Regan's; then the shadow of a smile.

"I was putting myself to sleep, too," Linda said, running a hand over Jeb's blond hair and straightening from Kenny's shoulder. Sam had begun, from his seat farther toward the front of the bus, to pick out the tune—his guitar muted, just audible above the soft snores of sleeping bodies—as Linda said, "A folk song from the sixties. Simon and Garfunkel. . . . I guess the tour made me think of it."

Kenny sat up with a yawn, stretching. "She knows every song ever written, Regan. She was going to be a singer herself."

"I was not."

"Until you met me . . ." He kissed her quickly on the mouth. "And surrendered your ambitions, too."

"Oh, Kenny—"

Blushing in the dim light, Linda turned toward Regan, easing Jeb into a new position close against her chest. When she began to sing again, Kenny voiced the harmony, soft, husky— he wasn't bad himself—pressing his cheek to Linda's temple. Regan recalled the words, too, adding a third part, and the song about being on the road, alone, welled up inside her. Missing someone, she thought, missing him so badly you could scarcely eat or sleep; wondering, always wondering, if he was missing you, too.

Her throat constricted. Love was a fine subject, she agreed with Clive—but so was loneliness. When the final chorus of the sweet-sad song had ended, she called out softly, "Sam? Tap Peter on the shoulder for me, will you? I think Linda's just turned the rest of this tour around for us."

The new medley, mostly of folk songs about the road, went over well. Dixon told her, "That's better, sugar. . . . Now you gettin' the idea. That last little ditty is plain sassy with a few tears wrung in for good measure, and it's a fine lead-in to our first number, too," though Regan didn't feel completely satisfied. Still, hadn't the Birmingham audience sprinkled in a few whistles—not related to a striptease—with the applause?

Maybe she would survive this tour after all and not be relegated at the age of nineteen to oblivion. After Birmingham came Jacksonville, then Tampa and New Orleans; a second stop in Nashville, on to Louisville, Cincinnati, Columbus, Pittsburgh, Harrisburg . . . and at last, New York.

If Kenny and Linda had come through trouble still loving each other, why couldn't she and Jake? If the tour could find its way through the darkness, too . . . why not?

* * *

On a dreary, leaden late afternoon that threatened Tampa with a brief, tropical storm before showtime, Regan slouched in her dressing room, staring at the vanity mirror. She felt exhausted from the day's travel. The bus had left Jacksonville that morning after two successful concerts, but the weather, even in air conditioning, had been hot and humid, and the highway had shimmered with waves of heat. Now, she needed a shower and shampoo, then something light to eat before she sang—but Regan couldn't move from her chair.

On the bus Jeb had been oddly fussy all afternoon, was screaming his head off by the time he and Linda were dropped at the hotel; and nobody had gotten much rest. "Sorry you invited the barbarian to keep you company?" Kenny had asked under his breath as they disembarked in front of the auditorium. "Or should I say—to keep you safe from temptation?" She wasn't sorry; but she didn't feel like singing in three hours, either.

Regan was yawning at her reflection in the mirror when someone knocked at the door. She supposed it might be Sam or Kenny, wondering if she wanted to eat; but a stranger stood in the hallway.

"Miss Reilly?" He looked like a purebred country boy, complete with freckles, a cowlick in his sandy-red hair, and large rawboned hands, one of which clutched a cheap black guitar case of imitation leather. But if he's straight off the farm, Regan wondered, why is he wearing designer jeans and a famous-label polo shirt? Regan could feel the anxiety radiating from him.

"Yes," she said. "Is there something I can do for you?"

She was sure in that instant that she'd seen him somewhere before. He looked to be about her age, but—

"I hope it's the other way around." Swallowing hard, he pulled a piece of paper from his pocket. "I have a note for you."

"Regan"—she could almost hear the drawn-out sound of the *e*—"this here is the brightest notion I ever had in my life! Clive."

She smiled at the boy, inviting him into the dressing room, watching in bewilderment as he removed a battered guitar from the scarred case, sat himself on her vacated chair by the dressing table, and began to adjust the strings with a delicate touch. "This used to be my dad's," he explained with a wide, uncertain smile before he began to play.

"But this is mine," he told her. "I hope—I hope you like it."

Regan stood as still as marble, her arms folded over her chest, while the music filled the small room and the boy's surprising voice offered the words like a priceless gift. My God, she thought in wonder, watching his eyes, seeing the same emotion she felt as he sang clearly, tenderly, with only a trace of soft Virginia drawl. A song of love and betrayal and the will to survive—the song Clive had told her she needed. A tough song, a gentle song, a woman's song. It was different from "All The Words I Know," not as lyrical but with a touch of (Yes, Clive) "sass"; and it affected Regan every bit as strongly as Jake's song had the first time she'd heard it. It touched her heart as much.

When the boy had ended the coda, Regan looked up from an intense study of his fingers on the guitar strings, their movements strangely graceful, to find Kenny and Sam standing just outside the door. The three of them began to grin like monkeys, and then the dressing room filled, not with music, but with exultation. Sam's came first.

"Regan, this is sensational stuff!"

"Just what we've needed—" Kenny began.

"A crossover," Regan cut him off. "A crossover hit!"

With this song, they would capture two markets at once. The traditional pop enthusiasts and the country people, too. If she was accepted by both, the sky for sales was the only limit!

Kenny's voice drew her thoughts back. "Regan, *I love this thing!* Songbird, don't you love it?"

Sam tried out the title. "'Nashville Nights,'" he said, and then over again. "It's gold for sure, folks."

"Kind of ironic, isn't it?" Regan asked. "I was miserable there." She subsided against Kenny, leaning in his arms, her back against his broad chest, the strong, sure beat of his heart.

"I'm sorry," she apologized with a smile from warm, green eyes, feeling guilty that the composer of the song she liked so much had been overlooked in the last few moments. "As you can see, we all like what you've written *very much,* and—oh, I'm sorry again, but I didn't catch your name."

She recognized his grin, though. And then, the rest wasn't really necessary. The note, either.

"Clive Dixon, Junior," the boy said. "By way of Virginia . . . and Yale University."

"Smart kid," Kenny pronounced that evening after the show. "That's the brightest idea Clive ever had—on two counts."

"Imagine, his father calling him at school and telling him—"

"'I got this pretty little gal on tour with me, needs some help in a hurry,'" Kenny finished with a laugh, imitating Clive perfectly. Lying beside him on the big hotel-room bed, Regan grinned first at Kenny, then at Linda.

"Sing it again," she asked, moving in time to the beat as she carefully laid out dress-pattern pieces of tissue on the carpet.

Regan had decided she needed a dress that didn't shout "New York nightclub" the minute she came onstage. If she wore the eyelet-ruffled blouse from the first weeks at the Birdcage with this new dark green gingham pinafore—long and gracefully cut—and the loden swatch of grosgrain ribbon in her hair, holding it back from her face but letting the mass of silk lie against her spine to the waist—yes, maybe the "Homeward Bound" medley would work even better, and they would love the new song.

"I think we should call it 'Country Torch,'" Regan said suddenly, bringing a smile to Linda's lips. "Don't you think so, Kenny?"

His hand held hers between them, but Linda didn't seem to mind.

Besides, Regan thought, with Jeb toddling around the room making an inspection tour of every surface he could reach and fussing when he couldn't, they were well-chaperoned. Kenny's eyes were closed as he spoke, and he was wearing his favorite after-hours attire: jeans, a pair of scuffed Wellington boots ("I've owned them for ten years, what do you expect?"), and an equally well-worn cowboy hat, now low over his forehead. No shirt, only an expanse of muscle and skin.

"I think we just call it number one on the charts for sixteen weeks, how's that?"

"Catchy," Regan said.

Linda laughed, too. "And having an Ivy League music major supplying custom material for your act," she said, "must mean you're really on the way." Then she warded off Jeb's approach as he tried to step across the fabric on the floor. "No, darling, you'll tear the paper, you can't walk here, *Jeb, please*"—when he began to whimper—"Mommy's busy now."

Great teardrops welled in the little boy's eyes.

"Oh, I wish he'd sleep for a while," Linda moaned, picking him up and rocking him in her arms. "The whole day howling on the bus . . . you'd think he'd collapse—Kenny, would you take him for me?"

But Regan sat up first, drawing her robe more tightly around her and securing the tie belt. "I'll be glad to hold him, Linda." She knew exactly how to distract Jeb from his misery. "Come on, sweetheart," Regan crooned to him. "There's somebody I want you to meet." Smiling, she got off the bed. Raggedy Ann, she thought. The doll had soothed more than a few tears in the past. But Linda objected, "You haven't heard the rest, Regan. I'm taking him to a doctor in the morning. I think it might be strep throat. If Kenny picks up the bug, he can take penicillin and still play drums—but I wouldn't want to risk your voice."

Regan reached for the baby, anyway. "Nonsense," she said. "We're all breathing the same air."

By the time Regan left the wings of the auditorium and took her place before the microphone in New Orleans, her temperature had climbed to 102°. The lights were blinding, and the audience seemed to weave in front of her as if they were swaying to the music even before it began. "You all right?" she heard Kenny whisper behind her, but Regan only nodded her head.

She had already sprayed her raging throat with a cooling, medicinal mist; taken three aspirin, which gave her stomach pains but might kill the fever; and patiently suffered the mentholated ointment Linda had slathered on her chest before she dressed. Its vapor wafted upward into her nostrils now. Thank heaven, she was standing on the stage, or the audience would think her choice of perfume for the evening most unusual.

Peter took his place at the piano; gave the signal. The house-lights dimmed. The spotlight, a soft rose, fell on Regan as she switched the microphone cord out behind her, freeing it from the green gingham fullness of her skirt. Flushed from fever, she knew she looked unnaturally radiant. A picture of country wholesomeness, freshness, innocence. With her left hand, Regan lifted the heavy mass of her hair, and with a light toss of her head (less than she wanted, but more than enough to make her dizzy), set the silken tresses shimmering down her back, catching the light.

She had saved Jake's song for next to last, ending the final chorus with a terrific surge of natural feeling, wanting him to be there, to know how much she cared.

". . . 'but of all the words I know, the only one I care to know is you.' . . ."

Soon, my love, she willed the thought to him on the last husky, trembling note, *soon I'll see you again.* The thrill of emotion ran down her back as if it were Jake's touch, his loving hand.

Catching her bottom lip between her teeth, Regan bent her head over the microphone as she finished, bowing to the applause, hearing the shrill whistles from the balcony of the red and gold auditorium.

"Give me just a moment, please," before lifting her head to smile tremulously at the footlights. When at last she spoke, her voice had steadied again. But her head still swam with fever and longing.

"Ladies and gentlemen, this next song is equally special. It was written for me, too, by a young man of exceptional talent. May I share with you now for the first time 'Nashville Nights' by Clive Dixon, Junior." Regan sent a smile toward the wings where Clive and his son stood together, grinning with pride . . . and apprehension.

They needn't have worried. As she had fully expected, the crowd loved the crossover ballad.

Regan, taking her bows to a torrent of clapping and shouting, acknowledged the songwriter. Then suddenly, she felt her arm seized by Clive Senior, who detained her. Speaking into the microphone, he said clearly, "Gentlemen and ladies, let's hear it again for *Regan Reilly* . . . who has just won herself a first, genuine gold record!" He turned her toward him, planting a sound kiss on Regan's cheek as a chill of disbelief flashed down her spine, and the applause thundered. "Thank you, little lady . . . it's been a pleasure."

"Thank you, Clive. Oh—thank you!"

Had she taken another bow? She didn't know. In a flush of fever and excitement, Regan ran offstage, straight into Manny Bertelli's waiting arms. "Manny, oh Manny! What are you doing here? Is it true?"

"You know it is." He was laughing, hugging her tightly to him. "Sweet, my God, what's all this complaining? You knocked 'em off the seats tonight—Listen, they're still wild out there"—though Clive and the boys had begun to play, and were toning down the noise at last. "Come on, let me look at you—"

Regan squirmed inwardly at the appraisal from her manager. She didn't want to encourage Bertelli, but she wouldn't alienate him, either. When Manny bent to her, Regan turned her head slightly. She had missed him, too—or was it only that she missed New York and the familiar? Gradually, she eased away from the kiss, which hadn't quite met her lips, and encountered Kenny's dark gray gaze. "Congratulations, songbird," as he ·passed, managing to jostle Manny's shoulder.

"You better keep your mouth to yourself, Manny," he added under his breath, "or the maestro's going to chain her to a wall back home and kill your fat percentage."

"What the hell's eating him?"

Regan followed Manny's glare toward Kenny's back.

"The boys have become very protective of me in your absence," she said pertly, which proved true enough as first Sam, then Peter and the other members of the band filed past, offering their congratulations, pressing her hand, kissing her cheek. But did Kenny still think there could be something between them?

"Come on, boss," Regan said, "my poor inflamed throat could certainly use some champagne—also, my soaring ego." She took a deep breath that racked her chest with pain. "Manny, a *gold record!*"

"Motto of the management," he told her with a grin. "We aim to please," and he did look a sight for sore eyes, in a well-cut beige summer suit. "But business first, sweet. There's someone I want you to meet." He was drawing her toward a woman with upswept platinum-blond hair, theatrical makeup, and a bright red dress.

Regan began to feel uncomfortable, not just sick. The woman was holding a notebook and pen, her black silk evening purse tucked under the other arm. A pair of brilliant blue eyes assessed Regan. A look like a vulture's.

She saw us kissing, was Regan's first thought. But the kiss hadn't meant anything beyond greeting and celebration.

Regan's head throbbed with pain. Why hadn't Manny coached her beforehand? She wasn't experienced at interviews; she'd only done a few. In the years ahead, Regan would know exactly how to deal with publicity in both its benign and malignant forms. Even now, she sensed which of the two she was facing. But what was she supposed to say? How could she answer this woman's predatory smile?

"Sweet, this is one of Ronnie Vance's stringers—you know her celebrity show from Hollywood, don't you?" Manny pulled Regan close, one arm around her shoulder, his fingers caressing her skin. "She'd like a few words. Let's give her something quotable, can't we?"

Chapter 15

"Close sources in New Orleans report that the latest singing rage, the oh-so-beautiful Regan Reilly, is far more than friends with her charismatic manager. When asked if the two will sing a very special song together, Bertelli replied, 'We're still negotiating' . . . but my dears—do I hear wedding bells? From Hollywood, this is—"

Veronica Vance signed off. The news returned. Jake lay without moving, concentrating on the pulses that threatened to shatter throughout his body.

Nobody's going to stop you, are they? And Bertelli could function in more than one capacity. Manager, friend, the father she was missing, star-maker . . . *lover.* Hadn't he known that months ago at the Birdcage? Even in the parking lot at Steven's, staring helplessly after Bertelli's limousine? *Don't try to talk yet, Jake . . . there's time.*

He tried to find excuses for her, feeling like a fool. He knew from Steven that she'd gone on tour, that she'd sent a ton of mail he couldn't read, having been—so to speak—under the influence most of the time. Until a few days ago, he hadn't cared. He still hurt like hell, but he'd been dealing with the pain on an increasingly rational basis. He even remembered gliding through the hallways yesterday in the wheelchair pushed by Denise, his nurse. He'd asked for less medication. A mixed blessing, Jake decided. The fact was, Regan wasn't here and there were no excuses.

Christ, how long had she and Bertelli been making it?

Jake nudged the button for the bedside light, plunging the room into darkness. Lucky it hadn't been a switch, or he would have had to call someone to turn it for him. *This is how it feels,* he thought, *when the bottom of the world drops out.*

"Jake, I'm going off duty now. Do you want anything?"

Denise's pert dark head poked in at his door. Don't look at her, don't let her see. Staring at her in silence, grateful for the darkness, Jake recalled the session with his doctor earlier that day. It had been bothering him ever since; not merely because the surgeon gave him no better than even chances: he'd already decided that 50–50 could as easily mean performing again as not. It was what he had to believe.

No, what puzzled him was Steiner's maddening Swiss coolness as he'd unwrapped Jake's bandages, inspecting the raw flesh. "Is better, yes," the doctor had pronounced. "But I will improve on this."

He'd tried not to wince while Steiner rotated, probed and prodded. "I hope so. I'll be playing piano the rest of my life just to pay your bill."

"The fee has been taken care of."

Jake's heart had jolted in shock. "By whom?"

"A friend . . . who wishes to remain anonymous."

Now, Jake's gaze sharpened as Denise repeated her question from the doorway. "Do you need something before I go?"

"Denise, who has financial responsibility for me? A top-notch plastic surgeon from Geneva doesn't work for free, but when I asked Steiner, he clammed up." If his mother had been given the same preferential treatment, Jake thought, she might still be alive . . . and if he hadn't betrayed her. He went on, "I've got to know, Denise," pleading with his eyes.

She took a moment to answer. "Well, I do know a few people in Accounting and Medical Records." She studied him, squinting against the dimness in the room. "But what happens if I lose my job for this?"

His heart was pounding furiously. "I'd take you with me

on tour and support you in the style to which you would like
to become accustomed."

"You get a helluva long way on charm, you know that?"
She arched an eyebrow at him. "I'll see what I can do, Jake."

He looked after her as she turned, showing him a trim behind
under the white nylon of her uniform. Good legs, too. A sure
sign of recovery, he'd thought only yesterday. But now, the
pain flashed through him again and he wasn't that certain.
Then he realized it was a different kind of pain.

And it got worse. Fifteen minutes later, in the nighttime
stillness that prevailed on the corridor, Denise slipped back
into his room. But long after she had disappeared for the second
time, leaving him alone with the information, he heard the
name tolling, clanging against the silence, like a death knell
deep inside him.

"Manny Bertelli." *Manny Bertelli. Manny Bertelli.*

He'd come up against a wall of brick. But wait, Bertelli
would never have paid a nickel for him; so Regan must have
talked him into it, salving her conscience. And Bertelli's, too?
The knowledge seemed to slam him against that wall.

Well, he'd never take another penny from either of them!
For the first time, Jake regretted signing away his rights to the
love song he'd written for Regan. The rights to financial security. If only he hadn't been so hasty . . . if only he had known
how brief her love for him would prove.

But at least she knew better than to drag out something that
should have ended the day he left on tour; while he'd made a
damn fool of himself for six more months. Hell, she was right.
Why get hung up on a woman? Jake asked himself. He never
had before. Why Regan, then?

I'll tell you why, he answered. Listen to the silky sound of
her voice, singing; or whispering to him in the night. Feel the
satin flesh, the soft swell of her breasts, the taut slenderness
of waist, that slightest rounding of her hips, still slim as a
boy's, the delicate anklebones like finest china, they ought to
be insured. Like the tawny fall of hair so fragrant in his nostrils,
and the misty green feline eyes. Her smile, her laugh, the way

she tipped her chin when she knew a fight was coming...a fight she didn't intend to lose.

Why fight it? For a little while, their lives had joined, his with Regan's; their paths had been similar before her career took off in the opposite direction. In the stillness now of midnight, he remembered what he had said to Regan in the beginning—promising help. But hadn't he also told her that he'd flunked physics? So how in hell did he ever hope to keep that rocket on the proper trajectory all the way to the moon?

But, Christ—his mind kept struggling with the truth—did she really think she could pay him for loving her?

The next night, Steven found Jake staring at the ceiling.

"Jake, Regan won't marry him," he began. "I won't believe for a second that she would."

"Well, I do. But it doesn't matter." Brown-gold eyes came to rest on Steven slumped in a chair beside the bed.

"Jake, she sat in the ICU every time they'd let her in, for days. The night you were hurt, she stayed in this hospital, not moving, not speaking—I swear, I was more scared for her than I was for you then, because nobody could help *her*, she looked like a lost kid."

God, he'd been afraid of this. All the way from Lancaster in the car, he'd known how it would be. He wondered what else Jake had learned.

"Look," Steven said desperately, pulling from beneath the chair a paper bag filled with mail he'd collected at the desk on his way in. Eight weeks–plus of cards from cities all over the South. "I've been waiting until you were stronger." Steven shoved them forward, remembering as they scattered that Jake couldn't take them in his hands. Embarrassed by his own clumsiness, Steven scooped them up again, sliding the cards from their envelopes one by one and opening them like a window display on the wheeled table by Jake's bed. No response. "Regan's been calling every day, too, Jake."

Jake's glance flickered over the bright greeting cards. "Wish you were here," he murmured. "Wish I was there."

"What?"

"Nothing."

"She didn't want to leave town, Jake. You should have seen her when she had to go, checking out of the Shelton. . . ."

"Looking like a lost kid?" Jake said softly. "We've all seen that look, haven't we?" His eyes met Steven's again. "Did you ever wonder how true it was?"

Not looking away, Steven drew a paper from his wallet.

"This is Regan's itinerary," he made another try. "She'll be in Cincinnati tomorrow. At the Ramada. I'll get a phone for you; then you can catch her before the show."

"I can't dial."

"I'll do it for you."

"I'm not going to her on my knees! Let's both get the message, all right, Steven? She wants the money, she wants the fame, she wants Bertelli. So let her, who the hell cares?"

"That pride of yours is a real ball-buster." Maybe getting Jake angry with him would work better than his lame attempts at reconciliation. As he'd expected, the brown eyes went dark with fury.

"Do you know what my mother went through to get me where I was before this happened?" He held up bandaged hands. "She worked herself to exhaustion, she sacrificed everything she had . . . and ended up sick. And when she was dying, in a crummy hospital not half as good as this one, with doctors who didn't care beyond giving her the next hypodermic to keep her *quiet,* for Christ's sake, what did *I* do for her? Goddamnit, the night she died, I—" Abruptly, he stopped.

"I know how hard she worked, Jake." Steven looked at his hands. "I know how much you loved her."

After a long silence, Jake said, "Nobody jumped me in that alley by accident. Bertelli warned me." When Steven's glance struck his, he added, "All right, maybe Regan didn't know; she never seems to see through him, but—"

"Jake, don't talk crazy. Why would Bertelli—"

"Crazy? What's crazy is me in this bed when I ought to be on tour myself! If I ever find out for sure that Bertelli was responsible—that I owe him for this, too—I'll kill him!" He

was breathing hard, using up strength. Steven closed his eyes briefly.

"You know about the money, then?"

"Blood money." Jake's eyes were like burning coals in his pale face. "But I'm not going to take it! She isn't going to buy me off—"

"Jake, you need that money. Right now you need his help."

And he saw Jake's body slacken, all the fight collapsing as if Steven had landed a blow to his stomach. He fell back against the pillow, his breathing audible in the quiet. "Oh Christ, I hate being useless, helpless." Jake stared for a moment at the thick bandages covering most of his hands. "More surgery," he murmured weakly, "and I haven't any choice, do I? Everything my mother worked for, died for . . . everything I always wanted to be is in somebody else's hands now, Steven, God—" He rolled his head from side to side in anguish. "Bertelli, Regan—"

"Jake, don't." Steven pressed the call button beside the bed. Then touched Jake's shoulder. "You'll be all right."

"I have to be, I have to be!"

When the nurse appeared, she saw Jake's agitation; immediately skillful hands eased him back on the bed when he tried to sit up, eyes dark and wild.

At her touch, Jake felt suddenly drained. He also felt like crying, but he was too tired to cry, too weak, and he hadn't done so in years, not since the night his mother died and he had helped to kill her. Because of someone's soft brown hair and hazel eyes. He looked up now into Denise's gentle gaze, saw the filled syringe in one hand. "Both our lives will be wasted otherwise," he told her as the drug flowed into his body. Denise smiled gently, indulgent. From far off, he heard Steven say, ". . . his mother." Then Jake's eyes drifted shut.

"I'm going to play, I'm going to play again. . . ."

Chapter 16

Regan stepped from the elevator at Jake's floor and walked toward the desk, clutching Kenny Williams' sleeve. She wore a tan safari-style dress with a multicolored scarf around her hair and a pair of large, dark glasses. Her heart pounded in her breast, hammering like the message that had brought her here.

"Kenny, I'm afraid..." without knowing exactly why. But Steven had said—

"Mr. Marsh underwent surgery this morning," the nurse informed them. "I'm sorry, but he can't be disturbed, the anesthetic..."

"We'd like you to make an exception. Miss Reilly has only a few hours in New York," Kenny coaxed. "Nobody's going to turn you in to the hospital director, Denise." He read her name from the tag on her breast pocket, making it sound as if he'd known her all his life. Regan slid a glance at him, almost smiling at the blatant charm—his white shirt unbuttoned at the throat showing a thatch of chestnut hair, his gray eyes dancing, his broad shoulders straining the denim blazer. Virile as the sky is blue, she thought; and it wasn't lost on the petite brunette.

Weakening slightly, she said, "Well, I don't know...."

"Please," Regan added. "I won't stay long."

Jake was lying perfectly still on the hospital bed; his coloring matched the sheets. Taking off her glasses, Regan immediately forgot the dark-haired nurse and Kenny standing at the door. She leaned over, touching the shadow of beard first, then his dark, glossy hair. There was only the faintest movement of his eyelids as he slept, some dream racing across his mind. *Oh my love, so pale. . . .*

Regan remembered Steven's words. They'd been brief, strangled.

"He's heard the report about you and Bertelli. He's down, Regan, rock-bottom. He's already lost so much." She'd heard the cracking tone of voice through the telephone wires. ". . . and now, the plastic surgery. I don't know if he can take it."

Regan had sat, holding the receiver; feeling fuzzy from illness and fever, which had since broken, leaving her just the raspy throat. But then, her stunned silence must have angered him. She didn't know what to say. How could Jake believe Manny's flippant comment, even if it was wishful thinking on Manny's part? She remembered Steven's irritation with her the day she'd left New York, and Jake.

"Steven, I don't know what—"

But he hadn't let her finish. "I'll tell you what to do, and you ought to listen for once. Break away from that tour some-how, anyhow, and get to New York!"

She'd guessed that tempers were running high and spirits very low, but when she'd stammered, "I—Steven, I—" Regan heard only a long, disheartened sigh.

"Congratulations on the gold record, princess."

And he'd hung up, as if he had no more faith in her.

Now, Regan bent closer to Jake and whispered his name. How could Steven ever have thought she wouldn't come? She'd been wanting to come back ever since she'd left. "Jake," she repeated, "I'm here." Her lips grazed his cheek, then the corner of his silent mouth. She kissed him gently, softly, but his lips stayed slack and unresponsive. *I love you,* she thought; *please, just for a moment, open your eyes.* Wanting to see that brown-gold gaze again, she waited. But nothing happened.

Regan's eyes went to his hands, lying palms downward on the blue wool blanket, everything bandaged except the tips of his fingers. She wanted to lift them, to kiss them; though she knew she couldn't. What had the doctors done this morning? Worked their miracles and made him whole again? She felt the tears trickle down her cheeks. She couldn't seem to look at him enough: the features she had known so well in health were different now, strained and gaunt. And yet, he was the Jake she loved so much, the only person in the world who had ever said he loved her too.

"Regan, we'd better go."

Kenny's deep voice startled her. "In a second," she said over her shoulder, showing him a pair of green eyes as luminous as the aurora borealis before she turned back again. "I thought I saw him move."

And then, as if in answer, Jake opened his eyes. Unfocused, they drifted over Regan's face, closed again, then came awake. Their color changed, turning hard and dark, as black as the marble of the floor. She stepped closer to the bed. He stared at her and asked: "Where's Bertelli?"

"Jake," she whispered, shocked. "You know there's nothing between Manny and me."

But he didn't believe her. She saw it in his eyes, and it wasn't the anesthetic, confusing his thoughts. In a slurred voice, he said, "Get away from me. I don't want you here," the syllables running together. "I don't love you anymore."

Regan's throat closed; her heart contracted. She drew back, recoiling. "But, Jake—" She felt his gaze slicing through her like a knife, wielded by loving hands, the absolute betrayal. "You said, remember when you promised—"

"Get away, don't you understand?" His breathing grew rapid.

"Miss Reilly—"

Jake cut through the nurse's plea. "I *hurt!* All I need is . . . I just want the music, to play the . . . piano." Jake swallowed dryly, gasping with the prolonged effort to speak. "Goddamnit, I don't want you—I want my music!" She was already taking backward steps.

"Regan, he doesn't mean it."

But Kenny's words didn't register clearly. Her mind and all her senses felt dazed, as if she'd taken Jake's anesthetic. Regan ran from the room, her heels clicking on the marble floor, her heart beating like a drum. He didn't want her, he didn't love her. And it wasn't a drug, coming through his words; it was Jake's struggle for balance, tipping, sliding like a seesaw, sending her crashing to the ground. *I don't love you anymore.*

Dry-eyed, Regan sat beside Kenny in the front seat of the rented Firebird, watching him drive and trying to make sense of what had happened. She felt numb, spiritless, and strangely tired, as if by simply resting her head against the seat back, she could fall instantly asleep for the rest of the trip. But she knew better. Jake's words would only circle madly, relentlessly through her brain. So she stayed upright, staring out the window or at Kenny's rugged profile, and tried to believe what he'd said.

How kind he'd been today, and since the call from Steven. He and Linda coddled her as they might have Jeb, supplying her with cold medicines, too, and attempting to ease her mind.

"Tell you what," Kenny had said. "Lin thinks you should see a doctor for that throat, and we know a good man in Manhattan; used to live in our building long before Jeb was born—when we were young and crazy. You could see John Thornen the same day. If you drive from New York, after you've seen Jake, it's only two hours to Philadelphia."

"I don't have a license, Kenny. I never learned to drive."

Thanks to Paul, she thought. He'd never let her take lessons.

But the rescue was immediate. "Remember that first car I told you about?" Kenny had asked. "Driving is my middle name, songbird."

"I thought it was 'accident.'"

Regan had smiled, but she'd been grateful for the company, too. And John Thornen had proved to be compassionate, with a wry humor and lots of common sense.

"Not much to be done for this virus," he had told her after the examination. "As much rest as possible, though if your life-style's much like Williams', I suppose that isn't likely. Hot

showers, then, to open up the pipes. And if you have a va-
porizer, run that at night. Otherwise, I'm sorry to tell you that
you'll have to wait it out."

Regan had smiled, giving a shrug of acceptance. "It can't
last forever," she'd said. "How much do I owe you, Dr.
Thornen?"

"John." A pair of twinkling blue eyes; a shock of light brown
hair. "Two tickets to your first New York concert?" he had
suggested in lieu of payment.

"You'll have them."

Now, Regan wondered if she could ever bear to come back
to New York again—for singing or anything else. Baltimore,
Atlanta, Alexandria, Nashville, Birmingham, Jacksonville,
Tampa, New Orleans. Never seeing him, never talking to him.
Louisville and Cincinnati, Columbus, Pittsburgh, Harrisburg.
The argument over Alyson had festered like a sore; Manny,
too. Late March through May. Had she sacrificed Jake after
all, just to be a *second act?* Oh God, the way he'd looked at
her . . .

"You'd feel better if you let it out, Regan." Kenny had
glanced over to find her staring straight ahead at the tumultuous
traffic racing, lane-changing, along the Garden State Parkway.
She saw his worried frown.

"Cry, you mean? I don't cry easily," she said, thinking of
all the nights at Paul's when she had willed herself not to. "But
that doesn't mean I don't hurt . . . inside," with a catch in her
voice that she hadn't wanted to let him hear.

The car sped down the road, hurtling around semi tractor-
trailers and camping rigs; seemed to barely slow for the next
tollgate, where Kenny slapped bills into the collector's hand.
It seemed only seconds later that he found the two-lane byway
winding through countryside, then the parking lot of a tiny,
green-shingled bar. Not that different from Steven's, she
thought, except for its size and the color of the paint. The
atmosphere might be the same inside. But Kenny went in
alone, her in the car at the side of the building. He came
back with a plastic cup half full of amber liquid. Two shots,
at least.

"Drink," he ordered. "Drink all of it."

Brandy, not very good. But it didn't matter. It burned like fire all the way down, and she wanted it to. Had Steven turned against her, after all? His voice on the phone, cold and distant, like his congratulations. At last, she leaned her head against the back of the seat and closed her eyes, holding out the empty cup to Kenny in shaking fingers. She heard him crumble it, throw it into the back on the floor.

"Nobody cares," she murmured, like a moan, feeling at last the sting of moisture behind her closed eyelids, the warm flame in her stomach, glowing like hot coals. "Nobody's ever cared."

Kenny hauled her across the bucket seat, lifting her into his arms. *"Oh, Kenny!"* Why wouldn't Jake's words go away? Why couldn't she see him as he used to be? Brown-gold eyes laughing, his mouth near hers, the strength of his arms, like those around her now? All the love words he'd whispered . . . when today, he'd said, oh God, he—

"Hush, songbird, hush."

She heard her own shuddering sobs, dry sobs without any tears, she'd squeezed them away, she couldn't cry. "He meant every word he said, Kenny, yes, he did."

She pressed her cheek to his white shirt, inhaled the fragrance of him, skin and tobacco and the lingering smell of brandy from the cup he'd crushed. "If he could have wiped his mouth," Regan whispered, "he would have wiped my kiss away." She felt Kenny's hands on her back, soothing as he had done at the hospital in the hall outside Jake's room, felt his mouth against her hair, the crooning words of comfort that soon turned to something else.

Then he began to use the words Jake whispered to her in the night, making her say, "Oh, please," his hands moving on her dress, holding her away, undoing the first buttons, his hands on her skin, his lips parting hers. Hot kisses with his tongue inside her mouth. "No," she said. His fingers on her breast, so gently kneading, making the nipple peak. "Linda," she murmured in protest, but it was feeble protest that wouldn't stop him.

"Don't you know how I feel about you?" His breathing

came fast, harsh. "I love you," he said, fiercely lowering his head to kiss the bare, rosy flesh. "I love you both, damnit—"

But with a violent effort, she wrenched away, covering herself with the gapped pieces of her dress. "Oh, God—where, Kenny?" Her eyes were wild, glazing green. "In the backseat of this car? In broad daylight in a parking lot?" With fumbling fingers, she managed to close the front buttons. "What good would it do?" She wouldn't ever forget those other words, forcing love away.

Kenny pushed away from her, jamming one shoulder against the drive door, balling his fist on the steering wheel. "What good does anything do?" Then she saw him reach into his blazer and pull out a small plastic vial.

Unscrewing the cap, he shook out several capsules, and a yellow tablet. It was Valium, Regan knew. When she said so, Kenny muttered, "The others are barbiturates . . . one won't kill you. Take your pick: it could be a long ride to Philly."

Regan swept a hand toward him, scattering the pills.

"I've got more," he said.

"I wish to God you wouldn't take them."

"Well, I wish I wouldn't, either. I wish a lot of things."

He stared at her in silence, the dark shadow on his features, the boyish smile gone, even the few moments of desire vanished. She wondered how many long, black nights before something terrible happened to Kenny Williams. Then he said, "Does that guy know how lucky he is?"

"Kenny, I love you," Regan murmured. His hand lifted a stray tendril of hair from her cheek and tucked it behind her ear, barely touching, sending the faintest shiver through her. "But I love Linda and Jeb, too . . . and Sam," she finished in a breaking voice. Hearing Jake's words again, she said, "You're my family now."

"As long as you want us, songbird," he said lightly, but his eyes missed meeting hers. Then, "Thank God Sam wasn't with us just now."

"If he had been," Regan pointed out softly, "we would both have behaved ourselves." Then she reached for his wrist, trying to read his watch, wanting to touch him without the other tensions between them, to show that she still would. "What time is it?"

He glanced down at her fingers on the back of his hand. "Nearly six."

"We've got a show in two hours. Can we make it, Kenny?"

With a smile that almost worked, he leaned over and gave her a lazy kiss. "Sure, nightingale." He twisted the ignition key. "You just hold on. We're both gonna make it."

Chapter 17

"Headlining?" Regan's shocked green gaze encountered Bertelli's as he appeared in the dressing room doorway, beaming. "But, Manny, I thought I was—" having my heart cut out tonight.

"Get dressed, sweet. Half an hour till curtain, and a new star is born." He assessed her features, not happy with what he saw. "Nothing wrong with that, is there?"

"Well, no, but—"

She couldn't seem to think. After the trip from New York, after Jake, that wasn't surprising; still, she hadn't counted on doing the entire show tonight herself. And her health at the moment, physical as well as mental, wasn't the best. But then, neither, apparently, was that of the lead singer's in tonight's top rock band. Chicken pox, she thought, shaking her head and suppressing a smile. With complications, yet. It was almost enough to shake the mood of the last few hours. And if it wasn't, having minutes to dress for a major concert in her life had to be. Headlining! Regan forced her personal feelings aside.

"I'm getting dressed, Manny," she answered his frowning look, and shooed him from the room.

When he returned, Bertelli's eyes swept over her with satisfaction. "Five minutes," he said.

The band had already begun to play an introductory medley of songs from the album, the cover of which had been photographed in a meadow of wildflowers, in the dress she wore tonight: sheer white lawn with a wide, sky-blue collar and matching tie belt; small blue buttons all the way down the front, on the cuffs of the long sleeves. Regan would carry a white straw hat with floppy brim, trimmed in the same pale blue. Manny said subliminal suggestion, the connection between the record and her costume—particularly against the impressionistic backdrop of painted white, yellow and blue flowers with dashes of green for stems and grass—would sell records like mad. That, and a good show, of course.

Regan stood up, arranging her gown. It was light and summery, and she only wondered what to do with the wide hat while she sang. Hold it in front of the microphone? Or would that muffle the sound? She'd have to try, and see. "Manny, I'm petrified," she said, lifting her gaze to him. "Do we have a long enough show? And what about the new ballad—I don't think it's ready...."

"It's ready." Bertelli walked toward her and swung Regan gently around in profile to the dressing-table mirror. "You're ready, sweet," he said. Picking up the brush from the table, he began to stroke it through the tawny gold silk of her hair, from the crown of her head to her waist.

"Who are you more pleased with, Manny?" she asked, glad to set aside her unhappiness for a while. "Yourself or me?"

"We're a team," he said promptly. "Inseparable. Incomparable."

Regan's glance sought his in the mirror, looking over her shoulder. "Yes," she said, "perhaps we are." Revolving in a slow circle, she let the long hair swing into place, then touched Manny's arm.

"To the conquest," he told her.

The houselights dimmed. The audience shifted. Peter Noel's thin body poised like a bird about to take flight. At his unobtrusive signal, the first notes came to life. Regan's heart somersaulted in panic. Giving her audience the well-known misty smile, radiating assurance she didn't begin to feel, Regan tossed back the long mane of tawny hair and flicked out behind her the trailing microphone cord: gestures that preceded the first song of every concert. There was only one song she wouldn't sing tonight.

Regan sang, her voice floating, amplified, over the theater and through the emotions of those hundreds of people who had paid to see her. She made small jokes between numbers, accepted applause, laughed and chatted with her audience, but her tone sounded brittle and into her consciousness drifted those moments in the hospital. Why didn't he want her anymore? Why had he left her alone again?

At the halfway point of the concert, Regan left the stage to switch costumes, exchanging the white lawn dress trimmed in blue for a more sophisticated length of teal-blue satin, envelope-slim. Its top made a blunted triangle, a slim rhinestone chain running through the fabric where the pointed peak had been turned under, and from there over her collarbones and around her neck. The sides of the dress slanted sleekly to the waist, barely covering the edges of her rounded breasts, and the back was bare. Ordinarily, Regan felt worldly the minute she stepped into the teal-blue satin; but now she only felt numb.

Until she began to sing again. The stage lights turned the teal-blue an even deeper, richer shade, changing each time she moved. And then, as if by some magic wand that could transform sorrow into joy, she felt the thrill of song itself: starting in her rib cage, the pit of her stomach and rising, ever upward, to her lips and teeth and tongue, then out into the air around her, to the people beyond the footlights. The shiver slid down her spine as the music soared. It was what she gave them in exchange for that which they sent back to her.

An hour later, the house roared approval of the finale, thousands of hands beating together, rhythmically as a song, rising in crescendo, deafening. People were on their feet, calling; someone in the front row threw red roses onto the stage.

"Go on, go back out there!" Manny shouted as she came offstage, the liquid movement of the teal-blue gown flowing about her. Regan's eyes shone; she was laughing, excited now.

She hugged Manny. "What should I do? Peter?" But he was motioning her back.

"Can't you hear? Can't you hear what they're yelling?" Manny cried hoarsely. "Go on, sweetheart, give them what they want!"

But they wanted her soul.

As their words registered, Regan walked more and more slowly toward the middle of the stage in an agony of indecision, reluctance. *Not tonight,* please. She faced the cheering crowd. *Oh, not tonight.* But the calling became a chant: first, the song's title; and then, "Encore!"; and at last, "Come on, Regan, sing it!"

Before she could prepare herself, the music had started and there was no way to avoid what she had purposely cut from the repertoire tonight.

"You are all the constellations of the stars, a roaring rocket ride to Mars. . . ." From the first phrase, tears began to well in her eyes. Thinking them a bit of stage business, the audience went wild, covering the skips and pauses in the lyric that came next by shouting, clapping.

By the time Regan reached the chorus, she was missing all but a word or two of every line, singing in a choked whisper of a voice, barely singing notes, the wetness making tracks down her cheeks. She didn't try to wipe the tears away. During the last chorus, she felt them slide along her throat and down inside the low neck of her gown, and for some unknown reason, the audience stilled—as if the people had finally read her pain.

"And you're . . . old and new," she sang. "But of all the words I know . . . care to know . . . *you.* . . ." Head bowed over the microphone, she finished; and the last notes, bittersweet and clear, faded. *Why did you stop loving me?*

The hush became a smattering of almost embarrassed applause, which grew bolder, more substantial as she raised her head to smile through her tears. Automatically, she whispered, "Thank you." She lifted her hand toward Peter and the orchestra, escaping while they took their bows.

* * *

The song began, a lullaby, low at first, then gaining volume until Regan could hear each and every word. "Sleep, my child, and peace attend thee, All through the night...." A gentle hand on her forehead brushed the golden hair as she gazed up into the face above hers. "Soft the drowsy hours are creeping, Hill and vale in slumber steeping ... I my loving vigil keeping, All through the night."

"I can't stay with you, darling," her mother said when she had finished. Her voice had been a flute, clear and true. "But when you wake up, I'll be here."

Wrapping thin arms around the person she loved most, Regan clung to the good smells of perfume and skin, to the soft blue print dress with its tiny off-white flowers. Then, content at last, she fell asleep. To awake at first light, alone. Regan called out, but there was no response.

Slipping to the cold floor, she padded on bare feet through the sparsely furnished rooms of the apartment: looking, calling, crying, then shouting her fear. Searching, searching. But the only answer was the throbbing of her heart. Where was the babysitter? Mama had said—

No one.

As panic made her shriek, suddenly the front door opened; she was scooped into strong arms, safe again, warm. She clung to his neck.

"I can't believe she left you alone, that snot-nosed kid! Why didn't she stay until someone came back?"

"Mama," Regan cried. "Mama!"

"You don't need her, missy." Paul's husky tone called her by the pet name. "We won't need her anymore."

The dream ended with the sound of his harsh tears, as it always had. Violently, Regan awoke and bolted upright in the bed. Cold air upon her thinly clad body, now as then; a child one second and a shivering young woman the next. Shaking not only from discomfort, but shock and a purity of love that had lost its source. Her own voice terrified her. "Mama!" quivering, and then, "Jake!"

Trembling, Regan wrapped the blankets tightly around her.

She hadn't had the dream in years. She remembered the early times in Paul's house, though—hiding her face in the pillow so Martha wouldn't hear, and scold, her tears. Now it seemed as if the power of the nightmare had been stored, and growing, between childhood and this night when Jake had thrown her out of his life.

Restless but dry-eyed, Regan got out of bed, slipping into a robe. She wasn't hungry, wasn't thirsty; but perhaps she'd call Room Service anyway, just for something to occupy her mind. She couldn't try sleep again. If she closed her eyes, the dream, like a reel-to-reel tape recording, would only rewind itself and play again. And again. All through the night.

Regan shuddered a sigh, turning her thoughts back to the evening's concert. To her surprise, Paul had been there, as he sometimes was now, waiting for some command of Manny's, an errand to run. But tonight he hadn't left as he usually did, after watching her solemnly for a few moments. Tonight he'd stayed, drawing Regan's glance from time to time as she tried to interpret the unreadable expression on his face. It hadn't helped to imagine she saw love there, and sadness, and then pride. It hadn't helped to remember the night he'd come to her room, looking just as haunted. Not when she felt the same way herself.

Forcing her gaze from his, she hadn't looked back again. But she felt his presence. He seemed to watch her reluctantly, obsessively. And when Regan had finished at last—Manny insisting that she return to take her bows at the standing ovation, the cheers—she'd come off the stage into the wings, and Paul.

Blocking her way, he'd stared at her for a long moment. Then, taking Regan's face in his calloused hands, he said, "I wish your mama could have seen you tonight," sensing, too, that there'd been something different, grander in the air. Competing with her heartbreak. Regan's gaze had held with his. Why, always, the fluctuating tensions between them? Paul's ever-changing mood where she was concerned?

"Uncle Paul—" she began.

But he cut her off. "She'd have been proud, too," he muttered.

Regan's heart soared. It meant so much, tonight, to hear him say it.

"Are you all right?" His eyes searched her face, showing Regan anger and tenderness at once. Slowly, she had nodded. Was that why he'd been watching her? What had Kenny told him?

"I'm real sorry you went there," Paul said.

"I'm sorry I did, too."

His hands leaving her face, he had pulled her briefly into his arms and the warmth she'd felt as a child when her mother left. Regan felt the tears crowding, succumbed for seconds to the embrace, then wrenched free of it. She didn't want to cry, to let go, to break down. Not in front of Paul, because of Jake. He would only say he'd been right from the beginning; and tonight she wasn't sure that he was wrong.

Now, Regan paced her hotel room. Twisting her hands. Room Service, she thought again: a snifter of brandy to warm her inside. She had her finger on the dial when someone rapped firmly at her door.

Peter Noel was standing in the hall, holding some papers and an air of hesitation.

"Is something wrong, Peter?" His normally pale face resembled plaster of Paris.

"I—I wanted to discuss some new numbers with you. I know it's late, but—"

"Come in. As you can see, I'm not sleeping."

Expectantly, she waited for him to hand over the pages of staff paper, neatly penned with songs. "I know I should have waited, but I saw the light under your door when I went to the elevator. I couldn't sleep, so I thought I'd work on these downstairs in the bar until it closed, but—"

"I'm glad to look at them. I'm a victim of insomnia myself tonight." And grateful for the distraction. But she had gotten through only the introduction to the first song when Peter blurted, "Regan, I'm sorry for tonight. Playing the song, I mean—"

"Well," she said plainly, meeting his dark eyes, "if you ever play it again, you'll be out of a job. That's between you and me and the dead of night."

"The audience was asking; I didn't know what else to do."

"Neither did I, and Manny insisted. But—"

She would never sing it again.

She didn't realize she was crying until Peter's hand touched her shoulder.

"I'm sorry," she tried to say, but the tears were coming too fast. Peter moved her to the sofa, awkwardly, his arm stiffly about her, and she forgot that she disliked him most of the time; that they rarely agreed; that they had become colleagues but not friends. She forgot everything but the constant echo of Jake's love song.

She subsided into Peter's arms, against his frame, so lithe and light and insubstantial, really; yet she wanted to be nowhere else at the moment. She had no relationship with Peter Noel beyond that of musical director to performer, and their distance protected her.

When the tears were spent, Peter brushed the tracks from her cheeks. "Perhaps I've been working you too hard."

Regan shook her head, managing a watery smile. "Not nearly hard enough," she said.

Remembering the applause tonight, the shouts and cheers, people standing at their seats, she knew how to survive this loss and heal the heartache over Jake. Nothing less would do. The love of her audience would drive out the grief inside, drive away the memory of those rejecting words, even the memory of her mother long ago. Just as the ever-present thrill down her spine when she sang would replace the warmth and strength of those loving hands upon her body, and her heart. Jake, her mother, even Paul. When she trusted someone not to hurt her— as Jake had promised; when she trusted someone's love . . . didn't that person turn upon her, run a knife blade through her soul? No more, no more . . .

If Peter and Manny were right, as tonight they seemed to be, she wasn't going to disappoint them. She would work like a slave if necessary, be the brightest star the world had ever seen. And then the nightmares would be gone . . . like her mother, like Jake.

Regan lifted her chin and squared her shoulders.

"Now," she said, readjusting the tie belt of her robe, "what have you brought me to sing?"

She had liked them! All six of them. He had worked enormously hard himself, every night after the concerts, every night on the road—in airplanes, on buses, in taxicabs—and the songs were good. As good as Jake Marsh's but without the sorrow. As good, she thought, as "Nashville Nights."

Peter carried the pages back to his room, where he changed the few bars of melody that Regan had objected to. He was still trembling as he wrote. Her perfumed scent lingered on the paper; her image stayed in his mind. So beautiful; unattainable. He knew perfectly well that he would never be anything more than a poor substitute for Jake. By virtue of his profession and the accident of timing, he could hardly be less.

But one day, Peter promised himself, one fine day, he would use the only edge he'd ever had—the constant striving for perfection—to give his love to Regan. Staring at the wall in front of the desk where he was working late into the night, he felt better. His thoughts took flight. He had in mind a musical, for Broadway. He could see her now, blond and beautiful, ethereal, almost floating across the stage. . . .

The communicating door of Regan's suite opened, and from the other bedroom Manny said, "I heard voices. Who was here, sweet?"

"Peter." She pulled the blankets closer, warming herself. "He's written some new ballads."

"And they made you cry?"

He must see the redness of her eyes; the drying tracks of tears. "No, of course not."

Manny leaned in the doorway, tilting his head to one side as he studied her. "Paul was worried about you tonight. Kenny told us something of what happened this afternoon . . . though he didn't want to at first." His eyes seemed to look into her soul. "You know that business in New York—"

"Is over," Regan finished for him, not wanting anyone else to say it.

"You're going to be a superstar," he said. "Sweet, I promise."

Slowly, thoroughly, the luminous green eyes searched his face. Fresh emerald tears welling. "Do you always keep your promises, Manny?"

"Yes." And he smiled, defusing the moment. He had known where it would lead. "Unless," Bertelli added softly, "you get a memo to other effect."

Chapter 18

Regan leaned forward, presenting a rounded view to the mirror as she gently prodded the dark circles under her eyes. Clad only in a sheerest white-on-white bra and panties, she wondered if she could sing tonight. Well, she often wondered that, because of nerves. But now, she told the image in the glass that she'd begin to look like Kenny if she didn't adopt sterner measures.

The first six weeks of the fall tour had proved exhausting. Also exhilarating. Astounded and delighted at the reception she'd received everywhere she went—such a contrast to last season in the South—Regan felt gratified, too, by the second gold record just received for "Nashville Nights." Manny expected platinum for her first album by the end of autumn; and last week the new album—entitled simply *Regan*—had climbed the charts to the number-two spot.

She especially liked the album's cover, a photograph taken of her on a bluff above the Pacific Ocean during the summer swing out West. It was an effective shot, a mist of fog and the gray water below; Regan herself poised at the edge of the rocks with her head up, facing into the stiff breeze off the ocean, her tawny hair rippling out behind her. Dressed in jeans with the cuffs rolled to her calves; a soft pink jersey; barefoot. All the colors were soft and muted, a rosy sunset streaking across the sky as if it had been painted on to harmonize with her shirt. "Looks like you're about to take off and fly, songbird," Kenny had said. Oh yes, they'd been doing that, all right.

Regan touched a dab of cream lightener to her shadowed skin now, blending it carefully until her eyes looked bright and clear again. She wasn't only tired from the tour; and neither was Kenny. She was worried. Regan had guessed—how could anyone have not noticed?—that Kenny was using drugs, just as Peter had once implied. More pills from the vial? Because of her? Regan didn't like to think so; but how to ignore her guilty feelings after that day in his car?

And certainly she couldn't ignore his obvious symptoms: the shifting moods, manic one day but silently withdrawn the next. That sometimes wild expression in his eyes, their pupils dilated—turning his clear gray irises a muddy charcoal—or so pinpoint-small that he had to be on something for them to look that bright, that glittering.

Perhaps, she thought, he only feels the pressure of prolonged touring. The physical fatigue, the emotional exhaustion, the artistic pounding. To be good, to be better, to be the best. Every night, every night . . . he'd stop, wouldn't he, when the pressure eased? Whenever that might be.

The nights, the days, the cities merged. Philadelphia had become Chicago, Denver, Houston, then L.A. and the Western states. After that first, surprising stint as a headliner, she had pushed herself and the band, too. And though she had thrived on it as an antidote to pain, Regan realized that the pace extracted its toll.

Sit-ups and push-ups, she told herself, mentally doubling her rigorous daily total, which wouldn't help Kenny, of course. The vitamins, either. Or the fresh fruit that everyone on the bus teased her about, just as they had done on the first tour. "Regan, you ought to learn to like demon rum," someone would say.

At least she had Linda on her side this time, and Jeb adored apples as much as Regan did, being partial to crunchy-sweet Red Delicious. "I wike 'em, Wegan," he would announce, cuddled beside her on the bus as they both munched away happily and pored over the pages of his latest colorful book together. Jeb had begun talking in short, choppy sentences— but he could never say the *r* in her name. Wegan. Like Elmer Fudd, she thought. It made her smile.

If only Jeb's laughter and his love—or Linda's—could make Kenny come to his senses again. If only she could stop blaming herself for that afternoon in the car with him, in the gravel parking lot of a bar off the Garden State Parkway.

With a sigh of temporary defeat, Regan had just turned away from the mirror when a commotion outside her door exploded.

"Kenny, Kenny!" It was Linda's voice, distraught and shrill. Then Sam, "Come on, man . . . get back to the dressing room and sit down. Linda's right—"

"Let go of me, damnit! I'll show 'em how good I can be—" Then came the slamming sound of a body hitting the wall, bouncing off, thudding against concrete again. "Think I can't? Don't come to see me, the hell with 'em, then they'll read it . . . made the New York papers, didn't we?"

"Damnit, Kenny—when are you gonna start thinking straight? Give up on those jerks back in Vermont—"

"What about Polly, huh? Have you given up, Henderson?"

"Stop, Kenny! *Please*. . . ." Linda cried.

Regan threw open the dressing room door. Linda was hanging on Kenny's arm, her face tear-streaked, her mouth distorted with crying, soundlessly. Sam held his other arm, as if the two of them were trying to chain a wild tiger—or the shaggy bear she had first likened him to. Now, Regan could see how agitated he was. Full of unfettered energy, shaking with it. Hardly any pupils at all showing in the silver-gray eyes.

"Songbird"—his voice came out a whisper as his gaze took her in, head to toe—"You tell 'em, will you? You tell 'em I'm all right."

With her eyes, Regan motioned Linda and Sam away. The hall echoed with their receding footsteps and Linda's quiet sobs. Unflinching as he examined her, Regan said, "I want you to tell me something. Kenny, *why do you do this?* Night after night? What have you been using? Those pills again?"

"I live the way I want to live!" Then he reached a hand to her, which she took, her anger softening as he said plaintively, "Regan."

"Oh, Kenny—do you really *like* the way that junk makes you feel, whatever it is—"

But he cut her off, his glance directed to the floor as he spoke.

"What I like, songbird, is the way it *doesn't* make me feel."

Regan pulled her hand away. She was trembling all over. *Does that guy know how lucky he is?* Regan swallowed convulsively, knowing what she had to say. "For the time being, do you think you can go out on that stage in ten minutes?" Her voice shook, too. "Eight thousand people waiting—and what do you think the gross is for this concert tonight?"

"Twelve, fourteen bucks a head . . . I haven't lost all my brain cells yet, I can multiply, you know—but is that all you care about now? You and Manny? What about your *friends,* lady?" he taunted. "That family you needed so badly?" He turned on his heel, surprisingly straight and steady as he began to walk the length of the hallway, the dark gray gaze gone with him. "You want *perfection,* nightingale, you got it . . . every night," he said over his shoulder. "You and the folks back in the Green Mountains of Vermont."

"Peter, you can't fire him!"

Regan cast a frantic look around her small but efficient dressing space—white walls and red-enameled table and chair; the track lighting over the small love seat upholstered in a tiny rosebud print. With an exasperated sigh, she looked back at her musical director. "Who do you suppose would play drums tonight?"

"There are two other guys in that band who could fill in. At least you wouldn't have to be edgy about Williams for the next few hours. Hell, *I* can fill in . . ." But he knew she had a point.

After the last moments in the hall, she was scared herself. Turning away to take her gown from its hanger in the closet, Regan draped it over the sofa.

"Regan, sooner or later—"

"Kenny's right, Peter! He happens to be one of the best drummers you could find—"

"When he isn't 'playing' the doper of all time himself!"

"And he's my friend," she said doggedly.

"*Friend?* Listen, lady, the bigger you get in this business, the more lonely you're going to be offstage. If there's one thing to be sacrificed, you can be damn sure it's friendship ... and the very last thing you can afford, Regan Reilly, is dragging someone like Williams along behind you." Peter took a deep breath. "He's going to end up on a street corner begging for pennies if he keeps this up!"

"Not while I'm around, Peter!"

But would he make a mistake tonight?

"*Ladies and gentlemen. . . .*"

Regan hurried into the hallway from her dressing room, hobbled by the narrow floor-length skirt she wore. That little lapse of timing, she thought. Too much volume, or conversely, none at all?

"*Miss . . . Regan . . . Reilly!*"

At the reassuring flourish of drums, she swept onto the stage with the announcer's introduction, brilliantly smiling, her dress a flash of silver light, her smile a beacon. Crossing her fingers behind her back, she reached with the other hand for the microphone. The dress, encrusted with thousands of bugle beads, seemed to weigh a ton. Her heart in her throat for the entire show, Regan kept glancing at Kenny, surprising a stupefied smile on his attractive face; then seeking Linda's worried gaze from the wings.

But during the final song, Regan decided she'd been mistaken. Peter was, as usual, too harsh in his judgments. Kenny had done nothing wrong, so she relaxed into the new ballad from Clive Dixon, Jr.—veering away from the country market toward the popular—entitled "Wildflower," its inspiration coming, he had said, from the cover of her first album.

Only the week before, she had introduced the record, just now hitting local stores. Still, already routine. The end notes, the final drumroll fading away with her voice, the soft finale, the start of loud applause seemed to come quickly. The song was going to be very popular. Peter, holding up his baton, almost smiling—which meant he was delighted. Peter, giving her, behind his back, a finger signal. Number One. His supreme accolade—except that the index finger used was, of course, slightly bent to indicate a minus.

Oh yes, Regan thought for him as she took her bows, I know what I did. Changed a few bars before the chorus, making a different harmony with his accompaniment. Me, not Kenny. It had worked, though; different from the record that people would buy, but fresh. Unique. She had let the thrill of performing take her to the heights, no interference tonight, no misery. Regan held up the microphone in her right hand, thanking the band, the audience, and, of course, "the city of Minneapolis itself for this beautiful auditorium, acoustically perfect. Will you bring us back again?" she asked, and the crowd roared. That shiver of accomplishment, acceptance, went down her spine like a lover's hand.

Flowers pelting the floor at her feet, Regan left the stage. She was already planning next year's visit, including two nights in the city, when the sudden, crashing noise put an end to woolgathering.

A loud gasp rose from the audience as if from one throat. Regan heard a simultaneous cry of pain, and running to the edge of the wooden stage from the wings, looked down. Kenny lay twisted on the concrete apron of the floor, thick carpet cushioning the aisles only a few feet away. She heard the commotion, saw it all, even recognized the wailing sirens from another time, the groaning man on the floor, Linda's sobbing instead of her own. Regan stood frozen in place, not even aware of the fans who surged onto the stage, clustered to her, touching her gown, her hair, her person, asking and demanding autographs in the middle of chaos.

"Let her be, let us through!" There were two guards, big and burly, with him, forcing their way through the crowd. Regan felt dazed; felt someone rip a piece of beaded fabric from the back of her dress.

Manny's arms came around her, his hand shoving someone away. "They're taking him to University Hospital," he announced, close to her ear. "We'll meet Linda there."

It was like the night Jake had been hurt. Regan's pulse pounded in panic. "Manny, how bad is he?"

But she was being dragged backstage, along the hall, jostled between the guards and Manny to the rear entrance and a waiting car. The crowd surged behind them. "We'll find out when we get there."

It could have been worse, the doctors told them. Much worse. A small laceration, a mild concussion requiring an overnight stay in the hospital for observation. He was lucky, a nurse said in the waiting room where Regan sat with Linda while Manny stalked the long hall, muttering to Peter who was complaining that the bus had to leave for Chicago by noon.

When Regan saw the forbidding expressions on both faces darkening like thunderclouds in argument, she forced her way into the conference.

"Kenny can meet us," she suggested. "There, or in Kansas City."

"He isn't meeting us anywhere," Peter said.

"Peter, there's no lip to that stage! You walk right up to it, and you fall off. I've almost done it myself."

He looked at her. "The point is, *you* didn't."

At the hotel, Manny snapped the tips of his fingers against the next morning's headline. "I've got one bitch of a day cut out for me. What do you think they found in that guy's bloodstream last night?" Regan didn't answer, focusing her attention on the lapels of her robe. "Well, it wasn't Tylenol, I'll say that much. The less you know, the better. And for God's sake, don't talk to the press yourself today—you hear me?" Regan only nodded, feeling the aftereffects of shock and too little sleep.

She kept thinking of Linda and Jeb; of the long bus rides when Kenny had talked with her about the past or made her laugh when she felt blue, missing Jake; and even when he had tried to love her. She thought of Linda sewing costumes on the thinly carpeted floors of hotel rooms while Jeb toddled through the mess. And of the baby, cuddled to her and calming for Regan when he fussed, sharing viruses and Red Delicious apples—and Raggedy Ann whom Jeb adored, torn petticoats and all.

She barely heard Manny say, "I've canceled Chicago—we'll just have to absorb the costs—on the pretext of Williams' injury. Peter's taking care of *him,* by the way." When her head came up and her eyes widened, Manny tossed the paper onto a chair. "And don't you interfere. As soon as I get back to New York, I'm putting his replacement on a plane."

"Manny—"

"Go ahead," he said, putting his back to her and zipping up his overnight bag at the end of the bed. "Hate me for the rest of the week, until you see I'm doing the best thing for you—and so is Peter. Save your soft heart for Denver, sweet. . . . I'll see you there when I get Chicago straightened out."

He had the good sense to leave her without saying more, leaving her with the newspapers and her snarled thoughts. He had come troubleshooting for Peter, on the first jet from New York straight to the concert, to Kenny's obvious addiction. Or had Kenny fallen, as she'd said, independent of drug influence? Regan didn't know. She only knew that Peter, and Manny, had taken the decision from her. For her own good, she was supposed to believe.

"Sent your hatchet man after me, did you?" Kenny stormed into her room an hour later. "Peter Noel with the friendly face and those beautiful manners? Because you didn't have the *guts* to fire me yourself? Regan, you can't do this to me!"

When he paused for breath, she looked up. The door had stood ajar as she had slowly made ready for the bus which would begin loading equipment first at the theater, then stopping by the hotel after dinner. Regan realized she'd been waiting for Jeb's light footsteps coming to visit. As if everything were still the same. But of course, it wasn't.

Regan looked down into the half-filled suitcase on her bed. "I disagreed with Peter—with Manny, too. I want you to know that." She swept a glance over his rumpled clothes, rumpled russet hair. No evidence of trouble today. Only the grayness of his skin, a dullness to his gaze that had nothing to do with last night's fall or the small square of bandage over his left eye: accumulated damage. Regan's heart sank. Manny and Peter weren't on opposite sides of her fence; she'd only wanted to think so. "Kenny, I wish I could change what's happened—" But he didn't want a civilized discussion.

"Then why don't you?" he challenged. "I've never been late, never missed a concert—and I've never messed you up—"

"Until last night!"

"That was *after* the show—"

"Oh, really? You've come darn close a dozen times before. Do you know what it's like, standing through a whole concert with my legs shaking, my heart pounding so loud I can't hear the music? You *said* you'd be all right, but *I* wasn't sure. I can't *work* like that, Kenny—every night, wondering if you'll make it through or—"

"Noel's going to turn you into a real *prima donna* yet, isn't he?"

Regan clenched her fists at her sides. She was angry now, as angry as she had once been with Jake for being stubborn about her career, not understanding where she had to go, what she had to become, when he wanted just as much for himself. And sad, too. "That's not fair!" Her eyes flashed at Kenny, but the answering gray held no light—not even fury.

"Kenny, my God, if you'd only stop, if you'd straighten out—for me . . . and Linda and Jeb, too," but she saw that he wouldn't. Grass, pills, cocaine . . . and what next? He had a history—Peter wasn't lying. If she didn't like the decision, she had to realize, looking at Kenny now, that she couldn't let the band down, the people who paid to see her.

"And how do I prove to you I'm straight, Regan?" His hand was gripping the doorknob, the knuckles white. "Who needs it?" he demanded. "If Noel hasn't smeared me from New York to California, there are plenty of bands out there—"

"*Good,* you want to waste your gifts, then go waste them

somewhere else so I don't have to watch!" Regan cried. "But when you decide to quit feeling sorry for yourself because your folks messed you up and you're not *happy* all the time, when you get off that *stuff* and stop poisoning your mind as well as your body—come see me for a job and you'll have one!"

"When hell turns to solid ice, lady." He glared at her, his voice soft as a whisper, a complete contrast to her own tormented shouting. It was a wonder the entire population of the hotel hadn't spilled into the hallways to listen. For long moments, they simply stared at each other, breathing fast. Regan's body felt rigid from holding herself in check. She didn't want it to end in shouting and misery. Did he feel as hurt as she had, living with Paul's suspicions? Losing Jake? Did he see her now as the enemy who had wounded him—like his parents, withholding love, inflicting pain? When he moved toward her suddenly in the silence with that odd grace she never expected from so large a man, Regan feared he might lash out at her.

But to her surprise, Kenny's hands came up, gently cradling her face the way Jake used to, something of the old clear light glowing briefly in his eyes. "Sing pretty, nightingale," he whispered, "because it's all you're gonna have." Then he gave her a slowly moving kiss to carry with her forever. *Don't leave me, oh, Kenny, don't leave me, too.*

"Linda, I didn't—*we* didn't—want to let him go," Regan was saying desperately half an hour later. She had sat staring at the suitcase on her bed for long moments after Kenny had gone, wondering what else she could have said or done. At last, she had decided that Linda might better listen to reason—but now, she wasn't so sure.

Linda kept her face turned away as she tipped the contents of dresser drawers haphazardly into a canvas valise in the middle of the floor. Regan wondered how she would ever get the case closed.

"I asked Kenny two or three times to stop, but . . . Linda, you've got to understand. You know better than anyone else that he's using again and—"

"I know you and Mr. Perfect don't want any mistakes!"

Linda concentrated on the packing, which was hampered by
Jeb's constant intrusions as he reached a small hand into the
growing pile, taking out the shirts that had just gone in, selecting a can of shaving cream, a half-bottle of cologne. "No
go bye-bye, Mommy," he declared solemnly as Linda wrestled
the objects from him, then set the boy aside on the rug once
more. "But yes, I've known . . . so how can I blame you? Is
that what you're trying to say?"

Regan winced at the tone of voice, so flat and strained.
Scooping Jeb onto her lap, she sat down on the big bed, which
was unmade. "Come here, darling, Mommy needs room to
work." The smell of Kenny's skin seemed to waft from the
orange-flowered sheets. "What I'm trying to say is—if Kenny
can get clean, his job will be as far away as the closest phone,
and I've told him that, too." She played idly with the silk of
Jeb's fair hair, making him giggle.

"He loves you," Linda said quietly, refolding a stack of
shirts she'd straightened a few seconds before. "You think I
don't know that? If it weren't for you . . . he didn't have to
travel. I knew what he'd do on the road when the nights got
to him again—and this is how you treat him?"

"Linda, if Kenny wants to join any rehabilitation program
in the country, I'll pay. I'm not trying to cast you both out, I
do want to help."

"You wouldn't help your own mother across the street,"
Linda said more fiercely. She spilled the last drawer of underwear into the valise.

"That's not true!" Regan pressed the little boy closely to
her, feeling his warm, damp skin and trusting weight against
her breast. "I love Kenny, and I love you, and Jeb—"

A pair of dark, clouded eyes met hers. "You love those
people clapping their hands for you every night! You don't
have to worry about your man falling apart in front of your
eyes—you didn't stay around when he did—or your baby
going hungry, because you only borrowed *mine*"—Linda lifted
the flap of the canvas bag and let it fall over the other half—
"so you just keep on being the big star, *Regan Reilly*—and
give me back my husband and my kid!" She snatched a squirm-

ing Jeb from Regan's embrace. "Nobody asked you to come and say good-bye after the hanging!"

Regan rose from the bed. Jeb was struggling in Linda's arms. "Let go, Mommy! Regan, let's play Raggedy Ann," every *r* and *l* in the words replaced by the Elmer Fudd sound that made her laugh; but now Regan could only feel her throat tighten as if she might choke. Her hands went cold and damp as Linda answered sharply, setting Jeb down. "Raggedy Ann belongs to Miss Reilly. Go and get the dolly, Jeb, and give it back to her."

"No! I want it, I want it!" The tears instantly in his bright gray eyes, as bright as Kenny's had been when she met him. Regan felt her own tears close to the surface as she watched Linda stride to the folding cot where Jeb slept, plucking the worn rag doll in its old pinafore from the covers. Jeb was screaming now, jumping up and down. "I want it, Mommy!"

"Please, Linda—let him keep her." Jeb was pulling at the long, floppy legs as Regan interceded, one hand on Jeb's hair and her eyes fixed to Linda's dark gaze. She could barely focus on the details of the face in front of her, which kept blurring.

She had never known a family life, three people she had loved as much, as if they were her own. How unfair to claim she'd borrowed them for selfish reasons. And to imply that *she'd* abandoned Jake . . .

"Linda, *please,*" she repeated above Jeb's continuing howls, "let him take the doll. Don't make a child suffer for our differences—we've been friends, all of us. . . ." But she didn't feel that much better, or relieved, when Linda thrust the carrot-haired rag at Jeb, quieting his cries.

"I told you some time ago, Regan—I have all the friends I need."

Her heart wasn't the only part of her that throbbed with pain. As Regan passed by them to the door, her hand ached to touch Jeb—but she didn't. Would she never see him again, never touch Jeb's silken hair? "Be a good boy, darling," she murmured in a shaken voice, for both of them: Jeb, and his giant teddy bear of a father, all the stuffing knocked loose.

"Take care of Raggy, Jeb."

"Wegan?" came the plaintive voice from his mother's skirt. She heard Linda's muffled sniffing, her face buried in her hands. *Don't leave me, don't let me leave like this.*

At the door, she made one final, futile try at apology.

"Linda? I *am* sorry, really sorry."

The stiff words were uttered without looking up.

"Regan, sorry doesn't pay the rent."

CHORUS

Chapter 19

On a blustery autumn afternoon with sharp November rain slashing against the glass, Jake closed the door on the last of his students for the day. With a heavy sigh, he sank down onto the piano bench and contemplated his hands.

Unless he looked closely for the tiny scar ridges where new skin joined old, he couldn't see the evidences of Steiner's surgical skill. Even the slight discolorations were fading after a year and a half. But he studied his hands again, as if looking for clues to his own slow progress; turning them, palms up first, then knuckles.

Why wasn't he doing better? If he looked the same—

Upon his release from the hospital, there had been no shocks, thank God, looking in the mirror. He'd been pale, and thinner, but the first summer had cured that; the worst mark on him still was the modest sunburst scar beneath his chin. Jake fingered it now. He could feel the blow that had caused it, and the imprint of the heavy ring. But the least of his problems, twenty months after the accident, was the state of his health. Or his appearance. If he couldn't play, if he couldn't walk out on a concert stage and send shivers along the spines of his audience—then he might as well have died in that alley. Every sacrifice his mother had made, giving him his chances, would only be more dirt on her grave. His fault, *his*.

Each day seemed to bring him closer to the realization that he didn't want to reach. The first panic had struck a year ago, in September. He'd been two months in this apartment, affordable and simple. He looked around now at the whitewashed brick walls of the living room; the bright-colored beanbag chairs he'd purchased, cheap and comfortable and warm; the homemade foam-slab sofa with puffy orange cushions. The rooms looked out on the street, and he could see the sky before he went outside—a definite plus in old New York buildings of residence.

He'd become a Murray Hill dweller, found a job nights playing piano bar nearby on East Thirty-sixth Street. Intimate and oak-paneled, the place attracted businessmen killing time before their trains from Grand Central to the suburbs; and high-class call girls hoping for an evening's employment.

Running scared because his music showed so little improvement, during the days Jake worked harder. What good was there, in being of a piece again, if he couldn't perform? Why else had he accepted Bertelli's money?

He remembered the weeks before his release from Special Surgery, shuffling along the hallways with Denise at his elbow, lending support. It astonished him how weak he'd become lying in bed; but day by day, his strength had returned. His recovery from the next skin grafts had been easier, quicker. Sooner than he'd expected, Jake was walking with Denise in the hospital gardens ablaze with summer color, the late-June sun a warm blessing on his face.

"What will you do when you're released, Jake?" she asked him.

He hadn't faced the logistics of freedom, health.

"I don't know." He'd renewed the tenant's lease on his house, Jake told her, "And Steven's got his own problems with the roadhouse losing a lot of money while I was sick. He doesn't need me in his way."

Not that he wouldn't be welcome; but there were memories for him there, too. Memories he wanted to avoid. Denise said after a moment's hesitation, "What about . . . that blonde . . . the singer?" Her eyes met his. He wondered, seeing her sympathy and confusion, how much she knew as the pain and anger shook him.

"There's just me now," Jake answered. "Just me."

"Then where will you go?"

He had looked at her gravely. "Anyplace that's got room for a piano."

Now, Jake left the piano bench and walked to the windows. He rubbed the back of his neck, trying to rid himself of tension. He wasn't happy with himself for this afternoon, any more than he felt proud of his own practice that morning.

After school, the girl had come again. Small and light-boned and timid, with a waist-length pair of golden braids. Jake had listened to her talentless preparations for the lesson, her slight hands fumbling with the keys. He'd found himself wanting desperately to still those fingers with his own, stronger—to cover the sound and silence it. Somehow he'd made it to the end of the hour; then, "The Chopin étude needs more attention. Make sure you can play it properly, perfectly, before next time." Or don't come back, his mind had added as she walked, head bowed, toward the door, as he closed it firmly behind her.

She would never be able to play it without mistake. And whom had he been angry with—the child or himself? He had no more patience, or inclination, for teaching than he'd had years ago. Even when he met Regan. And didn't the girl unpleasantly remind him of her, with that confinement of tawny silk in braids and rubber bands?

As if he needed reminding after his morning trip to the bank. An innocent errand—until he had rounded the corner at the newsstand. And there she was. Jake's heart had stalled out like his playing, as he stood, motionless, staring at the magazine.

It wasn't a major publication; but she'd gotten the cover. Backlighting brought a halo effect to her long swing of tawny hair, an almost frosted look, luminous. The picture had been snapped from the wings at some concert, making the most of angles and their opposites: her bared back and the deep-shadowed, curving column of her spine, the soft gleam of light off her right shoulder, and the gentle curve of breast in the slashed-down neckline of the sleek gold lamé gown. She was holding a microphone, about to sing, and the camera had managed to catch the catlike green of her eyes, the darker ring that made them so striking. Black lashes fanned velvet shadows along her cheek.

Loud and heavy, Jake's heart had begun to beat again. He'd tried to make sense of the article, but the words registered no meaning. Or the title, either—which should have. *Rising Star*. Something he'd said to her on the night of her debut at Steven's. *I'm glad I saw you, rising . . . rising.*

His bank deposit forgotten, Jake had walked home, thinking, Damn Regan, *damn her*. Nobody that faithless, no one that hell-bent on her own success, running over bodies, using and discarding, had any right to look that beautiful.

And what had he accomplished? Today, he'd spent hours at the piano, teaching kids who didn't want to learn—or couldn't—and working between lessons himself on the same piece until he felt limp. If he hadn't thrown away the rights to Regan's first gold record—the song he'd written from the heart—by now, he'd be a rich man. He wouldn't have to teach. He wouldn't owe Bertelli, either. As if money could help his playing. He was only resenting Regan's success.

Jake stopped watching the passersby in the street below his apartment window. Walking back to the used piano that had been his first purchase after he signed the lease, he sat down.

The same visions filled his mind in place of music.

Always, these concert stages in his head, and rows of people in evening dress: his constant companions. Were the replayed sonatas that he heard only part of the healing process, just as the levels of physical pain and awareness had been before? Or would they take the place forever of—

Jake took a deep breath, feeling his palms grow moist with the panic that had become too familiar as well. No, *no*. He placed his fingers resolutely on the keys, heart hammering, and played a quick passage with a number of lyrical trills. Schubert. But the notes stood out singly, stiff and measured, unblending.

Jake stopped. It took more, much more, to play lightly, with feeling, than to bring off the heavier stuff. More fine control ... but damnit, he hadn't any. Placing his hands in position again, he checked his reach. Ten keys, eleven, he remembered; now, he barely made the octave. Like the girl with golden braids and fine-boned fingers.

Over time, he'd been assured, flexibility would increase. But more than a year ... bones and tendons, muscles and nerves. Damaged! Damaged. It was never coming back, never going to happen.

And how would he repay his mother if it didn't? How would he write a check in full for Bertelli? When he didn't have the touch.

His reviews, if he'd had any, would now just read, "adequate." Even though he'd never put much store in them, the thought made his gut twist. The truth was, they'd be right. He played best when demonstrating for a handful of students— short passages, relatively simple ones. As for his own practice, progress ... well, there wasn't any tour, was there?

Getting up from the bench again, restless, Jake roamed into the tiny kitchen that served his needs. A small apartment, a smaller life. Opening a can of lemon-lime soda, he paused, staring at the wall above the sink. The clock. *In four more hours,* he thought, *I should be playing Brahms in San Francisco.*

Jake decided to go to work early. He often hung around The Grenadier before and after hours: talking with the bartender, playing when the place emptied late at night, when his fingers felt most flexible, loosened by hours of pop standards. The music came out smooth and easy, then; and classical once more.

He was caught somewhere between the two worlds when he looked up near closing that night and saw someone he thought he knew. Jake's pulse speeded up instantly. She'd come in with a second girl he'd seen before and dated once—the only kind of woman he bothered with now. A professed actress, though he had his doubts. An hour later when the girl left with a paunchy, middle-aged salesman, Jake felt neither disappointed nor surprised.

What startled him, as it had when he first looked up at the two women, taking a corner table out of the light, was that slight upturn of the first girl's nearly straight nose, the averted profile that confronted him each time he glanced over—more and more frequently as the moments passed. She was wearing a knitted cap pulled low, in a natural color that matched the sweater over her dark green skirt. She wore high-heeled black leather boots and a green plaid coat; and if she hadn't looked directly at him, Jake could have sworn it was—but no, the gaze wasn't the same. Nature had stopped at ice-blue on the palette of color; nature hadn't kept going to verdant green. And then, taking off the cap, she shook out her hair, letting him see auburn, not gold, frizzed in not-quite-current style, looking as if someone had run an eggbeater through it.

Only the family resemblance, Jake corrected; but still his heart wouldn't return to normal pace. You couldn't deny the influence of genes in that profile, the tilt of her head when she had been speaking to her friend; and her body had slimmed since he last saw her that fateful night. Five or ten pounds less again and she might have been—

But why should he care? As she moved over to the bar and ordered another drink, sliding onto the empty stool nearest him, Jake kept working at the Gershwin, trying to ignore her.

"I'm not leaving," she said after a while, blue eyes running quickly over his dark trousers, the blue shirt, the slate herringbone tweed of his sport jacket. He had undone his navy tie near the end of the evening. Only on weekends did he wear a suit for the more formal crowd, and her gaze rested briefly on the hollow of his neck. He hoped she couldn't see his pulse beating strongly. "I've spent far too much time tracking you down, Jake."

"What for?"

He stared at the keyboard, watching his fingers as he played, thinking that the scars showed hardly at all now, putting an extra flourish to the melody. His voice seemed to echo, bouncing off the walls, the piano.

Alyson Oldham tried a smile on him. "To say I'm sorry." The second time, the smile came out all right. He glanced up again, catching its full impact. Seeing Alyson as she'd been on another night, seeing her in the rust-colored robe so like the color of her hair, remembering the swell of her breasts, the line of her body in the shower. Remembering, "Hello, my love . . . Jake? I'm home"; then the shattered glass-green of Regan's eyes, the trembling mouth, the disbelief . . . and, *how good you are at letting people down.*

"Won't you let me explain?" Alyson asked. "You think everything then was my fault, Jake—but it wasn't."

He wanted to tell her to get lost; that he didn't believe her for a moment; that whatever she had done to separate him from Regan Reilly she surely didn't regret—but something wouldn't let him. How would he ever know unless he listened?

Jake ended the Gershwin rhapsody, pausing before he played again. And he thought about the late night and the empty streets, loneliness hugging him with the warmth of a corpse. But above all, the need to punish whomever he should. Was it really Alyson?

"Stick around for half an hour," he said. "Then we'll talk."

Jake would remember only one conversation with Alyson Oldham during the week they spent together. "Yes, I saw Manny that afternoon," she admitted, sitting up in bed, letting the covers fall away from her ample breasts, showing none of the modesty he had once associated with Regan.

"I went to his office," Alyson went on, "because Daddy and I didn't know Regan's address. We hadn't heard from her, and I wanted to check in while I was on spring vacation from school. I'd already told you that, hadn't I?" When he didn't bother to answer, eyes fixed coolly on her nakedness, she said, "Manny asked me to lunch. It was just noon, and he said Regan would be busy all day. We went somewhere fancy—I've forgotten the name—and drank a lot of wine, laughed a lot, too. He's really very nice, Manny. . . ."

During the meal Bertelli had remarked that, in fact, Regan would probably not be finished working until very late—the album was being taped, a difficult session, he thought—and that Jake Marsh was already straining at the bit to see her himself.

"I said, 'Maybe he'd like to have some company while he's waiting,'" Alyson reported, "but in a joking way, you know . . . and then Manny said, 'Don't tell me you're like all the rest'; that he didn't understand why women fell all over themselves for you." She smiled at Jake, as if she were sorry to repeat Bertelli's words, and put a hand on his abdomen. "Only, I think he did understand. He looked real irritated."

"You mean jealous." Well, Jake thought, he's got her now. "Then what?" he prompted.

"Manny said I had a clear chance for the evening if I wanted, probably as intimate as I wanted, too, because you were already mad at Regan, which I ought to make the most of, he said, being a very attractive girl myself"—she almost blushed— "and then he told me he knew how I must feel. Because— because he wanted more from Regan than her thanks when he booked her into a good club, more than his percentage, oh Jake, I don't want to—"

"*Go on.*"

"It wasn't the way it sounds when I tell it now. Nothing but lunchtime chatter, Jake, and probably too much wine; then later that night, I had more to drink with *you*, getting up my courage . . . hoping you'd like me a little. We weren't plotting, honestly we weren't . . . I wasn't, that's what I wanted to explain. What right did Regan have, getting self-righteous when she came in to find me there with you at the hotel. . . ." He would have sworn she was telling the truth. Blue eyes pleading, her hand fluttering over his belly. And what difference did it make now? But still—

"Manny was very kind to me, Jake. Getting me a room at the hotel; and when we left the restaurant, he even slipped me some money to buy a new dress, he said, or a pretty trinket," as if that might convince him. The only thing he really believed now was that Regan hadn't been aware of Bertelli's manipulations, either. He pushed Alyson's hand away, wondering how bright she was. "He still paying you?"

"He didn't pay me, Jake! That wasn't why—He cares about people, really he does. Manny told me when I finished college he might be able to help me with a job . . . and late this summer, after I auditioned for what seemed like a million parts, nothing right for me, he—he said he'd put me to work himself. You see?"

No answer.

Alyson drew his hand to the naked expanse of skin beneath the sheet. Her eyes were hungry again, wanting an end of talk and explanations. Jake stroked the silky flesh, closing his eyes for a second, his mind and memory. "He's giving me a chance doing promotional work—a steady salary and I'll get to be *seen,* noticed—"

He wondered if she ever got tired of sex; if she'd been lying to him. If Alyson and Bertelli had struck more of a bargain than that. A setup, nevertheless, even if he'd been susceptible to it.

Letting his hand slip lower now, Jake asked, "What do you know about my accident, Ali? Was Bertelli part of that, too? Who did he hire to get rid of me the next night?"

Her breath came faster, lighter. "All I did was go to the hotel—"

"I'm never going to *play* again! Don't you understand? I'm never going to get on a concert stage, oh, *goddamn*—"

"Jake, please!" She grabbed for him. There was no music in his head; no loneliness in his gut. Nothing, nothing. He was twenty-eight years old, with most of a lifetime of preparation behind him, and—he faced it now—no future that he could see, or even want. Nothing. Might as well find out again what he'd taken the pounding for.

Sliding lower in the bed beside Alyson Oldham, down lower, then lower still, his hands ungentle, his teeth sharply nipping until she cried out, Jake murmured, "Is this intimate enough for you?"

Slut.

Chapter 20

Regan finished the song, drawing out the last note, green eyes shining, a smile on her lips, and took her first bow, ignoring her inner disquiet. The tawny-gold hair swished about her, the lamé gown—one of her favorites—caught the lights and threw them back like a thousand gems, winking and sparkling. It was the dress of her daydreams. The applause became a storm, and calls for encore, a pelting of flowers, then a standing ovation. How could anything have been wrong tonight? In the wings she saw Manny, trying to catch her eye, making broad gestures for her to hurry. Instead, she took her time.

Circling to include the orchestra and Peter, who scowled as he made his own bow, at the rear of the stage she confronted a dozen images of herself: enormous blowups of black-and-white photographs that had been used for a backdrop. Regan from her album covers, in a field of summer flowers, at Big Sur, and in the forecourt of Lincoln Center; Regan running on a beach in shorts and top; Regan waving good-bye to fans as she boarded a plane.

She was laughing when she reached the wings of the stage. *The high after a concert*, she thought, *is like nothing else on earth;* the purest love she knew. The *only* love she had, and could count on. If there was disappointment ahead, it would come from within her. Though she didn't intend to let that happen. Not when every night she felt the warm affection flow from the audience to her. Why did Linda make it sound like such betrayal when it was the only love she had ever been allowed to keep? She hadn't wanted to leave Kenny, or Jeb ... or Jake for hundreds of hands, clapping.

Regan drew her bottom lip between her teeth, sharply enough to stop the unwanted memories. She concentrated on the applause still ringing through the air—as it had before in Sydney at the start of the tour, then in New Zealand and Japan, now back in Australia again—and focused all her attention upon their mutual joy, savoring it.

They loved her. And she loved them.

She had turned toward the stage again, was taking a first step toward another curtain call when Manny's hand stopped her. "What the hell—" He began to pull her gently but firmly in the opposite direction. "We're due at the hotel in five minutes. The limo's at the side entrance. Let's be in it before they decide to mob the car again tonight." Grasping her arm more tightly, he whisked her away. No time to remove makeup and refresh herself; no change of clothing; no rehash with Peter. Why, Regan asked herself again, had he looked so furious?

In the car, while Regan wondered about her musical director, Manny briefed her. Important names and occupations, influential connections and opportunity. Everyone, it seemed, had a gimmick. A promotional gambit. A money-making proposition. But Regan's thoughts kept whirling. Could Peter be angry because—

She tried to stop the droning in her ear. "Manny, you're making me dizzy!"

"The night's not over. Just because you've sent the musicians home doesn't mean you're finished working."

He was not in a good mood; in fact, he hadn't been civil in weeks.

With a sigh, Regan dug her spine into the plush rear seat of the Lincoln Continental limousine. Manny kept his distance, but she wondered what he was thinking. Hard to tell with that bland, polished expression on his olive-skinned features, the lids low over his jet-dark eyes.

Why did Regan balk at every opportunity, over every issue—not even wanting to hear while he reeled off the list of important contacts for tonight. Hadn't he done everything for her? But ever since he'd gotten rid of that lousy drummer—never anything but trouble, Williams—she'd challenged his smallest decision on her behalf. Manny hunched into the corner of the seat, staring out at the traffic.

Why did she prefer the status quo? He had offered her—repeatedly—what most women still wanted, damnit, even if they wouldn't always admit it readily. A ring on that left hand. Regan wouldn't take him any other way, apparently. Time enough. He was thirty-four years old, and had discovered a gray hair at his temple that morning; and Regan would turn twenty-one in the spring. She ought to know her mind by this time.

Bertelli glanced at her as the limousine neared the hotel entrance. Patience was a fine thing, valuable in its time, but he'd paid a high price for this beautiful package wrapped in gold lamé, and he'd sure as hell insure it.

Manny searched the increasingly famous profile for a clue to her feelings. If the pressure didn't work, he could end up another Jake Marsh himself, consigned to oblivion. The parallel struck a bit too close for comfort, and he began to have silent gnawings of anxiety—rats nibbling at his insides. To hide the realization from himself, Manny scowled. A word he had stricken from his vocabulary years ago came suddenly to mind. *Dames*, he thought derisively. And above all, Regan. Lately, he never knew how to read her; and for the first time, Manny Bertelli felt something close to pity for Jake Marsh.

Seeing the familiar blandness become a frown, Regan relented.

"Don't be cross." She leaned over to kiss him, giving Manny a brief, stirring glimpse of her breasts as the gold lamé gapped away from her skin. But he didn't smile. And she knew he wouldn't until the reviews came out later.

"Remember about the cowboy," he cautioned, supplying yet another name. "Money hanging out of his pockets, probably stuffed into his socks, he's in—"

"Sheep. Second largest station in the country."

Manny sent her a look of grudging admiration. "At least you listen when I talk," he said as the sleek, dark limousine drew to a stop.

Nearly two hundred people jammed their suite, which was ornately trimmed in gilt, upholstered in dark red velvets and creamy brocade. The carpet, thick and plush-cut, was palest ivory, getting filthier by the second, Regan noted, as she was instantly besieged by party-goers—prominent Australians, expatriate fans from America, and hangers-on, plus Manny's favorite members of the press—before she had a chance to scoop up the discarded cigar stump by the foyer entrance. She saw it ground into the rug as someone grabbed her arm.

"Regan, you look absolutely beaut!"

"That *dress,* darling . . . would you sing for us? Just a number or two?"

"I'm sorry, but I'm slightly hoarse." No free concerts, folks. Everybody pays.

Regan eased away from the pair of dowagers with the oddly tortured vowels that made her think of horses, the Outback, vast trackless spaces of grassland. Across the room she spied a tall man so astonishingly good-looking that Regan paused just to stare at him in appreciation. Good shoulders, a dark suit cut to show his athletic frame to perfect advantage, long, muscular legs, and a pair of well-shaped hands. But it was his coloring that arrested her progress through the suite. Golden, like a beautiful statue; and when he turned she saw his eyes, a lovely sea blue that most women would have killed to have themselves. When he suddenly smiled, the room seemed to brighten. It was an almost boyish smile, which surprised her; mischievous and secret-sharing.

But she didn't have the vaguest idea who he might be.

Returning his smile, Regan continued on her way, murmuring greetings to a dozen guests who tried to waylay her as she sought the bar and a cold drink. Regan watered hers. Sometimes these post-concert parties went on until she nearly dropped from fatigue; and she had quickly discovered that liquor *ad libitum* didn't help; in fact, meant an inexcusably bad performance the following night—and quite possibly the danger, too, of an unguarded remark.

"Miss Reilly . . . the folk-song medley tonight?" She looked up into a pair of watery eyes. "Brilliant," the man said. "And one of our own tunes as well."

"A waving of the flag, yes. I'm glad you enjoyed it."

"Regan, *angel,* my name is . . ."

"Do you think we might get together on this thing? Market the T-shirts in the States, too? Only a beginning, of course, a whole line of—" Cotton tops; posters; even plastic dolls, someone had said. Really? "We could all make millions."

Regan smiled noncommittally. Then smiled some more, until her head began to ache. Suddenly she was reminded of a small auditorium, and a recital, and Jake, standing about afterward, receiving adulation. As if it were his due, she had thought then; now, she knew better. The smile pasted on her lips, the gracious words uttered by rote, the neutral comments were not ego at all, but only protection. Regan excused herself, feeling an urgent need for escape.

"Please talk to Mr. Bertelli, won't you? He's the dark-haired man with the gray suit."

Manny was heading her way through the maze of people, using a lot of elbow and shoulder to do so, and holding two glasses of sparkling champagne aloft. Intercepted by someone as she watched, he paused for only a second. Passing the buck, Regan supposed. His secretary would be deluged in the morning with requests, demands, for appointments.

When he reached her at last, he let his strained arms down slowly, handing Regan the unsolicited tulip glass of crystal, then sipped from his own before he took a folded newspaper page from his inside pocket. *"Salut,* my sweet. *Prosit.* Have you seen this yet? You're taking the continent by storm, no," he said, "by tidal wave."

Hurriedly, Regan scanned the sheet. "Do you think so? That good?"

The review, the first one out, was totally favorable, full of superlatives, but she felt a sudden wave of uneasiness which she had experienced too often since Kenny and Linda had left. The review gave her pleasure, but it was fleeting. Peter had been frowning, she told Manny; then everyone at this party had swamped her with praise. Who was right? Whom should she believe?

How much simpler the first tour already seemed to her. And how she still missed the camaraderie, the warmth of people she had trusted. For months after Minneapolis, Regan had awakened trying to tell herself that Kenny and Linda and Jeb were just down the hall, still sleeping, Raggedy Ann tucked beside those fair blond strands of hair, that flush of pink cheeks, and sturdy, small boy's body.

Then had come the realization that the band would never be the same; and for a while, she'd hidden from that, too. Nobody calling her *songbird* and *nightingale,* just as no one called her *baby* anymore. Oh, she'd telephoned a few times, she and Sam—but Linda tersely claimed that Kenny wasn't home, and she didn't want to talk.

"No self-doubts, sweet. You were wonderful—as always," Manny said easily. "Besides, Noel never learned to smile . . . doesn't mean a thing."

His joke, such a standard among everyone in the band, made Regan smile. Then her eyes fixed on a face near the foyer door, and Regan began to see everything in the room through a red, shimmering haze. Not so much anger, she soon realized, as the dress itself.

A scarlet flow of chiffon undulating toward Manny and Regan through the crowd, turning people's heads to notice the cut-down front and back held together by only the thinnest of straps. The auburn hair, a spiral of curls in every direction, looked like a wildly flickering torch. And also as if she'd just gotten out of bed, Regan thought. Which was entirely possible.

"What's *she* doing here?"

Manny followed her gaze. "Working," he said after a pause. "Publicity."

"And what, may I ask, is her unique qualification for the job?"

"She has a drama degree, sweet—barely dry so far as the ink's concerned. An aspiring actress in a world of hopefuls— that is to say, out of work. She'll put a lot into promotional work for you, simply because it helps her to be seen." Manny's forefinger ran gently down Regan's arm, shoulder to elbow. She felt no response at all. She had begun to tremble, but not from desire.

"You may handle the business end, Manny; you may hire the people you think best suited to get *me* ahead—and that's the only reason for hiring them—but if Alyson Oldham is one of your staff, keep her out of my sight!" How dare he . . . *how dare he bring her here?*

"Sweet, people are staring—"

"Let them! I don't feel like smiling anymore tonight." Regan glared at her cousin, at Veronica Vance who had come closer, too, scenting news like a bloodhound; and when she would have run, there was no escape. She had been surrounded by Manny, the gossip columnist (who looked like a blond clone of the stringer who had interviewed her in New Orleans), a few curious onlookers—and now, Alyson.

"I'll deal with you later," Regan hissed in Bertelli's ear, wondering if he'd used some signal to gather the guard closer. Nothing possible but light talk, and this brittle posture, her back aching from the effort not to flee, her hand tight around the champagne glass. The old competition again. Manny saying once, "Your cousin reminds me of you, sweet . . . every now and then. Very pretty, in a bolder fashion." Regan stared now at the blazing red dress, the brilliant hair. Then down at herself. How could gold lamé seem plain and dull? The pain she remembered from Paul, Martha, that mustard frame house where she had never belonged swept through her. But this is my world now, Regan thought. Open your mouth, then. Say something, anything. Regan schooled her features to blankness.

"Hello, Ali. Welcome to Sydney in the summertime."

A quick, harder-than-necessary hug. "Regan, how long has it been? I must say, you know how to throw a party."

Then, Manny's introductions to the rest of the gathering; more talk she didn't hear; more liquor she didn't want. Regan used every ounce of willpower she possessed not to slap Manny's hand away from her waist. What did Alyson want this time? Why was Manny flashing her in Regan's face—without so much as a word of warning? Looking silently into her champagne glass, she studied the way the bubbles popped and rose to the golden surface then fizzed away; but in another fraction of a second, they all went flat at once.

Alyson had been talking about the States, the poor weather setting in. Then the words, gloating and well-timed, gained her complete attention, and there was no place to run. No one else to turn to. The mention of his name alone shocked Regan all the more for its suddenness, her own quick reaction.

"I saw Jake in New York before I left."

Her heart took up a measured pounding. Manny's fingers making white marks on her arm. She wanted to toss the glass of wine in Alyson's face, and his. Fine newspaper copy that would make. Veronica's bright eyes had become sharp as a hawk's, and Regan thanked whatever lucky stars she had that, when she and Jake had been together, she was an unknown. As casually as she could with everyone looking at her, Regan asked, "Oh? And how is he?" her throat tight and aching. She wanted to bury her face in someone's shoulder as the agonizing rush of memory overcame her. And why not that golden man's, still watching her from across the room, a slight puzzlement on his handsome face now?

"Magnificent. As always." Alyson smiled at the secret they shared. Everyone else speculating as to who he might be; and what was the connection she wouldn't supply. Then Alyson leaned closer to whisper in Regan's ear so the others couldn't hear. "But you really should have warned me that he was such a fierce lover. I told Jake he ought to register himself with the Manhattan police as a lethal weapon—like a handgun." *Bang*.

Regan straightened at the second shock wave. "Oh, my God," she breathed, not caring what anyone thought now. The room wavered about her. She wrenched her arm free of Manny's fingers and fled, dropping the glass, hearing the shatter of crystal as she ran, oblivious of the curious stares after her, the murmuring buzz of conversation; Veronica's imperious, "Regan?"; not caring who saw the suffering in her eyes. Blindly she ran, a golden blur of light and flying tawny hair, taking with her through the crowded room a vision of that ice-blue gloating gaze. And Jake.

In the bedroom, which had a reversed color scheme of gold accented by deep red, Regan found Peter Noel making a telephone call. Nowhere else to go, she thought, and sank into a velvet-cushioned armchair, waiting for him to be through. Her heart wouldn't slow down, though it stopped occasionally for a couple of breath-stealing palpitations that made Regan cough. She felt cold, even her muscles chilled.

Peter didn't appear any happier. He was talking softly but frowning—not in anger, she realized, but in concern. His mother? He never talked about his problems, but that didn't mean there weren't any. An invalid, he had told her. What a terrible word. *Invalid:* not valid, weak . . . having no force or strength. Enough to make you give up, she thought, just knowing the label. But if the woman was anything at all like Peter, she'd never surrender to any illness, not even to her own ruined heart.

And what about me? Regan asked herself, smoothing the gold lamé of her gown over her knee. Why let Alyson hurt her again? Why be reminded of the past? Paul and Martha, or Jake, either. Even his name summoned up memories she'd rather not think about.

Sighing, Regan glanced up, relieved that Peter—still wearing the same unhappy look—was ending his telephone conversation. She wanted solitude and silence. She didn't want to think anymore, or feel. Alyson, Manny, the sugarcoated reviews tonight. What did people want of her? And whom could she trust now? When Peter dropped the receiver in its cradle, she was hardly aware that he had turned his frown on her.

Taking out his frustrations on the nearest target, he demanded, "What in hell happened to you tonight?" Regan would have thought he meant Alyson, but he hadn't been in the living room for some time. "Do you realize you were a half-step off through most of the second chorus in the jazz piece?"

"Was I?"

"Yes! And you damn well know it, so stop—for Christ's sake, Regan—stop the smirking!"

She hadn't imagined she was beginning to smile, wouldn't have thought it possible; but all of a sudden her heart could beat again at normal speed, without interruption or racing. Regan murmured, "Peter, you have the most irascible disposition of anyone I've ever known," which sounded strangely like a compliment. "And besides, I have fun when I sing. You just reminded me of that."

"You're not out on that stage to have fun—if you do, that's incidental—or to have everybody in the other room pat you on the fanny afterward and tell you how terrific you were, either... particularly when parts of that show stank, if you want to know the truth."

He glowered at her smile, and Regan felt a weight lifting from her heart.

"I thought I was perfect now," she teased, unable to resist. Her gaze dropped away from his.

"Not by a long shot, goddamnit! You stumbled on the lyric in 'Wildflower,' too."

"But my dear musical director, you were the only one who noticed."

"Except yourself."

Impulsively, Regan hugged Peter. "Yes, yes, you're right!" his slight body stiffening at her touch as if to ward her off, then relaxing its guard ever so slowly. No one else would tell her now, Regan thought; no one but them had heard the mistakes, however small. Underneath, she had known what was wrong with the concert tonight, too. "Thank you for your searching honesty," she added.

"Bullshit."

But Regan only smiled more broadly as she drew away. "Peter, I like you."

"Bullshit again," though he almost smiled back. "Rehearsal at nine tomorrow. All day if we have to. Don't be late."

"I won't be." Regan touched his shoulder. "How's your mother, Peter?"

"Holding on," he said. "It's, uh, kind of you to ask." And he slipped from the room like some insubstantial shadow, as if he'd never been there; as if by disappearing he could erase the glimpse of gratitude and feeling she'd seen in his eyes.

Feeling better, Regan forced herself to return to the party, too. Smiling, nodding, constantly moving from one group to the next, she made simple conversation on safe topics and managed to avoid even the sight of Alyson Oldham.

But she couldn't seem to keep away from Manny. When his touch slid along her bare shoulder to cup the bone, his fingers cool against her skin, Regan forced herself to stand still. "Sweet, you've put Ronnie Vance's nose on tilt here tonight, sniffing for trouble. We wouldn't want to give the impression that there's discord between us."

The fingers tightened, and Regan found herself playing public relations as if it were a parlor game—giving the blond columnist in the pink-flowered organza dress and rubies just enough, but not too much. Smiling until her face felt like cracking in two.

"You'll be the first to know any news that's worth repeating, Ronnie."

Hating herself for the lie. It was going to be a frigid day in hell (as Kenny said) before Vance—or Manny, for that matter—heard wedding bells again. Bring Alyson all the way to Australia for promotion work? The truth was, Manny was trying, in his inimitable fashion, to show her who held the reins in their relationship. It was no accident, either, to find the reigning queen of gossip so far from her own Hollywood turf.

Regan turned slightly, including Manny in her smile. "You'll see that Ronnie gets tickets for tomorrow night's show, won't you?" at the same time easing out from under his hand. "Best in the house, of course."

"A few friends may want to join me," Veronica was saying.

"As many as you like."

With a final nod of dismissal, Regan turned away to bid some departing guests good-bye at the door, the tall, golden-haired man among them. Manny ought to have been more careful with his *investment*.

He's a manipulator, Jake's warning, Regan thought, as she moved across the room like a quicksilver flow of molten gold. *Not again, not me.*

"I've been watching you. Anything I can do to help?"

Regan looked up into those sea-blue eyes as the tall, golden man whose gaze had followed her all evening now took her hand. She smiled, shaking her head. "No, I think not. Are you always so perceptive?"

"I try to be. Feelings," he said, "are important to me. I'm an actor," giving her one of those boyishly innocent smiles. As if he were apologizing at the same time for having so apparently frivolous an occupation. "At least that's what I tell myself in the mirror every morning."

The smile widened to match Regan's.

"I'm a fan of the first order, by the way," he added, strong fingers lightly squeezing hers. They weren't quite shaking hands; it was more a loose holding that warmed her to the bone. "My name's David Sloan," he introduced himself.

"I wish I could say *I'm* a fan, but . . ." Regan let the sentence trail away.

"Nobody's a fan of mine yet, dear girl." Grinning, he at last released her hand, taking a step back. "In America, no one's even seen me on the screen." Regan smiled, imagining David Sloan in a British drawing-room comedy, wearing a tweed jacket with leather patches at the elbows and contemplatively sucking on a pipe. He had a refined, upper-class accent, delicate and civilized. The sort of accent that made dry wit seem second nature to him, as much a part of David as an arm or leg.

"I'm flying to Madrid tomorrow morning," he announced. "Just finished a docu-drama here for television, and then on to Italy by spring." He paused, holding her gaze with his. "B films," he explained. "The sort of thing that used to be called Spaghetti Westerns." And then, as if embarrassed by his credentials, "My agent thought tonight would be a good idea, making contacts . . . There are a number of film people here. I guess he was right. But more to the point, I'm glad I came. I've been wanting to meet you ever since your first record, 'All The Words I Know' . . . a fabulous sound."

Regan tensed slightly. "Thank you. I'm glad to meet you, David." Surprisingly reluctant, she walked him nearer to the door, aware that there were other people waiting to say good night. But she didn't want him to go, didn't understand why she felt such instant attraction . . . not physically, though he was beautiful, to be sure. It was something much deeper in him, warm and caring. As if she wanted to edge closer to a fire that would end the chill in her heart.

"Regan, darling—"

David blocked the insistent party-goer from Regan's path.

"Listen, I'll be in London this summer. I understand you're making a debut there in June." His words were rushed, and urgent. "May I call you? Perhaps we might have dinner together."

"Is London your home, David?" she asked, receiving a puzzled look in reply.

"I'm a damn Yank, the same as you, love."

Regan grinned in surprise. From the accent, she would have thought—Then she laughed, delighted. "I think you're going to make a fine actor," she said. "Yes, David, I'd love to have dinner. I'll be staying at the Connaught."

Much later that night, with no memory of having moved from bed, Regan found herself staring out the hotel windows at sleeping Sydney. From the high vantage of the hotel, she saw a cluster of new high-rise buildings. The growing, changing face of the city, forming dark silhouettes against a gradually lightening sky. But Regan took in the sight only with her eyes.

Her thoughts whirled, tangling memory. *Fierce, savage. Why didn't you warn me?* Regan gnawed gently at her bottom lip, trying to understand the emotional pain she felt. Oh God, he'd been telling the truth! Regan pulled her thin silk robe around her, feeling the nighttime chill in her bones, her spirit. Jake had been blameless. But if he hadn't let her down by using Alyson then, hadn't he sent Regan away when she tried to make amends? Hadn't he believed the worst of her?

His words echoed again inside her. *I don't love you anymore.* And if he had ever loved her, wouldn't he be here now, Regan asked herself—not ten thousand miles away, and more?

Chapter 21

In Palm Beach, perennial playground of the rich, Jake had found sanctuary; or so he liked to think. Heading for Florida after Alyson Oldham's visit to the Grenadier—he hadn't been proud of himself for that—he had discovered the season in full swing. By the end of a week he had a good-paying job at a posh piano bar, a reasonable apartment, and a deep, tropical tan he'd never had the opportunity or leisure to acquire before. It should have been a peaceful life. The days were his own, long and lazy, and the nights...

Tonight, for example. He might just as easily have been at home in bed; but as usual, Jake was only playing piano while his mind took a nap.

If he had wanted action, it was easy to find. The Pier One catered to divorcées, widows, neglected wives. Which wasn't what he wanted... as if he knew what was.

Cutting off the dark direction of his thoughts, Jake glanced around the large room. It had a heavy nautical theme—elegant brass captains' clocks and ships' wheels; a deep blue and white color scheme; and liberal doses of mahogany, polished to a high luster.

Steven would have turned a handsome profit here; and for a moment, Jake could see him behind the lesser bar in Lancaster, wielding a damp rag as he cleaned and waxed. Then

Jake looked again toward the bar in this room. Three times as long, and you could see your face in the finish.

But that wasn't what he saw now. Jake's eyes slid over a sleek female form, and he felt a gratifying rush of interest. He attacked the last chorus of "Autumn Leaves" with vigor, rippling the keyboard, watching her ass. Nice. Could hardly be nicer. He wondered if she had a ring on her finger.

Hell, that's all I need, he thought: a bored, restless woman looking to get laid. Which would make them, for the moment, anyway, more or less twins.

Flicking a glance at her again, Jake saw money, but style, too. It's amazing, he thought, how few women in this world have style. Her clothes, so deceptively cut, were top-designer with none of the garish display the older patrons of the place preferred. In a room full of leathery tans, her skin was pearly porcelain perfection. An ash-blond pageboy, collar-length, was pulled back on one side by a straight, diamond-studded clip. Very little makeup, but her deep-set azure eyes didn't need any. Matched the exact shade of her slim skirt; the sleeveless sweater she wore.

When he finished playing, she was standing by the piano. "Do you honor requests?"

"Sure," he said. "Name it."

"A late supper with me." She was smiling now, even white teeth without a flaw, and a soft, generous pink mouth.

"I'm sorry, I don't know that one." An old joke, maybe the oldest he knew as a musician—but great for making distance. If that was what he wanted.

To his great surprise, Jake saw her expression change, the blue-green eyes faltering briefly.

"I have some excellent salmon, flown in from Oregon this morning, and a very nice Muscadet—on ice," she added. "And my chef prepares superb *chocolat mousse.*"

"Is that what you're after?" Jake asked. "Someone to drink your wine?"

She gave him a long, level, destructive stare, then walked away, a picture of absolute dignity. And class. He went after her.

"Wait," Jake said, taking her gently by the arm. No ring on her hand. They stood in the center of the long, narrow room with interested eyes focused on them from every table. "Wait a minute, that was rude of me."

"I suppose your assumption was as natural as the joke." Her gaze swung around the bar and back to him again. She removed herself from his grasp. "Perhaps, too, your assumption is correct." The little-girl uncertainty disappeared again; in its place a self-assured, sophisticated woman of means who knew how to flirt. But Jake wondered if the sophistication was a veneer, like mahogany over pine; if underneath he would find the need he sensed in her. Wondered why he wanted to. When she said, "Do you dare to find out?" he didn't hesitate.

"Yes," Jake answered.

She touched his cheek with a lightning-swift movement of the hand, soft and smooth. Jake saw a woman at the nearest table smile. "Good. I'll make a call and say good night to my friends when you're finished here. I've been told you're a tremendous natural resource," she said, "and I can see why." Jake felt his blood beat faster. Her eyes slid over him as she smiled. "But I'm going to have to teach you some manners."

Her name was Cecily Ferris, and she lived on a yacht.

"I adore this little spit of land," she told Jake, "with Lake Worth on one side and the Atlantic on the other, fringed palms everywhere, brown pelicans frolicking in the surf. It's only a half-mile wide, you know—Palm Beach—in most places, very *intime*."

Trim and elegant like her, the yacht boasted an actual living room carpeted in white, with fresh flowers in elaborate arrangements on every table. The atmosphere, even mingled with salt air, seemed heavy with scent, like a funeral home. Because Cecily preferred a certain florist in New York, blossoms were flown from the city each morning.

"My friends tonight thought I'd gone mad," she said as he looked around the room. "Bringing you here, I mean." Jake had noted they were on a par with the other customers at Pier One, a quartet of aging women much older than she was, and he wondered what they had in common except money. "They won't set foot on the yacht themselves, but then . . . family friends. It was a social duty this evening having drinks with them. They don't understand why I keep this thing on the water, and they never have. But it's very private, and relaxes me. I bought the *Shearwater* when I was nineteen."

"On your allowance," Jake said with a bland smile.

"The year my father died," she answered. "With my inheritance." A small part of it, she added quite seriously. "I suppose you think I'm spoiled, but I can't help it. He owned just about everything and passed all of it to me." The azure eyes looked away, leaving Jake to wonder at the sudden hole in the conversation just before their food was served.

While they ate a late supper, Cecily told Jake she had rarely seen her father, and his heart went out to her at the matter-of-fact tone of voice. "But I had everything else," she went on. "And I had Charlie, who is in charge—normally"—with a smile for Jake—"of getting me what I want."

Charles Peyson had been her father's indispensable aide; Jake immediately considered him part of the inheritance. "Charlie is my financial adviser, friend, confidante, errand boy, and," this with a small laugh, "I suppose a blend of Ann Landers, Emily Post—"

"You forgot Don Juan," Jake went fishing.

"Charlie? Not the type, I'm afraid—much too dedicated to the family interests to bother chasing women. Or to marry, either." At fifty-two, she said, he probably never would.

Just turned thirty ("what used to be a rather desperate age for a woman unattached"), a pudgy adolescent duckling turned sleek swan, Cecily refused *chocolat mousse* after dinner. "I trained myself with great difficulty, or I was trained, you might say."

Fat farms and exercise clinics, she went on; Elizabeth Arden and Kenneth and Sassoon; Givenchy and St. Laurent, Pucci and Dior. "What wondrous miracles they do perform."

Jake laughed with her, but he didn't quite mean it. Cecily seemed a perfect example of quality control in one of her father's apparently ubiquitous industries, and it bothered him.

There was something about her, something defensive, and—for all her crisp chatter and smiles—quite lost. It struck a chord in him, but he couldn't say just why. They studied each other from opposite ends of the white sofa, sipping cognac and listening to the sea outside. Then she said, "What about you, Jake?"

"No money," he replied. "And no . . . attachments."

"That surprises me," though she looked, he thought, relieved—just as he had been to find no wedding band on her finger at Pier One. "Most of the good men are taken rather early, I've found."

"I considered getting married—once." He cut her off before the memory took hold of him, pushed it away as he rejected magazines—ever-increasing numbers of them—with stories of *her,* and the Arts section of the Sunday paper listing concerts. Another very good reason for his removal to Palm Beach. "Briefly considered," Jake added, then looked fixedly at a cluster of red peonies in a white porcelain vase on the coffee table. "It doesn't seem like a very attractive notion now. I wonder why it did then."

For the next week, Jake allowed Cecily Ferris to stalk him like a cool and sinewy golden lioness. She came nightly to Pier One, waiting until he finished work, then drove him in her Rolls Corniche to the *Shearwater.* She fed him food and compliments, sent expensive classical records to his apartment and a beautiful music book full of stunning color plates—the sort bought as coffee-table decor—and half a dozen hand-sewn shirts, which fit perfectly. It was, he soon learned, impossible to refuse her tokens of affection. Whether they watched a comedy at the Royal Poinciana Playhouse or enjoyed a swim and lunch—succulent crabmeat salad served on the terrace bedecked with umbrella tables—at the exclusive Bath & Tennis Club, Cecily paid.

Jake didn't mind at first because it seemed to please her, but what bothered him in time—a rather short space of time—was her habit of referring to him in front of her friends as, "my diamond in the rough," followed by a quick kiss to show possession. It reminded him of the night Alyson had wondered why he let Regan toy with him.

"You'd better stop this," he warned. "You're turning my head." But Cecily only laughed, a bright, clear laugh, and ran a slender finger along the top of the piano at Pier One, as if she were searching for dust—except that the motion looked more like a misplaced caress; felt like one. Soft as a butterfly kiss, she said, "I certainly hope so."

She seemed to be reorganizing his life, which Jake admitted could have used fewer cobwebs, a little more sweeping.

"You'll need a dinner jacket," Cecily decided.

"I've got several."

She flipped through the contents of the hangers in his closet.

"They're looking worn, and Palm Beach is very much a black-tie town, darling. We'll run over to Worth Avenue and have you fitted, shall we? I think three to start."

"Cecily, my concert days are over, and—"

"Saturday night," she explained as if to a backward child, then, "Didn't I mention the Heart Fund Ball at the Breakers?"

Three it was, then. In immaculate evening dress, ebony black and snowy white, Cecily beside him in the rear seat of the Corniche, in ruby taffeta that rustled when she moved, Jake leaned back to watch the long driveway unfold past the massive Old World fountain. At the two-story, colonnaded porte cochère of the opulent hotel, they were descended upon by uniformed staff, a doorman and the parking valet.

Inside the fairy-tale splendor of the place, they danced far into the night, whirling beneath gargantuan chandeliers of gleaming crystal, eating and drinking too much. After suffi-cient champagne, Jake was persuaded to play the piano during an orchestra break. Cecily qualified her lavish praise. "Darling, you were wonderful—but why so much Chopin? And I do feel the Schubert went sailing past."

"I thought you wanted the diamond to have some sparkle."

It was only on Sunday afternoon that she seemed to appre-ciate his sarcastic reference, saying with concern etched on her classic features, "Jake, I wouldn't want to do anything to ruin this." He saw a glint of moisture in her eyes that made him ashamed of his rudeness. Perhaps she was right about him.

"Neither would I. We'll have to both work harder at my manners, won't we?" Wrapping an arm around her shoulders, he directed her attention to the field. "Look, the line judge is waving the flag! There's a goal!"

They were watching a match on one of thirteen playing fields at the Palm Beach Polo & Country Club, and drinking mimosas as a remedy for last night's hangovers. He wasn't in the best of shape, Jake reminded himself as Cecily applauded her team's scoring, the tears glistening in her eyes; but he might be a little easier on her.

No mistaking how pretty she looked today, or how much she seemed to want him. It wouldn't be difficult responding to her body, if not her life-style. On some level he'd been resisting both, and he wondered why, when there were facets to her that so greatly intrigued him.

Looking bright and healthy in white linen pants and an aqua silk shirt, she hung on Jake's arm, her own skin perfectly smooth, untanned. "The beautiful people," her set were called. And wouldn't it be simple? As effortless in appearance as the next goal that rolled between the posts.

Jake grinned at her. "I'm about to owe you ten dollars," he said of their light betting. He had picked the opposite side, wearing yellow shirts against Ceci's navy blue team, and they were three goals down in the last chukker.

Easing her head into the hollow of his shoulder, Cecily smiled at him. "I think we can arrange easy terms."

Jake didn't realize it then, but he was never to make love to Cecily Ferris without the feeling—usually correct—that he was repaying her for something. Raised on one elbow to study her complexion, milky against the cream-colored background of flowered Porthault sheets, he couldn't help asking, "Why is this relationship ass-backwards?"

"Because I'm rich. And you're not."

He stared at her, gauging the smile. Was this what she

wanted of him, then, other than an escort properly groomed and dressed? Just someone in her bed?

He'd been telling himself to pull back; but then he'd have to think, feel, remember what he didn't want to, ever again. Alyson Oldham, the alley and the pain, Regan and Bertelli, his own ruined future. And there would be the unhappiness, too, in Ceci's azure eyes, that had made him think there could be something more between them. "Darling," she whispered now, running her hand over his chest, his shoulders, "it's only money. That's what it's for." And he knew he wasn't going anywhere.

He'd come here not to think about the past, and by Christ, he wouldn't. More slowly this time, Jake began to make love, not rushing for the end, losing himself in the cushion of Cecily's body. Some control, anyway. At least in bed.

That night they didn't sleep, rocking together violently in heat, then more gently as sex receded and the yacht dipped at its moorings, the quiet black water of the marina slapping against its sides like the tender movements of a lover.

Chapter 22

Regan eased a gown from her dressing room closet, tossing the white froth of fabric encrusted with imitation emeralds onto the brown velvet sofa. The evening promised to be abnormally warm for September in London, this last week of a summer-long European tour; and she wondered if the dress would be too hot.

Still, she shivered now in the air-conditioned chill of the starkly modern brown and silver room, which depressed her. In fact, a strange foreboding had been following her all day from Charles de Gaulle airport outside Paris to Heathrow's landing. She couldn't explain the feeling; but it wouldn't go away, either.

What could be wrong? Sitting at her dressing table to begin her makeup, Regan smiled into the mirror. Two platinum albums out of four; and the newest, *Encore,* moving up fast. Its cover used a photograph from the first concerts in Australia where she had met David Sloan, the shot taken onstage in the gold lamé gown of her daydreams, the lighting making a halo all around, the microphone held high. It was a lovely picture, which had been the illustration for a magazine article first, and Regan liked its sophistication.

She also liked the four gold records, including those for

"Nashville Nights" and "Wildflower." She didn't allow herself to think about Jake's song, the first. His song . . . their song. She never did.

Applying a mascara wand to her eyelashes, Regan forced her mind to dwell on more pleasant thoughts. Nothing was wrong, nothing. Slowly, she smiled away the frown that memories had brought.

In June, David Sloan had made good on his invitation to dinner that night in Sydney when they'd met. The evening had been the first of many. And David had proved a delightful guide to London's spectacular sights.

The intriguing Tower complex, bathed not in terror but by clear summer sunshine that morning; the Byzantine grandeur of St. Paul's Cathedral; the charm and elegance of Kensington Palace in the middle of the park; a day trip down the stately Thames to the splendor of Hampton Court. The Food Halls at Harrod's, hanging game birds suspended from the ceiling with their feathers still on. She'd seen the more traditional tourist spots as well—Parliament, the changing of the guard at Buckingham Palace, Trafalgar Square.

David's favorite had been the London Dungeon, however; a dank display of deadly torture devices and gore in a realistic wax museum that made Regan's skin crawl. She had preferred the awesome historical significance of Westminster Hall where monarchs, going clear back to the eleventh century, lay in state beneath the high, beamed Gothic ceiling.

She'd been only slightly less awed by the London traffic, everything coming from the wrong direction. If it hadn't been for David, she'd have stepped into the path of the first oncoming cab and been flattened instantly. "Watch yourself, dear girl!"

The Britishism always made her smile, and David asked what she was laughing about. *Dear girl,* the clipped English syllables from a man who looked like the epitome of the California surfer. "I'd love to have known you in Italy," she told him, imagining that he affected the accent of whatever country he was in—which still didn't explain Australia—but David answered, "I wish you had, my delicate little *ravioli*," kissing the tips of her fingers with a flourish, "my delightful *fettucine*," showing her that boyish grin when she laughed. "Well, come on, those are the only words I learned in more than three months—and sufficient they were."

Yet, no matter his affectations, Regan liked him. David made her laugh, and he treated her well. There was none of the game-playing she knew with Manny, nothing of the intensity with Jake.

Remembering those pleasant summer days now, she carefully outlined her eyes.

Their time together had been marred only a few times—the first, by Paul. Had she really seen him, loitering outside the entrance to Covent Garden when she and David arrived? The photographers' flashguns had made vision less than perfect, and Regan had decided it was certainly not Paul's sort of place to begin with. Backstage was one thing; in the wings, another (he'd been doing advance work for her concert tour); but the world-famous theater, a ballet? Regan doubted it.

But then—

"Are you sleeping with that guy?"

Manny had telephoned from New York in the middle of her night.

"You've been listening to Paul, haven't you?" Regan countered immediately. "Well, if I want to have an affair—which I'm not—I'll darn well have it!" Shaking with anger, she drew a steadying breath. "Manny," she said more gently, "this isn't working. I'm not going to marry you. I'm not thinking of marrying anyone right now and—"

Regan broke off, wondering what made her so sure about Manny. He'd asked with increasingly discomforting regularity. But she'd never envisioned him as a lover. It occurred to her that, although she could hardly blame Manny for Jake's interpretation of the Veronica Vance interview, he hadn't helped the problem. But he couldn't help it, either, that she didn't love him. And after Sydney, Alyson—

"I told you once, I'd make you want me," Bertelli muttered into the crackling static of the transatlantic connection. "But it isn't me, is it?" he asked. "It never was . . . and it never will be."

"Not that way, Manny." She ran a hand over her eyes, not wanting to hurt him. "I'm sorry, no."

The silence lasted only a few seconds. "You're not thinking about a new manager, are you?"

"You've never made a mistake where my career is concerned," Regan conceded. He might be manipulative, calculating; but he was one of the best in the business, and as promised, he'd made her a star. "We both know that, Manny," or she wouldn't have been in London on the eve of her debut. "Do you remember, after watching me for a week at Steven's, when you took me out for *croque monsieur* at that little inn nearby? Do you remember saying we should talk 'hard business'?"

"I remember."

"That was one of the most exciting nights of my life, Manny."

She heard the tension ease from his voice. "Well, there's a lot more to come, starting tomorrow. You're sold out for the opening." He paused. "I wish I could be there."

"So do I." There was a catch in her tone. "You always say we make a good team, Mr. Bertelli." It had always been the most important part of their relationship; and he had to know that, too.

"Hard business it is, then," he said gruffly, clearing his throat. He wished her well before saying good-bye. Regan felt a sadness pervade her spirits, the end of an era . . . but without regrets, unlike the time with Jake, or Kenny. And of course, not nearly so final.

As she replaced the receiver, Regan wondered if she had heard correctly. "I must have holes in my head," Manny's voice fainter, the overseas connection fading. "Why would a street punk want a class act in his bed, for Christ's sake?"

Then, the next time Regan talked to him, Manny had asked slyly, "You don't mind, do you, if I give your cousin a call?" easing her guilt and at the same moment making her smile in speculation. "With my blessing," she said.

Ever since, until tonight, she'd been feeling relieved and

buoyant, able to fully enjoy her growing friendship with David, no longer concerned that Paul noted their relationship. *Manny . . . and Alyson?*

When she and David dined at The Queen's Favourite, a sumptuous restaurant on a pristine side street in elegant Mayfair, Regan hadn't been prepared at all for the near ruination of the evening. But her reputation had grown overnight, the result of rave reviews for her opening. As soon as they sat down, someone asked for an autograph. And the interruptions grew constant. Some were insistent, aggressive.

"Look," David finally rose to his feet, "you know how to find the box office and—"

"Get your faggot hands off me!"

David had spun the heavyset man around just as the headwaiter moved toward them, and before Regan could push her chair back from the table. "If you want to see the lady, buy yourself a ticket for tomorrow night's show—and leave us the hell alone tonight!"

When the intruder had been hustled away, Regan tried to shut out the stares from everyone else in the room by playing with the buff-colored napkin in her lap.

"Regan, I'm sorry I lost my head with that idiot, but when he started name-calling—"

"Let's forget it, can we?"

"Can *you?*" he asked, looking up from his menu to study her.

With a rueful smile, Regan thought of the first southern tour in her own country where people had been no more polite. "If you'd ever gotten catcalls from an audience and loud requests to remove your clothes, believe me, David, this would seem relatively minor." But her hands were trembling. "You'll soon learn about publicity yourself."

David's eyes, the clear, bright blue of speedwells, wandered over her, making her say quickly, "I do appreciate your bravery with that man."

He laughed, leaning back in his chair against the heavy beige watered silk upholstery. "I doubt that guy had any more respect for my biceps than my father seems to," and Regan saw the quickly veiled discomfort in his eyes, though he smiled at her across the table set in softly gleaming pale blue damask with pewter service. He didn't elaborate, asking instead, "How do *you* see me, dear girl? As the ... potential heartthrob of millions?" The tone of voice wasn't quite teasing.

"I see you as my friend, David. I'm afraid my opinion is prejudiced."

She tried to keep his smile, but it vanished abruptly. Surely he hadn't taken that man seriously. Or had she wounded his male vanity herself? Under the soft glow of light from the chandelier, in the flickering shadows made by ivory tapers in sterling candlesticks, he looked undeniably handsome, virile, appealing. Regan felt a startling change between them, a rush of long-denied desire. "David...."

"Not to worry."

He kept his eyes downcast, beginning to peruse the menu again. The Dover sole had improved his mood, Regan remembered, until, by the end of the meal they were both laughing again. She'd gone that night to his suite on the floor above hers at the Connaught, but then—

A firm knock at her dressing room door interrupted Regan's reverie. Turning, she held a tube of lip gloss in one hand, calling out, "Come in!"

Sam Henderson's thin, ascetic features appeared, his darkly sorrowful eyes in the mahogany face looking even more so, and the strange foreboding Regan had felt all that day seemed to coldly embrace her again.

"Could I see you for a minute?"

Sam looked ill, and shaken. Dressed for the concert, he had neglected to fasten one of his shirt studs, and the black butterfly tie angled against his collar: Sam, so neat and precise and moralistic. Something *was* wrong.

"What's happened, Sam?" Regan waved him toward a seat.

For a long moment, he stared at her, but not at her face. His dark eyes moved over the persimmon-colored dressing gown, studied the tips of her white satin mules. As if he were trying to decide whether to speak at all. Then she saw his deep-set eyes fill. "Oh Regan, goddamnit—" His voice was husky, halting. "Oh, shit—it's Kenny!"

"Kenny," she repeated blankly. But the chill of certainty ran through her veins.

"Regan, Kenny's . . . *dead.*" The word hung, suspended, irrevocable, in the silent air. "He died in Chicago, he—" Sam broke off, shaking his head, gesturing helplessly with his finely boned hands.

An accident, she thought; an illness. Hepatitis, or pneumonia. He could be so careless with his health, his own welfare, and there was Jeb—Regan's mind kept racing with her heart—passing on viruses like the one she'd caught on the first road tour, that sore throat that wouldn't go away . . . how could he be—? There were people too much alive, far too vital to just . . . men like Kenny with that muscular frame and the shock of russet brown hair and the big laugh; the arms that held and kept the hurt away the day Jake had sent her out of his life, men like Kenny didn't die because—because, oh God, how could they help each other if he was *dead?* Uncomprehending, Regan looked up at Sam, barely understanding his words.

"Why did he mess with that crap? How many times did I tell him, Regan?" Sam ground the heel of his black patent dress shoe into the carpet, staring with disgust at the toe. But the tears were running down his face, and he didn't wipe them away. "Dirty smack, and something else. Higher than hell, he must have been, and the stuff stopped his heart, everything—"

"When did it happen? Who told you?"

Regan felt as cold as ice, as if her own lungs had stilled.

"Early this morning, London time. I got a call from Clive Dixon about twenty minutes ago—he's on tour up North, and caught the news on a local station; he thought . . . we'd want to know."

Clive. Regan tried to feel something at the mention of his name again. "That was kind of him," she said dully. Sam nodded, agreeing as she thought, Clive Dixon and his Country

Band. *You're just singin' over those people's heads, honey.*
Sending his son to her with a song. "He said he was awful
sorry, Regan, and if there's anything he can do..." Sam gave
up trying to speak, and shrugged.

"I don't know," she said. "I just don't know."

Linda. And Jeb. And Kenny. All she could do was say their
names to herself and think that she hadn't seen them in almost
two years now; that somehow she had known during those last,
bitter moments in the hotel with Linda that she'd never see
them again. That Kenny had died thinking she didn't care.

"Fifteen minutes, Miss Reilly!"

This time, she had barely heard the rap at the door. Oh
God, not dressed; and the news going through her like an
endless wave. How would she sing? Regan stared helplessly
at Sam.

"He was my best friend, Regan, even the night in the hall,
remember—when he came after me with the bottle? Remember?"

"Yes, Sam, I know."

"Listen, I'm sorry I laid this on you before the show. Peter's
going to have my ass for this."

"I'll talk to Peter. I'm grateful you told me, Sam. I wouldn't
have you keep it to yourself all night." She walked him to the
door, and when he paused, lifting a hand to her hair, rested
her head on his shoulder for a second. The first tour, she
remembered, and Clive Dixon and all the shows that didn't
work. *Chicken Little,* they had said. Regan wished she could
cry, anything but go onstage in a few minutes more. *The sky
has fallen,* she thought, murmuring against his jacket. "Oh,
Sam..."

Stepping back, he looked at her severely, and Regan was
sure that the same words had struck them both at once, like
the blow of Kenny's death.

What are we going to do?

"You sing good tonight," Sam told her. "Because I'm going
to play like a sonofabitch."

Sing pretty, nightingale....

* * *

For a long while, Regan didn't know what she was singing; but her voice rang true, in perfect pitch and clear as crystal, and the audience applauded loudly. She had worn the white dress with the U-shaped neckline and long sleeves, trimmed in green stones, not caring whether it might be too warm or whether the effect was too much against the beaded curtain—but her appearance, too, had been wildly cheered.

She did a medley of show tunes, which always went over well. "Wildflower," of course. Then an upbeat number, soft jazz that was usually great fun, which she had to force tonight. The thrill she always felt when she sang seemed to have died, too.

Regan stopped the song in the middle. Oh God, she had the feeling she was dancing on a grave. Or trying to. *Kenny, I didn't want to send you away.* "I'm sorry, I'm sorry, I can't—"

There was an immediate rustling from the audience, a buzz of speculation. She ignored Peter's glare, the sure question in his eyes—was she going crazy onstage?—turning briefly toward Sam, who sat hunched over his guitar. He glanced at her, and she saw that his eyes were moist. In the silence, someone called, "Come on, luv—what's the matter?" as Peter hissed, less generously, "For the love of God, Regan—"

She faced the microphone once more, head up and eyes on the crowd, the long shimmer of her gown flashing brilliance in every direction, turning her graceful body into a living statuette, gem-encrusted and shining. Like an award that moved and sang and smiled, made little jokes to hide the tears she couldn't cry. An award, she thought, for living.

Regan flicked the long microphone cord out behind her as she spoke.

"Ladies and gentlemen, the next is for a very dear . . . friend of ours, Sam Henderson's and mine." She gestured for him to come closer, waved Peter away. "And tonight, I want to do it as we first heard the song—because he won't be here again."

Regan didn't even have to signal after that. By instinct the same as her own, Sam began to play the opening notes, the two of them at center stage together, his monkish features transformed by the lights, softened; those wonderful, deep-set brown eyes looking almost saintly; his lean, dark fingers unerringly on the right strings, plucking the sweet, stirring melody to "Nashville Nights" from the satin-varnished guitar. And she was back again in another time, another place where she hadn't quite belonged.

I love it, she heard him say, *I love that thing,* while Clive Dixon, Jr. grinned at the reception for his song, his playing then. Hope and joy and life, so much alive, and—very nearly—loving each other, too, she and Kenny. Regan sang with her heart, as she had tried on another night of ending to sing the beautiful words to Jake's love song. But this time, she didn't miss a note or a phrase of the lyric; and when she had finished, she didn't think there was a dry eye in the house—except, still, her own.

Regan bowed her head over the microphone, and the curtain of tawny silk enveloped her, the sudden flash of cameras made her close her eyes against the light. The song had never sounded so good, not even the recording. She had never heard Sam play so beautifully, and as the applause began, she wouldn't look at him. She sensed that he was crying openly, unashamed. If only she could free the tears herself, if only—

But all she could manage was the husky whisper that rose, magnified by the magic of electronics, above the noise of clapping to fill the auditorium. A last benediction, from the heart.

"No more long, black nights, Kenny."

Then she backed slowly away from the stand, handing the mike to Peter, and left the stage, hiding her feelings as her lovely face had been hidden by her hair.

"You shouldn't be alone," Peter had told her after the final curtain call. "Isn't there someone—?"

"There's nobody," Regan answered. *Nobody cares,* she had cried to Kenny; and hadn't she made him feel, herself, that it was true?

"Why don't you call Sloan?"

"David?" She had been surprised that he'd noticed their

friendship. Then wondered why the surprise, when Peter seemed to see everything about her. Wondered, too, why Peter himself didn't offer to give comfort—though, of course, he knew how tenuous was their relationship; how much it was based on careful distance, even after that night in Philadelphia when she had sung Jake's song, even after the glimpse of feeling on his own face in Sydney. He would expect her to turn to someone else. Anyone else, Regan thought. "I haven't seen David since London," she said. "He's on the Coast, in California, shooting a film." His first stateside film.

And so, she was seated across from Sam Henderson in the ultramodern American Bar at the hotel, nursing a double whiskey while he toyed with a glass of Guinness Stout on which he had poured too deep a head, four inches of creamy foam. There were no words between them, but the silence shouted.

It was a hundred nights on the blue-and-silver bus, a thousand different stops—or so it seemed. Testing equipment, setting up, striking the next day to move on again. Like a traveling circus, Regan remembered. All the alien cities then—though she knew them now—and Kenny's voice murmuring to her in the green-lit darkness as they rode. That incredible chemistry overcoming the other tensions between them. Almost, she corrected. Almost.

"Sometimes I wonder," Regan mused in the stillness, "what would have happened if I hadn't called Linda to bring the baby on tour with us." She had had enough of the whiskey, was feeling just fuzzy enough, to broach the sensitive subject to Sam.

"Nothing good," he said, which didn't surprise her. "Sometimes things are better left alone." He stared into the glass of dark liquid, and tried to shake the foam down. "Listen, I wish my old lady hadn't walked out on me—or that I hadn't let her go. But hell, Regan, what would that have proved? I know it now. We'd have been miserable with each other for five, ten more years—but the end would have been the same."

"Do you really think so, Sam?" Regan asked gently. "Don't you imagine you'd have learned to live with each other's . . . I don't know, foibles? That's an odd word, isn't it? Bad qualities, maybe. Temper...." She thought of Jake's stubborn pride, her own impatience. Having trailed off, she tried again. "I used to envy Linda," Regan admitted. "Staying with Kenny no matter how serious their problems were, but when he couldn't face them any longer, she stuck by him, didn't she?" Regan twirled the swizzle stick in her glass, remembering how Linda had accused her of leaving Jake when he was ill, or borrowing Jeb because she wouldn't have a baby of her own. "I feel sorry for her tonight, I hurt for her so much," she said, "but at the very least, they had Jeb, didn't they, which is a lot to leave behind, Kenneth Williams, Junior—"

"His name isn't Williams."

The flatness of his tone made her look up, startled, to Sam's serious, deep brown eyes.

"Kenny never bothered to marry her! Why do you think I rode him all the time about how he treated her?" Grief and anger mixed in his tone. But why hadn't they married? Regan wondered. For Jeb's sake, if nothing more? "Christ," Sam went on, "she's been through all kinds of hell for him, the last year or so with the needle and no money left, Kenny crazy all the time . . . what's he left her with? I'll tell you," he said, not waiting for Regan's answer. "Nothing, except responsibility for Jeb. Zip. Zero. Zilch. *De nada*, lady—so you better thank God Above that you're working every night, making money, paying salaries, even if you are alone now because—"

"Sam!"

He stared at her miserably. "I'm sorry, Regan." He reached for her hand, covering it with his darker one. "I know you had troubles with Jake . . . and I'm sorry. But Regan, Kenny would only have made matters worse. You knew that as well as I did . . . or Peter."

Seeing the whiteness of her face, he didn't go on. Regan wondered if she had allowed Manny to send him away in order to save herself from the same fate, the endless dark nights that had finally destroyed him.

Kenny had needed her, and she had fired him instead of helping. There must have been something she could have done—not simply nod her head to Manny and Peter, hiding from bad publicity. You'll have a job, she'd told him, but Kenny had answered proudly, *when hell turns to solid ice*. And now, he was dead. She could ignore the painful reference to Jake, but she couldn't ignore that.

"Don't envy Linda," Sam was saying. "She never had it any better, and just like you, she's going to pick herself out of the dirt—without as much to start over as you had, Regan."

That didn't ring exactly true for Regan, but she couldn't think why. Tonight, she only knew how Linda must feel. How *she'd* felt once. And that part of Linda's sorrow was *her* fault made Regan's grief worse.

Forget loneliness, she thought. Forget the roaches in bad hotel rooms, the greasy food and little sleep; forget the pressures of performing, the physical and mental toll of artistic striving, the constant necessity of commercial appeal to a changing market. Forget everything Jake had told her when she was starting out, and couldn't believe him.

But how to forget the fact that you betrayed your friends— the few there were—and moved them, inched them, shoved them one step closer to death?

"Was there insurance, do you know?" Regan asked Sam in a hollow voice. "Did he leave anything for her and the baby?"

But Sam shook his head. "Whatever they had lapsed long ago. Linda told me that much the only time she'd talk to me after Kenny . . . left the band." Did Sam blame her, too? Regan wondered.

She rose to her feet, dropping some pound notes on the table. "I'm going upstairs to call Manny. Linda's going to have what she needs, Sam." Money every month, a trust fund for Jeb's schooling. She could do that now; it was all she could do.

"Linda won't accept help from you."

But he was staring at her with respect.

"Oh yes, she will." Regan gathered her evening bag and white lacy shawl. She hadn't bothered to change from the emerald-spangled gown. "Linda's a private person, but she's smart. Just now, she needs help badly, and I can't think of a better way to remember Kenny and our . . . friendship," she said, "than to provide for his child and the woman he loved. Can you?"

It was a challenge the way she said it, daring Sam to accuse her of self-aggrandizement when there was nothing of the kind involved. Oh yes, she could hear Linda, even now: *Sorry doesn't pay the rent.* Well, the rent was one problem Linda wouldn't have, because if she had to—for Jeb's sake—Regan would stuff the money down her throat.

Manny thought she was crazy, though he agreed to make the financial arrangements. "You want to throw money away," he said, "I can't stop you."

Hanging up, Regan paced the rooms of her riverfront suite, oblivious to the quiet Edwardian elegance, as she had been unable when she left the bar to appreciate the mellow mahogany foyer downstairs carpeted in deep pink, or the sweeping stair-case rising to her floor. Driven by desperation and unspent grief in the middle of the London night, she placed a second call; but David Sloan was not at home.

Dining with friends, she was informed by the concierge, in Laurel Canyon. He kept a busy social life, she knew that, one that didn't include waiting for a call from Regan Reilly. They had talked frequently by telephone since he'd left London for the States; his conversations had trailed her through France. But Regan wondered if—after that night in his hotel suite—he'd lost interest in anything but friendship.

Coming from the restaurant where they'd been so unpleas-antly accosted, David's spirits restored by white wine and anec-dotes over dinner, Regan had hesitated to go upstairs with him. Then, at last, relented.

David's suite, with the same decor Regan's had, was en-hanced by his own formidable array of *objets d'art:* Yes, there were identical sofas and chairs in rich Prussian blue, the same gold and ivory walls, and gilt-edged mirrors as Regan's, the heavy brocade spread on the elaborate bed, the same rich Ori-ental carpet picking up the color scheme. But there were also dozens of framed photographs of the great and famous, each one inscribed, and delicate Dresden figurines and small pieces of graceful statuary, even a Russian Easter egg containing a miniature military scene.

"You carry your home with you," Regan said, delighted, "like a turtle with its shell."

"Not a very flattering simile, dear girl." David tried to look reproachful, but couldn't manage it.

"Like a dashing Bedouin sheik, then."

Which pleased him more. Offering cognac, which Regan refused, David then decided to forego the drink himself. She wondered whether he felt light-headed, too, from all the wine as he began yet another anecdote. Something to do with a weekend at a duchess's country house in Kent and an amusing minor scandal that made the tabloids. At the first pause, some time later, Regan cried, "David, it's three A.M.! And I've got a show tomorrow!"

When she stood up, she slipped his arms around her gently, as if she were one of the china figurines on his dresser. "Stay with me, love."

He turned her face up to kiss her tenderly, and something stirred in her. The way he tilted her chin, the way his mouth moved lightly over hers. Suddenly, she was shaking. Regan let David draw her to the bedroom, felt his touch skimming the curves and hollows covered by the buttercup-yellow Halston silk jersey gown she wore, strapless and narrow-waisted with a graceful fall of skirt. "Beautiful," he murmured, meaning her, too; and she felt his hands at the long zipper, sliding it down. Her heart beat quickly, loudly. Peeling away the gown, then her undergarments, scraps of silk and lace upon the carpet, he touched her skillfully, reverently.

But when they had fallen onto the soft bed and wrapped the satin-covered eiderdown quilt around them, when their naked bodies had warmed and melted toward each other, David nuzzled Regan's neck. And nothing else happened. "David?" she whispered.

"Sorry." His hands stilled on her bare flesh. "So sorry, my dear girl, but I'm afraid . . . I've had far too much to drink."

And he fell promptly into a sound, profoundly disappointing sleep.

It must have been the wine, Regan agreed now, again. Which didn't help any more than it had the next morning. Neither of them had mentioned the failure, of course, They'd shared a massive breakfast, English kippers and American pancakes; and David had flown to New York that afternoon.

Now, she stared out into the damp London darkness, wondering if there would be anything more for them.

In the meantime, they'd become confidants as well as friends. Regan supposed she might have to settle for those midnight chats while she snuggled into bed in whatever hotel, enjoying the deep throb of David's voice across the ocean. Just as she'd once cherished the long-distance visits by telephone with Jake when he was on tour. One night, she'd even told David about him—that's how close they had grown.

And her voice had broken several times, so that he had to encourage her to continue. When she'd finished, Regan recognized anger in his silence, though all he'd said was a soft, "There's nothing the equal of a first love, is there? Whether it's good or bad." He hadn't needed to say which he considered Jake to be, and Regan hadn't mentioned him again.

Instead, she'd questioned David about his home, his family. To her surprise, she'd learned he was from Nebraska, a small town of fewer than five hundred people—about as far, Regan thought, from the Pacific Ocean surf where she'd once placed him as he'd been from the England of his acquired accent. His father was a farmer; his mother taught school. "A life as plain as apple pie," David said. "Hayrides and football . . . homecomings."

Regan had heard the edge in his tone. "You decided to find the bright lights instead."

"Yes."

Now, Regan stopped looking out into the London night that was rapidly lightening toward dawn. In the bedroom, she folded down the spread, smoothing soft blue sheets. But she knew she couldn't sleep. The thoughts of David had only been holding the other, painful ones at bay.

She sat on the edge of the bed, easing out of her robe, wondering what to do. But there was no way to stop the other nights from crashing in, the visions of booze and dope and fights with Linda behind closed doors, the black shadows hanging over Kenny's head and the loneliness he had never escaped; that she couldn't, either? Because she and Kenny were alike. Remembering, she felt terrified again, like the small child who had awakened, screaming, and alone.

Martha's cold hostility and Alyson's meanness of spirit. Paul's ever-changing treatment of her, loving, hateful, concerned and scornful. Her mother's leaving. And Jake . . . promising that he'd be different. She felt as if she'd died, too. Oh, Kenny, you said we'd make it; you were supposed to have the missing parts, damn you, damn Ja—

Where had he gone? *Where?* What had happened to him after that day in the hospital when he'd said he didn't want her anymore? Could he play, still, again? She hadn't asked Alyson in Sydney, couldn't bring herself to ask. But oh, please, she thought, please. . . .

And then, heard a wild, hoarse voice, a woman's voice, *her* voice crying brokenly, "He's gone," not knowing which of them she cried out for most, Kenny or Jake, wondering why there seemed to be so many dead men in her life . . . no matter that one of them still lived, breathed, moved . . . and loved. "He's dead, he's dead, *he's dead!*"

Morning had dawned chill and gray at some point she hadn't noticed. Whatever the time, there was no sunlight, and the large bedroom of the suite seemed to trap darkness in the covers, the heavy draperies, the flocked paper on the walls. Closing her eyes again, Regan fell back into a soft pocket of sleep, exhausted by her grief.

It seemed long hours later, and perhaps it was, when Regan woke again to someone's presence in the room. She hadn't heard the door open—had there been a murmur of voices in the hall?—but suddenly she felt a strong hand on her bare shoulder. Regan's heart slammed frantically with the touch. "No, no!"

Then the soft timbre of his voice, "It's me. David," made her collapse against the pillows, her arching body as weak as water. "David Sloan," he said gently, letting her go as soon as he was satisfied she wouldn't scream.

"Oh, David . . . David, hold me, please hold me!"

She was naked under the sheets, shivering. Obediently he sat on the edge of the bed, drawing her close, and cradled her body in his arms, wrapping the blanket tightly around to keep her warm, crooning to her. "Easy, love . . . there, there."

She didn't hear anything else he said; all she knew was that the tears had come at last. It was a long time before she could stop crying, long moments until her chest ached from sobs, longer still until she could speak half coherently. "Cold," she murmured. "I'm so cold, David."

Wrapping her in a comforter, he went to her bureau, and the closet. He selected soft, comfortable clothing: a raspberry cotton sweater, a pair of beige pants, some deeper berry-colored leather shoes with low heels. While she dressed, shivering, he didn't watch, though he seemed to sense, too, that she wanted him to stay close. When he silently brushed out her snarled hair with long, sure strokes as Manny used to do, holding the length against her skull with his other hand, Regan said, "You're treating me like a baby, David."

"We're all babies, one time or another. Enjoy your turn without a fuss, will you?"

"Yes, sir."

Over her shoulder, she gave him an almost normal smile, feeling the ice in her blood begin to thaw. But when David asked her if she would like to eat, she didn't answer.

"I'll order, then." He had already picked up the receiver. "California melon, please, sweet rolls, and a pot of coffee— you take sugar and cream, don't you?—yes, and some grape- fruit juice."

"Thank you, that sounds good."

She wasn't hungry in the least; but he was trying so hard. Then, suddenly, David was serving her coffee and rolls, pour- ing out the juice from a hammered silver pitcher. When had Room Service knocked at the door, the food arrived? How had she gotten in this chair? David's face looked extraordinarily grim, but then, it was a grim morning.

"What's happened to your filming, David?" she asked, clenching her jaw enough to keep from chattering when she spoke. But the cup rattled in the saucer when she took it from him. "They mustn't have liked your taking off in the middle of the night." And how had he known she needed him?

"I wish I'd left sooner," he said. "I didn't give them any choice—or explanations, either." He walked toward the windows and lifted the draperies, looking out at the gray day. "Sam and Peter had both called me within half an hour of each other, concerned at how you'd taken the news of Williams' death—or rather, weren't taking it, not showing your feelings, not able to cry—but I swear, I would scarcely have needed the plane to get here, anyway." He turned around and showed her those clear blue eyes. "I'm glad you called me, too. I've been thinking about you constantly for three months, my lovely little *canneloni*—"

"David, be serious."

But the quick spurt of weak laughter on both sides didn't last. He came back to her, taking the cup from her hands—she'd been holding it firmly to keep it still, without being able to drink—and set it on the table.

"I am serious," he said. "Totally. Completely. Absolutely serious. London then was more than good, for both of us, I think. And our telephone talks since then. Haven't you missed me? Yes, I thought you must." He put his hands around hers, pressed tightly together in her lap. "In fact, I'm so serious I can hardly say what I'm about to say. . . ." He cleared his throat. "Which is, that I want more than a few days of sightseeing, making jokes about my Spaghetti Westerns. I know, Regan, that I ought to give you time, wait until you've absorbed last night a bit more, but when I saw you this morning, I—" He stopped, flushing.

"Yes, David?"

"Well, I wanted very much to have you with me, that is" —he finished in a rush—"to have you end the rather arid years of my bachelorhood."

"*. . . Marry you?*"

He looked as puzzled as Regan by the proposal. Relief plain

in his smile, David said, "Yes. Yes, dear girl, that's exactly what I mean."

Regan gaped at him.

"I know what you're thinking, love. And it's only partly true. Friendship is a better start for marriage than most I've seen based entirely on . . . passion. What's wrong with being friends first? There are worse beginnings, you know, than being married to someone you don't *worship* with all your heart and soul." He didn't mention Jake; but he didn't have to. It was there in David's eyes. "Besides, we're decent to each other, aren't we?"

He was kneeling in front of her, his eyes on a level with Regan's.

"I live a very public life, David. It isn't easy," she said, "with the cameras all around, microphones thrust in your face every time you turn. The limo gets mobbed, your clothes get torn—"

"Terrible fate, fame," he murmured. "Why not let me worry about that?"

But he hadn't liked the aggressive fan in the restaurant that night; and *he'd* been only a minor incident, a moment in time.

"I work so much of the year now," Regan argued softly, playing devil's advocate while her heart began to warm at the look in his gentle blue eyes. Didn't she want more than telephone calls, and lonely nights?

"Thank God," David said, smiling. "And so will I. We'll have time together." His hands came up, holding her face lightly, as if he was afraid she'd draw away. "Everyone needs connection, love. A meaningful connection."

And she melted inside, knowing how much she'd been wanting exactly that. Again. Better, stronger, more lasting. *Sing pretty, nightingale,* Kenny's hands cradling her like this. *It's all you'll ever have.* And it was grand, beyond her wildest dreams. But it wasn't enough. No matter how hard she worked, how beautifully she sang—she needed someone to love, someone to love her in return. She'd felt it once with Jake. She felt very close to that now with David. Very close. As if she might belong, after all.

And still, she made the protest.

"But David, why ... me? I don't quite understand, I mean—"

His thumb glided over her lower lip, sealed it gently against the upper one. "Give me some credit for *wanting* to marry you," his eyes teasing now, "for reasons of my own."

But getting married? She had to think the words several times, they sounded so strange ... like love itself. *Getting married!*

Regan was unaware of the barely perceptible nod she'd given until David whispered, "Fine," and folded her into an embrace, lifting her with him to stand close together, his arms strong and sure and warm. He smelled like the faintest aroma of good leather, and she smiled into the buttery soft cashmere of his blue sweater. Maybe he was right, that something more would come of the commitment they were making. Then she heard the ragged edge to his voice, pulling her from thought and doubt.

"For God's sweet sake, dear girl"—she felt his mouth move against her hair—"when will you learn to trust the people who care for you?"

Chapter 23

There was no escape from it. Her. Lying in bed, Jake glanced up from his newspaper at the television announcer's words, and she was there, intruding on the careful blankness of his mind, cutting like a scalpel through a closed wound, drawing blood again when he'd hoped the scar had healed at last. But why expect to get away? She was famous now.

"... today, in a breathtaking ceremony of Gothic splendor, Hollywood's newest sex symbol, David Sloan, disappointed hordes of female fans by marrying America's nightingale, Regan Reilly."

Projection TV, no less, and it seemed to fill the entire stateroom with Regan's image, with David Sloan.

"Will you look at that spectacle!" Ceci murmured beside Jake, eyes fixed in fascination on the scene.

A few seconds' flash of the billowing white bridal gown, sleek golden hair encased in lacy mesh, those sparkling green eyes, a blond giant of a groom, the couple spilling down the cathedral steps to a waiting black limousine in that impressionistic autumn atmosphere that could only be Manhattan in October. Not long, but long enough.

Abruptly, Jake sat up in the elegance of Cecily Ferris's blue-and-white yacht, anchored off Palm Beach. Avoiding the images on the screen, he got off the bed, naked. "Enjoy the soap opera. I'm going to shower. I've got to go to work soon," regretting instantly that he'd turned around, as if he couldn't help himself, to see the happy couple—odd, he'd always thought it would be Manny—climbing into the big car amid shouts from curious onlookers.

"Congratulations!"

"Love you, Regan— Happy wedding day!"

"David, come on, give her a kiss—"

And Sloan, grinning, as they settled into the rear seat of the limousine. Obliging. The cameras moving, close against the windows. Regan laughing as he drew her into his arms. Big, blond beautiful male. Take that, Bertelli, Jake thought with a grim smile. How does it feel? Maybe they had something in common after all: heaped on the discard pile together, like worn-out shoes going to the trash.

He tried to shake the feeling. But he could sense her mouth parting under his instead, feel the narrow waist between his encircling hands. That exquisite moment, suspended time, before he closed the final distance to kiss her, and felt the flesh like warm, fine satin under his fingers. Would it be the same now, running his hands over her body—not as sensitive, his fingertips. Almost, but not quite. Maybe nothing could be the same. And now, Sloan with Regan.

"Pretty breathtaking themselves, aren't they?"

Jake slammed the bathroom door on the announcer's remark to the cameras. He turned on the shower full-blast, cold. He felt as if he'd fallen down a hole, slick-sided, mud-smooth, and he would never get out again. Twenty-nine years old, he told himself severely. Looking at thirty. Regan's nearly twenty-two. Feeling sorry for himself, he added months to both their ages.

And you're a has-been; but she's a star. She's mar—

"... Jake?"

He heard Cecily's voice, uncertain and half-amused as she reached into the shower to adjust the temperature from cold to warm. "You must be freezing." The glass door slid shut; she had stepped inside with him. *You can't imagine how cold I feel.*

"I'm going North," she said, which wasn't a new announcement. In the past months, March into October, she'd made a dozen trips to New York, jetting back to Palm Beach to be with him on the yacht, then flying off again. It had reminded him of the last tour when he'd taken every opportunity to be with Regan, and he had begun to see the same signs of fatigue in Cecily's azure eyes. "How would you like to live on land for a change?" she asked. "I'm on a dozen committees. With the debutante balls during Christmas season, I don't see how I can keep up this constant commuting."

The dual-career couple.

"I've got a job, Ceci," Jake said tautly.

"Leave it." In the shower, after soaping his back, the humid environment now redolent of sandalwood, she slipped her arms around him, murmuring contentment. She moved against him, fitting her front to his back, doing pleasant things with her hands down his chest, over the flatness of his abdomen, along his hard flanks. "Quit your job," she crooned.

His breath was beginning to come in short gasps, shallow and harsh, her hands roundly caressing him everywhere. What was she offering? Plush surroundings and no worries, pleasant company—they did get on well together most of the time—and athletic sex. More money than he'd ever thought to have, even indirectly.

But he thought of the night before, when they had lain in darkness, Jake asking about her mother. "She died the week after I was born," had been the soft answer. "An infection that couldn't be controlled. I know so little about her—though I think I resemble her. My father removed all the photos from the house. . . ." shrugging as if she would forgive him anything.

Jake doubted that many people had ever seen through her cheerful exterior, the polished poise, the beautiful clothes and belongings—Charlie Peyson, perhaps, whom he'd met a few times; but not many others. And he liked that part of Ceci best, the part other people couldn't see, that he'd seen last night.

"It's so wearisome, don't you think, having to work?" she whispered. Her hands moving, moving until he couldn't remember the midnight before, couldn't remember at all.

"Yes," Jake grunted, "boring as hell."

She turned at his urging into the embrace. "Then it's settled." And he thought money, no matter how it came packaged, was power, too. Feeling dazed by Ceci's hands, the offer she had made. But when he closed his eyes, a vision of that green gaze laughing into Sloan's made him open them again to deepening azure blue.

Not only one-sided, then. He wouldn't disappoint her. He knew what she needed from him, poor little rich girl, read the meaning of the unhappiness he wanted to remove from Ceci's eyes. He could give her that, the love she'd never known. He would try.

But in his hands, her breasts felt, all at once, identical—though he knew Ceci's were larger—the softness, the swell, the peaking of the dark nipples hardened by need, and water now, like—

"Jake, you're hurting me!"

"I'm sorry, I'm sorry, Ceci," as the billowing white skirts of lace filled his mind, like the rising of desire. He clasped her more tightly in his arms. "I love you." *Oh Jake, I feel like a bride.* "Ceci, I love you!" wondering why his voice sounded like a cry of pain, as if he were in the hospital still, begging for the blank release of Denise's medication.

In a sobbing, mournful voice, the pledge came, echoing.

"I love you, Jake, yes," as the steaming shower pelted them, a warm tropical rain, like paradise. "There's no need to be bored," Cecily said in a shaken tone, lifting her face to his, "and you won't be, darling, ever."

Jake let his hands wander then, arousing, their mouths and bodies slick. He wondered where Regan and Sloan had gone for their honeymoon.

Chapter 24

"The Greek Islands for the whole winter!" Regan groaned as she rooted through a cardboard carton. "Wouldn't that have been lovely?" Pushing a strand of hair from her face, she emerged from the box with the bulky fisherman's sweater she'd been hunting.

"What's that, love?"

David walked into the living room, and Regan slipped her arms around his waist, dropping the soft bundle of wool. He hadn't heard. "I said, why does the honeymoon have to end? Why should I spend three months away from you on tour?"

"Because I've got two commercials lined up, a profile as promising newcomer in *People,* and a screen test that will, hopefully, become a part." Releasing her with a smile, he strolled over to the window wall that overlooked the beach. "I do wish I could join you. I didn't expect to be this busy so quickly—not complaining, understand."

The light was such coming through the glass that David could catch his reflection in it. Regan assumed that he was giving himself one of those abstracted goings-over. She'd seen them before, almost as if he were looking for something so mundane as holes in his socks—more an inventory of his body as commercial extension of his talent than one of ego.

As he twisted slightly one way, then the other, he appeared

to be following something on the beach in the distance. Raising her eyebrows, Regan shrugged. Not only had their wedding trip been too brief, but seven days back weren't nearly enough to complete the adjustment to marriage. There was so much about David she didn't know.

Glancing around the large room, Regan realized that she didn't yet feel at home here, either. The house, low and modern, had been David's choice of a rental. But in the small town of Quogue on Long Island, its privacy suited her as did the quietly lavish decor—all the rooms done in shades of driftwood and bone, carpeted in a rich, lustrous grass-green. The openness of the floor plan achieved intimacy in small ways. The warm copper kitchen. The lovely turquoise bathroom fixtures and off-white rugs, the mirrored tiles there of walls and ceiling. The unexpected, always delightful, flashes of vivid color in artworks placed at exactly the right spot. It would be a house to love, in time; as she and David, Regan thought, would grow to love each other.

A love that she hoped would prove as enduring as David's fine sculptures of marble, alabaster, jade, and terra-cotta. For now, she wished that Manny hadn't scheduled her first winter concerts so soon—but then, she excused him: he hadn't known she was getting married.

Married. She hadn't known, herself! Regan looked back at David, utterly motionless now that he had finished his assessment. His back seemed unnaturally rigid, though Regan's eyes slid past to focus on the clean lines of his legs and arms, the perfect shape of his skull, that golden hair. Then he turned, the blue eyes warming as if a switch had been activated somewhere. "What are you thinking about?"

"How much I'll miss you." Regan flushed a little. The sight of him in the mornings, radiating vibrant masculinity. "Eating popcorn with you in bed, I mean," she added as he walked slowly toward her, his eyes unwavering on hers. Another of David's passions, like old movies. Her heart began to drum. *One* of his passions.

"Popcorn, huh? That's all you think I'm good for?"

The days in Greece flashed through her memory, the nights.

Not enough of the nights. And the sometimes perplexed light in David's eyes, the light she had seen just as he turned from the windows a moment ago. When she'd asked him about it, he'd said, "Only nerves about the screen test, love. I'll be fine when it's over. This is a big chance for me." Making a determined effort to change his mood. "I'll be fine."

Now, he drew her into his arms, nuzzling her throat and shoving aside the opening of her robe. Regan shivered as the sinuous silk fell from her shoulders. "Cold?" David whispered, lifting her. "Let's get warm," as he carried her across the grass-green carpet to the bedroom.

"Lovely," David murmured, *"bellisima,"* his lips on hers, firing every cell with newfound warmth, his thumb raising her nipple to a hardness that cold could never match. Regan gasped at the quick force of her response. When he raised his head at last, she saw the new promise in his eyes.

Regan's heart seemed to shudder in her breast, held now in David's heated hand—as if it were a small bird tenderly trapped there, released and given life after an overexposure to wind and ice; as if he were a one-man rescue team come to save her. Not from weather, but from loneliness and need and searching, always searching, for something she had never found.

Now, she didn't have to look any further. Whenever she came back to this house, there'd be David, waiting. David, loving. *David. . . .*

"David!"

Regan leaped from bed and, hearing the terrace door slide shut, ran to the window. David, in gray sweatpants and shirt, was jogging toward the beach. She'd fallen briefly asleep after lovemaking, and now it was late. With a smile of remembrance for the past hour, Regan pulled on jeans and a sweater and began to finish packing.

She hoped he wouldn't forget her three o'clock appointment with Linda for final fittings. He'd promised to drive into New York.

Linda. As she folded clothing, Regan's thoughts turned back to the even busier days before the wedding. And to renewal.

In the week after Kenny's death, while Regan was still grieving and at the same time adjusting to the notion of being engaged to David, a note had reached her from Iowa. Short and to the point, it had nevertheless bridged the long gap in communication. "Thanks for the help. I'll repay every cent when I can. I know you did what had to be done, firing Kenny, and didn't need to do anything further for *us*. Yet now, you have. Here's a picture, Regan, of 'your' boy, growing up fast."

Staring at the photo of the small blond child, so changed from when she'd known him, Regan had guessed how hard it was for Linda to write the apology and to take money offered through Manny. But why should it be charity, even temporarily? Within minutes, Regan had been on the phone, begging Linda to accept plane tickets to New York as she'd once asked her to join the tour.

"I need you," she had pleaded. "Who else could make my wedding gown exactly the way I envision it? *Please,* Linda."

"I don't know. I'm still out of sorts and Jeb's been a handful— though my parents would probably be glad to have the break. But how can I take responsibility for dressing you—it's such a special occasion! Everyone in the world will see that gown!"

Exactly, Regan had thought with a secret smile; but she'd kept her notions to herself for the time being.

A few days later, she'd been awash in tears and reunion.

"Linda! Linda, over here!"

Regan had waved frantically at the airport gate, her famous green eyes hidden behind huge sunglasses, her tawny hair secured beneath a floppy red bush hat she'd brought home from Australia. In jeans and a navy sweater, she looked like scores of other travelers crowding La Guardia. It had taken the dark-haired woman coming toward her another sweep of the crowd to find Regan.

Then all at once, after two years, they'd been face-to-face again. Regan stood motionless, looking into Linda's eyes deeply smudged by sorrow. She noted the loss of weight, the shapeless hang of mourning black on her thin frame. Even her wrists and ankles stuck out, sharp bones everywhere. "I'm so glad to see you again," Regan managed. "Oh, Linda . . . Kenny. . . ."

Tears filled both their eyes, were blinked away as she pulled Linda close. "Regan, I've cried so much in the last week or two, I thought there weren't any left."

"I've missed you, Linda—terribly, and I—"

"Mommy!"

The frantic cry forced them apart, Regan's eyes quickly searching the long corridor. "Jeb," she whispered. "Oh, my God, Linda—he's so big, bigger than the picture you sent!" and nothing could stop her.

Pushing aside a large man with a heavy briefcase in his hand, not feeling the bump of leather and metal against her thigh, Regan had run forward, never thinking that he might not know her. Halting at last when Jeb froze a dozen feet away, his gaze widening in alarm.

At three and a half, he showed signs of his father in the beautiful gray eyes, the shape of his face. Solemnly, Jeb studied Regan without a trace of a smile or any recognition. She felt her heart twist. "Don't you remember me, darling?" Oblivious to the pass of strangers on either side, Regan removed the large dark glasses and pulled off the bush hat, her hair tumbling free. "It's Regan." But he'd been a baby then, just eighteen months old and barely talking. Why would he remember what her own heart couldn't possibly forget? Certainly Linda wouldn't have mentioned her, certainly Kenny—

Then she noticed the reason he'd been lagging so far behind. Clutched in one arm, held in a death grip to the front of his neat blue blazer, was Raggedy Ann—as battered, as scarred, as ever—and just as loved. The torn pinafore peeked out, in need of further mending. Regan's vision blurred as she heard Linda say, "He wouldn't let me make her a new dress. The first months after we left your tour, he wouldn't give her up without a fight, even to take his bath—and at bedtime he slept with that doll, wrapped around her every night."

Regan took a step, then another. Reaching out, she tentatively touched the sagging ruffle, a red yarn curl that looked like a sprung wire.

Linda's voice trembled. "He cried until Kenny and I thought we'd go mad ... cried himself to sleep, saying your name the way he always did." And then, "Regan, it's the oddest thing, but since his father—this past week he's carried Raggy with him everywhere again."

"Linda—" She would have touched her for comfort, but Linda pulled slightly away, struggling for control.

"Jeb, aren't you going to say hello? Come on, darling—"

He tightened his hold on Raggedy Ann, his gray eyes meeting the navy sweater, then the jeans waistband. "Hello, Regan," he said with only a trace of imperfection at her name. Regan cried out, dropping to her knees in front of him as Jeb finished, "My Daddy couldn't come, so I brought Mommy on the plane to see you."

"Oh, sweetheart—"

And they were all three in each other's arms, the tears flowing freely, the old rag doll smothered between them, the months of grief and guilt torn away like the pages of Linda's drawing pad later as she tried one bridal rendering, then another until Regan's dream met paper.

The gown itself couldn't have pleased Regan more. The fine cream silk complemented the style she'd envisioned, modified from the Middle Ages: a neckline high and simple, the sleeves long and tapering to points at the wrist, trimmed to match the throat with tippets of costly Brussels lace as delicate as ivory gossamer webs. The dress molded to her slender figure, falling from the hip in graceful folds to the floor, to the cathedral train.

Standing in the rear of the Gothic church, carrying a single, ivory rose, her hair tucked into a caul of net in even finer lace than her gown's, she'd felt quite bridal, indeed. And scared to death.

Nervousness had not been in short supply, Regan noted. David, waiting at the altar, handsome and severe in his formal morning coat and trousers, had pushed his hair back repeatedly, when it was perfectly neat. And Paul's large hand trembled as he took hers for an instant, guiding Regan toward their starting place. "I'd be honored," he'd said stiffly when she asked him to give her away. As her only living relative, he made the logical choice, the most reasonable; and in a way, since he had raised her almost from infancy, she felt she owed it to him.

Not that Alyson had appeared to like the picture of them together. But Regan ignored her cousin's surly expression, the head turned to watch them from a front pew, as Paul kept her hand in his.

"You're gonna be okay now," he muttered. "You look . . . real beautiful, Regan. And David's just the man I always wanted you to meet, to *marry.*"

"Thank you, Uncle Paul."

Regan swallowed the tightness in her throat, remembering how David had charmed Paul Oldham. "Whatever did you say to him?" she'd asked. "He's positively glowing," and after a bad beginning, too.

"I told him I intended to make you a good husband. And a few other comforting words," he added. "That fathers of the bride—so to speak—like to hear, I'm told." Fidelity, Regan had surmised; stability. She could hardly blame Paul for wanting that: she wanted the same.

When Paul dropped her hand as the final strains of music before the processional sounded, Regan had looked into Manny's jet-dark gaze. On the way to his seat, he had stopped, a tight smile on his face. "Have you seen the press outside? There's a crowd to the corner, police barricades, minicams from the networks—"

Regan said dryly, "You should have charged admission, Manny," smoothing the skirt of her gown for the hundredth time. She'd been joking; was surprised to see his heart showing in his expression.

"I'm not that mercenary."

She felt tears sting her eyes. "I'm sorry."

Bertelli's lips grazed her cheek. "Well, I still love you, sweet. I probably always will."

Nerves, Regan had thought, swallowing again as she watched Manny walk away, flashing a grin of reassurance at Paul. Later, she'd seen Manny at the reception with Alyson. Anxiety made them all a little softer. So many days of planning when she'd been too busy to worry—yes, like preparing for a concert. Wardrobe, rehearsal, photographs, music—

The fluted Purcell filled the air, soaring toward the vaulted ceiling. Nerves, Regan thought, her hands becoming moist, were only for the wings; or the rear of a cathedral.

Linda flicked the long white train of Regan's gown into place with one deft motion of her wrist. The six young girls chosen for attendants, dressed in white silk jersey replicas of the bridal dress and carrying bouquets of rosebuds and baby's breath, formed the procession: the daughters of casual friends, of one member of her band. Jeb, as ring bearer, squirmed in blue velvet and lace ruffles. As matron of honor, Linda would walk behind the children.

Pausing, she had tucked a stray wisp of tawny-gold hair into Regan's lace caul, their eyes meeting. "Be happy, songbird."

The tears crowded close again. Regan almost wished she hadn't spoken. Remembering the night after the wedding rehearsal, she wondered that Linda had violated her own command. "I'll talk about anything, Regan . . . silk *peau de soie,* or why I picked oysters for dinner, or whether Jeb will lose the ring tomorrow going down the aisle"—then she had looked directly into Regan's face—"but I'll never talk about Kenny, *never.*"

Regan had her own topics to avoid. In that moment, the message that Kenny might have given—and her memories of Jake.

With the tremulous smile, Regan had taken Paul's arm, stepping onto the scarlet runner, following the bridal procession slowly past pews bedecked with hurricane lamps, their ivory candles flickering, and the soft light from stained glass windows brushing muted colors over the invited guests. Down the aisle Regan moved in splendor to the performance of her life, to David, and her future.

We'll be happy, David, we will. . . .

New York, as if to make the event more spectacular, had put on an elaborate display of brilliant blue-sky weather and the most impressive fall foliage in a decade—culminating on Regan's wedding day.

The honeymoon in Greece had proved equally spectacular: sun- and sea-washed days at a charming villa where meals were set in place then whisked away, rooms made up, fresh flowers and fruit arranged in the white stone villa, every comfort attended by unseen servant hands.

Yet David hadn't seemed to covet their privacy as Regan did. She would have been content to laze the mornings away in bed or on the patio beneath the olive trees, enjoying hot coffee and sweet, sticky buns slathered in butter. Would have loved walking the hot white beaches under an incomparably blue sky, the color reminding her of David's eyes. She could easily have slept, curled against the heat of his body, for their entire stay.

But David had kept her out half the night at parties. He seemed to know fascinating people in every corner of the world, the islands being no exception. Under other circumstances, Regan would have liked them, too. Only, bright lights and laughter, exotic food and drink, even the heady romance of a different culture, weren't what she wanted then. She had begun to wonder whether David found her strangely lacking.

Sighing now, Regan thought: *Maybe I've just caught post-honeymoon blues. We did have a good time; David's a tender lover; I'm going to miss him half an hour after the plane takes off tomorrow. I miss him already.*

Locking the last of her suitcases, Regan straightened from the task, easing the stiffness in her spine. A growling stomach reminded her that—because of the noontime lovemaking with David—she'd missed lunch. In the bedside table drawer, she fished for a chocolate crunch bar, ripped off the wrapper and, ignoring a twinge of guilt, consumed the candy in three bites. *Heaven.* On holiday, the old craving had resurfaced, and been indulged. Leaving on tour, she'd have to stop again.

Glancing at the clock, Regan swallowed the last of the chocolate. She'd better hurry. Linda's schedule was getting increasingly busy as well; since the wedding, she'd developed a small, but growing, clientele: Manny's female accountant, a band member's wife, a Broadway actress, and, most recently, a society debutante. Working from the small, two-bedroom apartment Regan had located in Chelsea, Linda now had her hands full—and her days. She'd also gained a few pounds, and Regan liked feeling partly responsible for the change. Maybe one day, Linda could put the past, and Kenny's death, behind her.

"Surprise me with some sketches for the tour when I get back from Greece," Regan had suggested. The results were waiting for her.

Regan slipped into the navy lightweight wool suit that she'd worn leaving the wedding reception at the Hotel Pierre. Severely tailored, it skimmed her slender frame, hugging the curves gently, the color relieved by a scarf of navy and white with green stripes. Hunting for her navy pumps, she called out, "David?" hopping across the room on one shoe, still looking for the other. He hadn't come back, then.

Fully dressed, Regan ran a slash of lipstick over her mouth, added mascara to her lashes. Binding her hair quickly into a soft knot at the nape of her neck, she walked into the living room and looked out the window wall toward the beach. There, a hundred yards off, she saw him. Not alone.

Regan frowned. He was talking to a tall, broad-shouldered man; black hair and what looked to be a perpetual tan. Dressed, too, in running clothes. Tall, and handsome. Yes, she remembered: a male model who had rented a house farther down the beach. He wanted to be an actor.

Sliding open the terrace doors, Regan called to David again.

"Sorry, love." He came jogging up from the beach a few minutes later, barely out of breath. "Won't take me a minute." He was shedding clothes as he strode into the bedroom. Regan couldn't stifle the giggle, which made him turn.

"What?"

She laughed again at the puzzled smile he gave her. "I'll never get used to those," she said, pointing at the tailored blue boxer shorts he wore. They struck her as remarkably unsexy for a romantic leading man.

David grinned. "My conservative side"; then he walked back to her, his cheeks ruddy from exercise, his hands cold as they cupped her cheeks, his body exuding heat. Regan looked at him questioningly. "Sexy as a centerfold," he murmured, "and as naughty as a child." He leaned closer. "That smear of chocolate on your chin," kissing it away.

"Guilty." Regan smiled into his eyes, forgetting the irritation she'd felt when gazing down at the beach, at David's lateness and—

"Um, you taste good." He tried a second kiss. Regan gave in to it. "Want to stay home and see if we can find something interesting to do?"

He knew what her answer would be. The tour leaving tomorrow; the gowns to finish today. Final arrangements, hundreds of them. Manny calling every five minutes from midnight until dawn, and Peter twice as often. Tickets that hadn't come from the travel agent; equipment that was lost; music that wouldn't— at the last minute—work. Regan groaned softly as her pulse sped up under David's lips. "I'd love to, but—"

Instantly, she was standing on her own, watching David walk away. "I'll only be a second, love." Why had she sensed relief in that moment? Relief as troubling as the perplexity sometimes in David's eyes? Why, Regan wondered, did she have the feeling that he was acting a part?

Chapter 25

"Play ball, goddamnit!"

Sprawled full-length on the soft-cushioned slate-blue sofa in Ceci's Southampton summer house, Jake glared at the television screen. He was avoiding both the heat outdoors at midday and the cutthroat backgammon tournament on the beach.

"Who's playing?"

The mild-mannered voice came from the doorway to the game room. Raising up on one elbow, Jake stared blankly at Charles Peyson, broad face wreathed in a smile of camaraderie. False. The sad brown basset eyes that followed Cecily around a room now stared unblinkingly back at him. "Yankees and Red Sox," Jake answered tautly. "Top of the seventh, five-to-three, Boston." He sank back onto the down-filled sofa.

"Mind if I join you?"

Charlie took a step into the room before Jake answered. As if he unquestionably belonged there. The cushions on which Jake reclined in white jeans and nothing else but a suntan blended eloquently with the Oriental carpet and the burnished gleam of dark hardwood flooring, the muted sand and buff and grayed-pink of the Andrew Wyeth original over the fireplace. The entire house, gables and glass and weathered shingles, had been finished in dusky pastels offset by winter white. Enormous as well as luxurious, and by his last count, full.

There were twenty-five extra people in residence this weekend. Charlie among them, as usual. All Jake wanted was some privacy, and the baseball game.

He said softly, "As a matter of fact, I do mind. Why do you think I closed the door?"

For a second, Peyson stared, as if making up his mind. Then with a shrug, he disappeared. Jake fiddled with the fine-tuning on the remote control. He wanted another drink, but didn't feel like getting up to fix it. He also knew that, after last night, he didn't need one. Staying very still during a commercial for low-cal beer, he began counting again. Seconds this time. When he reached twenty, Cecily said, breezing into the room, "Why did you speak like that to Charlie? He's been coming to this house since I was a child."

"He didn't want to watch the game, Ceci. He wants to grill me."

"About what?"

She was standing over him now, blocking his vision of the screen. "My intentions," Jake muttered.

"That's absurd, we're already married. Charlie's only interested in my happiness. He'd like to know my husband better."

"He'd like to know my—" He didn't finish. *Wife*. Sitting up abruptly, Jake pushed her lightly to one side. "Ceci, *Christ*— that was a perfect triple play and I only saw the end of it!"

"Then you'll catch it on replay. They show the same thing three or four times." She made a wide gesture, encompassing the elaborate electronics system, crowned by an expensive VCR. "You could have taped it for later."

"I want to watch it now."

"Do you realize we've had houseguests for two days, and you haven't stirred from this—this aerie of yours to help with the entertaining?"

People sleeping in his beds, eating his food, drinking his liquor. Jake might have laughed. It wasn't *his* liquor: nothing in this house was his. Nothing at the penthouse in Manhattan, either. It all belonged to Ceci. Including him.

"You're forgetting last night." Jake smiled lazily. "The party," he reminded her, "and afterward."

It had gone on until dawn: one of Ceci's treasure hunts, the drinking and gourmet food, midnight swimming and a couple locked in the sauna, the costly baize pool-table cover shredded by a careless bit of cue-stick handling, and then . . . "a continuation of our honeymoon, darling" just before the sun came up. He had a pounding headache.

Jake felt the partying, the post-nuptial celebrations had lasted long enough. How many months had they traveled, Italy to Switzerland to Majorca, Paris and Madrid and Tunis? Then the Caribbean. Someone's villa, and more good wishes. Luxury and languor. November to June before they reached home again. Home, he thought with a grim smile. Park Avenue; weekends at the shore. The beautiful people all around. And he didn't have to do a damn thing. Nothing, except learn to live with Cecily's wealth. It had been the longest, laziest, most indulgent six months of his life.

Eight months, Jake corrected. Now it was August.

"You're a good enough hostess for us both," he said, watching the hesitancy come into her eyes. That crack in the facade.

"Jake, don't you like my friends? They think you don't. The Harrises and the Daltons, especially. If you'd give them a chance—"

He glared at her. "Sue Dalton is a vicious woman, Ceci!" Feeling that he might as well continue what he'd started, Jake said, "And she's just one person. All of them simply tolerate me—and do you know why? Because I'm exactly what you've led them to believe I am." He stood up, trying to ignore the soft pink-and-yellow swimsuit she wore, the shadowed cleft between her breasts. "A possession . . . an escort." Jake softened his own impression: *stud.* "Christ, they go out of their way, every one of them, to point out the subtle fact that I don't *do* anything!"

Cecily couldn't help smiling. "Neither do most of my friends."

"No, but they do *nothing* with a hell of a lot of cash for backup."

Jake hated the sulky sound of his own words. But he felt

more useless than he had lying in a hospital bed, listening one night to Veronica Vance. And Bertelli. And learning from Denise that—

"I thought we had agreed that my money was to be used," she said. "That's all it means to me, Jake."

"Ceci, hell—" He looked away from the gentleness in her azure eyes. He didn't really care about the money. "I spent the first twenty-seven years of my life pounding the piano eight, ten, twelve hours a day...going to school, working. It's not easy to admit that I never have to get up at six A.M. again—"

"There are people who would die for that privilege."

He had to answer her smile. "Yeah, I know."

And his mother was one of them. Or had been. His smile went away.

"Jake, I want to make you happy." Cecily's hands warmed his bare shoulders; she pushed down lightly until he lay back again on the piled cushions. "Darling, about my friends..." that anxious note creeping into her voice.

He felt like a jerk. She was spoiling him; he didn't want her to; but just now, he was going to let her. "Forget it, I was blowing off steam—or maybe indulging my hangover." He trailed his hands from the blond sheen of her hair to the sleekness of her hips. He'd forgotten entirely about the baseball game. Even the crowd's roar didn't capture his attention as he eased Ceci down beside him. "They just find it easy to dismiss me," rolling over into the dominant position. "Because I'm not among all you bluebloods in the Social Register...or a member of the Fortune Two-fifty."

By Monday afternoon the weekend population had considerably diminished. Only the Daltons and Charles Peyson remained. After a slashing—and, he had decided as a concession to Ceci, obligatory—game of tennis with Andy Dalton, Jake excused himself to shower.

As he came out of the bathroom looking for a polo shirt he'd left on the bed, Ceci asked, "That wasn't so bad, was it?" She walked the room, pausing to finger the set of tortoise-shell hairbrushes with his initials set in 18-karat gold on Jake's dresser. She'd bought them in Spain.

"Dalton plays passable tennis." At least he wasn't a snob, and never talked business. Probably because he didn't have any, Jake thought. The fifth-generation fortune had been wisely invested; and though Sue Dalton's main occupation, other than gossip, was spending it, she had a long way to go before poverty set in. At least as long as Ceci.

"I'm glad your mood is better," she said. "And I'm sorry about the baseball game."

"We more than made up for it." Jake slipped his arms around her waist from behind, nuzzling Ceci's neck. He felt her shiver with pleasure. But then she drew away, smiling. "Which reminds me..."

From the pocket of her wraparound skirt, she took a pair of tickets. "Sunday at the stadium," she announced. "Double-header," with only a slight grimace. She didn't care for sporting events other than polo. "I'm planning to be brave, and to wear my most stoic smile."

And that wasn't all.

Walking away toward the wall of closets that held his extensive summer wardrobe, she began, "About that conversation yesterday, I really think that you ought to do something, Jake, with your training."

His heart vibrated for the space of several seconds. Jake felt his hands grow cold, as if he were preparing for a concert but hadn't learned the score well enough. "Ceci, you know I can't play—I mean, even considering the incredible Steinway in the penthouse. It's mostly brief illusion."

"I don't mean *perform*, darling," she interrupted in a reasonable tone. "But to *use* what you know. Business," she said simply. "Have you ever thought about it? Last night, Charlie and I were talking and—"

"Wait a minute." Jake waved her toward the low puff of cream-colored velvet that passed for a chair near the bed. "Run this by me again. You know I don't like Peyson mixing in our marriage!"

"But Charlie has access to my financial affairs." Cecily paused, studying Jake's set features. Hands clenched at his sides, he knew he must look pale, his brown eyes dark. "Please listen," she urged. "Yesterday when you mentioned how inadequate you feel, not being *involved* in something—"

"I don't recall using the word *inadequate*."

Turning his back, Jake pulled on the navy shirt that had been lying on the bronze satin comforter with his crisply pressed light gray pants. Cecily waited patiently while he tucked in the tail and fastened his belt. Then said gently, "We already own the company, darling. Magnum Publishing," she answered his spun-around posture, the look of amazement. "It's not as if I'd gone looking for it."

"Magnum?"

"A modest profit-making operation with potential." Jake looked down at her, slim legs attractively posed and a guileless expression in her sea-blue eyes. "Sheet music, instruction books." He wondered how innocent it really was. "Charlie says—I am sorry to keep quoting, but he is the source of information—that we've a small interest, ongoing, in performance music as well. A small firm, I think, that could easily be merged—"

"Jesus Christ."

Cecily's cheeks dotted with color. "Well, I know it doesn't sound like much—but you could do an absolutely first-rate series of classical records, darling, and—"

Jake's revulsion at Charlie's interference gave way to wonderment, then interest. He recalled those slow stages of healing after his accident, climbing one level to the next as pain receded; remembered later, the visions of row upon row of people in evening dress, the feel of a keyboard beneath his fingers, even the familiar ache in his back from playing too long. Healing. And he wondered if part of his irritation with Ceci's friends, her money, didn't come from inactivity and confinement. As if he were once again a patient, getting better; resenting the care of doctors and nurses. "Records," he repeated after a moment.

"There's a production facility somewhere in New Jersey; it

was never used after we acquired it. But the main office is in
New York, darling. We've a long-term lease in prime real
estate." She offered the final temptation. "The executive suite
is yours . . . if you want it."

Jake's pulse began to speed. A masterpiece collection, he'd
call it. The finest symphony orchestras, the best soloists. High-
tech, distortion-free. Laser-cut discs. "Maybe not a bad suggestion," he said as Cecily leapt from her chair, throwing her
arms around his neck.

"Darling, I knew you would!"

But he didn't want Charlie Peyson in control. He wanted
to do this himself—try, anyway. Jake trembled inwardly as
the idea shook him. "I'm going to need some help," he said.
"I don't know how to run a business, Ceci. I'll want people
around me who do. . . . Someone," he added, "of my own
choosing."

Cecily's azure eyes sparkled. "You may have whatever you
want, darling. You know that."

Feeling glad that he'd gotten up this morning, Jake smiled.
Someone he could trust, absolutely. As she covered his mouth
in a long, celebratory kiss, Jake murmured, "Steven Houghton."

Chapter 26

"I've always heard it pays to marry rich."

Twisting the gold band on his finger, Steven Houghton posed uneasily behind the broad expanse of teakwood desk in the huge and barren office he'd been assigned twenty minutes before. Immediately, he tried to take the words back. "I'm sorry. I didn't mean that the way it came out." He watched Jake stroll into the room, brown eyes clouded over his smile. "Cecily's a lovely woman. I liked her very much when we had dinner the other night."

"Yes, well, this is the woman who wipes out the disappointment over a bad game of tennis with a four-hundred-dollar racket. The generous soul who, noting my boredom one June evening, led me by the hand next morning to the driveway ... and a waiting Mercedes." The racy 450-SL, silver with a navy soft top and dark blue interior, had been his six months' anniversary present. Jake shrugged. "I don't know what to call all this," waving a hand at the elaborate surroundings. "Except," with a smile, "Magnum Multimedia Corporation."

He drifted toward the windows overlooking Fifth Avenue, thirty-four stories below. "Of course, you'll need furniture. We've got a design firm on retainer, but if you'd rather pick things yourself, that's fine too."

Steven shifted his weight from one foot to the other, looking unhappily at the mound of alien paper on his desk. Nothing much else in the room. He hadn't the vaguest idea what those memoranda contained, what Jake hoped to get from him. Least of all, what he—a small-time bar owner—might provide.

He was still in the daze that had formed when Jake stepped into his life two months ago. Fussing over the roadhouse accounts, his spirits had been steadily sinking with his profits. No relief in sight. Still, he saw Ellen everywhere; heard her voice, her laugh; felt her narrow body under his. When the door had opened in a glare of sudden sun, he'd barely looked up at the tall, lean silhouette walking with an economical grace of movement toward him.

"Sorry, we're not open until six."

"Can't a friend get a drink in this place without an appointment?"

The familiar voice cut through his curt dismissal, changing everything. Steven was on his feet, papers skidding to the floor. "*Jake,* holy Jesus!"

In the center of the room they'd met in that peculiar male combination of handshake and bear hug. "Where the hell've you been? God, it's great to see you!" He had felt tears sting his eyes, then render him speechless. He'd flinched under Jake's perusal as the firm grip on his upper arms held him off. A keenness to the brown-gold gaze that hadn't been there before. Or was there something missing?

"Don't look too close," Steven cautioned. "I've added ten pounds since you saw me. Too much beer behind the counter. I drink my own profits." He steered the greetings in another direction. "But Lord, look at you!" Jake's dark suit didn't shout, but whispered discreetly, *money.* Lots of it. "That European tailoring must have cost five hundred bucks." Or more.

Jake shrugged lightly. "I don't know, maybe so." Taking a chair, he indicated the mess on the table, scooped up papers from the floor. "What's this?"

"Disaster. Trying to make the month come out right for a change." Again, he took the offensive. "Where the hell have you been hiding? I haven't seen you since—"

"Special Surgery." At once, they both glanced at his hands.

Not a visible mark. The specialists had done superior work. "I got better," Jake said softly.

Restless, he stood up, as if flinching away from the pain, and went toward the silent piano in the corner where Steven had shoved it long ago. There was no weekend band now; no singer with a soaring voice, a shimmer of tawny hair. Jake ran his fingers over the dusty keys, not having to see them in the dimness. He struck a few chords, then the opening bars to a ballad Steven had heard many times in this room.

Jake stopped abruptly. It was the song Regan had sung, illuminated in a shaft of sun, that afternoon, auditioning. His voice was husky. "Christ, Steven, don't you ever have this thing tuned?" circling around, a look of consternation on his face as if he'd mentally prepared himself for this trip back in time, and the planning hadn't been adequate.

Did he see her there, too—by the piano, dressed in white and gold, and terrified? Then thrilling the audience with a first performance that Steven would never forget? "It hasn't been the same, Jake, since—"

"You're getting out of here." The tone harsh, interrupting. "I'll find a buyer for this place if I have to sell it to Ceci."

"Ceci?" Steven had questioned, clearly lost in an information gap. And with a smile, "Where do I go on the proceeds? To a nursing home?"

"I've been worse places."

Then had come the backtracking and filling-in of years; the news of Jake's surprising marriage to an heiress; the even more unexpected proposition about Magnum. Steven hadn't known what to say.

Standing in his new office now, the first morning on the job as Jake's executive assistant, high up in a Manhattan skyscraper and possessed of a five-room apartment a dozen blocks away, he still didn't know. How could his life have changed so drastically in months? Did he really want it to? "What am I doing here?" he asked aloud.

Jake turned from an apparently intense study of the traffic gridlock on East Fifty-fourth Street. "You're not starting that

again, are you?" Irritation sounded in his tone. "Try wading
into the pile for starters," indicating the desk. "Once you begin,
you won't have time for doubts."

Maybe, Steven thought. I wasn't exactly happy in Lancaster;
but at least it was familiar. And close to Ellen; the memories
they'd made. As for the roadhouse—

"We had a dream," he said slowly. "Ellen and I, from the
day we got married. That we'd be innkeepers in the traditional
sense, make an oasis of—"

"Jesus, Steven!"

"Jake, we put all our money into that little place, all our
hopes."

"And some guy opened a *rathskeller* across town, lured the
college kids and most of your regulars away, but you're still
wanting to make a go of something that—"

"Because it was my life, and Ellen's, too."

"Ellen's dead."

The flatly uttered words silenced him. Steven stared back
at Jake, remembering the pounding at his door one night. The
cold February wind sweeping in with the leather-jacketed highway patrolman. "Steve, better sit down," and the stark terror
clutching at his heart. In that instant, he'd already known. "It's
Ellen," and there had been no turning from it, no escape. *Ellen,
my God.*

"You're right," Steven said. "She's gone . . . but I've still
made a mistake." He looked hard at Jake. "I don't accept your
offer for the roadhouse, or for Magnum, either. Jake, you told
me years ago that all you knew was playing piano. Well, all
I know is standing behind a bar, for God's sake!" He gestured
at himself, an expanse of regulation gray flannel. "I haven't
been stuffed into a three-piece suit since the day I got married."

Jake's hand spun him around as Steven took a first step
toward the door. "You think I have any idea what to make of
all this myself? If you think the shit on your desk is overwhelming, you ought to come across the hall and look at mine,
hell, my new *secretary* knows more than I do!" He returned
the glare. "There's not a goddamn thing familiar to me about
this job, except that I can tell one composer from another for

our new classical record label. Half the staff along this hallway thinks I'm some nasty joke played on them by Charlie Peyson! You think it's easy for me, do you, taking money from my wife? Getting a pat on the head every morning as she sends me off to work—that's 'work' with quotes around it, by the way—*Christ*, I'm just as scared as you are!" Jake took a quick, deep breath. "But somebody's got to take charge."

He shook his head. "Jake, I—"

"Steven."

Panicky, he tried to move away; then felt himself hauled into an embrace no less awkward than that when they'd met again at the roadhouse. For a long moment, they held to each other before the awareness of intimacy crept in and their arms slackened. Steven blinked rapidly, looking past Jake's shoulder at the wall. Empty. No pictures. Nothing but the desk, a scarlet carpet as dense as the pile on a mink coat, two neutral armchairs. Jake cleared his throat. "Steven, I need help."

And he realized what had been wrong for him in Jake's smile that afternoon; why he had said *yes* to a fantastic proposal without taking time to think. Jake would never have asked for help before; but now, Steven thought, there's a hollowness inside him. Feeling the same himself, it was easy to identify. He looked away from the wall to Jake and saw the mirrored brightness of his own gaze. The light's missing from his eyes, though. It's gone, too. "Well," Steven said quietly, "I don't see anybody else in this room."

After a brief inspection of the carpet, a slow smile spread across Jake's face. "Come on, let's get started." He dragged a beige tweed chair opposite Steven's desk. "Maybe if we plow through this stuff together, it'll make sense. Jesus, it *has* to." When they were seated, suit jackets discarded and shirtsleeves rolled to the elbows, ties loosened, Jake said, "Let's make a pact right from the beginning." His gaze carefully measured Steven, noting the right hand that began to massage the ring finger of his left.

"What kind of pact?"

"Not to look behind," Jake said.

"Is that what I'm doing?"

"Yes."

Steven conceded the fact, adding, "Don't you?"

"Not when I can help it." Jake reached for the top folder in the pile. Their eyes met, holding for long seconds before Jake began scanning the first memorandum. "Forward movement," he said. "Eyes on the road. Now, I've had a couple of ideas. . . ."

Jake heard the penthouse elevator, then the click of Cecily's heels on the parquet floor of the entrance hall. Shoving aside the report he'd been reading, he reached for the next in the stack. It wasn't a bad investment, long-range; merging with the family-owned publishing house would increase Magnum's size by half and allow plenty of expansion room over the next five years. As Steven had suggested, branching out seemed overdue. Jake made a marginal note to have Steven supply figures on the literary classics series used as a teaching tool on college campuses. Would appealing to a wider audience make more sense? Colorful covers, a popular price, perhaps a few best-sellers to broaden its range? Providing Steven's projections looked solid, they could come up with an offer for Parsons & Son by—

The library door swung open, bringing a flood of light from the hall. Jake peered around the glare from his architect's lamp on the desk. "Ceci, I didn't hear you come in," which wasn't exactly true. He'd simply forgotten the sound of her footsteps as soon as he heard them.

"How long have you been home?" Pausing in the doorway, she stripped off black kid gloves and laid them on a leather-topped mahogany side table. Leaning back in his chair to ease the cramp in his back, Jake watched her shrug out of a full-length Blackglama mink, tossing it over a watered-silk upholstered chair the color of celadon porcelain.

"I don't know exactly," he admitted. "What time is it now?"

"Ten past eleven." She smoothed the skirt of her blue chiffon dress.

"A couple of hours, then." Too late, he remembered. "Christ, I'm sorry! Ceci, I completely forgot."

No wonder she hadn't been smiling.

"The Daltons send love. We missed you at dinner."

Their instruction had been to meet at Lutèce at eight o'clock. "Did you enjoy the meal?" Jake asked, staring at the telephone reminder his secretary had given him that afternoon. It had been stuffed in the side pocket of his briefcase.

Ceci said, "I wasn't very hungry. The *ris de veau,* I'm told, was incomparable."

Sweetbreads. Jake's stomach recoiled at the thought. "I'm sor—" he started to apologize again, but she cut him off.

"Must you bring home work every night?" The subdued tone of voice, the controlled motions of suppressed anger, disappeared. "Jake, this is the third social engagement you've 'missed' in the last two weeks. Do you know how long we waited—? Andy Dalton asking leading questions, the ones Sue didn't think of first. The next thing, we'll be in the papers as this season's surprising divorce!"

"Don't be ridiculous. And I don't give a damn what Andy Dalton or his snoop of a wife thinks of our marriage!"

Damnit, here we go. Jake ran a hand through his hair. She was right, of course. He'd been unforgivably rude. But her call had come in after four o'clock, just after Steven's announcement. By God, he'd actually signed what might prove the hottest new rock group in the world to an exclusive three-album contract with Magnum Records! After that, there'd been legal questions, more telephone calls, a first conference with marketing. . . .

In the first four months of their business relationship, Jake and Steven had developed a system all their own. Quickly, the strengths of each had shown themselves: Jake, the creative planner, insightful, with an eye to the future of the growing corporation; Steven, the handler of day-to-day detail, Magnum's crack troubleshooter already. They'd barely begun; but the experience had been exciting, far beyond expectation—and Jake not only brought work home. He could barely wait for nine o'clock every morning.

This evening, he'd left the office oblivious to anything but the paperwork in his briefcase.

"I'm sorry, Ceci," he tried for the third time, dropping the phone message on his desk. When he looked up, she was faintly smiling. Fortunately for him, she never stayed angry. With a warming of his brown eyes, he beckoned her closer, saw her hesitate only a few seconds before she slipped into his arms, sitting on his lap in the desk chair. He had wanted to ask her again the question from yesterday, but decided to wait. It was too soon, and he couldn't think how to make the California trip more palatable to her. Not yet.

"I like your new dress," he murmured, kissing beneath her ear at the most sensitive spot. "Linda Designs for You," Jake repeated the increasingly well-known label. "Did you know that I used to know Linda?"

"In what capacity?"

Jake smiled at the light display of jealousy, pushing away his own nostalgia. Linda's dark hair as she bent over her baby at the table across from him. The Birdcage. And the soaring sound of a voice. ". . . She was married to a friend of mine," Jake improvised. "A drummer in a band." Kenny Williams, big and broad, that flash of a smile and the darkness inside. Jake had read of the musician's death not long before he married Cecily. One more talent down the pipes, had been the epitaph in his mind. Not long before Regan married David Sloan. As if none of the past existed, for any of them.

"She's lovely in the fashion sense. . . ."

"Green eyes," Jake murmured. He shut his gaze, letting Cecily's hands wander over his shoulders, the nape of his neck, toying with the hair.

"I try to control myself," she whispered.

"A lady in public," Jake summed up the image, "but in bed . . ."

She wouldn't let him complete the old saying. A flush creeping into her cheeks, Ceci linked her fingers behind his collar. "Shall we . . . ?"

"So, what do you think?"

Lying beside her, Jake ran a hand over his bare chest.

"If you must know, I'm still angry with you."

Cecily moved closer, fitting her body against his. Jake put an arm around her shoulder, ran his fingers down her spine. "Well, I'm not going to apologize again." He grinned in the darkness. "I don't have the energy for reconciliation." He stifled a yawn. "I meant, what about the Grammys? You promised me an answer."

For the last week, he'd been asking; and she'd been holding him off. Tonight, of course, hadn't helped. If he'd been less forgetful about their social life—

"I'm not planning to attend," Cecily said, as if replying to a formal, engraved invitation.

"Reconsider."

"It isn't my sort of affair, Jake. All that blatant publicity, those horrid photographers everywhere. I leave that kind of thing to show-business people, comedians, singers. . . ."

Jake tensed. Show-business people," he repeated softly. "That covers most of my territory these days, you know." Magnum's newborn interests in popular music, records and cassettes; his increasing conviction that they should move into paperback publishing. Perhaps later, movies or television. Yes, he thought the entertainment industry extremely promising—creative and profitable. Magnum profits. He forced a smile she couldn't see. "Look, if you're carrying a grudge because of Lutèce—"

"I'd feel uncomfortable. There wouldn't be anyone I know there."

"You think I know those people? Ceci, that's part of the reason for going—to get to know them."

He heard the unhappiness in her tone. "I never thought you'd become a workaholic."

"What did you expect?"

"That you'd take a light interest, maintain an office . . . open mail several times a week. Not plunge your hands into Magnum, or bring Steven Houghton in to ride shotgun for you, and do your very best to destroy our home life, not to mention every friendship I've—"

Jake held up a hand. "You really imagined that curing boredom would be so simple? A few hours a week, and I'd be that

much more malleable to your social plans? You never antici-
pated my having the least success at Magnum, did you? No,"
Jake answered himself, "you thought Charlie would throw me
a bone, and I'd fetch it once in a while. Provide a little dinner-
party conversation. . . . Well, that's not going to be the case,
Ceci!"

"Obviously not."

Jake felt the slow roll of anger in him. He got off the bed,
shaking his head in exasperation. Park Avenue, this penthouse.
Entrance right off the private elevator. Costly carpets and even
more priceless oil paintings; the sheen of richly finished woods;
the finest fittings; room upon room—twelve of them—piled
to the ceilings with the riches that Cecily's money, and her
father's, had bought. Not one stick of furniture belonging to
Jake. Not an article of clothing she hadn't purchased, other
than the small core wardrobe he'd brought with him, that now
resided in the back of his walk-in closet. Old jeans that had
known the warm feel of grass on the ridge behind the Talbot
mansion . . . a warmup jacket from his school days. Nothing
more. Until Magnum.

And by God, Magnum was going to end the year with a
profit.

"Jake, I'm sorry."

"I'm getting sick of that word," he said. "From you or me."

He sat on the edge of the mattress, hands clasped between
his spread thighs.

He was tired of a lot of things. Magnum wasn't one of them.

Why couldn't she see his pride in achievement? Small, but
still . . . For someone who'd never been poor, never been out
in the cold or hitting bottom, Jake supposed the insensitivity
made some sense. But not to him. And the Grammys came up
once a year—why couldn't she go? Why couldn't she bend a
little?

He'd tried suggesting other ways to be close. Asked if they
might start a family soon, giving them a common bond that
couldn't be broken. But Ceci had rejected the idea. "Darling,
you are propositioning a woman who's spent the better part of
her life becoming thin, and staying thin. Why would I delib-

erately put on pounds again, so awkwardly, too?" Then she'd seen the hurt in his eyes. "Jake, I mean—can't we wait awhile longer? We're practically newlyweds, darling." She'd dismissed the matter with a kiss. "Another year or two, all right?"

Jake had the impression that the subject had been permanently shelved. *I could never want your baby.* The memory of Regan's cry came to him as clearly as if she'd been in this room. His pulse began to pound.

"Ceci, what's wrong with us?"

"Nothing's wrong." But when he turned his head, her azure eyes were troubled. "Perhaps . . . we're not spending enough time together. You've been at Magnum; I've had committee meetings virtually nonstop. . . ." She trailed off. Afraid he'd bring up California again? Afraid he'd ask something of her that she couldn't provide?

Jake frowned, looking away. He'd made enough errors in his life; he wouldn't compound them in his marriage. "Let's go away, then," he said abruptly. "I'll make the arrangements." He moved beside her on the bed again, running a hand down her back, the rounded rise of her buttocks in the silky-soft gown. "We'll leave all of this."

"Leave what, darling?"

He gestured at the rich room, the quilted satin bedspread and sheets of finest Egyptian cotton. "Materialism," Jake said. "Do you realize how much of our lives has gotten wrapped up in *things?* Clothes and parties and presents nobody needs, the S.L. as one example—"

"Next, you'll be telling me to cancel delivery on the Silver Shadow. Darling, I do think if you're to take your new position at Magnum so seriously—"

"I don't give a damn about the car! Order a thousand cars if you like, that isn't the point." He felt absolutely frustrated.

Cecily studied his face, Jake's torso above her. Why couldn't she see? What did she feel in his arms, when their bodies joined? Was that all it was? Their only connection, in this bed? The same shallowness he'd felt in Palm Beach, that he'd tried to convince himself was just in his mind, when he was overworked and tired? Why couldn't he reach the center of her?

"Ceci, please . . . listen." He smoothed the ash-blond hair at her temples. "I don't want to be a workaholic. I want us to feel right about each other. I want us to explore this marriage in privacy, somewhere quiet and . . . simple." Yes, completely away from people like the Daltons.

"But Jake, I don't see—"

"I'll rent a place," he said urgently. "A nice cabin— How does that sound? Nothing too rustic, but in the woods or the mountains with plenty of space around and freshness. We'll stock it with good food, wine, firewood. . . ." Books, he thought. And music—he could teach Ceci about the classical masters he'd revered for most of his life; she'd tell him about her childhood, her feelings. "Ceci, there won't be anyone around but you and me, just us—"

He broke off as her hands pushed into the thickness of his hair. For a moment, she studied it, as if analyzing the blend of colors. Then her gaze met his, pleading, as he had begged, for understanding.

"But darling," Ceci murmured as if she hadn't heard a word, "whatever would we do?"

Chapter 27

Regan dropped her caramel-colored shoulder bag onto the sofa, draped a toffee suede coat over a chair, and without breaking stride, hurried into the bedroom. "David? Come kiss me!" but there was no answer. Nor quite the feeling, either, of an empty hotel suite.

Bungalow, Regan corrected. The pink confection of the Beverly Hills Hotel, no less. She had the strange impression of someone else in the rooms; but a closer inspection of the second bedroom revealed no one. She glanced at the turmoil of sheets and blanket on the bed she would share tonight with David after the Awards ceremony. Why such an unkempt atmosphere in this world-famous mecca of hostelry? Regan grimaced at herself in the bathroom mirror.

Obviously, she was only feeling the aftereffects of a five-hour bumpy flight from the East Coast, and a rough landing in Los Angeles. Her mood not the best; her anticipation of seeing David now thwarted—and she couldn't seem to stop moving, either.

Forcing herself to stand still, Regan switched on the shower, adjusting the temperature as hot as she could bear it. She wanted to take the kinks out of her muscles after so much sitting. An hour stuck in traffic from the airport. And now

David wasn't here to keep the nervousness from overwhelming her.

Tonight. The Grammys!

It was like climbing a high cliff, reaching toward the top. But would she get to the plateau, a pinnacle of achievement? Or would someone else walk up those steps to the podium to claim an award she wanted with all her heart? Gold records, platinum albums. She wanted a Grammy, too.

Taking deep breaths to control her anxiety, Regan quickly stripped off her clothes and stood under the pulsating stream of hot water. In the bedroom she had left gray slacks and a taupe-colored crepe shirt, its matching brassiere thrown onto the carpet as well. The long gold chains she'd worn and three bangle bracelets had landed on the bathroom countertop.

When she emerged, half-relaxed at least, to vigorously towel her hair before using the blow-dryer, she wiped away steam from the mirror and peered at herself, assessing the ravages of travel. She wanted to look her best tonight, fresh-eyed and dewy-complexioned; but she had a lot of help in the gown she'd brought to wear.

Not too many evidences of tension, she decided. Perhaps the dress wouldn't have to do all the work after all. Flashing herself a thumbs-up signal in the glass, Regan picked up the gold jewelry and started for the bedroom. Then stopped. Her glance fell to the ceramic-tiled vanity. She saw a gold razor and onyx shaving mug she'd never seen before; a tiny mustache comb to match. *David doesn't have a mustache*.

As if she were being watched from cover, Regan whirled around, heart beating faster—but she was still alone. Still feeling the presence of some intruder, hurriedly pulling on a robe, she went to the sitting room to put on the chain. She had her hand on it when the door opened.

"My God, David!" Regan sagged weakly against him.

"Dear girl, I didn't quite expect you—" He held her off after a brief kiss. "I haven't had that greeting before."

He wasn't wearing a mustache; hadn't grown one in the month since she'd last seen him in Quogue. "David, who's been here? I thought you checked in just before I did, but—"

It was an innocent question. She didn't understand his defensiveness.

"I have a lot of friends," he said. "One of whom spent a day or two with me. I got a call for a quick commercial spot, and had the time to do it, so I came early. Midweek," he said. "Why do you ask?"

"It just seems odd that he'd be using ... our bathroom."

David walked toward the bedroom, not looking at her again.

"The other one's been acting up. Damned hotel maintenance hasn't got around to fixing it."

Another blot on the record, Regan thought. It didn't seem right. Nothing did. David's enthusiasm had been forced, even lackluster. It wasn't like him. Or the sliding-away glances, either.

Regan tried not to think about the unmade bed. She walked past it to apply her makeup at the dressing table. "You'd better hurry if we're to have dinner before the ceremonies." She slicked on a coat of clear scarlet lipstick, tempering the shade with a lighter gloss. Then eyeliner, mascara, foundation, shadow. Tonight, the works. Startime, and she'd better look the part.

Her heart hammered with expectation, dread. What if she didn't win, what if ... ? "We stayed here last year once, remember? When you tested for that comedy—the terrible one you wouldn't do?" she talked to David, dispelling her own nerves. "The staff was wonderful then," her voice followed him into the bathroom. "I can't recall a thing that wasn't tended to promptly."

"What the devil is this, an inquisition?" David came to the doorway, scowling, with his face half-covered by shaving cream. Regan would have laughed at the comic effect, but her heart was suddenly pattering and skipping; and David's eyes were darker than she'd ever seen them.

"No confessions by torture required, love," she soothed. "I was making conversation." Wondering why suspicion made her weak.

David disappeared. She heard the water rushing. He said above the sound, "I'm not sure I understand the topic."

Raising her eyebrows, Regan checked her makeup once

more in the mirror. *A friend,* as if she'd asked Linda to spend the week, keeping her company. Why not?

With a sigh, she abandoned the issue, pulled the two-piece gown she would wear tonight from the closet where efficient staff had hung it for her, and quickly eased into the long skirt, side-slit to the thigh; then into the matching sleeveless V-necked white silk georgette overblouse—both lavishly sewn with silver bugle beads in an intricate design. She smoothed the outfit into place, adjusting the hem of the top at her hip-bones, approving the shimmery dance of light at the slightest movement. It was the gown she'd worn in Minneapolis the night Kenny fell from the stage, the night before he'd been fired . . . in her best interests.

By the time David came out of the bathroom and began to dress, Regan was ready, running a brush through the long fall of tawny-gold hair. She'd decided to wear it loose. Rooting through her jewelry case, she asked, "What do you think? The silver earrings, or diamond studs?"

David appraised her with the critical eye of an artist.

"Diamonds are too flashy with the dress, silver's too plain. What else?"

Regan plunged back into the supply. "Garnets?"

"Perfect." Fastening his shirt, he dropped a kiss on her mouth. "Matches your lips tonight, clear and luscious. Nervous?"

Regan nodded. "At least I've picked the right dress to shake in. It'll certainly be noticed." She put on the left earring, smiling at David's pale yellow boxer shorts as she did, watching him grin back. He seemed more himself now; maybe she could relax.

Then she fumbled the second garnet, tiny, round, and simple in its silver mounting. Difficult to find. "Oh, damn." She could hear a car outside. *The limousine already?*

Falling to her knees cautiously in the tight gown, she didn't ask David to help her. He was hurriedly finishing the studs to his dress shirt, getting his trousers. Regan groped with one hand, sweeping back and forth under the bed, making a face at David's laugh as he shrugged into his dinner jacket. "America ought to see you now, love."

Regan's fingers closed around something soft, formless. But when she dragged it out, she didn't find one of David's athletic socks. "Come on, Miss Shoo-In for Best Album of the Year, we'll be la—"

She held up the pair of skimpy briefs known as posing trunks. Black. Her heart thumping wildly, frantically. David's smile died as she watched, his brows coming together in a frown. "Regan—" he began.

Struggling for dignity, she rose slowly to her feet, hampered by the narrow skirt and the weakness of her limbs. Her eyes on his, she dropped the black fabric into his outstretched hand.

Regan sailed into the foyer on a wave of grief and pain, slamming the closet door back on its track with a vicious motion and hauling a silver fox coat from its padded hanger. "The car's waiting, David," she said through gritted teeth that wanted to chatter in shock. "Are you coming, or did you have other plans?"

Utter silence held. Not a word, except politeness, throughout dinner—Regan couldn't remember where they'd eaten—and during the drive to the theater. She clutched the fox fur tightly around her, warding off the chill in her bones, her heart. Impossible. Ignoring the glances she sensed from David in the car.

Imagine, she told herself, that life is going on normally. But what had there ever been, except a strange masquerade? The cathedral, her gown, the conviction—only hers?—that they could make each other happy. But she remembered, too, the misery in his eyes when he'd asked if she saw him as a romantic leading man; the surly fan who'd called him an ugly name in the restaurant; David, falling asleep the first night they went to bed—more a pretense at being drunk, she realized now, than fact. Now, when it was too late.

What had made her trust this man sitting so quietly beside her? Why hadn't she guessed—about the male model in

Quogue? What made her want to listen now to explanations? Were they necessary—words that would wipe the rest of her world, their marriage, away? No, I don't want to hear them. Not tonight.

Turning her face away, Regan watched the darkness and the traffic flashing by the limousine.

At the Shrine Auditorium, Regan took her seat on the aisle, barely glancing at her husband. What else could she do but sit quietly, waiting—pretending that part of her dreams hadn't been blown apart?

Ronnie Vance flitted past, wearing petal-pink tulle, large ruffles at her crepey neck and the wrists of her long sleeves, a fussy sweep of skirt. "Darlings . . ." she addressed them both, asking David about his new film, then adding, "Best of luck, Regan," with a clawlike hand on her arm. "I'm confident you won't be disappointed tonight." And she floated down the aisle in search of other prey.

David ordered softly, "Look at me," one finger beneath her chin. "You know why."

There are more photographers in this place tonight than I've ever seen before, she thought, all looking for a story. Don't show them anything's wrong. Chin up, eyes full of love for David. As she glanced up, obeying, her lips tilted in a soft smile, the barrage of flashes exploded. When David's mouth touched hers, she clenched her hands together, trying not to flinch. "Later," he promised. "We'll get through this first."

Regan stared at her hands. The ceremonies began. The National Academy of Recording Arts and Sciences, six thousand voting members.

She didn't hear her name when it was called.

"That's it, love!" David's hand, urging her to stand up. "You!" The applause beginning as he grabbed her, kissing her hard. "Go on, it's yours, dear girl—the Grammy!"

Regan's knees went weak; her heart began to race. My God, dear God. She was halfway down the aisle, music and shouts and clapping ringing in her ears, when she saw him.

Regan's step faltered. In four years, she hadn't seen his

face. She'd had the memorandum, of course, from Manny's office. A few months ago. With a brief article about the small but growing media contender; creative management; raw talent. "Surprise," Manny had jotted across it. "Jake Marsh is Magnum Multimedia."

She'd been surprised, even stunned. Nothing like this. Why hadn't she thought—why assume he wouldn't attend tonight?

For a few long seconds, their gazes met. Then, tearing hers away, Regan continued down the aisle toward the stage. Or had the sense of unease been something more than nerves about the awards? More than suspicion about David? She'd picked her gown very carefully. Flash and dazzle. Perfected her makeup, left her hair free. Why? So he would know, if she saw him, that she hadn't been destroyed by his cruel rejection? *Best Album of the Year: In The Morning.*

Regan climbed the steps to the shrill sound of applause, whistles. Breathing quickly, she gave the presenters a brilliant smile, words of ritual she didn't hear. Then she stepped close to the microphone.

"I suppose the thing to say is, that I don't quite know what to say." A light rash of laughter. "But the truth is, I do . . . as most people must." Gently, she cleared her throat, her hands damp, her eyes carefully avoiding that one row in the center of the auditorium. "I do promise that I won't spoil the producer's timing by rambling. I simply wish to thank a few people by name."

Regan paused, collecting her thoughts. After David; after Jake's sudden appearance, she couldn't think at all. "My manager, of course . . . Manny Bertelli," she managed, "who's been with me for years, and the best musical director in the business, Peter Noel"—Regan smiled toward the footlights, knowing he was there in the crowd somewhere—"and that wonderful talent, Clive Dixon, Junior. Thank you, Clive. It was your song that clinched this for us all."

Regan held the statuette aloft to thunderous applause. And then, her throat closed tightly around the words she hadn't expected to say.

"There are others . . . who believed at the start when there was no reason to, except for faith in a young girl with no training. . . ."

She wanted to include David, but she couldn't. And it wasn't David she was thinking of.

Regan sat, frozen in her seat, for the rest of the ceremony. Except for a second trip to the podium. *Best Female Pop Vocalist.* She made a shorter acceptance, looking nowhere but at the microphone.

Afterward, she chafed to get outside, to be in the limousine, speeding away from the auditorium. But in the aisle, nothing moved very fast. David, with his arm draped around her shoulder, turned to saysomething to someone and was separated from her. Regan couldn't twist her head far enough to see whom he was talking to; but she heard him laughing as if nothing had happened tonight, as if they were still the same. Congratulations swirled around her, kisses bestowed by strangers; the continual flash of cameras had her seeing stars.

"Regan, tremendous!"

"Darling, I wasn't surprised at all—you deserve it!"

"Congratulations, doll!"

She didn't know more than a handful of them. Regan pushed her way toward the lobby, feeling panic rise in her. She had to get out of here, into the darkness, into the car. Where was David? Then someone touched her elbow, lightly but firmly, and the contact, though brief, warmed her entire body. She knew before she turned to face him who was standing there.

Her voice sounded breathless: such simple words after the space of years. "Jake, hello."

Her first thought was how blank he looked. Every vestige of expression had been wiped from his face. *Handsome, oh Lord, how handsome he is,* more than ever; but she might have been looking at a mannequin. Regan stared up into those brown-gold eyes, finding them curiously darker than she remembered. "Well, superstar . . ." His gaze ran over the glitter of her gown; she watched him suppress the flicker of some emotion. Regan sensed the maneuverings of photographers around them, and so did he.

Jake backed her into the lobby's corner, his body shielding her.

"I'll add my congratulations to the rest," he said. "No use pretending we didn't see each other. Despite the disclaimer," he added, "that was a pretty acceptance you made."

Driven by curiosity, still she couldn't look at his hands. "I would have mentioned you by name, but—I thought you might not want me to."

"No need," he said smoothly, his eyes steady on her face. "Small contributions. . . ."

Regan felt the sadness pervade her. "It wasn't small to me, Jake, you know that." Despite everything he'd said to her, she wouldn't have him believe his help hadn't mattered at the start.

"Do I?"

Having opened herself to him, Regan retreated. She hadn't expected the bitterness in his voice, the apparent dislike in his darkened eyes. Why not, considering their last meeting in his hospital room?

"Congratulations as well to you," Regan managed stiffly. But to her horror, he misunderstood.

"A different world, marriage . . . isn't it? I can't say I'm quite accustomed to it yet. What about you?" The little pauses as he spoke, his eyes watching her, guarded and cool.

Regan's pulse pounded with dismay. "A period of adjustment," she whispered, thinking of David and the scene they'd merely postponed for the awards tonight. *Later,* he'd said. Now, at this news from Jake, she felt another door slamming in her life. When had he married? What was his wife's name? Not long ago, she assumed. "Jake Marsh, married," Regan murmured. "She must be a special lady."

He smiled coldly. "Oh, she is. If she could have been here tonight—she's away on a trip, Austria—you could have met her." His eyes wandered over Regan's body, seemingly fascinated by the flash of bugle beads against her chest.

"I meant Magnum," she said. "Before. Your new company."

Humiliated, yet she didn't want this moment to end, anyway; wanted to stand here looking into his eyes, remembering what she had thought she wanted to forget. What she had been trying to find again with David.

The same emerald eyes, Jake thought, full of wistfulness and wonder. A shining vision, repeated over and over with the thousand memories running through his mind. He'd expected to see her tonight—was that why he'd wanted so badly for Ceci to attend? But nothing had prepared him for this dazzling spectacle. Why had he approached her, offering congratulations?

"It's a beginning," he said. "Magnum." What did he want of her? "You know Steven's with me?"

"Steven Houghton?"

And the soft mouth lifted in a smile, her lower lip trembling slightly. The warmth touched her eyes, made the green sparkle more brightly—a trace of tears?

"Yes," he went on. "I couldn't let him molder away in Lancaster; the roadhouse . . . well, you were there in, more or less, its twilight radiance." *Eyes on the road*, Jake told himself. "He's made a new life. My executive assistant, and climbing."

Regan stopped smiling. "Will you give him my love?"

He wondered about her, with Sloan. Something about her, wary and alone. "I'll try not to forget," Jake promised. For the first time, he gave her a genuine smile. "By the way, if you ever decide you're not happy with Worldwide, have Bertelli give Steven a call. We'll begin negotiations. You might like to do an album for us."

She couldn't tell whether he was baiting her. Regan caught her bottom lip between her teeth, Jake's gaze darting there. "I don't think so, I—"

Then the rough voice intruded. "David's looking for you, and Manny's hunting you inside. They want some pictures."

Regan glanced into Paul Oldham's icy blue eyes. Though Jake didn't turn around, she sensed his discomfort in the slight stiffening of his posture. "In a minute, Paul." Her gaze shifting, she said, "Jake, I'm—"

But there was nobody there. Looking toward the crush of

people near the doors, she saw him pushing his way out, shrugging off a greeting from a film producer she recognized. Shaking his head. Not looking back. Regan turned fiery green eyes on Paul.

"You didn't have to be so rude," she said.

His hand caught her arm, steering Regan from the corner. "You're lucky I was that polite."

"I guess we'd better have this out." David leaned against the just-closed door of the bungalow. When Regan didn't move to turn on the lamps, he said, "If the darkness makes it any easier—"

"Nothing would make it easier, David."

After the sequence of celebrations following the awards ceremony, they were home from a sunrise breakfast in Malibu. In the unlit room, Regan hugged her arms around her body, not taking off the fur coat she'd worn. She felt as if the words had been locked inside all night, and she didn't want to let them out.

"David, why did you marry me?"

She saw him glance toward the stack of film scripts on the coffee table. "Stop looking at me like that," he said. "I'm not depraved." But she thought one of them must be. "God knows, everyone else is out of the closet these days. Even men with children. If it weren't for my being a romantic lead..."

But Regan only continued to stare at him.

"Maybe I wanted you to find out," he confessed, raising wounded blue eyes to her for a second. "All evening at the Shrine, and later, at the parties, I kept telling myself that this was a tragic blunder on my part. But now I'm not so sure. I've been leading a kind of double life, knowing that I—"

"Why didn't you just *tell me?*" Regan cut in. "My God, tonight, walking in here, finding—"

"The classic plant," he supplied. "Not even subtle, though it wasn't intentional, either. I hope you'll believe that much at least. I didn't want to hurt you, Regan, I—"

"Didn't want to hurt me," she repeated. "Didn't want to—" She broke off, twisting away so he wouldn't see the tears in her eyes. What could have hurt her worse than this? David, sharing their room with another—Oh, God! She would have laughed at the bizarre reversal on that other night—finding Jake with Alyson at the Shelton suite—but this, *this*. . . .

"Why did you marry me?"

He hadn't answered before. What had he ever wanted from her? Someone pretty to walk next to, someone who could make him look *straight?* Was that all? Then she caught him looking fixedly at the scripts, half a dozen of them. Offers. Like the flurry of invitations they'd come home to from Greece—talk shows, interviews for magazines, the parts he'd been wanting while he made grade-B films abroad. Regan felt her bones chill. And he'd made his start, hadn't he?

She moved before she even thought to, knocking the pile of David's betrayal to the carpet, making his eyes lift to hers in shock. "This is why you came to see me in Sydney, isn't it? The reason you attended the party in the first place? The cheap movies weren't enough, the waiting—you wanted more, didn't you? Publicity, David!" She repeated the word in a low, hoarse tone. "Publicity. That's all you've ever wanted from me." His own reasons for marrying her, he'd said. "Your picture in the papers, Veronica Vance ringing the phone, stopping in the aisle tonight, producers with fat parts—"

Regan covered her mouth, making a small sound of despair. When David said her name, gently, she cried, "I believed in you, damnit! I trusted you! I thought . . . God, I actually thought we were happy!"

David's gaze shifted to the carpet, the littered scripts lying there. "You may have a divorce if you want one," he said after a silence. "As long as it's quiet."

Regan's green eyes widened. "Quiet?" Her voice, dulled now. "Oh, David, I assure you—there'll be nothing quiet about it."

He looked at her. Surprised, disappointed, afraid. She read all of that in his expression, but wouldn't care. Couldn't bring herself to care. She trembled with rage and sorrow, with the bruising pain of loss.

"You want the world to know?" he asked. "Why, Regan? Because you've been hurt? Well, I'm hurting, too. It won't do any good to broadcast the news!" He stepped toward her, cautiously. "You're a star now, much brighter than when we met in Australia, and all the more vulnerable, love." When he would have touched her cheek, she cringed from the endearment, too.

Given a good beginning, friendship and liking, hadn't she supposed they'd come to love each other? And look at the result, a hopeless travesty. Turning away, she remembered the brief moments tonight with Jake and felt closer to tears. How could she fight, what was she fighting?

"Don't ruin yourself, too." She tried not to hear David's desperate tone. Not looking at him, she walked slowly toward the bedroom. *America's golden couple,* the press called them. *America's nightingale.* Unfair, unfair . . . he made her feel less than a woman. Not a woman at all, but a thing. A joke. "Ruin myself," she said softly. "No, I suppose not."

David followed her. There were two bedrooms in the bungalow, and Regan stood in the open doorway, staring for a long moment at the unmade bed they would have shared. All right, he wanted to be a leading man; he was well on his way. But she wanted something, too.

"David, I'll be your wife in public, for the cameras and the press. For as long as this . . . charade does *both* of us some good. No one will ever suspect from me," she murmured, "that when the door closes on us late at night, we're not even friends."

She heard him take a breath. "Maybe you'll listen to my side one day," he said. He tried to turn her, but Regan moved out of reach. "You think there isn't another side, do you? You think I'm blind, too, about Regan Reilly—well, I'm not! I know the truth about *you,* love." At the connecting door, she circled on him. David's eyes blazed midnight blue, shot with sparks. "I know I'm not making the music you want to hear."

Regan felt his gaze burn her, and his words. "I don't know what you mean." Jake. The sight of him again, the white pleated shirt and black tuxedo. The face she always remembered, the darker brown-gold gaze. Not looking at his hands, as if she were guilty for the past. *Well, superstar* . . . With a shaking breath, Regan put her hand on the doorknob and pushed.

She didn't feel successful, couldn't appreciate that miniature Victrola she'd carried home tonight; two of them, in fact. She still saw Jake's dislike, felt David's absolute rejection now. Like one of his art objects at the house in Quogue, she thought, she had been tucked into a plaster niche, put on a pedestal, to be looked at when he wished, to be touched and displayed. And used.

"I'll be using the other room," she told him, giving David a long, even look that effectively held back her tears. "I don't suppose I'll have to lock my door."

"I'd divorce him if I were you," Linda told Regan.

Regan's smile was anything but happy as she handed some sketches back to her friend. "This may sound odd when I've just agreed to buy such a magnificent collection without batting my financial eye . . . but you're lucky you aren't." Then she stood up, wanting to be busy so the night of the Grammys didn't wash over her again in heart-pounding waves. The next morning David had put her on the plane for New York, the jumping-off point for a round of U.S. concerts that would keep them apart completely until summer. The new drawings she'd just examined were for the following autumn.

She didn't plan to see him unless she had to, for publicity purposes.

In Linda's small apartment now, Regan watched as the hem was pinned on a sheer white muslin Empire-style gown shot through with both gold and silver threads. A woven metallic braid underscored the bosom, the neckline deeply cut and the short sleeves softly puffed.

"You look marvelous in period pieces," Linda had told her before she designed the first tour gowns for Regan right after her honeymoon. And the adaptations she'd supplied since then had always brought compliments. Regan now included one historically inspired costume in every tour collection. But she wasn't quite sure about this one: wearing the pale body stocking underneath the dress, giving the impression that it was her own skin. Regan frowned slightly as she watched Linda working.

Her mouth full of pins, Linda said, "Well, David's certainly anything but fair to you," continuing the conversation. "Are you intending to go on as if nothing's happened? I mean, staying together and—"

"No." Regan sighed harshly, frustrated all over again. "Between us, I'm only in this marriage to provide exactly what David wanted in the first place. Mutual exposure."

"Which benefits him more than it does you, Regan."

"You think I'm wrong to stay at all?"

"I think I couldn't do it myself," Linda said. "Maybe I'm just projecting." Rising from her kneeling position in front of the dressmaker's dummy, she smoothed the skirt of the gown and, satisfied that it hung evenly, turned to Regan. "I couldn't go through another round of heartache with any man, darling. I don't understand how you can. After the suffering over Jake—"

"You know I saw him again?" Regan interrupted, not wanting to concentrate on her feelings that night. "At the Grammys. Did you know he's married?"

Linda nodded, surprising Regan. "I know his wife. Cecily Ferris . . . Marsh." Linda supplied the name reluctantly. "I don't know much more than that, except that she's loaded, and—" Linda walked briskly toward a file cabinet in the corner of her living room, pulling out a folder. "Here she is, a photo from *Women's Wear*. I did a dress for her."

Regan heard the tone of voice. "Don't apologize," she said, her eyes hungrily searching the picture. Fair-haired, meticulously groomed, looking self-assured. Pampered and indulged, all her life. Not lying awake in Paul's house—

"Regan, he made you so unhappy." Linda's voice drew her back, confused for a second until she realized that Jake, not her uncle, was the topic. She handed back the clipping. "I'll tell you, I wouldn't endure one bad moment myself, with Kenny . . . or anyone else!"

Linda's bitter-edged conviction surprised Regan.

"Do you know what Jeb had to *watch?*" Linda asked. "That

little boy, seeing his father—a man he *worshiped*—kill himself
by slow degrees, drawing farther away from us every day,
until—" She stopped, unable to continue. "No, I *couldn't!* I
don't want a man in my life again. I don't want to care that
much. I just need Jeb and, thanks to you, Regan, my work
now and—"

"But some day," Regan said softly. "Don't you think
that—"

"Oh, dinner with a friend of the male persuasion, yes."
Linda's eyes sparkled with unshed tears. Taking the fashion
article, she filed it in the cabinet. "But I don't need any involvements beyond a brief but pleasant evening. And when I
get home, I'll climb into bed alone."

There was a silence. Regan didn't know how to break it.
Maybe Linda was right, though she hadn't begun to suspect
how deep the wounds from Kenny had gone until now. She
felt the pain herself, the stunned acceptance when she'd gazed
at the photograph of Jake's wife. Remembered his cold appraisal at the Grammys, her own sadness that those hospital
memories of him hadn't been wrong after all. But why did she
think of him tenderly, with the background music of his song
still playing through her heart and senses?

He didn't care. David didn't care.

Broken promises. But wasn't there someplace in the world
where she truly belonged, someone who would love her?

If Linda was right, the answer had to be *no*. And after the
last night with David—

Regan said to Linda, "Let's finish the dress, shall we?" She
began to slip it from the dummy. "I'm worried about this body
stocking."

"The ladies of Napoleon's court"—Linda held the gown so
she could slip into the sleeves—"didn't wear anything
underneath. The design was quite shocking from what I've
read—but you wouldn't want to sing having the audience
actually see right through, would you?"

Regan smiled at the teasing. "I'd forget the lyrics pretty
fast, thinking of those awful nights down South when they
expected a striptease instead of a song!"

For a moment, there was a joining of memory before Linda looked away, asking about the concern Regan had expressed over a new song she'd just recorded. Peter had written the ballad, poignant and evocative, entitled, "Long Ago, My Love," but Regan thought the melody too complex for any hope of hitting the charts. "Peter likes it," Regan said, "although I suppose he could just as easily hate his own song."

Linda laughed, the lines of tension between her brows easing. "Jeb likes it, too. He thinks it's a winner."

"What would I do without him?" Regan asked lightly, but her throat constricted. "What would I do without both of you?"

"You didn't realize when you hired one reasonably fair dress designer, did you, that you'd be getting the future president of the Regan Reilly Fan Club, too?"

Regan left for Dallas with the shadow of a smile. It was true. Jeb knew every one of her records which had gone gold—five by now—and could recite the titles of her albums without mistake. *All The Words I Know. Regan. In Concert. Encore. In The Morning.* Three of the five had been platinum, the others gold. The last, a Grammy winner. The new one, with Peter's lead song, would be hyped during the tour.

"It's gonna be a diamond one," Jeb prophesied, those gray eyes of Kenny's smiling into hers as she hugged him goodbye.

Regan's tight control nearly slipped at this expression of faith in her. Were the awards, the applause, more important to her than the singing that produced them? That thrill running along her spine, that nearly sexual charge when she performed—which had caused it all this time? The singing, or the love she got back from it? The only love that wouldn't betray her.

She'd lost her mother. She'd wanted Paul to love her. She'd taken the risk with Jake, then with David. Always, she'd lost. *I'm not making the music you want to hear.*

"There's no such thing as diamond, I'm afraid." Regan forced her attention back to Jeb. A million discs to go gold, two for platinum. But from the vantage point of a nearly five-year-old's boundless enthusiasm, Jeb was undeterred by reality.

"You'll make a new one," he said. "Yes, Regan, you will."

"Diamond it is then, my love. . . . Take care of your mother and I'll bring you a present."

"Will you bring Raggy one, too?" Jeb didn't want his best friend to do without. Linda reported that he still slept with the old doll at his side every night.

"I'll certainly think about it. But you'll have to tell me when I call in a few days whether she's behaving."

With his giggle sounding in her ears, the moist kiss still on her cheek, Regan boarded the plane for Dallas, where she hoped work would sustain her, as it always had before.

It's gonna be a diamond one.

Chapter 28

Steven Houghton was midway through the International Arrivals Building at JFK when his attention was suddenly caught by the noisy whirring of electronic camera advances, and a barrage of photographers appeared out of nowhere to bar his path. What the hell—? he thought, coming to a halt. Steven stood on one side of the crush, the object of photographic curiosity on the other, so he couldn't see at first who had caused the fuss until, like the Red Sea, the crowd parted and he caught a glimpse of her.

"Regan! *Regan Reilly!*" he shouted over the din.

Finally she saw him, craning her head above the others, and she broke into a smile. More flashes went off. "Steven—wait!" But it took some moments until, with the help of several plain-suited men, possessed of wide shoulders and twice the normal complement of muscles, Regan managed to meet him halfway.

Whirr. Flash. Whirr.

"I'd kiss you," she whispered, "but if I did, these pictures would end up Page One tonight; and the current lady in your life wouldn't thank me for it."

Too noisy, Steven thought, to tell her there was no woman.

"Who's your friend, superstar?"

But Regan only shook her head at the reporter who thrust

the microphone into her face, and with a firm "That's all, ladies and gentlemen," turned to Steven. "Help," she said weakly under her breath. "I've escaped my traveling circus, but not the local paparazzi. Can we please get the hell out of here?"

Flanked by the two staff men, they were soon outside. Two long limousines waited at the curb. Regan conferred briefly with the drivers and her aides, but Steven heard nothing beyond, "You were told to meet the plane—at the gate! Mr. Bertelli will hear of this."

Steven grimaced at the hard, controlled tone of her voice; but when she had joined him inside the head car and the two musclemen were settled in the rear limousine to follow, Regan was smiling again. She waved to the rapacious reporters who had pursued them to the car itself.

"Frightening," Steven murmured as they pulled away from the curb, the chauffeur quickly accelerating, "but Lord, what luxury." He sank into the rich upholstery, and for the first time, was able to look closely at Regan.

She wore a fur coat, Canadian fisher, dark and rich, with a casual but costly silk cossack shirt and dark brown pants, full-cut and tucked into tight, cordovan leather boots. The tawny hair seemed the most familiar thing about her even disguised as it was in a loose knot at the nape of her neck. The hair, and of course, her eyes, looking at him warmly. "Where were you getting back from, Steven? Oh, it's so wonderful to see you!" The green gaze feasted on him, but with uncertainty.

He took her hand, wondering if she remembered that the last time they'd been together and the one time they'd talked by phone before Jake's surgery, he had not been happy with her. "Saint Thomas," he said. "I've been on a well-deserved vacation, fishing and loafing. Mainly loafing."

His doctor had advised the brief rest. He'd been working too hard. But reluctant to discuss Magnum—Steven didn't know what Jake had told her that night at the Grammys—he turned the conversation to her work. The first glow of meeting having worn off, he noted a wary look still in her eyes as she answered questions. As if he might expose her, something about her.

"Just a doting fan," Steven assured her.

She smiled. "Still? I'm glad. I wasn't sure." She stared out the window. Then, "I'm sorry. I'm a little edgy. I left Peter, baggage and frowns, in Europe."

As the big car pulled into the stream of airport traffic, she recalled that the last concert in Paris had thrown them both badly.

"Regan! Regan Reilly!"

She could hear the rhythmic chant of the overflow crowd, feel the hot lights again, the throbbing music. *Please, Peter, stop. I can't.* Limbs shaking with the effort to remain standing, she'd gripped the microphone in a stranglehold to match the imaginary fingers closing on her throat. Cold and clammy, somehow she'd finished. Stumbling on the lyrics. It hadn't been the first time.

Later that night, she'd sat at a table overlooking the coveted view of Notre Dame from Tour D'Argent, feeling ravenously hungry and avoiding Paul Oldham's eyes. Like a condemned prisoner, given a stay of execution. Sam had suggested dinner for the three of them, then immediately spied a guitarist friend across the room.

Regan looked down at her white pleated georgette shirt with wide, soft sleeves, at the black wool crepe trousers striped in satin, at the dulled gleam of lapels on the slim tuxedo jacket. Hair pulled sleekly back from her face in a fashion equally sophisticated and severe, the long golden braid as thick as Paul's wrist hung to her waist. She kept hearing the applause she hadn't deserved earlier; kept feeling the steady inspection of Paul's milky blue gaze.

"You having marital problems?" he'd ventured the guess.

Regan's startled glance met his. "And if I were," she said quietly, "what could you do about it, Paul?" watching him fidget with the crystal water glass.

"He's cheating on you? Has Sloan got himself another woman?"

Regan would have smiled, if she could. "No, Paul," shifting her gaze to Sam's back at the other table, "David doesn't have another woman."

Like a second reprieve, their food had arrived then, and Sam rejoined their party. While they dined on duck, the house specialty, and *pommes soufflés,* Regan listened to the drone of conversation, more English spoken than French, and gazed out across the Seine, at the lights of a city made for lovers, a city that made her sad because she didn't belong there, either. In a few days, she'd be flying to New York for the taping of David's television special, which she dreaded. Seeing him again, too. His popularity increased by the day, she had to give him that.

The unhappiness with the publicity marriage—two years now, a year since she'd learned the truth before the Grammys—added to the new anxiety when she sang. She felt such pressure, too many people depending on her, fans and staff alike; as Paul had used her paychecks long ago. Where was the old exhilaration, the pleasure she'd felt then? The easy camaraderie with her audiences? Now, they mobbed the limousine. And the choking came almost every time, each performance an agony. Until she left the stage and her throat relaxed so she could breathe, speak, eat and drink again, forget until tomorrow.

She had to be more careful not to show her feelings. Paul saw too much.

"I'm disappointed with the performance tonight," she told him over coffee. "You were backstage, you saw." Before he had turned away, as usual. "I'm not eager for the reviews."

They had been no less favorable than they always were. But Regan had carried with her to New York the image of Peter's dismal scowl, her own knowledge that something was going badly wrong. She and Peter, seeing the truth where no one else did. Now, she glanced at Steven with a sigh, confessing, "Frankly, I'm glad to get away. I feel sewn up in a little sack, cloth-of-gold, to be sure—but it's as if someone had dropped me in, then pulled the string tie nice and tight." Around her throat.

"Well, *I'm* glad you're getting a vacation, then."

"Not likely. I'm here to work, then back to the Continent to finish a tour by the start of summer."

"The high price of fame," Steven said with a smile. But Regan didn't answer the jest.

On the drive into Manhattan, they planned to meet for dinner. At Windows on the World in the Trade Tower, with the city spread out beneath them like a toy, Regan picked at her meal, leaving most of a prime steak on her plate. The conversation cautiously neutral. Did he like living in the City? The reviews on David's latest picture had been superb. Yes, but what had happened with the roadhouse?

Avoiding her own life, Regan edged closer to sensitive issues. "I sold it." Jake sold it for me. "Not a bad profit, considering its location in a section of town going rapidly to seed." No mention of Ellen.

After dinner, they took a cab uptown to Rockefeller Center, buttoning their coats tightly against the wind, watching the skaters on the ice. Taking in his changes—the new suit and camel's hair topcoat, the neatly styled hair—Regan gently teased him. "What exactly is your position with . . . Magnum?" she asked.

It had been a year since the Grammys, and he'd been promoted.

"Vice-president," Steven muttered, still embarrassed by the title. "Senior vice-president," he felt obliged to make the correction.

Regan laughed, delighted; sounding more open than she had since their first greetings. Taking his arm and saying, "How modest you've been! No wonder you're looking prosperous," she drew him away from the rink. They walked into the wind, their heads down, her blond hair flying. On Fifth Avenue, turning north toward the hotel where she was staying, Regan soon stopped. "Oh, Steven!"

He followed her gaze to the hansom cabs lined up across the street, waiting for fares on Central Park South in the cold night. The horses' breath made clouds in the air. "I've never had the time before. Do you think we could go for a ride now? Jake and I always meant to, but—"

She halted dead, mid-sentence, and looked at him like a small child caught mouthing obscenities in front of company.

Regan stayed silent for most of the ride. In early February, winter still hung in the air like the tension between them after the mention of Jake. Eyes straight ahead, Regan stared at the driver's back as he flicked his whip over the bay's head. There was a clip-clop of hooves on pavement, a comforting sound that made Steven think of another bygone era when life must have been simpler.

At last, with a sigh of resignation, Regan said, "I'm happy that you're together again, the two of you."

Steven smiled slightly. "He had to drag me into Magnum, kicking and screaming all the way. But it's been a good opportunity, a new life . . . and yes, I'm happy to be with him."

Regan was silent for a time. Then, "I saw him last year, you know . . . it was awkward, brief. He seemed to approach me reluctantly, in fact. Did he give you my message?"

"That you'd said hello? Yes, he told me."

She hadn't put it quite like that; but at least he hadn't "tried not to forget." And Regan realized that it felt good now just to ask about him, to ask someone who had loved him, too.

"What happened to his music?" And he had the feeling she held herself in check, wanted instead to rush on with a hundred inquiries, to hear him talk all night. "How is he, Steven? Really?"

He took his time. "Well, he'd lost so much momentum and, of course, most of his bookings. Physically, he didn't feel he could make up the time, couldn't be good enough again to gain the first rank—"

"And would never settle for less," Regan finished for him. "He was always such a perfectionist."

Steven said, "Funny thing, he keeps a piano in his office, blows off tension sometimes by playing. He sounds damn good to me." He glanced at her, finding Regan's eyes intently upon him. "He's changed, though. Quite a lot."

He worried about Jake. The day he'd come to the roadhouse,

like Lazarus risen from the dead, Steven hadn't begun to appreciate the hardness in him, the emptiness of his eyes. *We won't look behind us* . . . but Steven wondered how successfully he kept from it. And what went on with—

Regan seemed to read his thoughts.

"Will you tell me about . . . his wife?"

She was looking at her hands in her lap now. Her fingers red from the cold. Steven covered them. A fur coat, he thought— and no gloves. Vulnerable. Maybe she wasn't completely the hard-bitten professional: her eyes had been so guarded earlier; she'd been so glad to see someone from the past. . . .

He tried to pick his words carefully. "Blond, sleek, very classy. Lots of money from oil, finance, even a pineapple fortune in Hawaii, I've heard, through her mother's family, some cattle, I think, and—" Steven paused, knowing that wasn't what she'd need to know. "They seem to get along, except for Ceci's traveling when he thinks she ought to stay home . . . but I'd say they're . . . doing all right." *Does he love her?* He'd heard the silent words, and couldn't respond. *What about David?* When he'd mentioned her husband, she'd changed the subject.

Regan glanced at the bay's head bobbing up and down, his shoulders rhythmically moving. A long interval, with the click of hooves like thunderclaps. Then she murmured, "I'm glad."

Regan's back stayed so straight that she never touched the seat; her shoulders were squared, her head up and the chin thrust out slightly, pale moonlight casting her graceful neck in alabaster. A breathtaking woman, Steven thought, even more than classy, with an added dimension all her own. And nobody in the world, not even Jake, knew better than he that the past had to stay buried in order to live the present. Steven learned the same lesson every morning when he awoke to find the pillow next to his so empty.

Then why dig up the wintry soil tonight?

But, "Are you?" he demanded. "That glad?"

The horse had clopped to a sedate halt before the Plaza entrance at Central Park South, and was standing patiently, oblivious to the blare of traffic all around. Steven helped Regan out, tipping the driver generously. Silent and withdrawn, they rode the elevator to her suite. When she invited him in, he didn't hesitate.

Closing the door behind them, Regan switched on a single lamp. The rooms were much larger, more ornate than the Shelton, but the suite seemed crammed with Louis XV furnishings swathed in cream brocade draperies. Regan stood looking around, her eyes solemn, dark green, just as she had done the last day he saw her, before leaving on tour that first time, as if she were searching for something she'd left behind or lost. "Being here with you," she said, "it's like turning back the hands on a clock."

Steven poured sherry for them from the decanter she'd indicated on a handsome sideboard. From the corner of his eye, he saw her kick off her shoes—though he felt uncomfortable himself, on edge.

Regan looked at him over the rim of her glass. "What were you trying to make me say awhile ago?" seeming more defenseless to Steven than she had in the hansom cab. "That I miss him?"

"It's none of my business, Regan, I'm sorry. But I—I do wish your memories of . . . him were as uncomplicated as mine about Ellen."

Steven realized that neither of them had used Jake's name since the first slip by Regan before they'd hired the carriage.

He studied her carefully for a few seconds, then put his glass aside. He saw her chin quivering, though she lowered it against her chest to hide from him. As he had during their vigil for Jake, Steven took her in his arms, not meeting any resistance. She buried her face in his shoulder after giving him a glimpse of bright, glistening eyes. Her hand touched his cheek in a fluttering gesture. Then she began to whisper, brokenly, about Paul Oldham, threatening her long ago not to see Jake again before the tour; that if she did, something worse would happen to him. The words tumbled out, muffled and torn against his suit.

"Why didn't you tell me, Regan?" Steven asked. "I'd have helped you."

"I was afraid! I thought Manny might have sent Paul to warn me! I went on the road because I felt it would be safest for everyone, including you—that when Jake got better, he'd come to me. But then, in the hospital—"

She couldn't continue. Steven felt her body trembling against his.

"What about the hospital? When?"

"After you called me. I went there before I had to sing in Philadelphia, the day of Jake's surgery . . . and he sent me away. He said—that he didn't want me, just his music . . . that he didn't love me anymore." The last words were barely audible. God, Steven's heart wrenched.

"And you didn't see him again?"

"Until the Grammys last year, no."

"Regan, he was sick . . . and Bertelli—"

"Yes, I know." But she hadn't married Manny. "He still hates me, doesn't he? For leaving him. . . ."

Steven lifted her chin gently until her eyes met his, the green gaze looking at him bleakly with the brilliant clarity of emeralds. She whispered brokenly, "Don't you hate me too, Steven?"

And she was right: he *had* judged her unfairly. But he'd never stopped caring about her; or seeing Ellen's fineness in her. Silently, Steven cursed himself.

"Don't, princess, don't."

As the sobs were torn from her, he never meant for it to happen. But Steven just as quickly knew that he was the only person Regan could turn to for overdue understanding; that the comfort he offered, and received, was pure and ageless, even innocent. That when their mouths met, it wasn't *their* kiss, not really. The kiss belonged to Jake; and to Ellen, as it always had. "I love you," Steven murmured. "I love you, Regan Reilly," because whether the memories were good or bad, they were both still grieving for the same, impossible thing.

Chapter 29

"David, I don't think I can go through with this!"

Regan glanced up as the door to the studio's greenroom opened. David, smiling and confident, stepped inside, his blue gaze settling on her. "You can do it," he dismissed her fears, "as well as you do everything else. If you hadn't neglected your television exposure for such a long while, love, you'd be feeling no pain at the moment. Nervous, are you?" he asked. "Then take something. The producers have kindly supplied all the appropriate painkillers." He gestured toward the array of small porcelain dishes on the coffee table, freeing one of his hands from hers. "Even everyday aspirin . . . or would you like a drink?"

"No, thank you."

Regan's eyes swept the room. It wasn't green at all, but a soothing combination of sky blue and white. Had she rehearsed the production number enough? No, not nearly enough. She was no dancer, she had told David and his co-host, but it hadn't mattered to them. They would cover the weak spots. But it seemed odd, more awkward than anyone else could know, to be waiting here with David to do this show. And after the hours with Steven—

"What's the matter, love?" She hardly saw how trim and handsome he looked in an eggshell-colored V-neck pullover sweater and dark red trousers, a matching dress shirt. "It's more than nerves," and she heard the change of tone in his voice. It occurred to her that she hadn't seen him in more than three months this time; half a dozen times since the Grammys.

"My brain knows I'm going to be all right," Regan said, not looking into David's eyes, "but the rest of my insides are never that sure."

He didn't believe her. She saw it when she glanced at his face. The usual openness of expression was missing, and his blue eyes were searching her to find the lie. She turned her gaze quickly away, studied her hands twisting in her lap. Why did I let him talk me into this? she thought. And why wouldn't he stop staring at her as if he knew every secret of her heart? David said with soft determination, "What do you say we talk—since it's so difficult to gain your attention unless it's captive?"

"I don't know what you mean."

"I mean the rumors about us, in case you haven't taken the time to notice! Though, I assure you, everyone else has. I've had a dozen calls in the last month, and the stories are—"

She was on her feet, her back to him, striding the long length of the narrow room. She whirled, facing him. "I thought *stories* were what you wanted!"

"That's what *you* said I wanted, not me." He looked at her with angry, wounded eyes. "Regan, there's more to this than disappointment on your part—or injured vanity on mine, and you damn well know it. How much is because of 'the only man you ever loved,' I believe is how you put it on the phone one night?"

"I don't know what you're talking about!" Had she, really? In London, or France?

But he had heard her sharp intake of breath, and he gave her a long look of regret. "If you could see those green eyes of yours right now, saying 'Go to hell,'" David remarked, and then, "Regan, who are you really mad at? Me, for not being what you think I should . . . or him, because he hurt you even more by being exactly what you wanted?"

Unable to answer, she sank onto the sky-blue sofa and stared at the light wood of the cabinets along the opposite wall. David was fixing a tall glass of vodka with orange juice.

"When I was fourteen years old and a freshman," David said at last, "I joined the football team at school. My father wanted me to carry on a family tradition, three generations of beefy linebackers—and I was big for my age, already solid. How could I refuse?" He had taken several long swallows of the drink, and was looking at her steadily as he spoke. "After the long summer months of skillful bullying at home, I was willing to give it a try." David looked down into the glass. "I lasted through a month of practice and the first game, then I quit, and you could hear the echoes of my father's wrath in the neighborhood until Christmas. But my God—his anger seemed a worthwhile penance for what I had learned about myself . . . because I'd been racked with the daily guilt over my own reactions to the sight of bare skin in the locker room, the shower—"

"David, you don't have to tell me this," Regan interrupted.

"I want to tell you! So will you please listen for a change instead of shoving me aside?" He hadn't looked at her, but his voice was pleading. "It wasn't a new feeling for me," he continued after a pause. "I'd had it before . . . just didn't understand what it meant—except that I was obviously *different* somehow. Well, knowledge or ignorance"—giving her a quick, unhappy smile—"I have the feeling still that, if I told my father right this minute, he'd blow my head off."

David stared into his glass, his cheeks flushed at the confession. Where was he leading them? Regan wondered. Then he lifted his gaze, showing her troubled blue eyes. "When I met you," he said, "I felt I'd been given a real chance . . . to prove to myself that I could, well, control my feelings, the inclinations, I mean, and—" He stopped, then tried again. "I thought you needed me too, Regan. You were beautiful and talented, successful but alone. So alone, and that morning in London after your friend had died—"

"I was so grateful to have you there," Regan conceded.

Then later, she'd been angry and hurt, their beautiful wedding a sham, her trust destroyed all over again, their married lives nothing but a facade for public viewing. . . . She watched him come toward her.

"We all have to deal with who, and what, we are," David said. "That's the point of this, love. I'm not sure I've done that, you see. Certainly I hadn't when I married you . . . but believe me, you have to face up to yourself as well. To that uncle of yours and all the loveless years in his house . . . how that made you feel afraid, unsure—" And then he said, almost too softly to be heard, "And to *him,* Regan . . . Jake Marsh."

She looked up sharply, her green eyes wide. Last night seemed to flood over her, the strange comfort in Steven's arms. When David took her hands in his, she didn't pull away.

"You need to be taken care of sometimes," David said. "You mustn't keep going it alone. I can't help but see two different people when I look at you, love: Regan Reilly, the green and gold beauty who holds people captive to her talent . . . and the other, dear girl—that child with the wounded look in those same lovely eyes, so haunted and searching."

"You know me too well," she answered, remembering that Jake had once said much the same thing: that she was determined, yet vulnerable, wistful. "Where do we go from here, David?"

But he didn't answer her directly. "First," he said, "I want you to know something, and believe it. I didn't marry you for publicity, Regan. I'd have gotten these parts on my own . . . later, but I would have had them."

"I knew that, David. I was only—"

"Lashing out," he said for her. "I don't blame you. It was a pretty raw piece of news to be handed at that particular time, with the Grammy coming and all." He smiled at her, softly. "I married you, love," he said, "because I thought we could make it, where a lot of other people haven't." His sea-blue eyes held hers, and Regan's heart seemed to be squeezed in some tender vise. "We were friends once," David said quietly, "and I miss that." He wasn't going to press for more; she didn't know if he wanted more.

For several seconds, Regan saw him through a blur of moisture. Mascara, she thought. Eye shadow. Pancake makeup. All in place. *I mustn't cry.* But high on the list of sacrifices to be in this room, waiting to tape a first television appearance, had been friendship. Just as Peter said. As the months piled up like so many gate receipts, friendship seemed hard to find, harder to keep. And, the old guilt surfacing over Kenny, she knew how much she valued David's.

"I miss you, too, David"; then she fell silent with her hand still closed in his.

"What's the matter, love?" he asked again.

"I'm not sure." Regan looked at him gravely. "The applause, the kick of performing, the shiver that singing always sent down my spine, always. . . . I haven't been feeling that lately." Though she promised herself that no one in her audience would ever suspect.

"It'll be there today," David promised. "I'll see to it myself."

Chapter 30

Thirty-four stories below the executive suite of Magnum Multimedia Corporation, Manhattan was the usual nightime fairyland: a carnival of lights and noise. But Jake wasn't having any fun.

Leaning back in the curry brown leather Eames chair at his desk, he let the glass of bourbon and ice in his hand dangle over the side. He shut his eyes. Tonight he was working late— but on his second drink, not on the papers on his desk. He felt trapped and restless, unable to appreciate the challenge of meshing difficult ego demands with the clean legal language of contracts. Frankly, he wondered what the hell he would enjoy.

He supposed he was still irritated with Ceci, who'd been taking brief, but frequent junkets to fashionable watering holes: Montreal for a weekend of skiing, an impulse flight to Spain or Cozumel. Punishing him for overwork? "You'll hardly miss me, darling," she'd said, leaving this time. For a moment, Jake couldn't remember where she'd gone.

Basel, he thought. A friend was having a baby. Why the interest in someone else's child, when she wouldn't have one of theirs? But he knew what would happen. Ceci would fly home again, laden with cheerful smiles, and gifts; and Jake would put aside his resentments once again until the next trip—

anywhere, he told himself, but a quiet cabin for the two of them, and time for each other.

There were days—this being one of them—when he wondered where they would end. Not liking the burst of pessimism, he sighed harshly and shot a glance at the telephone. What in blazes was keeping Steven? The vice-president's amber button still glowed, a conference call with the Coast. Preferring the theoretical approach to Magnum himself, it amazed Jake that Steven didn't have a peptic ulcer by now.

Killing time, he pressed a button on the panel beneath his desk, and across the room, sliding doors on the white bookshelves glided open, and the color TV came on. Slumped, nursing his drink, Jake thought: God, the usual hoopla. Every variety special looked the same. Loud music, garish color, spangles on everything that moved and even things that didn't. The more pizzazz the better, was the theory in some network hierarchy.

The emcee had almost danced across the stage. Until he recognized him, Jake smiled slightly. A caricature of the stereotypic leading man—tall, solidly built; moved well. Classic features and beachboy hair; wide smile. A perfect set of high-gloss caps. Then he stopped smiling. *David Sloan.*

Sloan's opening gambit was a dramatic reading intended to titillate the ladies. It was sentimental claptrap, which Jake stopped listening to after the third sentence. He held his empty glass, smoothing rivulets of moisture, wondering why he kept watching. Some fascination with Sloan? Or only boredom?

He chose the latter. Then Jake slammed upright in his chair; the glass tumbled soundlessly to the carpet. Like an apparition from a bad dream, she appeared—as beautiful, as remote as the last time he'd seen her. A year ago, that cool demeanor at the Grammys. And now, again, those clean movements as she swept onto the stage followed by a pinpoint of peach-colored spotlight.

With that characteristic flip of the wrist, she flicked the mike cord out behind her, flashing her misty smile at the audience, right into the red eye of the TV camera, straight into him. Even with her hair tucked out of sight, Jake would have known her anywhere.

"... Miss ... Regan ... Reilly!"

She wore a slink of low-waisted dress, genuine flapper style, a continual flash of deep, bronzed-red beads from neckline to hem; matching shoes; and a skull-tight cloche of the same material, effectively hiding the long flow of tawny-gold hair. On any other woman, Jake thought, almost in detachment, the complete severity would look grotesque; but Regan's bone structure, the perfect hollows of her cheeks and the eye sockets, made the result breathtaking.

A helluva costume. But as the music swelled with the applause that greeted her, David Sloan came running.

"Wait! Wait, love. This is *my* show, remember?"

Laughter from the audience. Regan, looking prettily confused.

"Are you trying to tell me that I don't have equal billing?"

"Equal billing," David replied with a grin, "means you have to share with me for a change."

A cute display of theatrical ego. Regan smiled, too sweetly. "Then what am I supposed to do?"

"Well, as you're dressed for the part ..." David turned toward the wings. "Lights," he commanded. "Cameras." He pointed an index finger in one direction, then a second. "Action!"

At once, they were surrounded, flanked by a semicircle of dancers, all male, all blond like David, all-American, surely, Jake thought derisively, the eaters of apple pie; dressed in dark trousers that fit like skin and wearing light blue oxford shirts with V-necked eggshell sweaters; each one decked out in an authentic full-length raccoon coat, straw boaters on their heads, and mahogany walking sticks in hand, sharply rapping time to the twenties music.

David stopped the beat when Regan didn't join in.

"What's the matter, love?" David asked her. "Haven't you learned the latest dance craze?"

"I was only trying to decide which of these handsome young

men I should choose for a partner, David," Regan said guile-lessly. "I can't dance with *all* of them." A statement which was followed by a roar of carefully spaced, eager offers from the boys in the chorus.

Throwing his head back, Sloan laughed. "Well, dear girl, I'll have to be the deciding vote, then," joining his wife as the music rose again, staccato beat, loud and brassy, the rhythmic click of tap shoes echoing the beat. The Charleston. Upbeat, zippy, full of fun.

Jake stared at her legs in the brief dress, wondering why he didn't turn off the television set. Not wanting to. Sheer, dark hose to match the gown, an impressive display of ankle and calf and knee, a hint of luscious thigh. Where did she learn to dance like that? A pro.

When the number ended, Jake let out his breath, trying not to hear his own erratic heartbeat. The applause lasted a long while before Sloan left the stage and the noise began to quiet for Regan's announced "Musical Tour of the Twenties," a med-ley of songs, some funny, some wistful, all superb. The vul-nerability that had grabbed Jake long ago seemed only a professional gimmick now; but her voice, still so clear and precise, made him tremble inside. The ending was a rendition of "Five Foot Two, Eyes of Blue—Has Anybody Seen My Gal?", the gender and measurements changed for David Sloan, husband and host. Regan sang jauntily, and the audience began to clap in time to the beat.

Another, more deafening roar of applause greeted the finish; then into the gradual stillness Sloan stepped forward from the wings, taking both Regan's hands in his.

"The producers promised I could sing tonight, too, love," he teased, sobering at the introductory phrase of music. "If you were the only girl in the world, and I were the only boy. . . ." A soft, romantic ballad that brought a hush to the studio, and to Jake's heart.

Did he imagine the wounded touch of insecurity he had seen so often, leaping now into Regan's eyes?

"Nothing else would matter in the world today; we could go on loving in the same old way. . . ."

Tears in her eyes as she listened to her husband, his hands at her wrists, then her shoulders, and finally cradling her face. Not real the tears, if they ever were. "...I would say such wonderful things to you...there would be such wonderful things to do," his voice dropping to a whisper, "If I were the only *boy* in the world"—drawn out until the audience had to notice his tears, too—"and you were the only...*girl*...."

A hush before the applause this time, and Jake, frozen in his seat. Sloan, kissing Regan's softly parted mouth, the wide-open look of her eyes. Then without taking his gaze away, he lifted his hand ever so slightly, and into the emotional stillness at the end of the song came the quick, light strains of the dance again, a Charleston reprise as the stage filled with chorus boys, the studio with the tumultuous sound of clapping. For a moment, Regan had appeared surprised—as if the dancing, and Sloan's kiss, weren't part of the routine at all; then she leaned close to kiss his cheek, smiling, as she straightened to join the short burst of music, offering a surprise of her own.

With a deft, lightning-quick gesture, gyrating with the blur of ivory and blue dancers, beside David in his matching dark red, she reached up to remove the beaded ruby cloche from her hair, spilling gold silk from the crown of her head to her hips. Barely a strand out of place as it fell. Jake wondered how to take the next breath; if he could. "Now, darling," she told Sloan and the audience when the energetic Charleston ended, "let your wife get to work," and the light began to slowly change, the stage to empty, as the camera moved in for a tight closeup.

Regan's face filled the screen. Vibrant. The swing of tawny-gold hair even longer now, long enough to graze her backside; a heavy, straight silk curtain. Those green eyes he had never forgotten, either: the changing shades of the iris ringed and intensified by black, altered by emotion.

She was singing a ballad from her newest album, according to the announcer offstage, pouring her heart—or so it seemed—into the words, a beautiful, soul-stirring piece, "A New Romance," the best of its kind, a melody of the sort that, once heard, couldn't be forgotten. Like her eyes. The past washed over him in waves, and he remembered a hundred nights, dozens of shows, her panic before and her exhilaration after; he remembered the rooms they had shared, the sweet way she had with him, and ah, Christ, all the loving . . . only she hadn't loved him. She had sold him out, sold herself to Bertelli for the phenomenal success he was watching now on a twenty-five-inch screen. When the camera rolled back at last for a long shot halfway through the verse, Regan was wearing off-white instead of bronzed-red beads—the color softened to rose by the spot—with no frills and no jewelry, nothing flashing now except her talent—and the long, sinuous line of her supple body.

"*Jesus*, Jake, I—"

He gestured Steven to silence. He hadn't heard him come into the room and he didn't look up. Mesmerized, they watched Regan wind her audience around her fingers like a skein of yarn. He could imagine how she paced her act on the road, tight and thoroughly professional, without a second's worth of dead time. He hadn't heard Steven's approach, and he wouldn't have heard the entire building explode around him; nothing but the sound of her voice. How well she had learned her lessons. When she finished, tears glistened in her eyes as she took her bows, then was joined by Sloan who held their clasped hands aloft, and the crowd went wild. No applause cues necessary this time. Jake could feel his pulse coursing up the carotid, a drumbeat, heavy and primitive. And scary, that she could wring any response from him after so much time and pain.

"Jesus," Steven whispered again.

"That's Noel's handwriting in the new song, I'd bet on that."

"She's supposed to get another Grammy for that one," Steven said.

"Well, I don't see why not."

Slowly, Jake got up from the Eames chair at his desk and, taking a deep, cleansing breath, went to the windows. His heart was still going crazy. He thought of Regan in the sleekly sinuous white gown at the Grammys, the dazzle of bugle beads in some intricate design. *You should do an album for us.*

The lights outside twinkled like circuits on the finely wrought miniature board of the city down below. A sick feeling in his gut. Jake felt as if someone had yanked out all his wiring. Did his expression look as stiff as it felt?

Steven handed him a drink. "She sounds great, doesn't she?" his eyes darting over Jake's features.

Jake walked from the windows to the TV set, not answering. On the screen, Regan and Sloan were trading jokes, standard variety-show filler, but they brought it off extremely well. Look at that smile, the answering grin. "Big stuff, huh?" Jake asked, watching the gold band flash on Regan's finger.

"Tremendous box office. First class, remember when I said that?"

And the day of Regan's audition returned to him. Steven's predictions. Sunlight streaming through the motes of dust that filtered between the chinks and spaces of the drafty road-house—the ancient, battered piano that wouldn't stay in tune—but she had sounded good then, too, Steven was right. She always sounded good. Just as she still chewed up his insides.

Turning away from the set, Jake spoke softly, his voice steady. Once he made a decision, he rarely questioned his own judgment, and he knew he wouldn't back down now.

"Buy Worldwide," he said.

"What?"

"Worldwide's on the market." There had been a big spread in *Variety* during the past week. *The Wall Street Journal,* too. Bad management, money problems, overextended. "Double their best offer if you have to."

"We need board approval, Jake."

"Then get it. You're a damned good arm-twister when you set your mind to it, Steven."

"I don't know if I can, Jake. We're in deep on a lot of things right now ourselves, the merger with Pacific Films; you know how everybody felt at the last Board meeting—"

"*I said buy Worldwide.* It wasn't a question."

Jake looked at Steven's cherubic face, drawn now and gray, though as usual Steven was running even with him. Maybe slightly ahead.

"What for?" But he already knew at least part of the answer. "Because of Regan? But why, for God's sake? Jake, I—"

"I'm chief executive officer here! Just do as you're told." At the hostile silence, he smiled thinly, feeling weak and powerful at once. "I'm sorry—I mean, do as you're asked."

After Steven left, shaking his head, Jake picked up a P.R. release on a rock group Magnum Records had signed. He stared at it until, slipping out of focus, the letters blurred and joined. He put the paper down, unread. Then nudged the Off button for the set. Regan and David Sloan, taking final bows with the cast, disappeared.

But her voice kept ringing in his mind.

Seeing her tonight, tawny gold and green and ruby-red, the slender column of her throat tipped back to sing, the satin length of perfect limbs, the well-remembered roundness of her breasts, he knew the past wasn't so easy to forget.

Steven didn't talk about it often—as they'd agreed—but Jake wondered now if his friend worked so hard, if he'd joined Magnum in the first place not for friendship, but because of Ellen. Then Jake asked himself why *he* worked equally hard; not only because of Ceci's trips, the emotional distance she maintained as well.

Closing his eyes against the restlessness that grew and grew, he put his head in his hands, hearing again the timeworn romantic ballad from tonight's show. Listening with his mind, hearing with his heart. And the song seemed as old as time itself, like the pain that wouldn't end.

If you were the only girl in the world....

Chapter 31

On the green Astroturf terrace carpet next to the lounge sat a pile of manila folders, plainly labeled—except for one—a stack of contracts, and Jake's dictating machine with a fresh cassette in place. But he hadn't begun to work.

He kept fighting himself. The idea was outrageous. He'd never wanted anything from her before. It seemed a very long while since those flowered Porthault sheets on board the *Shearwater;* since he had first been spoiled by breakfast in bed served on silver trays under sterling dish covers; since she'd given him custom shirts and he'd repaid the generosity with sex. Now, the life-style was habit. And he had Magnum to save his pride. And damnit, he wouldn't ask!

Jake was staring glumly across the smoggy expanse of an April Sunday in Manhattan when Cecily joined him on the penthouse patio.

"If this lifts off," she began, "we should have a lovely afternoon." She went through her morning ritual, kissing Jake with a low sound of content, then sitting at the breakfast table to pour coffee, adding some to his cup, which was nearly full. "You're not going to toil, are you?" Her eyes swept over his bare torso, the brief swim trunks.

"We people of the working class..." He tried smiling at

387

her, but it didn't work. Jake shifted, finding a more comfortable spot on the lounge. White wrought iron with a heavy upholstered pad in persimmon, lime, and white, it was the most uncomfortable piece of furniture in the twelve-room apartment. Even a mild amount of sun trying to peek through the cloud layer made the cover slippery with sweat.

"You don't have to work."

"We settled that some time ago, didn't we?"

Cecily's wealth was functional, its sole purpose to keep her feeling useful, and loved. Jake noted that this morning she had on her hungry look, as heated about the azure eyes as her light blue dressing gown was cool and placid. "Anything in the paper today?" she asked as if changing the subject, acceding to his silence. But no, he could see she wanted to buy something. Something big. Her need was like some hormonal cycle, peaking regularly, like ovulation.

Jake's gut began to gnaw as he changed his mind again. He snatched up the brown file by his chair, afraid he'd lose his nerve if he hesitated, silently asking the question as he handed it to her. "Here, take a look at this instead."

"Oh?"

His pulse accelerated. Cecily opened the cover and leafed through, hunting for the details, scanning the lawyers' recommendation while he held his breath. She looked briefly at the photo Jake's secretary, Janie, had found. He didn't think Ceci had read much but stockholders' reports since her schooldays at Miss Porter's.

"Lovely," she commented. "Or could be." A slight pause, then the pleading, anxious look overwhelmed her features. He knew that look so well. She would do anything to make him happy, to get what she needed. "Do you want it?"

"Yes." He had said it before she put the interrogative tone to her question, realized how much he wanted to hear her ask; that for the first time he truly did want something from her. Good profits from Magnum, yes, and growing, but not that good, not yet; and the opportunity couldn't be missed. "Yes," he repeated.

"Are there grounds—decent ones?"

"Twenty-six and three-quarter acres. Woods, a stream, rolling hills, a beautiful view from the ridge above and behind the house."

"You sound as if you've been there," she said, but her eyes were amused by the enthusiasm in his voice, the very eagerness of his posture.

His heart was slamming. "In my dreams." Cecily smiled at him. He smiled back, hearing his own pulse in his ears. "They want well over a million," Jake said.

"I didn't ask." *If you could afford to live here, you wouldn't have to know the price.*

"I'll call Charlie." Cecily laughed, delighted. *If you're a good girl,* he had teased, *I'll buy it for you.* "He can make the bid for us today."

"Maybe they'll come down. The place has been empty for years, on the market six months, though I only just saw the listing." Called all over Connecticut to find it. "It needs work, Ceci, I understand—" *Stop,* she wants to, damnit. He thought about the money he would repay her soon for Magnum, whether she wanted it or not—she'd refused to even discuss the matter half a dozen times.

She said lightly, "We'll give them their asking price. So much simpler without the haggling, and no one bidding over us."

That easy. Cecily left the terrace, made the call and came back, smiling. "Done," she said. Christ, it had been so easy.

"Pretty fast," Jake muttered.

"Darling, I pay Charlie to do things quickly." Charles Peyson, the faithful family retainer-cum-errand boy. Cecily stood over the lounge. The sun, which had finally cleared away the haze, burned his body. She stripped off her dressing gown, then knelt over him. "What do you say?" she coaxed, laughing deep in her throat. Her eyes smoky with desire.

"Thank you."

Jake murmured it, kissing her throat, her bare shoulders, the pale skin between her breasts. He needed what she did now—to release the corkscrew tension inside. Cecily pushed him flat. His hands roved her body, caressing, probing. "Are you glad?" she moaned. "Do you really like . . . ohh—"

His fingers brushed her nipples, erecting them. "Yes, Ceci."

"I love this penthouse," she whispered fiercely. "No one can spy on us up here; we can do anything we want."

"It will be even better at the new house."

"'A stately pleasure palace.'"

Jake stopped. "What made you say that?"

"I didn't. Coleridge wrote it. 'Kublai Khan,' or something, I forget: one of those druggy things he penned."

"'A stately pleasure dome,'" Jake corrected.

"But we'll have a whole palace, won't we, darling?" His heart vibrated. *This room, this house were made for pleasure.* Then give it to me, give it to me; and the singing began again inside him, growing with his passion, *pianissimo* at first, as Cecily snaked off his navy swim trunks.

"God." He pulled her back against him, kissing her, his tongue busy, Ceci gasping with the unaccustomed force of his response. The house was a thousand gifts, and he paid in kind, was inside her quickly, deep inside, arching up and blinded by the sun over her shoulder.

"Jake," she groaned, asking for the only thing she wanted.

Again and again, he mouthed the simple words of gratitude she required, that he needed to give, thrusting until the voice inside and his arousal became one, indistinguishable, a crescendo of sound and sex. "Oh, baby, thank you, *thank you*"— *fortissimo . . . now!*

Crying out, Cecily came, and he followed, the plan forming in his mind at the instant of his own reaching for release. It was an explosive climax, a triumph, as if he had already paid the rest of the debt, a payment that was not business, not cold cash or even power, but totally personal—between him and Regan. At last, yes, he had found the prescription that could stop the singing, once and for all.

The Talbot mansion, Jake thought, *is mine.*

* * *

The invitation, heavily engraved, seemed to stare at him in challenge.

"Mr. and Mrs. James Harrod Marsh request the pleasure of your company at home, Manorwood, The King's Highway West, Lancaster, Connecticut, at eight o'clock on Saturday, the eleventh of June. Black tie preferred."

Steven Houghton, shrugging into his tuxedo jacket, wondered what kind of evening he was about to endure, dragging some total stranger to a party he didn't want to attend in the first place. Since he and Jake had become enmeshed with Magnum, he'd suffered through a fair number of these events. Dinners. Dances. Summertime weekend house parties on Long Island. Autumn fêtes at the penthouse in New York—but at least that was near his own apartment, and he could be home in minutes when he felt like escaping.

Tonight, and Lancaster, were question marks. "Connecticut," Steven grumbled to himself as he climbed into his car: an hour's drive, and having to make small talk. Possibly one of Ceci's *Sturm und Drang* galas. A female stranger, at that.

He should have made some excuse not to give her the ride, though Jake would have seen through it. "She's an old friend. And now, Ceci's dress designer—one of them. Anyway, you live near each other, why bring two cars?" Steven sighed harshly, making a second pass around the block as he looked in vain for a parking space at her building. What had made Jake buy into the right side of their hometown, anyway? *I'll just feel I ought to come in the back door,* Steven thought. *Or begin tending bar for the other guests.* God, a dress designer?

She terrified him on sight. Steven felt his breath catch at the vision in a silver gown, chic and high-style— One of her own? he wondered—her dark hair polished-looking, it was so shiny. For a moment, he panicked. Tongue-tied, he led her outside to the curb, letting her do the talking. He didn't hear a word. She was small and light and lovely, scaring him out of any wit he might have claimed.

"You're double-parked." Linda's voice startled him as he unlocked the car door, and he turned too quickly. "With two free spaces right in front of the lobby doors." Then she grinned at him, and the daunting sophistication seemed to vaporize in the air between them. "I'm shaking so hard myself that I think I'd better get in the car and sit down," Linda admitted. "Why did I ever accept this invitation?"

And Steven let out a long sigh of relief.

"I imagine we'll be very happy here."

Jake couldn't begin to count the number of times he'd said the words tonight. Standing in the receiving line beside Cecily, he thought how insincere they actually were.

Cecily despised the house.

"What a horrid wreck," she had pronounced on first seeing it, casting a look at the overgrowth on the drive, the lawns, at the broken windows and general attitude of decay.

"Wait until you see inside," Jake had soothed.

But the disrepair outside couldn't compare to the ruined interior. A few years had made an enormous difference. Even Jake felt his spirits sinking. He reminded both of them that she had agreed to buy, readily.

"Good Lord, I can see Bernice when I ask her to take *this* project," Cecily said. She tested the bottom step before she started upstairs, her hand resting gingerly on the dirty banister.

"No."

She turned around. "What do you mean, no? She is absolutely the best interior designer working, anywhere in the world. You like what she did with the penthouse, Jake—Bernice has always done my homes."

Not flinching, he had said, "But this house is mine."

Perhaps then he had made a tactical error. If only he had managed to say *ours,* Cecily might have developed some liking for the house, but she hadn't included him in ownership of the Park Avenue apartment or the summer house on the Island or the property in Palm Beach, not even in conversation; and he didn't think of joint ownership now.

The mansion was to be restored as closely as possible to original decor: colors, furnishings, draperies, even the tapestries. The improvements included for comfort, even luxury, would not detract from its basic character. Jake had agreed at last to let Bernice take her commission for ordering a few items and suggesting people to do necessary skilled work, thus placating Cecily and saving himself time.

He had been saving something else, too. At that particular instant, parading through the upstairs halls, Cecily flung open the door to that particular bedroom. Such a jolt to see it again, even knowing it was there, knowing he would have to. He stood stock-still. As on that day, sunlight poured through dirty windows to glance off the lovely old delft-tiled fireplace. *I'd have two wing chairs there, one on either side.* And for a single, wrenching moment, he had feared that if he looked too closely at the wooden floor he would see the muslin cover still spread where they had lain together. Regan's innocence spotted there, rusty with time, the scene of an ancient crime.

"Charming little room," Cecily noted, "with possibilities. Chippendale, perhaps, not too heavy or—"

"No!" Jake had reached out, pulling the door shut. "I have my own ideas."

Ceci looked at him oddly, measuring. "You seem to be having a number of them lately."

Now, Jake glanced at her in the receiving line at their housewarming. Why couldn't he think of it as their home, too? Not just for a party. Forcing away a frown, he saw that Steven had just arrived with Linda. He hadn't been wrong, after all. He hadn't seen Steven smile like that in years. Not since Ellen died.

Steven settled Linda in a corner of the library on a green velvet love seat, easing down beside her with his own plate of food. Mercifully, they were alone. The chatter and movement of the party echoed to them from a distance, down the long hallway; but it was quiet here.

"Well, what do you think?" he asked after a silence.

"About this house?" Linda grinned at him. "It's like something from a film, isn't it?"

Jake had taken them on a long tour, showing not only the elaborate Great Hall and public rooms, but bedrooms and baths, nooks and crannies; a lovely morning room where breakfast would be served—and all the new extras, too. Sauna and massage tables, an exercise room beside the indoor pool that boasted a skylight roof; the outdoor pool, set on a level between the upper and lower terraces; and the formal rose gardens, the Japanese garden with its terra-cotta figures charmingly displayed amid stones and plantings. They had finished in the billiard room, enjoying a couple of games before Jake excused himself to return to the line with Cecily.

Steven had the feeling that Jake had been relieved to get away for the tour, not only because he wanted to play the obvious matchmaker.

Glancing at Linda, he said, "I think I like my place better. Old books and furniture from the house I sold, tacky mementos. They spell home for me, always have."

He watched the firelight strike off her silver gown, off the sheen of her hair. "You're a gentleman, Steven," she said. "And, I think, a gentle man."

Shifting his gaze, embarrassed by the compliment, he contemplated the fire opposite them: reds and yellows crackling, licks of blue flame, smoke rising up the flue. Gentle? he wondered. Or meek? Sometimes he wished he were more like Jake—direct, forceful. Never holding back; not clinging to impossible times, or people. Jake seemed to be good at that. Or was he . . . ? Steven thought of the ongoing negotiations to buy Worldwide. What had been the real motive behind the acquisition? And that look on Jake's face the night of the variety special when it had first come up, just after Regan sang. *Buy Worldwide.*

Tonight, Steven thought, as usual Cecily looked the compleat wife, cool and graceful in palest blue. Jake, in midnight navy dinner jacket, white pleated shirt, a sapphire signet ring on his right hand. Every inch the perfect host and husband.

Yet from Steven's vantage, their marriage more closely resembled a business deal than a romantic merger. When the party ended, when the guests had gone, when there were no more hands to shake or smiles to be exchanged, what did Jake say to Cecily? What did they find to dream about, or to plan for? This perfect house, the model woman... yet he preferred—

"Linda," she said quietly.

"I'm sorry, I must have been muttering to myself."

She didn't say whose name he had used, but he could guess. Steven stood, and straightened his own correct but sedate black dinner jacket. He had been thinking of Ellen, yes, about simple women and good times, but he had also been thinking of Regan. Selfish of him when this lovely girl in cool gray was going to waste.

"Linda, how would you like to get out of here and forego any more small talk with people you won't ever see again?" At the suggestion, her face lit up. "I think I'll suffocate," Steven added, "if I have to spend ten more minutes in this lousy butterfly tie."

She offered him her hand. "I thought you'd never ask."

Driving toward the City, he asked himself why. Panicky again. He would buy her a cup of coffee or a drink, leave her in the lobby of her building or see her safely into the elevator, then go. But once inside, Steven heard himself ask, "May I come up for a while?"

He felt awkward, even furtive. As if Ellen were waiting for him at home and he was about to cheat on her. During their marriage he had never been unfaithful. As he had rarely been unfaithful to her memory. But then, he seldom wanted to be.

"Please," Linda urged, "stay as long as you like."

They sat in the living room, drinking triple sec. The conversation became strained again, and it was with relief that Steven glanced up to find the small boy standing at the edge of the living room. In brightly patterned Superman pajamas, he stared solemnly back, clear gray eyes unblinking in their fringe of dark lashes. "I think we have company," Steven gestured with his glass.

"Jeb, what are you doing out of bed?" Linda left the sofa instantly, going to him. Bending, she took the child's hand. "This is my son. And, sweetheart, this is Mr. Houghton."

Rising, Steven offered his hand. "How do you do, Jeb. It's nice to meet you."

There was no answering politeness. The gray gaze flicking from Steven to Linda's glittering silver gown, he took them both in, sensing something in the air that Steven himself hadn't wanted to examine closely. "You're not my daddy," he declared accusingly. Then turned on small bare feet, and with awesome dignity padded back down the hallway to his room without so much as a good night.

Steven shifted uncomfortably, still standing with his hand halfway out for the manly exchange of greetings. He dropped his arm to his side.

"Steven, I'm terribly sorry. I can't imagine why he—"

"No reason he ought to want me in his home well after midnight. He's the man of the house, isn't he?"

With a nod and a sigh, Linda acknowledged their situation. She gestured Steven toward his seat on the sofa again, offering to refill his drink. "Please don't run away. We were just getting acquainted."

Which wasn't quite true, but Steven sat down, realizing that he wanted to stay. "He's a handsome boy," he said of Jeb.

Linda smiled, all her love showing in her eyes. "I can't take credit for that. He's the image of his father."

"Jake told me that your husband died several years ago," he opened the delicate topic with a softly voiced show of concern. "It mustn't be easy for you, raising a child alone."

"It wasn't exactly easy when Kenny was alive."

But he didn't want to leave it there. "Tell me about it," Steven said. He listened to the reluctant tale, his heart going out to her. What devastation there had been in her life, what changes since her husband's death. Then he learned that Kenny hadn't made her his wife, either. And an anger he rarely felt burned through him. "I'm sorry you've had such a rough time, Linda. Even though you must have loved Kenny—"

Her tone was rage, subdued and all-consuming. "I shouldn't have loved him! Sometimes I wonder how I ever could have, seeing what Jeb went through when he was too small to understand at all. . . . I should have left Kenny when I had the chance, right after he lost his job with . . . with the band."

"He played for Regan Reilly, didn't he?" Steven asked. "She's a friend of mine."

"Regan? How lovely." For the first time in twenty minutes, she smiled. "I should have listened to her, then. Instead, I nearly ruined our friendship. . . ."

When she didn't go on, Steven murmured, "It's difficult, isn't it? Knowing the right thing to do, even how to continue sometimes. When I lost Ellen, I didn't think I . . . well, the mornings stopped appealing to me for a while. Quite a long while. If it hadn't been for Jake, and later, Regan, too . . ." He trailed off, lost in a haze of sad memory, until Linda urged him to talk about it. He found himself telling her in detail about the woman he had loved and had never stopped mourning.

Suddenly, the night had all but disappeared.

"Six years," Steven finished, twisting the gold wedding band around his finger. Then he flushed, remembering that he was sitting here with Linda. "Sorry. I guess there's nothing quite as boring as a man who talks endlessly about another woman." He rose, wishing he had left earlier, before the confidences on both sides.

Linda walked him to the door. "You loved her," she said softly. "I was glad to listen." She smiled faintly. "And thanks for hearing mine. I'm sorry it couldn't have had some lighter moments."

"Don't regret your love for Kenny, Linda," Steven said. "Love shouldn't have conditions on it." He realized they were holding hands as if this were something they did every night. Enclosed with her in the foyer, he could catch the light scent of her perfume, smell the natural sweetness of her skin. "Good night, and thanks . . . for making a pleasure out of a social obligation."

When Linda murmured, "Good night," it was inflected like a question, her pink mouth an invitation he couldn't hope to resist. Slowly, ever so slowly, Steven bent his head to kiss her, faintly shuddering as need shook him. Linda's arms went around his neck, her lithe body molded itself to his, and he forgot to breathe.

After a long, clinging moment, she loosened the embrace, gazing into Steven's darkening eyes with a tender smile. "I'm thinking what you're thinking," she whispered. "But it's too soon . . . and Jeb. . . ." She didn't finish.

Steven drew her close again for a last, leisurely kiss before he left. "I'm a patient man," he told her.

Chapter 32

Clawing, pulling, tugging, scraping, the hands grasped at her. And she was lost, cold, abandoned to the mercy of the surrounding throng: alone, in a writhing sea of people. Regan struggled through a crowd of thousands, faces grinning, hideous and grotesquely distorted. Her heart threatened to burst with every laboring breath. "Let me go, let go!" she cried, scrambling for the safety of the limousine, softness then pressing against her spine as she relaxed, relieved. Safe, safe. She looked down at her bare arms, and a sharp cry escaped her lips again. Red crescents in the clear shape of fingernails had deeply marred her flesh. The wounds began to sting and seep. Then a weight dipped the seat on which she sat, and the car started to rock. Back and forth, back and forth. "No, *No!*" Faces at the windows, at all the windows peering in, hands extended, banging at the glass. "Regan, Regan!" Applause? Or brutal demand? A tornado, with herself at its center in the whirling vortex. They would haul her from the limousine; tear her limbs from their sockets; her skin into strips. They would kill her!...

"Manny, I can't work tonight. My throat hurts."

"You've never missed a concert, sweet."

"But I'm ill. This time I'm really ill. The doctor said—"

"Do you see the house? There isn't a seat to be had in all

of Paris." His voice lowered dangerously. "You owe the good citizens of France your best tonight, sweet. Your life, if they want it." But she resisted; and Regan's gown ripped, the beautiful froth of silk organza turned blood-red in his fingers. "Stop screaming, sweet. If you'd only stop begging for rest, give up eating, drinking, and going to the bathroom like any *ordinary* person, you could sing four concerts a day instead of only one. Think how much money I'd make then. No weekends, no holidays. . . . Of course you can sing tonight. You can sing every night. All night."

Sleep, my child. . . .

"Let me sleep," she moaned.

But the hands took her again. She couldn't sing or breathe, or even swallow. She couldn't take in enough air. She felt as if the life were being choked from her again. She needed oxygen, she had to have—

"I need the song, Peter!" she pleaded; she would die without it. But he held the staff paper just out of reach. She grabbed, but he evaded the movement. He was smiling as she had never seen him smile before: not the faint upcurving of his thin lips, but a genuine grin. It frightened her. "Don't tell me you're writing for Alyson now. Even if she has been hanging around you for weeks, watching every note you've scribbled—I won't believe that of you."

Why was he turning her out now? The melody was exquisite; she tried to tell him the single would go gold in a week's time, but he wouldn't listen. "Don't worry about the music," he told her. "Perhaps I'll have a surprise for you one day soon."

He would leave her; work for someone else; take the song with him. Distracted, short-tempered—even for Peter—he had already closed her out with his smile.

Regan thrashed in bed, opening her eyes. The room was pitch-dark. She saw Steven's smile now, his blue eyes, watchful and caring. Four months ago, but it still haunted her as much as the dream from which she'd awakened.

Nothing seemed to work. Oh God, *nothing*.

Lying in the darkness, she blamed New York. After seeing Steven, she had returned to Paris—the TV special taped and scheduled for broadcast in April—but lugging a heavy cold that became bronchitis.

Regan had called her physician, John Thornen, in Manhattan. After issuing his own recommendations for antibiotic treatment and rest, he referred her to a colleague closer at hand.

"You are very much fatigued, mademoiselle," the French doctor had concurred. "You must curtail your demanding schedule, and soon."

But there was no way of doing so with Manny, and the rest of the tour. So she had lost a few pounds, but never a night's work. She felt easily irritated and just as easily moved to tears. Not even the kind reviews of David's variety special had helped.

The attacks of nameless panic seemed to come over her with increasing frequency, leaving her unable to breathe; the feeling of hands at her throat snuffed out her life.

The tour ended here in Paris tomorrow night. But Manny had arranged summer concerts in the States, then—

With a groan, Regan sat up. Had he always been so demanding, so insensitive? She got out of bed, switching on a lamp, then wrapped herself snugly in a silk robe that matched her lavender gown.

The walls seemed to close in around her. Tomorrow's commitments, appointments, rehearsal, display danced through her mind in double time, made her body tighten, her throat constrict again. She couldn't go on, she *couldn't*. Defenseless. Overworked, overwrought. Hadn't John Thornen said so? And the French physician, too?

Regan took a deep, unsteady breath. *Get a grip on yourself . . . nothing happened.*

But why this growing misery, when her career had always sustained her in the past? She had counted on applause, the love of her audience—just as she had counted on David, and their marriage. Why did nothing work as it should? What did she need? The discontent had been growing, with the nightly panic, ever since that late afternoon when she'd entered the bungalow at the Beverly Hills Hotel and learned the truth about David, about their marriage. Since that night when she'd received the coveted Grammy . . . and seen Jake again.

Regan walked from the sitting room of her suite, hugging her arms tightly to her middle to keep from trembling. She was a star, yes . . . as bright as she'd ever dreamed. She could demand as easily as Manny! *I'll go back to the States,* Regan decided, but not to work—except for a June concert too near to cancel. David was away on location out West. Perhaps she'd rent an apartment, buy a condominium: something separate from her public life, and marriage. The idea appealed to her.

Sleeping late and eating when she pleased—whatever she wished. Chocolates. Regan smiled at the possibility. She would think about color and texture and fabric, buy furniture. A home of her own, wasn't *that* what she needed? Where she could plant flowers and grow tomatoes in boxes on the terrace. A view, she imagined. A place with ample sun . . . a bedroom, with a shining brass bed. . . .

Alyson Oldham stepped into the living room, followed by her father, making Manny Bertelli look up from the *Post* he'd been reading to nod a curt greeting.

"Well?" Bertelli grunted as the two sat down next to each other on the matching plum silk brocade love seat across from his.

"You asked me to bring over the papers from the office," Paul said, "and I got some messages your secretary sent."

He handed over a small packet.

Since his return from the Coast the night before, Manny had been sleeping, trying to readjust his biological clock. The trip West never affected him very much, but flying East again was a killer. His telephone had been unplugged all day, and the maid given strict orders not to admit visitors.

But Alyson had come home from a disappointing day reading for a television part she hadn't won because of the producer's girl friend, she said, and then she reconnected the telephone, which promptly rang, Manny's office calling. While Paul was en route with the messages, Alyson had insisted upon climbing into bed for another purpose, despite Bertelli's feeble protest, "Your father'll be here any minute."

"Not with rush-hour traffic, lover. Besides, the element of danger adds spice."

It had been one hell of an hour in that bedroom: it was all he could do now to stay awake.

With mild interest, Manny leafed through the paperwork while Alyson fixed her father a ginger ale with ice. Perched on the edge of a sofa cushion, Oldham seemed uncomfortable in this house, a restored brownstone mansion with opulent Regency furnishings and nineteenth-century British landscapes, and he never stayed long.

Feeling half sorry for his discomfort—Manny didn't care for the paintings himself, but they added class—Bertelli glanced at Oldham's hands, looking for dirt under the nails. After all the years in the street, the richer the fabrics, the more costly the decor, the better Manny liked the result. It was too bad if Paul couldn't adapt to the surroundings as well as his daughter had.

Bertelli stopped looking for the grime—surprisingly, there wasn't any—and swept a final glance over the room with satisfaction, noting the soothing effect on his own psyche of its new colors, plum and daffodil and a faintly yellowed white. A bouquet of spring flowers—lavender irises and sunshiny tulips and crisp white hyacinths—on the marble mantel brought the room together. He wondered if Alyson had chosen the mauve satin dressing gown to go with it, or to pique her father if she could.

Then he remembered what she had said once: "If I stood in front of him in all my newborn glory he wouldn't notice, but let Regan show an inch of extra skin and he goes wild." So Bertelli doubted it. He glanced again at Oldham, leaning forward and holding the glass between his hands, his elbows resting on his knees.

"What's this?" Manny waved a torn page from *The Wall Street Journal*.

"Kind of an interesting paragraph there, Manny. Could mean big changes."

The article concerned Magnum Multimedia Corporation's

growth by leaps and bounds over the last year, including the acquisition of failing Worldwide Records during the past week. Bertelli snorted a laugh. "Tell me something I don't know." He'd wired the information to Regan before he left L.A. "Worldwide was in trouble. You get me out of bed for this?" He tossed the sheet aside. "What's one more for Magnum, Christ, they've bought half of New York already and a big chunk of the Coast, so they take Worldwide Records, small change—"

"And they get Regan."

It was Alyson who spoke, but her father quickly followed, still scowling over Bertelli's rebuke. "What if they decide not to promote her, Manny? What then?"

"They lose a lot of money." He dismissed the possibility. Oldham was always slightly off balance about Regan, protective one day and abusive the next. But Jake was nobody's fool; and Regan was important now, too. A star, not a novice; and not a young man's love, either. Her albums sold consistently well and—

"You think *he* cares?" Paul asked. "About money? With that fancy wife of his? You think he wouldn't step on Regan if he could?"

His eyes sparked with that same excitement Manny had become used to seeing in Oldham. Or was it excitement? Paul was practically twitching in his seat now, his hands so restless on the drink glass that Manny feared he might spill the contents on the creamy wool carpet. Was he worried about his own livelihood—or was Paul Oldham really concerned about his niece? Even with Alyson he couldn't tell, but the smile seemed to be fading. Manny had promised her a Christmas trip to Europe if profits held steady during a mild recession.

Bertelli's gaze switched back to Paul as he said, "Manny, I don't want Jake Marsh anywhere near her," his tone at once a plea and a command. *What the hell*—

"Listen, Oldham, I'm the boss—"

"I don't want him in her life again!"

Hell, maybe he had a point. Manny remembered the days before the first tour, and Regan's misplaced devotion. He'd been in love with her himself then; but always, she'd been business first. Just as they'd agreed when she took up with David Sloan. Hard business. And he had never liked—trusted— Jake, either. "All right, all right."

Manny reached behind him, grazing Alyson's breast with one hand. Such displays of possession in front of her father provoked precious little response from Paul, but his daughter welcomed them. "Get Steven Houghton on the line for me, will you, doll? He'll be at the office. Jake's right-hand man; his left testicle, in fact. Gossip has it those people at Magnum slave around the clock. We might as well see if the loyalty extends to our girl."

Steven hung up the phone and sat in the quiet of his office, staring at the wall. There was, he had assured Bertelli, no devious motive to Magnum's acquisition of Worldwide and Regan's contract. Nothing beyond a sound business venture. Magnum had wanted to get into recording on a larger scale. Where Regan Reilly was concerned, Magnum would take the greatest care—and Bertelli could count on that.

But why give Bertelli such peace of mind when he felt none himself? The nagging sense of something bad about to happen had been following him around all day, ever since he'd walked into Jake's office that morning and dropped the folder on his desk blotter.

"Worldwide," Steven had announced, his mood already sour before Jake said a word. "And Regan," he went on. "Signed, sealed, delivered. As *requested*."

"What the hell's eating you?"

Jake flipped through Steven's neatly written notes, pausing briefly at a page with Regan's handwriting, round and clear and feminine, on a suggestion for album promotion. Steven knew, because he'd stared at it for a long while himself. Then the figures. He slumped into a navy blue upholstered armchair, one of the pair in front of Jake's desk, watching as Jake skimmed an index finger along the page.

"Gold. Platinum. Platinum. Platinum. Gold," he read aloud. "More of the same. Two million, *three* million . . . no wonder they named the most recent album *Gold*—what else would do?" But his smile was grim, and Steven was remembering the album cover, a brilliant metallic display with the title itself in raised letters, and in the center of the jacket—a white oval like a picture frame—was Regan wearing a rich cranberry-colored gown.

"I thought it was very Christmas-y," Steven commented. "Worldwide released the album just before the holiday season."

"First-rate marketing strategy."

There must be at least eight albums now, if he remembered correctly. Before the last one had been *Presenting Regan Reilly,* a two-record set recorded live in Europe and Asia. *Long Ago, My Love,* a tender album with too many love songs on it, so that sales hadn't quite reached award levels. Surprising lapse. Good work, though. "That perfect blend," one reviewer had written, "of mature artist and top-notch material." And, of course, *In The Morning,* platinum in a shockingly short period of time. Steven didn't even count the gold singles, but for all he knew, she could be near a dozen by this time. And climbing. Yes, Bertelli knew what he was doing. So did she.

"I think part of the reason for her sales success, Jake, is that Regan's kept a very active role in all the albums, from choosing material to recording and advertising—you can see that—and, of course, personal promotion through the tours."

"Well, she can relax. From now on, she won't have to get so bothered by detail." Jake glanced up, closing the file. "Bertelli told her she was a phenomenon, he sure as hell wasn't joking."

Steven leaned forward to pick up the papers.

"Jake, I'm going to assure Manny that we'll keep her flags flying." He focused his gaze past Jake's shoulder, at the glare of light from the wide windows that formed one wall of the vast office. His voice seemed to echo, flat and hollow, in the space. "And when Regan gets back from Europe in a few days, I'm calling her." He could almost feel Jake stiffen. *She's coming home,* the air between them seemed to say.

"Why not call Linda instead?" Jake countered smoothly. "Take her to lunch today, my treat. I'll have Janie reserve a table at Twenty-One. Maybe it'll cure your mood." As Steven's glance found his, Jake forced a smile. "Yes, I know you've been seeing her since the housewarming, and glad of it. You should hear the secretaries buzzing." And then, "So why are you laying this guilt trip on me? I thought you were so busy walking on air—"

"That I'd let you off without a word? You asked me to split my loyalties on this one, Jake, you know that—and without explaining why. Well, I did the drudge work, so you can damn well listen!" He stood up, clutching the papers, trying to hold on to his patience. "Whatever road you're turning onto, wherever you think you're going with *her,* for God's sake, take it slow!" He looked into the dark brown eyes, unblinking and steady on his face. Jake hadn't moved a muscle. "You will, won't you?" Steven pressed.

And Jake was on his feet, a commanding presence in the vested gray pinstripe suit and pewter tie, executive issue. Like the placid, ungiving smile that, as usual, didn't touch his eyes. They might have been strangers, not friends. "You're the one who always wanted me to patch things up, remember? You worry too much, Steven."

"I don't know that I do."

After one last, searching look at his face, Steven had left the other office. But he hadn't been soothed that morning, and he wasn't now, sitting with the deed done and Bertelli mollified.

"You've got cold eyes, Jake," Steven had murmured earlier in the day, "and for some reason, I feel like Judas Iscariot."

The nagging truth was, he still did. He just didn't know why.

REPRISE

Chapter 33

Regan settled into the gleaming Rolls-Royce Silver Shadow that Magnum had sent for her, and smiled to herself, thinking that no one else could sense imminent harm in such creamy-soft leather upholstery, the quiet hum of the extravagant motor, the silent efficiency of the black-liveried chauffeur at the wheel. *Where were they going?*

Glancing down at her dress, made especially for her by Linda—bare in back, the front of the black crepe a deep, soft V angling at the waist into a graceful floor-length skirt—she tried to relax. Regan had worn little makeup other than smoky eye shadow and a dark liner with a transparent slip of lip gloss. No jewelry. Her eyes looking large and wide, jade-green tonight. So why worry?

It wasn't as if she were meeting a stranger.

Regan turned her gaze from the chauffeur, smoothing a hand across the leather seat. Why so anxious? After all, Steven would be there—as a buffer, if necessary.

But why would she need one? She'd been in New York for the past ten days, happily bursting with plans for her new apartment: a lemon-yellow carpet for her bedroom, perhaps refinishing the kitchen cabinets, which seemed too dark and—

"When may I see you?" Steven had asked.

"Could we arrange dinner sometime next week?"

She hadn't expected the invitation to come from Jake's office. Hadn't thought of refusing, either; considered it a good sign. Now, Regan gazed at the nighttime scenery flashing by, along the stretch of I-95 that had been so familiar once, the same route she and Jake had driven from New York, the Birdcage. She sat straighter in the seat, studying the reflection of her face in the glass, patting the artless Gibson hairstyle into place, willing her heart to slow.

It couldn't be. But the limousine had taken the Lancaster exit, and she didn't know whether to look or to close her eyes against the memories. She preferred to think how unfamiliar everything appeared, just a sweep of yellow headlight all around. Twisting, turning, winding—the sound shattering the night; the explosion of the blown tire which had torn apart their argument as well; and he was holding her while she thought, *we might have been killed*, kissing him . . . and in a way, she thought, we were.

The chauffeur's voice startled her from the bout with memory. "Here we are, ma'am." The big car braking, turning. The iron gates with their rusting Gothic-letter T's had been replaced by new ones, more classic and severe. They opened, smoothly, soundlessly, in front of the lights, then the Rolls ran the ribbon of gravel drive among the stand of pines, stopping before the wide stone steps.

Regan's breath caught. No, she thought, it can't be real. This is just another dream. But staring up at the mansion's facade, oak and stone and brick, she knew it was the same. Felt as if she were in some hypnotic trance with no one around to snap his fingers, bringing her out again.

The double front doors of walnut, with their brass pulls polished to a gleaming shine, opened quietly, too. A butler nodded the delicate indication that she should come inside, "Miss Reilly," blinking against the light as she vaguely heard the car draw away, looking around in wonder.

Why, it's like the pictures in my scrapbook.

The entry hall. Large and square and floored in buff Italian marble with a blush of pink, bare except for the solitary sideboard against the end wall; on it, a profusion of tulips in every permutation of pink and peach mixed with soft early yellow roses sprayed from a slender Meissen vase. Above the fragrant arrangement hung an exquisite oval mirror, also in mahogany, with beautiful inlays.

From somewhere deeper in the house, like an echo of beauty, a piano sounded softly. A Chopin nocturne which she recognized, sweet and stirring...

"Miss...? Follow me, please." The maid had startled her, appearing, it seemed, from nowhere to find Regan staring toward the source of that sound, her eyes wide, disbelieving. Though it was his house; and she recognized his playing.

At the entrance to the Great Hall, the servant stepped back.

"Sir, Miss Reilly," she announced, and left them. In the middle of a delicate phrase, the playing ceased, suspended notes hanging in the air. A shiver ran through her, dread and expectation and delight. And in a flash of pure feeling she wanted to run to him, to close the distance between them in this large room, and all the years with it.

But it was Jake who moved, rising slowly from the bench, turning to her.

"Forgive me. I don't play very well now."

And all the blame in the world, in those few words. Regan stood, staring at him. The dark suit, European cut to fit his lean frame beautifully, in a shade that passed from deep gray to navy with the light. His dark hair edging the collar of his shirt. A little longer, the style, more shaped than it used to be. And he was tanned, still, she saw—the kind of tan that follows the sun. A moneyed tan. He looked taller than she remembered, even from the Grammys, with the few pounds more of maturity, none of them badly placed. Handsome, and severe.

"Jake," she said weakly, then didn't go on. Her throat closed, making speech impossible. Regan's glance swept the large room, looking for salvation. She hadn't expected this to be so difficult. "Where's Steven?" she asked.

"Sorry, he couldn't be here. I hope you won't mind. He

had a business emergency in Las Vegas, and left on a five o'clock flight."

Regan's mind began to work again, a door on slightly rusted hinges.

"Did you send him?"

"Yes, I suppose I did." The smile was slight. He strode to the bar beside the massive stone fireplace with its carved motifs that she had once explained to him. Selecting two glasses, he studied the array of bottles, then opened a Chivas Regal and fixed their drinks, remembering that she liked only a splash of water and plenty of ice. When he handed it to her, Regan avoided his touch, already feeling her fingers stiff with cold.

"Thank you." She wondered if she could get the glass to her lips.

"Don't look so trapped," Jake said lightly. "I asked you here to welcome you to our little family. Appropriate, I should think—for a star of your magnitude." Jake saluted with his glass, then drank. But why were they alone? she wondered. And why wouldn't her heart slow down? Despite Manny's reassurance, she hadn't known quite how to interpret Magnum's buying up her contract.

"Let's dispense with business, shall we?" He looked at her with hard, unforgiving eyes. "You were with Worldwide, and now you're with Magnum." His voice hardened. "Count yourself lucky, by the way. In case Bertelli didn't tell you, your albums and those of one or two other artists were the only thing standing between Worldwide and bankruptcy, so you're far better off. Magnum is not going under. End of discussion."

She watched him toss off his drink. Why so coldly angry? "Since we're being honest," she said, "don't you think you ought to tell me why I'm really here . . . without Steven? When we met at the awards a year ago, I had the impression—"

"What impression?"

"That you . . . preferred a greater distance. I can't see why—"

"Let's say, for the sake of argument, that I wanted to give you a bonus, the same as Bertelli's for deserting— One," he said tautly, "that doesn't have a hell of a lot to do with singing!"

Surely he couldn't think— Regan's heart made extra beats.

"I'm not going to stand here so you can insult me—"

"Then sit down." His voice, deadly quiet, almost caressing.

Regan strode quickly to the ivory French phone on the black walnut table by the entryway. She didn't think she had even read the marked buttons before jabbing one, but she must have. "Garage? Yes, this is Miss Reilly at the house. Please send the car around, will you, I'm going back to— *What?* Well, why on earth not?" Then she turned slowly to find Jake looking at her from the center of the room, his head a little to one side, speculatively, as if he were considering bidding on something at auction. "Yes, I see," she said into the telephone. "Yes, of course." She slammed the receiver down. "Why? First, Steven, and now the car—"

Jake smiled. "I don't know why you persist in fancies of persecution. Our servants never respond for anyone but me or Ceci."

"Then please call for me."

"No, I don't think so. If you're that anxious to insult my hospitality, phone for a taxi." Then he glanced at his watch— needlessly, Regan was certain—and shook his head. "Though I'm afraid one of the disadvantages of living so far out is that our local transportation stops functioning quite early, around nine. . . . You've missed them by half an hour."

With jerky steps, Regan walked to the hall, her heels making a staccato click on the marble flooring. Her heart thundered.

"Yes," Jake said after her, "if you're willing to remove those slippers, you probably can hoof your way into Lancaster to the train station—it's a little over five miles and slow going in the dark, but I have every confidence you'll make it. You're used to getting where you want to go—any way you have to."

Taking long, deep breaths of air that didn't seem to help, Regan stopped, turning back to face him. He wasn't the only one who'd been hurt. She felt like sobbing, *Jake, it's me, don't you remember how much I loved you?* But she hadn't been prepared for such hostility, however quietly expressed. Not even at the Grammys. "Jake, *please,* if you want to talk about the past, let's—"

"I don't want to talk. Where did you get that idea?"

He was leaning now in the doorway to the Great Hall, arms crossed over his chest, and waiting. Jake, who had consumed her once. Jake, whom she had never forgotten. His dark hair—pooling light from the hall chandelier—the intense brown gaze, and the straight, lean body were the same as she remembered. The very familiarity of his appearance pushed her off balance as Jake smiled. His lips curved in the same gentle way: even teeth displayed against his tan like pearls on velvet. But with a single difference: the smile was quite contained; his eyes every bit as blank, as hard, as they had looked when he first turned from the piano to greet her.

She sensed the struggle to control himself; but he wouldn't let it show. "Tell me," he said in a conversational tone, "since you insist . . . do you like what we've done to the house?"

We. Regan looked around dutifully, as a hold on sanity. And where was she? Jake's reputed beauty of a wife. Not at the Grammys, not here. What part had she actually played in the restoration?

Were those the original tapestries on the side wall? Regan wondered. She thought they must be, the dark reds and blues washed out to such delicacy of shade. And the huge Kirman in a Tree of Life pattern, predominantly ivory and deeper red, carpeting the floor, its stone edges accented by the rug, was genuine—she could see that at a glance.

Yet, the furniture was different from that in the old photos Regan had kept: deep, pillowed, and comfortable, in neutral shades of beige and white so as not to detract from the rest, a successfully unobtrusive blend of the Middle Ages with the modern world. A room of elegance, she thought, and authenticity. The soaring, creamy stone fireplace, the high, darkly beamed ceiling. French doors along the terrace wall stood open to the summer night, to the sweet smell of flowers and freshly mown lawns.

Regan conceded, "It's very beautiful," but she wouldn't discuss interior design with him. That wasn't why she'd come.

Regan's gaze sought the doorway, wondering if Cecily might appear. "Jake—" she began.

But she couldn't ask why he'd bought this particular house, either. Of all the houses in the world . . . unless it had been to break her heart.

Did he see the dark confusion in her eyes, the loss of all they'd had once? When she didn't go on, he straightened from the door frame to press a button in a panel on the wall; and in seconds, a uniformed maid appeared—not the same one who'd shown her into the hall.

"We'll have dinner," Jake told her, still looking at Regan as he spoke. When the girl had gone, he added softly, "It would be a sin to waste the chateaubriand. I'm not that eager. I can wait. And you really should taste the asparagus tips, with lemon and sweet butter: they'll melt on your tongue." His eyes were watching her lips as she moistened them.

Regan felt as if he'd touched her. Her senses whirled; unbidden desire joined the blood in her veins, circulating through her body. My God, he couldn't be serious! If he still blamed her for the past, why would he want her now, tonight?

But as long as he wanted her to stay, she had the chance. The long years apart, the success and disappointment in her life—and maybe his?—their awkward meeting at the Grammys . . . during all that, yes, she had missed him, mourned the lack of explanations and forgiveness.

Looking up as Jake said her name, coming toward her, she saw that he was holding out his hand.

For a frozen second, Regan studied it, remembering with a flash of anguish how she had loved his hands. Remembering how important his music, Jake's playing, had been to him, and that his first words tonight had concerned his lack of ability now—which, as Steven had said, wasn't true. Remembering how he had tried to juggle his career and his unwilling love for her.

And she couldn't bear to have the past between them, unresolved and festering. Couldn't bear, really, to have anyone dislike her . . . especially not Jake. Feeling the first shock of warmth and fineness after so long, she placed her hand in his.

Feeling that she'd come in, not from a summer night, but out
of a cold, wintry darkness to warm herself at someone's fire.
Jake's fire.

Somehow, she would make him understand, find a way to
end his bitterness toward her. *Dear God,* she asked him silently,
don't hate me.

Chapter 34

"You've scarcely touched your food."

Jake stood up, scraping his chair, and dropped the white damask napkin beside his plate before he came around to Regan's place. "No," she agreed, making no excuses, but only shaking her head very slightly.

"You're certain you don't want dessert?" he asked, pausing behind her chair. "Not even a sliver of the Austrian torte... whipped cream and walnuts," he tempted, "seven or eight layers." But she refused with another negative motion of her head and sat rigid in the high-backed Jacobean chair, dwarfed by it, not turning to look at him.

She fixed her gaze on the snowy linen tablecloth, then the amethyst-and-crystal wall sconces that matched the enormous chandelier.

"A splash of brandy," Jake said to show her he didn't mean to rush. "I have some Armagnac that goes down like honeyed fire."

"No, nothing."

"Shall we have a look around, then? You haven't seen much of the house."

And she had no choices left. Preceding him from the dining room as he indicated, Regan moved with that fluid grace he always admired. Damnit, he had to admire her now. The dress,

just right; her hair with the sheen of heavy satin; the softly
agreeable voice she had used through dinner . . . and the silent
wariness with which she watched him. As if the table had been
some sacrificial altar, wafer-thin Bavarian china and Irish crystal somehow threatening her. And as if she feared physical
harm, she had left most of the Belgian endive salad, drunk
little of the rich Burgundy wine.

Had he imagined the quick flash of gladness in her eyes
when he turned from the piano in the Great Hall? Those eyes,
soon masked by shock at the accuracy of these surroundings,
this house she had coveted now lovingly restored—the scene
itself must have unnerved her.

She'd almost left, he knew. And that awesome presence,
star-quality, had proved difficult to handle. Speaking cool words
of challenge, he'd felt his heart hammering, his hands grow
cold when, now, he could barely contain his eagerness to touch
her again.

That melting glance at first; the faint tremble when he took
her hand. The incandescent beauty, the gleam of her bare back,
the shine of her hair as she walked in front of him now made
his reactions to her television special seem weak by comparison; made their brief encounter at the Grammys pale to in-
significance. He could hardly keep his hands off her, didn't
want her to guess how badly she had shaken him.

Slowly, they went up the wide stairs to the second floor,
Jake keeping his voice low and reassuring, their measured
footfalls identical, soundless, on the thick moss-green carpet.
What would Regan's reaction be to his surprise? Casually, he
pointed out the new plasterwork, intricately molded, of the
ceilings; the refinished linen-fold paneling Regan had liked so
well in years past.

But she didn't let down her defenses. As they walked the
cool hallway, her steps began to drag. Jake put his hand lightly
on the small of her back, his pulse rate instantly soaring. God,
the feel of her. Then, as if by some preappointed signal, they
both stopped halfway down the corridor, all the way back in
time. Over her shoulder, Regan sent him an asking glance.
Without explanation, Jake twisted the brass knob of the oak

door, letting it glide open, inscribing a semicircle of shadow across the gleaming floor. And he heard her strangled gasp.

"Oh, my God, Jake ... *dear God.*"

She had known about him, about Magnum and her contract; but she couldn't have known about the house itself, and this. His fingers closed upon her shoulders, preventing flight, holding her the barest distance from him, no more than half an inch of air between their bodies.

"Don't you like it?" She was quivering, her silken flesh trembling in his hands. Trembling, burning him. "If you don't, I'm disappointed."

Standing on the threshold, Regan took in every detail of the only room in the mansion not restored according to the Talbot plan, but hers. Her gaze moved slowly over the canopied bed, shining brass as she had always imagined it would be.

Yards and yards of snowy white batiste fabric, used to make the side curtains, were tied back to the four posts and softly draped, falling to the floor, blending with the skirt of the bedcover, quilted of matching batiste in a delicate design that looked almost like lace. The sheerest draperies, blowing gently in the summer-night breeze, matched the under curtains, the covering on the brass bed. It made an airy effect; the whole room seemed feminine; yet it was not a room in which a man might feel uneasy.

The silk wallpaper was a simple Directoire pattern, stripes on stripes of off-white and palest gold. The carpet had a light ground with a design of amber and deep blue, picking up the colors in the delft tiles of the fireplace—and the twin amber velvet wing chairs standing to either side.

The chairs, Regan thought ... he had remembered those, too. Everything she'd wanted. Faintly, she shook her head, but she couldn't stop looking, wondering, as if she were peeking into some forbidden book. Repulsed, yet fascinated. Jake allowed her a long moment before he spoke.

"Well?"

"All here," she acknowledged softly. "Intact," Regan murmured, "like a museum."

And he let his hands slide, circling the round shoulder bones, pulling her back against him until their bodies touched at last. She felt pain flash through her as swiftly as desire; but it wasn't physical pain. The house itself had awed her; this room made her want to cry.

"Jake, why?" she asked him. "Why?"

"Because I have an excellent memory."

Regan didn't have time to react to the ambiguity before he had moved. In a split second, his hand, clamping on her wrist, had yanked her around to him. Her eyes haunted, her face a mask of sudden fear, she felt him tangle his free hand in her hair. Forcing her head back, then setting his mouth on hers. She tried to twist away, but he held her still, kissing her hard, again, hard and bruising. *"Let me go!"*

An echo of her tortured breathing, Jake was panting too, the fantasy he had wanted to create seemed to go beyond itself at the first touch of her lips, taking him to a place he'd never been. Why had he wanted her off balance, why had he wanted her to fight him? The struggle continued, passionate, wordless, until he muttered, "You never found my kisses distasteful before, *my lady*"—and instantly, incredibly, Regan went limp, became dead weight in his arms. He had to tighten his hold to keep her from falling.

If you're going to come inside, my lord, you must play. . . .

Sagging against him, she buried her face in Jake's shoulder, shaking her head slowly, rhythmically, the movement causing her delicate perfume to waft upward, filling his senses: a clean, soft, faintly woodsy scent.

"Smart girl," Jake said quietly. His hand brushed hair from her temple, then moved to the Gibson knot and the pins hidden there, taking them one at a time, loosening the swirls of silk, freeing the length as his fingers, remembering, followed its waterfall: shimmering hair that long ago had wrapped them both in embrace.

At last she said, shuddering at the light touch of hair on her bare back, "When we were in this room before, you played my game, didn't you?" Her voice, sounding curiously resigned, was muffled against his shirt. "I suppose now I have to play yours." Her head came up. "Dealer's choice, Jake?"

"Strip."

At the single word of command, loud in the sudden silence, shocked green eyes met his, then lowered in submission. It wasn't what he'd expected, this giving in, this surging of his own blood, a strange flood of feeling he couldn't name. And for an instant, Jake thought he would stop her. Don't, *don't*. . . .

Then Regan stepped away from him, taking a deep, shaken breath. And her eyes, fixing on his, never faltered, not once, as she reached behind to unzip the silky black gown. It slid with Jake's glance to the carpet in graceful folds upon itself. Like the Wicked Witch of the West in *The Wizard of Oz,* he thought, the heap of material would disappear in a puff of smoke; then, when it didn't, his eyes dragged from Regan's slim ankles up the neat calves to slender knees and along firm thighs to lace panties.

It took much longer for his gaze to shift from round hips to narrow waist to her breasts, which were fuller now than he remembered; because, suddenly, mixed with desire, came the oddest impression that he was trespassing.

"Having second thoughts, Jake?"

Her voice came quietly, full of dignity. She never flinched, and her eyes had stayed wide, but they were much too bright, and with surprise he saw that slow tears were mapping her cheeks. Battered pride, or shame? She didn't cry easily, he knew that. Or was it—much more likely—an act, hoping for reprieve? Too late, too late. Let her entertain him, for once.

Jake dropped his suit coat onto one of the amber velvet wing chairs. "No," he murmured, "I've been waiting for this," unbuttoning his shirt with rapid motions, reaching for his belt. And more surprising to him than her tears had been, Regan began to help.

"I think I've been waiting too," she whispered in a tone he hadn't heard for a long, long time. "Oh, Jake," she cried softly, ". . . so many nights," but he covered her mouth with an angry kiss. Her fingers on him were swift and cool; but his skin felt warmed by fire.

"You," he whispered, his lips on her, then his hands, flying, slipping over her body. He couldn't seem to touch her enough.

"You tramp," as he followed her down onto the big bed, but the epithet came weakly, more a cry of passion.

Nothing was going the way he had planned, *nothing*. He had meant to shock, to hurt, to end the ceaseless yearning with one night. Now, this, *this*. Regan lay motionless, looking up at him and saying, "I'm not, oh God, I'm not," the muted moonlight coming through the windows reflected in her eyes, bottomless green eyes with the same misty look she'd worn for him; that she now took out for public occasions like the television special.

To shut it out, Jake kissed her with his eyes closed, stopping the words, too. His hands roved her flesh of their own will, disconnected from thought yet totally connected to his senses. He felt the first hunger of her mouth, light at first, then growing as he gentled the kiss, unable not to, and her lips parted, Regan's tongue meeting his, sending sabers of sharp desire through him. God, God. . . .

Then her body moved beneath his, consuming him once more. Easily, so smoothly, as if they were still Jake and Regan, coming together in her innocence again, shedding it like their unnecessary clothing.

"Jake," she whispered fiercely, shuddering as he began slowly, so familiarly, to move in her. He couldn't believe how right it felt to be there, deep inside, held tightly. *But it's not the same,* he tried to think; *it can't be.*

And still, he needed the sameness—to hear her, young and trusting, call his name, wanting him, sweet Christ, really wanting him and only him. He needed the tears he tasted, tracking her beautiful face, to be not from sorrow, but from love. As if she understood, Regan joined him in the quest, as helpless as he, both of them pressing on to end the spiraling excitement like no other he had ever known, heedless and united in a passion that neither could deny—that neither could control.

"Why did you come here tonight?" In the final, cresting surge of fulfillment, Jake cried out. "Why did you let me do this?"

* * *

Regan awakened quickly, incompletely, still feeling drugged by the lack of deep sleep, to find the side curtains of the bed drawn back. The sky outside had imperceptibly lightened, and the room was still dark. It couldn't have been more than an hour since she'd drifted off to sleep, her body naked and warm against Jake's.

Now he was standing beside the bed, wearing his white shirt open at the neck and dark trousers with no belt, and what had brought her swimming slowly, ineffectually, up from slumber was the soft weight of her black gown falling onto the covers.

"Get dressed."

"Not now, Jake," with a feeble groan, rolling over in bed, careless of the dress slithering to the floor, one arm thrown over her face to keep out the light as he switched on the lamp by the bed. "Sleep," she mumbled.

"Put this on," Jake told her coolly. "The car's coming around to the front. I've already called for it."

And she was wide awake. Furious, humiliated, stunned by the cold indifference of his tone after such heated passion, unable to meet his eyes, if he would have given her the chance, faced her long enough to exchange glances. He seemed very busy, reordering the room, straightening the dresser, the table, dropping Regan's jet earrings into her hand without touching— as if she were contaminated. She could imagine the can of Lysol in his pocket, ready to spray the room, the sheets, when she was gone.

"Are you the sort of person who cleans before the maid comes?"

She was surprised at the tremble of her voice, but he wouldn't rise to the fragile bait, said with a light shrug of his shoulders, "Don't forget your shoes. They're under the chair."

"Is your wife on her way home?"

Regan felt worse than a contamination: she felt bought and paid for. She wished she had worn the heaviest perfume Paris ever made, something to hang in the atmosphere of this room for part of a century no matter how many cans of disinfectant

Jake used to spray away her evidence. Who did he think he was?

Regan thrashed out of bed and began throwing on her clothes. He didn't look at her then, either—which was just as well. She was furious, and she didn't want to blush. Jake swept their wineglasses from the bedside table—he'd gone downstairs to the library for a bottle of Chablis and some ice earlier—then paused to look out the window before he put them on a small, round tray containing the remnants of the snacks that had accompanied the wine. Rye crackers and crisp wheat thins and a hunk of Jarlsberg cheese, sweet and nutty. She could still taste it.

"Are you ready?"

Regan zipped her black dress with a vicious motion. *Who the hell did he think he was?* She'd be damned if she'd even comb her hair. But in the next second, she was at the dresser, a lovely cherry piece with delicate lines, peering into the glass and trying to make some order out of the tangled tawny strands. Which made her all the more angry, that she cared what the chauffeur might think. Damn him. Jake. He was holding out her black lace shawl, which he must have brought from downstairs.

"Better check again," she said as she took it, holding the wisp of fabric by her fingertips. "Make certain you've gotten rid of all my traces."

But he was looking out the window again toward the stretch of rolling lawn, the drive that arced in front of the big house, saying that the car was here. He hadn't even heard her. "What?"

Regan marched toward the door. She could feel his eyes following her all the way to the hall before he moved, walking her down the stairs to the entrance. The house was silent, the hall lights were on—advertising her exit. At the front door, he looked at her for a moment in the same, assessing manner as he had before when she had wanted to leave. Which is what she should have done while she had the chance.

"If I had to get up at this absurd hour of the morning," Regan said with a scathing inspection of his features, "you might at least have given me something to eat," and she saw his glance falter. She didn't want him to know how mortified she really felt.

Until he spoke, Regan thought he looked apologetic. Then Jake informed her coldly, "I didn't invite you for breakfast."

Chapter 35

Regan blinked. The single spotlight rose, too bright, a white sun in a dead-black sky. She stared out over the empty rows of seats that spread, crescent-shaped, over the buff and blue auditorium.

"Where the hell were you this time?"

Peter rapped his baton sharply against the music stand, his voice shrill as Regan jerked her wandering attention back to him, suddenly aware that the orchestra had squawked away into silence.

"Here," she said, like a grammar-school student answering attendance. The musicians snickered, Sam grinned at her, and Regan felt like an idiot for allowing herself to be so preoccupied. In fact, she had been looking down at her old brown corduroy pants and faded orange sweatshirt, wondering whose clothing she had on. Seeing in her mind the black crepe gown she'd worn; feeling it slip, sinuously slow, the entire length of her body to the floor, leaving her naked, vulnerable.

"I wish I could believe you," Peter said. "May we begin? Yet again?"

In the first, agonizing hour of rehearsal, they hadn't once completed the song that was to replace another ballad with more difficult range. For this week of preparation around the

428

final concert of early summer—a performing arts festival in a New Jersey suburb not far from New York—Regan had been plagued not only by wayward thoughts, but by hoarseness, too.

Pages turned; the orchestra began the introduction to a ballad she had sung innumerable times. Regan couldn't remember the first phrase. She struggled for the words, then for air itself. That choking sensation again; the shortness of breath; the feeling of imminent strangulation. She swallowed and swallowed, gasping as if there were fingers at her throat squeezing, robbing her lungs of air. Her legs had begun to feel like rubber and the stage was swimming in front of her face. How could she go on tonight? She couldn't even breathe.

She missed her cue. Sam Henderson was the last to stop playing, trying to distract attention from her with a quick bit of improvisation on the guitar.

"I forgot the words," Regan said.

"I get the impression you've forgotten your own name!"

"Go to hell, Peter!"

But at least she was angry now, and that made the adrenaline flow. They stood glaring at each other until at last Regan realized that she was breathing and Peter had probably made her mad on purpose. "Are you going to do this, or not?" he challenged, dark eyes boring into her, unblinking. With a single, whipping motion of the page, he snapped the sheet music to her.

"I'm going to do it," she said. *I can't,* she wanted to shout. *I can't sing anymore,* she thought, not even this one night, and I don't know why; but when she opened her mouth, the notes came out. As wooden as they sounded, they were at least true, and she managed to finish. Perspiring and cold at once.

"I simply have no more patience," Peter said softly. "Let's try for a run-through around five o'clock. Until then, I intend to pray, continuously. I suggest you do the same, gentlemen"— he included the musicians with a gesture, then turning enough so Regan could see his tight and angry face, said, "And you, Miss Reilly, please try to get some sleep."

What was his excuse? she asked silently, furiously. Withholding new music from her, working on his own—whatever it was. He was only blaming his distractions on her. And vice versa, Regan admitted.

With her head down, she began walking off the stage to her dressing room. She was stopped by Peter's hand, thin but strong, on her shoulder.

"Wait," he said as the rest of the band filed past them. "I'm worried about you."

"Well, I'm worried about you, Peter."

"It's a damn good thing this date is the last until fall," he said, searching her features. "Showing up in that ghost costume this morning," as his hand touched her cheek. "You're white as that, you know. I think you should see a doctor, Regan. You've been having those spells again, haven't you?"

How did he know? Did he watch her that closely? Had he known this morning during rehearsal?

"Are you trying to say my mind is going, Peter? That I'm having a breakdown or something?" Her voice was taut, defensive.

"I'm saying you ought to take it easy for a while. And have a checkup right away."

"I think it's a touch of asthma," she said, frightened by his scrutiny.

"I don't think so," Peter told her, almost gently, then took his hand away. "Call me if you need me this afternoon . . . if you can't sing tonight."

"I can sing, damnit, Peter!"

And he damn well knew it.

Regan went back to her dressing room, not knowing whether to be angry all over again at Peter's innuendos or grateful for his concern. Maybe he was just trying to justify his resignation. She could almost see the neatly typed letter clutched in his hand after tonight's concert. The *prima donna*, falling apart. What else could he do? Hadn't she once said they couldn't work together? Unfortunately, she had proved to be right, and he had to think of his own future, his invalid mother. He was extremely sorry, but—

Regan flopped into a chair after slamming her door shut.

She felt like a reprimanded child; but Peter was right in one regard. She was exhausted, and she could hardly blame him for that. She had been up most of the night, and was ill-prepared for the concert she must struggle through tonight.

In fact, for most of the week, instead of her repertoire, those hours in the Talbot mansion had kept running through her mind; the shock of seeing that room, so perfectly planned. For her alone? And why?

The only thing he had said about her all that evening was, "Ceci does a lot of traveling," and his smile had been cold. "Sloan too, I imagine," he had added. No more communication between them than that, Regan thought. He'd been so harsh and unloving, such a stranger to her, until they went to bed. Was that all Jake had wanted from her, then? To punish her sexually?

And yet, everything had changed in those hours after dinner in the amber room with the brass bed. After the shock had worn away. Undressing for him, she had wanted to die of shame, but it hadn't been physical shame. It hadn't been one-sided, either, that evening in the Talbot house. Manorwood, they called it now. His house, and Cecily's.

Last night, too, in the fading darkness before morning, Regan had tossed in the quiet apartment, in her own room, wanting to wake up beside Jake; to make languid love for hours and hours more. How could she want him again?

I didn't invite you for breakfast.

Oh God, she hoped she never heard from him again! But as she castigated herself, Regan was also dialing the telephone in her dressing room. Why hadn't she thought of David until now?

He was on location in Arizona, and would be until mid-summer. Since the taping of the television show months before, they had enjoyed a series of friendly telephone chats, but Regan wasn't sure this would turn out to be one of them. "We're on lunch break," David assured her. "And I've just finished learning my new lines . . . an endless process on this film, it seems. Every morning there are rewrites for the script, and then the next day, rewrites for the rewrites."

Regan gave a small laugh, but it was more dutiful than real. And then, "David, I've done a rather foolish thing. . . ."

"What would you like me to say?" When she had finished, David's voice was as hushed as it had been the night she first told him about Jake, not much above a whisper from the other end of the line. "It isn't my place to forgive you, Regan."

It should be, she thought. *If we had a normal marriage. . . .*

"Oh, David, I know you can't. It's just that I'm so confused. It was even more like it used to be for us that night," she admitted, "than it really *was* long ago—if you can understand what I'm trying to say, because I can't."

"You enjoyed it," he said. "And so did he."

"He didn't want to, I know that much." She thought her voice sounded very small, and he wasn't helping. She felt even worse for his silences while she spoke, the soft tone of voice without the usual undercurrent of humor and acceptance, and the fact that he hadn't once called her *dear girl*. "Oh David— what should I *do?*"

"What do you want to do?" he asked mildly. "Are you seeing him again?"

"No!"

"Then why not simply forgive yourself, love. I've never met the man," he said, "but I can't say I care for his methods where you're concerned." She heard the slightest warming of his tone. "It's been a long time coming, we both know that."

"David?" after a long pause so that she wondered if he was still there. "I didn't know who else to call, and you're right, of course, but am I—is this hurting you?"

"Of course not, dear girl."

There. It was all right then, the smile in his voice again. He was only letting her work things out for herself, as she had to do, with a little sympathetic listening and the right questions. She was more disappointed in herself than David could possibly be. Should she fly to Arizona to see him after the concert tonight? But he refused her offer.

"Why don't we meet in Quogue? We'll lie on the beach and talk. There's no need to come out here: the heat is blistering." But she wondered if he was seeing someone there and didn't

want her around. Was that why he'd been so offhandedly understanding? She imagined he wasn't alone while they'd been
talking; maybe that was why he had sounded different, flat and
strained. "I'm flattered you want to see me," he added.

"We could do the museums together. That tiny gallery on
Seventy-ninth and Madison you like so well will be showing
some rare Chinese bronzes—"

"Send me a catalogue, will you?" She heard the first enthusiasm in the conversation.

"David, thanks for listening." They said good-bye, and he
wished her well on the concert.

Regan went to the dressing table and was running a quick
comb through her hair when someone knocked at the door.
What she had to do right now, this minute, was figure out how
to get through the performance later without strangling or forgetting the lyrics or inciting Peter to murder, onstage. "Come
in," she called, not very happy at the interruption. Her face
looked drawn; her body felt like lead. Then her features brightened, seeing Steven Houghton's reflection in the mirror.

"Hi there, princess."

Her expression fell as quickly as she had smiled. "I forgot,
I'm furious with you."

Steven shifted his weight. "I *am* sorry. I meant to drive up
with you to Lancaster for dinner, but—"

"I know. You were sent on a mission."

Steven smiled at the dry tone. "Fortunately, business went
quickly. Late that night, and over early breakfast. I hopped a
plane before eleven, and there I was and—and here I am."

"On another assignment," Regan deduced.

"I assumed you two were friends again." He looked the
question, but Regan only shook her head. "He promised me
he'd treat you well," Steven said, his smile changing to a
frown.

"Oh, he fed me a lovely meal I didn't want."

". . . and then?"

"A woman has her secrets, Steven." She wouldn't make it
easy for him. "If you want to know, why not ask your boss?
His version should be interesting."

Steven cleared his throat. "Jake wants you to come to Lancaster tonight after you sing, so it can't be that bad."

No response. Regan looked down at her hands, fidgeting with a jar of cold cream on the table. Why was her heart pounding so loud she could hear it? "You may jump when you hear your master's voice, Steven—but *I won't*," and then, looking up at him, "because whatever he told you, Jake's invitation has nothing to do with friendship."

"But Regan, maybe—"

"No!" Her voice snapped across his. "I love you, Steven, but I will not accept you as Jake's intermediary. If he wants to talk to me, tell him to get on the phone. If he really wants to see me, let him come." And explain away his marriage; hers, too, if he could. Explain why he wanted her this time. Apologize for last.

"I wish one of you was less stubborn than the other," Steven said, sighing. "Jake doesn't do things that way, Regan—not anymore."

"Tell him for me he'll have to."

On Sunday morning, Jake rang the doorbell at the apartment Regan had leased on Central Park South. Wearing an unbleached linen shift and no makeup, her tawny hair wild and loose, she looked caught unaware by his early visit, before she had a chance to put the guarded expression on her sleepy face. "Steven talks too much," she said, guessing correctly where he had procured her address.

"Good concert," Jake answered, gesturing at the newspapers under his arm.

"I've read them. And they're too generous," she said. She had choked up last night—again. If it hadn't been for Peter, the show would have ended after the first medley.

Dismissing her self-deprecations, he brushed past her into the apartment, which was large and airy with sun sweeping every corner of the square living room, bleaching the old brick fireplace to dusty rose, burnishing the plants that occupied the spaces. "Nice," he approved. "Very nice," though he thought she could use a few more plants.

Regan sighed. "Thank you." She hadn't bought a condominium after all, renting these eight spacious rooms instead: she hadn't been able to buy, couldn't bring herself to make such a commitment. She asked Jake not what he was doing there, as he might expect, but if he would like coffee.

"Please."

Murmuring something to the effect that they were both being civil this morning, she told him where to leave the Sunday papers, and disappeared into the kitchen. Jake wandered around, looking at the result of her new nesting instinct. That she loved primary colors seemed apparent from the profusion of bright patterns and cushions, yellow predominating. Though she had an oak desk piled high with books and papers, she owned more modern furnishings than antique. What did she read? What films did she see? Did she still sleep curled around herself in that tight, fetal position? A few nights ago, they hadn't slept much. *He* hadn't, anyway. He had stayed up watching her, feeling disgusted with himself. Why was he here now, damnit? Walking softly, hoping she wouldn't throw him out, feeling like a boy on a first date? *Vulnerable* was a word he had always applied to Regan, but this morning he felt raw and tentative and young himself. What the hell was he doing here?

"Well?" She had brought their coffee and suggested they sit on the sofa. But he couldn't relax. Regan sipped from her cup, looking at him warily over the rim as he sat stiffly on the edge of a cushion. "There must be some reason why you've paid me this sudden visit so far from home—other than last night's reviews, I mean."

"There is," he said, deciding. "Pack a bag. I want you to come home with me."

"I said no."

"That was yesterday."

"It was a blanket refusal, Jake."

"Why?"

She set her cup on the chrome-and-glass coffee table. "For one thing," Regan said slowly, "your wife."

"Ceci's in Europe; she will be all summer."

"Does that excuse you? How convenient. What sort of arrangement do you have with her, Jake—anything that keeps you occupied while she's gone?"

"How did you get so fucking brittle?"

"I only wish I were."

Regan looked at the floor. He stood up, angered by her goading; confused by both her self-assurance before and the quick flash of uncertainty that had just crossed her face. "What do we have here, anyway? Some sort of new double standard? Is that part of the feminist conspiracy?"

Regan glanced up, her eyes looking charged with green fire. "I just don't play with married men—it's a funny quirk of mine."

"I don't think it's funny."

"What's wrong, Jake? Are you bored? No society parties this weekend?"

He jerked her to her feet. "No parties," he grated, "except the one for you and me."

"You must not have heard what I said—"

His hands gripped her shoulders, hard. "I said *pack*. Want me to do it for you? You might not like my choice of clothing."

"Jake, damn you—" She tried to free herself, but he held fast against her struggle, their eyes locked. "I won't be rousted from a sound sleep and thrown out in the middle of the night—"

"You won't be."

His grasp on her shoulders eased the slightest bit. "I'm sorry for the other night." Jake was amazed that she'd cared so much when he sent her home; he'd thought her simply angry. And why had he forced her out? Because he hadn't trusted himself with her any longer, had felt a tremendous need to draw back and think things through, apart from the golden, glowing light of her in his bed. A whole week hadn't made the picture clearer, though; and now, he saw the hurt still in her green eyes. A hurt that wasn't only recent. "It won't happen again," Jake said. "I promise."

"I don't believe much in promises." Her voice low, throaty.

"Mine, you mean."

But she shook her head, saying, "Anybody's."

Lifting her chin with one hand, he made her look at him.

He sensed the same confusion in Regan, the pull and tug he felt. She wanted to go; was afraid to go. Just as he needed her with him, but wasn't sure why. All he knew was that he had to take her back now to Lancaster. "I shouldn't have sent Steven to Vegas," Jake added. "But I wanted to see you alone. And I want us to be together now."

"Why?" she asked, but he couldn't answer. Regan stared at him for a long moment of indecision. Certainly, the mutual attraction still remained; they'd both experienced how strong it was only a few nights ago. But underneath the passion, did Jake feel something else, too? Something even better, that they'd both lost long ago? Was it possible that—

"Regan, there's no trap this time."

Slowly, not to frighten her, Jake bent his head, moving closer to her mouth, which looked soft and warm and was slightly quivering; but she didn't try to pull away, and her protest was feeble.

"Jake, no, I don't—"

His mouth stopped her, his kiss hard yet coaxing, until he felt her begin to surrender in that same powerless fashion as she had before, at the mansion in the amber room. Regan's breath caught at the onslaught of Jake's kiss. *David is right,* she thought. *I have to find a way through all the feelings about him.* As Jake whispered, "Come with me," her mouth went soft and willing under his. "Please," he added; then breathed against her lips, melting the last hesitation, "I want you. I want you so much I ache all over."

He wanted her all the time. Let it run its course, Jake told himself, like a bad virus; but it never did. For her, either. "Why is it so strong?" she asked him late that first night, their arms around each other. "Jake, why is it still so strong?" but he had no answer. After they left her apartment, Regan didn't go back except to collect the rest of her summer wardrobe. Jake had offered to pay her rent. "I can pay it myself," she said. "I rented the apartment in the first place to have something all my own. I ought to be there now."

"Mi casa," he said pleasantly, *"es su casa."*

"Your accent is horrible," she said, remembering how he had offered his mother's house to her the night she moved in with him. "Besides, your house belongs to Cecily, not to me. What do you need, Jake? Someone waiting for you at the door in a red-checked apron? A substitute for your absent wife?" She had always accused him of being an outdated chauvinist.

"Ceci's never worn an apron in her life," he pointed out. "And I have servants to keep my house. No," he said softly, "I want exactly what I've got—I want a whore."

She appeared unruffled, but he wasn't sure. Sometimes it was hard for him to gauge her reactions. "Then pay me," she said lightly. "Me personally, I mean, not my bills. Each time— isn't that the way it's done?" as if he went to prostitutes all the time.

"How much?" But still, she didn't wince. She looked on the verge of smiling; she must think he was only teasing. Regan considered a moment, then did smile, a lovely smile that he wanted to erase.

"Something more lasting than money," she said. "More of an investment."

"Jewels," he replied. "Hard and brilliant and faceted . . . like you."

Regan looked away, and the smile disappeared. "Well, then . . . what do you think, Jake? Would you buy me diamonds for my favors?" with a catch to her voice.

"That depends," he answered, "on how good you are."

They argued, or they made love. Sometimes both at once. Jake felt the hormones raging in him, as strong as anger, desire a constant fire that needed tending with Regan's body, Regan's hands, Regan's mouth. She was very good. But had she known all this before; or learned it since?

Regan seemed his again, but only in the throes of sensual pleasure. She was two people at once, Jake thought: the Regan Reilly he had loved; and a different Regan, not a girl but a woman, surer and wiser, just as soft yet calloused. Above all, confusing.

Where, once he had wanted to protect her, more often now

he felt like hurting. And slashing at Regan, Jake always felt the wound himself.

"I loved you, you knew I did," she said in self-defense one evening.

Jake laughed harshly. "You sure as hell didn't stick around when I was down, did you? You sold me for a chance at the big time! And if the opportunity presented itself, you'd do it again right now." He paced the bedroom, then flung himself into one of the amber wing chairs to stare at the empty fireplace. It was a hot, humid July night; the central air-conditioning had broken down; and they had been quarreling since he came home from work in a mood.

"No," Regan said. "I wouldn't—and I didn't then."

"The *hell* you didn't, and don't think you did me any favors, fixing me up afterward. I'd rather have been on a charity ward than to have Bertelli pay for *this!*" He held out his hands. "If I'd known I would never play again—"

"*No,* you wouldn't have wanted that whether you could play or not, Jake! And whatever you think I did, I did because I had to."

"Jesus Christ, admit you wanted what you could get—however you had to get it!"

"And you didn't?" She spoke quietly. "If not, then why did you marry Cecily Ferris?"

Regan watched his expression, wondering, fearing what he'd say. Pride wouldn't let him admit he'd married to repay a debt, and honesty wasn't going to tell her he loved his wife—if, indeed, he didn't. After a long pause, Jake said softly, "Maybe I wanted to punish you. Don't forget, I'm the one who was still flat on my back when Veronica Vance started ringing wedding bells for you and Bertelli!"

"Do you really think I hadn't suffered, too? Being away from you when I wanted nothing more than to stay? To talk out the argument we'd had over Alyson and—"

"That was crap, and you know it!"

"Well, so was the gossip about Manny and me, Jake. But you never questioned that, did you? No, the day I came to the hospital, you—" She broke off, helplessly shaking her head.

"The hospital, when?"

She heard disbelief in his tone. Regan's eyes sought his again. Could he really not remember? "The day you had plastic surgery for your hands the first time, just before I had to sing in Philadelphia. I left the tour because Steven had telephoned to say how badly you'd taken Manny's thoughtless quote." Her voice slow and halting, Regan told him everything she could recall about that afternoon in his room, repeating Jake's words to her even though they still hurt. *I don't want you, I don't love you.* She stared down at her hands, finishing with the soft statement, "I knew then how much more important the music was to you. . . ."

For some moments, Regan couldn't look up. The silence in the room became all-encompassing, a sound in itself. When at last she did glance up, Jake was looking at her, thoughtful and abstracted, his eyes slipping over her as if he would remember every second of that day when they had last seen each other. "Regan"—his voice was hoarse—"I don't have a very clear memory of what you're saying. I think I remember your being there, or maybe the nurse telling me you were, but—" He ran a hand across his eyes, as if to clear the vision of long ago. "My God, I'd spent the morning heaving my guts in the recovery room; I was pretty much under the anesthetic all day; I—"

"Yes, I know how ill you were." She wouldn't forget the image of him, pale and beard-shadowed and so obviously in pain. But that he couldn't recall sending her out of his life— and he'd looked at her in such sharp focus . . . Regan's eyes misted with tears. "Why didn't you come after me then, later . . . why, Jake?" Even if he didn't remember, *especially* if he didn't. . . .

"I thought you'd made your choices, and I wasn't one of them." He smiled faintly in self-reproach. "God, I waited for you to marry him, and then *David* was on the television screen!" Jake raked his fingers through his hair, challenging her with darkened eyes. "*You* didn't come back," he said. "After that bus pulled out for the next town, you—"

"Because I was afraid! Afraid that you'd only say the same

thing again because you meant it, Jake, afraid for you because—"

Regan's heart raced. She couldn't tell him about Paul. He
wouldn't believe her if she did.

"I'm not one of your fans, you know." Jake stared at the
carpet, out the window, anywhere but at her. "Believing those
big green eyes—" His brown-gold gaze slid to her face. "When
the *hell* did you ever care about anybody but yourself? How
many days and nights do you think I spent, watching the *goddamn* doorway for you—"

"I couldn't," she cried. "I couldn't."

Things were no better after all than the first night she'd
come here. Underneath the passion, there was nothing—nothing, at least, for Jake. Only the bitterness she couldn't bear
any longer. What would it do in the end, except destroy her
own love for him?

Regan's pulse leapt in alarm. Rising from the other wing
chair in which she'd been sitting, she walked to the cherry
dresser, staring into the mirror above it. Wide, unhappy green
eyes stared back. She saw Jake's face in the reflection, his
accusing gaze. *She loved him, she still loved him.* She had
gotten her tenses wrong before. All the years, and nothing had
changed: no matter how she tried to push away the memories,
with work and David. The first day in this room, she had
thought there was no one else for her; and so far, there hadn't
been. Maybe there never would be.

A curse, she thought, far worse than Kenny's. *Sing pretty,
nightingale.* Far worse than Jake's complete rejection of her
in the hospital. Turning, she walked back to him, glad to be
on her feet while he was still sitting, as if it equalized the
strength between them. "Do you think it was easy for me? Oh,
yes, there've been bad hotel rooms and lousy food, the way
you always said, and the long, black nights that Kenny talked
about; audiences that didn't know a song from a dirty limerick,
people who threw trash on the stage and shouted obscenities
through the lyrics, fans who tore my clothes—"

Jake's voice was hard. "Don't tell me you don't want to be
where you are, Regan."

"And you blame me for that, don't you? For ruining your career, even for succeeding at my own!" She met his gaze steadily, unblinking so she wouldn't cry. "Do you know what success means to me right now? Not being able to sing anymore without choking in the middle of a song! Being scared to death that nobody will want to buy my next three-and-a-half minutes on a round piece of vinyl! It means losing what I've worked very hard to get, yes, at a cost, Jake . . . my friends, even you, and David who—" Swallowing, she couldn't go on for a moment. Wouldn't tell him that, either. "Oh God, I can't stay here, I—"

"You're not leaving."

But David was coming home, her friend if not her husband. And how could she stay? Regan felt panicky, remembering her promise to meet David in Quogue when he finished shooting. What had she accomplished by coming back to Jake when she'd told David she wouldn't? Told herself, too. He only wanted to hurt her. Physically, of course, he couldn't hold her here; but then, occupying a certain space, Regan realized, wasn't what either of them meant. "Jake, you're tearing me apart," she whispered. When he didn't answer, she drew a deep breath.

"Do you think I wouldn't go back to that moment when I stepped outside Manny's club and Paul—" She turned away, but Jake had left his chair and come after her. "I wasn't quite nineteen years old then! I'd spent all those years in his house, never knowing what his moods meant or when they might suddenly change!"

Regan felt Jake grip her shoulders from behind.

"What about Paul?" When she shook her head, he repeated the command.

"He—he warned me," she murmured so softly that he had to strain to hear. "That if . . . I didn't leave New York on tour as Manny wanted, he—he'd make you wish you'd died in that alley." Regan's voice broke. "Oh, Jake—"

"Manny's doing?"

She swore she could hear his heartbeat like the vibrant ticking of a clock.

"I don't think so, I was never sure. He'd warned me, too, about fulfilling my contracts, but—" Regan shrugged against Jake's hands. Her body began to tremble. "I don't know. All I knew was that you needed money to get well and Manny had that, where Steven and I didn't! Guilty or not, he made the bargain with me—and that was all I cared about! He'd have made me go away no matter what. And I just wanted you to get well!"

Regan turned to face him, surprising a look of anger and compassion on Jake's features. As if he'd let the balance tip in the argument; was seeing her side, too.

"Damn him, damn them both," he said too softly. He was still holding her shoulders loosely, and she felt his fingers shaking.

"Jake, I don't think Paul meant what he said that night, but then I wasn't sure! I was afraid," Regan cried. "I was so afraid for you!"

"Hush," she heard Jake whisper. She felt his muscles trembling. "Hush," he said in a raw tone. "He isn't here now."

And though his arms didn't release her completely, she drew back to stare up at him with huge, luminous green eyes misted with tears that were not for an audience to applaud now, as Jake thought in anguish: I'd kill him, just as I wanted to kill Bertelli years go, Bertelli or whoever smashed my hands in that alley. But all he could say was, "I'm here," as if it were an incantation against their pain. "I'm here, baby. . . ."

"Are you, Jake?" she whispered, her eyes so solemn. "Are you, really?"

His hands at her shoulders, he drew her closer with one convulsive motion. His voice was as thick as her own had been.

"Don't cry," he said. "Oh God, baby, don't cry . . . not for him, and Christ, not over me." He tried to raise her chin, tried to make his tone lighter; tried but couldn't. His hands at her face, his palms becoming wet as he tried to wipe away the tears that would not stop falling.

Turning her face in his hands, Regan put her lips against one palm, against the fine scar lines that could not be clearly seen but only felt; and when she would have surrendered, saying she *was* sorry for the part he had assigned her in the loss of his dream, Jake gently pulled her head back—as if he sensed what she might say and didn't want to hear—then threaded his fingers through her hair. "You're drowning us," he murmured. Lowering his head, he kissed her, cheeks and lips, transferring the salt taste of tears from his mouth to hers along with whatever remorse he felt. It was something, Regan thought. Something.

"Make love to me," she pleaded softly. "Make love to me, Jake," she said, "every way you know," the fear and the love warring in her heart.

Chapter 36

"What the hell do you mean, *she's gone?*"

Jerking the knot of his tie loose, Jake strode from the Great Hall back to the entrance foyer, glaring at the white-faced butler. "She was here this morning when I left!" as if she couldn't have moved in the meantime. She had waved to him from the bedroom window as the limousine pulled away down the drive. Her face relaxed from sleep, her long hair tangled from their lovemaking, slow and sweet again just before dawn. Why would she have gone, and where? After the first peaceful hours they had spent together.

"I believe Miss Reilly phoned for a taxi around ten o'clock, sir."

"A cab? To the railroad station?"

"I don't know, sir, she didn't say . . . but I put the suitcases in the car with the driver. There were four of them."

Most of her summer clothes, then. But Jake climbed the stairs to the bedroom, anyway, having to see for himself. The room was a shambles, drawers hanging open, the closet violated, clothing thrown over the unmade bed. She had left in a hurry, possessed of some demon. What had he done? He couldn't remember. A battle, yes, and his accusations—but the argument had ended with tenderness, and she had begged him to love her.

Jake stood staring around the room, at the empty top of the cherry dresser where her brushes had been, her perfume. One of the amber wing chairs had been shoved aside, out of place. Seven o'clock now, he consulted his watch. She might be halfway around the world by now, damnit.

"Why didn't you call me?" Jake whirled on the butler, standing almost at attention just inside the room, uncomfortable at being in the private quarters, seeing the mussed sheets. And why in hell hadn't the room been made up?

"I didn't think to, sir. I'm sorry, but *Mrs.* Marsh—"

"Comes and goes as she pleases! This is . . . different, you should have notified me immediately."

He sounded like a raving lunatic. What did he expect the man to do? Tie her to the bedposts? And why did he care that she was gone? He hadn't been sure he wanted her to stay before, and now he was coming apart in front of a servant because she'd decided to leave on her own. It seemed to be a habit of hers. Back to Sloan? he wondered. Or she might be at the apartment. Only, he didn't have the number, which was unlisted. Goddamnit to hell.

He looked at the butler, trim and slight with distinguished graying hair, breathing the fact that he was properly English from every pore. Censuring Jake. *Mrs. Marsh.* . . .

The butler cleared his throat. "Will there be anything else, sir?"

Jake pulled a small leather notebook from his inside jacket pocket, took out a pen and jotted down a number. "Call Mr. Houghton and keep calling until you get an answer. I'll talk to him whenever you do." Steven would have her numbers; and he'd damn well hand them over.

"Yes, sir. Very good, sir."

Regan sat on the wide bed, staring at the telephone. Would he try to find her? Did she want him to? Why had she run away after the long, passionately tender night with Jake? She'd fallen asleep in his arms, awakened to a gentle rain of kisses along her cheek, her throat. Then, as soon as he'd left for the office, she'd been alone with the aftermath of the night before, their argument, her own confessions of the past.

Jake hadn't offered much in return. Even the slight acceptance of her and his anger at Manny and Paul might be turned against her. The next time they fought—and yes, there was always another time—wouldn't he use her vulnerability as a weapon? The same way he might use her love for him, if he suspected how much she cared?

After those last hours in his bed, when Jake had answered her plea, inventing ways to please her . . . he must know. She had wanted to give everything of herself to him . . . but if she did, what would she have left? *Go back to David, go back.*

I want us to be together, he'd said. But he never spoke about tomorrow.

Unable to bear looking at the silent telephone a moment longer, Regan picked up the receiver to make a call herself. Linda didn't prove to be as sympathetic, however, as she'd wanted.

"Well?" Regan asked, finishing the gory details of her stay with Jake, the frantic flight that morning.

"What else are friends for?" Linda said. "I'm listening."

"But not approving." She shouldn't have gone to Jake in the first place.

"That isn't in the agreement, darling." A pause. "But at least you've corrected one mistake. When is David coming home?"

No more reassured than she'd been before the call, Regan hung up after brief pleasantries about Jeb, and Linda's sky-rocketing design firm. Even though Jake had told her—much to Regan's delight—that Linda was seeing Steven, the wounds left by Kenny were still fresh, apparently. Well, what did I expect? A shoulder to cry on? Or absolution?

Jumping from the bed, Regan roamed the rooms in Quogue until David's arrival that evening, looking brown from the Arizona sun, his eyes twice as blue against his tan. He wore snug jeans and a blue shirt open halfway to the waist, showing a broad expanse of chest—but thank God, no shining silver chains—and he had bought himself expensive Western boots, hand-tooled. *He's one of the most striking men I've ever seen,* Regan thought as he flung his navy blazer in a bone-colored easy chair; and the old sorrow flashed through her like desire when he took her in his arms, kissing her hello with a flourish.

"God, you look sensational!" David held her away, his gaze running over the cool green caftan she had put on after her shower. He ignored the shadows beneath her eyes now, giving her compliments like a nosegay of flowers. *If only we could really love each other,* she thought. "Wait until you see what I've brought you," he said.

Regan's voice rose in disbelief. *"Cowboy boots?"* Beautiful cordovan leather with an ivory scroll design to match his. "But where will I use them?" she asked, laughing as she held them up.

"Maybe we'll buy horses. I seem to spend a good portion of time on the beasts, I may as well learn to ride, God—"

And then they were both talking at once.

"Oh David, the most fascinating offer! A Christmas special for us, together; they want to use the house here in Quogue as a set, a fantastic production number on the beach—"

"And we'll ride off into the wintry sunset!" Laughing, he twirled her in his embrace, planting kisses on her cheeks as they invented one wild improbability after another for the show. "Wearing our boots, of course," Regan laughed.

"And nothing else but *bikinis*—" David answered. Then he stopped, and buried his face in the fragrance of her freshly washed hair, which she had dried outdoors in the sun. His breath shook, his voice quavered against the tawny silk. "Oh my beautiful, delectable little *canneloni*—Lord, it's good to be back, away from the smell of horseflesh and goats!"

The first gift arrived the next afternoon.

It was innocuous enough, and Regan tried not to mind, or even to take notice. But, "Why should he be sending you presents?" David wanted to know. "That's a very expensive book, all those color plates," as he checked the price printed on the inside of the jacket. "A comprehensive look at the world of popular music and its stupendous superstars," David read from the blurb. He leafed through the book. "The write-up on you is very nice," he remarked with barely any inflection to his voice. "Look at these photos. . . . This one's from the first concert in London, isn't it?"

"Yes." There was an old print from Manny's club, when she had first begun. "And this"—she pointed to a photo of herself wearing the stark black-and-white tuxedo, her hair tightly braided—"seems the opposite end of a spectrum, doesn't it? That was taken in Paris last spring." At Tour d'Argent with Paul. David's face was impassive.

"An effective bit of sophistication," he said, "the severity itself makes you even more beautiful," and then a pause. "Though you could hardly look otherwise," the fact not seeming to please him for once. Regan's discomfort began to grow. "You've been seeing him again, haven't you?"

"I didn't intend to, David." She looked away from the piercing glance he gave her. "When I talked to you on location, I meant what I said."

"And then?" He waited patiently for her answer, holding Jake's gift in his hands as if it were evidence from a crime. More than disappointed in her, Regan realized. He was angry.

"He apologized. I accepted. And I thought you were right, that I ought to try dealing with the past we'd shared."

"Unsuccessfully, I take it."

Regan looked around David's elegant living room before her gaze settled on the grass-green carpet. "Yes."

David threw the book aside, its cover shutting over the photographs of Regan in Paris. "Temporarily, I'm to understand . . . ?"

"Why, no, I don't—"

"Dear girl, if he buzzed the doorbell this very second, you'd be packing your overnight case." Regan's heart sank as he looked at her once more, a coolness in his blue eyes that she'd never seen there before; then he strolled away toward the broad windows overlooking the sea. "I don't suppose I can blame you," he murmured, as if to himself, "or that I could stop you . . . though I'd probably try."

"Oh, David. . . ." Feeling inadequate, Regan hunted for the right words. But they didn't have a regular marriage, like most people; and should she chastise herself for wanting a bit of happiness? Yet, she did; just as David seemed to. "I'm not proud of myself," she said, but he didn't answer.

When the silence lengthened, Regan rose from the sofa. "I—I think I'll check with the service for my calls." She paused in the doorway, clearing her throat. He didn't move from his contemplation of the beach, the gray water. "David, would you like to go out for dinner tonight? The little seafood place on the way to Patchogue that you like so well?"

"Yes, all right. I wouldn't mind."

With a last glance toward him as he stared through the glass, Regan left the room.

Jake had telephoned no fewer than a dozen times, leaving only his name. How had he known the unlisted number here, and the address? At least he hadn't shown up at the door—but what if he did?

Her heart had rolled like the surf outside when she opened the book from Jake. No message there, either, except for his name scrawled over the title page; but that had been sufficient to make her pulse beat double-time.

When the telephone roused Regan from a deep, satisfying sleep the next morning, her heart was racing instantly. She sat up in bed, trying not to see David's curious gaze as he turned his head on the pillow beside her. They'd gone to dinner in Patchogue, David's mood finally relenting; but after attracting too much attention, they'd been forced to leave. At the house, they'd settled into easy chairs, kicked off their shoes and listened to the sea while they sipped champagne; and well after the midpoint of the night they'd drifted to bed. They hadn't made love; but just being in his arms, warm and close, felt wonderful, safe. "I've missed you," David said, as if apologizing.

Now, she swept the hair back from her face as she answered the ringing phone. Good Lord, what if it was Jake? Why hadn't she let the service pick up the call?

"Hello? Miss Reilly?"

"Yes." Her blood pressure fell back to normal. It was the doorman at her apartment building in New York.

"The florist's van is here," he said, sounding perturbed, "double-parked, but I didn't know whether you wanted me to let them in. Your housekeeper hasn't arrived, and—"

"Florist? I didn't order any flowers."

Oh God, now what?

"Well, actually," he said, "they're plants."

"Plants?"

"Big ones," he told her. "Rubber plants and the driver says some Norfolk pines, a couple of fig trees about six feet high, and a kind of bushy green—"

"Yes, I get the idea. Will you ask the deliverymen whose order they've taken?"

But of course she knew the name without having to hear. Regan glanced at David, who was running a hand through his hair, so sun-streaked blond, and staring at her. She rolled her eyes toward the ceiling, mouthing, "Jake," by way of explanation. David's eyes were like hard blue stones, and she couldn't look at them.

The doorman was talking, but Regan had heard only half of what he said. ". . . if you want, I'll read them to you. There must be a dozen cards, but—"

"One or two will do," Regan said. How intimate could a message be, written on a piece of paper attached to a plant? And she might gain some idea of Jake's intentions in providing her with a jungle.

She remembered his looking around at her apartment that Sunday morning before he convinced her to leave with him. Was he telling her to stay where she was now, with her superstar life—a message from yesterday's book—and her new quarters?

But she heard a throat being cleared. "'Happy new house,'" the doorman read in a stilted tone so far removed from Jake's that for a moment, until the last, she wanted to laugh. "'When are you coming home?' . . . uh, there's no signature, Miss Reilly."

"Well, I think we've already solved that mystery. Thank you, John. I don't know what to tell you, except—oh God, have the plants taken upstairs, and when Maggie arrives to clean, will you tell her to ... arrange them where she thinks they'll look best and get the proper light?"

When she had hung up, David was sitting cross-legged next to her with his well-muscled forearms resting on his knees over the sheets.

"Well, I have to hand it to him," he said. "He's got flair. Most men would have sent you six dozen long-stemmed red roses."

"He'd never send me roses," Regan said. Or daisies either, now. But David wouldn't be convinced.

"First a book of flattery, then a horticultural display.... I can hardly wait for tomorrow." He got out of bed and gave himself one of those visual once-overs in the long mirror on her closet door. "But make no mistake about it," he said over his shoulder in that same flat tone. "By Christ, he's courting you."

Regan was glad she hadn't related the message on the card to him. Cards, she corrected; but all the same words, the doorman repeated again and again. Was David right? *When are you coming home?* And what would Jake send next?

She thought of calling, asking him to stop—but she knew he wouldn't, unless he wanted to. With a mental groan, Regan hoped the plants were the last of it.

But a huge carton of temptation arrived the following afternoon. David was away from the house, taking a swim to cool off because it was exceedingly humid, with temperatures hovering in the high 90's. Regan groaned as she opened the boxes inside, one after the other, each one wrapped in heavy embossed paper and tied with a bow—all different. Red, green, yellow, blue; a bow of eggshell lace; a wisp of black net made into a pom-pom. He knew she couldn't resist such sinful richness. A wealth of imported Swiss chocolates, laced with exotic liqueurs. Her mouth was already watering as she inspected the first gold-foil box.

For a while, she simply feasted her eyes on the chocolate-covered cherries, toffees, cream centers, the milky gleam of mounded nuts coated with heaven. "Oh darnit, Jake," she mur-

mured. "If I could, I'd send you an onion sandwich for this—
and wish you an important social engagement the same evening!" Then, casting a glance toward the patio doors, Regan
groaned again in defeat and plowed through the first layer,
finding one of her special favorites, a crunchy, butter-sweet
nougat. Better than an apple in the Garden of Eden, Regan
thought as that ultimate satisfaction of the chocoholic slid down
her throat.

"'You're past the age of consent,'" David recited from the
enclosed card later. "'So why not take a chance?'" then tossed
the paper onto the coffee table beside the litter of boxes.

"I'm, sorry, David... I should have—"

"Hidden these? Why bother? The evidence is written all
over your pretty, and I might add, *sated,* features. I feel like
I've stumbled onto the old set for *Tom Jones.*" Then he leaned
down to Regan, who had collapsed on the sofa, and kissed the
chocolate smudge from her chin. "Classic sexual foreplay," he
said. "All that eating of oysters and grapes and such... if I
remember right?"

"Yes, I think so." Regan didn't share his affinity for old
films. "But does this really bother you, David?"

She felt totally ashamed of herself. Gluttony, she thought.
And sloth. *Oh God, what would he send tomorrow?*

"No," David said after a moment, "this doesn't bother me,"
waving a hand at the brightly wrapped and still unopened boxes
of candy. "*He* bothers me, the arrogant bastard. Why doesn't
he simply drive out here—since he obviously knows exactly
where you are at all times—and snatch you away?"

"I wouldn't let him," Regan said, not as convincingly as
she wanted to.

She and David didn't own New York after five o'clock,
Regan told herself the next evening; and neither did anyone
else. Chez Phillipe being only one example. They were, after
all, in a public place, she insisted silently: a dining and dancing
place, a place with fine food and pleasant music and not too
many aggressive autograph-seekers, so why shouldn't he be
here, too? Trying to ignore the painful pulsing of her blood at

twice normal speed, Regan watched him coolly, wondering who the woman, a very young woman, was with him . . . not Cecily.

"Cover girl," David followed her glance across the room to the other table. "She's normally more athletic-looking, but tonight's glamour routine is equally pleasing. It appears we've been trailed, dear girl. Would you care to leave?"

She heard the tenseness in his voice, which rivaled her own. But Regan shook her head, twisting the gold damask napkin in her lap like a piece of rope. Chic and high-style, that girl: a sinuous whisper of silk from throat to ankles, a long column of porphyry, a shining cap of silver-blond hair. Opals, she thought from a distance. And yes, she recognized the smile now. Regan wondered if there was any color at all in her own face.

Her lips felt cold, blue. She said past their stiffness, "No, of course I don't want to go. And why would anyone want to follow us?" A line which might have been accompanied by giddy, hysterical laughter. It wasn't.

"Not just anyone," David said softly, with a slight emphasis. "Is he, Regan? You're as white as new-fallen snow, and you can't take your eyes off him."

Guilty, she glanced away from the set of his shoulders, the dazzling white of his formal shirt against the black tuxedo, the flashing wink of gold studs at his wrists, the gleam of dark hair.

"I'm sorry, David. Yes, you're right. It's Jake."

There was a brief silence that seemed to Regan much longer.

"Well, I suppose I can understand why dealing with the problem seems to be taking you such a long time, dear girl," he said at last. "Which isn't," David added, "to say that I'd like to make his acquaintance just now."

Regan's gaze shifted again, weaving through the crowded dance floor between them to Jake's table as if she were trying to waltz after too many cocktails. And what would Cecily think of your dinner companion? she asked him in silence, furious that the girl rankled her, too.

But David interrupted the start of a mental tirade. "Would

you like another drink?" he asked. "Your eyes are getting greener by the second... which is exactly what they're supposed to do, I'm sure."

Regan flushed at the truth. "Make it a double," she said. "And kick me under the table if you feel like it."

"Regan...."

"I would leave," she said, "this very instant... but I'll be damned if I'll give him the satisfaction of chasing me out."

They were halfway finished with newly ordered vodka-and-tonics when a pair of slender silhouettes suddenly shadowed the gold tablecloth. The restaurant, in ivory and gold velvet with dark mahogany paneling and trim, gave the effect of a comfortable turn-of-the-century town house; but Regan didn't feel very much at home. Keeping her gaze lowered and wishing fervently that she'd left when she had the chance, she heard him say in a too-cheerful tone, "Well, hello. I hope we're not intruding, but I see you haven't begun to eat yet." A swift upward glance confirmed the perfect smile, then a feminine one to match. "This is Cynthia Marlow, you've probably seen her work—"

"In *Seventeen*," David acknowledged, not very nicely, as he rose.

Regan regretted having looked up; her eyes locked immediately with Jake's dark brown gaze, which wasn't nearly as amused as he sounded. "Cindy, you know Regan Reilly," he made light introductions, smiling at Regan all the while, then turning again to David. "...and this, of course, is"—he stopped—"I'm sorry, the name won't come to me."

Cynthia's giggle made Regan blanch even more quickly than the stares of challenge being exchanged by the two men. "Oh Jake, I'd recognize David Sloan anywhere!" She held out a hand, which David took politely. But his jaw was working, the muscles clenching tautly.

"How do you do, Miss Marlow?" Regan, watching him, clenched her hand into a fist on the table, praying for a steak knife and the will to use it on Jake as David said, "I'd ask you to join us, but we've only a table for two."

"So have we, I'm afraid," Jake said. Thank heaven, Regan

thought. She couldn't imagine having to eat with that healthy, girlish face across from her and Jake's insulting grin. "That's the trouble with this place," he said. "It's a touch *too* intimate— but actually, Cynthia would love an exchange of dances before dinner. And as long as you two are showing them how it's done, David, I'll just"—with a pause of precisely the right length—*"borrow your wife, if I may."*

Absolute courtesy, though he didn't mean a word of it, Regan thought. She could feel David's anger as if he had actually raised a fist. And why hadn't he? God knew, Jake deserved it.

"Well," David said, "I don't think I—"

But she knew why he hadn't taken the well-deserved swing, and she covered his lame protest. The room was jammed with onlookers, and Jake had been counting on David's aversion to bad publicity. Not to mention hers.

"It's all right, darling," she said, rising to join the others. She laid the mangled napkin aside. "They're playing your song," with a smile that threatened to fall apart. The longer Jake stood there, mouthing his obviously planned repartee to irritate her, the tighter her stomach would curl into knots.

David said reluctantly, "If you're sure...."

"Absolutely."

The tune was from a Broadway show. With a brief backward glance, giving her the chance to say no, David held out his hand for Cynthia Marlow to take, then led her onto the small dance floor. But Jake's hand had barely touched her back when Regan pulled away, the motion so smooth no one else could have seen it. "I don't want to dance with you," she said under her breath. "Jake, you're behaving like an *idiot*—"

"Thank you for noticing," he replied. "Didn't you know I do impressions?"

"Oh for God's sake—"

"They're much better than your manners, incidentally." He had stopped smiling. They were standing close together by the table, and she could feel his body heat all but singeing the yellow silk of her gown. It was the Halston strapless she had first worn with David at dinner in London soon after they met, and he had requested she wear it tonight. Jake was staring down at the cleft between her breasts. "I send you greenery," he said, "and a few excellent photos of yourself at work, not to mention your very favorite excess in all the world ... *practically*, and what do I get—"

Regan glared at him, forcing his eyes to meet hers. "Thank you," she grated. "Thank you and thank you again ... now what else do you want, Jake?"

"This." To her astonishment, he tilted her chin and quickly kissed her mouth. "No chocolate," he pronounced as a flashgun fired somewhere in the room. "And no blemishes, either. I guess you have grown up, then."

Regan sank into her seat. "Now you've done it! That picture will—"

"Nothing to worry about." Jake's eyes had quickly searched the area. "Just a visiting fireman who's not likely to sell his film to the *Post*, so—"

But Regan's patience had fled. *"Why are you chasing me?"*

His answer surprised her. "To apologize," he said, turning a dark brown gaze upon her, his eyes completely serious. "For whatever it was I must have said that night. Why did you leave, Regan? I've been going over everything, but I don't know what the hell I did, or—"

"It wasn't you." The truth deserved truth in reply. Her voice barely a whisper, she looked down at her hands. "I—I decided on some distance. David was coming East and I—I didn't like having left myself so wide open. . . ."

Jake's glance followed Sloan and Cindy, the handsome man in black and the pretty girl wearing opals. "They dance well together, don't they?" he asked, not expecting a response. Then looked thoughtfully at Regan. "You mean, telling me about *Paul?*—I wanted to kill him—Christ, I'm not that much of a bastard, to throw him at you the next time we—" He broke off, sliding into the chair across from her. "Regan, come back and I'll prove it. You won't be sorry." He reached for her hand, but she quickly tucked it under the table, both hands in her lap, against the soft whisper of yellow silk on her thighs.

She was having trouble with this softer side of Jake. She

didn't know whether to trust him; what the last night between them had meant. "Why?" she asked warily. "Why should I? My husband isn't touring Europe this summer."

A flash of anger brightened his eyes, sparks of bronze so that she looked away as quickly as she had glanced at him.

"Your husband, *Miss* Reilly, was splattered all over the newspapers not a week ago with a very attractive redhead—"

"That was a premiere, damnit!"

"Still," Jake said softly, "they didn't do a very good brother and sister routine, too much electricity flowing for—"

"That's none of your business!"

"And Ceci isn't any of *yours,* so let's get that straight!" Then he ran a hand over his forehead, shut his eyes for a second. "Jesus," he said wearily, "why do you always make me angry?"

"We, both know why, Jake. We both know what you really want . . . an eighteen-year-old girl, the girl you used to know, who loved chocolates and thought the sun rose and set on you, who loved the shape of your hands"—which she tried now not to look at—"and the set of your mouth, your eyes, your laugh . . . the girl who thought you were Mr. Wonderful—"

"Which I'm obviously not any longer?"

There was an undertone to his voice; the argument had shifted, lowered. She looked up into the brown eyes she had loved before, loved still, wouldn't let him know she loved. "I don't know, Jake, what I think . . . or maybe, yes . . . you are . . . but I don't know why." And he leaned closer as the music started to wind down, as the orchestra went into the coda. "Dance with me," he said, "this dance. I want to touch you, hold you, feel you against me—"

"Don't, Jake, I can't," but his words had already sent the liquid fire through her vessels, heart to extremities, and back again. She went weak and full with longing. He whispered, "I want to kiss you," fervently, and she could feel his mouth drinking in her sweetness and her doubt, as if he'd really bruised her lips with his. "I want to—"

"Oh, Jake—"

"Come back, baby." His voice, his eyes, a rich intensity. Calling her by the special endearment he so rarely used; had, in fact, not used at all until the last night before she'd left him, fleeing to Quogue and David's safety. She wasn't sure Jake meant the tenderness now.

Regan tried to cringe away from the memory and the yearning. "That's hardly possible just now." Weakly, she added, "We're not alone."

He began to smile at her, seeing the change, seeing her mind begin to sort alternatives of action, almost deciding in his favor, feeling—above all, feeling—the yielding of her body against his again. "You liked the candy, didn't you?" he coaxed. "The next present's even better," and then, "Sloan will find someone to ease your absence ... the redhead maybe. He isn't that good an actor, Regan."

Wide green eyes looked at him steadily.

"You have no idea," she said slowly, "just how good David really is."

"So this is how you've decided to deal with him, is it? Go back so he can use you again for a punching bag? Can you stand fifteen rounds, dear girl?"

"I can take care of myself."

"Oh good God, how many times have I heard you say variations of the same damn thing?" David paced her bedroom the next morning while Regan nervously tossed clothing into a suitcase. The night before she hadn't found the courage to tell him she was leaving again. Not that she would have left without a word, but—

Minutes ago he had strolled into the room, smiling over something in the papers, then stopped dead to stare at the unmistakable activity. She hadn't begun to know how to apologize then for the surprise, or the omission. For hurting him, either; because obviously, she had.

"I'll be careful," Regan murmured.

"Sure."

"David, I'm sorry he embarrassed you last night. He was angry with me for running out. He didn't really forget your name."

But he turned on her, blue eyes cold. "I don't give a damn for embarrassment! What's he doing to you? What does he want from you?" His skin went pasty underneath the tan, washing out all his color. "There's another problem," David went on. "You don't know, my dear girl, when he's being sincere and when he's not!"

Having had the same thought herself, Regan stared at him with liquid green eyes, holding a frail slip of lace in her hands. "You're right. But I still can't help myself." Carefully, she placed the lingerie in the case. "Won't you welcome the time to . . . to do as you please for a while after all those weeks on loc—"

"Meaning what, exactly?"

Regan realized belatedly what she had implied; even though, in the past, it had been true. Still, they rarely discussed his private life. "Whatever you want it to mean," she said.

"Don't make neat excuses for yourself, or for him! My God—" David ran a hand through his blond hair; he didn't bother to flick it back into place as he usually did. "You think I'm enjoying this, do you? Well, I'm not! But I couldn't protect you last night, and you won't let me now. Apparently, you don't want my protection. I wish to God I could turn my back," he said fiercely. "You don't begin to know how badly I want that. To tell you to go and, yes, sleep in the bed you've made with him; forget about me dragging you out when the mattress catches fire next time . . . but damnit to hell, Regan, I *can't!*"

He shot her a quick, miserable glance, then walked to the door with his head down. "I can't ask you to stay, either—can I?"

She heard the rasp in his tone. "I'm sorry, David."

"So you say." After taking a step, he paused again. "He sure makes the world go around, doesn't he? . . . doesn't it?"

Her cheeks began to flame. "David." She reached out a hand imploringly, but he had turned away and didn't see.

"You'll be sure to call if you have need?"

"Yes, David. I'll call."

But Regan, biting her lower lip just hard enough to stop the tears in her eyes, wondered if she would, if she had the right. She felt suddenly that she'd burned her bridges behind her, and it would be a long while before she asked for David's help again. No matter how badly she needed it.

Chapter 37

The next gift, of course, had been Jake himself. Lying in his arms, Regan could almost convince herself that this summer was their first; that the people they had known, the events which had come between them, had never really happened. Cecily, and David. Alyson, Manny. . . . Because Jake had kept his promise to her this time. As their arguments grew less frequent, even became gentler, Regan began to dream again of the Talbot mansion for her own; to dream that she was loved.

"What for?"

The short question startled Regan from a reverie. She had just asked Jake if they could let the staff go for a few days. In reply, she had gotten a mildly curious look, and the two words.

"That is the voice of a man too used to luxury," she said decisively. "Because I want to cook, that's why. I want to fuss in the kitchen without Berthe hanging over my shoulder," lowering her voice as if the German cook might overhear. "I want you hanging over my shoulder."

Jake shook his head, but with a grin, and dismissed the servants.

On Saturday, long before rising time, Regan surveyed the big stainless steel kitchen, feeling physically lost among the enormous pots and pans, the huge double-doored refrigerators that lined one wall, the restaurant-issue range and ovens, but otherwise capable.

Eggs Benedict, she decided, smothered in hollandaise. At a slight sound, she glanced up from her study of the available cookbooks on a shelf, her eyes darting to where Jake lounged in the doorway.

"What in hell are you up to?" He was wearing only the faded jeans Regan had discovered in his closet and left lying at the foot of their bed: *Theirs?*

"This isn't much like your mother's kitchen," she said quickly, not wanting to pursue her thoughts. "Not cozy at all. You could cook for an army here," with a little laugh as she went by him to get a whisk from the rack. But Jake moved, drawing her close, and with a whispered greeting, nuzzled her neck.

"Sometimes we do," he said. Delicious shivers ran through her. She could ignore the pronoun as long as he was touching her like this.

"Um, good morning," she answered, running a hand through his thick, dark hair. "You look very boyish, uncombed."

"I'm not a boy, you tempting wench."

Regan answered his suggestive grin. "You can prove it again later, my lord. Right now I am trying to fix your breakfast, if I haven't forgotten how to light a stove—so why don't you go on the terrace where the table is already set? And enjoy your coffee?"

These were the moments she'd wished for earlier in the summer: a whole day ahead of them, and not a cloud in sight. She wouldn't allow herself to think about tomorrow. *Why can't I be happy for a while?* Collecting eggs and cream and butter from the refrigerator, Regan softly hummed a tune from her latest album. Because, yes, she did feel happy again. And free. And his. *Even if Jake isn't mine....*

For now, she was going to play the woman. She could be a star, Regan told herself firmly, in September.

After they had eaten, Jake took her driving, unleashing the

SL to race the narrow up-and-down lanes near the estate until Regan felt breathless, but excited. Then, he headed the sleek silver car for Lancaster.

"What if someone recognizes me?" she asked, feeling the first twinge of publicity in weeks.

"In that disguise?" Jake smiled at her huge dark glasses and the flower-printed lawn kerchief she was hastily wrapping around her hair. "I doubt that very much. Besides, didn't you know?— privacy is the local cult religion." He was right, too. Nobody stopped them. No one asked for an autograph or snapped a picture. No one even looked at them curiously.

In a small gallery, Jake bought her an expensive Japanese print, framed in silver and matted in soft rose. What did the gift mean?

To her dismay, Regan discovered that she was constantly looking for signs, omens, portents, then asking herself to what purpose.

If she needed any reminders that Jake had a wife, she found them easily enough: postcards in the daily mail, an occasional letter. Rome. Venice. Milan. And twice a week, Cecily telephoned, reaching Jake at breakfast.

At the first ring of the terrace extension on Tuesdays and Thursdays, Regan would rise from the table, as if cued, and quickly take her coffee to poolside, out of hearing. She tried not to see the smile on Jake's face as he talked.

Where was her pride? she had begun to ask herself.

One day, soon, Cecily would return; Regan would go back to work; and summer would end. What would the weeks together have proved? Questions, she thought as Jake tucked her into the car, without answers. She clutched her Japanese memento of this quiet Saturday.

On the way home, Jake pointed out various estates belonging to celebrities, to important businessmen—all of whom, he said, relished the anonymity that Lancaster so willingly provided. Regan wondered with discomfort if he was urging her to stay, when staying was so clearly impossible. But to illustrate his point further, Jake wheeled the car on impulse into the parking lot of a country inn. "I'll show you," he said. "Why not?"

They'd never gone out in public.

"I'm not dressed for dinner," Regan protested weakly, her pulse starting to pound.

"Don't worry. They'll take our money."

Jake removed her sunglasses, then the flowered scarf from her hair. The SL suddenly disappeared, driven away in a splash of stones by the waiting attendant, and Regan was standing at the restaurant entrance. She glanced at Jake. He had said *our* with absolutely no emphasis.

Grinning, he took her hand, leading her inside where the maitre d' did a superior job of pretending he had their reservation, even of lending the impression that their attire—Jake's navy-striped polo shirt and jeans, Regan's white pants and scarlet top—was *de rigueur* at the inn. Regan felt as if she were standing barefoot on the thick carpet. "You've been here before," she surmised.

When they were seated, Jake asked if he could order for her.

"Yes, please." Looking around at the tasteful light and dark blue room, touched by lavish oak, she couldn't begin to think of food. Couldn't stop staring at Jake, either, as he consulted the wine list next and chose one. She kept thinking of the old red VW and the run-down house they'd shared, of simple meals at home in the kitchen.

But tonight, there was pheasant in a rich but delicate cream sauce with green apples. She couldn't fault the wild rice, either, or the summer salad garnished with zucchini and yellow squash slices. The fresh peas in butter, even so late in the season, were delicious.

"Then finish," Jake said at last. "You keep searching the room as if you expect the press to explode from behind the draperies."

"I know, you told me, no one would dare."

She had been thinking that it had been a long while since she'd enjoyed a restaurant meal undisturbed, an afternoon of shopping without intrusions. A long while since she'd been devoid of appointments, people to see, places to be. Six years without a break; and now, Jake's luxurious privacy that couldn't be invaded.

After a few moments of silence, Jake glanced up from his plate again. Without his smile.

"They really hound you, don't they?" he said. "Photographers and the public, too? And what about Bertelli? I don't suppose he offers much protection."

"Yes, they do," she said softly. "And, no—he doesn't. But that's their business, Jake. And his." She gave him a small smile, not returned, as Jake's eyes slowly searched her face.

"No one ever gets to me," she said, though he was certainly the exception. "I travel with a pair of bodyguards."

"I'm glad you left them somewhere else tonight."

The husky tone took her by surprise. Wondering if he wanted to keep her safe, or to inflict more wounds, Regan ate every bite of food he had ordered and drank too much wine—easy enough with the dry, legendary Montrachet of the Cote d'Or.

After a moment, Jake said, "Your staff must be devoted to you."

Regan shrugged lightly, remembering the call she'd made to Jake's chauffeur who had refused to drive her home. "Probably not so much as yours. I think it may be more a matter of my meeting the payroll—for most of them." She excluded Sam and probably Peter—when he hadn't been planning to leave her—but few others. "Sometimes that scares me—men paying their mortgages, putting braces on their children's teeth, sending kids to college because of decisions *I've* made. Doesn't that bother you, that people survive—or struggle—as a result of *your* policies, *your* profits?"

"As long as there's a profit, no."

The even tone surprised her. "But then, I suppose my product isn't so removed as yours, a book or movie, even a hit record . . . still, my *voice* has to go on being clear and true, no laryngitis lasting more than a day or two . . . or people won't eat, eventually." She grew silent, then: "I *am* the product, really. A commodity in the marketplace. That never worried me before . . . until—"

Jake watched her face carefully. "The choking fits you mentioned."

"Yes. Funny," she mused, "I haven't felt like that in weeks, since—" She had moved in with Jake, away from the world. "Since the summer tour ended," she said instead.

"Fatigue," Jake suggested. "Simple anxiety."

"Peter assumed I was losing my mind."

He didn't quite smile at her. "Even if you couldn't sing again," he proposed the impossible, "you're not indispensable. Nobody is. Your people would find other jobs. That's a pretty simplistic notion, their not surviving without you."

"Egotistical," Regan said for him.

He raised his eyebrows slightly. "Well. . . ."

"I said it, not you." She toyed with the spoon on her saucer. The coffee, which had just been served, wafted its rich aroma upward, and Regan breathed deeply. "I'm not trying to be, though."

"Those gold records," Jake said softly, "are probably the most enduring part of your success." When her glance lifted to his, he added, "All I'm saying is, enjoy it while you've got the chance."

"Jake, don't you miss it?" To her horror, she hadn't been able to keep from asking. Regan saw the frown flicker across his face, then disappear. "Playing every night in a concert hall, the lights going down, people in evening dress, the music. . . ." She didn't know—having wondered so often—whether she wanted him to say *yes, it rips my soul to pieces* or *no, I've forgotten all about it*. Which was what he had seemed to want her to think.

But he said neither. "It's gone," Jake answered. "I've found something else to do. What more is there to say?"

She was sorry to have brought the topic to life again, trying to save herself; felt ashamed to have caused that shuttered look on his face, the darkness in his eyes. She wanted to stop, but couldn't seem to. The past, the need for understanding everything that had kept them apart, affected them, drove her on. "But on some unconscious level," Regan insisted, "I mean, all the training, Jake, and the standing ovation in Chicago. Solti's probably the best conductor with the finest symphony orchestra in the world—"

Abruptly, Jake's glance left hers.

Regan finished lamely, "You were wonderful." Why wouldn't he tell her how he felt? All she saw was that blankness of expression. "You were so wonderful, Jake."

And then he looked at her.

"You still are," he said. "What are you torturing yourself for?" *Me,* she could all but see the word flit through his mind, his gaze shifting away again. "You're going to rest your voice for the summer, then sing when you have to . . . superstar."

She flinched at the quiet tone of voice. No particular emphasis there, either; but his message was plain enough. He thought her selfish when she only wanted to understand; still blamed her for the pain he'd felt. Was feeling now. She was sure of it.

Regan watched Jake refill his coffee cup from the silver pot on the warming stand, stirring in the cream long after it was mixed through. "Jake, I'm sorry."

"Why?"

He took another moment, idly watching the sommelier open someone's wine, then said, "When I met Ceci, I felt pretty low . . . running from New York and myself, the fact that I couldn't play the way I wanted to. Wondering what to do with my life." He glanced up. "She gave me time and space to get my head together. For a while, I didn't *have* to do anything," which had nearly driven him crazy in six months, Jake admitted. "Until Magnum," he added. "I owe her a great deal more than the opportunity to become successful in a second career . . . which, I'm afraid, she never expected."

Regan wondered if he was warning her away; as if she'd humiliate herself by being around when Cecily came back from Italy.

Jake continued, "She grew up with everything money could

buy, but very little of her father's time or attention. She's insecure because of that, I think, and I've tried to make up for it—which sounds falsely noble, I imagine. She reminds me of you, in fact. Ceci lost her mother practically at birth." He looked at her steadily. "She never overcame the loss. But you have, haven't you?"

Superstar. "I'm not sure, Jake, I—"

But he hadn't been asking for a response. "You're strong, Regan. Ceci isn't, not underneath the smooth exterior, and very few people know that."

Then why was he sitting here with her in this public place? If he didn't want his wife to learn about her? People might not bother them; but that didn't mean they weren't seen. Regan swallowed, trying to ease the lump in her throat, staring beyond Jake at the draperies, pale blue, summery polished cotton drawn back to show a glorious sunset. *I ought to get up and leave,* she thought. But she didn't move.

She had asked more than once for frank conversation, for the truth. Why let him see how weak she became, what a coward, when she heard it?

"And Sloan?" Jake's inquiry drew her back. "Where does he fit?" He looked skeptical, and Regan glanced away from the intensity of his eyes. She stared into her coffee cup, thinking, *here it comes, I knew it would, sooner or later* as Jake went on: "He's good-looking, all right. Classic features, perfect build. He makes a damn fine escort, Regan . . . but what happens when the cameras stop rolling? My guess is, not much."

In defense, she said, "Would you like me to contradict you?"

But Jake continued doggedly, "You wouldn't have stayed with me the first night if things were good between you—and you sure as hell wouldn't be sitting here with me now—"

"I could say the same, you know." Her heart beat rapidly.

"Ceci doesn't know you're in Lancaster. David does."

"That only makes you dishonest, not a good husband."

She saw the muscle in Jake's jaw twitch. For a few seconds, he didn't speak, then he smiled faintly. "In business we call that 'transferring the monkey' . . . and I'm not going to let you do it." His eyes moved over her as if he could see the right answers. "Sloan relinquished you without more than an ice-blue glare in my direction, so—"

"We manage." Regan's hands were damp; she wiped them discreetly on her napkin.

"You implied once that he . . . fools around," Jake persisted.

"We manage," she said with finality, "as well as anybody else."

Restlessly, her pulse hammering, Regan looked around the restaurant. It had filled as the hour passed, and she felt a growing claustrophobia under Jake's persistent questioning. "Are you trying to clear your conscience for 'borrowing his wife'?"

In the abrupt silence, Jake signaled their waiter for the check.

Late dusk had cooled the heat of the day. The air had stayed damp, as if it were tightly trapped in a fist. They drove without speaking.

Then, "Why won't you tell me?"

Jake spun the wheel lightly, propelling the Mercedes through the iron gates at Manorwood, then slowing the powerful car as it breezed along the winding gravel drive through the majestic pines. Regan listened to the hum of the air-conditioner, imagining the sound to be that of the trees sighing in the wind.

She felt Jake's glance slide over her. "Try me," he said. "After all this time, I've got the hide of a rhinoceros."

Thinking to change the direction of the conversation, Regan murmured, "And the memory of an elephant, I suppose?"

"I leave that to the ladies. Ceci remembers every word I've ever said to her," when he could barely recall at the moment what she looked like. He wondered what sort of impression he had given Regan of his marriage. Not enough, obviously, to loosen her tongue about Sloan. And what would he have said? Since the housewarming for Manorwood, he hadn't spent half a dozen nights with her. Was it the same with Sloan? Did he want it to be? Jake wondered if that would make anything simpler.

"Well, you saw the wedding apparently, at least on the six o'clock news." Regan remembered his mentioning David on the screen. "Beautiful gown, beautiful day ... all ingredients necessary for happily-ever-after." Her voice lowered, becoming husky. "The honeymoon lasted a little more than a year, actually. A good year, David's roles improving, my career on the rise, lots of public appearances. And then, I won the Grammy. . . ." She spoke haltingly, unaware that Jake had stopped the car among the trees and cut the motor. When she had finished the story of that night, the months afterward when she and David had barely acknowledged each other in private, he couldn't fail to hear the heartbreak.

"I didn't count on *that* ugly afternoon, the kind of someone else that no woman knows how to fight and—" She broke off, burying her face in her hands.

Jake felt his stomach turn. "Why didn't you divorce him?"

She took a moment answering. "Because I ... oh, at first it was publicity, not wanting the scandal that would surely be uncovered. And then, oddly enough, David and I declared a truce, became friends again. This spring, when we did the television special together." Her green eyes met Jake's dark gaze in the dimness of the car. "I feel something for him, you know. I care what happens to him. I went into this marriage expecting too much, perhaps ... wanting to make something in both our lives, a continuity. . . ." Regan trailed off, shrugging away the unhappiness.

"I care about Ceci, too." Jake spoke gently. "That's what I was trying to tell you at the restaurant."

And what does that mean for us? Regan wondered.

"Jake, is your marriage—"

"We manage," he repeated her words. "Like everybody else."

"Let's walk."

After a shared silence, Jake got out of the car, coming around to open Regan's door. Without speaking, they laced hands to stroll the grounds of the estate, already wet with dew, and watched stars. Regan felt a mix of emotions even stranger than those she had experienced during dinner: closeness, yes; and a companionship they rarely enjoyed; but an odd, deep sadness, too. And she longed for the early days together when she and Jake had shared each other's hearts with no one else involved.

At last she told him, haltingly, "I know why I can't reconcile this summer with before." Thankful as she spoke that he couldn't see her features in the dark. "The setting is the same, and we look the same, but we're *not*, are we? Our changes are inside, too—like this house." She searched for the right words to tell him how she felt. "From here, in the night, it rises up as it used to, but its rooms are improved now, richer . . . *different*. When we met again," she said, "I imagined that once we'd forgiven each other, you'd be the Jake I first knew."

The great healer, so the sages said, was time—and lots of it; not a half dozen years that only made the fresh wounds easier to open. For her, anyway. She wanted him to leave now, to let her be, alone with the rising tears she hated so and wouldn't have him see again. She wanted to sink down on the cool grass, to lay her forehead on the dew-wet blades of dark green and cry in solitude until there weren't any tears left inside, ever. Ever.

"How foolish of me," she murmured, fighting the break in her voice, "trying to push the present back this weekend, fixing breakfast, putting on old jeans, trying to be—oh damnit, *damnit*, eighteen again. . . ."

Jake reached out, turning her with a hand at her shoulder. In the blackness, relieved only by a pale, yellow-gold slice of moon, in the cover of the birch *allée* at the far end of the house where they had been walking, it was difficult to see. As difficult as it was to understand him now. *My God, dear God, why can't I stop loving him, too?*

But when she tried to twist free, he held her, saying, "Regan," in a queer tone she'd never heard before. *I don't know how to stop it, I don't think I can.*

Again she struggled; and again, he wouldn't let her go. "Please," she said, asking favors of the executioner.

She peered up at him, begging with her eyes, looking harder into his face, which stunned her because he seemed to duplicate for a moment the original Jake, the feeling Jake. Or did she only imagine it in the long shadows of night? Unmoving, she waited. And if she let her mind go, she could invent a gaze for him, warm brown again and loving, flecked like long ago with bronze light.

Then Jake took her face in his hands, and after he said it, Regan wondered if she had only imagined that, too—his tone so low the words might not have existed. "Even inside, some things haven't changed." Putting his arm around her shoulder, he said nothing more, holding her close to his side, all the way back to the house. To the room. To the brass bed. And a lovemaking so tender—as if he really did not want to hurt her now, as if her fragility of emotion were one of physiology—that, when morning came, Regan supposed she had conjured up his gentle passion, too.

Chapter 38

Flipping idly through the Monday morning accumulation of mail on his desk, Jake found his attention sharply arrested by a morocco-bound script. Paper-clipped to the cover was a note from Allen Jenkins, in charge of Magnum's legitimate-theater interests.

> Jake, this guy tells me he knows you, but the piece speaks for itself. Take a close look.

A stunning portrayal of the last days of the Old South during Reconstruction, the play combined pageantry, romance, and sweeping characterizations with an excellent musical score.

Halfway through the book, Jake buzzed Janie, asking her to get Jenkins and Steven for lunch, then dialed the author to join them. Peter Noel, the steady supplier of tuneful ballads for Regan Reilly, had outdone himself.

Jake left the office that afternoon precisely at five o'clock—ignoring Janie's look of astonishment when he told her she could go home on time—and chafed all the way to Lancaster, mentally pushing his foot to the floor, cursing the chauffeur for obeying the speed limit. He was out of the limousine before it had fully stopped.

"Regan! Regan!"

Every evening he had come home with his heart thundering, so afraid that, once again, tonight, she wouldn't be waiting, would be gone like that other day, back to Sloan. . . .

And tonight, of all nights, when she had to be there—*oh Christ,* not at the door, not in the marble-floored entry hall. Taking the stairs two at a time, he felt as if his heart were in his throat, as it had been the night at Chez Phillipe when he almost hadn't won her over. *Oh Regan, God.* . . .

She was nowhere upstairs, either; but the room looked neat, the bed made, a lamp lit, the draperies drawn for evening, fresh bowls of yellow coreopsis blossoms on the tables. Down the steps again, the door slamming behind him, one hand still wrapped in a death grip around the handle of his briefcase, her perfume like a shawl around his shoulders, and where in hell were the servants when—

"Jake?" he heard her call in a tentative tone.

The library! He felt the tension wash from him. Why hadn't he looked there first? She was in the library, wearing the new honey tan and the sunstreaks through her tawny hair, a sensual tigress with eyes more catlike-green than ever, smiling at him as he crossed the room.

He loved this room, large and high-ceilinged, with long, leaded windows looking onto the rear terrace and the lawns; liked the rich quiet of its colors, the deepest of forest greens and generous splashes of luxurious, dark apricot lightened here and there by cream in the wool of the carpet, the draperies. All of these shades, and a few others, on the spines of books seemed to soften the room, the wall of shelves to mellow it. He had a green velvet sofa, deep and comfortable, and a large mahogany desk topped by the lustrous sheen of old leather, and Regan was just now curled into one of several apricot silk-upholstered armchairs near the stone fireplace, which was a smaller replica of that in the Great Hall.

Jake's pulse throbbed with relief and a mixture of excitements. Regan graced a cool, pale peach sundress of softest batiste that set off her tan, and her nipples worried the sheer material. Stretching lazily in the chair as he bent to kiss her, she fit right into his hands. "Ummm . . . I think I was nearly asleep," she said. "Lately, I can't seem to stay awake."

"What did you do today?" he asked, straightening with a smile of indulgence. "Other than doze over a fascinating novel."

"Nothing very much." She said this with immense satisfaction, then mentioned some gardening work she had directed on the English hedges, that was all, and maybe one day she'd learn to give orders without pitching in herself to do half the work. "Remember when I used to rip out weeds on Sunday afternoons?" and then, "But you're home early. I didn't expect you for hours. What's happened?"

She didn't seem to notice that her words implied some permanence for them, some ongoing relationship after summer.

"That plain, is it?" From his briefcase, Jake took the leather script he'd been carrying with such hope, silently handing it to Regan. His heart had begun to race again. "I won't have to tell you when you see this," he said, watching her face as she opened to the title page, at first curious; then, to his dismay, frowning.

"Peter?"

Her reaction had been explosive, angry. Jake watched her leaf through the pages with quick impatience, her green eyes scanning the words.

"Don't you like it?" he asked, feeling his heart sink.

"Not if I'm losing my musical director, no. I knew Peter was hiding something, but not what, or exactly his intention when it was finished." She pointed to a song, the major romantic duet between the daughter of the plantation owner and the Yankee carpetbagger hero that Jake had liked. "I saw this in Paris. Peter wouldn't tell me a thing about it, though." Then she glanced at him with sudden comprehension. "Has he offered this play to Magnum?"

"He wants to, badly. Seems Bertelli is standing in the way, more or less, but nothing's concrete or legal. He'd given Manny first refusal, but doesn't want him to have it now." Jake smiled. "He's afraid Bertelli would ruin the artistic quality of the production. He's also afraid of losing his job with you. But there's nothing in writing, so I doubt that—"

"With Manny, it doesn't have to be in writing," she interrupted, murmuring something about inducements being sufficient. With a frown, she went back to the script, and he saw her begin to smile. "Oh, but this is *good....*"

"If we can get the play, find the backers, and the right people for the leads, *Song of Dixie* means megabucks for everyone involved." He looked at her, pleased that her reaction matched his—almost, he thought, in spite of herself. Jake took a breath to steady his voice. "Regan, I want you to read for the part of the heroine—Marisa."

And her smile became amazement. *"Me?* But that's out of the question. Even if I wanted to try a play, I'm booked solid for next year already."

"But if you weren't—would you do it? Does the part interest you? Peter's knocked himself out for you, and—"

"How could this not interest me? Jake, it's grand, but I've never done anything remotely like Broadway before and—" Her voice was breathless. *"Peter?"*

"He wrote the play for you, superstar."

"And I thought he was looking for greener pastures of his own!" Smiling again, she looked rueful. But, "Jake, I know what I can do best, and—well, maybe it really doesn't matter if the whole world doesn't love me." Trying hard to laugh at herself.

Weak point, he thought. Jump on it.

"The whole world will, baby," he said patiently. "You've captured the concert stage, records, even television. Show the critics and the public you can do Broadway, and you're really on top then. You'll have the world in the palm of your hand."

He pushed her gently toward the library doors. "Read."

When Jake went up to bed that night—having worked in the study during the evening to give her time alone—Regan was dead out with the lights on, the script lying across her lap still open to the last scene. She was smiling in her sleep.

The next morning, just before seven, Jake awoke alone. Dressing hurriedly, he went downstairs. Yes, someone *was* playing the piano in the hall: Regan at the Steinway grand, trying to pick out one of the ballads from the show. As he came up behind her, she started over on the same phrase he had heard all the way down the stairs, missing the same note.

"Sharp the thing, for God's sake," he said, leaning over her shoulder and striking *F*. "I'm going to have to get you lessons. It's time you learned more than how to sing."

"More? As in *just?*" She made a face at him, comic but beautiful. He grinned and sat next to her on the crimson-upholstered bench to play the stirring melody line.

"Can you see the scene?" he asked. "Marisa walking beneath the willow trees, wishing on the moon? And slowly, faraway and delicate, like this, then growing, the music comes up... here..."

Regan took over, adding the words and melody while Jake played accompaniment. It was an odd moment, with everything working perfectly between them, reminding him of the long practice sessions during the first weeks he had known her, before Steven and the roadhouse, before other people moved in and Regan left him. Close together on the ebony bench, arms touching, Regan's head came down on his shoulder, her hair sweeping over him as the song ended and the final notes, voice and piano, died away. In the silence, he murmured, "Baby, I want you to do this play."

She lifted her head and half-smiled, her lip trembling. "Am I to understand that you have recovered some faith in me?" That soft look again; her eyes liquid. "No, don't answer that now. I'll audition, Jake, but if I fall on my face—"

"You won't," he said. "You never have before."

Like a monkey wrench thrust into his careful plans, Alyson Oldham came to see Jake late that same afternoon. "I *am* impressed," she said, looking around his office before she sat down uninvited. Then, coming right to business, "You've read Peter's play?"

"Possibly. What if I have?" He looked coldly at her, legs crossed on the white linen sofa opposite his desk.

"Don't be hostile, Jake. You have read it, you liked it, and you want Magnum to produce."

"Spies in my employ?" he asked mildly. What did she know?

Everything, or nothing? Peter's plans or merely her own scheme, whatever it was? Don't make it simple for her, he told himself—though he had begun to have a damn good idea why she was here, an uncomfortable idea that Peter Noel wouldn't like any better than Jake did; which was information she obviously didn't have.

"Peter doesn't hide his dislike of Manny as skillfully as he would like to think," Alyson went on. "Or his manuscripts, for that matter. The play is marvelous. And I'm perfect for Marisa, Jake. I intend to have the part."

He answered after a pause. "Well, what can I say? I only read it myself yesterday; Steven has it now. If he and Jenkins agree we ought to go ahead—"

Alyson leaned forward. Jake looked at the desk blotter to avoid seeing her exposed cleavage as she said, "I can find money for you. Is there any good reason why we can't work together, all of us? You and I were quite a match once, weren't we, Jake? I haven't forgotten." He avoided her eyes, too. He hadn't forgotten, either—though he often wished he could.

"Bertelli?" Jake asked.

"Why not? Everybody benefits. Both of us, Manny, Peter himself—I know he's scared to death he'll lose his job on a gamble. But I have influence with Manny."

"Go on," he said. Jake would see that the role of Marisa went to her, Alyson explained. In return, Alyson would have pledged production money, half the required total, within two weeks, if not sooner. Peter would approve the choice of lead because he wanted to see the play produced well and because he trusted Magnum. And after all, she added, Peter Noel had written the part for her; she had been watching his progress for months and offering encouragement.

"My people will want you to read for the role," Jake said.

"I'm not a novice. I do have a drama degree. I've read for dozens of parts."

But hadn't gotten any of them, Jake thought; and she wasn't about to have this one. He wondered what drove her to risk her relationship with Bertelli.

"Still," Jake said, "the formalities must be observed, I sup-

pose. You approach Manny. If he has no objection to our joining
forces to make some money, then we'll talk."

Satisfied, Alyson flashed Jake a dazzling smile.

"I knew you weren't carrying any grudges."

Jake kept his expression carefully neutral, his smile benign.
If Alyson thought for one second that the coveted role of Marisa
could be hers for a simple, rigged reading and a pile of cash
for the production, she was dumber than he'd ever imagined.
No grudges . . . and gamble what might well turn out to be the
smash play of the new season? He almost wanted to laugh.
Peter Noel would burn all copies of the script before he let the
lead go to anyone but his first choice.

"I'm sure we can work together," Alyson said, "every bit
as effectively as we played."

Like hell.

Jake and Manny met on neutral ground at a small Italian
restaurant in the East Fifties. After they had taken a corner
table and ordered wine, Manny said, "You look good, Jake.
Real good."

"Well, I'm not pushing so hard these days," came the answer
as Bertelli's gaze rested on Jake's hand, holding the glass of
red Lambrusco. "Should I say, thanks to you?"

Manny squirmed slightly in his seat. Jake was watching
him, a coolness to his eyes that had never been there before.
Obviously, he had learned to control himself. "No thanks necessary. I got your check."

Manny began to discuss safer topics, the play in general
and, at last, Alyson. "She's got some idea you promised her
the female lead."

"That's a matter of interpretation," Jake said.

"I figured it might be."

"She has as decent a chance as anyone else."

"And Regan?"

He felt a quick flash of triumph at the surprise in Jake's
eyes before the expression was veiled. "Regan, too." Manny
had been irritated with Alyson for going behind his back to
Jake, but perhaps it hadn't been a bad move after all. Jake and

Peter meshed better than *he* did with the talented conductor, possibly a matter of musician temperament. Bertelli and Noel looked at music from totally different viewpoints—money the important factor to Manny, artistic quality paramount to Peter. As head of Magnum, Jake should be able to find the balance between profit and style.

"So," Bertelli said when Jake remained silent, "are we in business?"

Jake nodded. "Partners," making Manny smile.

You couldn't say that Jake had double-crossed Alyson, only that he'd let her think what it suited him to have her think. She was going to be mad as hell about the audition—and Regan. If, Manny added to himself, he told her. Which might make for an interesting night: there were few things better between them than making up after a nasty fight. But then again—

"If Regan comes out on top," Manny said, "we might have problems. In less than a month she jumps off on the fall tour. Before that there's a new album to cut—for Magnum—and she ought to begin rehearsing soon, getting back into form. All in all, a very busy year." Manny smiled again. "I'm glad she's enjoyed such a peaceful summer."

This time the surprise on Jake's face was more quickly extinguished. When the waiter served their meal, he seemed to take a long time buttering his roll.

"Why don't you outline that year for me?" he suggested mildly. "If we're going to work together, there's no reason for one of us to be in the dark."

Pulling a narrow leather notebook from his inside pocket, Manny consulted a page, then reeled off the list of concert dates and places for the next several months. Jake raised his eyebrows.

"At that pace, no wonder she looked worn-out when I first saw her again. I'd say she deserved some peace."

"Regan didn't become a star sitting on her backside, Jake. She has to keep on working—even harder." Bertelli smiled grimly. "If she wouldn't keep playing the Good Samaritan," he said, "she might be able to take things easier now and then.

For instance, Williams. He was nothing but a junkie, shot himself so high he never came down again. I was right to fire him when I did, before he could dump all over Regan's career. But when the news came through that he'd died, what does she do? Calls me and tells me to start supporting his common-law wife, and the kid, too, he's—"

But Jake cut him off. "Linda and Jeb were always important to her."

"Sure, and so is the roadie on tour whose kid needs braces he can't afford, and half a dozen other hard-luck cases she's fallen for over the years. She isn't going to wind up with much if she doesn't learn to say no . . . so don't blame me, Jake, if she's got to work three hundred days out of every year!"

Though he could plainly see that Jake did blame him. And that he hadn't known about Kenny Williams, either. Jake pushed his plate away, the tender saltimbocca half-finished. If Manny had no objections, he said he would like to make a few timing changes. An understatement, Manny thought when he heard them. They were major contingency plans, and Bertelli could feel his digestive system rebel.

"You know, Jake, Paul Oldham had some wild notion you wanted to bring Regan down. He thought Magnum buying out Worldwide was just too much coincidence—he was so suspicious I had to send him away on advance work for the first concerts."

Jake frowned. "Are *you* worried?"

Manny smiled. "Magnum would have needed more leverage than a recording contract to do that kind of number on her." Like the play, he thought as his stomach turned again. A big roll of the dice. If it failed, there would be hundreds of thousands lost, no matter who ended up with the lead. But if Regan herself played Marisa, and *Song of Dixie* closed, and if Jake's plan were followed, there might well be at least temporary disaster for her. And for himself, Manny realized.

"Regan is my client," he went on, "and a very lucrative one. I won't take her out of circulation, as you suggest, without some financial guarantee."

Signaling the waiter, Jake hunted in his wallet for a credit card. Every movement was calm, smooth, calculated. Controlled, like the expression on his face and his flaring temper now. "Sorry," he said, "but I'm in a bit of a hurry. I've got a board meeting."

The tab quickly paid, the two men left the restaurant and went out into the muggy late-August heat of midday. Wearing dark glasses against the glare of sun, Jake presented no discernible expression, but his voice sounded perfectly amenable, his parting words yielding to Manny's request.

"Work it out, then give me a call," he said. "And name your figure, Bertelli."

Jake walked back to the office, feeling none of the rage he'd expected at seeing Manny. Perhaps because they met as equals. If he had to now, he could buy and sell Manny with ease. And it looked as if he might have to do just that.

"Who's going to tell her that the autumn tour's being canceled?" Manny had demanded. "Regan will scream bloody murder."

"I will. I'll tell her myself," buying time for them.

Right now, the important thing was for Regan to prepare for the reading; once she had secured the part, he could admit to the financial deal with Bertelli. Jake knew the amount itself would be astronomical.

But the money was secondary. If he had the resources to cover her lost earnings, why not use them? Regan's salary for the role would never equal the money from a tour; so Jake would contribute up to the level of Bertelli's estimate. If she got the part and the play closed instead of becoming a hit, he would pay her half-year's income, and Regan could rest as much as she wanted. Likewise, if Regan did not play Marisa, Jake had promised to reimburse her loss. She wouldn't lose a dime if he could help it.

And the investment on his part was worth every cent, Jake thought as he waited to cross at the corner of Fifth Avenue and Fifty-fourth Street. Bertelli was running her into the ground, Good Samaritan or not. Jake didn't want to see her looking as pale, as thin as she had when they met again at the end of

June. Or so damn tired, either; she could still fall asleep in seconds, "simply by staying in one position long enough," Regan joked.

Or was the fatigue lingering? Jake crossed the street and entered the lobby of his office building. More, it seemed to be enjoying a recurrence, and though he had wondered at first if she might be truly ill, in fact she looked wonderful. Filled-out again, tan and glowing. But it was more, too, Jake decided, than beauty. Regan seemed, in some indefinable fashion, to be powerfully . . . well, female. There was no other word he could put to it, and he liked believing that he'd had something to do with that himself.

Jake smiled. In these weeks of summer, she seemed to have mellowed him, too. Another reason why Bertelli hadn't bothered him? There were fewer angry words, more understanding—like the night when she had told him about David and the sorrow of their marriage; when Jake had confessed to a sense of obligation toward Ceci as well. What were they to do with each other, and the other people in their lives?

As he walked across the avenue, shouldering through the lunchtime crowd, Jake ran through the mental images of her: Regan, smiling at a small joke in a magazine, laughing with him; digging weeds in the garden, a smudge of dirt on her nose; Regan in Manorwood's vast kitchen, her green eyes dancing as she teased him about breakfast; Regan, kissing the palm of his hand and the scars there, her tears slippery on their skin, on his mouth. He saw her at the piano picking out the ballad from the play she was afraid to do.

They were happy images, loving ones. He had almost told her so the other night, walking among the birches in the darkness. But what could he offer her when their lives were so entangled, when he hadn't any reason sufficient to leave Ceci alone—except his own need of another woman whom he wasn't certain of? All he knew was that he didn't think he could let her go again.

If nothing else had told him, the deal with Bertelli made him sure.

But Manny, the play, and even Regan left his mind when

Jake entered the executive suite at Magnum. As he thumbed through his telephone messages, his heart sped up.

"Would you like me to put through the European call before the Board meets?" But he barely heard his secretary's voice. Giving himself time he no longer had, he stared at the first sheet again. The blood roared in his ears as Jake swore silently, viciously. "Yes," he said tightly, though the call wasn't necessary.

The number was Cecily's; and he already knew what she was going to say.

Chapter 39

You've never failed before, Jake had said; but like a church litany, Regan's mind kept supplying: *There's always a first time.* She still remembered those long-ago nights during the southern tour when she had come very close to disaster for her career. Rational or not, the idea of doing the play terrified her, and Regan decided that she needed to touch more familiar ground. "You must know how my last album is selling," she insisted when she had Steven on the phone. The record had been released while she was in France.

"I—I know I should, but I've been—tied up, princess. Magnum's constantly branching off, and the new play has me busy. Why don't you pin Jake down instead?"

Transferring the monkey, Regan thought. "I'm asking *you,* that's why." Desperation in Steven's tone, she was sure; and a growing fear inside herself. Maybe she ought to hang up, or have him switch the call to Jake's office, but he was so difficult to reach during the day, and probably still out to lunch. She would only get his secretary, some polite dismissal. And she didn't want to leave her name—it seemed indiscreet; but she didn't want to wait until Jake came home, either. "Steven, he won't know a single dollar sign more about *Gold* than you must, so—"

"Listen here, young lady"—patronizing tone—"you're supposed to be taking the summer off."

"Summer's almost over," Regan pointed out with a sinking feeling in the pit of her stomach. Something seemed very wrong. "And if it wouldn't inconvenience you too terribly, do you think you could locate the recording dates for the album I'm to do before I leave town?"

She would promote *Gold* in the States during the fall tour, not having been able to do so before; and at holiday time the new album would be released to coincide with the winter concerts. But it also seemed that someone else had different ideas.

"That's been, uh, postponed," she heard Steven say lamely. She could all but see him twisting the gold wedding band on his finger, a sure sign that he was perturbed. "The starting date, I mean," he added, as if that helped matters.

"Postponed? Until when—next winter when I'm in L.A.? Or Las Vegas? What good will that do me, the whole season—"

"I don't know. Let me check. I'm not sure." Putting her off, Regan thought, trying not to slam the phone down. Why the stall? The evasions? On whose order—as if she didn't know—and why? *You've never failed before.*

Regan spent the rest of the afternoon by the pool, turning restlessly from front to back, perspiring in the humid heat under the eye of the sun. Trying in vain to doze off—something that had been too easy for the entire summer—she found herself listening instead to the discordant inner jangle of incessant bells. She never heard from Steven.

"If you want to know what's going on at Magnum," Jake said reasonably, "ask me," his voice as taut as a wire. He set a glass on the bar in the library, crammed ice in it, then poured a double dose of Scotch. Regan had the feeling she was listening to a set piece, carefully rehearsed between Steven and Jake after her phone call. "The album is doing okay here— not as great as it was, but sales are down industry-wide just now. A hot summer: the entertainment's at the beach."

Regan smiled grimly to herself, not satisfied. Dismissed. "And my new one?"

"The date's been shifted," he repeated Steven's dodge. "I don't know when it will be, but try to be patient if you can. I know patience was never your strong suit, but Steven will pass the word as soon as he's able. I'll be glad to bring the actual sales figures on *Gold* home with me tomorrow if you really need them. But the album was platinum in June—what more do you want?"

"Why were you having lunch today for two and a half hours with Manny?"

The words fell like boulders. With a startled glance he couldn't cover, Jake held up a bottle of sherry to ask if she cared for some. Regan shook her head. Recently she seemed to have developed a nervous stomach—small wonder with days like today—and liquor, any kind of liquor, could be risky. Not wanting to dilute the moment with words, she stayed silent, waiting for Jake's explanation. After her call to Steven, she'd been so agitated that she had finally, against her own advice to herself, telephoned Jake, whose secretary had informed her of his luncheon with her manager. But why Manny—the last person with whom she expected Jake to be sharing a meal?

"Your manager has decided to co-produce the play," Jake announced, for all the world as if he expected her to turn cartwheels at the news. "I'm sure you're going to get the lead," he began, walking the library and holding his drink as he detailed the first plans for staging, lighting; the theater they hoped to obtain.

Regan watched him in growing horror until he came to a stop in front of her. "What's the matter? You look strange." He held the glass under her nose. "Here, take a sip of my Scotch, you're damned pasty-looking."

"For heaven's sake, I told you I'd audition, and that's the end of it!" She pulled back. The smell of the amber liquid had made her stomach turn, and Regan had to swallow before she could speak. "Why on earth you dragged Manny into this—"

"I *didn't*. He wants to be involved, you knew that."

"I don't know very much, do I? Except that you seem to

be doing your level best—with Manny's help—to stick me in a play I'm not even sure I could handle!"

"You can handle anything you have to, goddamnit!"

Regan tried to glare at Jake, but she felt tired and fragile and not quite well, disgusted by the aroma of his Scotch. She had never smelled anything so repulsive in her life. She felt close to tears. "I have no idea about my fall tour, which is the way I make my living, *damnit*, or—or about the new material Peter promised, either!" She was drained; she was jumpy. She could hardly make the words come out, and when they did, she wasn't sure they made sense. She had to work; no, she never wanted to sing again; oh God, she didn't have any idea what she wanted except, "Jake, I need my life back again!"

"What are you talking about?"

Jake was staring at her as if she'd gone crazy; and perhaps she had.

"I don't know!" she cried in frustration. "I don't know!" But if Jake didn't stop looking that way, so accusingly—

He did stop. Without a word, Jake let his breath out, walking away to pick up the mail from the desk top, and suddenly everything came into focus again. She remembered Sturgis bringing the mail to her that afternoon at the pool, his eyes smugly disapproving of her as always, but more . . . victorious, she had thought. Sorting letters, he had passed by the same pale green envelope that Regan recognized now in Jake's hand, having seen its duplicates with some regularity over the last two months. Which one this time? She knew all the postmarks: Venice, Milan, Rome, Turin, Naples. But the postmark didn't matter.

"She's coming home, isn't she?" Regan made herself ask, feeling a surge of hopelessness. Hadn't she known, hadn't she always known? Never more than one letter in a week, the last a few days ago.

Watching Jake now, she felt pale and cold, like death. Quickly, he slit the envelope with a pewter opener shaped like a dagger. She could feel it piercing her flesh as his eyes slipped over the pale green page. The now-familiar writing. Piercing her heart with the one word.

"Yes." Jake glanced at the calendar window of his wrist-watch, a motion as needless as the night she had come to dinner when he had already known the cabs were not running before he checked the time. "The day after tomorrow," he admitted, looking at Regan, then back at the desk top. Still holding the letter in his hand. "This is to confirm her flight."

"But you knew, didn't you? Before?"

"She phoned the office this afternoon while I was with Manny." She had wanted to make certain someone met her, he said; she suspected the letter might not reach Jake on time. Without expression, he read it over, more slowly; his eyes seemed to stop at every word; but he didn't look happy, he didn't look unhappy.

"Excuse me, please," Regan said, hoping her tone conveyed some shred of dignity. She took a first step toward the door.

Jake glanced up sharply. *"Oh, for God's sake!"* The letter fell to the desk. "Is this what you're in such a lather about tonight?" his tone all masculine impatience. "She isn't coming here!"

"But this is *her* house, Jake—*her* bedroom I'm sleeping in!" Had it amused him to furnish it according to Regan's dream? "After all, Jake, you said—"

"I want you here, damnit! I'll handle Cecily." But he hadn't moved toward her, and his stillness only hardened her resolve. "Let's drop this for now," he said. "You're upset without reason. You're probably wiped out from too much sun today. Let's have dinner, you'll feel better."

"I'm not hungry." At the mention of food, she shuddered. "I'm tired, but I feel queasy, too." Nauseated—and afraid of something she couldn't name. Was it the very fact that they'd been getting on so well? Because, Regan told herself, implicit in finding Jake again was the possibility of losing him. A possibility that, with Ceci's letter, had become terribly real. "I'm going upstairs," Regan murmured, and left the room.

Jake lay on his back, unable to sleep and, in the dark made deeper by the drawn side curtains of the bed, looking up at the gauzy white canopy, thinking. Cool and dry, the room hummed with air-conditioned comfort, soft as a whisper. Soft as Regan's breathing.

Jake let his hand go to her hair, smoothing the silken tawny strands back from her temple, over the neat shape of her skull. He hadn't known how to deal with her in the library, what to say. After she'd gone up to bed, he had stayed at his desk, forgetting dinner himself, working while his attention wandered and his ears strained for the upstairs sounds of packing and leaving.

Why couldn't Ceci have stayed away another month?

As if in agreement, Regan thrashed and groaned in her sleep. Then a scream brought Jake bolt upright in bed. He had to fight flailing limbs to hold her, wild-eyed.

"Baby, baby," he whispered, pulling her rigid body close, "what's the matter, baby? Bad dreams?" His own heart throbbed with alarm. She began to murmur about a dress with flowers of blue, and empty rooms, and someone singing a lullaby to her, and then, "Oh, Jake, *hold me!*—tighter! Don't let it happen again, please, not again . . . people always forget to come back for me!"

Her parents? Was the dream about her mother? About anyone who let her down? His specialty. *You come to me,* she had said long ago, and he had been disappointed that she wouldn't meet him halfway. But was she selfish, as he had thought then; or was she scared? Every night, on tour, she heard applause, the sound assuring her that she was loved. Maybe the panic tonight about leaving his house had been only the need to reassure herself through work. And hadn't hunger for love on a mass scale driven her away from him?

Rocking her in his arms, Jake said, "Nobody's forgotten you, baby. You'll see, Broadway will be the biggest high . . . and if you're uneasy about staying at the house, there's your apartment. We'll be together, Regan, do you understand? Rehearsals, every performance."

But in the moments after she finally drifted off to the lullaby of words, before sleep found him, Jake felt some of her panic.

Had he helped her? Or was he going to let her down? He couldn't; he wanted her to trust him; and (the thought amazed him when it came) he wanted to protect her.

Shielding her eyes against the sun, Regan sat up by the pool to refasten the top of her tangerine bikini. She squinted at the gold clock on the nearby umbrella table: a few minutes after four. Long shadows would begin to cover the deck soon.

She should go inside and shower . . . but then what? Jake wouldn't be home tonight. Home, she repeated bitterly. "I have to spend a few days with her," he had said, "probably on the Island. I'll get back as soon as I can."

In Jake's absence Regan had promised to read the playscript, working up the scene of conflict they'd selected between the hero, Jared Leslie, and the heroine, Marisa, for her audition.

But she kept thinking of the other pages she and Jake had practiced, lazily, the day before when he had stayed home from work. After her nightmare, Regan hadn't been fooled by his light mood. "No matter what September brings," she had said, "I'm glad for these weeks. Such a wonderful, idle summer."

Lying back in the grass on the ridge behind the mansion, Jake had corrected, "A summer idyll."

The scene they'd done had matched the day itself: a light, romantic exchange, happy and loving. "We're not bad," Jake said. "Are your misgivings lessened now?" And for a while, she *did* feel better. If she worked hard while he was gone—

But how could she work when she kept playing in her mind a third scene that had nothing to do with the Old South? Regan put her arms around her knees and leaned her head on them. In the airport, she envisioned Jake wearing a light summer suit, khaki-colored, with a Haitian print tie. Cecily walked through Customs toward him, her azure eyes sparkling, the little smile in place. Slowly, easily, Jake's wife would glide into his embrace, Regan imagined, and raise her face to him; their mouths would touch, hold—

God, how could she possibly work?

With a sigh, Regan raised her head and immediately caught sight of Jake's butler skirting the pool with a silver tray in hand. At least she had no reason to fear a pale green envelope today. Small blessings, she thought.

"There is a gentleman waiting for you in the library, madam. Will you see him?" He pushed the tray forward, within her reach.

Surprised that anyone would have come here to find her, Regan slipped into a gauze caftan that matched her bikini, then took the modest square of note paper: "Please, no refusals, my dear, dear girl. I must speak to you. Most urgent."

Regan stared at the words, feeling the tension behind them.

"Tell Mr. Sloan I'll be right in," she murmured.

And the summer's idyll came crashing to an end.

Chapter 40

Regan's first view was of David's back as he stood by the library windows, looking out onto the drive. At the sound of her approach, and the closing double doors, he turned, and she saw how white and sick he looked. "Thank God!" He had her in his arms, which were trembling, was holding her more tightly than necessary. "I didn't know what I'd do," he said, "if you wouldn't see me—"

"David, what is it? What's wrong?"

They hadn't been in touch since the morning she had left Quogue.

David released her and picked up a newspaper from the green velvet sofa. "You haven't seen this?"

The second page carried a large photograph of David, the kind of candid shot with which Regan was only too familiar herself. Grainy and overexposed. David, with his expression caught in surprise, giving his eyes an owlish look. And the headline was even less flattering:

HOLLYWOOD ACTOR LEADS LURID DOUBLE LIFE

Regan's disgust grew with each sentence of the article below. A purportedly factual account of David's homosexuality, it both stunned and horrified her—she, who knew the basic fact to be true. But oh God, the rest—

Unable to finish, she closed the newspaper, its pages rattling in the absolute stillness as if there were a high wind in the room; but the words were imprinted on her mind and she couldn't forget them. Nor could she look at David who was standing a foot or so away, motionless.

"You know what a—a *sensational* tabloid this is," she tried, but her voice sounded hoarse, unnatural.

He removed the newspaper from Regan's shaking hand, tossing it aside. "Who's going to believe me ever again, taking some actress in my arms, *kissing* her, for God's sake?... My phone's been ringing all day without a stop, even Ginny Randall—" who had been David's most recent co-star in Arizona. "Christ, she called me every name in the book. I couldn't get a word in, I—"

He broke off, running a hand through his sun-streaked hair, his blue eyes wild when she looked at him.

"Oh, don't even try to say anything... *My God, the photos!*" He was staring at her with such pain in his eyes, but she couldn't move, couldn't find any words of comfort. "Delivered to my doorstep," he said. "Copies, of course—and there are plenty more, I'm assured. Waiting for every columnist, director, and producer in the United States, Europe—"

"Photos?"

Regan had been thinking of the newspaper picture, awkward enough but innocuous, only a Hollywood nightlife pose in tuxedo and open mouth, David's tie askew—but she was wrong. There were a dozen pornographic shots of him, he had been advised, lewdness with a variety of young men, extremely young men, "*boys*, actually—but the pictures are pasteups or whatever, God, I *never* in my life—"

Regan fought the urge to stop her ears with her hands. "David, you needn't explain." *Boys?* "Who do you think might have done this?" she asked. "Sold the story, and sent you those pictures? And what are they asking for?"

"I don't know," he said. "I don't know." He began to stride the length of the library, combing his fingers through his hair. His whole body rumpled-looking, his dark pants unpressed when David was normally immaculate, even his white summer knit shirt mussed with creases now.

"But you must have *some* idea," Regan insisted. *"David, think!"*

Her own mind raced. Show business was filled with homosexuals, as were most other art forms; but for David Sloan, the article was disastrous. If anyone ever saw the photos— No wonder he looked white as flour, Regan thought. He wouldn't be laughed off screen; he'd never get the chance to film in the first place. There had to be someone who wanted to discredit his romantic image.

"I haven't been asked for a dime," he said, "not for anything." Then he whirled, facing her. "I'd bank my last dollar, Regan, that it's no one I know . . . not that way. My God," he said, "there's so much envy in this business, in any business where people succeed so enormously— Who the hell knows what I'm up against, or why? It might be some guy from an acting class years ago, someone who got stepped over for a role . . . a studio cameraman who thought I asked for too many retakes, getting the profiles right. . . . Christ, the telephone lineman in Tennessee whose wife thinks I'd be great in the hay—"

Regan stared at the oriental carpet, following its patterns, geometric and sane, blinking away her tears until she felt him next to her, standing just at her shoulder, though he didn't touch her. "None of this is your doing, but I didn't come here, either, because I wanted you to fix things—" It seemed a long while before he went on, his voice husky and drained of strength.

"It's just that when I'm alone sometimes, at night in some room, a motel on location—I've felt I could pick up the phone and find you in Chicago or Paris, and you'd talk to me, make me feel—not so restless and unhappy with myself, the things I've done—"

"David—"

"I don't mean the obvious, certainly not what's in this paper, which isn't true, or anything faintly like it. I mean the people I've hurt inadvertently and the paths I haven't taken when I should, even . . . regretting *us* sometimes, you and me. I haven't made you happy, and I—I'm sorry." She felt his hand on her shoulder, turning her. "I'm sorry to put you through this now."

She heard the soft rush of his breathing, felt the chill of his hand. During the entire speech he'd made her, neither of them had looked directly at the other. Just as they had never really shared their lives. It was an oblique approach to marriage, she thought sadly. And more than marriage . . . to each other.

"Oh David, *I'm* sorry—" Then she couldn't continue. Regan squared her shoulders and looked up into the sadness of his eyes, so blue and earnest. "You've always helped *me*."

She wasn't going to throw him to the wolves, as she felt she had done with Kenny. "There's only one way to handle this," Regan said decisively.

His fingers tightened on her shoulders. "My dear girl, I didn't come here for a publicity extravaganza."

"But David, nothing less will do."

She had begun to smile slightly. They would be seen together, laughing, talking, holding hands, exchanging public kisses . . . refuting every charge against him, making a ridiculous mockery of the story itself. Regan Reilly, who was best known for romantic ballads—married to a hideous pervert? The very notion would cause people to smile in disbelief, and— she was thinking now of Jake's accident: "In a day or so, hardly more," she said, "the press will go looking for another sensation, which, of course, they'll find. And you know how quickly, too, David."

With a grateful smile and a sigh, he sank down onto the velvet sofa, stretching out his legs. "You're really something," he said as some color washed back into his face.

Regan rang for a pot of coffee, lacing both their cups with Napoleon brandy from the decanter on Jake's desk. "You'll be helping me, too," she said. "Can you wait while I pack a few things?"

"Sure." David looked around as if seeing the library for the first time. "This is some setting," he said appreciatively, his glance approving the walls of books, the long windows, the late sun flooding in, the richness of tapestries and carpet and the colors themselves of Jake's library, his sanctuary and the hub of his territory. The beautiful green and apricot room Jake loved; where she felt his presence now. "Are you sure you want to leave?" Then his gaze flickered, too, over the tangerine bikini, visible under the gauze caftan, and he said, "I imagined he'd have hidden away all your clothes to keep you here. What will he think when he finds you gone again?"

Regan shrugged, her throat constricted.

"That may not be for a while," she said.

". . . I gathered he wasn't here, but are things all right between you? You haven't called me."

"I honestly don't know."

She sent an unhappy glance toward the large French clock on the mantel. "His wife landed at Kennedy fifteen minutes ago."

"You're not cut out for that game," David observed.

His eyes were gentle, and he was right. No matter how pleasant their domestic routine had been, how many nights Jake came home like a husband to find her waiting, no matter how strong their mutual attraction—Cecily's claim on him was stronger, legal and binding. Hadn't she known that for weeks? Jake had never mentioned divorce; or permanence for them, either, except casually. Even the nightmare had provoked strange words of comfort from him, about sharing her apartment.

The sharp agitation she had felt all day, trying to study the playscript, trying to relax by the pool and not think about him, turned crystal clear. Became Cecily's face again: her even features, her azure eyes, her smile. Regan felt her heart contract. She murmured, half to herself, "He said, 'Be here when I get back.'"

But she needed time in a more neutral setting, away from the rich lushness that belonged to him, away from his arms and his kisses. She disliked this new vision of herself: Cecily's rival. It was too much like Paul's worst impression of her, and it scared Regan. Frowning, she handed David the brandy decanter, ruby-and-amber cut glass with a faceted stopper.

"Please have more if you like. I'm going up to change. Did you bring a car?" He nodded, watching her. "Then I won't have to borrow one," she said. "Jake can wonder where I am for the next couple of days. Or read the papers if he wants to know. I think what *we* both need, David, is a very public evening . . . or three or four."

"Are you sure you want to do this, Regan? If he—"

But she didn't answer until she had reached the library doors; and David hadn't finished. "I am helping my *husband*," she said firmly, "and Jake is in no position to mind, or to make a fuss if he does," even though her heart was beating like a flock of birds trapped in a tiny cage.

Arms outstretched to recapture his freedom, she rushed toward him—and he was holding a stranger, kissing a ghost.

In the months of summer, Jake had all but forgotten her; yet here she was, softly fleshed and shorter by an inch or so than Regan, the light scent of flowers assaulting him by its very contrast to Regan's woodsy perfume and the natural aroma of her skin.

Something else he hadn't expected: the brightness of her smile. The genuine pleasure in her azure eyes. And he hadn't any reason to resent her, except that she'd come home too soon.

Cecily's arms clung tightly to his shoulders. "Oh, darling— you are much more wonderful than a brass band, or any other greeting I could imagine!"

Disengaging himself, Jake held her away. "You look as elegant as ever." Not a blond hair out of place; makeup exactly right, understated and casual; her clothes unrumpled by the long, transatlantic flight. She wore white linen suit, a soft jersey top, peach-colored, and a hat with snowy ribbon trim around the crown. A big straw tote bag that would have looked touristy if anyone but Ceci had been carrying it. As she hugged him again, the hat fell to the terminal floor.

Bending to retrieve it, Jake said, "Welcome home," wishing he had sent a brass band in his place. He wasn't looking forward to the next days in Southampton. *Great God,* Jake thought. *I hope she hasn't brought back any significant presents.*

Early the next morning, Regan awoke in her own apartment. Had the telephone just stopped ringing? Had David answered?

If so, either it wasn't for her or he had gotten rid of the caller so she could sleep. She wondered if it had been Jake. He would be angry—helplessly angry—when he saw her picture with David, plastered across the gossip columns.

It had been a long night, and hard work after so much rest at Manorwood, and she had paid the price. After dining on creamed crab and even richer pastry, she and David had gone dancing, polishing off the evening with several different liqueurs at several different nightspots. Then as soon as David brought her home, Regan had been sick.

How stupid, she thought, to have eaten so much and consumed such a quantity of liquor. All summer—and especially recently, because of her flighty stomach—she had eaten well, but sparingly: fruits and vegetables, salads; the small, thick filet mignon that Jake liked. She had become unused to sauces or rich desserts. And last night had paid dearly for indulgence.

Her stomach this morning felt as tentative as her relationship with Jake. But thank God, she had no headache. Getting out of bed slowly, carefully, Regan tiptoed into the bathroom, trying not to jar herself. She ran a hot bath, and sank, with a sigh, into the steaming water.

"How are you feeling?"

Her stomach uneasy even from the mild scent of the floral bath salts, she glanced up to see David, gently smiling, in the doorway. "Not as well as I ought to," she admitted with a wry smile. "Weren't the papers generous—if I remember right?"

"Except for one or two direct hits from the snipers who love such an easy target, I'd say we both fared nicely. I'm beginning to think I *may* live. How about you? Can I get you anything?"

"No," Regan answered too quickly. My God, if she saw a single bite of food, or even a glass of water— "Thank you, David, but I think I'll wait until dinner . . . at least."

He gave her a long, thorough look. "You're not the delicate type, in my experience. No vapors, no fainting spells, no traveler's indigestion. And it's not flu season yet, so—"

"It must have been the crab," she said.

"I ate it too," David pointed out softly. He was already turning away as he said, "Let me call John Thornen for you.

I'm sure he'll work you into his schedule today, and if it's nothing but the food or yesterday's strain . . . well, no harm done."

But what was he really thinking? "You're treating me like a child again," Regan protested, not very strongly. Perhaps a B-vitamin shot. As a matter of fact, she felt dreadful.

"And I had my turn yesterday," David said. "Enjoy your soak while I get you that appointment."

"Don't tell me you walked in here stone-cold." John Thornen rolled a ballpoint pen across the faded red blotter on his desk until Regan couldn't stand his confiding smile another instant. She hadn't liked the poking and prodding during the exam, either. At her nod and the widening of her green eyes, John's tone changed, softened. "You're not going to die. For heaven's sake, don't look so morose. I'm sorry I teased, but—" He pressed a finger to the bridge of his tortoiseshell glasses.

"*John.*"

He spread his hands, a gesture of innocence. "Regan, as the old saying has it, you're . . . slightly pregnant."

And the whole world fell in. Regan jumped up from the red leather armchair, scraping her elbow painfully on one of the brass studs.

"I can't be!"

"The tests don't lie. I was fairly certain without the specimens." He looked steadily into her eyes. "You're roughly eight weeks along," he said. "Getting late for anything relatively simple like vacuum curettage. I take it you and David—"

"Two months?" Wildly, Regan tried to make the necessary calculations, of which she seemed incapable at the moment. Pregnant! Dear God, she'd become pregnant as soon as she and Jake— "I didn't suspect anything," she murmured.

She'd taken precautions—inadequate, as it turned out. Regan began to pace the office. "What can I do?"

"Go home. Talk to David. And call me tomorrow when you've reached some decision, which you'll need to do quickly. You do know, for the record, how I view these things?"

"John, please don't stack the deck." Regan turned to look

at him. Why hadn't she known that the weight-gain wasn't simply because of rest? That the fullness in the bodice of her yellow linen dress wasn't just the result of good food all summer? "You're going to tell me that I'm an independent young woman with financial means, and astonishingly healthy."

John couldn't hide the grin. "And I'd much rather deliver you in seven months, yes. A nice, strapping infant. But if it's . . . something else, then I'll arrange that." He sobered as quickly as he'd smiled.

"Thank you."

Walking slowly west across Fifty-seventh Street, Regan barely heard the blare of traffic or saw the shimmering haze of heat rising from the pavement. *Talk to David,* John had said. Didn't he read the papers, or was he merely being considerate of her feelings? How was he to guess that her marriage was nothing but an ongoing public relations gimmick? One she couldn't abandon now.

Oh John, if you only knew . . . *this unfortunate child's father already has a wife.* What would Jake say if she told him? Their fragile beginnings of understanding were as embryonic as the life within her body. Could they even make a decision together? Or was she really—much more probable notion—in this quandary by herself? With a stubborn heart that balked at common sense. *If only he'd said he loved her.*

The decision, she realized, wouldn't be easy after all. Oh, why hadn't she known sooner? She cursed her own body's irregularity, blamed on nerves and exhaustion. A *baby.* Biological fact, yes, but as foreign to her as a different language. John Thornen would have to wait a few days more for her choice, Regan decided. It was about all the decision-making of which she felt capable at the moment.

David has his scandal, she thought; *and Regan Reilly has hers.*

"Miss Reilly, what a pleasure," said the young brunette at the desk, buzzing the intercom at the same time. "Mr. Bertelli is expecting you."

Well, of course, Mr. Bertelli was not. But John Thornen's

surprise had short-circuited rational thought. Regan had wandered along Fifty-seventh, down Madison, then over to Fifth Avenue, and was standing at the receptionist's desk before her mind focused again on everyday matters.

Regan missed most of the deferential treatment accorded her as well as the admiring stares from the several other clients waiting. Dazed by shock, she even failed to see Manny's grin as he came out of his inner sanctum. "How refreshed you're looking, sweet, such becoming roses in your cheeks."

Manny ushered her into his office and shut the door.

And what if I were to tell you why? Regan wondered, beginning to function at last. She groaned inwardly. But to Manny she said only a cool, "Thank you."

"I tried to call you earlier. Saw the spread in the papers, you and Sloan. Great publicity, even if he is—"

Oh, my God.

"Not to change this charming subject, Manny, but I do open the fall tour in less than three weeks—Detroit, I believe—and I would appreciate some rehearsal time." *Keep your mind off the baby, the decision.*

"Ah," Manny said, steepling his fingers, settling back in his desk chair, not looking at Regan but at some point on the wall behind her. "Well, there've been a number of changes. You may as well take a few more vacation weeks, prepare for the audition, then after *Dixie* has been cast—"

"Changes?" The concert dates were set months, sometimes years, in advance. Pouring water from the stainless steel carafe on the desk, Manny cleared his throat. "Cancellations," he corrected uneasily.

"I think you had better tell me exactly what they are."

Detroit, to begin with, he said uncomfortably, staring at his phone as if it could rescue him. And then Houston, the rest of the Texas circuit, the West Coast, Vegas.... "Six months," Regan repeated slowly. "You expect me to stay idle for half the year?" Idle; idyll. Oh Lord, a whole week of surprises: the album doing just "okay," the new one postponed; Cecily, and Jake going to her; then the baby. And now, the fall tour had collapsed, which didn't make sense. Or did it? Regan picked at the skirt of her linen dress, sunshine yellow when she felt more like black at the moment.

Manny excused himself from blame with all the ease of a greased pig. He had been assured that Regan would be informed in detail, that the schedule shifts were in her own best interest.

"Told by whom?"

"Don't yell at *me*," Manny said unhappily, although she hadn't raised her voice. Yet. "I told him this would happen. He promised he'd speak to you and explain our thinking—"

"*Peter?*"

"No," he said. "It was Jake . . . Jake made the suggestion."

Why? *Why?* Because he expected her to get the part, Manny went on, and if she did, the cancellations would have to be made closer to the actual dates, which wouldn't please anyone. But Regan had only promised Jake the reading to please him; she didn't expect the part. *And if I fail? You never have before.* Had he been trying to reassure her? Or to lull her into complacence? Was that what he'd wanted all along? Jake had blamed her for destroying his career. Why not ruin Regan Reilly's in return?

The first twinges of discomfort that she'd felt upon receiving Manny's cable—*Magnum's acquisition of Worldwide complete*—flashed through her mind again. And everything went cold inside.

She would fail, as alien to her as a knowledge of skydiving; she would have no tour, no salary, nothing.

Why else had Jake become partners so readily with Manny? To gain access to her schedule. He knew how self-serving Bertelli could be; if he thought Regan's starring in a play would make him more money than her being on the road, Manny would cancel any number of concerts. "He's duped you," Regan told him.

"Don't worry, sweet." He reached out to pat her hand. "About the reading—you couldn't do a bad job if you tried, and as miserable as your cousin will make my life for a few days afterward—"

"Alyson?"

Manny hesitated, flushing. "She's auditioning, too. Didn't you know?"

But naturally, she hadn't. For weeks, she'd known only what Jake wanted her to know: about the album, her single, Peter's play. Alyson! Even her cousin had more acting experience than Regan. A sick feeling that had nothing to do with eight weeks of pregnancy ran through her stomach. But she forced herself to sound calm.

"You're right, Manny. I'm being unreasonable. No, I didn't realize that Alyson was trying out, too—but I wish her well." Not charity, no. Regan wasn't feeling in the least charitable.

Defiance welled in her like tears. Damn him, Jake was controlling her again: sexually *and* professionally. One more irrefutable fact, Regan thought bitterly.

Standing, she walked slowly to the door of Manny's plush office, all dark maroon and fine wood with lavish touches of shining chrome, an office she had paid for with sweat and determination. The smile on her face felt carved from wood, like the heavy furniture around her; but she kept smiling because she wouldn't have Manny carrying tales of panic to Jake—sequestered on the Island. With his wife. Damn him, why did it hurt so much?

Yes, she assured Bertelli, she would talk to Jake herself. He needn't bother.

"Friends again?"

She allowed Manny to kiss her cheek, wondering if he could feel ice in place of flesh. "Friends."

She would prepare the audition and give her best effort, and then some. She wanted the offer of that part now, wanted it with every cell of her being. Because if Jake thought for one second that he could manipulate her career and her love and her body, then get away with it, back to the safety of his wife and Magnum . . . he was very much mistaken.

Oh why, Regan asked as she fought back the furious tears, why had she almost trusted him?

Chapter 41

Regan felt as if a cold, hard center had formed inside where her heart used to be. Well, she needed a heart of stone, as he used to say. Oh, she understood him now: the sudden mood swings, the solicitous insistence that she rest and read and lie beside the pool—and drop her guard. And of course he had never said he loved her, for one very basic reason: he didn't.

When she and David left that evening to go to dinner, the two of them seemed banded together more strongly than ever, like refugees in a strange land, outcasts far from home.

Regan determined to look as if she were having the time of her life, even though the smile slashed on her face like a wound made her cheeks feel stiff. Photographers seemed to come "from behind the draperies," as Jake had said. Smile, smile. Respond to the inane questions, sign autographs with a shaking hand, remember to lean against David, touching, always smiling.

The cameras followed them to a small club downtown that had a reputation as the best place in New York to hear fresh comedy. Sipping dry Blanc de Blanc, not to upset her testy stomach, Regan had blocked out the jokes when suddenly she heard her own name, then David's. And she was being coaxed onto the stage.

"I can't—" Regan began. "My voice—" throwing David a

look of horror. Her throat had begun to tighten at the first strains of music, and she swallowed convulsively, swallowed again. *"David, I can't sing!"*

But he had taken her by the hand, was leading her the few steps up to the small stage. Regan's palms grew moist, her tongue became dry. The spotlight shone on the green silk organza of her strapless gown, on the gleam of her shoulders, on the tawny-gold satin of her hair. Heart pounding, Regan faced the crowded club.

She heard the introduction ending, the verse to a ballad from her most recent album beginning. Nothing to do but try. She didn't want the wrong stories in the paper, she—

Caught the first note as it sailed by, and then the next. Soon, her voice was soaring, clear and true and stronger by the minute, and the song ended just when Regan had started to enjoy it.

"We're not letting you off so easy, are we, folks?" the emcee prompted the audience. "Give us another . . . Regan Reilly!"

And how could she refuse?

Acknowledging the burst of applause, Regan laughed. "Thank you all. I see I've had enough vacation." Her eyes searched the room as she flicked the microphone cord behind her, tossed the mane of golden hair. "This one's for David—my husband."

She sang "In The Morning," a tender love song from the album of the same title. It was a beautiful song that hadn't done as well as it should have, full of feeling and melody, the sort of ballad for which she had become famous, the kind she loved to do. The trademark that Jake had urged her never to abandon. And as Regan sang it now, once again she felt the shivers race along her spine, that exhilaration so like love itself. The look on David's face afterward seemed more than gratitude for the public display; more than pride that she'd been able to perform.

Coming back to their table, she kissed him in full view of a dozen photographers. Then Veronica Vance was suddenly leaning over them with her spun-sugar hair and a smile equally sweet.

"Hello, my darlings. . . . I was going to offer condolences, but I see there's been no harm done. I've been trying to phone you, dear. Regan, you look marvelous, in fact, *radiant*." She grinned at David, holding him responsible. "Word has it, my dear, that you're to test for the lead in next season's Broadway blockbuster," she said to Regan without looking at her.

"I'm to read for *Song of Dixie*, yes. But so are a lot of other people," including Alyson.

". . . but if you land the role as you're expected to—according to my usual reliable sources—who will play opposite? I understand the male lead's a plum."

Someone tall, someone dark, someone riveting. Someone, Regan added silently, who wanted her to fail.

"I have no idea," Regan answered. "I don't even know who's auditioning."

She only knew who had read, once, with her, in the warm grass on the ridge behind the Talbot mansion. Regan forced away the memory that made her heart twist. The brief illumination from a camera flash caught David's features, shining. A romantic hero, she thought suddenly, tarnished by bad press. Of course! Why hadn't she seen it before? It couldn't hurt—and since Ronnie wanted her story, why not let her have what she'd come for? She could almost see Jake's face when he opened his morning paper.

"David," she said deliberately, "have *you* ever done any stage work?"

Then Regan smiled for the cameras, for Veronica Vance, and for herself; smiled into the unexpectedly blue eyes of Jared Leslie.

Scowling, Jake sat at the breakfast table in the dining room that overlooked the ocean, trying to ease scalding coffee down his throat. The morning papers were appalling! Every one contained photographs of Regan with her husband: dancing, kissing at a ringside table in a downtown club, arms around each other as Sloan hailed the limo from a line of parked cars. "I've missed singing," she had commented to a reporter, "and

I look forward to the new season." It had been carefully noted that, despite persistent rumors to the contrary, she was in perfect voice.

Behind him, Jake heard a throat being gently cleared. "You don't mind, do you, darling," Cecily asked, "if I slip away for a few moments? With Charlie—to talk about these boring papers he's brought all the way from Manhattan?"

"Papers?"

Lost in his own problem, Jake expected her to comment on the pages he had hastily closed, but of course she said, "Business," and kissed his cheek. "I know this isn't fair, but I won't be long."

Jake felt a wave of relief wash over him. He could hardly wait until the two of them had disappeared over the crest of emerald lawn toward the beach before snatching up the telephone to dial. Under Cecily's watchful eye, there had been no opportunity to call before.

Had Regan gone with Sloan only because of his publicity? Why couldn't she just stay where he'd asked her to wait for him? Oh, hell. Jake spun the dial again, trying Sloan's house, then the apartment in Manhattan. Maybe he'd missed the number somehow. Missed seeing something in Regan, too.

A third try at the telephone.

How long would Ceci walk on the beach with Charlie Peyson? Discussing contracts and conglomerates, whatever the hell they talked about. Charlie's short brown hair brushed smooth against his head, the sad brown eyes that didn't go with his careful smile; his courtly way with Jake's wife virtually unnoticed by her as they strolled. He had watched the two of them often enough. Ceci talking; Charles listening, with that attentive, deferential incline of his head, and—

Answer the phone, damnit.

". . . Hello?"

"Jesus, there you are!" At the sound of her voice, he went weak. "What took you so long? Regan, what the hell is going on? Have you seen the papers? What is all that stuff? And on top of it, Sloan reading with you for *Song of Dixie*—that's a piece of excess responsibility, isn't it, trying to get him a job? Why are you dragging yourself through his *muck?* And why did you leave the house when—"

"I had to." She spoke in a subdued tone, as if she was unwell. "I was—I was in the shower just now; that's why I couldn't answer. I presume that was you before, ringing the phone off the hook."

"Yes. But listen—those pictures are the least of it. Vance's column this morning has you out of hiding, 'wherever you spent the summer,' and patched up with Sloan, but—"

"You don't think that's possible?" she said. "Well, the stories about David are untrue. You ought to believe what Ronnie has to say, Jake . . . or should I add, *again?"* which made his temper snap the rest of the way.

"Are you alone?"

"At the moment, yes." A pause. "Are you?"

"Look, I know you feel hurt about Ceci, but there isn't any reason to—"

"A masculine attitude."

She seemed to be waiting for some phrase from him, some message, but he couldn't find the words. What had happened to her in the last two days? It was like talking to a total stranger.

"Regan, I know my position just now doesn't strike you as very attractive—"

"No," she agreed.

"Meet me at the house later," he said in desperation. "I've been here long enough. I'll get loose somehow, and—"

"I'm staying with David tonight."

"Did he take you to bed last night, too?"

Silence. Jake caught sight of Charles Peyson and Cecily climbing the slight rise of lawn to the house at the same instant jealousy flashed through him over Sloan. Damnit. He thought Regan had hung up on him, but there'd been no click. And now, he heard her audibly breathing. "All right, I know. You could ask the same of me." He lowered his voice, wanting her so badly it was a craving. "Baby—"

"I'll see you at the audition, Jake. I'm . . . tired, and David and I have a lot of work before then."

Not too tired to go dancing, to drape herself over Sloan. They'd been husband and wife before; he wasn't all—

The sliding glass doors opened, and Cecily came inside with Charlie, her arm tucked through his, both of them chatting, unconcerned and relaxed.

Jake said grudgingly into the phone, "I'll expect great things from you."

Regan said he would get them, hanging up before he said good-bye. Jake wondered what he'd done; if there'd ever been a rift with Sloan. Her coolness was more than simple jealousy of Ceci. More than nerves about the play. He became aware of Cecily's questioning gaze.

"Business," Jake said ruefully, replacing the dead receiver. *The stories aren't true.* He felt as if they'd been apart for months instead of days. But why? And then suddenly he knew. Knew by the tone of her voice, the new devotion to Sloan.

Somehow, Regan felt he had let her down. The words revolved in Jake's mind, taking him back to a black night of pain, to his mother's wasted features . . . and then, to someone else. A woman he hadn't thought of in years because he never let himself remember those hazel eyes. *Enid,* Jake's mind at last formed the name. *My God, Enid, she needs me.*

But how could he possibly have betrayed Regan now?

"Something wrong, Jake?" Charlie Peyson was looking at him in an accusing fashion, but then, he usually did. Proper and severe. So at home in this house where the ghost of Cecily's father lingered in the rooms like a weekend guest who wouldn't go home. Fifty years from now, he would still be here—as Enid would stay deep in his own soul.

"No." Jake shook his head, praying that the words were right. "Nothing's wrong."

Waiting for the explosion, Manny Bertelli hunched into his seat next to Jake. "I'm sorry I let slip to Regan about the tour," he had said earlier. "I hope she's settled things with you since then. As you probably know, she wasn't happy." A placating smile, man-to-man. Hell, how was Manny to know that she'd stalk into his office first?

"I haven't seen her." Jake's eyes had gone hard as stone. "What about the money? Did you tell her that we'll put her people to work, too, while she's in New York?"

But there'd been no chance with Regan; and Manny didn't know what to say now. Jake hadn't spoken fifteen words to him since the first hour of auditions. He had declined lunch, and now was watching with fierce concentration as Alyson, the first actress to read in the afternoon session, took her place in front of the panel of backers and Peter Noel.

Alyson proved surprisingly effective in a physical way, even though her coloring was wrong for Marisa; but despite the drama degree, Manny thought, and her aspirations, she was no leading lady.

"Thank you, Miss Oldham," a voice intoned when she had finished. Looking slightly confused, she left the center of the room.

"Here she comes," Peter Noel whispered. He sat to the left of Manny, with Jake on the right. Manny looked up. He saw Alyson's eyes widen as Regan appeared wearing a long, gathered dirndl skirt in shades of blue and lavender; a simple white tucked shirtwaist with long sleeves puffed gracefully at the wrists and caught with lace; her hair casually pinned high on her head, stray tendrils escaping in a fetching way. She had used a bare minimum of makeup: moistened lips and a scrubbed look, with thick, dark lashes that wouldn't wash out under the lights. Stunning. Manny shot a look at Jake, gauging his reaction to Regan and her partner. David Sloan, in a colorful brocade vest, looked like a riverboat gambler, black pants and white shirt ruffled down the front. Both of them had dressed for their parts.

In the heated argument between Marisa and Jared, David Sloan exuded raw animal vitality, a ferocious sensuality tinged with sardonic amusement.

Superbly, Regan and Sloan battled with words. Their voices cut like swords. Their timing was flawless. They acted and reacted as if they had worked together for years; and when, at the height of their conflict, Sloan appeared to lose all patience with Marisa and pulled Regan violently to him for a kiss of searing passion, they told the world that they were lovers.

Jake hadn't moved. A vein throbbed at his temple; his jaw was tightly clenched; the knuckles of his hands showed white.

Regan broke the kiss and pulled away, breathing hard—or pretending to. Her eyes flashed green fire. Her cheeks were high with color. Every line of her slim body stood poised in justified outrage and affronted southern womanhood.

"You, sir, may leave! You will not call upon me again!" Her voice trembled on the verge of tears, but the pride was plainly heard. She had even managed a passable accent. "You, sir, are unwelcome in this house!"

"But not," added David very softly, "in your bed, madam"; then with a mocking bow, he straightened, turned smartly on his heel, and stalked away. Regan, advancing toward his retreating back, wrenched him around—as if with difficulty—and pasted a resounding slap across Sloan's face. Not much stage business in that one, Manny noted, wincing himself. A clear white imprint of her hand had already sprung up on David's cheek.

"Bully!" Regan hissed. "Every one of you northern vermin is nothing but a coward and a bully!"

With a maddening smile, Sloan replied that he hoped to change her mind. Bidding Marisa an unruffled good day, he exited with Regan following close behind.

There was an immediate buzzing among the backers. But Jake sat absolutely still with an expression on his face that defied description. "Jesus," he whispered, "Jesus." Then bolted from his seat, after Regan.

"Was that meant for me?"

She had been crying; had sent David and his solicitations for her welfare away, asking for a glass of water. Poor David, he'd been so patient during their rehearsals. "Relax, dear girl . . . every woman's an actress from birth." But today, from the instant she had walked into the hall, her emotions had been not manufactured, but devastatingly real.

Jake's eyes upon her, inquiring, probing, burning, had fired her responses to David . . . Dear God, how he could tear at her heartstrings—no matter what he did to her. When David had kissed her and she pulled back, Regan wasn't acting. She had hoped with all her soul that Jake felt the slap.

Now she whirled, teary-eyed as he asked the question; not daring to look into his brown-gold eyes. "Manny told me you know about the tour. I'm sorry, baby, I shouldn't have left you hanging—but it's not the way it sounds. The money—"

Regan looked at her shoes. "There is no money, thank you very much." Not if he had his way.

"There's plenty," Jake insisted, his tone changing. Hard business, Regan thought miserably. "You were unbelievably good just now; everybody thought so. But part or no part, I told Bertelli that I'd pay your earnings." Quickly, he detailed the arrangement with her manager, leaving Regan aghast.

"And that makes it right?" Wiping angrily at her tears, she stared at him. "Is that any better, Jake, than Manny paying your hospital bills? Do you think I feel any less compromised than you did? Any less humiliated, or—*managed?*"

"I don't want you to leave," he said. "Do you think that's trying for control?"

It is, Regan thought, if you can't give me the words I waited to hear the other day when you called, and all the days before. She couldn't believe what he was saying now; that he wanted his own way at any cost. Covering her salary to keep her in New York—that is, for whenever he felt like spending the night with her. Or dragging her to Connecticut for a furtive weekend together. No, she wanted no more half-life, no waiting for the phone to ring—or Cecily to come home and claim him. As David had said, it was a game she couldn't play. "Is it a crime to help you stay near me?"

"I don't know. Why not ask Cecily?"

"I'm asking you!"

Jake was reaching for her, his eyes dark with irritation when David stepped between them, handing Regan the glass of cold water. "Drink this." Over his shoulder he addressed Jake, who stood frozen in astonishment. "Can't you see she's upset?" and then, "Come on, love. Sit down."

"You stay out of this, Sloan!"

But Regan ended the confrontation. "He's my husband, Jake. Leave us alone." She stared past David's rigidly controlled expression and added, "You can keep your money. I don't want it."

Then she let David quickly steer her from the rehearsal hall, the only image in her mind that of Jake's chalk-white face. Which must have matched her own.

In the lobby of a nearby restaurant, while David ordered stiff doses of brandy for them, Regan excused herself to make a telephone call. She took one deep breath, then plunged into the long, uncertain future.

"John, this is Regan Reilly." Her heart raced on with the words. "Will you reserve a suite for me at Lying-In Hospital? For the appropriate date—seven months from now."

After hanging up, Regan rested her cheek against the telephone's bulk, listening again in her mind to the relieved sigh that had come from John Thornen, and his single comment, "Done."

In the privacy of the phone booth, Regan felt the withheld tears squeeze from her closed eyes and begin to slide down her cheeks. Yes, she thought. It was done. But in this child, she and Jake were joined, as they could never be in any other way. And in his daughter, or his son, she kept a part of him: perhaps, Regan told herself as the tears continued to fall, the best part.

Chapter 42

"Are you all right?" David asked, coming across the hall from his bedroom to Regan's. He held out his arm for her to fasten the pearl studs on his shirt. Half-dressed herself, she stood in front of him, concentrating on her task to avoid his eyes. But when she had finished the second sleeve, Regan felt a hand under her chin, tipping it upward until their gazes met. "Well, love? You haven't answered my question."

"I feel fine." She pulled away, turning her back and feeling the long silk skirt of her evening slip swirl around her legs with the movement. "John said there was nothing the matter with me," she said, stretching out the truth. She hadn't told anybody about the baby. She'd been sick the morning Jake called and sick most mornings since—including the ten days after the audition—but she kept the information to herself, running the shower hard to delude David until she felt better. In Quogue, her own bathroom was far removed from his.

"Then I have to conclude you're still angry with me," David persisted as she retrieved her dress from the closet and lowered the long zipper. Slipping the gown over her head, she heard him say, "I could hardly invite the big guns from Magnum without including Jake, you know. As one of the backers, he'd have been glaringly absent. Bertelli won't be here, though

516

Alyson's representing, I understand. He's in Zurich, if that helps."

"Slightly."

She *was* annoyed—and a bit panicky around the edges, too. Jake's being at the party meant Cecily as well; and though a picture was one thing, flesh was quite another. Regan wasn't looking forward to the meeting; and she didn't particularly want to see Jake, either.

Regan ran a hand over the fabric of her dress and adjusted the bodice. Figure-skimming, with a deep U-shaped neckline that showed the newly generous swell of her breasts—well, there's *one* way to get them, she thought, remembering her old insecurity over her anatomy—the gown nipped at her waist then gently rounded her slim hips before reaching to the floor in a series of soft, fluid vertical folds. It was a dress for dancing, easy to move in and nice to watch; but she wasn't concerned tonight with dancing. And though the slight cap sleeves gave a winsome air, there was nothing innocent about the deep ruby color of the lightweight satin. It was a go-to-hell dress, Regan thought, the sort of thing she wouldn't be wearing much longer; and if the message screamed was *femme fatale,* so much the better.

"Here," David offered. "Let me zip you."

She added a pair of matching, heeled sandals, and an inch-wide velvet choker with an ivory cameo at its center, and she was as ready as she would ever be. About as ready as any opening night. After fastening the necklace for her, David stood back and gave a long, low, exaggerated wolf whistle.

"You may not feel equal to the task," he said, "but you look as if you're ready to party with the whole lot of them."

Regan's green eyes softened. "Oh David, thank you—I'm sorry that I've been doing my best to ruin your birthday." Didn't he have a perfect right to celebrate? And why not add a smattering of guests political—from Magnum and the play—if he felt his chances for Jared Leslie might be strengthened?

"I doubt very much that you could ruin this party, love," he said. "And besides, you'll have to face him sometime or

other—the world's even smaller than we think—so it might
as well be here."

And it was, far sooner than Regan would have wished. She
and David had left her bedroom, walked along the hallway
lined with watercolors and carpeted in the rich grass-green
that had been used throughout the house, were rounding the
corner at the edge of the large, square foyer, just about to step
down into the sunken living room level and the crush of party-
goers there when they met. Her eyes restlessly searching the
room in front of her, she had failed to see Jake coming at her—
heading, she supposed, for the dining room where the bar had
been set up—and ran almost literally straight into him.

Putting a quick arm around Regan's shoulder, David drew
her back at the last instant, avoiding collision. "I'm going to
have to install stop signs at strategic intersections," David
joked, and the four of them laughed politely but without conviction. Regan wanted to die.

Unwillingly, her glance slid to the woman on Jake's arm,
her fingers firmly fixed to the sleeve of his jacket, a camel-
colored corduroy, the sort with practically no wale so that it
looked more like velvet, its color changing subtly with the
light. Like the amber wing chairs at the mansion, Regan thought
with a twist of fresh misery. He was wearing chocolate brown
slacks and a silk shirt without a tie.

But as casually elegant as he looked, he couldn't over-
shadow that perfectly manicured third finger of the left hand
clutching at his sleeve—or the largest, brightest, most amazing
pear-shaped blue diamond Regan had ever seen. Carats and
carats. Its size and brilliance barely escaped gaudiness; yet,
escape it did; and beautifully. Matching the gleaming setting
was a simple platinum wedding band: the only other jewelry
she wore. But then, she didn't need any.

Jake said softly, "Ceci, I don't believe you've met David
Sloan, or . . . Miss Reilly."

She thought he had been holding her gaze by the greatest
effort of will, holding his own smile with as much difficulty
as Regan did hers.

In a simple, wintry white chiffon cut low to expose the roundness of her breasts, Cecily Ferris Marsh looked nothing less than a queen. The one photograph Regan had seen hadn't captured the poise that seemed inborn and the breeding that had to be. Gracious as royalty, she smiled. "I'm a tremendous fan of yours. Regan"—extending a slender hand—"if I may use your given name."

"Yes. Of course."

The warmth of azure eyes in that serene expression. The soft touch of her skin when they shook hands. The bell of satiny ash-blond hair perfectly framing her face. Regan wanted to run and hide. She felt like the king's strumpet in her dark red dress, her hair loose and, in her mind's eye, tumbled no matter how sleek and well-brushed it actually might be. She was going to hell, all right, with this gown, being presented to the royal consort.

It's a beautiful dress, Regan insisted to herself, but that didn't help, either. Or Jake's unspoken but apparent approval as he let his glance slip over her for the barest fraction of a second. She tried to shut out everything from her mind but the conversation being directed to her, without success. How long could she stand here, practically shrinking against David for protection? If she hadn't felt his body warmth, she would have turned into a solid block of ice.

Regan kept her eyes away from Jake's, focused them on Cecily's ring flashing light in every direction.

"The absolute miracle of the human voice," Cecily was saying. "Jake, you must have Steven send some of Regan's albums to the house. I don't believe we have any."

"I didn't realize you were so interested in popular music," Jake replied. At his dry tone, Regan wondered with a tripping of her pulse whether Cecily's words had been genuine or laced with sarcasm. *How much could she know of the summer?*

"Why, darling, I'm fascinated by music in any form." An undercurrent to the well-modulated voice. "You'll have her signing her next recording contract elsewhere," Cecily said. "Not to mention the play. I think you'll be ideal for Marisa; everyone is so pleased that—"

"Ceci, let's not conduct business tonight," Jake cut in.

"Oh, I'm sorry, but I thought—"

"Have you found time to look around the house?" David asked hastily. "After your extensive travel in the last few months, I think you'd enjoy—"

Regan didn't hear the rest.

There is a lot of frantic conversation in this room, she thought. Why didn't David stop the art lecture and take her away? She didn't feel like a prominent celebrity who could handle hecklers in an audience with skill and sophistication: she felt schoolgirlish and diminished. As if Paul were reprimanding her again. Caught. Cheapened.

Jake was studying her, Regan noted, with frowning impatience. *Why?* Why had he stopped Cecily's chatter about the play? And David, too? It was the only time she'd seen them joined in a common cause. With that realization, the room started to tilt, and her unsteady-at-the-best-of-times stomach made its own threat. Ears humming, Regan could hear nothing but a meaningless buzz of words. Her hands felt cool and clammy; but the room seemed stiflingly hot. "Excuse me, *please,*" she choked out beneath the conversation and fled.

When Jake reached her, Regan was standing beside the swimming pool, taking quick, deep gulps of evening air. Miraculously, they were the only two people outside, away from the house just now; no one swimming after the season, and because the night was cool. Later, when alcohol had lowered inhibitions, he couldn't have guaranteed their privacy; but at the moment, he was grateful for it.

Jake went around in front of her, Regan's back to the water, and lifted her chin to see her face better in the silver light; the moon tilted, too, hanging in the sky like a Christmas ornament. "I'm sorry," he said. "But it seemed better to let Ceci go on. I'm sure she doesn't know anything, that was just her way." Regan pulled free from his hand.

"What Ceci almost let out of the bag in there was news I wanted to give you myself." He paused, waiting for her eyes to meet his again. "Marisa," Jake said softly. "The part's yours, Regan. Unanimous."

"I don't want it."

There had been no hesitation whatsoever. "The contracts are being drawn for your signature."

"Jake, I won't sign."

She had been waiting, he realized, for the chance to refuse. Regan looked up at the stars flung against a black velvet sky.

Relentless, he tried again. "Baby, the play won't be the same without you ... and Sloan." When she glanced at him, Jake said with a smile, "We're offering David the Leslie role tonight, though it won't be much of a surprise. He's known for several days."

And had graciously granted Jake permission to approach Regan himself, thereby surprising Jake and inching his estimation of Sloan up several inches.

Now, Regan's face reflected shock. "David ...?" And then, determined, "I still can't."

"But why? Regan, you're not making sense. Why would you make such a brilliant tryout only to say no?"

She looked at him bleakly. "I was wrong to audition. I never should have."

"Because of me? The guarantee with Bertelli and the jobs for your staff ... ?"

"No, Jake."

"Because I wasn't trying to—to manage you, none of that."

"Jake, it won't do any good," Regan said. "I'm not taking the part."

"You don't sound very happy about that," he pointed out. "You know what I think?" He didn't wait for her answer. "I think you went into that audition mad as a hornet, wanting to show me you could do the role, then tell me to go to hell when you got it ... am I right?"

He saw the faint shadow of a smile.

"Then you realized how good it felt, to be onstage, speaking lines with David ... so what's the holdup? If you still want, I'll cancel the agreement with Bertelli ... and I—I'll keep clear of the production, too. Is that it? You feel awkward, having me around while you work with him?"

"No." She offered nothing more.

Leigh Riker

"Jesus, help me out, will you? I'm not very good at mind-reading!"

"I have my reasons," Regan said vaguely, "and I'm asking you to respect them."

"Well, that's pretty damn hard when I don't even know what they are!" She looked at him again, her eyes wide and dark and bright, and the took her face in his hands, his fingers finding the thick silken warmth of her hair. But when he had moved to touch her, she had obviously been fighting not to cringe. "What's the matter, baby?" he whispered, feeling the stiffness all through her as she looked away.

"Jake, let me go."

She was obviously fighting not to cry, too.

"You can't still think you're going to fail with this play. It has everything going for it—and so do you, Regan. Listen to me," he said, feeling the first tremor of resistance in her body. "Come on, look at me. Please." He smoothed the light strands of hair from her temples, ran his fingers along her cheeks, her mouth. He felt her shiver. But she wouldn't glance at him again. "Do you remember," he said, "when you were first beginning—doing a week here, two weeks there, out in the Midwest, while I was on the last tour before . . . before I had to quit?"

"Yes." Her voice trembled, and she was staring at some point beyond his shoulder.

"You told me that I was making a competition of our relationship, and you were right. As proud as I was of what you'd done, I was scared inside, too—scared of exactly what did happen in the end. That you'd keep going, and I'd wind up nowhere. I was pretty quick-tempered in those days, worse than now—and afraid about Bertelli. You told me I was only helping things along there, too. . . ."

"I sound like the voice of wisdom," she murmured.

She could hear his smile. "The point is this: that we're different now in some ways, yes . . . and we don't have to compete. This summer I've stopped blaming you for what happened to me. If I told you that I don't miss the concert hall and wearing white tie and tails to play, that wouldn't be the truth—you've made me see that, too—because I do miss what might have been. But I can live with it. Because I get another kind of kick from Magnum, a sense of achievement."

Her gaze met his at last, and he saw the sheen of moisture in her eyes.

"Oh, Jake . . . I'd have changed places with you if I could."

His voice was hoarse. "I don't want you to change places, baby. I just want you to do this play. It's yours, and—"

"You traitor!"

At the stridently uttered words, Regan and Jake whirled around. Alyson Oldham came striding across the flagstone patio to the pool deck, her eyes dark and glittering in the night. Her peacock-blue chiffon dress swirled around her slim legs as she walked. *How long had she been listening?* "You promised me the reading, Jake! And you promised me the role! *It's mine, Jake*—"

"The producers of this play think otherwise."

"Did Manny know about this?"

Jake said yes, that an open audition had been necessary. He was certain that when Bertelli returned, he'd explain to her—

But Alyson turned on Regan. "No wonder you're so successful!" she hissed between her teeth. "There's always some man paving the path for you, isn't there? Jake and Manny, David Sloan, even my father—"

"Ali, I don't want—"

"Do you know how hard I've worked at dance lessons, singing lessons—all those years in school slaving for my degree? We could have been a team, Regan, when you were working Steven Houghton's roadhouse—but no, you were selfish even then! Grabbing what you wanted, using people to get ahead, using *me* when we were children— My God, when I think of the clothes and the toys you got from *me*, and you didn't even belong in our house! If she hadn't left you behind, that whore of a mother—"

"Stop it! Stop, Ali." Regan's voice shook. "Please, that's not true. I didn't take from you—"

"You cheap little liar! You took what I wanted most, and you're trying the same thing now!" Alyson gasped for breath, her chest heaving as she struggled to get the words out. "You took my father's love—"

"Ali, he's never cared about me. How can you say that? Paul made me feel terrible about myself, he was always changing from one mood to the next; even when he was trying to be nice, I couldn't trust him! He kept me confused and afraid." Regan made a move to touch her cousin's arm in reassurance, but Alyson stepped back. "Ali, when I worked at Steven's, Paul kept my pay. How can you think that—"

"He loves you," Alyson insisted. "He always loved you more than he did me.... From the day you came into our house, he preferred *you*—and why not? With that sweet little smile and those wistful green eyes...." She trailed off, helplessly clenching her hands, then letting them loose again. "If it hadn't been for my mother—"

Jake cut across the broken tone, his voice quiet. "Alyson, Regan had nothing to do with the decision about Marisa."

Cold blue eyes stared back at him, unforgiving. "Whether you're honest enough to admit it or not, Jake—you promised me this part!" She began to turn away. "And *she's* not going to have it!" Taking a step, Alyson halted. With her back to them, she said, low and vicious, "If Regan Reilly steps on a stage as Marisa in *Song of Dixie,* you're both going to be very, very sorry!"

Her footsteps echoed across the stone patio in the stillness. Jake and Regan stood looking after her until the swish of brilliant blue-green fabric had disappeared into the house. "I don't envy Manny his homecoming," Jake broke the silence. But he hadn't noticed Regan's shivering.

"I never knew how much she hated me," she whispered. "I never understood why." But the very notion that Paul would love her instead of his own daughter...

"The aggressive exterior hides a lot of, well, sibling envy, doesn't it?"

Regan glanced at him. She had to hug herself tightly to keep from shaking harder. All the years in Paul's house seemed to rush over her in an instant: Martha's resentment, the confused memories of her uncle's kindness before Regan's mother left, Alyson's thrown-away toys . . . Raggedy Ann. She swallowed, trying to clear her throat of the painful tautness there.

"Regan. . . ."

"No, it's all right." She twisted away before Jake could touch her. "Maybe—maybe it's better knowing where I stand, even if she is wrong about Paul." Regan forced a tepid smile. "Why doesn't she see that he stays around now, working for Manny, because of his own greed?" And then, "Well, there's no problem, considering that I'm not going to take this part, anyway, so—"

"Why are you running from it?"

"I don't want to play Marisa! Jake, how many ways do I—"

Regan broke off, feeling the tightness begin to choke her air supply. Convulsively, she swallowed again. Glancing at Jake, she saw the puzzlement in his darkened eyes. It was no less than her own confusion. Regan thought of her fear—Paul's fear—that the Worldwide acquisition meant harm from Jake for her career. She thought about the slow sales for her album—no more than that summer slump?—and the delayed recording for fall, the canceled tour . . . and then Jake's proposal to Bertelli, covering her earnings. Should she believe his motives innocent, believe that he wanted her near because he cared?

But what future did she have with Jake, who seemed to want her but not to love her? What if she told him now about the baby she carried? His baby. For a moment, looking into his dark eyes, Regan weakened.

Then she saw the motion of his hand, saw him pull a small package from his inside pocket. "You might as well have this," thrusting it at her.

Regan stared at the slate-blue paper and white satin ribbon. "Open it," Jake said, his eyes expectantly watching hers.

Pulling the wrapping off, she exposed the matching blue box inside. The lid was carefully removed, her heart beating heavily for some unknown reason, to reveal a cushion of thick blue velvet nesting a delicate pin: fragile platinum petals and stem gleamed in the darkness; dazzling light ricocheted off the cluster of diamonds that centered the jeweled flower.

"I don't understand—" Regan began.

But then she did. And thought she might faint.

"Hard and brilliant and faceted." Her gaze took in every detail of the beautifully crafted evidence of Jake's contempt. "Like me," Regan murmured. "As you said." And of course, it had to be a daisy—because roses were not her flower. "Tiffany's," she said, the blaze of diamonds blurring.

"Regan, wait." He was about to say he didn't remember saying anything of the kind; but too late, he cursed himself. Like Ceci, she had an elephant's memory. The beginning of summer, an argument laced with bitter sarcasm. He'd had the pin specially made, but not because—

Oh, Christ. What could he say that wouldn't make things worse? This had been his last-ditch attempt to convince her about the play; and all he'd done was turn her more firmly against it. Him, as well. Helplessly, Jake watched her chin come up, her shoulders straighten.

How could he tell her that he'd put the angry past behind him, with her help? He'd tried to convince himself he was buying Worldwide to slow her down; but he'd only wanted to see her again, to have the excuse. *You ought to do an album for us,* his heart slamming that night at the Grammys as he looked into her wide green eyes. How to let her know at this impossible moment that he'd intended the Talbot mansion, her imagined room, as a punishment, to wipe her from his memory—and had ended up wanting that one night to become endless thousands?

Jake had opened his mouth to try when he felt two things at once: the piercing anguish from Regan's liquid green gaze, her eyes swimming with tears; and the stab of the ten-thousand-dollar pin's catch in the skin of his palm. *Something more lasting than money,* he had said. *Jewels for your favors.*

"I'll never wear your payment!" Regan cried. "Never, Jake!"

He folded his hand around the coldness of gems and precious metal, watching her flee into David's house.

*   *   *

David handed Regan a glass of water, which was all she felt she could safely manage. In the handsome fruitwood-paneled study of his house, he stood over her like a father in front of a naughty child.

"It's impossible for me to play Marisa," Regan said for the tenth time. Impossible to forget Jake's watchful eyes; the payment he had offered. Retribution, swift and painful, going through her like a blade. "I promised only to read, not to sign contracts."

"You wanted to do a super job, and you did. You asked me to help make that possible. Why? Only to watch him squirm?"

"David, I—"

"I'm not blaming you, understand. I think you have reason, in some ways. He's been careless of your feelings."

Regan sipped at her water, then put it aside. "Well, one good thing has come of this," she tried. "You've gotten a marvelous chance with the Leslie role."

"Not unless you change your mind."

She heard the finality in his tone. "You mean you won't do the play if *I* don't?" She used her green gaze imploringly. "But David, you must . . . I didn't mean to back out on you!"

"Then why are you? Regan, *you* are Marisa and *I* am Jared Leslie." He used his most persuasive tone. "Please sign—we'll have a smashing time."

Regan looked down at her hands. Yes, they could have if—

"What's the matter, love?" David asked. "Your tour is out of the way, whether you do the play or not. What are you planning to do for the next six months? Eat chocolates and watch soap operas or—"

"Have a baby!"

Regan heard the short phrase crash against the four walls of the room, tinkle like a shattered crystal into awesome silence. David gaped at her. With a trembling hand, Regan pushed the hair back from her eyes. "Yes, David, you heard correctly. I'm pregnant." Which statement was followed by an even heavier stillness.

"My God," he murmured at last, "when you play house, dear girl, you play for keeps." His bewildered smile made her

look away. After a pause, David said, "A *baby*," as if to make
the news more concrete somehow, and then he added, "How
far along are you?"

"Ten weeks or so, a little more."

She could feel him watching her, and she wanted to slip
between the cushions of the bone-colored sofa. It must have
been a shade, Regan thought, to match her skin just now.

"And you've already decided to keep the child?"

"Yes."

"Does *he* know about this?"

"Of course not."

David turned aside, brushed the blond hair from his forehead
with that familiar, snapping motion of his hand. "Well," he
said, "I should have guessed. Your visit to John a few weeks
back, all that bathroom time every morning . . . are you feeling
any better?"

"A little." Then more truthfully, "Now and then."

"That stuff ends, doesn't it?" he said. "The morning sickness—isn't that what they call it?—I mean, you won't have
to go the whole way with your stomach giving you fits?"

"No." She almost wanted to smile at the sound of his voice:
a bit embarrassed by the physical complaints, by reality; but
even more, concerned, as if *he* had the responsibility. "I'll be
fine in a couple of weeks, so John promised."

"And your health otherwise . . . ?"

"I'm as sturdy as a peasant, David."

When at last he turned toward her, he was half-smiling, and
his eyes looked very blue.

"Well, then," he said decisively, "it looks as if we've got
ourselves a relatively minor problem. You can do the play, I'm
sure of that—a few skillful tucks and pleats from the wardrobe
wizards. We'll get Marsh and Bertelli to hire Linda to dress
you; then some legal protection in your contracts, perhaps a
month or six weeks' leave—but that won't come until we've
opened. . . ." He bent to kiss her hand. "And," David said,
"some personal insurance as well. That's where I come in."
And when Regan gave him a look as blank as the one he'd
given her a few moments before, "I am able to play more than

one role at a time, you know. Or have you forgotten again that you already have a husband with a perfectly respectable name that he's ready to—"

"You'd claim Jake's baby as your own?" Regan asked, astonished.

"If you'll play Marisa, yes."

"That's blackmail, David."

But he was smiling.

"Only if you choose to think of it that way," he said.

"But why would you—"

"Please don't ascribe any noble notions to me, dear girl. I'm not the first to take another man's child and give it a name—and I do so willingly, Regan." He had stopped smiling and was beside her on the sofa, holding both her hands in his.

He glanced at her face.

"Oh, you think I'm after a fat part on Broadway and a lot of rich publicity to save my skin after that other mess, do you? Well, I won't deny that fathering a child—as far as the press is concerned—would do me a world of good, but it can't hurt you, either . . . though that isn't why I want to, anyway."

"But David—"

"Look, my dear, dear girl, there are marriages all over the place that last for lifetimes without . . . sex being all that important. I don't know if we can last or not, but I think it's time we ought to try. Really living together," he said, "doing the play, and watching you grow great with child—"

"Oh, David."

"What do you say?" he asked, and she reached up to touch his face, looking into the grave blueness of his eyes. This man, to whom she'd been married for three years, was practically proposing again. Was it possible, after all, that they could make some kind of life together? Regan smiled softly.

"I say *yes.*"

"But I don't want you to see *him,*" David continued. "And I won't see . . . anyone, either. We'll just make it a day at a time, shall we?"

"Yes, David."

"There's one more thing. If you think I haven't been jealous of Marsh," he went on, "all summer, you're very wrong. I think you have a lot of trouble, my delectable little *canneloni"* —trying to lighten the tone of what he said—"seeing me as a normal human being, let alone a normal man, and you've been wrong there, too."

"David, I don't mean to—"

"I haven't loved you any less for not being able to understand. After all, we've had a rather hit-or-miss arrangement till now, haven't we?" Then he took her face between his hands. "Don't look so stunned," he said, reading her features accurately enough. "I love you very, very much, Mrs. Sloan—and you're going to have to believe that sooner or later. For now, let's just take it on faith, shall we? And get back to our guests?"

"I think we should, yes."

David leaned close, still holding her face, and gently kissed her smile, brushing her lips lightly as he always did. "My dear, dear girl," he said, "there are so many kinds of love—you can't begin to imagine them all."

Chapter 43

"*What are you staring at?*"

Regan had agreed to meet Linda at her studio in the West Thirties on a Saturday morning, having begged off for the weekend in Quogue on the pretext of needing time for wardrobe fittings and an intensive study of Act Two.

The first rehearsals—a chaos of wooden dialogue and jerky action—had terrified her. But the truth was, Regan didn't want another house party with David's friends.

Now, in the jumble of dressmaker dummies, bolts of fabric, and Linda's drawing board, she watched the mouth rounded in a circle of surprise as dark eyes slipped again, north to south and back, over Regan's form. Her heart began to pound.

"When's the happy event?"

Before she stopped to think, Regan had whirled to the full-length mirror on the back of Linda's office door and was turning back and forth to catch her silhouette, much as she had done in her girlhood room, wondering if her hips were obvious enough, if she had a chest at all.

"Am I really showing? Oh God, it's so soon—"

The hand over her mouth came too late.

"When did you say it was, Regan?"

"The doctor tells me March."

She sank into a dark blue paisley armchair in front of the

desk and stretched out her legs, which ached from yesterday's dance routines, rehearsed until dark. What she craved now was a hot bath with bubbles—not a cross-examination from Linda. *I should have gone with David to the Island*, Regan thought in dismay.

But she'd been so tired, not wanting to smile and make conversation. And feel, as always, that she was simply in the way. Then, last night in bed, she'd been thinking about today's appointment with Linda, smoothing a hand across the slight mound of her stomach. And Regan had suddenly stopped.

She felt something: not indigestion, not the butterflies of anxiety before a concert. Her heart rate surged with excitement. The time was right—if anything, overdue. There, she felt it again—that tiny, feeble fluttering, under water. The baby! Again it had moved, then once more while she lay still, lest she couldn't feel it the next time. Alive! The baby was alive inside her body! And in the quiet darkness, she had rejoiced.

"Have you told him?"

Regan didn't pretend to misunderstand Linda. "Are you crazy? There is a stopping point, you know." She regretted her confidences during the summer. If she hadn't told Linda about Jake— "As you once said, things are better ended than running in circles. . . ."

"Oh, now it's *my* fault, is it, that you're knocked up?"

Regan straightened in the chair, ignoring Linda's grin.

"I am not 'knocked up'—what a disgusting phrase! I happen to have a bona fide husband—"

"Pardon me, but I didn't have that impression . . . which isn't to say I don't like David." Then Linda's teasing grin began to fade. "You mean to tell me, he's taken responsibility? He *knows?*"

Regan said patiently, "We live together, don't we?"

There was something to be said for platonic marriage. No jealousies, no petty quarrels, very little of the male-female power struggle. Once she had accepted the limitations of their relationship, Regan decided that she and David were well-attuned roommates; even, she told Linda, best friends.

"Holy Moses. . . ."

"Well, what would you have me do?"

No answer for a long moment. Linda sat down on the other chair, propping her feet up on the littered desk. "This place is a shambles, isn't it? It ought to be declared a disaster area. I don't know how I get a thing done."

"Linda."

"He'd make a damn good father, if you want to know what I think! Remember at the Birdcage"—she smiled softly—"how gentle he was with Jeb; how wonderful Jake looked holding the baby while he finished his own drink and—"

Remembering how he had looked, arriving at the club fresh from his tour, a raincoat slung over his shoulder and his dark hair shining, Jake's brown eyes dancing at first sight of her, she wanted to cry now. Why hadn't they stayed so happy with each other?

Regan said flatly, "Jake's *forte* these days is taking over smaller, weaker companies for Magnum, making himself a tidy fortune, not babies—"

Linda touched her arm, so that Regan looked up into sympathetic brown eyes. "But he has made one. With you, darling. And I really do think you ought to tell him so."

"Why? Do you have any idea how we ended up this time? Not only with me pregnant!" Quickly, she told Linda about her canceled tour and Jake's suggestion to cover her earnings. She finished with the diamond pin shaped like a daisy. Exhausted to even think about the past few weeks, let alone the rest of the summer, Regan covered her face with a hand.

Linda's voice was compassionate, but questioning.

"Maybe he did want to help you; maybe . . . you took his gift the wrong way. When he handed you that Tiffany box he might have been saying—"

"Linda, stop! You're only fantasizing some romance that you can't complete for yourself with Kenny, so *please*—"

Regan's hand dropped to her lap at the sharp intake of breath from Linda. She stared at her friend, horrified by what she'd said. Just because she'd felt threatened— "Oh, Linda, *God*, I'm sorry!"

But Linda looked away, fixing her gaze on the drawing

534 Leigh Riker

board against the wall. There was nothing on it but a blank sheet of paper.

"No, you're right. Romance doesn't seem to be my *forte*." Glancing back at Regan, she smiled weakly. "At least not where Steven Houghton's concerned."

"Steven's one of my favorite people—and so are you." Regan tried to make amends for her thoughtless slip of the tongue. "Linda, what is it? I thought you were having fun together. Steven's looking younger than ever, alive again...."

A flicker of interest in the dark, troubled eyes. "Do you think so? Listen to *me*," Linda said wryly. "This is the woman who promised she'd have nothing more to do with the male of the species, excepting Jeb... certainly nothing more serious than accepting a dinner invitation." She looked again at the blank drawing board. "I think Jeb's the strong one in our house, Regan. If it hadn't been for him, I'd never have pushed Steven out the door the night of Jake's housewarming when we met."

"And now?"

Linda looked at her. "Status quo.... But Steven doesn't seem to mind very much." Eyebrows lifted slightly beneath the fringe of dark, glossy hair. "Oh, he's wonderful about taking me places, even eager to help out at home; and he's been trailing after, with great good spirits, while I house-hunt for a bigger place...."

"But?" Regan prompted when she didn't continue.

With a heavy sigh, Linda threw up her hands. "When the time comes to head for his own apartment, he goes. Not looking terribly unhappy, which makes *me* the only miserable one at this point." She grimaced slightly. "Jeb's barely polite when Steven's around. The resentment rises from him in visible waves."

"It can't be easy for a little boy who's lost his father," Regan said. "But don't let Steven get away. He's completely monogamous, you know. I think he may have invented marriage." Trying to make Linda smile, she'd forgotten about the painful past. About Ellen.

"A one-woman man," Linda said softly, her eyes getting moist. "And I thought I was the mortally injured party."

Regan covered Linda's hand. "Let me talk to him, Lin. Maybe he just doesn't see how you feel—"

"No, Regan. Don't." She studied their hands. "He's right, that love shouldn't be a mess of terms and conditions. It either works—or it doesn't." Linda smiled faintly. ". . . but when it does," she softened her gaze, looking back into memory. No matter what happened with Steven, Regan thought, Linda's bitterness over the last years with Kenny seemed to be lessening. Maybe that's all anyone could hope for: to have the loss become poignant instead of wrenching.

"You're not sorry you loved Kenny now, are you?" Regan asked.

"No."

The word had been whispered into the silence between them. Linda pulled her hand free, wiping quickly at her tears. She forced the smile. "Regan, it's a pretty dramatic bit of stuff, giving a man you love his son, or daughter; having him with you when that new life comes into the world, all pink and slick and yelling at the top of its lungs."

"Jake isn't going to hold my hand while I'm in labor, Linda."

"Maybe he would," she said gently, "if you asked him."

"Well, I'm not going to—so you might as well save any more breath you were willing to waste!" Regan stood up abruptly. "He already told me, for your information, that he isn't about to leave his wife . . . a frail-natured beauty compared to my own squat-in-the-fields-and-drop-it sort of peasant strength, so—"

"Don't be bitchy, Regan."

"Oh, *damnit,* I'm not as strong as he thinks, I'm not—" She turned away, biting her lip and then running a hand over the skirt of a basted gown that adorned one of the dressmaker's dummies. "This is too bunchy. Can you take out some yardage without making my stomach show—so I can move during the production number? And let's finish the fitting, can we? I've got a whole act to memorize by Monday; and if I don't get it down, David will wonder why I didn't go with him to Quogue."

Although there were always couples present—and a few unattached women, Regan excused herself—most of David's guests were male. Men in the arts; some who were lawyers or doctors, who designed scenery or clothing or bridges. Geoff, for instance, an account executive on Madison Avenue, red-haired with deep blue eyes, who smiled at her every time they passed in the hall—then sought David's gaze across the room.

One weekend David would be attracted to Geoff, or some-one like him—and then what? Already, in self-protection, Regan felt herself drawing inward, focusing on the baby she carried. Not even the play could gain her full attention.

With a resigned sigh, Regan watched Linda pin the new dress along a different seam allowance. "Keep your weight down, or I'll have work I can't afford with the new collection starting, and a move coming up." Pinning, writing measure-ments, correcting a sketch in silence.

But when Regan had tried on the gown, a red-sprigged muslin, Linda's hand smoothed the front pleats, tentatively touching Regan's abdomen. She asked gently, "Has it moved yet?"

Regan smiled, thinking of the night before. She'd been relieved as well as overjoyed; glad in mid-November that, although John Thornen assured her the baby was healthy, she needn't worry any longer that it was on the small side. She felt life within her—after all, a gift of love from Jake.

"Yes, last night," Regan whispered. "Oh, Linda, it's like . . . like a ripple in a stream, so light and shivery."

"Just wait awhile." And their eyes met, full of shared ex-perience and forgiveness. "It's going to kick like a mule." Then Linda grinned as if she couldn't resist. "I'm sure it will, songbird, considering—"

"Considering what?"

But Linda only shook her head.

"He's a good-looker, too, that man," she said huskily, pat-ting the slight roundness once again before she turned to hunt for more pins. "But I sure hope this kid comes out the image of its mother."

It wasn't long before Linda's first prediction came true. When Regan fell asleep at night, often the kicking of the baby wakened her. The movements were anything but gentle now, not light and fluttering like some frail swimmer, but strong and vigorous, as Linda had said they'd be, a minuscule hand or foot sending well-aimed thrusts at her abdomen.

"In the next few months that kid is going to do plenty of dancing," John Thornen soon told her, smiling hugely. "Get used to it."

"Just like a man," she groaned, trying not to smile back. "No sympathy at all."

"Having a mommy and daddy in show business, what else would you expect? That fetus is spending half of its time every day on a stage."

Though only one parent, Regan corrected him in silence, was acting in a rehearsal hall, singing and dancing. The other had done his performing behind closed doors, for a private audience of one, in the elegant setting of a medieval mansion.

Chapter 44

"Too bad you haven't found time to stop in at rehearsal," Manny Bertelli said, dropping some paperwork at Jake's office. "Peter's whipped that cast into shape already. No conflicts, no flak—just one big family," he said. "...except they all get along."

Bertelli laughed; Alyson smiled. She was draped in a chinchilla coat bought to appease her loss of Marisa, and wearing a deep wine dress that clung. Jake didn't like her smile. He was too much of an expert himself at the same type: lips and teeth, with no eye involvement.

Chinchilla coat or not, she hadn't forgotten the part. And the less he had to do with her, he decided, the better. Alyson wasn't a schemer, Jake thought, not clever or strong-willed enough. But she would damn well take advantage of her opportunities.

Jake said, "I'll get these papers to Steven. He's handling detail on *Dixie*. He and Allen Jenkins."

After Sloan's party, Jake had washed his hands of the project.

Bertelli said, "Tell Houghton to give me a call soon. This little girl and I are going to Paris for the holidays."

When they had gone, Jake looked for Steven, but his secretary said he was out of town. Like Ceci, he was always out of town. Shrugging, Jake left the papers and took the down elevator.

Outside, it was cold, choppy with wind; raw and bitter. He wasn't particularly hungry. Jake headed west, walking without purpose, or so he assumed, letting the cold eat into him; but he had been walking with more direction than he thought. Broadway, and the hustle of traffic, the blasting horns, the jostling crowd assaulted him. He found himself standing in front of the rehearsal hall, not far from the Browning Theater where the play would open.

Inside, the vast room was alight and alive, filled with bustle and people. His eyes adjusting to the rush of brightness, Jake stayed just inside the door, in the shadows, and cursed himself for coming to the hall.

Peter Noel called for quiet. "All right, people, picnic's over, let's get to work. Where's my script? Where's the goddamned script?"

Everyone scattered. There was shuffling and coughing. Then David Sloan sauntered in, wearing jeans and a sweatshirt—and that slim gold band of possession on his finger. Sloan turned and motioned. He had stage presence, Jake reaffirmed; he would sell tickets and pack the house, even if he appeared by himself.

But he would not. His gesture answered, Regan came out from a side room. Her tawny hair shone softly, swinging lightly against her back. Her jeans matched Sloan's, but she wore a loose velour shirt of rich copper color.

The scene began. *Damn*, it was the only scene Jake knew himself, almost by heart.

Marisa and Jared had taken a ride over the plantation, war-ravaged and nearly barren, and had stopped to rest their horses—"tethered" offstage. Although the ultimate setting would be elaborate and realistic, today a faded quilt represented the grass, and there was no tree to sit beneath.

Leslie's language was at first light, then testing and flirtatious. ". . . and you heard every word, *ma belle*."

"I am not your beauty, Mr. Leslie, and if you become too forward, sir, I shall insist that we return to the house,"

Regan answered like a true coquette. "I do believe—"

I believe, my love, that we know each other well enough—
"for you to call me by my name," finished David, smiling
wickedly.

For a second, Marisa seemed startled. She appeared to weigh
this northerner's blatant approach against the subtler formalities
of southern culture. "Mr. Leslie," she began with strong emphasis.

Jared. "Jared," David intervened.

(His hand takes her chin.)

David held Regan's face. Her eyes debating, she let him.
Then the smile she had been trying to hide broke through in
all its glory.

"Jared Leslie . . . Jared," the syllables rolled, her voice and
accent even better than during the tryout, as Sloan's face moved
closer to hers with each repetition of his name. "You do need
me, you will. . . ." And he kissed her. As Jake had kissed Regan
on the ridge behind the mansion, play and reality blended like
the two cultures of hero and heroine. The conflict over Cecily's
return had been forgotten in that last afternoon together. In the
moments of their own joining on the hill. *I need you.*

"Marvelous." Peter Noel clapped his hands, and a startled
shiver rippled down Jake's back.

There was laughter from the cast. Regan and David grinned
at each other, then exchanged a kiss of triumph. But when she
moved away, the velour shirt caught between them, tightening
around her middle. No, he thought, I'm seeing things. She
can't be . . .

Pregnant!

His heart pounded, thick with blood. Pregnant how long?
He couldn't be mistaken. The rounding was small, but obvious
enough. How the hell would Marisa look waddling across the
stage with a stomach like a watermelon, singing under a southern moon, wishing for Jared Leslie to come back to her? Oh,
Christ.

Jake's mind spun. There must be some kind of clause in
her contract. Let Steven find it, and explain the foul-up. Find
a clause, a release, and Regan's replacement.

* * *

A band of pain pressed at his temples. No, not exactly a pain, but more a pressure—as if some remembrance inside kept pushing to get out.

Jake sat in the darkened den of the penthouse late that night while Cecily moved about in the living room, straightening the glass and ashtray clutter from the evening; two other couples had joined them for drinks and conversation, most of which Jake had missed.

Not that he minded missing the Harrises, or the Daltons. Particularly Sue, with that endless prattle of gossip. Planning to spend the holidays in Paris where one daughter attended the Sorbonne, then on to Switzerland for a week of skiing. Would the Marshes reconsider? Jake closed his eyes against the notion, against the whole day from beginning to end.

Why had he gone to rehearsal for one glimpse of rounding belly that still made his own stomach twist?

You do need me, Jared told Marisa.

She needs me, Jake had said so long ago. *But I need you, too,* she had answered. Hazel eyes and soft brown hair and kindness. Eyes that drowned him like Regan's green ones, seeming to offer when they were really taking—forcing him from duty, forcing him to disappoint.

Now he leaned his head back against the chair. *She needs me.* Long ago, those words had been the only prayer he knew.

Jake opened his eyes to darkness in the den of the penthouse. The wallpaper, he remembered, had been faded—once a wine color with stripes of off-white between, and some unidentifiable pattern, also wine, on the light background. Like Alyson's dress that morning, he realized. Funny, the connections the mind would make. So long ago, that other night. And today, Sloan's line had helped to trigger the remembrance. *You do need me, you must realize, you will. . . .*

"I wondered where you were." Cecily switched on the light. Jake's eyes snapped shut briefly at the painful rush of brilliance, then, opening again, focused on her. She was dressed for bed in a long gown of sea-foam lace with a matching peignoir and floaty sleeves.

"Were you all right when the Daltons were here, and the Harrises? You were so quiet, so remote."

"I had a bad day," he said truthfully.

"Poor darling." *Poor baby.* Cecily settled on his lap, wound her arms around his neck.

"What did you want to say, Ceci?"

She kissed him again, lingering until he pulled away. "I would like to elicit some interest on your part in going to Gstaad for the holidays. I mentioned it last week. And tonight, Sue—"

"Is that all you think about? Traveling?"

"Well, at least you know what I'm concerned about. You're either preoccupied or uncivil. I thought it might bring us together again."

Together where? Jake wondered. In the Hamptons, here at the penthouse, on the moon?

When he didn't answer, Ceci went on, "But as soon as I got home last summer, I knew something was different, Jake."

The little-girl pout puckered her features. Her arms clung to him. "Couldn't we spend Christmas at home?" Jake asked.

"But it's so cold on the Island then—the wind goes right through. Switzerland is . . . invigorating, much dryer."

"I meant Lancaster." A huge tree with silver tinsel, fragile glass ornaments and lovely lights, an angel on the top. A corny, old-fashioned Christmas in the country. "A roaring fire," he said, playing with her pale blond hair, "and lots of packages to open. What would you like, Ceci?"

"Gstaad," she answered promptly. Jet-set Santa Claus.

He fell back on the old excuse. "I don't want to go to Switzerland in December. Or January or February. I want to work. I've got backlog up to my—"

"If you won't fly with me, I'll go alone."

"What's new about that?" he asked, suddenly angry. "Go ahead, if you want. Or take Charlie."

"Maybe I will." She slid from his lap and walked swiftly to the door. "At least Charles Peyson has a pleasant word once in a while."

"Ceci—" Christ, his head had begun to throb.

"Sometimes I wonder if you care about me at all, Jake." The petulant tone made his pain, and aggravation, all the worse. For an instant, she had sounded like a six-year-old.

"I care," Jake told her, "when you let me."

"Let you?" The sulky voice broke. "Oh, that's funny!"

The lacy nightgown swished and disappeared, like a final comment of its own.

Jake rested his head against the chair, rubbing his temples with the thumb and middle finger of his left hand. Why the hell wouldn't she let him give; make a Christmas this once for the two of them; stop running in such frantic, stylish circles? A wealthy—and professional—nomad. As if she was afraid to stop. Why couldn't Ceci offer something less than hard cash? And yet, something so much more.

Chapter 45

The following morning, Jake found Charles Peyson waiting for him in his office. "Cecily mentioned the trip, I believe?"

"And you're here practically at dawn to ask permission to join my wife?"

"Not exactly."

"Charlie, why don't we stop circling each other?"

"Cecily told me you were annoyed."

So she had run from the den last night to the telephone, whining to Charlie about her marriage. Jake felt his thin patience begin to go. He had come straight to the office this morning, prepared to do battle with Steven over Regan's contract, the vision of her pregnancy still painted in wild colors on his mind—as that disturbing memory of Enid also was— and now *this*.

"Not so much annoyed," he said with a sigh, "as curious." Peyson's gaze fell first. He turned away, studying the seascape over the linen sofa. "Why, Charlie? You've had it in for me since the day I married her."

"I . . . feel a certain responsibility for Cecily, you must know that. From the time she was a small girl. Her father was not a very demonstrative man. He left Cecily alone with governesses and tutors—and later, of course, me." Charles turned around to look at Jake.

Little daubs of color stood out on Peyson's face, and at the tips of his ears. "I was there and he never was. I'm a longtime habit, Jake. But she does... depend on me for many things. Good sound business sense, mostly; but every now and then, a shoulder to cry on, too—if you get my meaning."

"You think I'm a prick."

"I think you don't give a damn!" Charles fixed him with a furious stare, the most emotion Jake had ever seen the man display. "I'm asking that you mend your marital fences. Be there for her, *listen,* care about her, for God's sake—"

"Charlie, you are a selfless man," Jake said softly. "Giving up the chance to jet off to Switzerland for Christmas, humbling yourself on Ceci's behalf—"

"She has no idea I've come here! May we keep it that way?"

Jake was spinning on a number of mental levels. He wanted to pitch Charles Peyson out of his office for telling him how to conduct his marriage. Didn't he realize how selfish *she* could be, how much unnecessary flight she undertook? But he also knew that he had given up trying very hard to keep her home. Last night, confused by his own reliving of the past, by his hunger for a better present, by the twist of his gut at first sight of Regan's rounding belly, Jake had tried his wife's ploy. Offering Lancaster as an ultimatum, he had forced Ceci to throw Charles at him to save her pride. Why blame Peyson for coming to see him, then?

"I won't tell her you were here," Jake conceded.

Charles Peyson twirled his homburg in his hand. The hat didn't go with his hairstyle, but somehow Charlie carried it off, as he also managed what amounted to a warning. "Whatever you do, Marsh," he said, "don't hurt her any more."

Jake had barely time to begin sorting his feelings and solutions when Steven rapped at the office door only minutes after Charlie had left.

"Answering the summons to council," he said with a breezy smile. Steven had a mug of coffee in one hand, Jake's curt command on paper in the other. "God, you should see the

Midwest. First snowstorm of the winter; everything's socked in. I was damn lucky to get out of O'Hare last night."

Jake motioned him to a chair.

"Did you know Regan's pregnant?"

Steven's eyebrows went up. He sipped at his coffee. "I heard rumors. Evidently, so have you."

"They're true."

"But how did—"

"Never mind." Jake wondered if Steven was buying time with pretended innocence: but if he was, it didn't matter. "Get rid of her," he said.

Steven's protest was immediate, and informed. Though he carried no contract in hand, Steven had come prepared.

"So we're stuck, is that what you're saying?" Jake demanded. "She's covered 'in the event of pregnancy during the production'? What about the last few months? And right after the birth?"

"She gets a leave of absence. Six to eight weeks."

"And who plays Marisa then?"

"The understudy, of course. She's good, Jake. Not too different in coloring or size. The costumes fit. She knows the role."

Jake rejected Steven's sensible explanations. "We're not going to make a penny, you know that? We'll be laughed off Broadway the second Marisa moves her supposedly virginal self across the stage like *that*. A month and a half . . . two. It isn't enough. And nobody's paying to see an understudy right after opening, they want Regan Reilly!"

The gowns were superb, Steven argued, hiding her condition in modified Empire waistlines and hoopskirts and crinolines and capes, but Jake wouldn't listen. Steven tried to switch strategy. Regan was doing a tremendous job; the contract was solid as rock; but no, he didn't for a moment think she and Sloan had been planning a child. Accidents happen, he said with a smile.

But Jake wasn't smiling. "Like hell." He frowned fixedly at his desk top. "Regan Reilly doesn't have accidents."

*   *   *

Jake didn't look up again until he heard his door close.

Why had he done it, for God's sake? The whole damned summer . . . chasing Regan from Lancaster to New York and back again. Feeling guilty because he'd given her the diamond pin. Christ, it was a good thing he hadn't volunteered his feelings, too.

Now she and Sloan were going to light up the Great White Way with their talents, their beauty; dazzle the whole world with what would soon be a very public pregnancy and—

Jake propped his feet on the walnut desk and studied the tips of his new Gucci loafers. He wasn't a complete idiot. The thought had occurred to him when Regan turned, showing him the rounded profile: there was an even chance. Sloan's spawn, he wondered, or *his* child? Christ. He thought back over July and August; no scarcity of opportunity, more his than Sloan's, and she'd told him—

Reconciliation. Apparently, it was true.

And as he'd told Steven, she was careful. Never made a misstep in her career. Or anywhere else. She'd only been using him again.

I don't want anything from you. Five years ago in the hotel room, she'd said it; and the words still sliced him to pieces. *I could never want your baby.* No, Jake decided. Her body, as strong and determined as her mind, would never accept his seed. She didn't want anything of his, and probably she never had.

Suddenly, his foot seemed to move forward, independent of any mental directive, jamming the heavy bronze bookends, sending a half dozen legal volumes to the thick carpet in a series of muffled thuds.

Had she gotten pregnant to sabotage the play? He'd have thought so; but she was too far gone.

Jake punched the intercom, speaking into it before Janie had a chance to answer. "Clear my schedule for this afternoon, will you? Tell Steven to deal with L.A. I'm going to have some skis fitted."

The least he could do, Jake told himself. Try to make this marriage work before *it* was too far gone. He would please

Ceci by going to Gstaad, to the chateau she'd already rented. To the Daltons. He didn't relish the notion of Christmas by himself, without her; and he had to try.

Whoever said bells rang, or the earth moved? Why should they; why should it? Once, on a night he wished had never happened, he had wasted his mother's life and been betrayed by a woman with soft eyes and softer hair. Then, promising himself that would never happen again, he had fallen for a luminous green gaze and tawny hair that wound around him like a silken cocoon. He and Regan had gone around twice. And always, always, as with Enid, the pain was what he remembered; the pleasure what he tried to forget. No more. Not ever. No more faith, he made a silent promise, and no more lies.

It wouldn't kill him to go to Switzerland. To make Ceci happy.

Pretend, Regan used to say, and Jake thought, oh yes. Pretend she never happened.

Answering the insistent ring of the doorbell at her apartment, Regan wondered for a startled second if she was hallucinating. The only occupant of the hallway seemed to be an immense, shaggy blue spruce that talked. "Believe me, I paid a veritable fortune," it began. Then Regan started to laugh.

"Where are you?"

"Behind this thing." David peered from the branches with a grin. "A Christmas tree you wanted, and a Christmas tree you shall certainly have."

Between them, laughing, they forced the huge bulk of greenery into the living room where they studied the tree from every angle, finally satisfied to place it in the corner between the windows and the fireplace. "Excessive," Regan had to agree, "but lovely."

"Now," David said, sawing with a small tool bought for the occasion at the trunk—because, upright, the tree had jammed itself against the high ceiling. "A few thousand dollars for ornaments, and you'll have somewhere to display those packages you've been wrapping for weeks."

"Not thousands," Regan said. She touched David's shoulder. "But do you think we could go out now, even though you've just gotten home, and pick up a few things to start? Some tinsel, and a really fancy gadget for the top?"

"Would I dare to tell you no?" David wiped his sweating forehead with the back of his hand, stood up, and having anchored the tree in its stand, tipped it right again. Shorter by several inches, it fit the space nicely. "Ohhhh," Regan murmured, eyes shining.

"Christmas," he said, putting an arm around her. "The season of peace and domestic tranquility."

She smiled at his gentle sarcasm, but Regan loved the entire season: the beautiful store windows at Saks, and roaming through F.A.O. Schwarz to look at the toys she would buy next year for the baby, and hearing carols sung at unexpected moments on street corners. To her further delight and gratitude, David indulged her, laughing when she rattled his presents to her and warning that every single one would be broken to bits before opening. Regan couldn't fathom how he kept his hands off the extravagantly wrapped packages she had placed beneath the finished tree.

"Simple, dearest girl," David said. "I've had Christmas before, and you haven't."

It was true. For the first time, she wasn't on tour, not in a hotel room—even talking to Jake long-distance—nor at Paul Oldham's, feeling left out, nor onstage as she had been more than one Christmas night.

The play rehearsals were different, a community effort. And at home, in the evenings, she had David's company. The script between them on the bed, they practiced lines and developed scenes until at last Regan threw the pages aside. "Enough!" Throwing out her arms, she would laugh. "David, I have this perfectly violent craving—"

"For ice cream and pickles? *Gefilte*-fish sandwiches?"

"No, for popcorn!" An impish grin told him she was half teasing. "Will you make some, please?"

Bundled back into bed, they flicked on the television set to watch one of the ancient movies David adored, licking butter from their fingers, sharing a Coke and laughing like naughty children staying up too late. The child she'd never been.

But she had so much to be thankful for now. The play was progressing toward dress rehearsal the second week of the new year, and the baby was growing inside her. In preparation, Regan had bought a crib and dresser and a changing table and a matching toy box—for next year's bounty. Mahogany, with white trim. And bookshelves too, for the future. David helped her paint the extra bedroom a pale yellow, and Regan ordered yellow gingham curtains.

"Maybe you should wait," he had suggested, "until the baby comes. Boy or girl . . . pink or blue?"

But she didn't want to wait. Or to use more traditional colors. She wanted to walk into the room and see it ready. One Sunday afternoon just before Christmas, Regan stood there watching the sun through the windows and the gleam of light on wood surfaces. She placed a hand over her abdomen, more prominent now. And the baby kicked in greeting against her palm. Regan smiled, thinking they were already friends.

Even now, she felt as if she knew this child: recognized its will and some habits; the shape of hands and the color of eyes. Having lived with it for nine months by birth, she might be as well acquainted with her son or daughter at the instant of delivery as she had been with its father. Or thought she'd been. Correcting herself, Regan wondered what their baby would become: a poet, a painter, a business tycoon; the first female to win some coveted prize in medicine; a singer, operatic . . . or a concert pianist.

"The baby's iron-willed," she had told John Thornen during one of her checkup visits. "Demanding, but very talented. I can tell," she said, "by the way it moves." Just as she knew what the baby would look like.

"Well, I wouldn't be awfully surprised," John said, "to see blue eyes and blond hair . . . unless David's taken to the peroxide bottle."

But she wouldn't acknowledge that. "Brown eyes," Regan said again, "and dark hair that shines like silk."

scoffed. "Even *I've* never heard an old wives' tale to that effect," as he looked at her curiously, then with indulgence. *Pregnant women often have strange notions all their own,* Regan had read in his expression while he prepared to take new measurements with the stainless steel calipers, checking the baby's growth.

Now, as she felt a stronger kick, she took her hand away and the smile became a sheen of tears. She had so much, so very much. David's kindness, the new challenge of Peter's play, and new life too. And she had recorded at last the overdue album that Steven was timing for release at the baby's birth. The songs selected were gentle, the tone of the album quieter than any she had done in several years. There were two lullabies, one written by Peter and the other the old Welsh tune that had haunted yet touched her since childhood. *All Through the Night.* Regan liked the album greatly.

But still . . . Running a forefinger along the top of the dresser, she met her green-eyed gaze in the mirror, her image blurred through the unshed tears. Soft, like the airbrushed pictures the magazines printed and the jackets of her albums. The beautiful photographs she competed against—heightened reality against the truer vision of herself. As she had once competed with Jake, so long ago.

That was over now, he said; and hadn't she tried to believe him? Over. Yes, she supposed in another way, too. Hadn't the diamond pin said so plainly enough? Far more sharply than her own, pregnant image in the glass. A child that was David's now . . . no matter what the future held for them. She stood staring at herself, blinking back the tears, thinking: no matter whom it looked like.

What more could she want now? And why, standing in this bright room on a clear winter day in the happiest season of the year, did she still feel as if she didn't belong?

The next evening, David came home late. After rehearsal, he had an hour of voice-coaching, so Regan normally went ahead to the apartment by herself. Usually, by the time she had showered and changed and started something for them to eat—unless Maggie had left a requested casserole—David was home. But not tonight. It was well after ten o'clock when he finally fitted his key into the lock.

"I'm sorry to have missed dinner," he began, making a business of hanging up his overcoat and scarf. "I did try to call, but there wasn't any answer. I thought you might be in the bathroom; then I got tied up. . . ."

Wordlessly, Regan went into the living room, leaving him to follow with the last of his explanation. She sat down on the sofa—an off-white slubbed linen pile with vivid green and yellow cushions—and stared at the Christmas tree, at its softly winking lights of various colors and the brightness glancing off the tinsel.

"You'll never guess, not in a million years, who I ran into."

David sank down beside her, waiting for the try, but Regan said she didn't have the faintest idea. "You'd remember him. He used to talk to you all the time at the house in Quogue, dear girl—that account exec, the sharp dresser, remember, the one who—"

"You mean Geoff."

Dark red hair and blue eyes, tall and smiling all the time. Confusing her, making her wonder.

"That was fast," David said with a smile. "Anyway"—continuing in a bluff, hearty tone—"it was too damn cold to stand around on a street corner. Geoff suggested a drink or two; then, well, one thing and another, we decided on a light meal. . . . I tried to phone," he finished weakly.

Elaborate excuses, true or false. Would they become more and more a part of this marriage? Regan could feel David's eyes watching her. She wasn't surprised—she'd even been expecting Geoff, or someone like him—so why should she feel deflated, depressed?

"I *am* sorry," David murmured. "Were you lonely? Not sitting here all night, were you, staring at your tree?"

Regan smiled wanly. "No, I made myself a salad and finished last night's chicken, then wrapped a few gifts."

He was still studying her, then tentatively placed his right hand over the roundness of her stomach. "That's a pretty top," he said. "I like you in such a quiet blue, with those touches of white. You manage to make maternity a fashion," his eyes taking in the dark blue slacks, too, and the wide white grosgrain ribbon holding back her hair. "Am I forgiven?" he asked, seeing her smile more naturally.

"Is there something to forgive?"

She saw his face change; and she knew. The drink, the snack they had shared tonight. It was only a matter of time before David's promise scattered to the winds. He looked away.

"I'm trying," he said. "I really am trying. It can't be easy for you, either, Regan," but she had her distractions now. When the baby was born, how would she deal with her own needs again?

"I'm not going to stop trying," David was saying.

She gave him a tremulous smile as he took her hand, holding it between them on the sofa cushions. After a silence, she said, "How would you like to call your parents? Wouldn't you like to tell them about the baby?"

"Yes," he agreed. "I suppose that would be a good idea before the media gets the news first."

"Can't you hear your mother now?" she asked him. "And your dad? Will they be pleased at becoming grandparents?"

He looked at her oddly. "Grandparents," he said softly. "Yes, I suppose they will, dear girl. Mom will think you're the eighth wonder of the world—though she does already. As for him," he said, "at least he'll think I'm prone to the more human inclinations."

His hand tightened in hers, and Regan didn't know what else to say. Was David having qualms about taking Jake's child for his own? He was frowning at the carpet as if he could find answers, too, in the rich, creamy yellow pile. Regan sighed and looked toward the Christmas tree, so luminous, even magical, in the dim light.

What if she could tell Jake? What if Linda's defense of him was true? Why could she still feel his thick brown-gold hair in her fingers, feel that dark gaze going through her, feel his lips on hers, and the sweet, hot thrust of love. . . .

"You're thinking about *him*, aren't you?" David's voice was quiet, startling. She looked into his blue eyes, full of pain. "I can always tell by your face. God, I'd give anything to be able to give you reason to look at me like that, but—"

She squeezed his hand gently to make him stop.

They were looking into each other's eyes, into confusion and regret, and suddenly she longed for the simpler days in London, the hours of sightseeing and silly jokes, David's Italian endearments, and even the night when they had almost made love, before she knew—

"David, it isn't fair!" she cried, gripping both his hands. "I do love you, but I don't know how we—"

"Hush." He had gathered her close, into the circle of his arms, was smoothing the long, tawny hair with one large hand still wearing the remnants of his summer tan. His hand trembling. "Hush, love," and she heard the thickness in his voice too, knew he didn't want her to look at him. Regan kept her eyes fixed on the beautiful green tree shining with ornaments and tinsel, shining with colored lights, shining and symbolic of the season. Domestic tranquility. After a while, she heard him say with a faint quaver in his tone, "You're absolutely right, dear girl . . . none of it is fair."

The following day, in high spirits, Steven was preparing to leave his office. He had promised Linda and Jeb a long holiday, including Christmas, somewhere north ("with mountains and clean snow" had been the request), and he'd taken a condominium in New Hampshire for the week.

Looking forward to the trip, he paused in his paper-shuffling. How would he and Jeb fare in each other's company? The boy still didn't completely trust him—not even after moving day. Or because of it.

Linda had at last settled upon the perfect apartment, eight high-ceilinged rooms on East End Avenue near the mayor's residence at Gracie Mansion. The building itself was close to Carl Schurz Park where Jeb could play after school, and Linda had crammed their space with his toys, an eclectic mixture of furniture, and an unusual color scheme that reminded Steven of nothing so much as Christmas. Bright red and dark green seemed to predominate with generous splotches of white.

He'd offered to help—insisted upon helping—several weeks before. There hadn't been much to do, the movers having completed the heavy work, of course, but plenty of cartons had been unpacked in the new kitchen; bookshelves had been loaded on either side of the marble fireplace. And Steven had, with only minor profanity and abrasions, managed to install a can opener and a bathroom lighting fixture.

"Steven, the maintenance people can do that on Monday," Linda had said.

"If you're lucky." Continuing to dig through the tools he'd brought, looking for the right screwdriver. "I'd like to see you settled myself."

What did he really want? They'd been dating—formal term—since Jake's housewarming. Slowly getting to know each other's bad habits and good qualities, never progressing beyond the holding of hands or a few good-night kisses in the foyer. Jeb, never accepting him. Steven, still feeling guilty that Linda attracted him so; not doing a damn thing about it. He wasn't sure she wanted him.

Then, evening. And a riotous first meal at the kitchen counter in Linda's new home—all three of them laughing as they demolished a huge pizza and half a container of Neapolitan ice cream. While Linda put Jeb to bed, Steven had coaxed a fire into a cozy blaze and poured them after-dinner Irish cream liqueurs. He hadn't spoken when Linda joined him, mutely offering her glass. "To your new digs," he'd toasted the apartment.

Linda smiled. "Thanks for the generous donation of blood so we can open the orange juice without a crowbar in the morning."

Steven examined his scraped fingers. "I've always been handy around the house." He had grinned at her, the expression fading at the sudden softness in Linda's eyes. "I don't like living on my own, either," she murmured. "Oh, I have Jeb, but—"

Rising from the sofa, she'd put distance between them. Her

cheeks flushed, her gaze uncertain. A woman who was becoming one of New York's most in-demand designers—one look around the enormous apartment would tell him how well she survived—but she looked like a young girl at that moment. Steven had felt his heart turn over.

"You kicked me out the first night," he heard himself say, his bruised finger worrying the gold wedding band on his other hand. "Want me to go home tonight?" He didn't look at her; and when he glanced up at the quiet, no one was in the room. Then he'd heard her voice calling him softly from the other end of the hallway that bisected the apartment.

He didn't remember getting to the bedroom, still cluttered with unhung clothing and boxes; didn't recall the first touch, the first kissing; only dimly registered the separate sensations of their joining, the quick flashes of desire, the urgency to be one with her. Everything melded into a unity of pleasure he hadn't felt in years . . . perhaps had never felt. It seemed that new, that special.

Remembering now, Steven smiled as he tossed a memorandum into his Out basket. In the middle of the night, Linda had curled against him, whispering: "I never thought it would be so good again. Life," she meant, correcting herself. "Oh, Steven. . . ."

They'd been teasing in the kitchen, Steven playfully manhandling her the next morning while they fixed breakfast, when Jeb appeared suddenly in their midst. A quick sweep of charcoal eyes over his mother's casually draped robe; Steven's bare chest above beltless trousers.

"Jeb!"

Linda's cry came seconds after they were alone again with only the sound of light footsteps running down the bare hall. The apartment had seemed to echo his reproach. "I'll talk to him." Steven held her back with a firm grip on her arm.

"No, he won't let—"

"I want to. Please."

His knock at the boy's door had gone unanswered. Steven rapped again, then pushed it open. Jeb lay in bed, staring at the ceiling, his eyes fixated to hold back tears.

"You're not my Daddy! Why don't you go home?"

Steven crossed the room, his heart hammering. They *had* been careless; after all this time, how could either of them forget Jeb's resentment? But the night, God—

"Jeb, I know I'm not your father. I'm not trying to be."

The boy glared at him.

"You know, my wife and I . . . we never had children. There wasn't enough time for us before she—" He stopped, watching Jeb shift away as he sat down on the edge of the bed. "Well, she died . . . in an accident and—"

"Like my Daddy?"

Steven shook his head. "It was a car accident . . . a long time ago. I still miss her," he said softly, "just as you do your father, Jeb. I don't want to take his place—that wouldn't be right." He saw the boy's gaze soften fractionally, the gray lighten in intensity. "But . . . I've been a lonely man since I lost Ellen; and Jeb, I like your mother very much."

Jeb looked away, frowning. It was such an obviously jealous look that Steven would have smiled—if he hadn't felt a network of relationships hanging in the balance. "It's hard for me to come here, wanting to spend time with her," he continued, "and knowing that you don't want me here. I promise you, Jeb, I won't take your mother away from you. She loves you, but I think she likes me a little, too. I would never do anything to hurt her." When the boy remained silent, he said, "Do you believe me?"

Jeb shrugged, thin shoulders moving under his Superman pajamas. "Maybe, I don't know."

"I'd like for us to be friends, too," Steven offered. "Hey, I'm not such a bad guy once you get to know me." He had ventured a smile, noting for the first time that Jeb was crushing a worn rag doll in one armpit. Nothing much was visible with the embrace except a torn pinafore and a riot of red yarn hair; but Steven would have known her anywhere.

He began to feel like a man holding a handful of aces.

"I see we've got common friends." When Jeb glanced at him, Steven explained, "Raggedy Ann . . . and Regan Reilly."

"You know Regan?"

"I've known her for years. I knew her when she carried that doll everywhere. You just ask her about me, Jeb. I think she'll give me a good recommendation."

Jeb's gray eyes moved slowly over him, warming as they had talked of Regan. "In fact, the first singing job she ever had was with me. I used to run a small club," Steven said, "the kind of place your father might have played in, too, when he began."

Taking the information into consideration, Jeb—who in months hadn't asked Steven a single question—stared at him solemnly. "What's a recommendation?"

Remembering the peacemaking scene now, Steven lifted his eyebrows slightly. It had been a beginning; but they had a long way to go. Perhaps if he took Jeb snowmobiling on the trip, built an ice fortress with him, showed him how to chop wood—

And what was he hoping for himself, with Linda? Frowning at his own uncertainties, Steven couldn't say. But as the hours shortened until they left New York, his anticipation soared.

Whistling as he worked, Steven hastily shoved papers aside on his desk—anything that could wait, must until New Year's. Then he came across the cover for Regan's newest album. The whistle tapered into silence. He wanted to find another category for the picture, but no . . . couldn't wait. Top priority. Yesterday, of course.

With a heavy sigh and a heavier sense of doom, Steven carried his burden into Jake's executive suite. They were both leaving late that afternoon—Jake headed for Europe. With a pang of apprehension, Steven wished fervently that it were tomorrow morning already.

"Need your approval," he muttered, shoving the photo across the wide desk.

Jake glanced at the picture, which Steven had decided would always stay in his memory as one of her best: Regan stood in profile, wearing an elegant hooded monk's robe of rich forest green satin that drank in light, the gentle rounding of her stomach noticeable but graceful. The color she wore matched the luminous green of her eyes in the softly focused shot backlit in warm gold. There was, he thought, a kind of Rembrandt glow to it, and there was no doubt in his mind that the album would attract immediate attention on that basis alone.

But after the most cursory appraisal, and only the time necessary to scrawl his initials in the corner, Jake tossed it back.

"'Madonna,'" he said scornfully of the title, to be printed in raised gold letters against the lighter background. "Whose brainstorm was that? Hers? Yours?" Then not waiting for his confession, added: "When will you learn, Steven? She's no saint—she's a bitch."

Chapter 46

Bitch ... ditch ... switch ... witch, Jake recited silently. He lay propped on cushions that littered the floor of the chalet. Except for a fire crackling in the rough stone hearth, the room was in darkness. Outside, the mountains reared up jagged against a crystalline night sky. All evening long he had been playing ridiculous rhyming games with himself and drinking, but so far the liquor hadn't blunted the pain in his right ankle. Or, for that matter, any other part of him.

"Two days on the slopes," he had complained to Cecily. "One damn fall on a tricky curve, and I'm flat on my back."

"And lucky you didn't break anything," she said. "Now. You have your pillows; your medicine is there by the sofa if you need it, and the brandy you like—clean glasses on the tray. Would you like a book?"

"I'll get it. I can get it." Hobbling, favoring the sprain, cursing. "But do you have to go?" he asked, then smiled. "Why not stay? We'll put more wood on the fire, we could play nymph and satyr all night and—"

"Darling, you tempt me. But I did promise. . . . Don't fall asleep, I'll try not to be late." She kissed him, and she had left, for night skiing with friends who wouldn't miss him.

Why had she gone? Everything seemed to be downhill, like one of the more difficult slopes, even the one that had crippled him for the rest of the trip. Slipping down the hill . . . down to hell. He couldn't seem to stop it. Down . . . frown . . . gown, he was going out of his mind. Gown. . . .

That forest green monk's robe of satin with the hood framing her features. And Regan. Looking beautiful and so pregnant in the picture for the new album Steven had shown him. No matter how fast he had slung the photo back, Jake had seen every last detail.

He sighed heavily, then grunted at the sharp pain thrusting from his ankle up his leg as he eased himself along the cushions to pour more brandy from the decanter on the coffee table.

He was still toying with the snifter when Cecily swept into the chalet on a whirl of fresh snow. The minute she closed the door and shrugged off the Russian sable flight jacket he had given her that morning, Jake knew something was wrong. She wasn't late, but early—far sooner than she had promised. Trying to smile, Jake leaned up on one elbow.

"All the revelers in their cups, Ceci?" They often joked about the debauchery of such celebrations, but she didn't laugh now. "No pagan rituals tonight?"

She flung the fur onto the sofa.

"Shut up."

He couldn't remember her ever saying anything remotely as sharp to him before: if Ceci was angry or offended, she became more articulate, her language precise.

"What have I done?" Because whatever was wrong centered on him. Otherwise, she would have entertained him with witty, acid stories about who had picked a fight at the après-ski party, or which young Nordic instructor had attracted whose wife, or whose husband had been caught cheating with—

Jake's heart began to race. She poked viciously at the last whole log in the fireplace, sending a shower of sparks onto the carpet.

She took a deep breath. "The Daltons were at the party tonight. They arrived from Paris late this afternoon. With fascinating information. It seems," she said, "that while in France they encountered Mr. Bertelli and his . . . shall we say, companion, such a rude woman."

"Alyson?" He could just picture the cocktail party in Paris, and Sue Dalton who loved nothing more than a piece of juicy gossip to chew on, even if—particularly if—it concerned one of her dearest friends. Jake barely heard what Ceci was saying. His own images were far more frightening, sharper. Alyson Oldham, trying to fit into a crowd where she didn't belong, and with two or three drinks under her belt, growing dangerously talkative.

Once the connection to Magnum and *Song of Dixie* had been established, Sue Dalton must have pounced on it. Drawing Alyson away from Bertelli. Asking if she knew Cecily and Jake Marsh. The Daltons would be seeing them Christmas week in Gstaad, she'd have said, and she hoped they were having a wonderful time, because Ceci had seemed unhappy lately. *"He's* quite the moody one," Jake could hear Sue Dalton saying. "Why, the last time we were at their apartment in New York, he hardly said a word all evening." And then Alyson's answer, "Well, if you want to know why. . . ."

Taking advantage of the opportunity.

"I have *never* been so mortified in all my life," Cecily was saying.

"If you wouldn't listen to cheap gossip—"

"And why shouldn't a friend let me know what's been going on under my own nose?" she demanded, her tone rising. "What was she supposed to do? Let me continue making an idiot of myself for how many more months, years . . . ?"

"Ceci, Alyson Oldham is—she's unstable. Don't believe a word she says—"

Her voice sank to a throaty whisper. "Not even about your interesting summer?"

The title of a school composition. Jake struggled to his feet, watching Cecily, whose hand was wrapped around the fireplace poker, her knuckles the color of chalk.

"Not even," she added softly, "about Regan Reilly?"

He lost the power of speech.

"Jake, how could you subject me to such total humiliation? Tonight wasn't bad enough, but that—that party at David Sloan's when you let me make a fool of myself. 'We must have Miss

Reilly's recordings sent to the house, darling.' 'I'm a great fan of yours, Regan'—" She choked on the name.

"Stop," he managed, but she wouldn't.

"Buying her contract from Worldwide; merging with the company in the first place just to get it, I suppose, and *her;* putting up money for that play so she could have the lead and—"

"She *read* for the role, goddamnit!"

". . . though it doesn't appear anyone else had much of a chance."

Jake drew in a deep, steadying breath. "Did she tell you that, too?" He shook his head in disgust. "Of course she did, Alyson and Sue Dalton, one embellishing what the other left out— Well, it so happens that nearly a hundred other actresses auditioned, and while Alyson wanted the part, she isn't much of an actress herself and—"

"Regan Reilly is?"

"Well, no, but she is a professional and—"

"Yes, I'm sure of that."

"Oh Ceci, Christ."

"Whether Miss Oldham can act is not the point, Jake, or whether she had any chance at all for the part—what matters is your ensconcing *her* in *our home*—"

"You hate it, for God's sake, you never go to Lancaster!"

As if that made it right, he and Regan; but he was angry now, on the defensive as well. Cecily ignored the outburst. "Nearly three months that I know of for certain," she went on. "As soon as I left for Rome you went after her, didn't you— or was it before, Jake?"

For a moment he thought she might brain him with the poker, but suddenly he didn't give a damn. In Ceci's crowd, he had quickly learned, everyone played around; it was almost expected. Without broadcasting the particulars, he added— which seemed to be the only rule. Jake and Cecily had never discussed their own roles in this scheme, but he supposed his wife in her travels had done her share of bed-roaming: How could she think he wouldn't eventually turn to someone else?

"If you didn't travel so damned much—"

But she cut him off. "I travel because you're never home, Jake! You're at Magnum day and night; we never—"

"Does it occur to you to wonder *why?* Damnit, I'm thirty-two years old; we're not newlyweds! I'd like a family, Ceci—a feeling of commitment—"

"This doesn't seem exactly the time for that statement, darling." Her voice, deadly soft. Her hand, white around the poker.

"I've made the statements before, and so have you. Ceci, don't blame this on a third party. I want something from you; I want to give in return, but—"

"You've given everything to Magnum." She looked at him gravely. "Or has it been *her,* instead, all along?"

Jake shifted his weight, easing the pain in his ankle. This trip had been his compromise, an attempt to break the circle of disappointment in each other. It sure as hell wasn't working, he thought in angry resignation.

"Why don't you cut the injured wife routine!" he shouted. "That's nothing but damned forced naiveté, for Christ's sake! You file me away in some mental drawer under *h* for husband—that's all right, isn't it—and when you have nowhere else to go and no friends to play with and absolutely nothing left to amuse you, then you command me to meet you at the airport. With the right phrases of welcome. You take me to *your* house, on *your* terms, and throw expensive presents at me. Oh yes, you do, and why? To collect the suitable thank-you's. Well, what the goddamned hell do you expect *me* to do ninety percent of my time? Jerk off to your picture on my *desk?"*

Cecily turned as pale as her tightened knuckles. Then gently, carefully, she replaced the brass poker in its stand. Softly, so softly, she said, "I—I thought you—liked the gifts." And me, he heard. Unspoken.

She walked to the windows. God, he thought. Not now when I've been trying so hard. With difficulty, Jake limped to stand behind her. "Ceci, come on," he said lamely. "You and I—we've led pretty independent lives in this marriage, haven't we? I thought that was what you wanted. I thought as long as we didn't hurt each other—"

"I've never hurt you."

He remembered Charles Peyson's warning. "You mean to tell me that in three years of marriage, flitting around the world with your friends, who are a pretty lively set of people—morally speaking—that you've never hopped in the—"

"No!"

At the one word, so full of grief and desperation, Jake recoiled. It stunned him, if she was telling the truth. And she usually did. When she turned around, her face seemed etched with sorrow, engraved in gray and silver, her eyes colorless: yet asking, pleading. She was not so much the wounded wife, he realized, as the unloved child she had once been. Still was, he knew. Sleek and sophisticated outside, yet plump inside. Cecily would always be the fat little rich girl she had told him about in the beginning—forever ten years old and ludicrous in ruffly dresses with tight puffed sleeves that pinched the flesh on her arms. No matter how many years she stayed thin as a blade of grass, no matter how many semiannual trips she took to expensive retreats to remain so, she would always be fat. And pastel. Buying friends and love. And expecting—why hadn't he seen this as clearly before?—total loyalty, fidelity, devotion for her investment. From him, too. Oh Christ, especially from him.

Her money was to be used, yes; but it also took the place of love.

She looked at him a few seconds more; then, easing past him, crossed the room. He didn't know what to say. He felt sorry for her and for himself, too. He stayed still, watched her pick up the brandy snifter he had left on the table. Looking down into it, then lifting it to her lips, she drained the inch of liquid in it.

"Are you in love with *her?*" she asked then, in a tone that begged for his denial. "Are you, Jake?"

His heart pounded. Why didn't he answer? Why not say *no,* it was only sex, pure and simple and meaningless; why not coax her from this dangerous mood of hurt and humiliation into something lighter. But how? *Try,* he told himself. *Try, damn you.* But he didn't want to be owned by her, either.

"I don't know that for a fact," he said slowly, tentatively. "And neither do you or Alyson Oldham or Bertelli or the Daltons, whoever the hell made your evening and mine such a smashing success—"

He caught, in that instant, at the edge of his peripheral vision, the flash of the brandy snifter. Before Jake even thought to duck, the glass had struck him. The tissue-thin crystal shattered against his left temple. The room spun, wavered between light and dark, then stopped.

"Oh!" Cecily cried. "I'm sorry. Are you all right, Jake?" She looked horrified. "I'm so sorry!"

Blood trickled from the gash and became a stream. Down the side of his face. Soaking his shirt collar. Staining his sleeve.

"I'm sorry, too," he said. Feeling dazed. His breathing came quick and light.

She mopped at the wound with a lacy handkerchief until he took her hand away. "I'll call the doctor," she said. "You'll need stitches." She went into the bedroom. Through a haze of consciousness he heard her on the telephone, her voice low and calm.

Jake walked to the window, to his own reflection in the glass and the image of the shattered snifter in pieces on the rug. He felt increasingly light-headed. He put his hand to his temple, just left of the eyebrow. The glass had missed his eye by half an inch, no more. He pressed the cut. Blood flowed between his fingers and down the back of his hand, the rivulets running, like so many exterior veins, over the face of the brushed gold Chopard wristwatch Ceci had given him earlier. The color of the blood, he noted in detachment, matched the ruby chips marking the hours. Then, slowly and with precision, Jake placed his palm against the windowpane.

Type O, he thought, watch it go . . . draining him, bleaching, exsanguinating his marriage. Coagulating, sticky and darkening, on the cold black glass. "Merry Christmas," he whispered to the empty room.

Chapter 47

Cecily stayed in Gstaad. "I suppose," she said as Jake packed the next morning, "that I haven't been honest with myself over the last few years. But I learned something last night, Jake." She regarded him gravely. "I *am* my father's daughter, aren't I? I've used his patterns of behavior as my own. I don't know how to give without expecting some return. The difference is, *he* expected my silence for gratitude, while I—I keep hoping someone will really care for me . . . despite the money . . . just for myself."

"That isn't anything to be ashamed of," Jake said.

During the doctor's visit the night before, she had been the very model of good breeding. Not one of them had made reference to Jake's curious accident. Taking neat stitches, the Swiss physician—reminding him of Steiner—avoided eye contact with either Jake or Cecily. The domestic squabble, his demeanor stated, was none of *his* affair. After all, what wife hadn't thrown, or been tempted to throw, some object at her husband in the long course of a marriage?

But as soon as the doctor had gone, Cecily had given Jake a long, even look. "You seem rather shocked," she said, indicating the living room sofa. "You'd better lie down." And she had gone into the bedroom, shutting the door.

Now, they spoke in polite and formal sentences, the marriage ended, the fight to be resolved by divorce; but Jake had the feeling that Cecily knew something else she wasn't about to confide, some revelation of Alyson Oldham's so violating to Ceci's emotions that she could never say the words aloud. During the night, when the procaine had worn off and his sprain began to pulse dully in sympathy with the temple sutures near his eye, he had gone to Cecily who lay drawn up in the enormous bed beneath a feather tester, pretending sleep.

"I'm sorry," he had said again. "I wish I could have spared you this evening—all of it," but she wouldn't answer. From the start, their relationship had been backward, Ceci calling the shots—something he had complained about in jest long ago. It occurred to Jake now that this was the first time he had felt completely inclined to let her.

"Is there something you haven't told me," he said, "anything Alyson dredged up that might . . . clear this thing up?"

"It seems clear enough."

"Ceci, what do you want me to do?"

She stiffened at his light touch on her shoulder. Then she said, "What I don't want is for you to touch me, Jake. Ever again." And there was nothing left for him but to fly back to New York on the first available morning flight.

Silent, Jake latched his suitcase. When he turned around to look for his coat, she was staring at him with an expression in her azure eyes he had seen before. In the beginning. An appeal that had reminded him then of Regan, such a look of naked need that it was almost a pleading . . . but he had only let Ceci down, too.

He stepped closer to her, still not touching. "It's a long time," he said, "three years."

"I promised myself late last night—after you'd come to the room—that I wouldn't blame you, Jake. And I don't." The azure eyes searched his face, his guilt. "Did you know," she said, "that when I was graduated from boarding school, my father didn't come to the ceremonies? Did I ever tell you that?"

"No," he said.

"He sent Charlie instead. With a brand-new car for me." She turned aside, picking his gray herringbone coat from the bed, handing it to him. "I don't wonder," she said, "that you wearied of that kind of love, Jake. So did I. . . ."

He felt sadness rise up in his throat as he shrugged the coat on over his suit jacket. It was too late, he thought. If she had let him see the fragility underneath that he always knew was there, the need . . . but she had been too proud, as proud as he was.

He put his collar up against the chill outside, taking his suitcase in a gloved hand as she walked him to the door. The hired car was waiting, the exhaust making plumes of white cloud in the air. He had never felt so bad in his life, except for the night he quarreled with Regan over Alyson Oldham— and the time in the hospital when he had learned about Bertelli. Ceci was standing by the open car door when he straightened, having shoved his bag across the backseat. Her eyes were sorrowful, but her voice was strong.

"Good-bye, Jake," she said with finality, even though they would have to meet again, if only over legalities. He was amazed when she said it for him, what he hadn't been able to put into words himself: "I wish we could have given each other the right things, too."

There were several things he ought to do as soon as he reached New York, Jake decided when his plane was airborne—all of which involved Charles Peyson. The legal proceedings must be instituted, of course, and he'd tell Charlie that repayment would be forthcoming on Ceci's remaining loans to him for Magnum and the house in Lancaster. It wouldn't be easy to raise that much cash, but he'd get it. And all at once, there was an even more satisfying item on the agenda, too. Why hadn't he thought of it before? It seemed so simple, logical, now.

Charlie knew Cecily's strengths, her insecurities, her weaknesses, and the reasons for them. Just as he understood the coldness of her father and what it had done to her. Her friends were Charlie's, too. He enjoyed the beachfront mausoleum on the Island. The backgammon tournaments. And the world-ranging trips. Their world, Jake thought; never his.

No wonder Peyson had been jealous of him from the start. But how many years, he wondered, had Charlie, with his quiet good manners and proper bearing, pretended that his concern for Cecily Ferris sprang only from association with her father or from his own sense of responsibility toward a lonely young woman? How many lonely years of loving her in silence?

Jake leaned back in his seat, closing his eyes. Feeling better than he had in the last twenty-four hours. One telephone call, he thought, and Charlie Peyson would be on the next jet to Switzerland. Despite his own failures, the very rightness of it made Jake smile.

Three days later Regan read the first news of Jake's pending divorce. She was stunned, then relieved that whatever had torn Jake and his wife apart overseas had happened after *she* was out of his life. Irreconcilable differences, the papers said. It would have made her regrets about the summer all the worse to have read otherwise; but there was no mention of scandal— just a single, discreet sentence in a popular column devoted to jet-set doings. *Irreconcilable differences,* Regan repeated grimly, thinking of Jake and her few weeks with him. There was, in those two words, no requirement of marriage.

The grim gray weather of January depressed Steven—getting close to February and his yearly doldrums—and the rehearsal for *Dixie* was going badly, and he had begun to wish he hadn't come to watch. Tomorrow night was dress rehearsal. Sure, he knew any production looked its utter worst just before opening, and this one would be no exception. But it seemed more than that.

Tension hung thick and heavy in the air, as if some of the winter day had come into the theater when Steven opened the door. The cast had moved from the rehearsal hall into the Browning Theater only the day before, and the new location, the different acoustics and space, had thrown everyone's timing off balance in the run-through. But it was more than that, too.

Steven wished he might simply blame the theater or the weather, even hangovers from holiday revelry, but at the end of January's second week, he knew he couldn't.

Trying to refresh his mind by taking his eyes from the scene in rehearsal, he focused on Regan, waiting in the wings for her cue. In slacks and a man-tailored pink shirt, she looked delicate. She was carrying the baby well and had gained little weight. But Steven made a mental note to tell Wardrobe she must wear over her dresses the capes and apronlike coverups that had been made as insurance. And oh yes—

Somebody fluffed another line. Peter Noel interrupted Steven's concentration with a shouted, *"Goddamnit,* start the whole *goddamned* scene over again!

Regan's voice was low but firm in defense of her understudy, who played Marisa's sister. "Peter, she's had the flu. Could we please take a ten-minute break?"

Grumbling his reluctant agreement, Peter slung his script into a vacant seat.

Steven grimaced as Noel passed his row with a curt nod of acknowledgment. Then he got up and walked to the stage, across it, and through the wings to the backstage area. And ruined the rest of his day when he spied Paul Oldham: glowering, irascible, his small, watery blue eyes following Regan as she marched down the hall to her dressing room. Why was he in town again? Bertelli kept him occupied, mostly out of state. Just now, of course, there was no advance work to be done, so perhaps Manny had brought him to New York for whatever chores he might be able to handle during the frantic opening week for *Dixie*. But was he hounding Regan again?

Suddenly, she whirled to continue an argument they had obviously been having before Steven's arrival. *"You are wrong!"* she told Paul, her voice shaking with rage, "and I will not listen to any more of your paranoid notions!"

She slammed the dressing room door shut behind her. Oldham said nothing. He merely turned slightly, redirecting his attention to where David Sloan stood with a man of slighter build, arrestingly attractive. The two men were talking quietly, in murmurs, with intense eye contact.

Oldham nudged Steven, whose glance had automatically followed his. "Take a look for yourself, Houghton. You tell me if I don't know what I'm talking about."

A chill ran through Steven. He hadn't believed the smear stories before. But at that instant, the man, his hair that richest shade of deep, deep red, put a hand on Sloan's forearm, and his face became urgent, pleading as he touched David's cheek.

"David," the voice said plainly, "you have to tell her. I am tired of waiting!"

"Lookit those two, like a couple of—"

"Oldham, go to hell!" Steven rounded, checking the hall. Empty, thank God. No one else except them and the two actors.

Steven walked away, his steps sounding on the bare floorboards. He heard Oldham whining in the background, "You don't believe me, Houghton, or plain sight, you ask Alyson. She knows, and she made sure that Marsh's wi—"

Steven nearly wrenched the door to Regan's dressing room off the hinges, he pushed against it so violently. At his abrupt entrance, Regan jumped.

She was at her makeup mirror. Her eyes were wide and darkest green and pained. Picking up her hairbrush, she began to pull it through the long, honeyed strands. The hair crackled with static electricity.

Steven closed the door, almost softly. She said, "He says the ugliest things. I—I have no idea why."

"And I have no idea what's been going on." He took a chair and, reversing it, straddled the seat, leaning his arms on the back. "Let's begin," Steven said severely, "with your wedding."

"Oh, Steven," Linda murmured.

"Oh, yes," he said bitterly. "I'm sure every last word is true—every lousy, stinking word."

He couldn't sit still. He felt as if he had worn a path in the rug on Linda's living room floor in the twenty minutes he had been there. He couldn't forget Regan's face, either, tear-strained and taut, or her voice, so dull and emotionless in contrast as she recited the details of her marriage to Sloan.

"'He's so kind,' she kept saying. Can you beat that?" Steven demanded.

"Well, he is kind." When he glared at her, Linda gave a small shrug. "I like David. And there is the fact that he's stayed married to her to—to give the baby—"

"A name that, for Christ's sake, doesn't belong to it! Him. Her." Steven ran a hand through his hair.

"There isn't anything to be done, Steven."

He glared at Linda again. So calm and reasonable. Well, he thought angrily, she hadn't been there. "Many homosexuals marry and have families," Regan had argued when he made his first protest.

"They do. And is your child his, then?"

She had looked at his rigid features. Then down at her hands, admitting, "I won't lie to you, Steven," and she had looked up again, despair in her green eyes. "No, but, oh God, I don't want anyone else to know that, either."

"Nothing to be done, is there?" he asked Linda now. Anger boiled in him. "Jake's nearly free. I'll go to him, I swear I will; I'll tell him whose baby this is; he can damn well marry her. He should have long ago!"

"You think he should have." Linda's voice quavered. "But are you so furious now because David disappoints your notion of the perfect husband? Or for a reason all your own?"

Steven stopped wearing out the carpet and stared at her. "What reason?"

"Ellen." She didn't flinch as she said, "Sometimes I—I think you buy her immortality through Regan Reilly." Her eyes, so steady, asked him something, but Steven was too shocked to try to find the answer.

Stunned, he only wanted to lash out.

"And what about Kenny? I waited long enough for you to bury him, didn't I?"

"Steven!"

There were tears sliding down her cheeks, but she kept her gaze upon him. He wanted, truly wanted, to put his arms around her; but the whole damned day was solidly planted, as substantial as the Great Wall of China, between them.

"Please, Steven—don't say anything to Jake! It won't do any good. Didn't you tell me that love shouldn't have conditions to it? *Anybody's* conditions? You can't change people's lives for them, Steven!" She took a shaky breath. "Promise me you won't try. Please," she said. "Regan doesn't *want* him to know about the baby—" Then she broke off, and the tears flowed.

He looked at her even more unhappily. Her tears aside, Linda confused him; she had pushed him just now to some invisible limit he wasn't at all sure he had wanted to reach. *Ellen,* he thought, and then—*Am* I going to grieve for the rest of my life? Am I? And for the first time, he didn't think he could handle such an abysmal future. Though he didn't want to face the present right now, either. What he wanted was to get away—from Linda, and from feeling. From the day itself somehow, if he could. At the moment, tolerance didn't seem a virtue to him.

"I have to be in the office early," Steven said. "I think I'll go home, stay at my place tonight. Not because of you," he added. "It's—it's just me."

Linda didn't speak until he touched the doorknob; then her voice called him back.

"Promise, Steven? You didn't answer."

"Yes," he said harshly, blowing out the word. "I promise."

And felt even worse. Because he had never lied to her before.

Chapter 48

"I want to talk."

Standing in Jake's doorway, Steven decided to use the same gambit he had with Regan the day before, though he doubted this time it would work.

"Sure," came the surprising reply. "Sit down."

Steven remained standing, needing an advantage. He ignored Jake's expression of mild amusement at his uncharacteristic sternness. Steven twisted his wedding band, cleared his throat. "About Regan," he began. He knew what would happen, of course. Every time her name came up—when he dared—there was the same well-practiced shutter-snap of Jake's emotions.

"Some trouble with *Dixie?*" Jake inquired mildly. Steven was thrown off balance twice as badly by the straight response. He had spent most of the night before rehearsing his arguments, selecting and rejecting information. He didn't want to break his word to Linda, but he'd also known when he made the promise that he couldn't keep standing by, not after seeing such unhappiness in Regan's eyes. Linda was wrong; something could be done, had to be done, or he was no friend at all.

"No trouble," he said. "This is personal."

And, late but effective, the shutter finally closed. "Steven, let's keep business in the office and our private lives outside."

"Then talk to Regan yourself."

"We have nothing to talk about."

"You sound like Linda," he said, hearing the rise of anger again in his voice. Jake looked surprised, but not amused this time.

"Well, she's right. Now—is there anything else you wanted?"

Dismissed. But Steven stood firm. "You know something? Neither one of you has the answer. What's the harm in trying? Doesn't it ever occur to you that you might be wrong?"

Jake studied him for a few seconds. Then he said evenly, "No."

It wasn't bad enough that he'd been unable to break through Jake's defense network, or that he felt miserable over the night before and whatever he had said—or hadn't said—to make Linda cry. It wasn't even Regan, or Ellen, or the tangled feelings that intensified his agony and maybe always would. But more, Steven thought, he loved his job. Magnum Multimedia Corporation. Senior Vice-President. The topper was, he had really loved his job.

Within the hour most of his office clutter had been packed into a dozen cardboard cartons strewn over the floor around Steven's desk. The old school trophies were there, and the glass paperweight from Steuben with his name embedded in Gothic script, a present from Regan at Christmas. As he packed, he tried not to see the room around him, because he liked that, too. The earnest brown leather of the couch and chairs, not the curry color of Jake's office, but quieter, more in keeping with his own personality, as were the white draperies and neutral walls. The touches of scarlet had been inspired by Ellen, the pair of needlepoint pillows she had made him for Valentine's Day one year, the shade repeated in small splashes around the room, in the spines of books, a picture frame, the blotter on his desk.

He didn't notice that Jake had appeared in the doorway.

"What in hell are you doing?"

Steven fumbled in the center drawer, sorting paper clips, rubber bands, scrap paper furiously without looking up.

"Leaving? I don't believe this. You can't walk out on an association like ours, after everything we've worked so hard to build—"

"You built. I'm only here," Steven said softly, "to follow orders."

"Oh, Christ, listen—just because I blew my top a few times . . ." He watched a spray of paper clips hit-and-miss one of the boxes. "Jesus, you're in a mood." He was certainly right there. But Steven felt the momentum of years of meekness, years of taking the backseat even when he felt the driver was headed for disaster.

"All right," Jake said with a sigh, "all right, what did she have to say? What's of such concern? Why should I see her?"

Steven shrugged. "If you want to find out, ask Regan. If you don't, don't. I've done my talking. A friendship can absorb a lot of crap and survive, because you allow margins—wide ones—but there's no room left, Jake. You were right. Time I learned to keep my mouth shut."

"Steven, *Jesus*—"

Not trusting speech, Steven shook his head. Then picked up the picture from his desk. "I never saw a photo of her," he managed hoarsely at last, "without this smile. You could always see the humor in her eyes, around her mouth. Remember? Look." He held out the scuffed red-leather frame, worn from years of handling as if he might make her alive again by daily touching. A stupid ritual that never worked; never would. He kept his arm extended until Jake took the picture.

"She was a fine woman," he agreed.

"Hell, yes." Their eyes met. "And you know something else? If *she* were alive today, anywhere in this world, I'd find her, and no matter what we'd done to each other, I'd ask her— no, I'd beg her—to come back." Steven blinked rapidly several times. "I'd beg her, Jake," he continued thickly, "because nothing else counts, not when you reduce life to basics."

Jake set the photograph on the desk top. "I thought you were through talking," he said, though the words appeared to have hit home. "Christ, Steven, *look*—every damned time Regan and I come near each other, it's like putting a fuse to a bomb. Somebody, *something*, strikes the match and everything goes . . . You know, I tried this summer. I thought she was trying, too. But then—" He stopped, shaking his head. Since the breakup with Ceci, he'd been looking tired and drawn; now, Steven saw a pallor that seemed left over from Jake's stay in the hospital. An utter weariness. "You know how I feel right now? I never want to see *her* again, touch her again; I don't want anything more to do with her—" He challenged Steven with a glare. "Did I forget anything?"

Deliberately, Steven put Ellen's picture in a cardboard box, cramming, rearranging the contents until they seemed snug. Why couldn't he cram events, and their interpretation, the same way? By brute force, as Jake tried to? But he wondered if he imagined pain underneath the defiance. Steven carefully sealed the carton with strapping tape, then stacked it on another box. Boxes and boxes, he thought. Pictures and paperweights. Objects: all that remained of the time together, everything they'd shared. The three of them. He looked hard at Jake.

"Yes," he said. "You forgot something." His voice shook. "Tell me you never loved her, Jake. Those nights after she sang, when we'd sit around talking, drinking, eating, when she seemed to shine with life—with *you*—tell me you didn't care!"

"Oh, I cared," Jake said softly. "I loved her."

He looked suddenly transparent, like one of those lucite figures kids got for Christmas, a physiology model—only Steven saw not a vascular system or musculature, but a deep slash through his emotions that Jake didn't seem to recognize for what it was. His gaze was fierce.

"Steven, I'm through being part of your life fantasy. What about Linda? A living, breathing woman, damnit! You think the only way to lose someone forever is through illness or an accident on an icy road? Take a good look sometime, Steven— sometime soon—before you lose Linda to a memory!"

The best defense, Steven thought viciously, is a strong offense. But what did he want from Linda? How did he really feel about her? They were questions he didn't want to examine. "I thought this conversation was about Regan, not me."

"What would you have me do, Steven? Ride onstage tonight on a white stallion to rescue her?" When he spoke again, his voice was taut, thinned by strain. "I tried that once, with Oldham." He paused. "Why now, with Sloan?"

Steven watched him for a moment before he said, "Maybe the pact wasn't such a good idea, Jake. Maybe we *have* to look behind us . . . before we really move ahead."

"From what I've seen, they look domestic as hell together. Yes, I went to rehearsal once, out of dumb curiosity. That's how I learned she was pregnant. So leave it alone, Steven— What good is talking now? What could we find to talk about?" Jake pressed. "Natural childbirth?" There was a catch in his voice. "Her baby?"

Forgive me, Regan, Steven told her silently. And Linda. And Ellen, too. He was guilty of the sin of meddling. Because he couldn't seem to separate his loves; even now, after all this time. Because he heard, he knew he did, the plea in Jake's tone. Looking straight into his drawn expression, Steven spoke very softly.

"Better you," he said, "than Sloan."

The office door closed, and Jake was alone. He stared for a long moment at the packing job Steven had done: the cartons; the top of the desk cleared so that the faint dust outlines showed of bookends and blotter and the in-out basket. Then, walking to the long windows, he stood watching the snow fall, not thinking. Because he couldn't think now; all he could do was feel: a breath-stopping, incapacitating pain.

He felt as if Steven had kicked him in the balls.

CODA

CODA

Chapter 49

"Is it mine?"

Jake closed the door to the dressing room behind him, eyes fixed upon Regan who was seated at the mirror, applying smoky eye shadow. Coming crosstown to Forty-eighth Street and the theater, he had practiced what to say; but the soft radiance of her, the mere sight of her after months wiped out every carefully planned phrase except the one. Blunt, and out of context. One glimpse of her, he thought, on the album cover photograph; another twenty minutes watching her rehearse with Sloan. Nothing more but his mental imagery—and those echoes in the still of night. Apparently, Regan didn't share his confusion.

"Well," she said, "you always did believe in the direct approach."

Avoiding his gaze—she had glanced up for the barest, shocked instant when the door opened—she drew a slender finger across the open pot of cream shadow, then over her eyelid, blending the color. She touched the pewter shadow lightly beneath her lower lashes, intensifying the size and shape of her eyes. He hadn't been quite right. Her hand was trembling as she dipped into a second jar, stroking sage-green above the gray on her lids until the emerald clarity of her irises seemed dazzling.

"David Sloan is my husband," she said, and her voice trembled, too. She seemed to be addressing the mirror instead of him.

"That's no answer," he said. "It's a non sequitur."

"There's usually a connection between marriage and babies, Jake."

"Not necessarily."

She stood, jerked upright by his words like a lovely marionette, and as the graceful folds of her long, full skirt shook free, the length of her stunned him. Jake's eyes strayed to the living cradle of her abdomen, barely obvious in the flowered dress of voile: Empire-waisted, with forest-green ribbon trimming the green-and-straw colored gown, the yellow straw picture hat lying on the dressing table. She wore her hair pulled back with ringlets gathered at the crown and the shimmering length of tawny-gold hanging loose down her back.

A look that was delicate and blossoming and fragile.

"Did you come here to argue?" She bit her lower lip, nervous as always before an opening—even dress rehearsal. Probably queasy, too. He might have smiled—but was that why she had reacted barely at all to his intrusion? Why, after three months of separation and his divorce, she asked him nothing?

Or did she simply want him to leave?

Jake glanced away from her, trying not to see how she had pressed both hands protectively to her stomach, as if he meant to harm her. The dressing room, which he hadn't noticed before, was a far cry from Steven's roadhouse with its makeshift curtain and sagging sofa. Here, in the Browning Theatre, were two Queen Anne side chairs and a small love seat, upholstered in a fabric with off-white ground and darker beige fleur-de-lys for the pattern, a neat slipper chair to match at the dressing table; wall-to-wall carpet the color of café au lait; light beige walls and tasteful art prints framed in gold; a neat, but tiny, bathroom visible through a partly opened door. Bowls of flowers, lavender and white, on the tables. Everything in keeping with the old-fashioned beauty of the theater itself. And he felt suddenly weary, thinking how much time and effort it had taken to get to this room, this night.

"I don't want to argue," Jake said. Steven had gutted him

as thoroughly as someone cleaning a fish. "I'm not going to hurt you," his eyes meeting hers as he stood by the love seat, Regan with her back to the dressing table. "I only want to know if this baby is mine, too—"

"I didn't think for one minute that kid belonged to David—"

Regan gave a hoarse cry. Paul Oldham had stepped into the room without either of them hearing him open the door. How long had he been standing in the hall, listening?

"Paul, I told you yesterday that I won't tolerate your prying!"

"What's so secret you got to whisper in corners? Alyson guessed weeks ago. We figured Regan looked pregnant enough that she must have been caught before rehearsals even started. Living with you all summer, Marsh—it didn't take us long to figure out. When Alyson went to Paris—"

"She just had to tell Sue Dalton," Jake said tautly. The missing part of Ceci's hurt and anger, he realized.

"She only knew the half of it then, didn't she, miss? What about yesterday when—"

Color had flooded Regan's face. "Get out," she said softly at first, then louder. *"Get out now, Paul!* I can't stand the sight of you—accusing, watching, *spying!"*

"That's what *she* said. *Her."* The odd tone of voice made both Regan and Jake stare at Paul Oldham. "Didn't she know I wouldn't hurt her?" He looked squarely at Regan, but his eyes seemed to focus elsewhere. "Lizabeth, I wouldn't harm you."

Regan's face was ashen. "Lizabeth was my mother."

"Allan and me, we was close as brothers until he brought Lizabeth home. She was so pretty, she was *beautiful."*

Instinctively, Regan drew closer to Jake until their bodies almost touched. He could feel her heat, and her fear.

"Long blond hair," Paul went on, remembering, "and green eyes and those thick, dark lashes— She never wore cheap makeup then, she didn't need any, but—"

"Uncle Paul—"

"Let him talk."

Regan began to shiver. Oldham's eyes slipped back farther

into some strange inner focus. "I told Martha how I loved Lizabeth, but then she wouldn't leave Allan like she promised. They had a baby, and Lizabeth wanted them to stay together. Until Allan shot himself, climbing over a fence. Lizabeth never believed it was an accident, though." He looked at Jake and Regan more clearly for a moment.

"Lizabeth went crazy after he died," Paul said. "She started running with other men. I spent as much time as I could with her and the girl; it was almost better than before. Nobody between us . . . but Lizabeth had a real bad feeling about Martha, who wouldn't even talk to her. Said it was Lizabeth's fault that her brother had died—that he was heartbroke because of me and Lizabeth." Paul cleared his throat, looking away. "I tried to watch her, tried so hard . . . but she got herself in trouble." He circled the dressing table, his arms moving agitatedly. "She wanted me then. 'Paul,' she said, 'you got to help me. There's no money, and my little girl. . . .'"

Regan buried her face in Jake's shoulder.

"What happened, Oldham?"

Paul sucked in a breath. "I got some woman for her, like she wanted—only . . . only something went wrong and—oh God, Lizabeth started bleeding real bad—"

"Don't!" Regan cried. "Please don't say any more."

She felt Jake's hand on her back, calming as Paul continued despite her protest. "My fault," he explained, almost gently. "My fault, letting her run free, thinking she'd come to her senses and come back to me. If I'd stayed closer, maybe nothing bad would have happened to her."

His face twisted in anguish.

"What happened to Lizabeth's child?" Jake asked. "She was about three years old then, wasn't she?"

Paul's head nodded. "Sweet thing," he said. "Lizabeth put her to bed that night, told me she sang before she left—"

"'Sleep my child, and peace attend thee. . . .'" Regan whispered a phrase of the old lullaby. "And she wore the blue dress I liked so much, with flowers."

"But she never came home again from that hotel." Paul's voice broke. "Martha didn't want Regan, poor little thing; said she'd have no reminders of that woman; but I promised Lizabeth to care for her child. I said she was the child of Martha's only brother! I told Martha if she didn't raise her, I'd leave *flat,* without a cent for her and Alyson."

"Oh, my God," Regan breathed weakly. "My God. . . ."

Paul glared at Jake, whose blood was pumping thick and heavy. His eyes were suddenly sharp and clear. "I watched her child, loved her better than my own. I kept her clean . . . until *you* came, and ruined her, and made her *filth!* You done it when you took her from my house, and you done it again this summer! I thought once Manny would save her, even Sloan . . . but I know better now. I know whose fault it is she's turned out just like her Ma! *Look at her—*"

Jake had barely time to push Regan aside. Paul lunged so suddenly that Jake was thrown off balance as Paul caught him in the stomach with a balled-up fist. The breath rushed from him, but Jake recovered, shaking his head to clear it as he moved.

He slammed Paul up against the nearest wall. That night in the alley, someone had delivered a nasty uppercut, splitting his skin at the jawline with a heavy ring. Destroying his career with a beating he didn't deserve. Smashing his hands; twisting his insides. And he saw that ring now on Paul Oldham's thick finger, clawing at his own throat, trying to free Jake's grip.

Abruptly, Jake released his hold. "Come on, Oldham! This time, the fight's fair—and I've got nothing to lose."

An expensive kind of satisfaction, he had said. But no more. In the hospital he had made himself a promise. And he was going to keep it now. If he ever found the man responsible for his destruction, he would kill him . . . *kill him.*

Regan barely recognized the street words Jake threw at Paul Oldham like blows, too, as again and again and again his fist smashed into flesh. Jake's anger had won him the advantage. But when she thought the fight had ended, Paul broke free. He landed a solid right to Jake's midsection, doubling him over.

The two men fell, rolled, until it became impossible to tell which of them was grunting, swearing, panting.

Regan couldn't seem to tear her eyes from the scene.

"Did you threaten her?" Jake demanded.

"No, I—"

A fist crashed into jawbone. Paul went down again, pinned to the floor by Jake's weight. Rasping, audible breath. "Did you warn Regan? Not to see me after you and your goons worked me over? Did you tell her to keep away, or you'd get to me again?"

Bright red spurted from Paul's nose. "Yes . . . *Yes!*" He tried to free himself. "But I was only trying to scare her a little!"

Regan was over them before she was aware of her own intention. Her body awkward with the long, impeding gown, the added bulk of pregnancy and her altered center of gravity, she tugged ineffectually at Jake's contracted bicep. She felt the muscle ripple with each movement of his arm, and his skin seemed to burn through the cloth of his shirt, his jacket as he shouted: *"Let go, damnit!"*

But she clawed at his shoulders, crying and terrified of his rage. Later, she would remember that he had called for her to move, but when he threw out his left arm, catching her hard across the chest, Regan was surprisingly unprepared for the blow. The momentum of force sent her halfway across the small room. She fell onto her hip, pain shooting through her, hot and sharp. And still, Jake hammered at Paul with his fists.

"You'll kill him!" she cried. "You can't want to kill him, Jake—"

For one stunned second of horror as Jake stopped, Regan thought Paul Oldham was really dead. Then, as Jake pushed off him and got to his feet, Paul began to moan.

"Lizabeth. . . ."

As if he had forgotten she was there, Jake turned in surprise and saw Regan trying to sit up, her legs and arms weak from shock and the grinding pain that traveled through her body. She had been lying in water and broken pottery, the flowers knocked from the table when she fell.

"Stay where you are, Regan!"

"What the hell's going on in here?"

Manny Bertelli appeared, then members of the cast, heads

and shoulders crowding behind him, the buzz of speculation.

"Get an ambulance," Jake said.

Manny disappeared as Paul struggled to his knees. "Why can't you see how much I love you?"

He lurched to his feet, planting his legs apart to steady himself. Jake's voice warned, "No farther, Oldham!"

But Regan shook her head. "He won't hurt me, Jake."

She could almost feel the night breeze again, blowing gently through her girlhood room, sense his presence beside her bed, the touch of his hand on her skin, gently, longingly. She could hear his voice then, calling as he had called a moment ago. And a shiver ran down her back. The three syllables she hadn't been able to identify that night, as she had never understood his treatment of her.

Growing up, he had told her with a look in his china-blue eyes that was both love and hate. And the look on his face that night in the hall when he had struck her. He had lost the one woman in his life he deeply loved—then saw her face, her eyes, her hair, her smile in that small girl she had left behind. Every day, the reminder growing with the years. Lizabeth's smile; and her rejection.

Glimpsing his twisted longings, his terrible guilt, Regan understood at last why she had been such a constant torment to him. And why he had confused her for so long about herself.

He was close to her, standing above her now, and trying to smile. The swollen lip made it a chilling grin, but Regan was more afraid of Jake's tenseness, which she felt nearby as if it were a separate, physical presence. If he moved—

"Paul," she said softly.

He knelt down beside her, awkwardly. "Lizabeth?" She heard pain in his voice, and his blue eyes were filled with the strange love so long denied. "I'm taking care of you," he said, his voice a rising singsong. "I wont lose you again—I love you. Did any of the others love you, Lizabeth?"

Manny came around the door frame from the hall. "They're here." Two white-coated attendants carried a stretcher into the room. On top lay a canvas straitjacket. The straps were made of heavy leather. Regan shuddered, but until the men knelt beside them, Paul hadn't taken his gaze from Regan. Then he began to struggle.

Held back by Jake's hand at her wrist, Regan felt an awful sympathy as the attendants fought Paul into the jacket. His protests became whimpers, then mewling tears. Wrestled onto the stretcher, he was quickly strapped down; but the milky blue eyes pleaded with her.

Regan took a deep breath, managing to gain her feet. Weakly, she pushed aside Jake's hand and the attendant's advice: "Better sit down, Miss Reilly. When we settle him, we'll take a look at you."

She bent over the stretcher.

"Lizabeth, I love you. . . ."

Regan brushed a strand of reddish hair from his forehead, trying to ignore the flash of pain through her, down low in her stomach when she moved. "Don't be scared now . . . don't be scared," he said as if she were that three-year-old child waking up alone. "You're mine," he said. "Regan . . . you're my baby."

"I know, Paul. It will be all right now." Then he was gone, a wild fright in his eyes replacing the brief acceptance when her hand had touched his face.

"Crazy," Bertelli muttered. "The guy looked like a Halloween pumpkin . . . that funny gleam. Like somebody scooped him out, then put a candle inside, behind his eyes."

Regan said sadly, "Somebody did."

"I'm sorry, baby. I'm sorry." Jake searched her body carefully, tenderly for broken bones. Regan sat in the slipper chair beside her dressing table—as she had been ordered to do after the room was cleared—and tried not to respond to his touch. Or to his endearment for her.

Seeing him in her dressing room tonight, asking the one question she had hoped to avoid, Regan had felt numb at first. How could she answer him truthfully now, when her existence had become focused upon playing out the charade begun with David's help? But hadn't she felt a wild leaping of her heart that Jake had come to find her, and beg forgiveness, to say he loved her?

"Baby, I'm sorry," he whispered again now, and she felt tenderness well in her like tears. She noted the blue swelling on his cheek and the knuckles of his hands scraped raw, oozing blood.

"It was Paul in the alley, Jake, wasn't it?" she asked in order to save herself, for his hands were upon her now, checking for fractures, sending the old, sweet lethargy seeping through every unbroken bone. But nothing could block the sensations— just as nothing ever had before. "You weren't guessing?"

But he only shook his head, continuing his ministrations. Why had he chosen this night to come to her? For weeks, Jake had avoided any involvement with the play. Had Steven gone back on his word to her? She stared at the top of Jake's head— bent over her as his hands kept moving, slowly, gently—at the shine of his dark hair.

"Was it really because of me, Jake?" she asked. "I feel responsible."

"You saw him tonight," he said in a rough, husky tone. "It wasn't your fault. It never was."

Then he glanced up at her, and neither of them seemed able to look away. She wanted to touch his cheek, his mouth, to kiss away the hurt she saw. If she moved toward Jake, would he only push her away? The gentleness had gone from his voice, from the touch of his hands, stilled now as they rested lightly on her shoulders.

Feeling the warmth of her, watching the tender green of her gaze, Jake was seeing Regan's nightmare of abandonment as she must always have dreamed it. Looking at her in the same thoughtful manner as that first afternoon at the Talbot mansion when she had told him, *No one's ever wanted me before.* Whatever she had done since, or was guilty of in his own heart, he hadn't loved her enough to make up for that awful lack in her life.

And for a moment, he remembered Steven saying, *Maybe we have to look back before we can go ahead.*

"Jake . . . ?" she said, the wide green eyes unwavering.

And he wondered if Steven could be right about him? That he had closed his heart to anyone's reasoning but his own.

Jake broke the stare, glancing at the dark beige carpet where a broken white porcelain bowl lay in a puddle of water and flowers, their green stems crushed, the white and amethyst blossoms mangled. Crocuses, he realized. My God, the crocuses of spring. Jake took a deep breath and said brusquely, "I want you to see a doctor."

"I only bruised my shoulder." She leaned over to inspect the discoloration in the mirror, her breast brushing against his arm, not seeing what the movement did to Jake's expression. She only knew that he sounded harsh. "You took a bad fall, and this far along—"

He broke off. Regan wondered if he might ask the same question again and demand a truthful answer, but before he spoke again, someone rapped at the door.

"Miss Reilly?"

Jake didn't wait for her reply. "You don't think you're going onstage after this?" He jerked open the door and spoke in low tones to the stage manager.

Feeling acquiescent, Regan leaned her head against the back of the chair and closed her eyes. Only for a few seconds, she promised herself. She hadn't wanted to tell Jake, but as she rested, a long, cramping pain began to roll once more through her body. She put her hands to her abdomen, pressing down lightly, and waited it out. Think of something else, she told herself. But that something didn't prove soothing, or helpful.

"I don't want you suffering," David had said the night before, broaching another topic, just as painful, "but I do like Geoff enormously. He returns that feeling, Regan, and if we want to meet after rehearsal, share a laugh or two and a few rounds of drinks, I can't see the harm."

"After Paul practically shouted his interpretation of you two together to the entire cast! My God, David, everything we've worked for these last months could be lost in a second if—"

"Perhaps our acting should be confined to the stage," David suggested with an unfamiliar edge to his tone.

"David, Geoff is the kind of man people notice! Please, until we know what will happen with *Dixie*, until the baby comes—" But his friendship with Geoff was far more than that already, Regan guessed. She had never seen David so unreasonable and trapped-looking; but hadn't she foreseen his temptations—and the frustration she had supposed was only hers?

"Well, I've never seen *you* so nearly resembling an ill-tempered shrew!" he had thrown at her. "God, Regan, I'm sorry—but I will keep seeing him, discreetly, and as often as I can, because—oh hell, I have to!" He was striding toward the door. "I had patience with you, didn't I? Kept my mouth shut when I wanted to scream how wrong it was for you to go to *him?* Well, maybe you weren't so wrong after all—and you ought to feel free now to enjoy another dalliance with your sometime lover! Frankly, I think we'd both be getting what we need!" He had stalked from the apartment, leaving Regan with the memory of a dozen surreptitious phone calls over the last few weeks, a small series of late nights when she had waited dinner, to no avail. Geoff, of course. It had been a vicious, wounding quarrel; and the unaccustomed argument was no more stale for the passage of the long night when David had stayed away, and all of today as well.

David had no lines until the end of the second scene. With the delay, there would be plenty of time yet for him to arrive, make up, and dress. But Regan wondered if he would come at all.

At least with the memory she had outlasted the pain. Opening her eyes, she looked up at the sound of the door closing, though it was Jake who walked toward her, not David, and she was jarred back to the present. "The cast physician's been called," Jake said. "Dress rehearsal is canceled." When she began to protest, he pointed a finger at her. "No objections. Put your feet up and rest."

Regan watched him bring a small, ornamental footstool close to the Queen Anne chair and prop her legs, which ached as if she'd been dancing all day. Her entire body seemed to be hurting now, and she didn't say a word when Jake proposed a cold compress for her shoulder. It was like the day he'd first loved her, after Paul's bruising. Perhaps someone should look at her—just to be sure. Not that anything was really wrong, but—oh God, she hurt.

Jake had just started for the bathroom when Regan felt another, sharper stab of agony through her middle. It seemed to split her in two, like a cleaver wielded with great force. Regan cried out involuntarily.

"Ohhhh!"

But before Jake could even turn, the pain withdrew in a hot rush of escaping water—as if, somewhere deep inside her own body, a dam had broken.

Chapter 50

Steven watched Linda put down the telephone receiver, her cheeks unnaturally pale. "Who was that?" he ventured, sensing immediately that something was very wrong, though he wondered if she'd tell him what it was. They had found little to say to each other since the night before—especially since Steven's announcement that he had left Magnum.

"It was Jake," Linda said, frowning. She kept her eyes from his. "There's been some trouble at the theater ... with Paul Oldham," she added flatly. "He's been taken to Bellevue for observation, and—and Regan was slightly injured during some sort of scuffle. A fall, Jake said. Some bruises, but now—she's gone into labor."

Steven's pulse leaped, and he felt the color drain from his face, too. "Holy God," he said, "it's too early!"

"Six months," Linda told him. "The baby has a chance."

"Where is she?"

"Lying-In Hospital. But Jake said not to come over. It looks like a long night."

"What made you think I was going?" Steven's gaze must have seemed to her more plea than challenge, and he couldn't control his tone of voice. "I quit my job, didn't I?"

Then he began to pace, restlessly, from the living room to the bedroom and back again. Running a hand through his sandy brown hair, he realized how much he was going to miss Magnum, this cheerful apartment, and Linda. He hadn't had time to think before. Now, he turned to peer at her.

She was furious, he knew, but wouldn't say so. She wasn't going to reproach him for breaking his promise; not even for leaving Jake. Or missing dress rehearsal, now canceled, apparently. Just as she wouldn't press him for commitment. It was just as well that there had been no talk. They would only have fought again, leaving him more confused by his anger, leaving Linda in tears. *Take a good look*, Jake said. *You think the only way to lose someone is by violent death?*

Closing his eyes in anguish, Steven saw flames rolling from a burning automobile in a snowy field; he saw death and grief and unremitting loss. But then, the image changed into a woman with a silver dress on a night when, for once, he hadn't wanted to say good-bye outside the door. And he saw all the nights since, the shared thoughts that didn't have to find a voice to be understood. Did her eyes say now what he thought they must?

I lost one man. If I have to lose another, I won't make a fool of myself telling him how I feel before he goes.

Today, giving Jake advice he wouldn't accept, Steven had tried to shame him into going after Regan. And by God, hadn't Jake gone to the theater? He was with Regan now at the hospital, Linda had just said so; the message had gotten through somehow. And maybe, just maybe—

Linda interrupted his thoughts. "Steven, why not go?" He heard finality in her voice. "To the hospital . . . or wherever."

He stared back at her—afraid. Twisting, twisting the wedding band on his finger.

But he wasn't married any longer; and the realization hit him like thunder. Going on seven years, Steven thought. Every spring the same, long and bleak—except for the brief spell after Jake had pried him from the roadhouse. Except for Linda. How he had fought to keep from seeing the future with clear eyes again. Even that strange night with Regan, he'd been fighting—they both had—clinging to a past that could never

be again. Shouldn't be. And he felt a swift surge of exhilaration—quite possibly, Steven acknowledged, premature.

"Well, that's where you're wrong," he said.

Jake had reached him, too. Watching the dark eyes, rounded
in expectation, skepticism, he remembered packing his office
and showing Jake the old picture of Ellen. Seven years, and
her brown hair with the out-of-fashion style—as if she were
telling him something, too, with that smile: that Linda was
here, and simply herself, with no reason to equate her to the
past and another woman. If he'd learned one thing from grief,
he'd learned that there was no scale of measurement for loss;
and if he let Linda go—

"We've got a lot to talk about," Steven said.

When she would have moved away, he stopped her.

"If I told you that I've forgotten my wife," he said, taking
Linda firmly by the shoulders, "or that I won't keep her memory the rest of my life, I'd be less than honest. Immortality
isn't a bad notion—"

Linda tried to escape his grasp. "Steven, I had no right to
say that."

"But you're alive," he went on, "and so am I, thank God.
And if I let you go on believing that I care for you in a casual,
temporary way—I haven't felt casual about you since the night
we drove to Lancaster."

"I won't hold you to that." Linda's voice was husky.

"Hold me," he said. "I didn't need Jake today to convince
me, though he did give me hell about you. I only needed your
face last night, saying good-bye. I've been seeing that all day."
He looked deeply into her eyes. "Linda, I don't want to say
good-bye to you."

Her face seemed to compose itself with effort. "You can't
make someone love you."

"Or keep them from it." Undaunted, he tipped her chin up
with a finger. The tears brimmed over and raced down her
cheeks. Looking away, she shook her head, and for a moment
Steven was afraid he had waited too long, was even certain
that he deserved to wallow in his own past forever, to lose this

soft and pliant future. Then courage found him. Or he stumbled over it.

Steven said, "Linda." And when she looked up at him once more, he began carefully to twist the gold band again, slowly easing it from his finger. "I haven't removed this," he said, "since the day I was married"; then he placed it in her hand, which he lifted, pressing the ring against her open palm. "High time I put it away somewhere," he said. "More than time. Do you think you can find a safe place?"

Mutely, she nodded, staring at the still-warm gold circle in her hand, closing her fingers around it. "I'll put it away with mine." And to Steven's dismay, he saw more tears.

"Linda, I love you"; then he had her in his arms, held tightly and without reservation, his mouth on hers—soft, almost willing.

"But Steven, I—I—"

He kissed her again, then a third time, until she relaxed at last, drawing away to smile at him. The demand coming clearly, "Say it again."

When he did, Linda leaned back in his arms, looking pale and shaken from the night before, from this day of separation, but with eyes as bright as morning, as blue as a clear sky. "Once more," she commanded, beginning to sound as if she believed him.

"I love you," Steven murmured obediently. "I love you, I love you, I—"

And she was laughing, wiping at the tears.

Steven's exasperation burst from him. "Is this some sort of female torture? What are you making me wait for?"

"Fair is fair," Linda said, and then, "I love you, Steven. I thought you knew."

For long moments, he knew nothing but the feel of her in his arms, the fresh smell of her hair, the softness of her lips. Then she pulled back again and touched his face, her eyes full of love, brimming with hope. And he knew precisely what she was waiting for next. Steven forced a sigh, trying not to smile.

Resigned, he said gently, "Get your coat," tracing her cheek with a fingertip.

"Where are we going?"

"Exactly where you thought I should go," he said with exaggerated patience. "To the hospital. I have to tell that stubborn jackass I want my job back, don't I, and—"

He saw her slip the ring into the pocket of her skirt. He watched her collect her coat, run a brush through her pert, glossy hair at the mirror above the sofa. He couldn't stop the smile.

"A healthy raise," Steven said, half to himself. "God knows, I do enough at Magnum to have earned one. And besides," he added, "a man has to be able to support his wife. . . ."

"I've got a job, Steven."

He tried again. "A family, then?"

Linda beamed at him.

"But you will accept the offer?" he asked; and she nodded, grinning as she came toward him, buttoning her navy coat. A look, he thought, of pure joy. Steven smacked her on the bottom, smartly. "Get moving, or we'll miss opening night."

"Opening night—?"

With a broad grin of his own, Steven explained. "We're going to see a baby come into this world," feeling as if he'd been reborn himself. At last, at last.

Crossing the terrazzo floor to her bed, Jake saw Regan smile weakly in greeting. The large private room was dimly lit, the blue draperies drawn, her face colorless against the white sheets. He smiled back, or imagined that he did. He hated the hospital smells; that aura of illness and suffering filled him like a bad memory. "I thought you could use some company for a while," he said. Nobody had been able to find Sloan, damn him; but Jake didn't know whether that made him relieved or angry. He still felt shaken from the fight with Oldham, by Regan's outcry and those first pains, the interminable wait for the limousine to be brought around at the Browning, the endless ride to the hospital.

Now Jake took her hand, thinking how small and fragile it seemed now, dry and too cool. His mother's hand. But when the contraction hit, those slight, brittle fingers crushed his, already bruised and twingeing, as she rode the crest of a wave, saying, "Ooooohhhh...." on a long, sighing moan. Finally, it eased and she said lightly, "Hard work, but at least I can eat on the job," faintly lifting one arm. Inserted in a vein at the inner bend of her elbow was a needle attached to a tube leading to a bottle of clear glucose.

Jake tried another smile, only slightly more successful than the last. "Tasty, isn't it?" He wondered how she could be so jaunty; remembered the jars of sugar water pumped into his own body.

Regan looked at him briefly—with sympathy, he thought, as if she remembered too. Then far down the hall someone cried out sharply, and Regan's expression mixed with anxiety, as if the suffering were communicable, like disease.

"Listen," she said urgently, "I'm supposed to breath quickly and lightly through my mouth when I hurt, somehow it takes the edge off. But if I forget, Jake, would you—please—just . . . say something?"

He was a bit startled by the request, far less prepared for this than she, but he nodded; and no sooner had she recorded the gesture than he heard her say, "Oh, no," very softly, could see her rising, rising in crescendo to a peak, holding, then slipping off the edge and down, down again. Silent the whole way except for a groan that was more nearly a sigh. A song, he thought, of pain. Absorbed in the pressure of her hand, he gave the command automatically, as if it were nothing more than a musical direction. "Don't forget to breathe . . . that's good, that's fine."

When she lay back, victorious against the pain, a little smile on her pale lips, Regan looked at him for a long moment with those green eyes fringed in black.

"What?" Jake asked gently.

"Nothing," she answered, then with the smile nearly reaching her eyes: "Or rather, something Linda said once—" And finally, looking away, "I'm glad you're here, Jake. Will you— will you stay with me?"

"Yes. Of course I will."

Until Sloan decides to make an entrance, Jake added to

himself. Then mentally cursed his own sarcasm as Regan drew his hand slowly to her belly, under the sheet, to the taut melon skin that had once been satin. "Feel," she commanded softly. "No more secret places," and his guilt increased, such guilty pleasure at touching her again, touching this life that wasn't his to share.

The navel was distended, nonexistent. Regan held his palm over her as the next contraction hit; the amazing steel rigidity of uterine muscle seemed to leap against his hand. He murmured, "God," feeling his stomach turn, and then, "Easy, Regan," when she groaned, forgetting what he said to her until the wave of agony receded; feeling useless.

After the next one—he stopped using the word *pain*—or was it the one after that, she said, "Oh Jake, I hurt . . . and I'm scared." The green eyes pleaded with him to do something. But what? Feeling his own gut tighten, he lifted a strand of tawny-gold hair and let it sift through his trembling fingers. He smoothed a damp tendril from her forehead. The bed sheets had turned clammy, too, with sweat.

"You're always scared," he reminded her of opening nights, "but you always do a beautiful job."

Regan smiled wanly. "Sometimes you say very nice things."

But then, other times . . .

"I'm scared now in a different way," she admitted. "There's no song and no applause, is there? And I guess I can't walk off the stage."

"You get to hear the applause for the next twenty years," he said. "You get to keep the baby." Whomever it belonged to. "Hospital policy," Jake added. But he hadn't quelled her anxiety, after all.

"Oh God, do you think he's all right? No one says a word. They come in to see how I'm progressing, but nobody tells me a thing, Jake—"

"I'll try to find Thornen." But with the offer, he didn't know whether he wanted to help quite as much as he wanted to escape from suffering. Regan's pain came too close to his own; and to his mother's. Jake stepped into the hall and almost into

Linda's embrace. She was standing near Regan's door with a questioning gaze. "How is she?"

"I don't know," he admitted. Avoiding Steven's eyes, he focused instead on Linda's, which were strangely bright—not only, he thought in a detached observation, from concern. Happy, Jake realized. He wondered what had transpired between Linda and Steven, but only for a second. There was definitely something different, changed, but—

"I'm looking for her doctor," he interrupted his own thought, feeling Regan's unease transfer itself to him. "Why isn't there any exchange of information around here? She's—oh, *Christ*, I don't know—"

"Who's her physician, Jake?" Steven spoke for the first time.

"John Thornen. She's known him for years," he answered, as if to reassure himself of a good outcome based solely on familiarity.

Linda smiled. "I'm sure he's excellent. I wouldn't worry, Jake."

"Who said I was worried? I'm not her husband, or the father of this child." He tried not to glare at Steven. "And that's from Regan, in case you were wondering."

A horde of reporters, the doctor informed Jake, had gathered in the main lobby. Hungry for news. A big feature story in the making. He wanted to know precisely who Jake might be.

"I don't mean to come on like the Spanish Inquisition," he explained, relaxing slightly, "but I need to be extremely careful where my 'celebrity patients' are concerned. Especially Regan," he said. "She's a favorite of mine," looking at Jake all the while as if he were a museum specimen of rare interest. Seeming to note the color of his eyes, then his hair, sensing the quality of his determination.

"Then do something," Jake countered. "She's in a lot of pain."

"Sedation is tricky. The baby's early, and even so, on the small side . . . two- to three-pound range, probably the low end. I'd be amazed much over two. We're talking about a survival rate of roughly forty-five percent."

Jake's mind flashed over another consultation with Steiner, who had not given him figures. Maybe a good thing, Jake thought grimly. Thornen wouldn't put even money on this baby's chances. And his mind lurched at the next thought.

"Regan is tired; she hasn't slowed down during this pregnancy," John continued. "And the fetal heart isn't as strong as I'd like to hear it. She's taken a bad fall, and though I won't blame labor on that alone, every week that baby stays put is to its advantage—and ours. Unfortunately, nature has decided to force an early appearance."

"Can't you stop labor somehow? Drugs, keep her in bed for a few weeks—?" Jake's heart pounded.

"Not at this point, no. Her water's broken, as you know, and Regan is already dilated about halfway. But I would appreciate it if you'd not tell her about the risks involved. We need all the faith we can get tonight." But he would order an injection for her, John said, the dose to be balanced between comfort and safety. Then he briskly dispatched Steven to the main lobby to issue a noncommittal statement to the press.

"If there's anything else," Jake said, "the cost doesn't matter. I'll pay," though Regan and Sloan were hardly paupers. But it seemed to be the only gesture left to make, so he made it.

"Money won't help," Thornen confirmed with a smile. "If the odds are against us, nothing will." He put a hand on Jake's shoulder. "Stay with her. We're still looking for David, but in the meantime you're a strong-looking specimen . . . and she wants you here. Let her squeeze your hands." When he looked intently into his face, Jake still couldn't read the message.

"Doctor—" he began.

But Linda gently dragged him away. "Jake, he knows what he's doing."

She was holding her own—Thornen hadn't said she wasn't, Jake reminded himself when he was back in Regan's room. Young, healthy, enduring a normal process . . . just weary, that was all. Not terminally ill; not, for God's sake, out of time.

Jake repeated these phrases like a litany of reassurance for himself, and when she was lucid, for Regan too—an edited version; but the Demerol-scopolamine cocktail had made her fuzzy, and most of the time she cycled through the pains, sliding up then down a scale played by her body's inner timing. Or rambled through a garden of remembrance in spoken thoughts she would probably regret later.

"Do you ever think," she asked him drowsily, "of the day we met— Oh, it seems so long ago, but it wasn't, really, was it? Do you remember the very first time we ever . . . I mean, at the mansion, at your house?"

He closed his eyes at the memory. Sun glancing off the shining wood floor. The dusty muslin cover. The unyielding bed; Regan's body yielding.

"The best day of my life," she said. He was bending close to hear, close enough to feel the heat of her labor, to see the beads of sweat that filmed her skin. "We were happy, weren't we, Jake? Weren't we mostly happy then?"

"Yes." Like a dying declaration, he thought. Oh Christ, did she have some insane presentiment of death? His mother had. But Regan couldn't. "Yes," he said, "we were very happy." And for a while she seemed comforted enough to rest.

But he was wrong. Only gathering strength, he realized soon—for the contractions came again, closer and harder, harder and closer, until there seemed to be no space or time between them. The force of their assault on her slim body, turning, writhing, oblivious to his consolation, racked him too—just as every fine bone, every bit of cartilage and tendon, protested the incredible pressure of Regan's fingers.

Though he didn't understand why, Jake damned David Sloan for not being there, and he damned John Thornen because there must be something more to do for her, darting in and out of consciousness with her eyes glazed, looking up at him without seeing, her breathing erratic, as labored as the rest of her body. "Help me, Jake—*help me!*" she cried; and then he damned himself because he did not know how.

"Pant," he urged, sweating too. "Come on, baby, you can do it. Don't lose control . . . !" But soon, the helpless cries, the measured breathing through her mouth, his tepid pleas, wouldn't work. Regan twisted under his touch, smoothing her taut abdomen at each contraction, bucked away from his hand.

"Oh God, Jake. It's different now, I—I think I have to"— a primitive growl that sounded more like rage to him than pain escaped her dry lips—"I have to *puuusshhhh!*"

Before he could press the buzzer, John Thornen appeared like the answer to a prayer, and sent Jake from the room. Everything happened in an instant. Standing in the hall, feeling even more helpless, he watched an orderly run the wheeled stretcher through the door, emerge again, rushing Regan away, as Jake had been rolled to surgery once; as his mother had been taken from him forever that long-ago night. His presence, then and now, seemed utterly superfluous. "Jake," she had called. His mother? Regan? But he couldn't go with her— they wouldn't let him. Thornen's steely grip on his forearm, holding back his first, impulsive step. Then he was alone, wandering instead to Regan's empty bed, slumping onto the chair beside it, leaning his elbows on his knees, his head down.

Help me, his mother had pleaded. *Jake, help me to die.*

No, Mommy, no!
Regan's dream began, disturbing, familiar; and yet, not the same. She smelled soap and perfume; but the soap had a harsh aroma, medicinal. She felt the flowered blue dress sweep her cheek as her mother pulled the curtains closed, leaning over. Again she slept, awakened to find the room empty, the lullaby's strains lingering in the chill dawn: "Sleep my child, and peace attend thee, all through the night. . . ."

Cold and frightened in the dream, she roamed the apartment, finding no one; but then, the child became a woman, hunting, seeking, with the same icy fear inside. Until she saw him.

Smiling, his warm brown eyes flecked bronze and gold, Jake took her hand, his fingers comforting and strong as she squeezed them, hard, harder, making her wonder that he didn't draw away in pain. Holding gently to her, lightly, he led her to a room she was certain she knew yet couldn't seem to place.

Like a prop from a movie set, the door stood by itself without

surrounding walls. Inside, a nursery, but not the yellow room
she had furnished for her baby. Not the same room at all. Then
why so familiar? she wondered, unable to form the answer.
Moving away from Jake, Regan seemed to float, to drift in
slow motion, brushing her fingers along the walls, which turned
a soft, grayed blue as she touched them. At the windows, white
curtains appeared when she passed by, their tiebacks a gay
patchwork pattern to match the curtain borders. In one corner
of the room hung a cascading asparagus fern, a froth of green
above the white Jenny Lind crib with its patchwork comforter.

Regan peeked inside and felt a rush of love. Nestled beneath
the blanket was a small baby. Eyes closed, sleeping, its skin
a healthy blush-pink, the infant had dark and silken hair. *Oh
my baby, you're here at last.* She wanted to touch, to pluck
the child from its bed, to hold it close against her breast. But
she was so tired and Jake kept saying her name, his voice
urgent, as fatigued as her own. "Come on," he said. "You can
. . . oh baby, I know you can."

She tried to reach him, but she couldn't. A blue plush carpet
covered the floor, but when she tried to walk, it was like
crossing a stream at spring flood, her limbs impeded as if by
churning waters. *Jake, wait, I'm coming, wait . . .* She bumped
heavily against the antique oak dresser that shared the side wall
with some matching shelves, already filled with toys. On one
shelf, she saw, there was an enormous white stuffed rabbit with
floppy pink ears and a comical expression. But for some reason,
the rabbit made her cry. She felt the hot tears scald her cheeks,
roll down her neck. *I can't. I'm trying, but I can't, Jake. . . .*

He called her again. She could hardly catch his words, his
voice had grown so faint. Fighting back her tears, the sadness
in his tone, Regan turned to the crib again. *Wait, please.* She
would show the baby to him, tell Jake it was theirs; but when
she reached the crib, it was empty, like the room around her,
the rooms in her dream.

She cried out, "Help me, help me!" but Jake was gone too,
and she was alone. The room was no longer a room full of
warmth and color and love, but only a door standing by itself
again; nothing remained except the same feelings of helpless-

ness, the overwhelming loss and abandonment the childhood dream had always left behind. And this time, struggle as she would against the insurmountable sadness, Regan didn't come awake, could not escape in sunlight and consciousness the unbearable, endless pain.

"You are *not* going to die," Jake had answered his mother. Or was he only reassuring himself again, years later, in a different waiting room, another red Naugahyde chair?

Stretching his body out, his head against the chair back, he stared at the flickering television screen across the room. "You may wait in the lounge, Mr. Sloan," the nurse had told him, stripping the damp bedding from Regan's mattress. And feeling numb, he'd obeyed. The waxed floor of the hall had mirrored his image like glass, the lights overhead too bright, spotlights on an abandoned stage. The waiting room was empty, too. He might have wished for company, except for the crowding of his thoughts.

Jake couldn't seem to shake the conviction that money, enough of it, would help. Hadn't he learned that long ago? His mother would have been admitted to one of the private pavilions—similar to this one—given round-the-clock nursing, consults of every sort if he had had the limitless cash to make her well again. Like Bertelli, paying for him.

There must be something....

"You'll be better tomorrow, like all the other times. You'll see." But he had said it later, long after Catherine needed him and he wasn't there. Because of Enid. Because that evening her house had been safe and inviting, full of life....

On the sagging sofa, her hand tucks into his with an electrifying touch of smooth skin, soft, satiny, like a girl's. The night grows older. And the inside tension, slowly mounting toward some strange inevitability, makes him turn at last to Enid's expected-unanticipated kiss: gentle, light, stirring him completely.

Pulling free from the long kiss that leaves him shaking, she gives a small sigh of resignation and, rising from the cushions, takes him by the hand, leading him like a child into the room with its cream and burgundy paper in stripes and undistinguishable pattern. And lies down upon her bed.

There is no preliminary play, not a trace of teasing or adolescent groping in the dark; no talk. There is only grim purpose and desperate affirmation of life—two people, overwhelmed and clinging—and finally, Jake's initiation: a wine-red passion of the blood and senses. The fullness of her breasts in his eager hands, the first hard male thrust of his body burying itself in hers. An hour of respite; sixty minutes or so of pleasure. Until the telephone rings.

"It's Catherine," Enid manages. "They've taken her to the hospital, Jake."

Her hand upon his forearm; her touch, telling him what he doesn't want to know. He shakes it off, jamming himself into jeans, then shirt, his fingers in spasms on the buttons. "You were wrong to make me stay. You were wrong to say she won't get well—"

"This evening we needed each other . . . yes, that way, too. If you blame me, then you will. But I'm going with you."

"No! I don't want you there."

"Catherine's my friend, Jake. I'll drive; you're upset; and I—I have to say—"

"Say it on your own time—tomorrow!"

Her voice ringing in his ears, he runs the three blocks home: her hands still burning his skin, his flesh on fire with the memory of what they've done. He throws open the garage door, revs the old sedan and tears through the quiet streets of night to the hospital where his mother lies betrayed. Betrayed, but still alive.

There was no more to be done, they said when he begged her doctors for *something*, their voices as calm and full of reason as Enid's had been full of tears. Powerful, competent men—and a helpless boy unable to save her, the very reason for his music; his mother, his anchor. She had, literally then, given her life for him. And how did he repay her? He, and Enid?

Sitting that night, all night, beside the bed, holding to the fragile hand, he had been glad she could no longer see him. Crying hard, he was not the man she wanted him to be. Needed him to be. Wrong again, Enid. It was no figure of speech.

In the hospital lounge now, Jake switched off the television's chatter and picked up an old issue of *Time* magazine and checked the clock on the wall a hundred times in ten minutes, the doorway twice as often—a caricature of the expectant father, he told himself. Only, the father Regan claimed for her baby was absent. Why hadn't it occurred to him, then, to tell the nurse *he* was not her husband?

Once, he might have been. The thought tugged at his heart, and Jake felt the gradually weakening grip of her fingers in his tonight, heard her cry, heard her shriek. He saw those green eyes glowing with warmth, then growing dark and jade-opaque with fear. Felt again the endless cascade of tawny silk, the way it sifted through his fingers when they made love; its dampness tonight in labor. Sensed the fierce spirit of her that, yes, if the truth were told, had always frightened him a little; that he prayed for now to see her through. My God, the terrible hard contractions torturing her body . . . *help me*, she had pleaded tonight. *Help me*, she had asked the first day. But in between were all the other days when he had let her down.

Guilty, Jake made the judgment of himself. Guilty on all counts: blind jealousy of Bertelli; believing the worst of Regan when she left the first time, magnifying things the second; not making choices of his own; trying to keep his marriage and Regan too. Above all, failing to consider the depth of her need. He'd treated her no better than Paul Oldham with his threats— canceling the tour and offering money for her commitment to him instead. No wonder she had left him.

Why had he geared his life not to caring, but to the competence and power he had envied once? None of it worked; and Jake felt as if the floor to the vacant lounge had suddenly opened into a dark, yawning void. He wasn't a sixteen-year-old boy without a father now—not poor or unsophisticated. And yet, tonight the man he had become felt every bit as impotent as the boy still within him, raging silently, realizing

that lives—and love—could not be controlled, that life itself
was capricious. Enid *had* been right; his mother's doctors; John
Thornen, too. There was nothing he could do but wait. Like
that other night. And wait some more. And let the warm tears
he was no longer ashamed of slip from him onto the open,
meaningless page of the magazine in his hands.

What if the determinaton that had made Regan a star—and
taken her from him—wasn't enough tonight? What if she—

". . . Jake? Do you hear me?"

Dazed by his thoughts running wild, he glanced up and was
unable to focus his eyes for a moment. Linda was holding out
a cup of coffee to him, Steven standing behind her with a
fading smile.

"She's in Delivery," Jake said, taking the Styrofoam container and tossing the magazine aside. He drank, but tasted
only hot water and cardboard. "She's so tired, Linda." He
couldn't seem to make more words come out, and shrugged,
then swallowed.

Sitting beside him, Linda put her arm around his slumped
shoulders. "That's natural, to be worn out near the end. So
was I, with Jeb. It won't be long. She's through the worst—
really, she is, Jake." But he only looked at her as if she were
lying.

Why had he counted on Regan's strength, wanting to believe
her when she said *I can take care of myself.* Ignored the old
nightmare, and the wide green eyes that asked for his approval,
the soft mouth that told him, *People always forget to come
back for me.* Why did he need her to be that strong, in such
contrast to Ceci? Because, Jake answered himself, he couldn't
bear the other thought: that it was possible to really lose her
. . . as his mother had been lost, without any chances left.

And for the first time, he understood Regan's bargain years
ago with Manny Bertelli: any price—including separation—
to see that he got well. Because of what they'd shared. Christ,
he thought, still shared. Tonight. For he recognized, at last,
in this lonely place of waiting, what was really between them—
and always, always had been.

Jake felt his throat tighten around the words. "There's so much I want to tell her."

"And you will." Linda's voice was firm, her arm around him reassuring. He saw her glance toward Steven, who was standing across the room by the television set, with a private smile. What was he seeing? Jake wondered. He looked closely at Linda, then at Steven with renewed curiosity. They were both vibrating, barely able to contain some secret he didn't share.

At last Steven supplied the answer with a tentative grin.

"We're getting married," he said, as if it were a challenge. Jake noted the bare ring finger of Steven's left hand. "What do you think?"

After a pause, Jake began to smile. He thought about Ellen and the lonely stretch of time without her, and he thought of his argument earlier that day with Steven, the mountain of cardboard boxes around the empty desk. Then Jake said slowly, "I think you'd better unpack that crap in your office." He turned, taking Linda in his arms to kiss her soundly, quickly. "Are you sure you know what you're taking on, pretty lady? This guy's not so easy to—"

"I'm sure." She answered his shaky smile, brilliantly. "Oh Jake, yes—I'm sure!" He held her for a moment, looking over Linda's head at Steven and exchanging silent apologies with their handshakes.

Steven lowered his glance to Linda's bent head, the glossy cap of hair. "If we can make it," he added with a tender smile, "so can you."

"But if she, if they—" In an instant, all his doubts came rushing back, full force. *Make it all right*, he prayed; please don't make it be too late. He seemed always to be too late, to fail Regan as he had failed his mother and Ceci . . . to fail Regan most of all. *Please*, he thought, not caring whose baby this was now: he only cared that they both survived.

"They'll be all right, Jake," he heard Linda murmur against his shirt collar. He tightened his embrace in answer, as if he were holding Regan, too. "Everything will be fine." But the

words were only further prayers that might not work, either.
Still, they were all that could.

Dear God, don't let them die. Dear God, don't let them
die. Dear God, *please*, don't let them die....

Chapter 51

"I'm sorry, we did everything possible."

In green surgical garb, rumpled and blood-spattered, his mask dangling around his neck, John Thornen looked pallid with exhaustion. Compassionate eyes behind the tortoiseshell glasses watched Jake with the same interest as before—and a great deal more sympathy—moving slowly over a dark suit that appeared slept in, though Jake only wished it were true. The night had passed minute by slow minute, without a wink of rest or ease. And now—

"I wish it could have been more," John added, touching Jake's shoulder. No one had mentioned David Sloan for hours, and he hadn't shown up. "I've given her a strong sedative," John said. "They'll be bringing her down to her room, and she'll drop off pretty quickly, but you can stay until she does." He glanced along the hall, still silent at dawn.

Jake leaned his head back against the wall where he was standing and murmured, "Regan knew it was a boy," closing his eyes. They felt gritty from lack of sleep, but he wasn't thinking of rest. Not yet. "She kept saying *him*...."

Regan clutched at the blanket covering the hard mattress of the gurney stretcher that rolled soundlessly along the corridor from the recovery room and into the elevator for a swift plunge down two floors, taking the bottom of her stomach with it. A disorienting swing around several corners, the ceiling turning in dizzying arcs above her, and she was in another room, quiet, dim. There were no more harsh overhead lights, and all the strange noises had disappeared, replaced by the soft murmur of a nurse's voice giving commands to an orderly. When had the odd beeps and buzzes of operating-room equipment, the monitors, stopped? How long had she been in limbo somewhere, awaking with a start, clearheaded, to the white glare of the recovery cubicle? Was everything a dream, like the nightmare? Had she really given birth?

Eased from the stretcher onto the high bed, she heard the criblike rails snap into place. But there seemed to be so little feeling—physical or emotional—as if her mind and body had rejected any further involvement with pain. Nothing in the past hours seemed to have really happened—certainly John's masked face hadn't loomed above her, talking softly to such brutal effect. Enough, enough. . . . no more.

True, though. Everything. *Fight it if you will, but the dream is no longer a dream*. She knew this as Jake walked slowly from the shadows by the window where he had been waiting, and she saw his expression, unsmiling, more like deep night than dawn.

Briefly, gently, as if he were afraid she might break in his arms, he held her, leaning over the bed rail in an awkward stance, then released her almost before they had touched, tucking the sheets about her, parentlike.

"Regan," he whispered, "I'm sorry—I'm so sorry . . . about the baby," his voice shaking. "If I hadn't pushed you—"

"Oh Jake, he was just too small," she said reasonably, a statement of fact which she hoped would be comforting, for he seemed to need comfort more than she did. Strange, that she felt almost nothing now. "It wasn't because I fell. And his lungs, John said—"

But he looked away. "They were taking him to the neonatal unit here, it's a good one, constant monitoring and all the right sorts of intervention . . . but he never made it."

It wasn't Jake's voice she heard, so thick and rasping, was it? As unlikely as the rumpled clothes he wore, like a parody of Dale Lester. Only it *was* Jake standing by her bed; and she didn't want to smile, either.

"Did you see him, Jake?" she asked.

And he nodded. "He looked exactly as you thought he would," he said as their eyes met. "With dark hair, and eyes that would probably have turned brown...."

"Did John tell you that?"

"Yes. But he didn't need to. He kept staring at me before, until I—"

"Oh Jake, I shouldn't have kept him from you," she said softly. Now, when she wanted to give him something, she couldn't. "There just didn't seem to be any other course last summer ... when Cecily came home, and I went back to David. I promised him, and—I'm sorry, Jake."

"Well," he said, "we weren't on the best of terms then."

"Tonight we were. Last night, I mean."

He tried to smile, but she read the whole night in his eyes. And now she was losing track of time, even of the dimensions of the room. She felt as if she were falling, slowly, backward, as she had the first afternoon singing for Jake; only this time the sensation seemed entirely devoid of promise. In drifting snatches of thought she remembered his being there during labor the night before, remembered holding so tightly to him that he must have been in pain.

"Poor Jake," she whispered, "so bruised and sore, you shouldn't have let me wring your hands."

He took a deep, sharp breath as if someone had hit him the way Paul had, and he couldn't get enough air. How powerless he must have felt. She saw all at once that his eyes were wet, the dark lashes shining in the morning light.

"I thought ... you were going to die," he admitted.

And Regan realized that, although she had John Thornen's drug to dull her senses now, Jake had nothing but the long hours, alone and waiting; nothing but the sight of their baby— and his own emotion, scraped as raw as the knuckles of his hands. She would almost have preferred the familiar mask he often wore.

"Do you know how fragile life is?" he said. *"Christ,* I hate that. . . . It sounds corny as hell, but when you're up against it by yourself, it's a giant truth, and brand-new."

"That's how I used to feel," she told him, "when you were so ill, lying in the hospital after Paul—oh God, I can't believe last night happened, that he said—" Paul, almost breaking through the haze.

"Don't think about him now," Jake said.

"I feel sorry for him. It's easy, isn't it?" he said. "So damned easy to make the mistakes . . . but so hard to correct them." And he began to talk, slowly, tentatively, of his fears last night; then of his mother long ago—in a rush, headlong, as if the words had been held back too long—and finally, of Enid.

When he paused, Regan spoke in a voice full of reassurance. "If you were a disappointment to anyone, Jake, if you ever let anyone down, it must have been Enid. Your mother *did* have time to be proud of you—not on one night, or in a single day, but all the days you shared. She must have known, somehow, that you were with her, too, the last night. Just as I felt you here with me. . . ." She reached for his hand. "Did Enid ever get to see your mother?"

"No."

"And you haven't spoken with her since?"

He shook his head. "Well, you ought to," Regan said.

". . . I wouldn't know where to find her."

"Yes, you would." She smiled, a trifle sleepy, feeling dizzy. His voice had begun to sound distant, as he'd been in her dream, as if he were standing by the door or even in the hall; and through the haze of sedative, she felt vaguely afraid again. But Jake was still beside her, his handsome features carved in relief by the silver shaft of dawn piercing the windows off the East River. Still, there was something so changed in his face.

"Maybe this isn't the right time, or the proper place," he began softly. "God knows, we've both had enough . . . but then, perhaps any place is right and any time to tell you what I've kept hidden from myself—from you—for such a long while." He took her face between his hands, his gaze searching hers as he said, "Regan, I love you. I loved you the first day I saw you; I love you now, this minute; and God help me, I'll love you the day I die."

Silk and satin and soft, the words, the utter gentleness in his tone, rushed over her, an old caress she had never thought to have from him again. So much time, so much hurt. And now, these beautiful words she had longed to hear, prayed and waited for, that should have touched her more. Instead, they were as confusing as Paul's treatment of her. Did he really mean them? She felt that he did.

But why, in the space of one second, did the words send such happiness through her, almost through the film over her feelings—and in the next second, terrify her?

Why? Dear God, it was so hard to think....

Regan let her eyes wander, trying to concentrate on the corner of her room, on sharp, geometric shadows and the texture of plaster; but the shapes kept shifting. "Oh, Jake, how can you forget the awful things we've done and said to each other? Don't you see what will happen? Again? Tomorrow or next week or next year when this morning fades away? And you're more yourself again? You'll manipulate me, or try to, even if you give it some higher motive, like *Dixie*."

"No," he said, "I won't."

But she couldn't believe him, no matter how she tried. Maybe the love wasn't enough.

"What about the other people we've harmed, Jake?" she asked. "Cecily must have learned about us—"

"Only because Alyson made sure of that through a third party. We didn't split up, Regan, because of last summer. It would have come at some point, without any provocation." A pause. "So that leaves David, doesn't it?"

Regan didn't answer. She couldn't seem to find the words. "Jake, please . . . I can't."

"Don't you care about *me*, is that it? Jesus, I'm trying to talk about the rest of our *lives*—"

His shoulders slumped, and he walked away, to the window, bracing one arm against the frame. "Oh Christ, I'm sorry." He stared at the water below and the small islands in the river, clumps of land that had once been barren, but were now built up, busy and expensive residential enclaves. Regan could hear his breathing. "It's the dope talking," he pronounced at last, as if to himself. As if that made perfect sense, and nothing else would. "I'm sorry to push you. We'll wait until you're stronger, then we'll talk." He turned around, his face pale. "You're feeling spacey, aren't you? I don't feel so hot myself. It's the drug now, isn't it, baby?"

But she said, "Only partly."

Because she couldn't lie to him. The changes must be temporary; he was, in his own way, as drugged as she. By too much emotion. Pushing her now, yes, but later, the force of Jake's will would be stronger, not weaker. As strong as the hard pains of her labor. With the same sort of ending, just as Linda said. Oh God, how could she send him away? But how could she not? The next time, the feelings would destroy her, Jake would destroy her, and she couldn't let that happen, she couldn't believe him—

"Don't you trust me, Regan?" Jake said softly.

He had come back to her, his face completely serious; but she focused on him with difficulty. The world was beginning to drift away, in slow circles that increasingly demanded her attention, turned inward even more than in the months of pregnancy just past. Still, she tried to stay. She felt loss and the sense of abandonment briefly penetrate the sedative haze that was enveloping her.

"Can't you trust me?" Jake repeated.

And she knew the answer, making her voice tremble.

"Neither of us."

For if there had always been love, there had never been trust between them, and without it—temporary, don't you see, Jake?—I can never belong . . . anywhere.

Then, dimly, she heard another voice.

"Is she asleep?"

Recognizing his footsteps, too, Regan wondered when the door had opened—and why so long for him to come, to save her; to offer, yes, another kind of love?

"Almost." Jake then, the one word hard and tight. "I'd better go," he said, though she didn't feel that he had moved yet from her bed. Regan's eyes opened, then closed again. Heavy, so very heavy. "I—I'll leave her in your care, Sloan," and an added murmur, "I'm sorry about... your son."

Still, she sensed the warmth of his body near her, the tautness of him, as if he would touch her but held himself back. And Regan, fighting oblivion, had one last, flickering glimpse of those serious brown eyes from which the flecks of gold and bronze had disappeared forever, their color dark enough to nearly match the pupils, shut down not against the morning light, but like the lens of a camera. As if—she went sliding into sleep with the thought—Jake were photographing memories to last a lifetime.

Chapter 52

Electronic flash units washed the entry hall of the mansion with pulsing white light—a photographic tide that ebbed and flowed with the waves of shouted demands from reporters.

"Please," Regan tried again to move away, "I'm here to attend the wedding reception of close friends, not—"

"One question, Miss Reilly!"

"Regan, just one . . . please!"

"How about it, superstar?"

And then, she had to smile—even though she didn't feel that happy herself today. She glanced with resignation toward the Great Hall of Manorwood where Linda and Steven were greeting guests, accepting congratulations and best wishes before a cheerily blazing fire in the huge sandstone hearth.

It had been a lovely wedding, the small, nondenominational chapel in Lancaster providing the perfect setting: a bit of quaint New England with its white clapboard siding and dark blue shutters, the simple altar inside banked with daffodils and crocuses and first tulips, a riot of spring color. Linda, fragile and breathtaking, had been a Dresden figurine of a bride, wearing Regan's own gown. Linda's first design.

"It's even more the height of fashion than when I wore it," Regan had told her, making the offer. "Thanks to your influence—I won't wear it again. Take it, Linda, please."

A gown from Regan; an elegant reception from Jake. She had already glimpsed, on her way in—before the press found her—the towering wedding cake decorated with doves and confectionery flowers in the dining room. There was to be dancing in the ballroom as well, the orchestra just now warming up—that delightful cacophony she knew so intimately. The reception, Regan thought, put her own wedding to shame—but for a greater difference than the size of this party. Loving each other, for all the right reasons, the bride and groom were happy.

Which made Regan think not only of Linda's radiant smile and Steven's constant grin today, but of David and last night after *Dixie*'s opening. Barely seeing the nod of Steven's head toward her in greeting, she turned her attention from the couple back to the reporters clustered around her in a semicircle. She supposed they would ask about David. Might as well get it over with, she thought.

"Yes, all right," Regan agreed, trying to smile. "One question." Then was taken by surprise, not at all what she expected.

"Has your doctor given you a clean bill of health, Miss Reilly? You look sensational!"

"Yes. He has," she said. Then glancing at her gown, "And thank you."

One month after the loss of her baby, she felt physically normal. Released from the hospital, Regan had gone home with David, the very model of the contrite, errant husband. Apologizing for the night of dress rehearsal when they'd quarreled, he had then hovered around her for days, waiting on Regan, fretting.

"You have to eat more," he would say. "John's order, too, or you'll waste away to a shadow."

"Not true." There were slight, but becoming, hollows in her cheeks. Her features seemed, if anything, more refined now. Her figure looked fuller, rounder, more womanly; her stomach flat again.

But the pale yellow nursery stood empty. David had stored its furnishings before she left the hospital. He said he thought seeing the readied room would be too painful for her. But it was more a curse. And anyway, it was the wrong room. But still, she couldn't cry.

As if sleep might compensate for the lack of feeling, Regan tried to rest. She read a score of books and took long baths in her favorite salts, soaping her body with the same luscious violet fragrance of Roger & Gallet, soaking until she nearly fell asleep again. Each day she tested her returning strength on long walks; and after ten days at home in such subdued mourning, had announced to David that, "I feel ready to cope with Peter. Will you tell him I'll be back to work tomorrow?"

She didn't want the production to lose money on her account, to keep paying theater rent and salaries; and what useful purpose could there be in sitting in the apartment when there was still—thank God—work to be done?

At the Browning, Peter had seemed in rare form, even for Peter—hammering endlessly at the cast. Few people escaped his bludgeoning that first day, except for Regan with whom he seemed to be exercising special caution; and yet, at his one criticism, as if it were a driven nail in her heart, Regan had run from the stage. Outside. To lean her forehead against the sooty brick wall of the theater, the smell of rotting garbage in the narrow alley filling her senses. *My God, my God....*

She was suddenly shaking, shaken with feeling and reaction, and she almost didn't hear him, as she hadn't heard the door close again.

"Do you want me to speak to Peter? I will, if you like."

Then she felt his strong hands on her shoulders, his hands turning her slowly, firmly, gently into his arms. His voice quiet and full. Not David's voice, not David's hands holding her close, one finger wiping the dirt from her forehead. "Oh dear God, Jake...." Regan buried her face against his sweater, needing strength. "It isn't Peter," she began, but then the tears came, nothing else. Days and weeks when she couldn't cry, and now she couldn't stop. "The baby," she whispered, "...the baby...dear God, *why?*"

She felt him swallow, but he never said a word. He held her until she had cried herself out, then cleaned her face with his handkerchief and smoothed her tousled hair, looking for a moment into her swollen eyes—surely there hadn't been any color to them, no green left against the black—before he took her inside. He had called rehearsal for the day, and sent her home with David. And in all the days since, until this very moment, Jake hadn't said a thing about that afternoon when she had cried for their baby, for Paul, for herself... and for them, too. Which unaccountably troubled her.

Regan tried not to notice that Jake's new behavior toward her—whether temporary or not—seemed harder to take than any of his previous attitudes. Never anything but gentle and solicitous and nearly formal, he would ask, "How are you feeling today?" his hand touching her arm so briefly she was never sure he actually had.

"Fine, thanks, Jake." Waiting for more.

"Well, don't overdo. You look a trifle pale"; then he would walk away, a distracted half-smile on his face. That mask of politeness like a wall between them, he had overseen every rehearsal before the play opened, while Regan could still feel his arms holding her close in the alley, her tears soaking his chest.

Last night in the wings she had wanted to cry again from anxiety, not grief; but instead of Jake beside her—as he had been at Steven's, and the first night at Manny's—it was David who clutched her hand, trying to smile, as nervous as she. Jake, reassuring Peter Noel in a quiet corner, not her. And why should he not maintain his distance when that was what she wanted? Why should her opening nights matter to him now?

"Regan! Were you pleased with your performance last night?"

Another reporter had stepped forward, thrusting a microphone in her face as the cameras took their shots. More flashing light.

"Very much so." How could she not be? Opening night, only four weeks late at that, had been everything anyone could have hoped for. Far beyond her own expectations.

After the final curtain calls, Regan had been mobbed by well-wishers. She reeled from excitement and applause. David kissed her in triumph, circling her in his arms just offstage while Regan recalled another night and a victory that did not require so much staging, but only a slow, joyous waltz around a tiny dressing room and the silky feel of fabric sliding the length of Jake's body. His arms, his mouth, his kiss of surrender—but their war, she kept reminding herself, had ended.

Regan stopped in David's embrace as Peter Noel walked over to them, stood and stared at her so that she wasn't even aware of David's leaving them alone. It was the first time Regan had ever seen Peter at a loss for words, and it made her ask, "What did I do wrong tonight?"

"Not a damn thing."

And suddenly, she was grinning. "You mean, I'm perfect now?"

"As close as anyone ever gets," he said.

"Thank you, Peter." She slipped into his arms. "For *Dixie* tonight, and for all the years." How slight and frail he felt; but she knew better. "It's been a long trip, but you've made the traveling"—she couldn't call it easy—"worthwhile." Regan smiled through her tears. "Will you keep holding to me with one hand, and cracking the whip with the other?"

"How could I not? My mother's your greatest fan—except, I suppose, for little Jeb." His smile wasn't quite firm; but then, she hadn't expected tears, either.

How she had resented him once for not being Jake; but as she watched his dark eyes last night, slowly searching her face, she had known that, for Peter, dislike had never entered the picture. Not at the height of his shouting and criticism. "Regan, I want to say—"

But she saved him embarrassment, planting a quick, light kiss on his mouth and tightening her arms around his slim waist. "No need," she murmured. *I love you, too.*

The moment had to break, and it did. She saw Peter look beyond her, an easy smile on his lips that she had never seen before.

"Here comes my replacement."

And she turned, feeling awkward and shaky in an instant, to Jake's grin. "Miss Reilly, what can I say?"

Her heart beat painfully. "You might try 'I told you so.'"

"Not before the papers come out."

"You don't believe the reviews, remember?"

Why did she need him to remember; to make the evening right? Her pulse had kept pounding in heavy strokes, waiting for his answer.

"No," he said softly, "but you do."

The reviews had been flawless.

"... 'Miss Reilly delights the senses ... dancing, singing, and—amazing plus—acting! A four-star performance from a four-star performer. ...'"

The reviews should have made her ecstatic; but they didn't. At the cast party, where everyone but Regan had seemed quite drunk, she dutifully read the newspapers and learned from their early editions that *Dixie* was officially a smash.

"I told you so."

The print blurred in front of her eyes as Regan's glance swept upward to find Jake with a girl from the chorus; Jake bending down for an instant as they passed the sofa where Regan was sitting; Jake carrying both their drinks and stopping so briefly that he appeared not to break his stride. Jake, whispering, "I told you so," then moving on before Regan could answer.

You've never failed before. You always do a beautiful job. Regan sat by herself, surrounded by party noise, wrapped in a cocoon of numbness. He had told her so many things. And she had believed so few of them.

"What did you think of your reviews, Miss Reilly?" came the question now.

Regan smiled cautiously. "I think the critics should always be taken with the proverbial grain of salt." And there was sprinkled laughter which she felt obliged to join.

Then from the rear of the group, yet another reporter raised his voice: *"Will you stay for the run of the play, songbird?"*

Regan knew him to be brash to the point of rudeness, and she knew, with a suddenly pounding pulse, what was coming next. "After the breakup with David—won't it be difficult, co-starring?"

"Our separation does not affect the play." Regan's hands were cold, and she clasped them together.

But the memory of late last night made her sad again. He had waited until they got home to tell her, waited through the weeks of rehearsal and her unhappiness about the baby. Until she had all but forgotten Geoff.

"We're going to live together," David said. He had been turned away from her, she remembered, fixing himself a brandy, though he didn't need another; but she supposed it made him braver, and she envied him his courage. "I think we've taken our own drama, you and I, to its logical conclusion. With *Dixie* under way, the last of our . . . reasons for staying with each other is gone. Proper exit, wouldn't you say, dear girl?" He had turned back to see her face, his own blue eyes full of sadness. "This isn't easy for me, either, you understand . . . but I—I want to do this more than I've ever wanted anything else in my life."

Not knowing what to say, she asked about their contracts.

"No need for our divorce to interfere. I hope we can agree to keep on as Marisa and Jared."

"Yes," she said. "All right, David."

"You see," he went on, "all my life I've been looking over my shoulder, expecting to find my father behind . . . chasing me, if you will, because—because I wouldn't play football for him or . . . or flex my muscles in any of the usual ways. Even the movies I made at first, Regan, were macho attempts to get his favor. And how absurd I felt doing them, too . . . but Geoff has helped me to see how wrong I was, living my life for someone else. Can you understand, that I want to be as honest with myself as I can be, to accept myself—"

"What about your other films? The . . . romantic comedies? And even *Dixie?* What if people know about—about your life and stop buying tickets because of it, David?"

"I'd be unhappy about that," he confessed with a slight smile. "But maybe we can't have everything. We won't— Geoff and I, that is—make a show of our relationship. We'll live rather quietly, use his place in the City when I'm working.

And if the public learns that"—he took a breath—"that I'm a homosexual, then, well, either the world takes me as I am, dear girl . . . and my father, too . . . or everyone in it, and he as well, can simply go to blazes!"

"Oh, David—"

He had made her laugh again, but then he sobered and set his brandy snifter aside, untouched. When he took her face in his hands, she didn't pull away, but watched him with luminous gem-green eyes.

"You see what I'm saying, don't you?" he asked gravely. "We've been all right together, haven't we? But it's time now, my delicious, my lovely little *canneloni,*" with absolutely no smile on his lips, in his tone, "for us both to be happy."

Regan wouldn't smile, either. She wondered what she was going to do without him. David, she thought. And Geoff. Regan Reilly . . . and no one.

She turned from under his hands and walked to the sofa, needlessly plumping the yellow and green cushions into place.

"Funny," she said, feeling the tears gather in a lump at the base of her throat. "It was always I who thought about divorce. Now, I don't know what to do with it."

She thought about London, the first days after they had met, the sightseeing junkets, the dinners, the hand-holding and laughter. She remembered Greece, and bitter disappointment before the Grammys, and how, after a stretch of time, she and David had become friends again. But now—

Regan felt David's hands at her shoulders, slowly turning her around. "Of course you know what to do," he said. "You won't need me for that, Regan." He smiled at her, but his eyes were serious. "You never listened to me, anyway, where he was concerned." His fingers tightened on her shoulders. "That morning . . . when you had the baby and I wasn't there with you . . . but *he* was . . . Regan, I've never seen such a look of pain on anyone's face—"

"David, it's over! Please *don't*—"

She couldn't believe the pain that flashed through her own body then, through her heart.

"Is it?" he asked.

"Yes!"

His hands dropped away from her, and he shook his head. "I think not," he said. "Dear girl, I think not."

But he wouldn't pursue the argument. It was up to her, his posture told her as he walked toward the bedroom. It had been a long night, he said, and he needed sleep. Regan stood in the center of the living room, digging her stockinged toes into the plush, creamy yellow carpet that she loved for its perfect color of freshly churned butter, and she wanted to stop him, stop what was happening to them at last.

"David—"

She had flown across the room then, halting him, throwing her arms around his neck, clinging until he pried her away as Jake had done the morning before Ceci came home from Europe.

"David, *please!*"

His warm hands, as warm as Jake's, on her face again, and then he was bending to her, brushing her mouth a last time with his lips, lightly lingering. "I want you to understand," he said.

"I do. I do, David...."

"That I love you—in my way?"

"Yes," she whispered.

"And that I'm there if you should need me?"

"In the middle of the night?" she asked. She remembered that the tears had begun to fall then, like a fine spring rain.

"Especially in the middle of the night," he said. "Does that apply to me, as well?"

"Oh, yes . . . I love you, David."

He pretended not to see her hands, smearing the wetness on her cheeks, and chose to smile at her instead. David's grin, so boyish and even; his blue eyes smiling, too. "Then I shall feel free to call you any time, day or night," he said. "And to take you regularly out to dinner, my still-delectable *fettucini*."

The remembrance of last night in its entirety made Regan smile now, until the same reporter glanced up from his notes, and she realized that she was standing in the marble-floored foyer of Jake's house, at Steven's wedding. Alone again ... alone with the constant stream of questions, the companion to her success.

With a mocking smile, the journalist looked beyond her as he spoke. "You and Jake Marsh ... *Dixie*'s producer, were close—very close—when he was a touring concert pianist several years ago." To Regan's murmured, "Yes," he went on: "With the play a hit, and David Sloan out of your private life—how do chances strike you for another ... alliance?"

A few intakes of breath in surprise, a stifled laugh or two. Another alliance, Regan thought. No chance. None. Her heart tripped out of rhythm as she heard Jake answer for her, his voice smooth and even and icy. How long had he been standing there?

"This is a social occasion, not a press conference. And this is also my home, which I invite you to enjoy, so if you please ... Mr. and Mrs. Houghton have just opened the dancing in the ballroom. Food and champagne in the dining room; the bar's in the library—"

A number of flashes went off, blinding Regan.

"No more pictures," Jake said. His first suggestion had been graciously given, considering the cool tone; but none of the uninvited press could fail to see the intention behind his smile. Either they put notebooks and cameras away—or the guards in neat black suits, mingling like Secret Service agents with the guests, would invite them, less gently, to leave. When Regan turned slightly, she found Jake's smile fading. Then his brown eyes sought her green gaze as he held out his hand. "As an example, Miss Reilly, shall we join the dancing?"

Music filled the huge ballroom with beauty and movement and the vibrant splash of gowns. Jake led Regan into a waltz. He held her loosely, bodies apart and hands barely clasped, as proper as a waltz could be, and she couldn't think of a thing to say.

Regan glanced around the room. She saw Manny, and Alyson in a soft yellow spring suit piped in white, her hair newly styled and much more classic. Why, he's good for her, she thought. And there was Linda, in Sam's arms, both of them laughing at some nonsense.

"Having a good time, aren't they?" Jake had followed her gaze.

"Sam's brought a stunning black model today, *Harper*'s newest sensation from Haiti, which of all the miracles I could imagine seems the most amazing. . . ." Then there was nothing else, and Regan was left with the violin music, the swish of dresses passing by, and her own thoughts of Linda.

"Well. what else could I do?" Regan had asked.

"Anything in this world but send him away— *Regan, how could you?"*

She had been paid a cheer-up visit one morning at the apartment nearly a week after her release from the hospital, while David was at rehearsal, and this was how she had been rewarded for hospitality.

"Oh, I know, you think I'm pounding you again—"

"Linda, my God— Wasn't it you who said that the endings were too hard, and—"

"I also thought you should have told him about . . . the baby."

A silence. Linda, stirring the cold coffee in her flowered, bone-china cup, and Regan, picking at imaginary lint on her pearl-gray wool pants. "Regan, I'm sorry," she heard after a moment. "I never meant to give you glib advice . . . but I didn't mean for you to take my experience for your own, either. So I think . . . I want you to know something I've never told anyone else."

Regan glanced up to a pair of tear-bright brown eyes. "Kenny didn't die in that hotel room in Chicago of an overdose," Linda said softly. "Not accidental, anyway. He wanted . . . to kill himself, and he did."

"Oh God, no—"

"I don't need a pathologist's report, I could see it in his eyes when he left home the last time. Regan, the minute I saw Kenny, I loved him! It does happen, doesn't it? But he was basically self-destructive, too. I couldn't have helped him; you couldn't have helped him. It took me a long while to understand that. He could never be happy, don't you see? It wasn't in him to be happy."

"He sometimes gave a good impression," Regan managed.

"Oh, yes! Wasn't he big and solid, with the jokes and the laughing? But, Regan, he wasn't solid inside—the way Jake is." The tears had streamed down Linda's face. Regan had been speechless. "Why do you want it to be finished?" Linda asked. "So you can spend the rest of your life being *miserable*? Like *Kenny?*" She grasped Regan's arm as if she wanted to shake her. "You're not like him, darling! You had a bad beginning too, but you've gotten through—and you always will! Because there are so many people who love you, Regan, don't you know that—?"

"Jake, you mean?" She had felt as if she were strangling again, in the middle of a concert that wasn't going right. "But only sometimes, Linda," Regan insisted, feeling the wrenching pain in her heart again. She looked away from her friend's tearful face. "Only sometimes."

"You've been like that for him, too. Yes, darling, you have. But love is like a deep, still pool of water, and you just have to jump in with both feet, break the surface, and then"—she forced a smile—"then hope you can swim. As I'm doing now with Steven. I'm scared; but it's like climbing a mountain because it's there," she said. "Because you have to."

"I can't," Regan had murmured. "I don't know why, but I can't."

Now, she saw Linda glance their way and smile, but Regan wouldn't answer. *We'll be better off, he and I,* she repeated to herself as she had done most of last night. *Both of us.* But still, she couldn't forget Linda's last words, or the quiet resignation in her tone, echoing David's.

"What are you more afraid of, darling?" Linda asked. "That he'll leave you in the end . . . or that he'll really love you in the first place?"

But Linda didn't understand. Regan remembered that look in his eyes, the one David talked about, and she knew how final it had been.

Look how he held her now, as if he didn't want to touch.

Listen to the silence between them. Look how everyone else is staring.

Everywhere they danced, people watched. Stopped their own stiffer versions of the old-fashioned patterns of the waltz to follow Jake and Regan with admiring glances. Regan's Grecian-style dress, made of white chiffon shot with gold, caught the sun pouring through the long windows of the ballroom and sent golden splinters of light about the room, overshadowing the candle glow in the amethyst-and-crystal sconces, the giant chandelier. She wore golden bracelets and little heeled sandals strapped in slivers of white; and her tawny-gold hair swung to her hips like a broad ribbon of creamy satin.

Jake wore a navy vested pinstripe suit with a pale blue shirt and a navy tie bearing a subtle monogram in slightly different blue upon the silk. His hair gleamed softly, and his smile shone—but his eyes stayed neutral, darker than they ought to be.

More and more people had ceased moving, until now only Regan and Jake remained, she in the hard warmth of his embrace, gliding and circling around the highly polished glisten of parquet floor, past the gilt-edged chairs along the wall with their gold velvet cushions, past the watching smiles. Dancing together as if they always had. Except that the only other time she could remember was at Steven's... another time, another dance, another Jake.

The dance, he thought, like the play itself, would go on and on and on for a thousand years. A millennium. Until the last shreds of his soul had been torn away. That bastard reporter, linking them together. And Regan in his arms now, looking like a goddess. Or a classical statue. Acting like one. Didn't she know? He would not approach her, hold her, touch her without invitation or social excuse. An excuse he regretted using now, when he had said all he had to say.

Why in hell was everyone watching them? Why didn't he stop dancing and release Regan from his embrace? Why wouldn't the music end? Why couldn't he simply let her go—as she wished him to?

"Thank you for rescuing me," she said suddenly. "I'm afraid the press will have a fine time with David and me." She looked up at him with liquid green eyes. *Please,* they seemed to be saying, *don't tell me that you're sorry.*

Throwing him a bone, Jake thought. If she had changed her mind, if she wanted him, wouldn't she say so now? But there was only silence, and she seemed to be concentrating mostly on following his lead as they danced.

"We're quite a pair, aren't we?" he asked. "Ceci and Charles Peyson will be married as soon as our papers are finalized. On board someone's yacht, I think, in the Mediterranean."

She gave him a quick smile that failed. Then she missed a step, but the break in timing became a graceful turn in his supporting arms.

"I never realized you were such a good dancer," Regan said, covering her immediate embarrassment at the compliment she'd given by adding, "Oh, Jake, doesn't the house look magnificent today?" her green eyes taking in the swirl of golden light, the flash of color, with the measured strains of Strauss. "It really is a place for tremendous parties, fancy-dress balls, *weddings*—don't you think?"

"Yes," he said, looking away from the brilliance of her eyes. "Yes, I suppose it was," then couldn't bear the quiet, couldn't bear his own thoughts. "Regan, I went to see my mother's friend the other day."

And she smiled expectantly. "Please, tell me about it." Probably relieved, he thought, that at last they had something safe to talk about. He smiled, too, remembering the visit with Enid.

"Catherine and I," she had told him, "said our good-byes every time we met for two long years. That night belonged to you, Jake, and it didn't take me very long to understand that. Not as long," she said, "as it took you to come back and see me." Enid's eyes sparkling.

He had apologized even more profusely then, until she stopped him, asking if he could stay for a cup of coffee. Her hair was graying now, but still soft and shining, like her eyes, clear and hazel with the remembered kindness in them. She sat across from him in her sunny kitchen as Regan had in his mother's house their first afternoon, catching up in talk. Enid's husband had died, and she was teaching again at the junior high school. She managed well enough, "though I always think I should do something with this house—like a face-lift."

She had been sorry to hear about his concert career, but Magnum's ever-growing success was a fascination. "So much responsibility," she teased, "and the power that goes with it," then a smile. "There must be a woman," she said. "Are you married, Jake?"

"Divorced."

"Children?"

He had hesitated. "No," he said. "No children."

The constant ache in his heart that had begun at the hospital with Regan had been with him, too, at Enid's. It still was. Now, Jake looked down at Regan and saw that her eyes were clouded, that people were staring. He tried to ignore them, using a matter-of-fact tone that he hadn't felt at the time and didn't feel now.

"I told her I loved her," he said of Enid, "and that's true. It was even easy to say, after all these years."

But sometimes, Jake admitted sadly to himself, the words had no effect. Like strangers, he and Regan glided, slowly, effortlessly, in the beautiful intricacies of the dance. "I'm glad," she murmured with a smile that broke his heart. "I am glad, Jake."

And he wished he might have *her* forgiveness as easily as Enid's, her trust, and her love without his pounding her into submission. But he knew not to try again for control. After tonight, after one final self-indulgence in the gold and amber room so full of memories, torturing him with the old pain and pleasure—like Regan in his arms for these last moments— his plans were made; and he wasn't going to change them. As if there were an alternative.

When the music stopped, Jake saw Bertelli walking toward them, and the moment hung, suspended from another time. He wanted to tighten his embrace at the same instant he loosened it, to keep this from happening. Looking deep into her eyes, those twin pools of jade-green, he felt the loss of her again as keenly as the first time; remembered Regan as a girl, the afternoon together in this house, that same silken waterfall of hair he wouldn't touch again. The absolute beauty of bared flesh, the pure perfection of her. She hadn't known how pretty she was, then. He wondered if she really knew it now.

The strange tenderness she had always roused in him swept through Jake like a warm breeze. He felt as if they were once again standing in some far-off airport, by the gate before her flight. Even now, there were so many things to say, things for which he had no words, and never enough time. Hearing Bertelli's approach, Jake let his hands linger on her shoulders, already feeling her slip away. *What is there about her?* he wondered; *some part of her I couldn't have.*

Briefly, he stopped her from moving; held her face lightly between his hands. "Did I ever tell you," he whispered, "that you have the most incredible eyes?" It was all he could say. The orchestra had begun a sedate fox-trot, and Jake was handing Regan to Manny Bertelli for the next dance. *Good-bye,* he told her silently. *Good-bye, baby. . . .*

She couldn't move, couldn't make her legs work. Regan stood staring after Jake as he crossed the wide room, watched him get a glass of champagne from a waiter's tray, say something to a man she didn't know. With a smile that wasn't his. Why had he said that to her? About her eyes? Looked at her as if he were saying—

"Come on, sweet. You're cheating me out of my dance."

Startled from her thoughts, she looked up and saw that Manny was only teasing—though he was right, too. They began keeping choppy time to the music, but all the while he was slowly edging her toward the side of the ballroom, and Alyson standing by a gilt chair.

"She's got something to say," Manny prompted, coming to a stop. "Haven't you, doll?"

Silence, and a shaky smile, her blue eyes not quite meeting Regan's gaze. "What is it, Ali?"

"Go on," Manny said again, in a warning tone.

"I—I wanted to tell you I'm sorry about the trouble over

Dixie, and that—that I'm grateful for what you've done for Daddy. That's all." She threw a grudging look at Manny, whose arm had settled around Regan's shoulders. Obviously, it had been a command performance.

"I'm glad I can help. The doctors haven't given up, I talked to one of them the other day and—"

But Alyson interrupted. "When my mother died . . . I tried so hard to make him love me more. I was—I was so afraid that I'd have no one."

And her success had been no greater than Regan's. The events of years before had ruined whatever home life there was to begin with. Alyson, living with her mother's bitterness about Lizabeth, her resentment of Lizabeth's child. And Paul himself, walking a shaky fence in his marriage, loving and hating at the same time, always remembering. It hadn't been Regan's fault; but she could hardly blame Alyson, either, for resenting her in turn.

"Ali," she said gently, "neither one of us ever knew what Paul was going to do or say next."

At the words, Regan felt a great weight lifting from her shoulders: that enduring need to make Alyson love her, and Paul. All the long years in that mustard frame house, the dull brown living room, the dingy pink bedroom that had been hers.

She watched her cousin's features slowly relax. Regan let her eyes slip over the yellow linen suit and the newly styled auburn hair, so neat and shining.

"Manny," she said, "why don't you dance with Alyson? I think I'll catch Steven. I haven't seen the groom alone since I arrived." Then Regan smiled at the other girl. "By the way, you look very pretty, Ali."

And got the shock of her life.

"So do you, Regan."

What sort of lure, Regan wondered, had Manny thrown out to gain such cooperation? Then she chided herself for suspicion. If Manny's methods worked with her cousin—and they obviously did—so much the better; she wasn't about to question them again.

Tapping Steven briskly on the shoulder, Regan gave him a dazzling smile as he turned away from a conversation with Linda's maid of honor. "I believe this is our dance. I insist on it."

He grinned at her, nothing on his face except sheer happiness.

"Take me, I'm yours."

"I'm ecstatic for you both, Steven," she said, moving into his arms.

Dancing, chatting, flirting in the harmless fashion they both enjoyed, Regan glanced toward Linda, radiant and smiling, her dark head tilted back, looking up and saying something to Jake. Not as distracted now, he inclined his head toward her with a smile. Sharing a joke, she supposed, while with Regan he hadn't spoken at all for the longest time.

Steven saw her staring and said, "You two made quite a picture yourselves before, dancing," as his gaze followed Jake and Linda.

"Jake was only dancing with me," she said tautly, "because he felt he had to." He'd been living up to his social responsibility: sharing a duty dance with *Dixie*'s star, that was all; and he couldn't wait for it to end, never mind what his eyes had seemed to be saying.

But Steven laughed harshly. "Oh yes, the same as I 'had to' marry Linda today." Freeing her hand for a second, he held his hand up. "And before you make some cute remark, I'll remind you *that* notion went out with birth control for the masses, so you can save the teasing attempt to change the subject."

Regan began to sense, in the hard tone of voice and the sudden absence of his smile, that she wouldn't like the next few moments.

"I think we've come far enough, princess, since that night at the Plaza, don't you? We don't have to hide any more, either of us. Or keep looking backward instead of going on— *My God*, Regan," Steven murmured, holding her gaze when she wanted to look away. "He's *miserable*, and I'm feeling damn guilty for being so happy, if you want to know the truth!"

Regan's step faltered, but Steven ignored her, continuing to dance and to lecture, to not notice her sudden pallor. "He can barely get up in the morning, damnit, and I think you ought to know this, too, since *he* won't tell you—he's leaving, Regan. Tomorrow morning, first flight, to L.A."

"He often does," she said. On business. But she found it difficult to breathe.

"This time," Steven went on, "he'll be staying. He's dumped the play, the record and book end of things on me. He'll develop Magnum's television and film interests on the Coast." She felt Steven's hand clamp more tightly around her waist; heard the infuriating patience in his tone, as if he were explaining a matter of utmost simplicity to a slow-witted child. "He's selling the house, Regan," and her legs felt suddenly made of wood, without hinges at the knees. Her heart began to pound, almost in terror.

"But he—but, Steven, he can't leave!"

Yet she knew he would; that she was hearing the truth, and would hear even more; that she had seen it moments ago in Jake's regretful eyes.

"What's keeping him?" Steven asked, falsely mild. "For four weeks I've been watching my best friend hold himself together like someone just out of surgery—trying to walk without pulling out the stitches. Careful, cautious, do the right things . . . but for *you*, Regan." Steven's eyes were hard blue glass, cutting through her. "Jake's been paving the way for you since that night in the hospital. Watching over you at rehearsal, protecting you from Peter's wrath . . . Regan, how in *hell* can you end it like this?"

Regan stared back with huge bright eyes at Steven's fury, his confusion. Linda, she thought. David. And now, Steven. But none of them understood why that brown-gold gaze frightened her so, why the words had terrified her in that hospital room. They didn't know how, in one instant and the next, she could yearn to keep him close, then send him away.

Clutching at Steven's shoulders, she tried to keep the fear, as fresh now as it had been then, from her voice. *Don't you turn away from me too, please, oh please—*

"Steven, don't look at me like that!" she cried. "Steven, I have to because"—the tears rose in her throat, threatened to choke off what she had to tell him—"because he wouldn't love me, either, not if he really knew me, Steven. Nobody would, when my mother—when *my mother didn't want me, she*—"

"*Regan!*" He pulled her close, stopping the tearful rush, shielding her sorrow with his body. "Regan, oh my God, sweetheart—is that what you've been feeling all these years?" He held her tightly, her face pressed to his shoulder, both of them oblivious as they stood stock-still on the dance floor, to the moving crowd around them and the music. "She didn't mean to leave you, and she certainly didn't intend to die. And how could she have known what it would be like for you in Paul's house?"

Are you more afraid that he'll leave you, Linda had wanted to know; *or that he'll love you in the first place?* And at last she knew the answer for herself, felt the trembling of her heart.

Steven's voice was gentle. "I don't blame you for hurting, princess. But you've got to stop running sometime. You're so scared of getting left behind, like that three-year-old girl you used to be, that you never stay long enough with anyone to risk it. You never trust yourself enough to love." She felt his hand sweep lightly over her hair. "Don't you see, Regan? At the first sign of trouble, *you* take off instead, then later tell yourself you've been abandoned again. Am I right?" He forced Regan's chin up with a brief pressure of one fingertip, not really needing her response because he saw it in her eyes, brimming, a flood of emeralds.

"Steven—"

"It's true," he said, "but so is this," making a quick gesture behind her, "You won't hate me, will you? It was always my favorite, princess." And she became aware of a sudden change in the music.

The slow ballad they'd forgotten had trailed away, and with Steven's words the orchestra began another song, one she knew so well. For an instant, Regan was thrust back to a warm September morning, before the steady run of platinum albums and the ever-increasing number of shining million-seller discs that now lined the walls of Manny's Midtown office. Again, she could see the words written on the staff paper, the music; but she saw them in her heart now. A love song, and a hit. Her very first. *Mine,* she thought, *and Jake's,* as the melody, sweet and molten, seemed to pour over her like liquid gold.

". . . all the constellations of the stars. . . ."

"Oh Steven, God—" She shook her head, uncomprehending. "How could you?"

Then, horrified, she saw Jake stop dancing with Linda and swiftly leave the ballroom, pushing people out of his way. Steven's hands held her face tightly, forcing her attention to him, his eyes searching hers.

"How could I not?" he asked. "For God's sake, don't you know yet that you belong to each other? Regan, make him stay. If you don't, you know as well as I do—princess, this time he isn't coming back!"

At the faintest hint of pressure from her, Steven let go, and Regan was free. *Coming back,* her pulse throbbed, *coming back.* Heart pounding, she ran past Linda, past the throng of guests. Across the marble hall and up the wide stairs carpeted in green, the chiffon folds of her gold and white gown floating, riffling, streaming. *Jake,* her heart seemed to shout as the music pursued her, *Jake!*

". . . a roaring rocket ride to Mars. . . ."

He was going away. He wasn't coming back. But hadn't he promised? *I'll always come back.* True, she had wanted an end to his manipulation of her; but she didn't want to lose the rest as well. Not the darkening look in those brown-gold eyes, not the warmth of strong hands upon her skin, the teasing note in his voice or the building up of passion. Long, lazy afternoons on the ridge behind the house. Walking together in the cool evening. Sharing a drink on the terrace under sharp stars. Breakfast in jeans and sun. Arguing; laughing; talking; loving. The heights and the depths, she thought. Oh God, yes. The darkness and the light.

But what if Jake never looked at her again with that special glow in his brown-gold eyes? She wouldn't believe it. In a month or two or three, wouldn't he be himself again?

"Now that Sloan's out of the picture," he would say ... but what if he didn't? What if he never looked at her again with tenderness, and humor ... and love? What if the distance between them, so cool and polite, lasted forever?

Steven was wrong, of course; she would see Jake again. At a matinee of *Dixie*, when he was in town on other business; at a party some night. Even in the jungle of Manhattan she might spot him on Madison or Fifth, his dark hair blown by wind, his tall frame visible above the others in the crowd around him. Lesser mortals, Regan thought with a tugging at her heart. And would she have nothing of him after all but a glimpse or two, a memory?

She was on the landing now, the next flight of stairs ahead, while her mind drifted back years ago, to an image in the clouded mirror above her dresser: a young girl with long blond hair and wide green eyes, her body twisting and turning back and forth, trying to see if she was pretty, yearning to know if she could sing. The notes of the bittersweet song Jake had written for her seemed to rise up the stairs as she went, and she heard herself again, as she had been so long ago, testing that clear voice, using an old hairbrush for a microphone. Dreaming of a closetful of shoes, a hundred dresses in all the colors of the rainbow, silks and satins and laces, the golden gown she had worn in Australia and on the cover of *Encore*, her fourth album. Dreaming of stardom, with that almost sexual exhilaration racing through her body while she sang.

She had risked everything for the success she'd earned from those dreams. Her own life, and Jake's; even, she thought, yes, a heart of stone. And the dreams had come true: money and recognition, that place in center stage. Her beauty was legendary; her talent without limits, so they said; the applause never-ending. All the dreams but one, she realized. A place, and someone to belong to.

But who could feel sorry for Regan Reilly, who owned the world, whose career had been a series of meteoric ascents, straight up, without stopping, into orbit? Jake's promise long ago *had* come true. A rocket ride to the moon . . . but without him, most of the way, without him.

". . . and you're all the words I know, old and new. . . ."

She had thought she knew where to find him, but the door to the room they had shared was locked.

Alone, Regan leaned against it, overcome. He wasn't there. He wasn't there. She could feel no give at all to the brass knob, so cool in the palm of her hand. The strains of the song filled her with longing. He would never be there again. Had he already slipped away from the house, the party? But then, from the next room on the hall, she heard the slightest sound of movement. She saw that the door stood ajar—like an old movie set—and Regan's heart twisted in remembrance. This door! Yes, the nursery in her dream, the nursery she had seen on that far-off summer day of first love. With pulse-pounding anticipation, she ran to it. What if—like that other room, with its brass bed and velvet chairs—what if here, their baby—

But when she pushed the door open, of course the room was bare. Barren. There would never be a child in this room, never the dark, silky hair and soft skin and blue eyes turning brown. No baby of ours, she thought, in its crib, sleeping. *I'm sorry about your son.* She heard Jake's sad hesitation, felt her own slipping-away into a dreamless void. The tears welled in Regan's eyes, the song lyric tore anew at her memories.

". . . but of all the words I know, the only one I care to know is you. . . ."

And then she saw him. In the glare of light, he stood near the window, his head tipped back slightly, his eyes focused on the ceiling in that classic attitude of silent despair. Oh God, the pain that David had seen, too, the pain she'd caused. Hearing her footsteps, Jake looked around; and she saw the anguish for herself.

"Was that your idea? To have them play that cursed song? Damnit, tell them to stop!"

"Steven asked for it," she said.

"*Christ,* I wish to hell I'd never heard it—" His voice rang with harsh disbelief. "I wish to God I'd never written it!"

Given this chance, so unexpected, Regan didn't know what to say to him. He seemed so closed in, rejecting her; his face as tight and hard as she had ever seen it. Worse than the worst of their senseless arguments. Dear God, she thought, please. At the recital that first day she couldn't imagine how to approach him, yet somehow she had found the words. But now?

Regan blurted everything, unprepared.

"Jake, you can't leave! You can't sell this house, please don't!" But he only gave her that flat, blank look she had come to know so well.

"Why not? Do you want it? I'll give it to you," he said coolly. "A gift of parting," looking away as if the sight of her was too much to bear. "It was always yours, anyway."

"But you love the house," she tried, feeling cold and lifeless, sculpted in marble by the hard, ungiving tone of his voice.

"*I hate it, do you hear me?* Do you think I could stay here one day longer, trying to cover your echoes in these empty rooms? Imagining you beside the pool, laughing? Smelling the fragrance of you every time I open the door to that *room?*" He waved a hand at the connecting door to the bedroom they'd shared, an image in her mind of gold and white and amber, the colors of loving.

Regan stood unmoving, stunned by his admission. Did he still care for her, then? In a whisper, she said, "You should write songs, Jake," touched to her soul by the poetry of his words.

"And you should sing them."

He said it in a shaken tone to match her own, his dark eyes focused hard on the door to the hallway beyond her left shoulder. She tried to discern more bitterness in his words, but found none as the heart song downstairs swelled in crescendo into the final chorus, toward its end. *Coda,* she thought. From our first time, that first year, to last summer. And now . . . An urgency seized her; Regan willed Jake to look at her again.

"I wish we could," she said gently. "You playing and composing, me learning and singing. I wish everything between us were fresh and new. I wish we *could* go back and start over—wipe out all the bad parts. . . ."

"We can't."

He hadn't looked at her, and she wondered if Steven was wrong about him, if she had killed Jake's feeling for her that morning in the hospital when she'd sent him away.

"But if we could," she persisted. "Oh Jake, would you?"

And his gaze flickered in her direction, slid away.

"Maybe."

"And find another red VW like the one we used to drive?"

He almost smiled. "A real piece of junk," he said fondly, his eyes warming with remembrance. "Still running strong after a hundred and fifty thousand miles."

Regan pressed the advantage. "Would you buy back your old house, too? And grow mushrooms under the sink?"

"Yes," he said. And then, "Toadstools."

"What?"

"They were toadstools, not mushrooms." He looked at her. "There's a difference."

"Like bricks and gold?" Regan asked. "And roads made from them?"

For an instant, she wondered where the reference had sprung from. Then she remembered. Once, she'd told Jake that she felt like Dorothy in *The Wizard of Oz*, stepping onto a golden highway of opportunity—the start of her singing career—and she'd been so disappointed when Jake pointed out that the road was really brick. Now she said softly, "You were kind enough one night not to tell me what the girl in that story wanted on the road. Not adventure and excitement—but to find her way home, back to the people she loved, the people who loved her."

He didn't answer, his features tensing as she watched.

Afraid he'd turn away, leave and shut her out forever—even more afraid because she trembled on the edge of a discovery that would change everything—Regan spoke in a whisper.

"Let me come home, Jake. Please."

Something happened in his face, and with the change, wary as it was, Regan moved closer. "For how long?" he said.

"To stay. I promise."

Inches more, and she had wrapped her arms around him; but still his body stayed unbending in her light embrace.

"You never believed in promises," Jake said.

"Oh, but I have to, don't I? I have to believe, Jake, and so do you!" She looked up into his face, her eyes a soft, liquid green. "When I was a girl," she murmured, "lying across my bed . . . and daydreaming by myself about the future, I thought about finding someone to love, too. And I wondered then how I'd know he meant it when a man said he loved *me* because—because, living at Paul's, I didn't have any experience to call on and—"

Jake interrupted. "Nobody does at eighteen."

"But I haven't that excuse now," Regan insisted. "And I think I understand my feelings better than I did then—and my mistakes."

She held his gaze with hers, wondering if she dared to take such a big step, one she'd never taken before.

"You've always come to me, Jake," she went on, haltingly at first, her voice gaining strength as he continued. "I never wanted to take the chances, did I? I left you for Manny and told myself I was doing the best thing for us, which was only partly true. I went for *me*, too . . . for my career, Jake. I felt deep in my heart that you'd take care of the rest, the way you always had—that you'd come for me when you got well, and keep on coming whenever I needed you. Even after Cecily had ended your marriage and I was back with David, pregnant, I hoped you'd come." She told Jake about her feelings of abandonment and what Steven had said about always running away and then how hard the old habits would be to break, "but I *will* break them," she finished. "I will."

"We both made mistakes, Regan," Jake conceded, his dark eyes fixed on her troubled features. "We hurt each other."

She shook her head. "I hurt you more," she whispered. "Steven said so today, and it's true. Maybe until now, a few moments ago, hearing your song again . . . maybe I didn't realize how much I'd hurt you, or that I had to give, too, in equal measure—" She felt as if she were babbling, wondered if she made any sense to him at all, and Jake's immobility didn't help. In her arms, he hadn't moved. Why couldn't she reach him? What more could she say?

You'll always know where to find me, she had told him before their first parting, when Jake had left on what was to be his final tour; but he was in her heart as well.

Men will be falling in love with you all your life, Kenny had said. But ever since the afternoon with Jake in the room next to this one, with the sun shafting Jake's body, since that first passion on the dusty muslin covering the dirty wooden floor... hadn't she been looking for the same thing? Home, yes.

But home wasn't simply a place, not even a magnificent house like this—the one she'd dreamed about—its rooms so full of treasure, its protective bulk built to stand a thousand years. It was a state of mind, of heart, Regan thought as she looked up into those deep brown eyes that studied her so cautiously. It was this man she had never, ever stopped wanting.

And if she didn't turn her back now, this minute, on Paul Oldham and the childhood nightmare, if she didn't forgive her mother for leaving, she would never be whole. She would live as wretchedly as Paul had; be as lonely and loveless in the years to come. *Don't be scared,* she heard him say, *don't be scared.*

Regan took a deep, shuddering breath.

"In the hospital when you said you loved me, Jake, I was terrified. Because that was something I'd never had to count on in my life... something I'd only sampled once, with you, then lost; and I felt too scared to try again. Linda says that I'm more frightened of loving than I am of losing you—and David told me that I'm afraid of the very fact that you're exactly the man I want; that it was easier for me to marry someone I didn't love—but I'm trying, Jake. I'm trying not to be afraid."

She was shaking now, trembling on the edge of a high cliff, much more dangerous than the one she'd tumbled over that spring afternoon in Jake's living room when he heard her sing. Then she felt his arms go around her, slowly, tentatively. Sensed the muscles of his body relaxing. Accepting. And with the motion, her heart soared. But still, she didn't know. All she really knew was that she hadn't run, that she was here in Jake's arms again, that she had found the courage to stay. It wasn't any easier to ask the question; but somehow, she did that, too.

"Do you love me, Jake? Can you still love me?"

His answer came without hesitation, filling her with relief, and joy.

"Yes," he whispered. "Always."

Downstairs, their song had faded away, another had begun; and from below drifted the rise and fall of voices they hadn't noticed until now, the clatter of silver against china, the tinkle of crystal. Silent, they held each other close. After long moments Jake said, "I love you, Regan," his voice shaken as he rubbed his cheek against her hair. The warmth of his fingers at last penetrated the thin chiffon of her dress, comforted her back. She leaned into him with a sigh of contentment, feeling lulled by his body and his love, and they were quiet for a long while, no need of anything but each other's presence.

Then Regan asked idly, "Is there a great deal of champagne downstairs?"

"Cases," Jake said, nuzzling her earlobe and the satiny curve of her throat.

"And enough food?"

"Tons," he murmured. "Staggering amounts." She could feel his smile against her skin. "Obscene quantities."

"And these people in the house—they're not really your guests, are they, but Steven and Linda's?"

Jake whispered yes, she could say that, and why did she ask? His breath tickled her neck. A shiver of happiness, not unlike that when she sang, raced down her spine. Regan felt she deserved every bit of it. "Because," she said slyly, "I think we should let them enjoy their reception—while we tend to our honeymoon first."

He held her away, smiling, with the steady, amused regard that had puzzled her long ago, and later, when she understood its meaning, delighted. The smile grew, and in Jake's eyes she saw once more the bright flecks of gold and bronze. "Is that a proposal?"

"A very honorable one, my lord. If somewhat reversed."

Then she stepped from his embrace with a sense of purpose, moving before Jake could tighten his hold. As she reached for the brass knob, he said quickly, "Don't open that!" but she had already pushed wide the connecting door from the empty nursery. She thought she heard a soft groan as Jake followed.

"I'm not grandstanding," he said just behind her. "I wasn't trying to pull anything, Regan. This was for myself—to remember you; I didn't plan for you to see—"

But she stopped the awkward rush of explanation.

"I know," she said. "I know you weren't."

Her voice was hushed with wonder, a feeling as delicate and strong as on that first afternoon together in this room, at the beginning, before the long years of searching. David had been so right, that there were many kinds of love: David's friendship and protection; Linda and Jeb and Kenny, Manny, too . . . even Peter. And Sam. She had come to know them all, even—in some ways—Paul. But always, always, there had been the one love she failed to understand, the most important of all, the one she couldn't do without.

It was the one love she had to trust in, to believe. And she did. Oh yes, she did! The necessary changes in him were permanent, just as hers would be. Regan looked around her slowly, the green eyes wide and luminous with love. The sweep of tawny-gold hair shimmered with the movement, and she thought, with an upward rising of her spirit: *Oh Kenny, I'm going to make it for us both. We're going to make it, Jake and I. . . .*

Beyond the threshold, the room gleamed gold and amber. The wing chairs, deep velvet, flanked the fireplace, its blue-and-white delft tiles shining; and in the hearth, logs crackled as they burned with the fragrant smell of apple wood. One window stood ajar—the cool, first breeze of spring wafting through to fan the fire, lifting the gossamer white curtains and the filmy batiste hangings of the bed. But it was not the ready fire or the chairs or the bright brass bed that made her certain of him, and of herself.

It was the flowers. Vases and baskets and delicate china pots of every shape and size held masses of them. Not diamond not hard or faceted or sparkling. Not artificial, but real. As real, Regan thought, as their love had always been, from the day of Jake's recital and the first minutes in this room. Dozens of them. White daisies.

"Oh, baby," Jake murmured, "even to me this room looks like a shrine. What a cornball thing to have done."

But she turned with a happy smile into his arms, and found him grinning back. "No," she said. "No, James Harrod Marsh ... it wasn't." Then she was laughing with him, the tears misting her clear emerald eyes. After seven years, she thought. Almost seven years. Tears without sadness or loss, and no more seeking.

"Or maybe it was," she conceded, "a *little* corny—but I love you for it—*oh Jake, how I love you!*"

Hadn't he told her, one confusing night, that *even inside, some things haven't changed?* They never would, Regan made the silent promise, and raised her face to his kiss, the taste of Jake's mouth her homecoming, and their beginning.

Neither of them heard the rest of the party.

The Best Of
Warner Romances